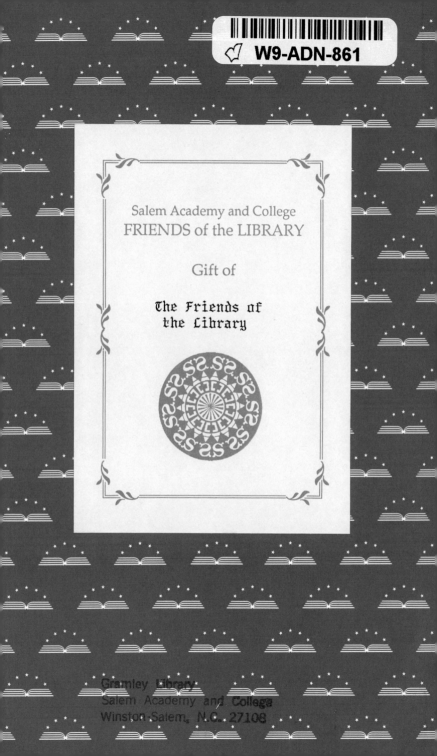

sent Paltiel a radiogram giving our new time of arrival, but we missed even that.

When the ship finally docked in Santos, there was no one to meet me. The ship would remain in port for only twenty-four hours. I tried to telephone from the harbor, but I couldn't get a connection. One time, someone did answer, but he spoke only Portuguese, which I did not understand. For some reason, I couldn't bring myself to disappoint Paltiel Gerstendrescher. The tone in which he had written about this visit implied that all his hopes depended upon it. After brief deliberation, I boarded a bus that went to Rio, and from there took a taxi to his address. It turned out to be quite far from the city, in a desolate section that the driver had trouble finding. The narrow road, full of pits and potholes, lay partially flooded under broad puddles.

I knocked at a house that was a half ruin, and a woman opened the door. To my surprise, I recognized her from Warsaw—Lena Stempler, an obscure actress, singer, and monologuist. She painted as well. I had met her at the Writers' Club. She was then a young brunette and the sweetheart of the well-known writer David Hesheles, who later perished under the Nazis. Lena had vanished from sight years before I left Warsaw. All kinds of slanders were spread about her in the Writers' Club. It was said that she had divorced four husbands and had offered her body to a theater critic in exchange for a favorable review. Someone told me that she suffered from syphilis. As I looked at her now, I was impressed at how girlish her figure had remained. Her short-trimmed hair was still black, though it showed the dullness of dye. Wrinkles could be seen through makeup. Lena had a snub nose, light-brown eyes, a wide mouth with loosely spaced teeth. The butt of a cigarette stuck out from between her lips. She wore a kimono of some flimsy material and high-heeled slippers.

When she saw me, she spat out the butt, smiled with an expression suggesting that she knew more about me than I imagined, and said, "I am Mrs. Gerstendrescher. Unexpected, eh?" And she kissed me. Her breath smelled of tobacco, alcohol, and something putrid.

She took my arm and led me into a huge room that seemed to be everything at once—a living room, a dining room, a

One Night in Brazil

I HAD never heard of the man before, but in a long letter he wrote me from Rio de Janeiro he represented himself as a Yiddish writer who had become "lost and ground up in the hot desert of Brazil." His name was Paltiel Gerstendrescher. A few months after the letter, one of his books arrived. It was put out by the Myself Publications, printed on gray paper and bound in covers crimped at the side from the time it had been in the mail. A mixture of autobiography and essays about God, the world, man, and the aimlessness of creation, it was written in a turgid style and unusually lengthy sentences. It teemed with typographical errors, and some of the pages were transposed. Its title was *The Confession of an Agnostic*.

I skimmed through it and wrote the author a thank-you note. That began a correspondence consisting of three or four incredibly long letters from him, and a brief note from me apologizing for not writing sooner and in greater detail.

I don't know how, but Paltiel Gerstendrescher found out that I was preparing to go to Argentina for a series of lectures, and he began to send me special-delivery letters and even telegrams asking me to spend a few days in Rio de Janeiro. At that time I wasn't flying, and it just so happened that the Argentinian ship I boarded was scheduled to stop over for two days at Santos, twelve days after its departure from New York.

The ship was nearly deserted, and someone confided to me that this was its last trip from North America. I had obtained a luxury cabin at a reduced rate, and in the dining hall I had my own wine waiter, even though I took only a sip of wine to give him something to do.

That spring—spring in Brazil and fall in New York—a hurricane swept over the Atlantic, with violent rains and gale-force winds. The ship lurched dismally. Its horn blew day and night, in warning. Waves pounded the hull like mighty sledgehammers. In my cabin I had hung my tie over the mirror and it executed acrobatic stunts. The toothbrush in the glass clinked without stopping. The ship fell behind schedule, and I

Contents

One Night in Brazil 7

Yochna and Shmelke 21

Two 30

The Psychic Journey 44

Elka and Meir 59

A Party in Miami Beach 73

Two Weddings and One Divorce 87

A Cage for Satan 98

Brother Beetle 104

The Boy Knows the Truth 114

There Are No Coincidences 126

Not for the Sabbath 143

The Safe Deposit 154

The Betrayer of Israel 168

Tanhum 177

The Manuscript 188

The Power of Darkness 197

The Bus 208

Author's Note

Although the story "Old Love" appeared in *Passions*, my last collection of stories, I have decided to use this title for the present book. The love of the old and the middle-aged is a theme that is recurring more and more in my works of fiction. Literature has neglected the old and their emotions. The novelists never told us that in love, as in other matters, the young are just beginners and that the art of loving matures with age and experience. Furthermore, while many of the young believe that the world can be made better by sudden changes in social order and by bloody and exhausting revolutions, most older people have learned that hatred and cruelty never produce anything but their own kind. The only hope of mankind is love in its various forms and manifestations—the source of them all being love of life, which, as we know, increases and ripens with the years.

Of the eighteen stories I offer here, fourteen were published in *The New Yorker* and edited by my great and beloved editor, Rachel MacKenzie. One of them, "Tanhum," was edited by William Maxwell, and another, "The Betrayer of Israel," by my new editor, Robert McGrat, following Rachel MacKenzie's recent retirement. Of the other stories, two appeared in *New York Arts Journal*, one in *Playboy*, and one in *The Saturday Evening Post* some fourteen years ago. All of them were edited by my good friend and editor of almost all my works, Robert Giroux. My gratitude goes to all of them, as well as to the many readers who write and encourage me in my creative efforts. While I don't have the time and strength to answer them personally, I read all their letters and often make use of their important remarks.

I.B.S.

OLD LOVE

Hershele and Hanele, or the Power of a Dream, 775
Pity, 785
The Angry Man, 793
The Mathematician, 799
The Building Project, 808
The Painting, 821
Morris and Timna, 834
Two, 844
Eulogy to a Shoelace, 858

Chronology, 863
Note on the Texts, 884
Glossary and Notes, 891

Loshikl, 396
The Pocket Remembered, 406
The Secret, 424
A Nest Egg for Paradise, 436
The Conference, 459
Miracles, 465
The Litigants, 481
A Telephone Call on Yom Kippur, 485
Strangers, 497
The Mistake, 504
Confused, 514
The Image, 535

from *Gifts* (1985)
The Trap, 564
The Smuggler, 576
Gifts, 581

from *The Death of Methuselah and Other Stories* (1988)
The Jew from Babylon, 593
The House Friend, 600
Burial at Sea, 607
The Recluse, 614
Disguised, 622
The Accuser and the Accused, 631
A Peephole in the Gate, 636
The Bitter Truth, 655
The Impresario, 662
Logarithms, 672
Runners to Nowhere, 679
The Missing Line, 687
The Hotel, 693
Dazzled, 703
Sabbath in Gehenna, 711
The Last Gaze, 716
The Death of Methuselah, 725

Uncollected Stories
The Bird, 737
"My Adventures as an Idealist", 745
Exes, 759
Between Shadows, 772

Contents

Old Love (1979)
    One Night in Brazil, 7
    Yochna and Shmelke, 21
    Two, 30
    The Psychic Journey, 44
    Elka and Meier, 59
    A Party in Miami Beach, 73
    Two Weddings and One Divorce, 87
    A Cage for Satan, 98
    Brother Beetle, 104
    The Boy Knows the Truth, 114
    There Are No Coincidences, 126
    Not for the Sabbath, 143
    The Safe Deposit, 154
    The Betrayer of Israel, 168
    Tanhum, 177
    The Manuscript, 188
    The Power of Darkness, 197
    The Bus, 208

from *The Collected Stories* (1982)
    A Night in the Poorhouse, 241
    Escape from Civilization, 253
    Vanvild Kava, 260
    The Reencounter, 268
    Moon and Madness, 274

The Image and Other Stories (1985)
    Advice, 293
    One Day of Happiness, 302
    The Bond, 317
    The Interview, 325
    The Divorce, 339
    Strong as Death Is Love, 349
    Why Heisherik Was Born, 357
    The Enemy, 366
    Remnants, 375
    On the Way to the Poorhouse, 387

———

First Printing
The Library of America—151

ISAAC BASHEVIS SINGER

COLLECTED STORIES:
ONE NIGHT IN BRAZIL
to
THE DEATH OF METHUSELAH

Old Love
The Collected Stories
The Image & Other Stories
Gifts
The Death of Methuselah & Other Stories
Uncollected Stories

THE LIBRARY OF AMERICA

ISAAC BASHEVIS SINGER

bedroom, a studio. A table stood here, set with plates and glasses, and a wide divan of the kind that serves as a sofa by day and a bed by night. Unframed canvases hung on the walls. On the floor lay piles of books and stacks of *The Confession of an Agnostic.*

Lena said, "Paltiel went to meet you in Santos. You missed each other. He called. I hope you remember me. We rarely exchanged a word, but I used to see you every day at the Writers' Club. In Rio, I read sketches you had written to audiences a few times. I married Paltiel in Brazil. We're together going on eight years already. Take off your jacket. It's hot as hell in here."

Lena seized my jacket by the sleeve and pulled it off. Afterward, she loosened my tie. She fussed around me like some relative, but also with an aggressiveness I didn't care for.

She put out refreshments on a small table—a pitcher of lemonade, a bottle of liqueur, a plate of cookies, a bowl of fruit. We sat down in wicker chairs, and drank and ate, and from time to time Lena took a puff on a cigarette. She said, "If I told you that Paltiel looked forward to your coming as one looks forward to the Messiah, this would be no exaggeration. He's been talking about you non-stop for years. When a letter comes from you, he goes berserk. He's crazy about you and he's made me crazy, too. Here, we are both trapped in a dilemma. Everything is against us—the climate, the local Jewish society, our nerves. Paltiel is a genius at making enemies. Here, if you quarrel with two or three of the community leaders you're as good as excommunicated. Because of him, I've been ostracized, too. We would starve to death if it weren't for a small stipend I get from my ex-husband. To hear the whole story, you'd have to sit and listen for days on end. Paltiel used to be a fantastic lover. All of a sudden, he became impotent. I, on the other hand, have become possessed by a dybbuk."

"A dybbuk?"

"Yes, a dybbuk. Why do you look so frightened? You write about dybbuks constantly. Apparently they are nothing more than fiction to you, but dybbuks do exist. Everything you conjure up about them is the truth. A dybbuk sits inside you, too, but you don't recognize it. It's better that way. Your dybbuk is creative, but mine wants to torture me. If he lets me live, it's only because you can't torture a corpse. Don't stare at me that way. I'm not crazy."

"What does he do to you?"

"He does exactly what you describe in your stories. I had saved up a little money, and I spent it all on psychiatrists and psychoanalysts. In Brazil they're a rare breed—and in addition maybe third- or tenth-rate. But when you're drowning you clutch at even a tenth-rate straw. Here is Paltiel."

The door opened and in came a little man wearing a short raincoat and a hat covered with plastic, an umbrella in one hand and a briefcase in the other. I had pictured him as tall, maybe because of his long name.

When he saw me, he appeared dumbfounded. In those days, my picture was seldom printed in newspapers and magazines. He stood there studying me up and down and even sideways. An angry smile showed on his pointed face. He had a high forehead, sunken cheeks, a sharp chin. "So it's *you*," he said. His tone implied, *You aren't what I wanted you to be, but I must accept the facts as they are.* Soon he added, "Lena, today it's a holiday by us!"

We ate a vegetarian meal, drank papaya juice and strong Brazilian coffee, and for desert Lena served a cake she had baked herself in my honor.

She threw open the door to a large and overgrown yard behind the house. The rain had stopped the previous day, and the evening was fresh with tropical scents and ocean breezes. The sun rolled toward the west like a coal, turning the remnants of clouds from the hurricane a fiery red. Lena switched on the radio and listened to the news for a while, and I cocked my ear to the song of birds that had flown in for the evening to roost on the branches of the trees. Some stayed where they landed, others shifted about, flying from tree to tree with a flapping of wings and a rustle. I had never seen birds of such color out of captivity. The force of Genesis still functioned here undisturbed.

Paltiel spoke to me about literature, about his own writing. "A creator should also be a critic," he said, "but the criticism must come later. My trouble is that before I even write three words I'm already filled with questions about what my pen wants to express and I try in advance to justify and smooth over everything. You asked me in one of your letters why I use such long sentences and enclose so many comments in parentheses. It's my critical nature. Actually, analysis is the sickness of man. When Adam and Eve ate of the tree of knowledge, they became critics and analysts and perceived that they were naked. All the current works written about sex have evoked an epidemic of impotence. Economists have interfered with the world economy until they've brought about inflation in every country. It's the same with the so-called exact sciences. I don't believe in all those particles of atoms they keep discovering. The human brain has imposed its own lunacies upon Nature, or Nature herself has eaten of the tree of knowledge and gone crazy. Who knows? It may be that God has gone into psychoanalysis and therefore—"

"Paltiel, I know your theories already," Lena interrupted. "I'd rather hear what our guest has to say."

"No, go on. It's interesting," I said.

I glanced toward the windows. Just a moment ago it had been day; abruptly, night had fallen as if a celestial light had been extinguished. The air inside the room filled with gnats, mites, midges. Huge beetles emerged from cracks in the walls and floor.

Lena said, "Life here is so plentiful you can't stop anything with nets. I was taught in Gymnasium that matter can't pass through matter, but that was true for Poland, not for Brazil."

"Tell me about your dybbuk," I said.

Lena cast a questioning glance at Paltiel. "Where shall I begin? If you want us to be open with him, we'll have to tell him the truth."

"All right, tell him," Paltiel replied.

"The truth is that we are both cursed or enchanted—call it what you will," Lena said after some hesitation. "Paltiel came here from Canada. On account of me he divorced a wife and left two children. We met in your New York. He wanted to be a writer, not a lawyer. He came to New York for some Yiddishist conference. I had the good fortune, as you might call it, to come here before the Holocaust, but I wasn't lucky in Warsaw, nor have I been lucky here. You remember me from Warsaw. I was raised in a house where Polish was spoken,

not Yiddish. I came to Warsaw to study at a Polish drama
school, not to become a hanger-on in the Yiddish theater.
It was your friend David Hesheles who made a Yiddishist
out of me. They probably said terrible things about me at
the Writers' Club. I was an alien element there from the
beginning, and I remained one until the last day. The men
were all after me and their slatterns despised me as they would
a spider. What David Hesheles did to me, how he tormented
me, is something I'd best not say, because he is already in the
other world, a victim of human cruelty. Just one thing—he
would only agree to be my lover if I was married. Crazy, isn't
it? First of all, he was tempted by the thought of possessing
another man's wife. Second, he was afraid that if I was alone
I'd be looking around for someone else. He gave himself
every freedom, but he burned with jealousy over me. He manipulated things so that when he saw I was growing attached
to one husband he arranged for me to be divorced and found
me another. How and in what circumstances I came to South
America is a chapter in itself. I arrived physically and spiritually ill, and, once here, I married again—this time allegedly
of my own will but actually for a piece of bread and a roof
over my head. My new husband was forty years older than I
and it was then that I met Paltiel and made another woman
miserable."

"Lena, you're digressing," Paltiel said.

"So? If I'm digressing, I'm digressing. You begin writing
about Yehupetz and end up in Boiberik but me you don't allow to come to the point. Because of your wild digression,
Parness has stopped publishing your work."

"Lena, this has nothing to do with Parness."

"In that case, I'll shut up and you can do the speaking."

"The fact is, she has talked herself into the lunacy that David
Hesheles comes to her, tickles her, pinches her, pushes her,
chokes her. He has taken up a position inside her belly. You
know from my book that I'm no atheist. A real agnostic allows
for all possibilities, even for your demons and hobgoblins. If in
the twentieth century there could emerge a Hitler and a Stalin
and other such savageries, then anything is possible. But even
you will admit that not every case of hysteria is a dybbuk. The
nuns who exhibited stigmata on the week of Jesus's anguish

weren't possessed by dybbuks. Today even the Pope would concede this—"

"Only yesterday you said that our house was haunted and that what I'm going through couldn't be explained away in natural terms," Lena broke in. "Those were your very words."

"It is impossible to explain anything—even why an apple falls from a tree or why a magnet draws iron, not butter."

"You said that only our honored guest would be capable of exorcising this dybbuk."

"I said it because I know that you admire him, love him, and all the rest. I admire him myself, and I would be in seventh heaven if he would stay with us and have a look at my writing. But your dybbuk is nothing more than hysteria."

Lena sprang from her chair. She nearly overturned a wineglass and caught it just as it was falling. She thrust out a finger with a red nail and said, "Paltiel, the second you came back I noticed a complete change in you. What did you expect—that our guest goes around with a crown on his head? Certainly I would like him to stay with us, but since he can't, that's my misfortune. You can ask him to take along your manuscripts to read on the ship. He still has six days left to travel. But me he can't take along. I wish he could. You know I'm choking here."

"You're a free person. I told you that from the very first day." And they switched over to Portuguese.

I had fallen in with a couple caught up in an ongoing controversy—one of those quarrels that drag on for years and make couples shameless. The few hours I had spent here had made me fully aware of the situation. Paltiel Gerstendrescher was an intellectual, not an artist. He read and spoke a correct, even an idiomatic Yiddish, but he completely lacked the mentality of the Yiddishist. He had probably gone to Canada as a child. He belonged to that breed of people who exile themselves to an alien environment, choose a profession for which they're unsuitable, and quite frequently an unsuitable mate as well. The same thing held true for Lena. Even the house where they lived—in a forsaken, non-Jewish neighborhood—was unsuitable for them. They had turned away from the only circle from which they might have drawn a livelihood; and besides, Paltiel had involved himself in experimenting with language, indulging in elaborate wordplays and mannerisms that had small hope of interesting the Yiddish reader and that could never be translated.

Well, but why *would* a husband and wife so thoroughly sabotage their interests? And what was it they expected of me and of a visit that would last at most a day? I had a momentary urge to try to speak about their situation to them, but I knew that it was already too late. Lena's words about her dybbuk had piqued my curiosity, but although hysteria itself is exaggeration and lying, I knew that hers was entirely artificial—a literary dybbuk, perhaps borrowed from one of my stories. The real victim here was Paltiel, I told myself. He bowed his head and was listening to Lena's complaints with bewilderment. From time to time he shot a look of suspicion at me. It was obvious from the moment we met that he was disappointed in me, but as far as I knew I hadn't spoken any words that might have displeased him. It could only be the way I looked. For all my embarrassment, I tried to come to a decision as to the color of his eyes. They weren't blue or brown or gray but yellow and set wide apart. It occurred to me that if I found myself in a situation like this in America I could simply get up and walk out. But there was no escape in an alien land far from a city.

Paltiel stood up. "Well, good," he said in Yiddish. "I'm going." In a moment, he had closed the door behind him.

For a while Lena kept speaking in Portuguese, but she realized her mistake and broke into laughter. She said, "I am so confused I no longer know what's happening to me."

"Where has he gone in the middle of the night?"

"Don't fear, he won't get lost. From looking at my neglected garden you might get the impression that we live in a jungle. Actually, we're only a few steps from the road and no more than twenty kilometers from Rio. It's not the first time he's done this. Every time I tell him the truth he runs away. He has an old widow in Rio who plays the role of his patron. She is also his only reader and he goes to her to bewail his fate. He stops a car and they take him. This isn't New York. People here aren't afraid to pick you up, especially such a runt as him."

"Is he having an affair with her?" I asked.

"An affair? No. Maybe. God grant he would and leave *me* alone."

"Who will take me to Santos in case he doesn't come back?"

"I'll take you. I have a schedule and all the rest of it. Don't worry. The ship won't leave without you. When they say four in the afternoon, they don't leave till ten at night. The whole way of life in these countries consists of putting everything off till tomorrow, till the day after, till next year. I see by your face that you want to hear more about my dybbuk. Yes, my dybbuk is David Hesheles. He caused me anguish when he was alive, and now that he's dead he wants to do me in. Not all of a sudden, mind you, but gradually. The only time he has left me alone was during the few years I was with my former husband, the old man. He was apparently not jealous of him. But since I'm with Paltiel I have had no peace. David Hesheles tells me frankly that he'll drag me down to him in his grave, though, to be factual, there is no grave. There is only a heap of ashes."

"He talks to you in a real voice?"

"Yes, in a voice, but I'm the only one who can hear him. Sometimes he makes noises that even Paltiel can hear, but he won't admit it. He plays the rationalist, but he's afraid of his own shadow. He has seen Hesheles's apparition walking down the steps of our cellar. He has heard him slam doors and open faucets in the middle of the night. David Hesheles has settled himself inside my stomach. I've always done calisthenics and I had a flat belly, almost like a man's. All of a sudden, I got up one morning with a huge swelling there. It's actually a head, *his* head. Don't look at me that way. Paltiel and the local doctors all have the same answer for it: neurosis, complex. When an X-ray shows nothing, it doesn't exist. But a head has settled inside my stomach. I can feel his nose, his brow, his skull. When he speaks, his mouth moves. As long as he is down there it's bearable, but when he falls into a rage he begins to edge up higher toward the throat. Then I can't breathe. I used to hear back home that if you did someone harm and he died, the corpse came back to strangle you. But I did him no wrong. He wronged me. At first I considered this an old wives' tale—folklore. I'll be frank with you: if someone were to tell me what I'm telling you now, I would tell him to commit himself to an asylum. If you want, you can feel the head with your own hands."

For a moment, a childish fear came over me, along with a re-vulsion against touching her flesh. I had not the slightest urge for this female. I recalled what I had been told—that she suf-fered from a venereal disease. I myself would have become im-potent with her. I began seeking a pretext to get myself out of this intimacy, but I felt ashamed of my fear. For the first time I was offered something the psychic researchers call physical evi-dence. I said, "Your husband may come back, and—"

"Don't be afraid. He won't come back. He undoubtedly went to her. Even if he did come, you wouldn't be in any trouble—we're both determined to show you the truth. I have an idea. There's a hammock outside. It's a dark night. We have no neighbors. The mosquitoes will attack us, but there is no malaria here. Besides, there's a net above it. Come!"

Lena took my arm. She flicked a switch and all the lights went out. She opened the door to the garden and a wave of heat struck me like heat from an oven. The sky hovered low, thickly strewn with southern constellations. The stars appeared as large as bunches of grapes in a cosmic vineyard. Crickets sawed unseen trees with invisible saws. Frogs croaked with human voices. From the banana trees, the wild flowers, and thickets of grass and leaves rose a scorching heat that pene-trated my clothes and warmed my insides like a hot compress. Lena led me through the darkness as if I were blind. She men-tioned the fact that lizards and snakes crawled here, but not of poisonous varieties.

Someone on the ship had told me the joke that what the government in Brazil stole during the day grew back at night. It seemed to me now that I could hear juices flowing to the roots and being transformed into mangoes, bananas, papayas, pineapples. Lena tilted the hammock so I could get in and gave it a playful push. Soon she slid in beside me. She opened the kimono that covered her naked body, took my hand, and placed it on her abdomen. She did everything quickly, with the skill of a medium accustomed to séances. I did, in fact, feel something inside her belly, protruding and long in shape. It began under the breasts and extended to the pubic hair. Lena guided my hand upward. She directed my forefinger to a small bump and asked, "You feel the nose?"

"The nose? No. Yes. Maybe."

"Don't be so scared. I'm not a witch. From the way you write about dybbuks, I assumed you were used to such mysteries."

"You don't get used to mysteries."

"Really, you've remained a boy. Maybe that's where your strength lies. David Hesheles is mad at me, not at you. He liked you. He always praised your talent. I kept seeking opportunities to meet you, but you fled from women like a Hasid. When I started reading your things here in Brazil, I couldn't believe that the writer was really you."

"Sometimes I don't believe it myself."

"Feel his forehead. You won't have many such opportunities."

Lena lifted my hand and I touched a pointed nipple. I jerked my finger away so that she shouldn't think I was trying to arouse her. For all the weirdness of the situation, I told myself that neither David Hesheles—that cynic, may he rest in peace —nor his soul had any connection with this game. Lena suffered from a tumor, or maybe it was the result of a practiced self-deception. If you desire something strongly enough, you can train the muscles to perform all sorts of stunts and contortions. But why should she want this so badly?

"What do you say now?" Lena asked.

"Truly, I don't know what to say."

"Don't be so nervous. Paltiel won't come back. I suspect that he started arguing with me on purpose so I could be alone with you."

"Why do you say that?"

"Why? Because he's half crazy, and because we are both trapped in a dark corner—physically, spiritually, in every respect. I've had husbands and I know. No matter how great a love may be, there comes a crisis that is just as much an enigma as love itself—or as death. You still love each other, but you have to part, or a new person comes along and introduces a new approach. I'll tell you something, but don't take it badly —in our fantasies, *you* were that person."

"Oh, but unfortunately I'm leaving the first thing tomorrow. I have my own complications. Why did you settle so far from everything and everyone?" I asked, changing my tone. "Paltiel is highly intelligent; he possesses lots of knowledge. In New York he could easily become a professor. Your chances would be better there, too."

"Yes, you are right. But here I have the house. I receive alimony from my former husband. This house would be hard to sell. Besides, it's not altogether mine. He wouldn't send me the cruzeiros to New York, either. Paltiel has grown completely apathetic. He sits day and night and writes these novels in which there isn't one interesting character. He is trying to become a Yiddish Joyce, or something of the sort. I hear that in New York the Yiddish theater is going under."

"I'm sorry, yes."

"Sometimes I want the dybbuk to go up to my throat and finish me off. I'm too tired to begin all over—especially since there is nothing to begin. I'm ripe for death, but I lack the courage to act. Don't laugh at me, but I still dream of love."

"So do I. I've heard this from sick and old people literally a day before they died."

"What sense does it make? I lie in bed loaded down with troubles and fantasize about a great love—something unique that probably doesn't exist. Whether my dybbuk will strangle me or I'll die from heart failure, one thing is sure: I'll die with this dream."

"Yes, true."

"How do *you* understand it?"

I wanted to say that I didn't understand it. Instead, I said, "It seems that life and death have no common border. Life is total truth and death is total lie."

"What do you mean—that we live forever?"

"Life is God's chariot and death is only the shadow of His whip."

"Who said that?"

"I don't know. Maybe I did myself. I'm just babbling."

"I told you—a dybbuk sits within you, too. Tell your dybbuk to kiss me. I'm not so old or so ugly."

I'm not going to start anything with her, I decided. This woman is a liar, an exhibitionist, and mad to boot. Her husband showed me hostility. I had had dealings with people of this sort. One minute they idolize you, the next they scold you. They are invariably out for some favor that is as impossible and crackpot as they are themselves. But even while I made this firm decision I put my arms around Lena. I was always intrigued by those who chose failure, wallowed in its complexities, sacrificed themselves to its deceptions. I kissed Lena now, and she bit into my mouth. I heard myself calling her endearing names and telling her that our meeting was an act of fate. We were rolling and struggling. She tried to cover us with the mosquito net and we fumbled to tuck it around us. Suddenly the hammock tore away from the tree and we fell into a swamp full of nettles, rotten roots, slime. I tried to get up, but I was trapped in the net. At that moment Lena let out a ghastly scream. Mosquitoes had descended upon us, as dense as a swarm of locusts. I had been bitten by mosquitoes before, but never by so many and with such ferocity. I somehow managed to disentangle myself and help Lena up. We tried to run to the door but were caught in thorns, branches, prickly weeds. Lena kept on screaming. Only now did I realize that she was naked and had lost one of her shoes. I tried to lift her up, but she resisted.

When we finally reached the house and the light was turned on, I saw that we were both covered with bites and with living mosquitoes. They had attached themselves to us like leeches. We began to slap one another to kill these parasites whose blood had been our blood only an instant before. We jumped against each other in a crazy dance. My shirt was soaked with blood. Lena tore it off and pulled me into a bathroom with a long bathtub over which hung a copper tank and a shower. She let the water run and we stood under it, holding one another to keep our balance. Lena opened a medicine chest, took out a bottle of fluid, and began to rub down our bodies. I saw in a mirror that the skin of my face was half peeled off. Still wailing, Lena led me back to the living room, where she pulled a sheet from a chest, spread it over the broad couch, and wrapped me up like a corpse in a shroud. Then she wrapped herself in a sheet. She bent over me and cried out, "God loves us. He has sent the punishment before the sin!"

She threw herself on me with a lament, and in an instant my

face became wet and salty. She put out the light, but it went on immediately—Paltiel had returned.

The next morning Paltiel took me on a bus to Santos. Lena had to remain in bed. Paltiel and I didn't speak a word. We avoided looking each other in the eye. I was so exhausted that I dozed most of the time, my head dropping again and again. I was too numb even to be ashamed. Before I entered the ship, Paltiel handed me two huge envelopes full of manuscripts and said, "We both gained a lot from your visit: I gained a true reader and Lena gained a true dybbuk."

I hoped that this would be the end of my bizarre encounter, but when I returned to New York from my South American journey I found three more manuscripts and two forty-page letters from Lena—one in Yiddish, one in Polish. Lena revealed to me that her love for me had begun when we were still in Warsaw and that she received vibrations and telepathic messages about my coming to her long before Paltiel knew of my trip. I tried to read what the two of them had written, but the manuscripts and letters arrived in such quick succession I realized that no time would be left for anything else. From glancing here and there into Lena's letters I learned that the widow, Paltiel's Maecenas, had died, leaving him quite a large sum of money, and that he was spending it to publish all his works through Myself Publications. Soon the books started to arrive at unbelievably short intervals. It was more than I could do to open their mail any more, but this did not deter them from continuing to send books and letters for a long time. Some years later I learned that Lena had died from cancer and that Paltiel had been put away in a mental institution. I had to dispose of the mass of their writings. I kept only one large book by Paltiel, written in an atrocious style, mad, unreadable, and a few letters from Lena—frightening documents of what loneliness can do to such people and what they can do to themselves.

Translated by Joseph Singer

Yochna and Shmelke

THROUGHOUT all his years Reb Piniele Dlusker had devoted himself to Hasidism. He traveled to the courts of
the Zanz Rabbi, the Belz Rabbi, the Trisk Rabbi. Hasidim argued with him that one rabbi was enough, but Reb Piniele
said, "Why can a mother love a dozen children? Why do rich
men live in many rooms? Why does the emperor have a lot of
soldiers? My pleasure is wonder rabbis."

Reb Piniele visited his rabbis on every holiday, even on
Passover, although the most fervent Hasidim made it a custom
to spend the Passover seders at home with their families. In the
first years of their marriage, his wife, Shprintza Pesha, had objected. Her mother had even advised her to get a divorce. Matters had come close to this when Shprintza Pesha lost a set of
twins to scarlet fever, which she took as punishment from
Heaven for having caused her Piniele grief. In later years, other
children died—whooping cough, diphtheria, measles—until
Reb Piniele and Shprintza Pesha were left with one daughter,
Yochna, named after Shprintza Pesha's great-aunt.

Yochna grew up healthy. She seldom cried and was forever
smiling, revealing the dimples in her cheeks. Shprintza Pesha,
the breadwinner, had a store where she sold yard goods and
notions—sackcloth, lining material, thread, buttons. Yochna
virtually raised herself. Reb Piniele wanted his only child to
grow up a pious Jewish daughter, and when Yochna turned
four he engaged a rabbi's wife to teach her the alphabet, and
later prayers, and even how to write a line or two in Yiddish.
But Yochna had no head for learning. She ate a lot and quickly
grew plump. Other girls played tag, hide-and-seek, and
danced in circles, but Yochna sat in front of the house in the
summers and made mud pies. At mealtime her mother
brought her fatty meats, groats, soup, bread with honey, and
Sabbath cookies. Yochna finished every bite, and always demanded more. She was as blond as a little Gentile, her hair pale
as flax and her eyes blue as cornflowers.

At eleven, Yochna became a woman, and Shprintza Pesha
brought her a little pouch containing a wolf's tooth to ward

off the evil eye and a talisman to drive away intruding spirits. She had the breasts of an adult, and Shprintza Pesha paid a seamstress to make her daughter camisoles and drawers with lace.

Yochna never learned to read from a prayer book, but she had committed to memory the prayer said upon rising, the benediction said before each meal, as well as other graces. Yochna loved Jewishness. She insisted that her mother take her to the women's section of the synagogue on Sabbaths, and like the pious matrons, she took care to say "Blessed be He and blessed be His name" and "Amen" when the cantor in the men's section recited the Eighteen Benedictions. She also listened to the supervisor of the women's services reciting the prayers for those who didn't know the alphabet. Whenever a traveling preacher came to town, Yochna went to hear his sermon. She cried as he described the tortures in Gehenna: the beds of nails, the whippings by the avenging demons, the glowing coals upon which sinners were rolled. Her eyes gleamed when the preacher told how in Paradise Godfearing women became the footstools for their husbands and were made privy, along with the men, to the secrets of the Torah.

When Yochna turned twelve, she was besieged by marriage brokers offering matches, but her father, Reb Piniele, brought her a groom from Trisk, a yeshiva student, an orphan, who studied seventeen hours a day. His name was Shmelke, and he was three years older than Yochna. He slept and ate at an inn. The couple would first face each other at the wedding ceremony during the unveiling of the bride, but Yochna cared for him without having seen him. She began to embroider a velvet prayer-shawl sack for him of gold and silver thread, as well as a bag for the phylacteries, a Sabbath-loaf cover, and a case for matzos. A rebbetzin came to teach Yochna how to count off the days following her period to determine when she could lie with her husband, and how to maintain marital purity by taking the prescribed ablutions in the ritual bath. Yochna learned it all, and the rebbetzin praised her diligence.

Shprintza Pesha ordered a trousseau for her daughter. It wasn't easy to fit her, since she had grown like dough made with lots of yeast. The tailor's assistants joked that she had a bosom like a wet nurse. They compared her thighs to butcher's blocks. But her feet were small and her fair hair hung to her hips. Shprintza Pesha spared no wool, silk, or satin to adorn Yochna.

The whole town attended the wedding, and Shprintza Pesha baked huge cakes and cooked caldrons of meats and soups. When Yochna was led to the ritual bath, the musicians played a good-night tune. The riffraff who hung around the taverns had plenty to mock. When the bath attendant snipped off Yochna's hair and then shaved her skull with a razor, the young matrons at the bath burst into tears, but Yochna said, "What are you bawling for? Since God ordered it, it's fine and proper."

On the night of their wedding, Shmelke lifted the veil from Yochna's face. She glanced up and was filled with a great love for him. He was short, slight, dark, with black earlocks twisted like horns and sunken cheeks that bore no trace of a beard. His gaberdine hung too long and too loose upon him. The fur cap he wore had slipped over his dark eyes, and he trembled and sweated. "Oh, does he look starved, my treasure, the crown upon my head," Yochna said to herself. "God willing, I'll fatten him up."

Under the canopy, Shmelke had trodden upon her foot—a symbol that he would be the head of the house—and a shudder ran down Yochna's back. She felt an urge to cry out, "Yes, rule over me, my lord! Do with me whatever your heart desires!"

Following the virtue dance, her two escorts, her mother and an aunt, led Yochna to the wedding chamber. Both women commanded her to give herself to her husband willingly, since to be fruitful and multiply was the first commandment in the Torah. Yochna undressed in the dark and put on a lacy nightgown that hung to the ankles. She got into bed and waited patiently for Shmelke to come to her. A bliss she had not known coursed through every limb. She was a wedded wife. Already she wore a night bonnet on her head and a wedding ring on her finger. Yochna prayed God to grant her a houseful of healthy children that she could bring up to serve Him.

After a while, Piniele and a respected town elder escorted Shmelke to the room and closed the door. Yochna cocked her ears for any movement. He had been let in like a fowl into a cage. It was pitch-black. How, she worried, could a stranger undress here? How could he find her bed? He stood there and mumbled. She heard him bump against the chest of drawers. He's likely to hurt himself, God forbid, or fall, Yochna thought with a tremor. She began whispering to him—he could drape his clothes over a chair. He didn't answer. She could hear his teeth chatter—he was shaking with fear, the poor thing.

Yochna forgot that she was a bride, who must act modest. She got out of bed to try to help him, but he jerked when she touched him and drew back. Gradually, she calmed him with words. He took off his gaberdine, the ritual garment, the slippers. The whole time he didn't cease murmuring. Was he reciting a prayer? Was he intoning an incantation? After a long hesitation he stepped out of his pants, and she half led, half pushed him toward her bed. Now he tossed about as if in a fever. An urge to weep came over Yochna, but she held back her tears. The attendant had told her that according to law the husband and wife were allowed to come together in bed and even kiss and embrace. She put her arms around him and kissed his forehead, his cheeks, his Adam's apple. She pressed him to her bosom. Suddenly she heard his voice: "Where is my skullcap?"

He must have lost it, and Yochna felt around on the cover, on the sheet. To avoid the sin of being bareheaded, he covered his skull with both hands.

"Oh, he has a sacred soul," Yochna said to herself. "What did I do to deserve such a saint?"

She got out of bed to look for the skullcap. She tapped about in the dark like a blind person. "Father in Heaven, help me find the skullcap!" she pleaded. Mentally she pledged eighteen groschen to charity. At that moment, she stepped on something soft. It was Shmelke's skullcap. Yochna picked it up and kissed it as if it were a page torn from a holy book. "Shmelke, here it is."

She could scarcely believe that she had the courage to do all this and even to call him by name.

Shmelke put on the skullcap and began uttering pious words to Yochna. The coupling of husband and wife, he said, was intended to bring forth sacred souls who waited by the Throne of Glory to be purified and, through a body, offered an opportunity to perform good deeds. He recalled virtuous women from the past. Even though Yochna didn't understand the scholarly language he used, it rang sweet in her ears. After he had finished, he mounted her. The bath attendant and her escorts had warned her that he was likely to hurt her and that she must accept this pain with gratitude and joy. But she felt no pain. He was as light as a child upon her. Soon he left her bed and went to his own bed, as the law dictated. When the women came at dawn, they found blood on Yochna's sheet and they took it along to display in the kosher dance.

Later in the day, the women and Shprintza Pesha led Yochna to visit esteemed matrons of the town, who all welcomed the guests with cake and wine or almond bread and cherry brandy. Yochna glanced in the mirror. How different she looked in the bonnet with beads and ribbons and in a dress with a train! Without her hair, her head seemed oddly light. Her skull felt cool. A married woman doesn't dare reveal her bare head lest it rouse the lust of strange men.

In the seven days following the wedding, guests came each night to visit, and Yochna's father, Reb Piniele, treated each one to a cup of ceremonial wine. Shmelke sat beside his father-in-law, and from time to time Yochna glanced at him through the open door—he looked as slight and bashful as a boy in cheder. The men discussed learned matters with him. He replied briefly and in a quiet voice. Shprintza Pesha brought him an appetizer, noodles with soup, meat-and-carrot stew, but he left most of it on the plate and his mother-in-law chided him, saying that for studying the Torah one needed to keep up one's strength.

As long as Yochna had been single, she had properly not had any girl friends, but now young matrons came to discuss housekeeping matters with her—how to sew, darn, knit; how to get bargains at stores; how to do needlepoint of trees, flowers, deer, and lions on canvas. The women taught her how to play knucklebones, wolf-and-goats, and even checkers. They insisted that Yochna show them her jewelry and the dresses that had been sewn for her trousseau. Shprintza Pesha had given her daughter all her jewelry, leaving herself only a gold medallion with a charm. The young women praised Yochna's jewelry but hinted that it was old-fashioned. Her chain, the bracelet, the brooch, even the earrings and rings were too heavy. A new fad had evolved—light jewelry. Yochna nodded and smiled. What did all these vanities matter to her? Her finest adornment was Shmelke.

The wedding had taken place on the Sabbath night following the Feast of Shevuot. In the month of Elul, Reb Piniele began talking of spending the holidays with his rabbis—Rosh Hashanah with one, Yom Kippur with another, Succoth with a third. He proposed to Shmelke that he accompany him. He wanted to show off his son-in-law, the scholar. But Shmelke demurred. Shmelke had his own rabbi. His father, blessed be his memory, had visited the court of the Warka Rabbi. When, after some hesitation, Shmelke told Reb Piniele that he wished to spend Rosh Hashanah in Warka, Reb Piniele struck a bargain. On Rosh Hashanah and Yom Kippur Shmelke would accompany him to Belz and to Trisk, and Shmelke would then go on to Warka for Succoth. And that's how it was settled.

At the news that Shmelke would be going away for the holidays, Yochna felt like crying. Most young husbands remained with their wives for the holidays. But a Jewish daughter had to do what her father said and what her husband wanted. Yochna began to prepare the things Shmelke would need for the trip: shirts, drawers, socks, fringed ritual garments, handkerchiefs. Around Succoth the weather begins to turn cool, and Yochna saw to it that Shmelke took along a wool jacket and an overcoat. What Yochna did for Shmelke, Shprintza Pesha did for Piniele. Shprintza Pesha was used to Piniele's travels, but Yochna began to long for Shmelke even before he left. She begged her father to keep an eye on him. Piniele replied, "Don't carry on, daughter. Those who travel in the service of God aren't harmed."

Piniele and Shmelke rode off in a wagon to a village by the Austrian border, where they were helped to smuggle themselves across. The border patrol was bribed in advance. To obtain a foreign passport and a visa cost too much and required a long wait. The Russians, Prussians, and Austrians had divided Poland among themselves, but the Russian Hasidim visited

Austrian rabbis and Austrian Hasidim visited their rabbis in Russia.

Once their husbands left, Shprintza Pesha and Yochna began to prepare for the holidays. On Rosh Hashanah night, Shprintza Pesha and Yochna lit candles in silver holders. Later, Shprintza Pesha pronounced a benediction over a goblet of wine and started to cut the Rosh Hashanah loaf, which resembled a bird. Mother and daughter each ate a slice, with honey, a carp's head, and carrots. Yochna remembered the correct Hebrew words to say.

The next morning, Yochna put on a gold dress and a headband with gems, and, even though she could not read, she took along to the synagogue a Hebrew prayer book with its copper clasp and a Yiddish supplication book, the title embossed in gold. When Shprintza Pesha bowed, hopped about, or cried, Yochna bowed, hopped, and cried along. Thus Rosh Hashanah and Yom Kippur went by. All the women wished Yochna a good year that would include a circumcision celebration.

During the intermediary days of Succoth, sudden heavy winds rose. Their force blew away the branches of fir that had been used for roofs for the Succoth booths, knocked over the walls, scattering chairs and tables as well as the holiday decorations. On the night of Hoshana Rabba, the seventh day of Succoth, thunder shook the air, the sky flashed with lightning, and rain mixed with hail fell in a torrent. Old people couldn't recall a storm of such intensity this time of the year. Water roared down Bridge Street, and the paupers who lived there had to leave with their children to sleep on higher ground in the house of worship or in the poorhouse. Gusts of wind sent shingles flying over the town. In the middle of the eighth day of Succoth it grew so dark it seemed as if the world might be coming to an end. Shprintza Pesha and Yochna had invited some women and girls over for Simchas Torah. Mother and daughter had prepared great pots of cabbage with cream of tartar and raisins, roast goose, and baked flat cakes and tarts, but no one could wade through the streets. Bad news came to the magistrate from many cities and villages that the rivers San, Bug, and Vistula had overflowed their banks. Herds of cattle had drowned, rafts that lumber merchants floated to Danzig had shattered, and those who worked them were lost. Pious women said that the disaster was punishment from the Almighty; the responsibility lay with the big-city heretics, as well as with the wanton women who went around bareheaded, failed to attend the ritual bath, and wore dresses with short sleeves that exposed their flesh.

Normally, Reb Piniele came home on the day after the holiday, but two weeks passed with not a word from him or from Shmelke. The rains had stopped by then and the frosts had started. Because the roads were covered with ice, the peasants couldn't deliver wood and grain to the villages and towns. During the gales, sluices had torn in the water mills and the mill wheels had broken. Children collapsed in illness, and mothers ran to the synagogue to clutch at the holy ark and pray for their recovery.

One night, Piniele came home. Shprintza Pesha barely recognized him. He looked emaciated, sick, stooped. He brought bad tidings. He had detained Shmelke in Trisk until the sixth day of Succoth. A day before Hoshana Rabba, Shmelke had started out for Warka. The wagon on which he was traveling had reached a wooden bridge. A fierce blast of wind came up. The bridge collapsed and Shmelke had drowned, along with the other passengers. The driver and horses had perished, too. The townsmen searched for the bodies for three days, but the current had carried them off to who knows where. Yochna had been left a deserted wife. She knew the law: if Shmelke's body was not found and recognized, she could never remarry.

Shprintza Pesha erupted in howls and Yochna howled along. Shprintza Pesha wrung her hands, and Yochna followed suit. Mother and daughter wept and wailed. Piniele spoke of Shmelke's greatness for hours. On the way to Belz and Trisk Shmelke had sat up all night in the wagon, chanting the Mishnah by heart. Both rabbis they visited had promptly acknowledged Shmelke's reverence for God and had called him a sage. Each report of praise caused mother and daughter to burst out anew. At daybreak, Yochna fell asleep in her clothes, her mouth open.

Shprintza Pesha woke her later in the morning. "Daughter, enough," she said. "It is God's decree."

"Shall I observe the seven days of mourning?" Yochna asked.

"Yes, Daughter, observe the mourning."

"I'll ask the rabbi's advice," Reb Piniele said.

Reb Piniele went off to consult the rabbi and stayed away a long time. Yochna took off her shoes and sat down on a footstool in her stocking feet. Her luck had glowed briefly, then been extinguished. What had she done to be so afflicted? She was deserted forever, albeit she would not want to marry again. Sitting there bewailing her fate, it struck Yochna that she should have got her period between Rosh Hashanah and Yom Kippur. How was it she had forgotten about it? And how was it that her mother had said nothing? Usually she kept track of the days. Yochna glanced up toward the window. The sky hovered low, gray. Across the way a crow clung to a chimney. It was hard to tell if it was alive or frozen there. Minutes went by and it didn't move either its head or wing. It had fulfilled its mission here on earth and was already in God's hands, Yochna thought. She closed her eyes and delivered herself completely into God's power. She listened to her own body. Had Shmelke really left an heir? God has dominion over the living and the dead and over those yet to be born.

Shprintza Pesha came in from the kitchen with a slice of bread and a cup of coffee with chicory. "Daughter, wash your hands and eat," she said. "The little saint in your womb is hungry."

Translated by Joseph Singer

Two

FOR almost ten years after the wedding Reb Yomtov's wife, Menuha, did not bear a child. Already it was rumored in Frampol that she was barren and a divorce was imminent. But she became pregnant and both Yomtov and Menuha referred to the coming child as "she."

The father wanted a girl because the Gemara says, "A daughter first is a good omen for the children to come." The mother wanted a daughter because she had it in mind to name her after her dead mother. When she entered her late months, her belly didn't become high and pointy but round and broad—a sign that she was carrying a female child. Accordingly, she prepared a layette of little shirts and jackets festooned with lacework and embroidery, and a pillow with ribbons. The father put aside in a box the first gulden toward a dowry.

Actually, Reb Yomtov had other reasons for wanting a daughter. He, a Talmudic scholar entrusted with removing the impure fat and veins from kosher meat, had the soul of a female. When he prayed, he didn't appeal so much to the Almighty as to the Shechinah, the female counterpart of God. According to the cabala, the virtues of men bring about the union of God and the Shechinah as well as the copulations of angels, cherubim, seraphim, and sacred souls in Heaven. Full union on high will take place only after the redemption, the coming of the Messiah. In the midst of the Eighteen Benedictions Yomtov would exclaim, "Oh, Mama!" When he was still a boy studying the Pentateuch in cheder, he was drawn more to the matriarchs than to the patriarchs. He preferred to glance into such volumes as the *Ze'enah u-Re'enah* and *The Lamp of Light* rather than the Gemara, the commentaries, and the Responsa. Yomtov was small and stout, with a sparse beard and small hands and feet. At home he wore silk dressing gowns and slippers with pom-poms. He curled his earlocks, primped before the mirror, and carried all kinds of trinkets—a carved snuffbox, a pearl-handled penknife, and a little ivory hand, a charm, left him by a grandmother. On Simchas Torah or during banquets he didn't drink strong spirits but demanded sweet brandy. The people made fun of him. "You're a softy, Yomtov! Worse than a woman."

Well, for all that Menuha and Yomtov expected a girl, the powers that decide such things saw to it that they had a boy. True, the midwife made a mistake and announced to the mother that the baby was a girl, but she soon acknowledged her mistake. Menuha grew terribly upset that between a yes and a no a daughter had turned into a son. Yomtov couldn't bring himself to believe it and demanded to be shown. Just the same, people were invited to the pre-circumcision party and cheder boys came to recite the Shema. Zissel being a name for both a man and a woman, the boy was named that after a great-aunt. Since his gowns, jackets, and bonnets had already been prepared, the infant was dressed in them, and when the mother carried Zissel in the street, strangers assumed he was a girl.

It is the custom that when a boy turns three his hair is cut, he is wrapped in a prayer shawl and carried to cheder. But Zissel had such elegant curls that his mother refused to trim them. The parents carried their precious offspring to cheder, but when the child spied the old teacher with his white beard, the whipping bench and the whip he began to howl. His slate with the alphabet printed for him to read was strewn with candy, raisins, and nuts he was told had been left there by an angel from Heaven, but the child would not be appeased. The next morning he was brought again to cheder and given a honey cake. This time Zissel carried on so that he suffered a convulsion and turned blue. Thereupon the parents decided to keep him at home until the following term. A rebbetzin who tutored girls at home taught him his alphabet. Zissel studied with her willingly. The rest of the time he played with other children. Since his hair was long and he didn't go to cheder, boys his age avoided him. He spent most of his time with girls and enjoyed their ways and their games. The boys played with sticks, barrel hoops, and rusty nails. They fought, got dirty, and tore their clothes, but the girls picked flowers in the orchards, sang songs, danced in circles, rocked their dolls, and their dresses and aprons stayed clean.

"Why can't I be a girl?" he asked his mother.

"You were supposed to be a girl," his mother replied. She kissed and fondled him and wove his hair into a braid for a joke, and added, "What a shame, you would have made such a lovely girl."

Time, which often is the implement of destiny, did its work. Zissel grew up and against his will began attending cheder. He was stripped of his dresses and made to put on a gaberdine, pants, a ritual garment, and a skullcap. He was taught reading —the Pentateuch, Rashi's commentaries, and the Gemara. The matchmakers early began to plan matches for him. But Zissel remained a girlish boy. He couldn't stand the brawls and recklessness of the daredevil boys, and he couldn't climb trees, whistle, tease dogs, or chase the community billy goat. When the cheder boys quarreled with him, they called him "girl" and tried to lift the skirts of his gaberdine as if he were really female. The teacher and his assistant refrained from whipping him because the few times they did he promptly burst into tears. Also, his skin was delicate. They overlooked it when he came late or left before the others. On Fridays, the boys accompanied their fathers to the steam bath. In the summer, they bathed in the river and learned to swim. But Zissel was bashful and never undressed before strangers. The truth was that he suffered anxiety and all kinds of doubts. He already was convinced that to be a male was unworthy and that the signs of manhood were a disgrace.

When no one was home, Zissel put on his mother's dress, her high-heeled shoes, camisole, and bonnet, and admired his reflection in the mirror. On Sabbaths in the house of prayer, he gazed up at the section where the women sat and he envied them looking on from behind the grate, all dressed up in their furs and jackets, jewels, colored ribbons, tassels, and frills. He liked their pierced earlobes and tried to pierce his own with a needle. His parents grasped that something was not right about their Zissel. They took to punishing him and calling him a dunce. This only made things worse for him. He often locked himself in his room, cried, and said a prayer in Yiddish from his mother's prayer book with its gold-embossed covers and copper clasp. His tears burned, and he dabbed his eyes with the edge of a kerchief, as women do.

■

When Zissel turned fifteen, matches were proposed for him in earnest. A quiet, handsome boy and an only son besides, he was offered girls from wealthy homes. His mother occasionally went to look over the proposed brides and she later described to Zissel their conduct and appearance. One was tall and thin with a deep voice and a wart on her upper lip; another was short and stout with big breasts and almost no neck; a third was red-haired, marked with freckles, and had the green eyes of a cat. Each time, Zissel found some pretext not to become engaged. He was afraid to marry, sure that a wife would forsake him the first day after the wedding. Suddenly he began to find virtues in his own sex. He saw the rascals of his childhood grown into respectable youths who recited the Gemara and the commentaries in a chant, discussed serious things among themselves, paced to and fro across the study house in deep deliberation. The girls on the other hand had become frivolous. Their laughter was loud; they flirted, danced wantonly, and it seemed to Zissel that they were mocking him.

Of all the youths, Zissel liked best one called Ezriel Dvorahs. Ezriel came from Lublin and behaved in big-city fashion. He was tall, slim, and dark, with earlocks tucked behind his ears and black eyes with brows that grew together over his nose. His gaberdine was always spotless, and he polished his kid boots daily. Although he wasn't engaged yet, he already wore a silver watch in his vest pocket. The marriage brokers assailed him with prospective matches, and the other students competed to be his study partner. When Ezriel spoke, everyone stopped reading the text to listen. When it was time to take a walk along Synagogue Street, several boys were always ready to accompany him. When he strolled past the marketplace, girls rushed to the windows and stared at him from behind drawn curtains as if he had just arrived from Lublin.

It happened that Ezriel, who was two years older than Zissel, chose him to be his study partner. Zissel accepted it as an honor. On Sabbaths he wished it were the weekday again so that he might study together with Ezriel. When it occurred some morning that Ezriel didn't show up at the study house, Zissel walked around steeped in longing. At times, Ezriel took Zissel with him to the baker's, where they ate prune rolls for their second breakfast. Ezriel confided in Zissel about the matches he was being offered and told him stories of Lublin. But sometimes Ezriel acted friendly toward the other boys and then Zissel felt a pang of resentment—he wanted Ezriel to think better of him than of anyone else.

After a while, Ezriel chose another partner. Out of distress, to show Ezriel that he could get along without him, Zissel agreed to become engaged. The bride-to-be was a beauty from Tomaszów, slender and fair, with blue eyes and a braid hanging to her waist. Zissel's mother couldn't stop praising her good looks. The articles of betrothal were signed in Tomaszów, and his prospective father-in-law, a timber merchant, gave Zissel a gold watch as an engagement present.

When Zissel came home after the betrothal, the youths at the study house gave him a friendly reception. He treated them to cake and brandy, as was the custom, and they offered him congratulations and questioned him discreetly about the bride. They had heard of her loveliness and envied Zissel his good luck. Ezriel joined in wishing him mazel tov, but he didn't ask for details. He didn't even ask Zissel to show him the gold watch with the engraved inscription on the back.

Ezriel was on the verge of being engaged himself, and shortly this was arranged. The prospective bride, a local girl, was homely. Her father was fairly well off and had promised a handsome dowry; still, the people of Frampol wondered why a gifted youth like Ezriel should settle for such a match. Apparently Ezriel regretted his decision, too, since he didn't show up at the study house for a few days and even failed to treat his fellow students to the customary brandy and cake. From the day of Zissel's engagement, Ezriel had grown cool toward him and avoided him.

Zissel wanted to delay his marriage a year or two; making Ezriel jealous was sweeter to him than becoming the husband of the Tomaszów belle. But the bride's parents were in a hurry for the wedding, since the bride had already turned eighteen. Zissel was taken to Tomaszów and the wedding was held. During the Virtue Dance when first the bride, then the groom was led to the wedding chamber, Zissel was overcome by trembling. With hesitation he went to his bride lying in the bed, but he could not do what he knew he was supposed to. In

the morning the women came to examine the sheet and perform the Kosher Dance of Consummation; they did not find
what they were looking for.

The following night, attendants again escorted the couple
to their wedding bed, accompanied by musicians and the wedding jester, and this was repeated on each of the Seven Days of
the Benedictions. Since both sets of parents felt that a spell had
been cast over the couple, the groom's mother went to the
rabbi, who gave her an amulet, an amber over which an incantation had been said, and a list of suggestions. The bride's
mother secretly consulted a witch, who supplied her own devices. In fact, the cures recommended by both the rabbi and
the witch were the same.

Within a few weeks Ezriel married, but his match, too, was
unsuccessful. Soon after the wedding he and his bride began
to quarrel, and within a few months Ezriel went back to his
mother. One day Zissel, who was boarding at his father-in-
law's in Tomaszów, received a letter from Ezriel in Frampol,
and as he read it he marveled. In an elaborate handwriting and
a Hebrew full of flowery phrases Ezriel described his anguish;
he called Zissel "my beloved and the desire of my soul," he reminded him of how pleasant it had been in the old days, when
they had studied the Gemara, strolled down Synagogue Street
together, eaten prune rolls at the baker's, and confided to
each other the secrets of their hearts. If he had the fare, he
would come to Tomaszów as swiftly as an arrow shot from a
bow.

When Zissel finished reading, he was overcome with joy and
he forgave Ezriel all his past neglect. He answered in a long
letter full of words of affection, confessed that his wedding had
caused him heartache and shame, and so that Ezriel could
come to visit him he enclosed a banknote he took from his
dowry without telling his father-in-law.

Without business in Tomaszów, Ezriel had no excuse to go
there, but letters between the friends went back and forth frequently. Ezriel was an ardent correspondent. His words often
rhymed and were full of insinuations and puns. Zissel answered in the same vein. Both quoted passages from the Song

of Songs. They compared their love to that between Jacob and Joseph or David and Jonathan. The fact was, they yearned one for the other. Ezriel began to call Zissel Zissa.

This correspondence continued until they decided to meet at an inn lying between Tomaszów and Frampol. Ezriel told his mother that he was going to inquire about a teaching position. He took along his prayer shawl and phylacteries and a satchel. It was hard for Zissel to find an excuse for leaving, and he therefore decided on a trick. In the morning, after his father-in-law had gone to his business, his mother-in-law had gone to the drygoods store, and his dainty wife had gone to the butcher shop, Zissel opened the wardrobe, put on a pair of women's drawers, a camisole, a dress, and shoes with high heels. He draped a shawl over his shoulders and covered his head with a kerchief. His beard had not yet grown. When he caught a glimpse of himself in the mirror, he hardly knew his own face and he was certain that no one would recognize him. The Spirit of Perversity had whispered in his ear that he shouldn't be a fool—to take from his father-in-law and mother-in-law whatever was handy. After brief deliberation, he obeyed. He took the dowry from its place of safekeeping, along with his wife's jewelry, and hid them in a hand basket, which he covered with a cloth. Then he went outside. When the women in the street saw him, they assumed that a strange woman had come to town on a visit.

Thus, Zissel walked past the market and saw from afar his wife pushing her way toward the butcher's block. He pitied her, but he had already broken the commandments that forbid a man to dress in women's clothes and to steal, and he hurried along.

On Church Street, Zissel found a peasant cart heading for Frampol and for a trifle the peasant let him ride as far as the inn. There Zissel got off and asked for Ezriel. He said that he was Ezriel's wife and the proprietor exclaimed, "He just told me he was about to meet his partner!"

"A wife is the best partner," Zissel replied, and the innkeeper pointed to Ezriel's room.

Ezriel was pacing back and forth as is the way of the impatient. When Zissel came in, Ezriel looked with bewilderment at the young woman who was smiling at him so coquettishly.

"Who are you?" he asked, and Zissel answered, "You don't know? I'm Zissa!"

They fell into each other's arms, kissed, and laughed in rapture. They vowed never to part again. After a while Ezriel said, "It wouldn't be safe to stay around here too long. When your in-laws find out what you've done they'll send police after you and we would both fall into the net."

So next morning they bade farewell to the innkeeper, telling him they were going back to Frampol. Instead, they turned off into a side road and hired a wagon to take them to Kraśnik, and from Kraśnik they went on to Lublin.

Since they had money, and jewelry besides, they quickly rented an apartment in Lublin, bought furniture and everything needed to maintain a household. Lublin is a big city and no one asked the couple who they were or checked whether Ezriel's wife went to the ritual bath. Thus the pair lived for several years together, indulging themselves to their hearts' desire. In Frampol and Tomaszów, the two missing husbands were sought for a time, but since they couldn't be found, it was assumed that they had gone off somewhere to the other side of the ocean. Both wives were adjudged deserted.

Zissel, known as Zissa, made friends with matrons and even maidens. They gave him advice on cooking, baking, sewing, darning, and embroidering. They also confided their womanly secrets to him. Zissel's beard had begun to sprout by now, but it was merely a fuzz. He plucked some of it, singed the rest, and from time to time committed the transgression of shaving. In order that the women shouldn't become suspicious, Zissel told them that he had stopped menstruating early, which was the reason he couldn't become pregnant. The comforted their poor sister, shed a tear over her fate, and kissed her. Zissel became so involved with his female cronies he often forgot what he was. He turned into an expert cook and prepared broths and groats for Ezriel and baked him delicious pastries. Each Friday he made the challah offering, said the benediction over the candles, went on the Sabbath to the women's section of the synagogue, as women must, and read the Pentateuch in Yiddish.

The money Zissel had stolen from his father-in-law was finally exhausted. Ezriel opened a store and at first it appeared that he might prosper, but he sat for days behind the counter and not a customer showed up. When one did come in, it was to demand goods at less than cost. No matter how Ezriel strained, he couldn't eke out a living. He developed wrinkles in his forehead and sprouted gray threads in his beard. He fell into debt. Things went so badly it came to pass that Zissel didn't have enough to celebrate the Sabbath properly, and he was forced to make Sabbath dinner without meat or pudding. On Fridays, he left pots of water boiling on the stove so that the neighbors would think that Sabbath dishes were cooking. Tears ran down his face. Following the Friday-night services, Ezriel came home from the synagogue in a patched gaberdine and a ratty fur hat. In a sorrowful voice he began to chant the hymn of greeting the angels and recite the "Woman of Virtue." Zissel had lit the candles and covered the table. He wore a Sabbath dress adorned with arabesques, slippers, white stockings, and a silk head kerchief. He gazed into a Yiddish prayer book. It was true that the two had broken the law, but they hadn't abandoned their faith in God and the Torah.

When the women who were fond of Zissa learned that Ezriel was on the verge of bankruptcy and that Zissa's pantry was empty, they began to seek means of helping the couple. They collected money and tried to give it to Ezriel, but he refused to accept it, as is the habit of the proud, who would rather suffer than hold out a hand for assistance. Zissel would have accepted the money, but Ezriel sternly forbade him to do so. When her friends saw that Zissa couldn't be helped with generosity, they offered suggestions—that Zissa peddle goods door to door; that, since she was so versed in studies, she become a rebbetzin who teaches girls to write a letter in Yiddish; that, being such a marvelous cook, she open a soup kitchen. It just so happened that the attendant at the local ritual bath died at this time, which seemed to Zissa's chums an omen that she had been fated to take the other's place. They went to the community leaders with this request, and when women persist they manage to get their way. At first Zissa refused to take the job, but Ezriel had to have someone support him. Zissa became the bath attendant.

In a ritual bathhouse, the attendant's work is to shave the women's heads, to trim their fingernails and toenails, to scrub and clean them before they immerse themselves. The attendant is also responsible for seeing to it that her charges immerse themselves completely, so that no part, even the shaved scalp, sticks out. The attendant also lets blood, applies leeches and cupping glasses. Because the women are on such intimate terms with the attendant, they reveal to her the most private matters about themselves, their husbands, and their families. It is therefore important that she be a person who can keep her lips sealed. She needs to be particularly skilled with brides, who are usually bashful and often frightened.

Well, it turned out that Zissa became the most adroit bath attendant in Lublin. The women loved it when she attended them and they gossiped with her. Zissa was especially gentle with brides. This was soon known, and they came from all over the city. Besides her wages Zissa received tips, and sometimes when the pair was rich a small percentage of the dowry. Ezriel could now sit around in idleness. He tried to pass time playing cards but this wasn't in his nature. Gradually, he turned into a glutton and a slugabed. He would wake in the middle of the night to eat a second supper. During the day he took naps under the feather bed. He became so lazy he even stopped going to services. He was not yet forty, but he had fallen into melancholy.

When Zissel came home from the ritual bath late at night, he tried to cheer Ezriel up with kind words and tales about the women, but instead of cheering him up he only depressed him further. Ezriel accused Zissel of having accepted his masculinity, of committing treacherous offenses against him. Sometimes the two wrangled all night and at times came to blows. The words they uttered during their outbursts and while making up astounded them.

One time an important wedding was held in Lublin. The bride was a ravishing virgin of seventeen, the daughter of a rich and distinguished family. The groom was a wealthy youth from Zamość. It was said that the groom would receive as a wedding present a silver Hanukkah lamp with stairs to climb for lighting the candles, it was so tall. Well, but the girl was shy and it came hard for her mother and sisters-in-law to introduce her into the ways of womanhood. Zissa was called in to study "The Pure Well" with the bride, and patiently to instruct her in her wifely duties. The bride quickly grew so attached to Zissa that she clung to her as to a sister. On the night before the wedding she came to immerse herself in the ritual bath where Zissa was the attendant. Zissa saw to it that the old habitués of the bath didn't tease the young bride or mock her, as they often did newcomers. It was the custom for musicians to escort the prospective bride to the ritual bath and to play for her on that special night.

When the bride—Reizl was her name—undressed and Zissel saw her dazzling flesh, what Ezriel most feared came to be. For the first time in his life Zissel felt desire for a woman. Soon desire turned to passion. He tried to conceal this from Ezriel but Ezriel was aware that a change had come over Zissel. Zissel now counted the days until Reizl would come to the bath again, and he fretted lest she promptly become pregnant and he would not see her until after the birth. When Reizl was there, Zissel devoted so much time to her that it aroused resentment among the other matrons. Reizl herself was perplexed by the bath attendant's attentiveness and suddenly she grew ashamed before her. As the Gemara says, "The person sees not, but his star sees," and so it was with Reizl.

One winter day a blizzard struck Lublin the like of which its oldest residents could not remember. Wind swept the snow from the gutters, heaped it in piles on roofs, pounded it against windows, howled around corners as if a thousand witches had hanged themselves. Chimneys collapsed, shutters were torn off, windowpanes were blown from their frames. Although ovens were heated and no wood was spared, the houses were almost as cold inside as outside. Women due to cleanse themselves after menstruation put off their visit to the ritual bath until the following day. Ezriel warned Zissel not to leave the house since demons were afoot outside, but Zissel replied that the bath attendant could not neglect her duties. One newly wed woman might want to use the bath. In fact, Zissel knew that Reizl was scheduled to come to the bath that evening.

Zissel wrapped himself up, took a stick in hand, and went outside, putting himself at God's mercy. The wind pushed and drove him along. Finally it lifted him and tossed him into a pile of snow. As he lay there, a sleigh drawn by a team of horses came by. Inside were Reizl and her husband, both wrapped in furs and covered with blankets. Reizl saw the plight of the bath attendant and called to the coachman to stop. In short, they rescued Zissel and revived him with spirits, and all three rode on to the bathhouse. Reizl's mother had begged her daughter not to risk her life by going out, but Reizl and her husband didn't want to lose a night. Her husband and the coachman went to the study house nearby to wait, and Reizl was turned over to Zissel's care.

That evening Reizl was the only woman in the bathhouse, and she was afraid of the dismal powers that hold sway over such places, but gradually Zissa calmed her, soaping and washing her gently and longer than was usual. From time to time the bath attendant kissed Reizl and addressed her in terms of endearment.

After Reizl had immersed herself and climbed the steps, ready for the bath attendant to wrap her in a towel sheet and dry her, Satan's voice rang in Zissel's ears: "Seize the while! Assail and defile!" The words had all the force bestowed upon the Tempter, and Zissel hurled himself at Reizl. For a moment Reizl was stricken dumb with terror. Then she erupted in violent screams, but there was no one to hear and come to her rescue. As they struggled they fell down the slippery steps into the water. Zissel tried to break loose from Reizl, but in her frenzy Reizl would not let go. Their heads soon sank to the bottom of the bath; only their feet showed on the surface of the water.

The coachman kept going from the study house to the sleigh to check on the horses, which stood covered with hides, and see if Reizl had come from the bath. The wind had stopped and the moon had emerged, pale as the face of a corpse after ablution, its light congealed upon the shrouds of the night.

According to the coachman's calculations, it was past time for Reizl to have come out, and he went to discuss her absence with her husband. After some deliberation, the men decided to go into the bath and see if anything could be wrong. They walked through the anteroom, calling Reizl's name. The echoes of their voices sounded as hollow as if they came from a ruin. They went on into the room where the ritual bath was located. Except for a single candle flickering in an earthen holder and reflected in the puddles on the stone floor, the place was empty. Suddenly the husband glanced down into the water and screamed. The coachman cried out in a terrible shout. They pulled the bodies from the water; Reizl and Zissel were both dead. The coachman rushed to alarm the people, and the neighborhood filled with commotion and turmoil. It happened that two members of the Burial Society were warming themselves in the study house. When they removed Zissa's body, a fresh tumult erupted. The secret was out that the bath attendant was male.

When the ruffians in a tavern close by realized the shameless farce Zissel had been playing, they seized whatever weapon they could find and ran to beat Ezriel. Ezriel was sitting wrapped in his caftan, searching his soul. It was cold in the house and the flame of the candle cast ominous shadows. Although he did not foresee that his end was at hand, he was consumed by gloom. Suddenly he heard violent voices, heavy steps on the stairs, the crashing in of his door. Before he could stand up, the crowd fell upon him. One man tore out half his beard, another snatched off his ritual garment, a third beat him with a cudgel. Soon his limp body fell forward upon his attackers.

Reizl had a funeral such as Lublin had never seen. Ezriel and Zissel were quickly put to rights and buried behind the fence late at night without anyone to follow their hearses or to say Kaddish. Only the gravedigger recited the passages which are said while the corpse is covered with earth. Oddly enough, like every housewife Zissel had put aside a little nest egg, which the members of the Burial Society found among the Passover dishes and used as payment for the cleansing and the plot.

The mound under which Ezriel and Zissel lay was soon overgrown with weeds. But one morning the cemetery watchman saw a board there with an inscription from the Second Book of Samuel: "Lovely and pleasant in their lives and in their deaths they were not divided." Who put the board up was never discovered. If the rains haven't washed it away, mold hasn't rotted it, wind hasn't broken it, the zealots haven't torn it out, it still stands there to this day.

Translated by Joseph Singer

The Psychic Journey

IT HAPPENED like this. I stood one hot day uptown on Broadway before a fenced-in plot of grass and began to throw food to the pigeons. The pigeons knew me, and ordinarily when they saw me with my bag of seed they surrounded me. The police had told me it was forbidden to feed pigeons outdoors, but that was as far as they went. One time a huge cop even came up to me and said, "Why is it everybody brings food for the pigeons and no one stops to think that they might need a drink? It hasn't rained in New York for weeks, and pigeons are dying of thirst." To hear this from a policeman was quite an experience! I went straight home and brought out a bowl of water, but half of it spilled in the elevator and the pigeons spilled the rest.

This day, on my way to the fenced-in plot I noticed the new issue of *The Unknown* at a newspaper stand and I bought a copy, since the magazine was snatched up in my neighborhood almost as soon as it appeared. For some reason, many readers on uptown Broadway are interested in telepathy, clairvoyance, psychokinesis, and the immortality of the soul.

For once, the pigeons did not crowd around me. I looked up and saw that a few steps away stood a woman who was also throwing out handfuls of grain. I started to laugh—under her arm she carried a copy of the new issue of *The Unknown*. Despite the hot summer day, she was wearing a black dress and a black, broad-brimmed hat. Her shoes and stockings were black. She must be a foreigner, I thought; no American would dress in such clothes in this weather, not even to attend a funeral. She raised her head and I saw a face that seemed young —or, at least, not old. She was lean and swarthy, with a narrow nose, a long chin, and thin lips.

I said, "Competition, eh?"

She smiled, showing long false teeth, but her black eyes remained stern. She said, "Don't worry, sir. There will be more pigeons. Enough for us both. Here they are now!" She pointed prophetically to the sky.

Yes, a whole flock was flying in from downtown. The plot

grew so full that the birds hopped and fluttered to force their way to the food. Pigeons, like Hasidim, enjoy jostling each other.

When our bags were emptied, we walked over to the litter can. "After you," I said, and I added, "I see we read the same magazine."

She replied in a deep voice and a foreign accent, "I've seen you often feeding the pigeons, and I want you to know that those who feed pigeons never know need. The few cents you spend on these lovely birds will bring you lots of luck."

"How can you be sure of that?"

She began to explain, and we walked away together. I invited her to have a drink with me and she said, "Gladly, but I don't drink alcoholic beverages, only fruit juices and vegetable juices."

"Come. Since you read *The Unknown*, you're one of my people."

"Yes, my greatest interest is in the occult. I read similar publications from England, Canada, Australia, India. I used to read them back in Hungary, where I come from, but today for believing in the higher powers over there you go to jail. Is there such a magazine in Hebrew?"

"Are you Jewish?"

"On my mother's side, but for me separate races and religions don't exist, only the one species of man. We lost the sources of our spiritual energy, and this has given rise to a disharmony in our psychic evolution. The divisions are the result. When we emit waves of brotherliness, reciprocal help, and peace, these vibrations create a sense of identification among all of God's creatures. You saw how the pigeons flew in. They congregate around the Central Savings Bank on Broadway and Seventy-third Street, which is too far for pigeons to see what's happening in the Eighties. But the cosmic consciousness within them is in perfect balance and therefore . . ."

We had gone into a coffee shop that was air-conditioned, and we sat down in a booth. She introduced herself as Margaret Fugazy.

"It's remarkable," she said. "I've observed that you always feed the pigeons at one o'clock when you go out for lunch, while I feed them in the mornings. I fed them as usual this morning. All of a sudden a voice ordered me to feed them again. Now, at six o'clock pigeons aren't particularly eager to eat. They're starting to adjust to their nightly rhythm. The days are growing shorter and we're in another constellation of the solar cycle. But when a voice repeats the same admonition over and over, this is a message from the world powers. I came out and found you too about to feed the pigeons. How is it you were late?"

"I also heard a voice."

"Are you psychic?"

"I was only fooling."

"You mustn't fool about such things!"

After three-quarters of an hour, I had heard a lot of particulars. Margaret Fugazy had come to the United States in the nineteen-fifties. Her father had been a doctor; her parents were no longer living. Here in New York she had grown close to a woman who was past ninety, a medium, and half blind. They had lived together for a time. The old lady had died at the age of a hundred and two, and now Margaret supported herself by giving courses in Yoga, concentration, mind stimulation, bio-rhythm, awareness, and the I Am.

She said, "I watched you feeding the pigeons a long time before I learned that you're a writer and a vegetarian. I started reading you. This led to a telepathic communication between us, even if it has been one-sided. I went so far as to visit you at home several times—not physically but in astral form. I would have liked to catch your attention, but you were sound asleep. I leave my body usually around dawn. I found you awake only once and you spoke to me about the mysteries of the cabala. When I had to go back I gave you a kiss."

"You know my address?"

"The astral body has no need for addresses!"

Neither of us spoke for a time. Then Margaret said, "You might give me your phone number. These astral visits involve terrible dangers. If the silver cord should break, then—"

She didn't finish, apparently in fear of her own words.

2

On my way home at one o'clock that morning, I told myself I could not risk getting mixed up with Margaret Fugazy. My stomach hurt from the soybeans, raw carrots, molasses, sunflower seeds, and celery juice she had served me for supper. My head ached from her advice on how to avoid spiritual tension, how to control dreams, and how to send out alpha rays of relaxation and beta rays of intellectual activity and theta rays of trance. It's all Dora's fault, I brooded. If she hadn't left me and run off to the kibbutz where her daughter Sandra was having her first baby, I'd be together with her now in a hotel in pollen-free Bethlehem, New Hampshire, instead of suffering from hay fever in polluted New York. True, Dora had begged me to accompany her to Israel, but I had no intention of sitting in some forsaken kibbutz near the Syrian border waiting for Sandra to give birth.

I was afraid walking the few blocks from Columbus Avenue and Ninety-sixth Street to my studio apartment in the West Eighties, but no taxi would stop for me. Riding up in the elevator, I was assailed by fears. Maybe I had been burglarized while I was away? Maybe out of spite for not finding any money or jewelry the thieves had torn up my manuscripts? I opened the door and was struck by a wave of heat. I had neglected to lower the venetian blinds and the sun had baked the apartment all day. No one had cleaned here since Dora left, and the dust started me sneezing. I undressed and lay down, but I couldn't fall asleep. My nose was stuffed up, my throat scratchy, and my ears full of water. My anger at Dora grew, and in fantasy I worked out all kinds of revenges against her. Maybe marry this Hungarian miracle worker and send Dora a cable announcing the good tidings.

Day was dawning by the time I dropped off. I was wakened by the phone ringing. The clock on the bedside table showed twenty past ten. I picked up the receiver and grunted, *"Nu?"*

I heard a deep female voice. "I woke you, eh? It's Margaret, Margaret Fugazy. Morris—may I call you Morris?"

"You can even call me Potiphar."

"Oh, listen to him! What I want to say is that this morning a sign has been given that our meeting yesterday wasn't simply some coincidence but an act of fate, ordained and executed by the hand of Providence. First let me tell you that after you left me I was deeply worried about you. You promised me to take a cab but I knew—don't ask me how—that you didn't. Just before daybreak I found myself in your apartment again. What a mess. The dust! And when I saw your pale face and heard your choked breathing I decided that you absolutely cannot remain in the city. On the other hand, it would not be good that our relationship should start off with a long separation. Well, early this morning an old friend of mine called—Lily Wolfner, also a Hungarian. I hadn't heard from her in over a year, but last night before going to sleep I suddenly thought about her and this to me is always a signal I will soon be hearing from that individual. Precisely at nine my phone rang, and I was so sure I answered with 'Hello, Lily.' Lily Wolfner is a travel agent. She arranges tours to Europe, Africa, Japan, and Israel, too. Her tours always have a cultural program. The guides are psychologists, psychiatrists, writers, artists, rabbis. I was twice the guide of such tours interested in psychic research, and some other time I'll tell you of my remarkable experiences with them.

"I said, 'Lily, what made you think of me?' and she told me she had a group that wanted to combine a visit to the State of Israel on the High Holidays with an advanced course in awareness. She offered me the job as guide. I don't remember how, but I mentioned your name to her and the fact that you had promised to give me an esoteric insight into the cabala. I beg you, don't interrupt me. As soon as she heard your name, she became simply hysterical. 'What? He really exists? He lives right here in New York City and you had supper with him?' I'll cut it short—she proposed that we both be guides for this tour. She'll accede to your every demand. These are rich women, many of them probably your readers. I told her I'd speak with you, but first she had to check with the women. A half hour didn't go by when she called me back. She had already reached her clients and they were as excited by the idea as she was. My dear, one would have to be blind not to see the hand of destiny in all this. Lily is a businesswoman, not some mystic, but she told me that you and I together would make a fantastic pair! I want you to know that in the past months I've faced deep crisis in my life—spiritual, physical, financial. I was closer to suicide than you can imagine. When I came up next to you yesterday, I knew somehow that my life was in your hands, strange as this may sound. I beg you therefore and plead on my knees—don't say no, because this would be my death sentence. Literally."

Margaret had not let me get a word in edgewise. I wanted to tell her that I wasn't a specialist in the cabala and that I had no urge to wander around Israel with a flock of women who would try to combine sightseeing with mysticism, but somehow I hesitated, bewildered by my own weakness.

Margaret exclaimed, "Morris, wait for me. I'm coming to you!"

"Astrally?" I asked.

"Cynic! With my body and soul!"

3

Who said it—perhaps no one: every person's drama is a melodrama. I both performed in this melodrama and observed it as a spectator.

I sat in an air-conditioned bus speeding from Haifa to Tel Aviv. We had spent Rosh Hashanah in Jerusalem. We had visited Sodom, Elath, Safad, the occupied regions around the Suez Canal and the Golan Heights, a number of kibbutzim. Wherever we stopped, I lectured about the cabala and Margaret gave advice on love, health, and business; on how to use the subconscious for buying stocks, betting on horses, finding jobs, husbands; on how to meditate. She spoke about the delta of the brain waves and the resonance of the Tantrist personality, the dimensions of the Shambala and the panorama of cybertronic evocations. She conducted astrochemical analyses, showed how to locate the third eye, the pineal eye, revealed the mysteries of Lemuria and Mt. Shasta. I attended séances at which she hypnotized the ladies, most of whom went to sleep—or at least pretended to. She swore that my mother had revealed herself to her and urged her to keep an eye on me; I had been born a Sagittarian and a Scorpio might start a fatal conflict with me.

I was enmeshed in a situation that made me ashamed of

myself. Thank God, until now I hadn't met Dora or anyone else I knew, but the tour was to be in Israel almost another full week. It could easily happen that someone might recognize me. Also, the group had become quarrelsome—disappointed in the hotels, the meals, the merchandise for sale in the gift shops—and increasingly critical of its guides. Many had turned cool toward Margaret and her lessons, and their enthusiasm for the cabala had diminished. One woman suggested that my interpretation of the cabala was too subjective and was actually a kind of poetic hodgepodge.

According to schedule, we were to stop over a few days in Tel Aviv to give the women time to shop. They would observe Yom Kippur in Jerusalem and on the next day fly from Lod Airport for America. I had intended to surprise Dora at the end of the tour, and before leaving New York I had demanded from Lily Wolfner an open ticket so that I would not have to return with the group. I told her I had some literary business to take care of in Israel. To avoid complications, I had not mentioned this to Margaret.

Following breakfast on the day before the group was to go to Jerusalem to pray at the Wailing Wall, I had to reveal my secret. I wanted to remain in Tel Aviv for the holiday, at the very hotel where we were now registered. I was weary from the constant traveling and the company of others, and I yearned for a day by myself.

I had been prepared for resentment, but not for the scene that Margaret kicked up. She wept, accused Lily Wolfner and me of hatching a plot against her, and threatened me with retributions by the higher powers. A mighty catastrophe would befall me for my duplicity.

Suddenly she cried, "If you stay in Tel Aviv I'm staying, too! I don't have to pray at the holy places on Yom Kippur. My job is finished as much as yours is!"

"You must go along with the group; otherwise you'll forfeit your ticket," I pointed out to her.

"The morning after Yom Kippur I'll take a taxi to Lod straight from here."

When the women heard that their two guides would be in Tel Aviv for Yom Kippur, they made sarcastic remarks, but there was no time for lengthy explanations; the bus was waiting in front of the hotel. Margaret assured the women that she would meet them at the airport early on the day after Yom Kippur, and she saw them off. I was too embarrassed even to apologize. I had done damage not only to my own prestige but to the cabala's as well.

Afterward, I showed Margaret my contract, which stated that my job had ended the night before; I had every right to stay on in Israel for as long as I wanted.

Margaret refused to look at it. "You've got some female here," she pronounced, "but your plans will come to naught!" She pointed a finger at me, mumbled, and I sensed that she was trying to bring the powers of evil down upon me. Baffled by my own superstition, I tried to soothe her with promises, but she told me she had lost all trust in me and called me vile names. When she finally went off to unpack her things, I used the time trying to call the kibbutz near the Golan Heights where Dora was staying. I wasn't able to make the connection.

So many guests had gone to Jerusalem that no preparations for the pre-holiday feast were being made at the hotel. Margaret and I had to find a restaurant. Although I am not a synagogue-goer, I do fast on Yom Kippur.

"I will fast with you," Margaret announced when I told her. "If God has chosen to castigate me with such humiliations, I have surely sinned grievously."

"You say you're half a Gentile, yet you carry on like a complete yenta," I chided her.

"I'm more Jewish in my smallest fingernail than you are in your whole being."

We had in mind to buy provisions to fill up on before commencing our fast, but by the time we finished lunch the stores were closed. The streets were deserted. Even the American Embassy, which stood not far from the hotel, appeared festively silent. Margaret came into my room and we went onto the balcony to gaze out to sea. The sun bowed to the west. The beach was empty. Large birds I had never seen before walked on the sand. Whatever intimacy had existed between Margaret and me had been severed; we were like a married couple that has already decided on a divorce. We leaned away from each other as we watched the setting sun cast fiery nets across the waves.

Margaret's swarthy face grew brick-red, and her black eyes exuded the melancholy of those who estrange themselves from their own environment and can never be at home in another. She said, "The air here is full of ghosts."

4

That evening we stayed up late over the Ouija board, which told one woeful prophecy after another. From sheer boredom, or perhaps once and for all to end our false relationship, I confessed to Margaret the truth about Dora. She was too weary to make a scene all over again.

The next morning we went for a walk—along Ben-Yehuda Street; on Rothschild Boulevard. We considered going into a synagogue, but those we passed were packed with worshippers. Men stood outside in their prayer shawls. Around ten o'clock we returned to the hotel. We had talked ourselves out, and I lay down to read a book on Houdini, who I had always considered possessed mysterious powers despite the fact that he opposed the spiritists. Margaret sat at the table and dealt tarot cards. From time to time she arched her brows and gave me a dismal look. Then she said that because of my treachery she had had no sleep the night before, and she left to go to her room. She warned me not to disturb her.

In the middle of the day I heard a long-drawn-out siren, and I wondered at the military's conducting tests on Yom Kippur. I had had nothing to eat since two the afternoon before and I was hungry. I read, napped, and indulged in a bit of Day of Atonement introspection. All my life I had chased after pleasure, but my sweethearts became too serious and acquired the bitterness of neglected wives. This last journey had degraded and exhausted me. Not even my hay fever had been alleviated.

I fell asleep and wakened after the sun had set. According to my reckoning, the Jews in the synagogues would be concluding the services. One star appeared in the sky and soon a second and then a third, when it is permitted to break the fast. The door opened and Margaret slithered in like a phantom. We had fasted not twenty-four hours but thirty. Margaret looked haggard. We took the elevator down. The lobby was half dark, the glass door at the entrance covered by a black sheet. Behind the desk sat an elderly man who didn't look like a hotel employee. He was reading an old Yiddish newspaper. I went over to him and asked, "Why is it so quiet?"

He looked up with annoyance. "What do you want—that there should be dancing?"

"Why is it so dark?"

The man scratched his beard. "Are you playing dumb or what? The country is at war."

He explained. The Egyptians had crossed the Suez Canal, the Syrians had invaded the Golan Heights. Margaret must have understood some Yiddish, for she cried, "I knew it! The punishment!"

I opened the front door and we went out. Yarkon Street lay wrapped in darkness; every window was draped in sheets. Far from the usual gay end of Yom Kippur in Tel Aviv, when restaurants and movie houses are jammed, it was more like the night of the Ninth Day of Ab in some Polish shtetl. Headlights of the few cars that moved by slowly were either turned off or covered with blue paint. We walked the few steps to Ben-Yehuda Street hoping to buy food, but the stores were closed. We went back to my room and Margaret discovered a radio set into the night table. The news was all of war; civilian communication had been suspended. The armed forces had been mobilized. The broadcaster appealed to the people not to give in to panic. I found a bag of cookies and two apples in my valise, and Margaret and I broke our fast. Margaret had engaged a taxi to take her to Lod Airport at five this coming morning, but would the taxi come? And would there be a plane leaving for America? Based on the news from the Golan front, I had a feeling that the kibbutz where Dora was now lay in Arab hands. Who knew if Dora was alive? There was a possibility that the Syrians or Egyptians would reach Tel Aviv tomorrow. Margaret urged me to go with her to Lod if the taxi showed up, but I wasn't about to while away my days and nights at an airport where thousands of tourists would have congregated from every corner of the land.

Margaret asked, "And to perish here would be better?"

"Yes, better."

We listened to the radio until two o'clock. Margaret seemed to be more shocked by what she called my base conspiracy than by the war. Her only comfort, she told me, was the fact that she had known it in the depths of her soul. She now forecast that Dora and I would never meet again. She even maintained that this war was one of the calamities Providence had prepared for me. Since time is an illusion and all events are predetermined, she argued, judgment often precedes the transgression. Her life was filled with examples—enemies prevented from accomplishing their evil aims by circumstances her guardian angel had arranged months or years in advance. Those who did succeed in hurting her were later killed, maimed, or afflicted with insanity. Before going to her room, Margaret said she would pray that I be forgiven. She kissed me good night. She hinted that though the Day of Atonement was over, the doors of repentance were left open to me.

I had fallen into a deep sleep. I opened my eyes as someone shook my shoulder. It was dark, and for a moment I didn't know where I was or who was waking me.

I heard Margaret say in a solemn voice, "The taxi is here!"

"What taxi? Oh!"

"Come with me!"

"No, Margaret, I'm staying here."

"In that case, be well. Forgive me!"

She kissed me with rusty lips. Her breath smelled of the fast. She closed the door behind her and I knew that we had parted forever. Only after she had gone did I realize the motives behind my decision. I didn't have a reservation, as she had, but an open ticket. Besides, I had told the women of the tour that I would be staying on; it would not be right in their eyes or mine to flee like a coward. Once, Dora and I had toyed with the notion that we were stranded together on a sinking ship. The other passengers screamed, wept, and fought to get to the lifeboats, but she and I lingered in the dining hall with a bottle of wine. We would relish our happiness and go under rather than push, scramble, and beg for a bit of life. Now this fantasy had assumed a tinge of reality.

It was dawn. The sun had not yet risen, but several men and women were performing calisthenics on the beach. In the dim light they looked like shadows. I wanted to laugh at these optimists who were developing their muscles on the day before their deaths.

I thrust my hand into the pocket of my jacket hanging on the chair and tapped my passport and traveler's checks. I had had no special reason to bring along a large amount of money, but I had—more than two thousand dollars in traveler's checks and a bankbook besides. No one had stolen them, and I went back to bed to catch up on my sleep. I had a number of acquaintances in Tel Aviv and some who could even be described as friends, but I was determined to show myself to nobody. What could I say I was doing here? When had I arrived? It would only entangle me in new lies. I turned on the radio. The enemy was advancing and our casualties were severe. Other Arab nations were preparing to invade.

I tried again to put through a call to Dora's kibbutz and was told that this was impossible. The fact that the telephone and electricity were working and that there was hot water in the bathroom seemed incredible.

I rode in the elevator down to the lobby. The day before, it had been my impression that the hotel was empty, but here were men and women conversing among themselves in English. All the male employees of the hotel had been called up and their places had been taken by women. Breakfast was being served in the dining room. Bakeries had baked rolls during the night—they were still warm from the oven. I ordered an omelette, and the waitress who brought it to me said, "Eat as long as the food is there." Even though the day was bright, I imagined that layers of shadows were falling from above as at the beginning of a solar eclipse. I did not approach the other Americans. I had no urge to speak to them or listen to their comments. Besides, they talked so loudly I could hear them anyhow—at Lod Airport, they were saying, people hovered outside with their luggage and no help was available. I could see Margaret among them, murmuring spells, conjuring up the spirits of revenge.

After breakfast I strolled along Ben-Yehuda Street. Trucks full of soldiers roared by. A man with a white beard, wearing a long coat and a rabbinical hat, carried a palm branch and a citron for the Succoth holiday. Another old man struggled to erect a Succoth on a balcony. Emaciated newspapers had been printed during the night. I bought one, took a table at a sidewalk café, and ordered cake with coffee. All my life I had

considered myself timid. I was constantly burdened with worries. I was sure that if I were in New York now reading about
what was happening in Israel I would be overcome by anxiety.
But everything within me was calm. Overnight I had been
transformed into a fatalist. I had brought sleeping pills from
America; I also had razor blades I could use to slit my wrists
should this situation become desperate. Meanwhile, I nibbled
at the cake and drank the thick coffee. A pigeon came up to
my chair and I threw it a crumb. This was a Holy Land pigeon
—small, brown, slight. It nodded its tiny head as if it were as-
senting to a truth as old as the very land: If it is fated to live,
you live, and if it is fated to die, it's no misfortune, either. Is
there such a thing as death? This is something invented by human cowardice.

The day passed in walking aimlessly, reading the book about
Houdini, sleeping. The supermarket on Ben-Yehuda Street
had opened and was crowded with customers. Waiting lines
stretched outside; housewives were buying up everything in
sight. But I was able to get stale bread, cheese, and unripe fruit
in the smaller stores. During the day, peace seemed to reign,
but at night the war returned. Again the city was dark, its
streets empty. At the hotel, guests sat in the bar watching television in tense silence. The danger was far from over.

About eleven I rode up to my room and went out onto the
balcony. The sea swayed, foamed, purred the muffled growl of
a lion that is sated briefly but may grow ferocious any moment.
Military jets roared by. The stars seemed ominously near. A
cool breeze was blowing. It smelled of tar, sulphur, and Biblical battles that time had never ended. They were all still here,
the hosts of Edom and Amalek, Gog and Magog, Ammon and
Moab—the lords of Esau and the priests of Baal—waging the
eternal war of the idolators against God and the seed of Jacob.
I could hear the clanging of their swords and the din of their
chariots. I sat down in a wicker chair and breathed the acrid
scent of eternity.

Sirens wailing a long and breathless warning wakened me
from a doze. The sound was like the blast of a thousand rams'
horns, but I knew that the hotel had no shelter. If bombs fell
on this building there would be no rescue. The door to my

room opened by itself. I went in and sat on my bed, ready to live, ready to die.

5

Eight days later, I flew back to the United States. The following week Dora arrived. How strange, but on Yom Kippur Dora had escaped with her daughter and the newborn baby to Tel Aviv, and they had stayed in a hotel on Allenby Road only a few blocks from my hotel. The circumcision had been performed the day before Succoth. I told Dora that I had spent a few weeks as writer-in-residence at some college in California. Dora had the habit of questioning me closely whenever I returned from a trip, probing for contradictions. She believed that my lectures were nothing but a means to meet other women and deceive her. This time she accepted my words without suspicion.

I went back to feeding the pigeons every day, but I never met Margaret. She neither called nor wrote, and as far as I knew she did not visit me astrally.

Then one day in December when I was walking with Dora on Amsterdam Avenue—she was looking for a secondhand bookcase—a young man pushed a leaflet into my hand. Although it was cold and snow was falling, he was coatless and hatless and his shirt collar was open. He looked Spanish to me or Puerto Rican. Usually I refuse to accept such leaflets. But there was something in the young man's appearance that made me take the wet paper—an expression of ardor in his black eyes. This was not just a hired distributor of leaflets but a believer in a cause. I stopped and glanced down to see the name Margaret Fugazy in large letters above her picture as she might have looked twenty years ago. "Are you lovelorn?" I read. "Have you lost a near and dear relative? Are you sick? Do you have business trouble, family trouble? Are you in an inextricable dilemma? Come and see Madame Margaret Fugazy, because she is the only one who can help you. Madame Margaret Fugazy, the famous medium, has studied yoga in India, the cabala in Jerusalem, specializes in ESP, subliminal prayers, Yahweh power, UFO mysteries, self-hypnosis, cosmic wisdom, spiritual healing, and reincarnation. All consultations private. Results guaranteed. Introductory reading $2."

Dora pulled my sleeve. "Why did you stop? Throw it away."

"Wait, Dora. Where has he gone?" I looked around. The young man had disappeared. Was he waiting just for me?

Dora asked, "Why are you so interested? Who is Margaret Fugazy? Do you know her?"

"Yes, I do," I answered, not understanding why.

"Who is she—one of your witches?"

"Yes, a witch."

"How do you know her? Did you fly with her to a Black Mass on a broomstick?"

"You remember Yom Kippur when you went to the Golan kibbutz? While you were there I flew with her to Jerusalem, to Safad, to Rachel's Tomb, and we studied the cabala together," I said.

Dora was used to my playful chatter and absurdities. She chimed in, "Is that so? What else?"

"When the war broke out the witch got frightened and flew away."

"She left you alone, eh?"

"Yes, alone."

"Why didn't you come to me? I am something of a witch myself."

"You too had vanished."

"You poor boy. Abandoned by all your witches. But you can get her back. She advertises. Isn't that a miracle?"

We stood there pondering. The snow fell dry and heavy. It hit my face like hail. Dora's dark coat turned white. A single pigeon tried to fly, flapping its wings but falling back. Then Dora said, "That young man seemed strange. He must be a sorcerer. And all this for two dollars! Come, let's go home—by subway, not by psychic journey."

Translated by Joseph Singer

Elka and Meir

ON THE NIGHTS that Meir Bontz could allow himself to sleep, his head would hit the pillow like a stone and, if undisturbed, he could pound away for twelve hours straight. But this night he awoke at dawn. His eyelids popped open and he could not close them again. His big, burly body heaved and jerked. He felt overcome with passion and worry. Meir Bontz was hardly a timid man. In his youth he had been a thief and a safecracker. In the thieves' den where the toughs congregated, he demonstrated his strength. None of them could bend his arm. Meir would often bet on his capacity for food and drink. He could put away half a goose and wash it down with a dozen mugs of beer. On the rare occasions that he was arrested, he would snap his handcuffs or smash the door of the patrol wagon.

After he married and was given a job at the Warsaw Benevolent Burial Society, which provided shrouds and burial plots for the indigent dead, Meir Bontz went straight. He received a salary of twenty rubles a week so long as the Russians ruled Poland, and later, when the Germans came in, a comparable sum in marks. He stopped associating with thieves, fences, and pimps. He had fallen in love with a beauty, Beilka Litvak, a cook in a wealthy house on Marszalkowska Street. But with time he perceived that he had made a mistake in his marriage. For one thing, Beilka didn't become pregnant. For another, she spat blood. For a third, he could never get used to her pronunciation—"Pig Litvak," he called it. She lost her looks as well. When she got angry, she cursed him with oaths the like of which he had never heard. She could read, and each day she read the serialized novels in the Yiddish newspaper about duped ladies, scheming counts, and seduced orphans. During meals, Meir Bontz liked to listen to the gramophone play theater melodies, duets, and cantorial pieces, but Beilka complained that the gramophone gave her a headache. A quarrel would often break out on Friday evening just because Meir liked his gefilte fish prepared with sugar as his dead mother used to fix it, and Beilka prepared it with pepper. The few

times that Meir hit her, Beilka fainted, and Zeitag the healer or
Dr. Kniaster had to be called.

He would have run away from Warsaw if God hadn't sent
along Red Elka. It was Red Elka's job in the Society to look
after the female corpses, sew their shrouds, and wash them on
the ablution board. Red Elka had no luck. She had trapped
herself in a union with a sick husband who was surly and half
crazy to boot. In addition, he turned out to be lazy. His name
was Yontche. He was a bookbinder by trade. On Bloody Wednesday, in 1905, when the Cossacks killed dozens of revolutionaries who had converged on the town hall to demand a
constitution from the czar, Yontche caught a bullet in the
spine. Afterward, he had a kidney removed in the hospital on
Czysta Street, and he never completely recovered. Elka had
two children by him, both of whom died of scarlet fever. Although Elka had already passed forty—she was three years
older than Meir—she still looked like a girl. Her red hair cut in
a Dutch bob didn't have a gray strand in it. Elka was small and
slim. Her eyes were green, her nose beaklike, her cheeks red as
apples. Elka's power lay in her mouth. When she laughed, you
could hear her halfway down the street. When she abused
somebody, words and phrases shot from her sharp tongue
until you didn't know whether to laugh or cry. Elka had strong
teeth, and in a fight she would bite like a bitch.

When Elka first came to the Society and Meir Bontz observed her antics, he was frightened of her. She bantered with
the dead as if they were still alive. "Lie quiet there, hush!" she
would admonish a corpse. "Don't play any of your tricks. We'll
pack you in a shipping crate and send you off. You danced
away your few years and now it's time to go nighty-night."

Once, Meir saw Elka take a cigarette from her mouth and
stick it between a corpse's lips. Meir told her that one must not
do such things. "Don't fret your head about it," she said. "I'll
get so many whippings in Gehenna anyhow, it'll only mean
one lash more." And she slapped her own buttock.

It wasn't long before Meir Bontz fell in love with Elka, with
a passion he would not have thought possible. He yearned for
her even when they were together. He could never get enough
of her spicy talk.

As a boy, and even later, Meir Bontz had often boasted that

he would never be tied to a woman's apron strings. When a wench started to play hard to get or to nag him, he would tell her to go to blazes. He used to say that in the dark all cats are gray. But he couldn't resist Elka. She made fun of his size and bulk, his enormous appetite, his huge feet, his rumbling voice—all in good nature. She called him "buffalo," "bear," "bull." Playfully, she tried to plait braids in his mop of bristly hair, as Delilah had done to Samson. It wasn't easy for Meir and Elka to have the time with each other they wanted. He couldn't come to her house or she to his. They tried to seek out rooms where you could spend the night without registering. Often they couldn't even do this; before they left their houses they would be summoned to the scene of a tragedy—someone had been run over, or had hanged himself, or jumped out of a window, or been burned to death. In such cases autopsies were demanded by the police, who had to be outwitted or bribed, since autopsies were against Jewish law. Red Elka always found a way. She spoke Russian and Polish, and after the Germans occupied Warsaw in 1915 she learned to converse with their policemen in German-Yiddish. She would flirt with the krauts and skillfully slip banknotes into their pockets.

Red Elka eventually managed it so that Meir Bontz became her assistant and her coachman, and later her chauffeur. The Society had acquired a car that was dispatched to bring in corpses from the outskirts and the resort towns on the Otwock line, and Meir learned to drive. Sometimes the couple had to ride at night through fields and forests, and this provided them the best opportunity to make love. Red Elka would sit beside Meir and with the eyes of a hawk search out a spot where they could lie down undisturbed. She would say, "The corpse will have to wait. What's his hurry? The grave won't go sour."

Elka smoked as Meir kissed her and at times even as she gave herself to him. Her time for childbearing had passed, but lust had grown within her over the years. When Meir Bontz was with her, he wanted to forget that he worked for a burial society, but Elka wouldn't let him forget. She would say, "Oy, Meir, when you kick the bucket what a heavy corpse you'll be! You'll need eight sets of pallbearers."

"Shut your yap!"

"You're trembling, eh? No one can avoid it."

Red Elka developed such power over Meir that things which had once seemed repellent now attracted him. He used her expressions, began smoking her brand of cigarettes, and ate only her favorite dishes. Elka never got drunk, but after a drink she became more flippant than ever. She blasphemed, made fun of the Angel of Death, the destroying demons, of Gehenna, and the saints in Heaven. One time Meir heard her say to a corpse, "Don't fret, corpse, rest in peace. You left your wife a pretty dowry and your successor will be in clover with her." And she gave the dead man a tickle under the armpit.

It wasn't Meir Bontz's way to think too much. As soon as he started to concentrate, his brain would cloud over and he'd get sleepy. He realized well enough that Elka's conduct toward the dead came from some idiotic urge stuck in her mind like a wedge, but he reminded himself that every woman he had known had had her peculiarities. Meir had even had one who ordered him to beat her with a strap and spit on her. During his few stays in prison, he heard stories from other convicts that made his hair stand on end.

Well, since he had commenced his affair with Elka, thoughts assailed Meir like locusts. Tonight, he slept at home—he in one bed and Beilka in the other. He had slept several hours when suddenly he awoke with the anxiety of one who has fallen into a dilemma. Beilka snored, whistled through her nose, sighed. Meir had proposed a divorce—he offered to go on supporting her—but Beilka refused. In the dark, he could see only Elka before his eyes. She joked with him and called him outlandish names. Elka was far from virtuous. For years she had worked in a brothel on Grzybowska Street. She had undoubtedly had more men in her life than Meir had hairs on his head. She had enjoyed a passionate affair with a panderer, Leibele Marvicher, who had been stabbed to death by Blind Feivel. Elka still cried when she talked about this pimp. Just the same, Meir was ready to marry her if she was free from Yontche. Someone had told him that in America there were private funeral parlors and one could get rich there from operating such an enterprise. Meir had a fantasy: he and Elka went to America and opened a funeral parlor. Yontche the consumptive died, and Meir got rid of Beilka. In the New Land no one knew of his criminal activities or of Elka's whoring. The whole day they would be busy with the corpses, and in the evenings they would go to the theater. Meir would become a member of a rich synagogue. They had sons and daughters and lived in their own house. The wealthiest corpses in all New York were brought to their funeral parlor. A wild notion flashed through Meir's brain—they did not have to wait. He could make away with Beilka in half a minute; all he had to do was give her throat one squeeze. Elka could slip Yontche a pill. Since they were both sick anyhow, what difference did it make if they went a year sooner or a year later?

A fear fell over Meir from his own thoughts, and he began to grunt and scratch. He sat up with such force that the bed springs squealed.

Beilka awoke. "Why are you squirming around like a snake? Let me sleep!"

"Sleep, Litvak pig."

"You've got the itch, have you? So long as I breathe she'll never be your wife. A tart is what she'll stay, a slut, a tramp, a whore from 6 Krochmalna Street, may she burn like a fire, dear Father in Heaven!"

"Shut up, or you're a dead one on the spot!"

"You want to kill me, eh? Take a knife and stab away. Compared to this life, death would be Paradise." Beilka began to cough, cry, spit.

Meir got out of bed. He knew that Elka had wallowed in a brothel on Grzybowska Street, but 6 Krochmalna Street was news to him. Apparently Beilka knew more about Elka than he did. He was overcome with rage and a need to shout, to drag Beilka around by her hair. He knew the brothel at 6 Krochmalna—a windowless cellar, a living grave. *No, it couldn't be—she's making it up.* He felt about to retch.

The years passed, and Meir Bontz didn't rightly know where. Beilka suffered one hemorrhage after another, and he had to put her in a sanatorium in Otwock. The doctors said that she wasn't long for the world, but somehow there in the fresh air they kept her soul flickering. Meir had to pay her expenses. He now had the apartment to himself, and Elka was free to come to him. Elka's husband, Yontche, ailed at home.

But the lovers didn't have the time to be together. After the war broke out on that day of Ab in 1914, the shootings, stabbings, and suicides multiplied. Refugees converged upon the city from half of Poland. The black car was constantly in use collecting corpses. Meir and Elka could seldom give up an hour to pleasure. Their affair consisted of talk, kisses, plans. When the Germans occupied Warsaw, hunger and typhus emptied whole buildings. Still, Elka lost none of her light-mindedness. Death remained a joke to her—an opportunity to revile God and man, to repeat over and over that life hung on a hair, that hopes were spiderwebs, that all the promises about the world to come, the Messiah, and Resurrection were lies, and that whatever wasn't seized now was lost forever. But to seize you needed time. Elka would complain, "You'll see, Meir, we won't even have time to die."

Elka had almost stopped eating. She nibbled on a cookie, a sausage, a bar of chocolate. She drank vodka and smoked. Meir got along on uncooked food. In the middle of the night the telephone would ring and they would be summoned to police headquarters, to the Jewish Hospital on Czysta Street, to the Hospital for Epidemic Diseases on Pokorna Street, to the morgue. They no longer even took off Sabbaths and holidays. The other employees of the Society got summer vacations, but no one could or would substitute for Elka or Meir. They were the only ones who had established connections with the police, the civil authorities, the military, the officials of the Gesia and the Praga Cemeteries.

Meir's apartment had grown dusty and neglected. Plaster fell from the walls. Since tenants had stopped paying rent, landlords had ceased making repairs. Pipes that burst from the frosts were not fixed. Toilets became clogged. On the rare occasions Elka prepared to spend the night at Meir's, she tried to straighten up, but the telephone always interrupted her. The couple was called in to attend victims of shootings, of fires, of heart attacks in the street. As the telephone rang, Elka would exclaim, "Congratulations. It's the Angel of Death!" And before Meir could ask what had happened she would be throwing on her clothes.

In Russia, the czar had abdicated. The Germans had begun to suffer setbacks at the front. Somehow Poland had become independent, but this didn't slow the sickness and deaths. For a short time peace prevailed; then the Bolsheviks invaded Poland, and once again refugees from the provinces invaded Warsaw. In the towns they captured, the Bolsheviks shot rabbis and wealthy men. The Poles hanged Communists. Elka's husband, Yontche, died, but Elka didn't observe shivah. Meir couldn't read or write, and she was needed to read documents, to sign papers, and mark down names and addresses. Because the two worked long hours, they earned a lot of money, but inflation had made it worthless. The several hundred rubles Meir had saved up for a rainy day were now worthless and lay in an open drawer—no thief would bother to touch them. Elka had bought jewelry, but she had no opportunity to wear it. When Meir asked one time why she didn't put on her trinkets, she said "When? You'll place them in the pockets of my shrouds." She was referring to the proverb that shrouds have no pockets.

Meir had long since gathered that Elka didn't only make fun of other corpses—her own death too seemed to her a game, a jest, or the Devil knew what. Meir disliked talking of death, but Elka brought up at every opportunity that what she was doing would undoubtedly be done to her. She had already arranged for a plot at the Gesia Cemetery—the Society had given her a bargain on it. She had made Meir vow that when he died he would be put to rest not next to Beilka but next to her, Elka. Meir would often lose his temper at her: she was just beginning to live; what kind of talk was this?

But Elka would counter, "You're scared, eh, Meirl? No one knows what his tomorrow will be. Death doesn't look at the calendar." Everyone in her family had died young—her father, her mother, her sister Reitza, her brother Chaim Fishl. How was she any better than the others?

Meir received a phone call from Otwock telling him that Beilka had died. She had eaten breakfast that morning as on any other day. She had even tried reading the novel in the Yiddish newspaper, but at lunchtime when the nurse came to take her temperature she found Beilka dead. Meir wanted to go to Otwock by himself, but Elka insisted she come with him. As always, she got her way. Since Meir had arranged for a plot for himself next to Elka, Beilka was buried in Karczew, a village near Otwock. Although the women of the Karczew Burial Society considered this a sacrilege, Elka fussed over Beilka's body, washed her with an egg yolk, and sewed her shrouds.

She shouted down into Beilka's grave, "We will come to you, not you to us. May you intercede for us on High!"

It seemed now that Meir and Elka would immediately marry. Why keep two apartments? Why maintain two households? But Elka kept putting it off. She refused to marry until a year had passed. She had read somewhere that until the first anniversary the soul still hovered among those close to it. After the year passed, Elka found new excuses. She wanted to change apartments, to buy new furniture, to get herself a wardrobe, to take a long leave of absence (she had years of vacation coming) and go to Paris. She talked this way and that—now seriously, now in jest. Meir Bontz hadn't forgotten his fantasies about America, but Elka argued, "What do you need with America? You don't live there forever either."

One night when Meir and Elka managed to get away and Meir was staying at her place, Elka took Meir's hand and guided it to her left breast. "Feel. Right there," she said.

Meir felt something hard. "What is it?"

"A growth. My mother died of the same thing. So did my Aunt Gittel."

"Go to the doctor first thing tomorrow."

"A doctor, eh? If my mother hadn't rushed to the doctors, she would have died an easy death. Those butchers hacked her to pieces. Meir, I'm not such a dunce."

"But it may turn out to be nothing."

"No, Meirl, it's a summons from up there."

These words served to arouse her, and the petting and kissing commenced. Elka liked to talk in bed, to question Meir about his former mistresses, his adventures with married women. She always demanded that he compare her with the others and describe in which ways she was better. At first, Meir hadn't liked this interrogation, but as always with Elka he got used to it. This time, she talked about the fact that neither the Society nor Meir would be able to get along without her. She would have to train a woman to replace her, teach her the trade. And while she was at it, the new woman could take Elka's place with Meir too.

Meir laid a heavy hand over Elka's mouth but she cried, "Take away your paw!" and she bit his palm.

From then on, by night and even by day as they drove around, Elka kept up her talk about dying. When Meir complained that he didn't want to hear such gabbing, Elka would say, "What's the big fuss? I'm no calf to be afraid of the slaughterer."

Elka didn't stop with words. Suddenly a cousin of hers materialized—a girl from a small town, who was black as a crow and slanty-eyed as a Tartar. She told Meir that she was twenty-seven, but she appeared to him to be past thirty. Like Elka, she drank vodka and smoked cigarettes. Her name was Dishka. It was hard to believe that she and Elka were related. Where Elka was loquacious and playful, Dishka measured her words. No smile ever showed on her mouth or in her sulky dark eyes. Meir hated her on sight. Elka took her along to the funerals. She helped Elka wash down the corpses and sew shrouds. Dishka had been a seamstress in the sticks where she came from and she was even more skillful than Elka at tearing the linen—scissors were not allowed—and basting with broad stitches. One time when Elka had some business to attend to in the city, Dishka accompanied Meir in the hearse to a suburb where a slain Jew had been found. The entire way there Dishka didn't utter a word. Suddenly she laid her hand on Meir's knee and began to tickle him and arouse him. He took her hand and put it back in her lap. That night, Meir lay awake until dawn. His skull nearly burst from all the thinking he did. He both sweated and felt chills run up and down his spine. Should he force Elka to get rid of Dishka? Should he leave everything behind him and run off by himself to America? Should he wait till Elka passed on and then slit his throat over her grave? Should he leave the Burial Society and become a porter or teamster? Without Elka, the thought of everything seemed to be hollow. Meir had never drunk by himself, but now he uncorked a bottle in the dark and downed half of it. For the first time, he felt terror come over him. He knew that Dishka would bring misfortune upon him. No one could take Elka's place. Meir stationed himself by the window, gazed out into the night, and said to himself, "The whole damned thing isn't worth a penny any more."

■

Elka was confined to bed. The growth in her breast had spread and the other breast had developed growths as if overnight. Elka suffered such pain the doctors kept her going with morphine. Professor Mintz tried to persuade Elka to enter the Jewish Hospital, where she could be treated with radium therapy. Maybe she could be operated on and saved from a quick death. But Elka told him, "To me, a quick death is better than a lingering illness. I'm ready for the journey."

Sick as she was, Elka remained employed by the Society. Meir had to report every corpse, every burial to her. Even though he despised Dishka—that country yokel—he had to admit she had her good points. When Elka became bedridden, Meir moved in with her, while Dishka moved into his place. She swept the rooms, took it upon herself to throw out all the old dishes and broken pots Beilka had left—she even persuaded the landlord to have the place painted, the ceiling patched, and new floors laid. In the mornings, when Meir met Dishka at the Society or at work, she always brought him food—not the cookies or chocolate on which Elka sustained herself, but chicken, beefsteak, meatballs. Elka needed only one drink to commence babbling her nonsense, but Dishka could drink a lot and remain sober. Meir could never make her out. How was it that such a piece could emerge from some godforsaken village? From where did she draw her strength? His own experience had taught Meir that small-town creatures were all miserable cowards, foolish mollycoddles, always sniveling, complaining.

One day the woman who watched over Elka became sick herself, and the one who was supposed to substitute for her had gone to spend the night with a daughter in Pelcowizna. Elka had got an injection from Zeitag the healer, and Meir sat by her bed until it took hold. Just before she fell asleep, she demanded Meir's solemn vow that after her death he would marry Dishka, but Meir refused. Early in the morning he was wakened by the telephone. An actor who for many years had played the role of a lover on the Yiddish stage, first at the Muranow Theater and later at other theaters and on the road, had died in the sanatorium in Otwock. On Smocza Street an alcohol cooker had caused a fire, killing five children. A young man on Nowolipki Street had hanged himself and the police wanted his body for dissection. Meir washed and shaved. Elka heard the news and wanted details. She had known the actor and admired his acting, singing, and jokes. All those deaths in one day revived her spirits, and for a while she conversed in a healthy voice. The woman who watched over her wasn't due till ten and Meir was loath to leave her alone, but Elka said, "What more can happen to me?" She smiled and winked.

The whole day, Meir and Dishka were so busy they didn't have time to eat. Meir tried to speak to her about the tragedy of the children. Dishka said nothing. Meir remembered that in similar circumstances Elka was always ready with an appropriate comment. He couldn't live with a grouch like Dishka for even two weeks.

The custom in the sanatorium was to keep a corpse all day in cold storage and release it late at night in order not to alarm the other patients. The whole day, Meir and Dishka were occupied in the city and it was late evening by the time they started out for Otwock. The night was dark and rainy, with no moon or stars. Meir tried again and again to strike up a conversation with Dishka but she replied so curtly that soon there was nothing left for him to say. What does she think about the whole time, Meir wondered. Surliness—it's nothing else. Doing you a favor by sitting beside you.

They drove past the Praga Cemetery. Against the big-city red sky the tombstones resembled a forest of wild toadstools. Meir began to speak in Elka's tone: "A city of the dead, eh? Wore themselves out and lay down. You believe in God?"

"I don't know," Dishka replied after a long pause.

"Who then created the world?"

Dishka didn't answer and Meir became enraged. He said, "What point is there in being born if this is how it ends? On Karmelicka Street there's a workers' house, that's what it's called, and a big shot was giving a speech there. I happened to be walking by and I went inside to listen. He said that there is no God. Everything had made itself. How can everything just come from itself? Stupid!"

Dishka still didn't respond, and Meir resolved not to say

another word to her that night. He felt a deep longing for Elka. "She dare not die!" he mumbled. "She dare not! If it's fated that one of us must go, let it be me."

The car passed Wawer, a village full of Gentiles; then Miedzeszyn, which was being built; then Falenica, where rabbis, Hasidim, and plain pious Jews came out for the summers; and later Michalin, Jozefow, Swider, where the intelligentsia gathered—Zionists, Bundists, Communists, and those who no longer wanted to speak Yiddish but only Polish.

Elka's sickness had stirred Meir Bontz's brain and he began pondering things. What, for instance, had this Dishka done in that village she came from? No doubt in the war years she had been a smuggler or a whore. Suddenly he thought of Beilka. At first she hadn't wanted him, and he had knelt before her and sworn eternal love. He had found her Lithuanian accent especially endearing. Years later, when she got sick, every word she spoke irritated him. He had one request of her: that she be silent. Yet with Elka the more she talked the more he wanted to hear.

Meir drove up to the cold-storage room at the sanatorium. Everything went off quickly, quietly, like a conspiracy. A door opened and two individuals transferred a box into his hearse. He didn't even see their faces. Not a word was spoken. In the brief time the door to the cold-storage room stood open, Meir caught a glimpse of two more such boxes. Before a long table on which burning candles spluttered and dripped tallow sat an old man reciting Psalms. A blast of cold like that from an ice cellar issued from the room. Meir grabbed the bottle of vodka he carried in his pocket and in one gulp drained it. As he headed back toward Warsaw, his life flashed before him— the poverty-stricken home, the thefts, the fights, the brothels, the whores, the arrests. "How was I able to endure such a Gehenna?" he asked himself, and he recalled a saying of his mother's: "God preserve us from all the things one can get used to."

The car entered a forest. Meir drove fast and in zigzags. He wanted Dishka to plead with him to slow down but she sat obstinately silent, staring out into the darkness.

Meir said, "Don't be afraid. I won't kill the corpse."

A whim to be spiteful came over him, along with an impulse

to test his luck, like the reckless desire of a gambler who grows tired of the game and risks all he possesses. The headlights cast a glare upon the pines, houses, gardens, pumps, balconies. From time to time Meir cast a sidelong glance at Dishka. "Life is apparently not worth a pinch of snuff to her," he said to himself.

The hearse came out onto a stretch of road running through a clearing. It skidded as if going downhill, carried along by its own impetus. At once Meir felt gay and lighthearted. Nothing to worry about, he thought. Things will take care of themselves. He almost forgot his sullen passenger. It's good to live. One day I may even go to America. There is no lack of females and corpses there. He drove and dreamed. Elka rode with him, disguised as someone else, joking and frolicking, challenging his prowess. Suddenly a tree materialized before his eyes. A tree in the middle of the road? No, he had gone off the highway. It's one of her tricks, Meir thought. He wanted to step on the brake, but his foot pressed the accelerator. "That's it!" something within him shouted. He heard a tremendous crash and everything went silent.

The next day, a peasant going to work early found a smashed car with three dead. The back door of the hearse had been torn off and the box containing the actor's body had fallen out. A crowd gathered; the police were called. From Warsaw the Benevolent Burial Society sent out two other hearses to pick up the bodies. The president and the warden decided not to let Elka know, but a female member who was watching over her learned the news on the radio and told Elka. When Elka heard it she began to laugh and couldn't stop. Soon the laughter turned into hiccups. When they had stopped, she got out of bed and said, "Hand me my clothes."

In the two days it took to arrange the funerals Elka regained her strength. Everyone in the Society observed her liveliness with amazement. She cleansed Dishka and prepared shrouds for her and Meir. She ran from room to room, slammed doors, issued orders. She talked to the bodies with her usual teasing: "Ready for the journey? Packed away in the shipping crate?"

Warsaw had two big funerals. Actors, writers, and theater lovers gathered around the actor's coffin. Around Meir's and Dishka's came the thieves, pimps, whores, fences from Krochmalna, Smocza, Pocezjow, and Tamki Streets. The war, the typhus epidemics, starvation had almost destroyed the city's underworld. The Communists had taken over their taverns, their dens, the square on Krochmalna Street, but enough of the old-timers remained to pay their final respects to Meir. Elka rode with them. She looked quite youthful and pretty in her black suit and black-veiled hat. Meir Bontz and Red Elka were still remembered. The droshkies stretched from Iron Street to Gnoyna Street. Meir Bontz had supported a Talmud Torah, and a teacher with dozens of students walked before the hearse crying, "Justice shall walk before him."

At the cemetery, two coachmen lifted Elka up onto a tombstone and she made a short eulogy: "My Meir, stay well. I'll come to you. Don't forget me, Meir. I've got a plot right next to yours. What we had together no one can ever take away from us, not even God!"

She addressed herself to Dishka: "Rest in peace, my sister. I wanted to give you everything, but it wasn't fated." With these words, Elka collapsed.

She was finally taken to a hospital, but the cancer had spread too far for there to be any hope of saving her. Elka sat up in bed propped against two pillows while the women from the Burial Society came to ask about her and to pass along word of what was going on. New people had been hired, but the Angel of Death remained the same. Linen had gone up, the community demanded more money for the plots, the headstone carvers had raised their prices. Jewish sculptors had begun to carve all kinds of designs on the tombstones of the rich—lions, deer, even faces of birds, almost like the practice of the Gentiles. Elka listened, asked questions. Her face had turned yellow, but her eyes remained as green as gooseberries. Now that Meir was in the beyond, Elka had nothing to regret. Everything was ready for her—a plot, shrouds, shards for her eyelids, and a branch of myrtle with which she, together with Meir, would dig their way through the caves and roll to the Land of Israel when the Messiah came.

Translated by Joseph Singer

A Party in Miami Beach

MY FRIEND the humorist Reuben Kazarsky called me on the telephone in my apartment in Miami Beach and asked, "Menashe, for the first time in your life, do you want to perform a mitzvah?"

"Me a mitzvah?" I countered. "What kind of word is that—Hebrew? Aramaic? Chinese? You know I don't do mitzvahs, particularly here in Florida."

"Menashe, it's not a plain mitzvah. The man is a multimillionaire. A few months ago he lost his whole family in a car accident—a wife, a daughter, a son-in-law, and a baby grandchild of two. He is completely broken. He has built here in Miami Beach, in Hollywood, and in Fort Lauderdale maybe a dozen condominiums and rental houses. He is a devoted reader of yours. He wants to make a party for you, and if you don't want a party, he simply wants to meet you. He comes from somewhere around your area—Lublin, or how do you call it? To this day, he speaks a broken English. He came here from the camps without a stitch to his back, but within fifteen years he became a millionaire. How they manage this I'll never know. It's an instinct like for a hen to lay eggs or for you to scribble novels."

"Thanks a lot for the compliment. What can come out of this mitzvah?"

"In the other world, a huge portion of the leviathan and a Platonic affair with Sarah, daughter of Tovim. On this lousy planet, he's liable to sell you a condominium at half price. He is loaded and he's been left without heirs. He wants to write his memoirs and for you to edit them. He has a bad heart; they've implanted a pacemaker. He goes to mediums or they come to him."

"When does he want to meet me?"

"It could even be tomorrow. He'll pick you up in his Cadillac."

At five the next afternoon, my house phone began to buzz and the Irish doorman announced that a gentleman was waiting downstairs. I rode down in the elevator and saw a tiny man in a yellow shirt, green trousers, and violet shoes with gilt buckles. The sparse hair remaining around his bald pate was the color of silver, but the round face reminded me of a red apple. A long cigar thrust out of the tiny mouth. He held out a small, damp palm; pressed my hand once, twice, three times; then said in a piping voice: "This is a pleasure and an honor! My name is Max Flederbush."

At the same time, he studied me with smiling brown eyes that were too big for his size—womanly eyes. The chauffeur opened the door to a huge Cadillac and we got in. The seat was upholstered in red plush and was as soft as a down pillow. As I sank down into it, Max Flederbush pressed a button and the window rolled down. He spat out his cigar, pressed the button again, and the window closed.

He said, "I'm allowed to smoke as much as I'm allowed to eat pork on Yom Kippur, but habit is a powerful force. It says somewhere that a habit is second nature. Does this come from the Gemara? The Midrash? Or is it simply a proverb?"

"I really don't know."

"How can that be? You're supposed to know everything. I have a Talmudic concordance, but it's in New York, not here. I'll phone my friend Rabbi Stempel and ask him to look it up. I have three apartments—one here in Miami, one in New York, and one in Tel Aviv—and my library is scattered all over. I look for a volume here and it turns out to be in Israel. Luckily, there is such a thing as a telephone, so one can call. I have a friend in Tel Aviv, a professor at Bar-Ilan University, who stays at my place—for free, naturally—and it's easier to call Tel Aviv than New York or even someone right here in Miami. It goes through a little moon, a Sputnik or whatever. Yes, a satellite. I forget words. I put things down and I don't remember where. Our mutual friend, Reuben Kazarsky, no doubt told you what happened to me. One minute I had a family, the next —I was left as bereft as Job. Job was apparently still young and God rewarded him with new daughters, new camels, and new asses, but I'm too old for such blessings. I'm sick, too. Each day that I live is a miracle from Heaven. I have to guard myself with every bite. The doctor does allow me a nip of whiskey, but only a drop. My wife and daughter wanted to take me along on that ride, but I wasn't in the mood. It actually happened right here in Miami. They were going to Disney World. Suddenly a truck driven by some drunk shattered my world. The drunk lost both his legs. Do you believe in Special Providence?"

"I don't know how to answer you."

"According to your writings, it seems you do believe."

"Somewhere deep inside, I do."

"Had you lived through what I have, you'd grow firm in your beliefs. Well, but that's how man is—he believes and he doubts."

The Cadillac had pulled up and a parking attendant had taken it over. We walked inside a lobby that reminded me of a Hollywood supercolossal production—rugs, mirrors, lamps, paintings. The apartment was in the same vein. The rugs felt as soft as the upholstery in the car. The paintings were all abstract. I stopped before one that reminded me of a Warsaw rubbish bin on the eve of a holiday when the garbage lay heaped in huge piles.

I asked Mr. Flederbush what and by whom this was, and he replied: "Trash like the other trash. Pissako or some other bluffer."

"Who is this Pissako?"

Out of somewhere materialized Reuben Kazarsky, who said, "That's what he calls Picasso."

"What's the difference? They're all fakers," Max Flederbush said. "My wife, may she rest in peace, was the expert, not me."

Kazarsky winked at me and smiled. He had been my friend even back in Poland. He had written a half-dozen Yiddish comedies, but they had all failed. He had published a collection of vignettes, but the critics had torn it to shreds and he had stopped writing. He had come to America in 1939 and later had married a widow twenty years older than he. The widow died and Kazarsky inherited her money. He hung around rich people. He dyed his hair and dressed in corduroy jackets and hand-painted ties. He declared his love to every woman from fifteen to seventy-five. Kazarsky was in his sixties, but he looked no more than fifty. He let his hair grow long and wore side whiskers. His black eyes reflected the mockery and abnegation of one who has broken with everything and everybody. In the cafeteria on the Lower East Side, he excelled at mimicking writers, rabbis, and party leaders. He boasted of his talents as a sponger. Reuben Kazarsky suffered from hypochondria, and because he was by nature a sexual philanthropist, he had convinced himself that he was impotent. We were friends, but he had never introduced me to his benefactors. It seemed that Max Flederbush had insisted that Reuben bring us together.

He now complained to me: "Where do you hide yourself? I've asked Reuben again and again to get us together, but according to him, you were always in Europe, in Israel, or who knows where. All of a sudden it comes out that you're in Miami Beach. I'm in such a state that I can't be alone for a minute. The moment I'm alone, I'm overcome by a gloom that's worse than madness. This fine apartment you see here turns suddenly into a funeral parlor. Sometimes I think that the real heroes aren't those who get medals in wartime but the bachelors who live out their years alone."

"Do you have a bathroom in this palace?" I asked.

"More than one, more than two, more than three," Max answered. He took my arm and led me to a bathroom that bedazzled me by its size and elegance. The lid of the toilet seat was transparent, set with semiprecious stones and a two-dollar bill implanted in the center. Facing the mirror hung a picture of a little boy urinating in an arc while a little girl looked on admiringly. When I lifted the toilet-seat lid, music began to play. After a while, I stepped out onto the balcony, which looked directly out to sea. The rays of the setting sun scampered over the waves. Gulls still hunted for fish. Far off in the distance, on the edge of the horizon, a ship swayed. On the beach, I spotted some animal that from my vantage point, sixteen floors high, appeared to be a calf or a huge dog. But it couldn't be a dog, and what would a calf be doing in Miami Beach? Suddenly the shape straightened up and turned out to be a woman in a long bathrobe digging for clams in the sand.

After a while, Kazarsky joined me on the balcony. He said, "That's Miami. It wasn't he but his wife who chased after all these trinkets. She was the business lady and the boss at home. On the other hand, he isn't quite the idle dreamer he pretends to be. He has an uncanny knack for making money. They dealt in everything—buildings, lots, stocks, diamonds, and eventually she got involved in art, too. When he said buy, she bought; and when he said sell, she sold. When she showed him a painting, he'd glance at it, spit, and say, 'It's junk, they'll snatch it out of your hands. Buy!' Whatever they touched turned to money. They flew to Israel, established yeshivas, and donated prizes toward all kinds of endeavors—cultural, religious. Naturally, they wrote it all off in taxes. Their daughter, that pampered brat, was half crazy. Any complex you can find in Freud, Jung, and Adler, she had it. She was born in a DP camp in Germany. Her parents wanted her to marry a chief rabbi or an Israeli prime minister. But she fell in love with a Gentile, an archaeology professor with a wife and five children. His wife wouldn't divorce him and she had to be bought off with a quarter-million-dollar settlement and a fantastic alimony besides. Four weeks after the wedding, the professor left for a dig for a new Peking man. He drank like a fish. It was he who was drunk, not the truck driver. Come, you'll soon see something!"

Kazarsky opened the door to the living room and it was filled with people. In one day, Max Flederbush had managed to arrange a party. Not all the guests could fit into the large living room. Kazarsky and Max Flederbush led me from room to room, and the party was going on all over. Within minutes, maybe two hundred people had gathered, mostly women. It was a fashion show of jewelry, dresses, pants, caftans, hairdos, shoes, bags, makeup, as well as men's jackets, shirts, and ties. Spotlights illuminated every painting. Waiters served drinks. Black and white maids offered trays of hors d'oeuvres.

In all this commotion, I could scarcely hear what was being said to me. The compliments started, the handshakes and the kisses. A stout lady seized me and pressed me to her enormous bosom. She shouted into my ear, "I read you! I come from the towns you describe. My grandfather came here from Ishishok. He was a wagon driver there, and here in America he went into the freight business. If my parents wanted to say something I wouldn't understand, they spoke Yiddish, and that's how I learned a little of the language."

I caught a glimpse of myself in the mirror. My face was smeared with lipstick. Even as I stood there, trying to wipe it off, I received all kinds of proposals. A cantor offered to set one of my stories to music. A musician demanded I adapt an opera libretto from one of my novels. A president of an adult-education program invited me to speak a year hence at his synagogue. I would be given a plaque. A young man with hair down to his shoulders asked that I recommend a publisher, or at least an agent, to him. He declared, "I *must* create. This is a physical need with me."

One minute all the rooms were full, the next all the guests were gone, leaving only Reuben Kazarsky and myself. Just as quickly and efficiently, the help cleaned up the leftover food and half-drunk cocktails, dumped all the ashtrays, and replaced all the chairs in their rightful places. I had never before witnessed such perfection. Out of somewhere Max Flederbush dug out a white tie with gold polka dots and put it on.

He said, "Time for dinner."

"I ate so much I haven't the least appetite," I said.

"You must have dinner with us. I reserved a table at the best restaurant in Miami."

After a while, the three of us, Max Flederbush, Reuben Kazarsky, and I, got into the Cadillac and the same chauffeur drove us. Night had fallen and I no longer saw or tried to determine where I was being taken. We drove for only a few minutes and pulled up in front of a hotel resplendent with lights and uniformed attendants. One opened the car door ceremoniously, a second fawningly opened the glass front door. The lobby of this hotel wasn't merely supercolossal but super-supercolossal—complete to light effects, tropical plants in huge planters, vases, sculptures, a parrot in a cage. We were escorted into a nearly dark hall and greeted by a headwaiter who was expecting us and led us to our reserved table. He bowed and scraped, seemingly overcome with joy that we had arrived safely. Soon another individual came up. Both men wore tuxedos, patent-leather shoes, bow ties, and ruffled shirts. They looked to me like twins. They spoke with foreign accents that I suspected weren't genuine. A lengthy discussion evolved concerning our choice of foods and drinks. When the two heard I was a vegetarian, they looked at each other in chagrin, but only for a second. Soon they assured me they would serve me the best dish a vegetarian had ever tasted. One took our orders and the other wrote them down. Max Flederbush announced in his broken English that he really wasn't hungry, but if something tempting could be dredged up for him, he was prepared to give it a try. He interjected Yiddish expressions, but the two waiters apparently understood him. He gave precise instructions on how to roast his fish and prepare his vegetables. He specified spices and seasonings. Reuben Kazarsky ordered a steak and what I was to get, which in plain English was a fruit salad with cottage cheese.

When the two men finally left, Max Flederbush said, "There were times if you would have told me I'd be sitting in such a place eating such food, I would have considered it a joke. I had one fantasy—one time before I died to get enough dry bread to fill me. Suddenly I'm a rich man, alas, and people dance attendance on me. Well, but flesh and blood isn't fated to enjoy any rest. The angels in Heaven are jealous. Satan is the accuser and the Almighty is easily convinced. He nurses a longtime resentment against us Jews. He still can't forgive the fact that our great-great-grandfathers worshipped the golden calf. Let's have our picture taken."

A man with a camera materialized. "Smile!" he ordered us.

Max Flederbush tried to smile. One eye laughed, the other cried. Reuben Kazarsky began to twinkle. I didn't even make the effort. The photographer said he was going to develop the film and that he'd be back in three-quarters of an hour.

Max Flederbush asked, "What was I talking about, eh? Yes, I live in apparent luxury, but a woe upon this luxury. As rich and elegant as the house is, it's also a Gehenna. I'll tell you something: in a certain sense, it's worse here than in the camps. There, at least, we all hoped. A hundred times a day we comforted ourselves with the fact that the Hitler madness couldn't go on for long. When we heard the sound of an airplane, we thought the invasion had started. We were all young then and our whole lives were before us. Rarely did anyone commit suicide. Here hundreds of people sit, waiting for death. A week doesn't go by that someone doesn't give up the ghost. They're all rich. The men have accumulated fortunes, turned worlds upside down, maybe swindled to get there. Now they don't know what to do with their money. They're all on diets. There is no one to dress for. Outside of the financial page in the newspaper, they read nothing. As soon as they finish their breakfasts, they start playing cards. Can you play cards forever? They have to, or die from boredom. When they get tired of playing, they start slandering one another. Bitter feuds are waged. Today they elect a president, the next day they try to impeach him. If he decides to move a chair in the lobby, a revolution breaks out. There is one touch of consolation for them—the mail. An hour before the postman is due, the lobby is crowded. They stand with their keys in hand, waiting as if for the Messiah. If the postman is late, a hubbub erupts. If one opens his mailbox and it's empty, he starts to grope and burrow inside, trying to create something out of thin air. They are all past seventy-two and they receive checks from Social Security. If the check doesn't come on time, they worry about it more than those who need it for bread. They're always suspicious of the mailman. Before they mail a letter, they shake the cover three times. The women mumble incantations.

"It says somewhere in the Book of Morals that if man will remember his dying day, he won't sin. Here you can forget about death as much as you can forget to breathe. Today I meet someone by the swimming pool and we chat. Tomorrow I hear he's in the other world. The moment a man or a woman dies, the widow or widower starts looking for a new mate. They can barely sit out the shivah. Often, they marry from the same building. Yesterday they maligned each other with every curse in the book, today they're husband and wife. They throw a party and try to dance on their shaky legs. The wills and insurance policies are speedily rewritten and the game begins anew. Hardly a month or two goes by and the bridegroom is in the hospital. The heart, the kidneys, the prostate.

"I'm not ashamed before you—I'm every bit as silly as they are, but I'm not such a fool as to look for another wife. I neither can nor do I want to. I have a doctor here. He's a firm believer in the benefits of walking and I take a walk each day after breakfast. On the way back, I stop at the Bache brokerage house. I open the door and there they sit, the oldsters, staring at the ticker, watching their stocks jump around like imps. They know full well that they won't make use of these stocks. It's all to leave in the inheritance, and their children and grandchildren are often as rich as they are. But if a stock goes up, they grow optimistic and buy more of it.

"Our friend, Reuben, wants me to write my memoirs. I have a story to tell, yes, I do. I went through not only one Gehenna but ten. This very person who sits here beside you sipping champagne spent three-quarters of a year behind a cellar wall, waiting for death. I wasn't the only one—there were six of us men there and one woman. I know what you're going to ask. A man is only a man, even on the brink of the grave. She couldn't live with all six of us, but she did live with two—her husband and her lover—and she satisfied the others as best as she could. If there had been a machine to record what went on there, the things that were said and the dreams that were played out, our greatest writers would be made to look like dunces by comparison. In such circumstances, the souls strip themselves bare and no one has yet adequately described a naked soul. The *szmalcowniks*, the informers, knew about us and they had to be constantly bribed. We each had a little money or some valuable objects, and as long as they lasted, we kept buying pieces of life. It came to it that these informers brought us bread, cheese, whatever was available—everything for ten times the actual price.

"Yes, I could describe all this in pure facts, but to give it flavor requires the pen of a genius. Besides, one forgets. If you would ask me now what these men were called, I'll be damned if I could tell you. But the woman's name was Hilda. One of the men was called Edek, Edek Saperstein, and the other—Sigmunt, but Sigmunt what? When I lie in bed and can't sleep, it all comes back as vividly as if it happened yesterday. Not everything, mind you.

"Yes, memoirs. But who needs them? There are hundreds of such books written by simple people, not writers. They send them to me and I send them a check. But I can't read them. Each one of these books is poison, and how much poison can a person swallow? Why is it taking so long for my fish? It's probably still swimming in the ocean. And your fruit salad first has to be planted. I'll give you a rule to follow—when you go into a restaurant and it's dark, know that this is only to deceive. The headwaiter is one of the Polish children of Israel, but he poses as a native Frenchman. He might even be a refugee himself. When you come here, you have to sit and wait for your meal, so that later on the bill won't seem too excessive. I'm neither a writer nor a philosopher, but I lie awake half the nights, and when you can't sleep, the brain churns like a mill. The wildest notions come to me. Ah, here is the photographer! A fast worker. Well, let's have a look!"

The photographer handed each of us two photos in color and we sat there quietly studying them.

Max Flederbush asked me, "Why did you come out looking so frightened? That you write about ghosts, this I know. But you look here as if you'd seen a real ghost. If you did, I want to know about it."

"I hear you go to séances," I said.

"Eh? I go. Or to put it more accurately, they come to me. This is all bluff, too, but I *want* to be fooled. The woman turns off the lights and starts talking, allegedly in my wife's voice. I'm not such a dummy, but I listen. Here they come with our food, the Miami *szmalcowniks.*"

The door opened and the headwaiter came in leading three men. All I could see in the darkness was that one was short and fat, with a square head of white hair that sat directly on his broad shoulders, and with an enormous belly. He wore a pink shirt and red trousers. The two others were taller and slimmer. When the headwaiter pointed to our table, the heavyset man broke away from the others, came toward us, and shouted in a deep voice: "Mr. Flederbush!"

Max Flederbush jumped up from his seat. "Mr. Alberghini!"

They began to heap praises upon each other. Alberghini spoke in broken English with an Italian accent.

Max Flederbush said, "Mr. Alberghini, you know my good friend Kazarsky, here. And this man is a writer, a Yiddish writer. He writes everything in Yiddish. I was told that you understand Yiddish!"

Alberghini interrupted him. "*A gezunt oyf dein kepele . . . Hock nisht kein tcheinik . . . A gut boychik . . .* My parents lived on Rivington Street and all my friends spoke Yiddish. On Sabbath, they invited me for gefilte fish, *cholent*, kugel. Who do you write for—the papers?"

"He writes books."

"Books, eh? Good! We need books, too. My son-in-law has three rooms full of books. He knows French, German. He's a foot doctor, but he first had to study math, philosophy, and all the rest. Welcome! Welcome! I've got to get back to my friends, but later on we'll——"

He held out a heavy, sweaty hand to me. He breathed asthmatically and smelled of alcohol and hair tonic. The words rumbled out deep and grating from his throat.

After he left, Max said: "You know who he is? One of the Family."

"Family?"

"You don't know who the Family is? Oh! You've remained a greenhorn! The Mafia. Half Miami Beach belongs to them. Don't laugh, they keep order here. Uncle Sam has saddled himself with a million laws that, instead of protecting the people, protect the criminal. When I was a boy studying about Sodom in cheder, I couldn't understand how a whole city or a whole country could become corrupt. Lately, I've begun to understand. Sodom had a constitution and our nephew, Lot, and the other lawyers reworked it so that right became wrong and wrong right. Mr. Alberghini actually lives in my building. When the tragedy struck me, he sent me a bouquet of flowers so big it couldn't fit through the door."

"Tell me about the cellar where you sat with the other men and the only woman," I said.

"Eh? I thought that would intrigue you. I talked to one of the writers about my memoirs and when I told him about this, he said, 'God forbid! You must leave this part out. Martyrdom and sex don't mix. You must write only good things about them.' That's the reason I lost the urge for the memoirs. The Jews in Poland were people, not angels. They were flesh and blood just like you and me. We suffered, but we were men with manly desires. One of the five was her husband. Sigmunt. This Sigmunt was in contact with the *szmalcowniks*. He had all kinds of dealings with them. He had two revolvers and we resolved that if it looked like we were about to fall into murderers' hands, we would kill as many of them as possible, then put an end to our own lives. It was one of our illusions.

When it comes down to it, you can't manage things so exactly.
Sigmunt had been a sergeant in the Polish Army in 1920. He
had volunteered for Pilsudski's legion. He got a medal for
marksmanship. Later on, he owned a garage and imported
automobile parts. A giant, six foot tall or more. One of the
szmalcowniks had once worked for him. If I was to tell you
how it came about that we all ended up together in that cellar,
we'd have to sit here till morning. His wife, Hilda, was a decent woman. She swore that she had been faithful to him
throughout their marriage. Now, I will tell you who her lover
was. No one but yours truly. She was seventeen years older
than me and could have been my mother. She treated me as if
she were my mother, too. 'The child,' that's what she called
me. The child this and the child that. Her husband was in-
sanely jealous. He warned us he'd kill us both if we started
anything. He threatened to castrate me. He could have easily
done it, too. But gradually, she wore him down. How this
came about you could neither describe nor write, even if you
possessed the talent of a Tolstoy or a Zeromski. She persuaded
him, hypnotized him like Delilah did Samson. I didn't want
any part of it. The other four men were furious with me. I
wasn't up to it, either. I had become impotent. What it means
to spend twenty-four hours out of the day locked in a cold,
damp cellar in the company of five men and one woman,
words cannot describe. We had to cast off all shame. At night
we barely had enough room to stretch our legs. From sitting
in one place, we developed constipation. We had to do everything in front of witnesses and this is an anguish Satan himself
couldn't endure. We had to become cynical. We had to speak
in coarse terms to conceal our shame. It was then I discovered
that profanity had its purpose. I have to take a little drink. So
. . . *L'chaim!*

"Yes, it didn't come easy. First she had to break down his
resistance, then she had to revive my lust. We did it when he
was asleep, or he only pretended. Two of the group had
turned to homosexuality. The whole shame of being human
emerged there. If man is formed in God's image, I don't envy
God . . .

"We endured all the degradation one can only imagine, but
we never lost hope. Later, we left the cellar and went off, each

his own way. The murderers captured Sigmunt and tortured him to death. His wife—my mistress, so to speak—made her way to Russia, married some refugee there, then died of cancer in Israel. One of the other four is now a rich man in Brooklyn. He became a penitent, of all things, and he gives money to the Bobow rabbi or to some other rabbi. What happened to the other three, I don't know. If they lived, I would have heard from them. That writer I mentioned—he's a kind of critic— claims that our literature has to concentrate only on holiness and martyrdom. What nonsense! Foolish lies!"

"Write the whole truth," I said.

"First of all, I don't know how. Secondly, I would be stoned. I generally am unable to write. As soon as I pick up a pen, I get a pain in the wrist. I become drowsy, too. I'd rather read what you write. At times, it seems to me you're stealing my thoughts.

"I shouldn't say this, but I'll say it anyway. Miami Beach is full of widows and when they heard that I'm alone, the phone calls and the visits started. They haven't stopped yet. A man alone and something of a millionaire besides! I've become such a success I'm literally ashamed of myself. I'd like to cling to another person. Between another's funeral and your own, you still want to snatch a bit of that swinish material called pleasure. But the women are not for me. Some yenta came to me and complained, 'I don't want to go around like my mother with a guilt complex. I want to take everything from life I can, even more than I can.' I said to her, 'The trouble is, one cannot . . .' With men and women, it's like with Jacob and Esau: when one rises, the other falls. When the females turn so wanton, the men become like frightened virgins. It's just like the prophet said, 'Seven women shall take hold of one man.' What will come of all this, eh? What, for instance, will the writers write about in five hundred years?"

"Essentially, about the same things as today," I replied.

"Well, and what about in a thousand years? In ten thousand years? It's scary to think the human species will last so long. How will Miami Beach look then? How much will a condominium cost?"

"Miami Beach will be under water," Reuben Kazarsky said, "and a condominium with one bedroom for the fish will cost five trillion dollars."

"And what will be in New York? In Paris? In Moscow? Will there still be Jews?"

"There'll be only Jews," Kazarsky said.

"What kind of Jews?"

"Crazy Jews, just like you."

Translated by Joseph Singer

Two Weddings and One Divorce

O NE DAY in autumn, a shoemaker's apprentice committed suicide on Krochmalna Street because his bride to be, a seamstress, betrayed him and married a widower. Krochmalna Street could speak of nothing else. The case was even discussed by the Hasidim in the Radzyminer study house. They were all three there—Meyer the Eunuch, who was sane two weeks each month and deranged the other two; old Levi Yitzchok, who suffered from trachoma and wore sunglasses night and day; and Zalman the glazier, a simple man who recited fifty pages of the Zohar every day though he did not know Aramaic. One young man was saying, "These love affairs are a result of ungodly books—the novels. In former times, when such heathenish books did not exist, there were no mishaps like this."

"Not true at all," said Levi Yitzchok. "The Talmud tells us of the heretic Elisha ben Avuyah that secular books fell from his cloak. Blasphemers and mockers lived even in the time of Abraham."

Zalman the glazier lifted his index finger, with its horny nail. "There were also love affairs among those who feared God. In our village of Radoszyce, a Hasidic boy fell madly in love with a wench unworthy of him in every way. He was the only son of a wealthy man, an ardent Hasid, Reb Shraga Kutner. Reb Shraga's other children had died. His wife had also passed away, and in his old age he had married a girl of seventeen, an orphan. She died giving birth to this son, Aaron David. Reb Shraga became weaker from day to day and he yearned to lead his son to the wedding canopy before he died. He asked the matchmakers to find a suitable girl, even though his son was too young for marriage.

"In those years no match was arranged until the parents of the girl sent teachers to examine the boy's knowledge of the Torah. Aaron David was known as a good scholar. The rabbi had predicted that he might become the head of a yeshiva one day. But somehow Aaron David failed to answer correctly the questions put to him. He seemed to know little of the Bible.

He made blatant mistakes in the interpretation of the Mishnah and the Gemara. At the beginning, Reb Shraga assumed that his son was afraid of the examiners and their verdicts and became mixed up. He therefore pleaded with the examiners to be patient. He also explained to Aaron David that examiners are not eager to have a student fail. They get a small percentage of the dowry if things go right, and they want him to succeed. But all this was no use. Some of the examiners became so disgusted with the boy that they told the townspeople of the stupid errors he made, and there was much to laugh at and malign. Reb Shraga felt utterly disgraced.

"Then, during an examination, Aaron David translated a Hebrew passage in a way so ridiculously wrong that Reb Shraga began to suspect his son was acting deliberately. But why should a young student wish to play the ignoramus and be shamed? He locked himself with his son into his library and said, 'My son, your father is old and sick, he is already with one foot in his grave. A single desire is left him—to get some joy from you. Now, tell me the truth, why do you spoil each match that is proposed?'

"When the boy heard these words he burst out crying. He confessed to his father that he had fallen in love with a girl and if he couldn't have her for his wife he preferred to remain alone. Reb Shraga couldn't believe his ears—such talk from a youngster who was barely fourteen. 'Who is the girl?' he asked. The boy answered, 'If you hear who she is, you will think I am crazy and you will be right, too, but I cannot get her out of my thoughts.'

"I'll make it short. Aaron David had fallen in love with a water carrier's daughter, a cripple born without hands and feet. Instead, she had sort of fins, like a fish. Her name was Fradl. Because she was unable to use crutches, she could not take a step. She had to be drawn on a cart with wheels. I knew her quite well. Her father, Shimmele Icicle, carried water to Reb Shraga and also to my parents. When there was frost in winter, icicles formed in his beard and sometimes they would drop into his pails or into the water barrel of the customer. From this he got his nickname. He was known as a coarse creature and a little pixilated. His wife had left him and he brought up his freakish daughter himself. Her face was quite pretty, with black fiery eyes. She had a sharp tongue and used foul language. They lived in a half-ruined hut on Bridge Street.

"It came about this way. Once, on Purim, Shimmele brought a Purim gift to Reb Shraga. Reb Shraga was out of the house. Aaron David thought that it was a gift from a householder in town to his father and that Shimmele was the messenger. He wanted to give him a penny for his errand, but Shimmele said, 'This is a present from my sweet little daughter to you, my boy.' 'Why to me?' asked Aaron David, astounded, and Shimmele replied, 'Because of your blue eyes and curly sidelocks.' I knew the whole story, for Aaron David told it later to my Uncle Leibush. She had sent a red apple, some St.-John's-bread, a peppermint candy. Shimmele said, 'Don't tell your father about it—he might whip you. Mum's the word. It could give you a reputation as a girl chaser.' When Shimmele left, the boy pondered. Who had ever heard of a girl sending a gift to a boy she did not know? After a while he decided he should give Fradl a Purim gift in return. But how? If he sent it by a servant, the whole town would know. So he put an orange, some cookies, and a slice of honey cake on a plate, covered it with a napkin, and carried it to Fradl himself. It seemed that the sly creature spoke to him ticklish words and worked a charm on him. There is a proverb: The Evil One is not choosy. Who knows? Perhaps she treated him with a potion that makes the blood hot. When a female washes her breasts in a mixture of water and Sabbath wine and gives some of it to a man to drink, she kindles his longing for her. Many loves are the result of such doings.

"I don't need to tell you that Reb Shraga was shocked and warned his son against such a pitfall. The boy had not told him about the Purim gift; he just said that he saw her through a window. The whole thing was a terrible blow to Reb Shraga. Shimmele was known as a ruffian and a blabbermouth. Reb Shraga went to his rabbi for advice on how to free the boy from his infatuation. The rabbi gave Reb Shraga a blessing and a talisman, but to no avail. Aaron David insisted that he marry Fradl or no one. Reb Shraga, realizing that his end was near and that the boy would never get over his madness, decided that perhaps it was a punishment from God or simply a curse to which one must submit. How does the saying go? 'If you can't go over, you go under.' He took off his shame cap and told his relatives to prepare for a wedding.

"When the people of Radoszyce heard of this match there was a commotion. Some cried, others laughed and spat. The women all insisted that the cunning Fradl had bewitched an innocent boy. But in time one gets accustomed to the most weird events. There was a wedding, and the wedding canopy was set up in the court of the synagogue as always when the bride is a virgin. Not only Fradl had to be carried but also Reb Shraga. From grief he had lost the power of his legs. Just the same, musicians played and the wedding jester cracked jokes. The riffraff of both sexes considered this marriage the high point of their lives. They danced, sang, and got drunk. Reb Shraga had ordered a festive meal for the paupers of the poorhouse. They sat at a long table, ate challah with carp, and drank mead. Shimmele lifted up the wings of his gaberdine and danced a kosatzke.

"Shortly after the wedding Reb Shraga died. People predicted that a cripple like Fradl would not get pregnant. But she was soon with child. In the years that followed she gave birth to five daughters, one more beautiful than the other. She turned out to be a diligent housewife. Aaron David hired for her two maids, and Fradl gave orders from her couch. Everything in her home had to sparkle. Her copper vessels shone like gold. When they grew up, her daughters indulged her every whim. The women from Bridge Street used to visit her and bring her all the gossip from the village. They took her to the marketplace. She was fond of bargains and bedecked herself with trinkets. There was plenty of money. Reb Shraga had been an able merchant even in his older years. He had a large drygoods store and visited fairs in Lublin, Nałęczów, Lemberg. As for Aaron David, he remained an unworldly Talmud scholar. He lived on his inheritance from his father. He must have loved his wife truly, because after her death he did not remarry.

"Fradl died in a very queer way. I've already told you that instead of hands and feet she had fins. Suddenly her skin began to grow scales. Aaron David summoned doctors from Lublin and even from Warsaw. Professors came to investigate the nature of her malady. They tried to remove the scales by surgery, but they grew so rapidly that soon her whole body was covered with them. Some of the town's wags joked that she had become a kosher fish, since that's what a fish must have to be kosher—fins and scales. The sickness did not last more than three months. I didn't see her in this stage, but I know that the curious came to look at her from neighboring towns. There were those who believed that her mother had sinned with a fish and Fradl was the offspring."

"What?" said Levi Yitzchok. "Such perversions were not practiced even by the Generation of the Flood."

For a long time there was silence in the study house. Only the wind could be heard. Meyer the Eunuch clutched his chin, seeming to search for the root of a hair. Levi Yitzchok poked his nose into his wooden snuffbox, took a whiff, and said, "Such a passion is sheer illusion; a foolish idea gets stuck in the mind like a wedge. Or it might have been the work of Satan. The Evil Ones have their power. The daughters of Lilith fly around at night like bats and tempt men to commit abominations. Even saints suffer the defilement of nocturnal emission. But true love has a holy origin.

"In the town of Parysow there was a Talmudist, an affluent man, Reb Pinchos Edelweiss. He came from a distinguished lineage—from Rabbi Moshe Isserles and from Rashi. The town elders wanted to make him their rabbi, but he refused. Why did he need to be a rabbi? He possessed forests, a sawmill, and I think a water mill, too. He sent rafts on the Vistula to Danzig. Reb Pinchos divided his days into two parts. From sunrise to noon he studied the Talmud, the Responsa, the Midrash, the Zohar. He prayed early in the morning with the first quorum. After lunch he conducted his business. He drove around in a carriage, like a squire. He employed a bookkeeper, a cashier, and lumberjacks who cut the trees into logs. His wife, Ada Zillah, came from an even more noble house than he. She spoke Polish and German and could write a letter in Hebrew. The only blessing denied the pair was children. Oh, I forgot to mention that Reb Pinchos had a younger brother who had deviated from the path of righteousness. He had swindled and forged a signature, and had had to run away to America. In those times to have someone in America was like having a convert or a suicide in the family.

"One day Reb Pinchos became ill, and no medicine helped him. He traveled to Vienna to the great doctors, but they all gave him up. Reb Pinchos knew that when he died childless his widow would have to go through the ceremony of Chalitzah with her brother-in-law in order to be allowed to marry again. Now, it is not an easy thing to go and search for someone in America—especially a person of an adventurous nature. Therefore Reb Pinchos decided that before he died he would divorce his wife, so that she could remarry without a release from his brother. Husband and wife loved one another with a great love, and when Ada Zillah heard about his plans for the divorce she began to cry bitterly, insisting that she would never have another man. Reb Pinchos said, 'Why should you live out your years alone? You are still young, and with another husband you might yet be able to have children.' Still she refused. When Reb Pinchos realized that she would not consent, he went to the rabbi without her knowledge and ordered a scribe to write a bill of divorce. He also made out a will wherein he left Ada Zillah half of his fortune and the other half to various charities. Everything was done in secrecy. The next day he called for two of his employees to serve as witnesses and for his wife. He handed her the divorce papers, reciting the proper words. Ada Zillah listened to the words and saw the divorce papers, and she fainted dead away. As soon as she was revived, she took a Pentateuch from the bookcase, raised her hand, and said, 'Pinchos, I swear by God Almighty and the Holy Book that I will never belong to another man.' And she cried convulsively.

"You know the law that a divorced man and woman are not permitted to stay under the same roof. Reb Pinchos had prepared for himself a room in another house, but so great was Ada Zillah's anguish that she seized her prayer book and her book of supplications, packed some linen into a bundle, and ran to the poorhouse. When the paupers in the poorhouse saw the wellborn Ada Zillah with her bundle and heard her say that she had come to stay, there arose a terrible lament. They all knew Ada Zillah. Every day she sent chicken soup and groats to the sick. Often she went herself to comfort the depressed and to dole out charity. Now important men and women of the town rushed to her to plead that she not ruin her life. In answer, Ada Zillah quoted to them the words of Job: 'Naked came I out of my mother's womb, and naked shall I return thither.' She had torn her husband's last will to shreds.

"When the poorhouse attendant saw that Ada Zillah was adamant, he wanted to put up a bed with linen for her, but Ada Zillah said, 'My bed will be a bundle of straw the same as for all the others.' She was given a hay pillow and a bundle of straw and she sat down on it in her silk dress and began to recite the chapters that are used in times of distress and illness: 'O Lord God of my salvation I have cried day and night before Thee . . . For my soul is full of troubles: and my life draweth nigh unto the grave . . . Have mercy upon me, O Lord; for I am weak: O Lord, heal me for my bones are vexed.'

"A prayer in such circumstances can split the heavens. Or perhaps the cure had already been decreed. That day Reb Pinchos became better. He was supposed to have had an ulcer in his throat, and he coughed so long and hard that whatever it was burst and the pus drained out. The threat to his life was over and the people started to say that Reb Pinchos could now remarry Ada Zillah. But they were reminded that Reb Pinchos was of priestly caste—a Cohen, who is not permitted to marry a divorcée even though she be his former spouse. So great was Reb Pinchos's despair that when his friends who visited him wished him a quick recovery he said, 'Better wish me a speedy death.' But they don't ask in Heaven a man's judgment on whether he deserves life or death. Reb Pinchos recovered completely. After witnessing such a miracle, the town healer, who used to be a heretic, became an ardent believer.

"Reb Pinchos went to Ada Zillah in the poorhouse and fell at her feet, beseeching her to take over his house and marry someone else. The rabbi was willing to revoke her oath, which had been given in a moment of desperation and possibly with an unclear mind. But Ada Zillah said, 'My oath stands, and I am not in need of a house. You, Pinchos, remarry. It is quite possible that I am barren, not you. Heaven wanted you to bring forth a generation, therefore this affliction was visited upon us. It is my wish that you find a young woman capable of giving birth and take her as a wife. Your children will be as dear to me as if they were my own.'"

"Did he remarry?" Zalman the glazier asked.

"No. The truth is that he broke the law. A man who has not fulfilled the commandment to be fruitful and multiply may not remain without a wife. The rabbi told Reb Pinchos that he transgressed, but he answered, 'Gehenna is for people, not for animals.' He withdrew from all business and became a recluse. He gave away most of his possessions, though he kept his house and garden, still hoping to provide a home for Ada Zillah. He even proposed to send her to the Holy Land in the hope that she would find solace there among the sacred places. But Ada Zillah said, 'I am not permitted to be with you under one roof; let me at least be with you under one sky.' Reb Pinchos went to the rabbi and said, 'Rabbi, as long as I live I am forbidden to be near Ada Zillah, but it is my will that when we both part from this earth we should be allowed to lie in our graves one next the other.' The rabbi could not decide this matter by himself and he took the question to the council of three rabbis. The verdict was that after their demise the former husband and wife could have adjoining graves.

"And so it happened. Reb Pinchos died before Ada Zillah. I no longer lived in town then. But I was told that when he fell ill she attended him, gave him his medicines, and cooked for him the dishes the doctor prescribed. Whether she acted strictly according to the law I am not sure. But behind each law mercy is concealed. In the few years Ada Zillah outlived Reb Pinchos, she went to the cemetery every weekday, summer and winter, and prostrated herself on his grave. On the plot next to his, she had her own headstone put up, engraved with the words 'Here lies Ada Zillah, the devoted wife of the pious Reb Pinchos.' Space was left for the date of her death. I heard that not long after she was buried a willow tree began to sprout from her grave. It grew rapidly into a large tree, and its branches drooped to cover both graves and to make them one. The law of divorce is only for bodies. Souls cannot be divorced."

For a while it seemed that Meyer did not listen. He sat there deep in thought. He grimaced and shook his head as if puzzled by something that he could neither solve nor forget. Then he said, "What you told, Zalman, happens every day. People marry blind ones, mute ones, hunchbacks, even lepers. When the Angel calls out forty days before birth that the daughter of one man is to marry the son of another man, this comes to pass. Providence joins the strangest bedfellows and works in a way that appears the doing of matchmakers. If Providence did not hide behind the laws of nature, all people would be saints and there would be no free choice. From your story, Levi Yitzchok, I like best the saying 'Gehenna is for people, not for animals.' Gehenna cleanses souls, and cleansing is benevolence. The body loves only itself, and even this is an illusion. Flesh is nothing but a garment. When the soul requires a new garment, the old one turns to dust. This is the mystery of reincarnation. We have already been males, females, cattle, trees, grass. They call me Eunuch. I am not a eunuch but androgynous. Adam, who was created perfect in God's image, was androgynous. There are hints of this in the Book of Genesis. Adam and Eve copulated from within.

"This story I heard from my grandfather and he heard it from his grandfather. In the city of Praga lived a man, Reb Bezalel Ashkenazi. He had an only son, Eliakim, a yenuka, a prodigy. At four the yenuka already knew the Bible, the Mishnah, and parts of the Gemara. At seven he gave a sermon in the Praga synagogue and scholars came to listen to him. It happens quite often that a yenuka is born androgynous, and according to the cabala this is right, because all great souls are a union of both sexes. Since Eliakim grew up wise, many matches were proposed for him. But he said, 'When the time comes, the right spouse will be with me.' He had long hair and did not grow a beard. He sang tunes that had never been heard in this world, and with two voices—male and female. A yenuka descends to Earth to correct a blunder made in a former existence, and when his mission is accomplished he is ready to ascend to the Mansions of Heaven. One day Eliakim's hair was black, the next day it turned white. Although he had no wife and it was not the custom for a bachelor to wear the prayer shawl, he sat all day long wrapped in a prayer shawl and with phylacteries on his arm and head like one of the ancients. His parents had died. There were no Hasidim at this time—certainly not in Praga—but people came to him as to a wonder rabbi. He pronounced incantations over pieces of amber. Mothers waited outside his house for him to bless their infants. Witnesses testified that when the yenuka studied the Book of Creation the pages turned by themselves. When he wanted to write some footnote on the margin of a scroll, the quill jumped into his hand. Those who are rooted in the primeval source of life enliven everything that surrounds them. In the winter the beadle did not need to heat the stove in the yenuka's house, because a fiery radiance emanated from him as from a seraph.

"He ate almost nothing. He slept never longer than sixty breaths at a time. He seemed more in Heaven than on earth.

"One day the yenuka let it be known that he was about to marry. His followers were all astonished. How can the androgynous marry? And what earthly woman could deserve to be his wife? He asked that only ten old men be invited to the wedding—all cabalists and servants of the Almighty. One of them was to officiate at the ceremony. On the appointed day, the beadle kept watch through the window for carriages bearing the bride and her relatives. None arrived. Just the same, after the evening prayers the ten invited elders gathered in the yenuka's house. One of them wrote out the ketuba, leaving only a blank space for the name of the bride. Four others set up a canopy supported by four posts. Wax candles were lit and a goblet was filled with wine. Through it all, the yenuka remained locked in his room. Some of the men listened at the door. Nothing could be heard. They began to wonder if because of his holy remoteness he had forgotten about the wedding. But just then the door of his room opened and the yenuka came out clad in a white robe and a white cowl, like a corpse in shrouds, and beside him the bride in a white wedding dress and a heavy veil. Her face could not be seen, but her garments shone with the colors of lightning. The few old men were overcome by awe; they could barely stand on their feet. Nevertheless, the one who wrote the ketuba took courage and asked the bride her name. 'Eliakim,' she said. 'The daughter of Bezalel.' The bride and groom had the same name and the same father's name.

"The ceremony was performed according to law. The one who officiated read the ketuba and recited the first benedictions. The bridegroom put a ring on the index finger of the bride's right hand and said, 'Thou art sanctified to me with this ring according to the law of Moses and Israel.' When the bride was about to drink from the goblet, she lifted her veil and they all saw two yenukas, their faces as white as mother-of-pearl and their eyes luminous with the glory of love. They resembled one another as closely as twins. After the second benedictions they were wished mazel tov, but they returned to their room in silence."

"Wasn't a wedding like this against the strict letter of the law?" Levi Yitzchok asked.

"There are copulations in Heaven that would be incest on earth," Meyer replied.

"What happened then?"

"The yenuka joined the Yeshiva On High the same night."

"And what happened to the bride?" Zalman the glazier asked. "She died also?"

Meyer shrugged. He closed his eyes and seemed to have fallen asleep. Then he rose and began to pace back and forth on the floor of the study house. He rubbed the palms of his hands and murmured to himself. Once in a while he burst out laughing. The kerosene lamp went out and a single candle burned in the candelabra. It flickered and sputtered. The room filled with shadows.

Zalman looked out through the window. "The moon is full," he said. "The half month begins when Meyer is confused."

Translated by the author and Alma Singer

A Cage for Satan

IN the forty years that Rabbi Naphtali Sencyminer had waged war against the evil spirits, he contended with imps, demons, dybbuks, and harpies, and sooner or later he vanquished them all—with incantations, with amulets, with the power of his voice, his cane, the stomping of his feet, and his curses. A single passion still consumed him—to capture one of these impure spirits, to bind it and lock it up in a cage like a wild beast. The rabbi had a cage suited to the purpose in his attic. One of his Hasidim, an iron merchant, had had it constructed for him in secret. It was made of heavy bars surrounded by thick wire mesh and had a door with two locks. On the mesh the rabbi had hung incantations written in a scribal hand on parchment, as well as a ram's horn and a prayer shawl that had once belonged to the Kozienice Preacher. On its floor lay the chains the famous saint Joseph della Reyna had used to shackle Satan. Rabbi Joseph hadn't managed to keep Satan prisoner, for he took pity on him and gave him a pinch of snuff. Two fires shot from Satan's nostrils and the chains fell from him. Rabbi Naphtali was determined to show the Devil no mercy. He planned to keep him in the dark without food or water, surrounded by the holy names of God and angels. Rabbis and even righteous Gentiles from all over the world would come to Sencymin to witness Rabbi Naphtali's triumph.

Well, but no matter how many traps Rabbi Naphtali set for Satan and his hosts they managed to elude him. One time he seized a wraith by the beard and a Lilith by its hair, but before he could imprison them they wriggled away. These fiends came back in the night to taunt the rabbi, to whistle in his ear and spit upon him. A sprite with the face of a billy goat deposited a pile of dung upon the rabbi's sacred book. It left behind the stench of galbanum.

By the time the rabbi passed his seventies, he began to despair. His wife had died. The cage in the attic was covered with spiderwebs and the chains had rusted.

But one summer night late in the month of Ab something occurred that impressed the rabbi as a miracle. It happened this way. The rabbi's beadle, Reb Gronam Getz, a patriarch who had served Rabbi Naphtali's father, fell sick for the first time in his eighty-seven years and was taken to the hospital. From the day the rabbi became a widower, Gronam Getz had stayed in the rabbi's bedroom to guard him from the spirits and their revenge. Now the rabbi slept alone; he had no faith in the young beadles. That night before he went to bed, the rabbi not only read the prayers of the holy Isaac Luria, as usual, but he recited those psalms specifically intended to drive away nocturnal trespassers. He had placed a Book of Creation under his pillow, and a long-bladed knife such as pregnant women kept under their pillows to ward off Shibta, the arch-enemy of the newly born. He also left a wax candle burning in a holder.

The rabbi slept in a white cloak belted with a sash; white stockings; and two skullcaps—one at his forehead, one at the back of his skull—as well as a ritual garment with special eight-fold twisted fringes. The moment he laid his head on the pillow and recited "Thou who makest the bands of sleep fall upon mine eyes and slumber upon mine eyelids," he fell into a deep sleep.

He awoke in alarm in the middle of the night. The candle had gone out. He heard quiet footsteps nearby. He felt an urge to cry, "Shaddai, destroy Satan!," but it struck him that perhaps his prayers had been answered in Heaven—this might be his opportunity to capture the evil intruder. A strength that astounded him surged through Rabbi Naphtali. He leaped out of bed with such force that the slats beneath his straw pallet broke. A dark presence stood outlined against the shuttered window. He lunged toward it with the ferocity of a lion. In a flash he had seized it and pressed it to him so violently that he felt ribs snap. Only now did the spirit begin to resist. It shouted something unintelligible, but the rabbi threw it to the floor, clasped it between his knees, clamped its mouth shut with one hand and clutched its throat with the other. He could feel a jerking, hear muffled words, a gurgling. Then it ceased to struggle and was silent. The rabbi had vanquished the demon. As he bound its feet with his sash, Rabbi Naphtali trembled, slavered, and stammered incantations: "*Kuzu Bemuchzus Kuzu* . . . An arrow in the eye of Satan . . . Yahweh's war with Amalek . . . Thou shalt utterly detest it, and thou shalt utterly abhor it."

Although the entity of the netherworld lay quiet, Rabbi Naphtali knew its submission was a sham. Until it was shackled and confined in the cage, it could regain its powers, stick its tongue out as far as its navel, burst into mad laughter, and fly away like a bat.

The rabbi tried to stand, but his legs felt as if they had been chopped off. Sparks flashed before his eyes. His ears rang. "I dare not give in!" he warned himself. "Asmodeus and his companions are merely waiting for me to show weakness."

The rabbi would have to drag the messenger of destruction up to the attic stealthily, so that no one in the house would learn what was going on. Had Gronam Getz been with him, he would have lent a hand—Gronam Getz was familiar with the cabala and knew all the spells and incantations. But the young beadles slept in their own homes, and even if they had been standing guard in the courtyard the rabbi would not have trusted them to help him with a mission of such gravity.

After a while, Rabbi Naphtali revived somewhat and was able to rise. He leaned down and picked up the creature of the darkness, slung it over one shoulder, and began to move toward the anteroom and the stairs leading to the attic. He knew full well that he was overtaxing his strength, but there were times when one could not yield to the body. He crept along the corridor, praying that he would not collapse under his load, God forbid, lest its allies find out and swarm all over him. Several times he bumped against doors and walls. His cloak caught on a hook. When he reached the narrow attic stairs, he was drenched in sweat and could hear the snorting of his own nose. But he refused to take a rest. At any moment his adversary might come to and drag him away to beyond the dark regions, to the gates of Hell, to the ruins of Sodom, to Mount Seir, where Naamah, Mahalath, and Lilith reigned. The rabbi could no longer remember any psalms or conjurations—his brain was dulled and his tongue thick as wood.

By the time he had climbed to the attic, day was dawning. The blaze of the rising sun shone through the cracks in the eastern side of the shingled roof. The cage could be seen through purplish columns of dust. The rabbi stepped toward it, but he banged against a wooden box full of old books and fell back. In the second before he fainted, he caught a glimpse of the burden under which he had fallen—a boy in a short jacket, his mouth and nose bloodied. Woe is me, it's a human, I've killed him! the rabbi thought as everything went dark.

2

When Rabbi Naphtali opened his eyes again, the sun still shone through the cracks in the roof, but now the light came not from the east but from the west. It took him a long time to grasp this. His bones ached, and his head hurt with a piercing pain. Next to him lay a corpse with eyes glazed, bloody mouth open, face yellow as clay. Only now did he realize what had happened—a youngster had come to rob him. Rabbi Naphtali didn't accept paper money for his services—only silver coins or gold ducats, which he kept in earthen jugs as well as in oak coffers lined with hide and bound with iron hoops. For years he had been making plans to go to the Holy Land to build a study house there, a ritual bath and a yeshiva, and to erect a tabernacle over the grave of his grandfather Reb Menahem Kintzker, who had died in Jerusalem forty years before. "God Almighty, why did this happen to me?" the rabbi mumbled. "My punishment is greater than I can bear."

He stuck out his hand and felt the body's forehead. The brightness of the sunset through the shingles soon dimmed and the attic filled with shadows. A great fear came over the rabbi. He rose with effort and began to shuffle toward the door. If at least he might have died along with his victim! But it had been decreed in Heaven that he suffer Cain's fate. At the head of the stairs he was forced to sit down. He had to consider his situation. His followers had undoubtedly been looking for him all day, but it would never have occurred to them that he might be up in the attic. There was no sound of movement in the house. They must have given up hope for him, or perhaps they assumed he had ascended to Heaven alive, like Enoch. Rabbi Naphtali had suffered many misfortunes—he had been left in his old age without wife or child—but during all his calamities he had been able to pray and to justify the harsh judgments passed upon him. This day, the first since he became thirteen, he had missed putting on his phylacteries. It was the hour to say the evening prayers, but he could not bring himself to allow sacred words to pass through the lips of a murderer. Of all possible disasters, he had suffered the worst —and at what a time in his life: on the brink of the grave!

Ordinarily, the spirits of good and evil fought a constant battle within Rabbi Naphtali, but now both remained silent. Night fell and the rabbi sat enveloped in a gloom like that of the abyss. "Whither shall I go from thy Spirit? Or whither shall I flee from thy presence?" he recited. Should he do away with himself? he thought. Since he had already lost the world to come, what difference would it make? Should he go off somewhere and vanish? Well, but if the thief is a Jew he must be given a Jewish burial. A corpse cannot be left to rot in an attic without ablution, without shrouds, without a mourner's prayer said over it . . .

The rabbi's head sank ever lower and lower. Compared to his ordeal, Job's had been a trifle. Rabbi Naphtali had but one request of the Almighty—to die. He now understood the words of the Sages: " 'Very good'—that is death."

The rabbi had fallen asleep and was awakened by voices, noises, the sound of feet. The beadles were running up the stairs to him. The light of a lantern dazzled his eyes. They lifted him in their arms and carried him away. He heard women weeping, men shouting. Am I dead? the rabbi wondered. Is this my funeral? They carried him to a room and put him to bed. They revived him with cold water and rubbed his temples with vinegar. Everyone talked at once, but he made no response. Suddenly a new lament rose and at that instant the rabbi understood what had happened. They had found the body in the attic. Someone called out a name: Haiml Cake.

How could this be, the rabbi asked himself. Haiml Cake is no longer a youngster. Soon after, they called another name: Bentze Lip. For all his distress the rabbi realized the connection between these names. Haiml Cake, a horse thief whom the police had beaten so badly that he could no longer steal horses, had become a teacher of young thieves. He must have sent out one of the gang, Bentze Lip, to rob him. Instead of capturing Satan, he, Naphtali Sencyminer, had murdered a young burglar—perhaps an orphan besides. In the midst of the turmoil the rabbi muttered, "Satan has captured *me*."

They were the last words his followers heard from the rabbi. In the three weeks that he lingered, he did not speak to those who came to visit him. The beadles dressed him in his prayer shawl and phylacteries, and he mumbled. They handed him a book, and he glanced into it, but no one saw him turn a page. Two days before the rabbi's demise, Gronam Getz came from the hospital and he alone stayed with the rabbi until the end. The rabbi ordered him to burn his manuscripts, not to save so much as a single page, and Gronam Getz did as he was told. The rabbi also dictated a will to him, leaving his entire fortune to the community, with enough put aside to erect a tombstone over Bentze Lip's grave, to hire someone to say the Kaddish over him, and to subsidize men to study the Mishnah in Bentze's name. The rabbi decreed that he himself be buried behind the fence, where heretics and suicides were laid to rest. He warned of severe punishment for any who defied his last wishes. Rabbi Naphtali Sencyminer had killed a human being and he had forfeited the right to lie alongside decent Jews. However, the Hasidim and members of the Burial Society dared to disregard his demands. Many rabbis gathered for the funeral, and they ordained that since Rabbi Naphtali had done what he did unintentionally and had atoned for it with a self-mortification that brought about his decease, he should be given a burial with all the honors accruing to a saint and a martyr. The eldest among them, an author of many holy books and a patriarch of eighty, said, "Those who love God more than the soul and heart can bear attempts to destroy the world. So long as there is a world there will also be a Satan."

Translated by Joseph Singer

Brother Beetle

I BEGAN to dream about this trip when I was five years old. At that time my teacher, Moses Alter, read to me from the Pentateuch about Jacob crossing the Jordan while carrying only his staff. But a week after my arrival in Israel, at the age of fifty, there were few marvels left for me to see. I had visited Jerusalem, the Knesset, Mount Zion, the kibbutzim in Galilee, the ruins of Safad, the remains of the fortification of Acre, and all the other sights. I even made the at-that-time dangerous trip from Beersheba to Sodom, and on the way saw camels harnessed to the plows of Arabs. Israel was even smaller than I had imagined it to be. The tourist car in which I traveled seemed to be going in circles. For three days wherever we went we played hide-and-seek with the Sea of Galilee. During the day, the car was continually overheating. I wore two pairs of sunglasses, one on top of the other, as protection against the glare of the sun. At night, a hot wind blew in from somewhere. In Tel Aviv, in my hotel room, they taught me to maneuver the shutters, but in the one moment it took me to get out on the balcony, the thin sand carried by the khamsin wind managed to cover the linens of my bed. With the wind came locusts, flies, and butterflies of all sizes and colors, along with beetles larger than any I had ever seen before. The humming and buzzing was unusually loud. The moths beat against the walls with unbelievable strength, as if in preparation for the final war between man and insect. The tepid breath of the sea stank of rotten fish and excrement. That late summer, electricity failures were frequent in Tel Aviv. A suburban darkness covered the city. The sky filled with stars. The setting sun had left behind the redness of a heavenly slaughter.

On a balcony across the street, an old man with a small white beard, a silken skullcap partly covering his high forehead, half sat, half reclined on a bed, reading a book through a magnifying glass. A young woman kept bringing him refreshments. He was making notes in the book's margins. On the street below, girls laughed, shrieked, picked fights with boys, just as I had seen them do in Brooklyn, and in Madrid, where

I had stopped en route. They teased one another in Hebrew slang. After a week of seeing everything a tourist must see in the Holy Land, I had my fill of holiness and went out to look for some unholy adventure.

I had many friends and acquaintances from Warsaw in Tel Aviv, even a former mistress. The greatest part of those who had been close to me had perished in Hitler's concentration camps or had died of hunger and typhoid in Soviet Middle Asia. But some of my friends had been saved. I found them sitting in the outdoor cafés, sipping lemonade through straws and carrying on the same old conversations. What are seventeen years, after all? The men had become a little grayer. The women dyed their hair; heavy makeup hid their wrinkles. The hot climate had not wilted their desires. The widows and widowers had remarried. Those recently divorced were looking for new mates or lovers. They still wrote books, painted pictures, tried to get parts in plays, worked for all kinds of newspapers and magazines. All had managed to learn at least some Hebrew. In their years of wandering, many of them had taught themselves Russian, German, English, and even Hungarian and Uzbek.

They immediately made room for me at their tables, and began reminding me of episodes I could not possibly forget. They asked my advice on American visas, literary agents, and impresarios. We were even able to joke about friends who had long since become ashes. Every now and then a woman would wipe away a tear with the point of her handkerchief so as not to smear her mascara.

I didn't look for Dosha, but I knew that we would meet. How could I have avoided her? That evening I happened to be sitting in a café frequented by merchants, not artists. At the surrounding tables the subject was business. Diamond merchants brought out small bags of gems and their jeweler's loupes. A stone passed quickly from table to table. It was inspected, fingered, and then given to another, with a nod of the head. It seemed to me that I was in Warsaw, on Krolewska Street. Suddenly I saw her. She glanced around, looking for someone, as if she had an appointment. I noticed everything at once: the dyed hair, the bags under her eyes, the rouge on her cheeks. One thing only had remained unchanged—her slim figure. We embraced and uttered the same lie: "You haven't changed." And when she sat down at my table, the difference between what she had been then and what she was now began to disappear, as if some hidden power were quickly retouching her face to the image which had remained in my memory.

I sat there listening to her jumbled conversation. She mixed countries, cities, years, marriages. One husband had perished; she had divorced another. He now lived nearby with another woman. Her third husband, from whom she was separated, more or less, lived in Paris, but he expected to come to Israel soon. They had met in a labor camp in Tashkent. Yes, she was still painting. What else could she do? She had changed her style, was no longer an impressionist. Where could old-fashioned realism lead today? The artist must create something new and entirely his own. If not, art was bankrupt. I reminded her of the time when she had considered Picasso and Chagall frauds. Yes, that was true, but later she herself had reached a dead end. Now her painting was really different, original. But who needed paintings here? In Safad there was an artists' colony, but she had not been able to adjust herself to the life there. She had had enough of wandering about through all kinds of Godforsaken villages in Russia. She needed to breathe city air.

"Where is your daughter?"

"Carola is in London."

"Married?"

"Yes, I'm a sabta, a grandmother."

She smiled shyly, as if to say: "Why shouldn't I tell you? I can't fool you, anyhow." I noticed her newly capped teeth. When the waiter came over, she ordered coffee. We sat for a while in silence. Time had battered us. It had robbed us of our parents, our relatives, had destroyed our homes. It had mocked our fantasies, our dreams of greatness, fame, riches.

I had had news of Dosha while I was still in New York. Some mutual friends wrote to me that her paintings were not exhibited; her name was never mentioned in the press. Because she had had a nervous breakdown, she had spent some time in either a clinic or an asylum.

In Tel Aviv, women seldom wear hats, and almost never in the evening, but Dosha had on a wide-brimmed straw hat which was trimmed with a violet ribbon and slanted over one eye. Though her hair was dyed auburn, there were traces of other colors in it. Here and there, it even had a bluish cast. Still, her face had retained its girlish narrowness. Her nose was thin, her chin pointed. Her eyes—sometimes green, sometimes yellow—had the youthful intensity of the unjaded, still ready to struggle and hope to the last minute. How else could she have survived?

I asked, "Do you have a man, at least?"

Her eyes filled with laughter. "Starting all over again? The first minute?"

"Why wait?"

"You haven't changed."

She took a sip of coffee and said, "Of course I have a man. You know I can't live without one. But he's crazy, and I am not speaking figuratively. He's so mad about me that he destroys me. He follows me on the street, knocks at my door in the middle of the night, and embarrasses me in front of my neighbors. I've even called the police, but I can't get rid of him. Luckily, he is in Eilat at the moment. I've seriously thought of taking a gun and shooting him."

"Who is he? What does he do?"

"He says he is an engineer, but he's really an electrician. He's intelligent, but mentally sick. Sometimes I think that the only way out for me is to commit suicide."

"Does he at least satisfy you?"

"Yes and no. I hate savages and I'm tired of him. He bores me, keeps everybody away from me. I'm convinced that someday he'll kill me. I'm as certain of that as that it's night now. But what can I do? The Tel Aviv police are like the police everywhere. 'After he kills you,' they say, 'we'll put him in jail.' He should be committed. If I had somewhere to go, I would leave, but the foreign consulates aren't exactly handing out visas. At least I have an apartment here. Some apartment! But it's a place to sleep. And what can I do with my paintings? They're just gathering dust. Even if I wanted to leave, I don't have the fare. The alimony I get from my former husband, the doctor, is a few pounds, and he's always behind in his payments. They don't know what it's all about here. It's not America. I'm starving and that's the bitter truth. Don't grab your wallet; it's not really that bad. I've lived alone and I'll die alone. I'm proud of it, and besides, it's my fate. What I'm going through and what I've been through, nobody knows, not even God. There's not a day without some catastrophe. But suddenly I walk into a café and there you are. That's really something."

"Didn't you know that I was here?"

"Yes, but how did I know what you'd be like after all these years? I haven't changed a bit, and that's my tragedy. I've remained the same. I've the same desires, the same dreams—the people persecute me here, just as they did twenty years ago in Poland. They are all my enemies, and I don't know why. I've read your books. I've forgotten nothing. I've always thought about you, even when I lay swollen from hunger in Kazakhstan and looked into the eyes of death. You wrote somewhere that one sins in another world, and that this world is hell. For you, that may have been just a phrase, but it's the truth. I am the reincarnation of some wicked man from another planet. Gehenna is *in* me. This climate sickens me. The men here become impotent; the women are consumed with passion. Why did God pick out this land for the Jews? When the khamsin begins, my brains rattle. Here the winds don't blow; they wail like jackals. Sometimes I stay in bed all day because I don't have the strength to get up, but at night I roam about like a beast of prey. How long can I go on like this? But that I'm alive and seeing you makes it a holiday for me."

She pushed her chair away from the table, almost overturning it. "These mosquitoes are driving me crazy."

2

Although I had already had dinner, I ate again with Dosha and drank Carmel wine with her. Then I went to her home. On the way, she kept apologizing for the poorness of her apartment. We passed a park. Though lit by street lamps, it was covered by darkness which no light could penetrate. The motionless leaves of the trees seem petrified. We walked through dim streets, each bearing the name of a Hebrew writer or scholar. I read the signs over women's clothing stores. The commission for modernizing Hebrew had created a terminology for brassieres, nylons, corsets, ladies' coiffures, and cosmetics. They had found the sources for such worldly terms in the Bible, the Babylonian Talmud, the Jerusalem Talmud, the Midrash, and even the Zohar. It was already late in the evening, but buildings and asphalt still exuded the heat of the day. The humid air smelled of garbage and fish.

I felt the age of the earth beneath me, the lost civilizations lying in layers. Somewhere below lay hidden golden calves, the jewelry of temple harlots, and images of Baal and Astarte. Here prophets foretold disasters. From a nearby harbor, Jonah had fled to Tarshish rather than prophesy the doom of Nineveh. In the daylight these events seemed remote, but at night the dead walked again. I heard the whisperings of phantoms. An awakening bird had uttered a shrill alarm. Insects beat against the glass of the street lamps, crazed with lust.

Dosha took my arm with a loyalty unprofaned by any past betrayal. She led me up the stairway of a building. Her apartment was actually a separate structure on the roof. As she opened the door, a blast of heat, combined with the smell of paint and of alcohol used for a primus stove, hit me. The single room served as studio, bedroom, kitchen. Dosha did not switch on the lights. Our past had accustomed us both to undress and dress in the dark. She opened the shutters and the night shone in with its street lamps and stars. A painting stood propped against the wall. I knew that in the daylight its bizarre lines and colors would have little meaning for me. Still, I found it intriguing now. We kissed without speaking.

After years of living in the United States, I had forgotten that there could be an apartment without a bathroom. But Dosha's had none. There was only a sink with running water. The toilet was on the roof. Dosha opened a glass door to the roof and showed me where to go. I could find neither switch nor cord to turn on the light. In the dark I felt a hook with pieces of torn newspaper stuck to it. As I was returning, I saw through the curtains of the glass door that Dosha had turned on the lamp.

Suddenly the silhouette of a man crossed the window. He was tall and broad-shouldered. I heard voices and realized immediately what had happened. Her mad lover had returned. Though terrified, I felt like laughing. My clothes were in her room; I had walked out naked.

I knew there was no escape. The house was not attached to any other building. Even if I managed to climb down the four stories to the street, I could not return to my hotel without clothes. It occurred to me that Dosha might have hidden my things quickly when she heard her lover's steps on the stairs. But he might come outside at any minute. I began to look around the roof for some stick or other object with which to defend myself. I found nothing. I stood against the outside wall of the toilet, hoping he wouldn't see me. But how long could I stay there? In a few hours it would be daybreak.

I crouched like an animal at bay waiting for the hunter to shoot. Cool breezes from the sea mingled with the heat rising from the roof. I shivered and could barely keep my teeth from chattering. I realized that my only way of escape would be to climb down the balconies to the street. But when I looked, I saw that I could not even reach the nearest one. If I jumped I might break a leg or even fracture my skull. Besides, I might be arrested and taken to a madhouse.

Despite my anxiety, I was aware of the ridiculousness of my situation. I could hear them giggling at my ill-fated tryst in the cafés of Tel Aviv. I began to pray to God, against whom I had sinned. "Father, have mercy on me. Don't let me perish in this preposterous way." I promised a sum of money for charity if only I could get out of this trap. I looked up to the numberless stars that hovered strangely near, to the cosmos spreading out with all its suns, planets, comets, nebulae, asteroids, and who-knows-what-other powers and spirits, which are either God himself or that which He has formed from His substance. I imagined that there was a touch of compassion in the stars as they gazed at me in the midst of their midnight gaiety. They seemed to be saying to me, "Just wait, child of Adam, we know of your predicament and are taking counsel."

For a long time I stood staring at the sky and at the tangle of houses which make up Tel Aviv. An occasional horn, the bark of a dog, the shout of a human being erupted from the sleeping city. I thought I heard the surf and a ringing bell.

I learned that insects do not sleep at night. Every moment some tiny creature fluttered by, some with one pair of wings, others with two. A huge beetle crawled at my feet. It stopped, changed its direction, as if it realized it had gone astray on this strange roof. I had never felt so close to a crawling creature as in those minutes. I shared its fate. Neither of us knew why he had been born and why he must die. "Brother Beetle," I muttered, "what do they want of us?"

I was overcome by a kind of religious fervor. I was standing on a roof in a land which God had given back to that half of his people that had not been annihilated. I found myself in infinite space, amid myriads of galaxies, between two eternities, one already past and one still to come. Or perhaps nothing had passed, and all that was or ever will be was unrolled across the universe like one vast scroll. I apologized to my parents, wherever they were, against whom I had once rebelled and whom I was now disgracing. I asked God's forgiveness. For instead of returning to His promised land with renewed will to study the Torah and to heed His commandments, I had gone with a wanton who had lost herself in the vanity of art. "Father, help me!" I called out in despair.

Growing weary, I sat down. Because it was getting colder, I leaned against the wall to protect myself. My throat was scratchy, and in my nose I felt the acrid dryness that precedes a cold. "Has anyone else ever been in such a situation?" I asked myself. I was numbed by that silence that accompanies danger. I might freeze to death on this hot summer night.

I dozed. I had sat down, placing my chin on my chest, the palms of my hands against my ribs, like some fakir who has vowed to remain in that position forever. Now and then I tried to warm my knees with my breath. I listened, and heard only the mewing of a cat on a neighboring roof. It yowled first with the thin cry of a child and then with that of a woman in labor. I don't know how long I slept—perhaps a minute, perhaps twenty. My mind became empty. My worries vanished. I found myself in a graveyard where children were playing—they had come out of their graves. Among them was a tiny girl in a pleated skirt. Through her blond curls, boils could be seen on her skull. I knew who she was, Jochebed, our neighbor's

daughter at 10 Krochmalna Street, who had caught scarlet
fever and had been carried out to a children's hearse one
morning. The hearse was drawn by a single horse and had
many compartments that looked like drawers. Some of the
children danced in a circle, others played on swings. It was a
recurring dream which began in my childhood. The children,
seeming to know that they were dead, neither talked nor sang.
Their yellowish faces wore that otherworld melancholy revealed only in dreams.

I heard a rustling and then felt someone's touch. Opening
my eyes, I saw Dosha wearing a housecoat and slippers. She
was carrying my clothes. My suspenders dragged along the
rooftop together with a sleeve of my jacket. She put my shoes
down and, placing her finger on her lips, indicated silence. She
grimaced and stuck out her tongue in mockery. She backed
away and, to my amazement, opened a trapdoor leading to
the stairway. I almost stepped on my glasses, which had fallen
out of my pocket. In my confusion, I wasn't aware of Dosha
leaving. I saw a booklet lying near me—my American passport. I began to search for my money, my traveler's checks. I
dressed quickly, and in my haste I put my jacket on inside out.
My legs became shaky. I climbed through the trapdoor and
found myself on the steps.

On the ground floor, I found the door chained and locked.
I tried to force it like a thief. At last, the latch opened. Having
closed it quietly behind me, I walked rapidly away, without
once looking back at the house where I had so recently been
imprisoned.

I came to an alley which seemed to be newly constructed
because it was not yet paved. I followed whatever street I came
to just to get as far away as possible. I walked and I talked to
myself. I stopped an elderly passerby, addressing him in English, and he said to me, "Speak Hebrew," and then showed
me how to reach my hotel. There was fatherly reproach in his
eyes, embedded in shadow, as if he knew me and had guessed
my plight. He vanished before I could thank him.

I remained where he left me, meditating on what had happened. As I stood alone in the stillness, shivering in the cold of
dawn, I felt something moving in the cuff of my pants. I bent
down, and saw a huge beetle which ran out and disappeared

in an instant. Was it the same beetle I had seen on the roof? Entrapped in my clothes, it had managed to free itself. We had both been granted another chance by the powers that rule the universe.

Translated by the author and Elizabeth Shub

The Boy Knows the Truth

WHEN Rabbi Gabriel Klintower took over his late father's chair, he let his beadles know that he would not accept women and their petitions to intercede in Heaven for them. True, his father and grandfather had accepted women and many other wonder rabbis did, but he could not put himself on the same plane as those saints whose thoughts were always pure. Rabbi Gabriel had a sensual body. His blood boiled in his veins. In the middle of his prayers impure thoughts assailed him like locusts. The Evil One spoke to him insolently: "There is no judge and no judgment; seize your pleasure as long as you can." The rabbi bit his nails down to the quick. With his fists he beat his head. He tore at his sidelocks and called himself outcast, betrayer of God. He looked continually for advice in sacred books, until finally he concluded that an imp had attached itself to him. What irony! Devoted Jews came to him to learn the fear of God; scholars copied his sermons; every day he lectured to chosen yeshiva students—all at the very time he was sunk to his neck in a passion for flesh. Studying *The Beginning of Wisdom*, *The Tree of Life*, *The Pillar of Service*, he thought about Rahab the Harlot and lusted for Abishag the Shunammite. It was said in the books of the cabala that in the higher spheres unions still take place between Adam and Eve, Jacob and Rachel, David and Bathsheba. Of course the cabalists referred to souls, not bodies. But the moment the rabbi dozed off he saw those ancient females stark naked. They sang lascivious songs and danced in a seductive way. The rabbi woke up shaken. "Woe is me. I am drowning in iniquity," Rabbi Gabriel said to himself. "Well, this world is a world of falsehood, where evil powers hold dominion." Many times he wanted to call in his Hasidim and tell them that he did not deserve to be their spiritual leader. But the rabbi knew that the moment he resigned from his position, took off his sable hat and silk robe, and stopped pretending, he would fall into the pit of Satan, since men like him are more ashamed of the opinion of people than they fear the Almighty.

The rabbi had a wife, Menucha Alte, named after the

daughter of the famous rabbi from Ropczyca. Menucha Alte was conceived and born in saintliness, just as Gabriel was given the nature of a wanton. He was tall, broad-shouldered, with the voice of a lion and an appetite to match. Although he was fifty-seven, his beard remained bright red, without a gray hair. He had a full mouth of teeth strong enough to crack walnuts. Once when there was a fire in his court, Rabbi Gabriel broke down the doors of the synagogue with his bare hands, wrenched off locks and carried out all the scrolls and later all the volumes from the study house. His beadle, Avigdor, fainted from the smoke and Rabbi Gabriel carried him down two flights of stairs. Then he ran to the well and for hours pumped water, working with the firemen to extinguish the flames.

Menucha Alte was small and as scrawny as a consumptive. She lived on medicines and incantations. Every few months she fell dangerously ill. She took upon herself acts of piety that even the most rigorous Jews had long given up. She had three kitchens—one for meat dishes, one for milk meals, one for *pareve* foods. She wore two bonnets to prevent a single hair from showing to a male. On Passover, she put stockings on her cat so that, God forbid, it should not drag in any crumbs of leavened bread under its claws. As long as Menucha Alte was young and still had her periods, she had problems with the ritual ablutions and Rabbi Gabriel was not allowed to have intercourse with her for months. When he finally came to her, her body was cold and she smelled of toothache and valerian drops. She whined that he was too heavy on her, and hurting. Rabbi Gabriel used to remind her that, even according to the strictest letter of the law, kissing and embracing are permitted and that tannaim and amoraim frolicked with their spouses in bed. But Menucha Alte groaned and sighed.

How strange that this broken shard gave birth to five children. Twins died from typhoid fever. Of the three who lived, two daughters took after their father: they were tall, with blue eyes and red hair. Both had husbands and children and lived far from Klintow, on the other side of the Vistula. Shmaya, the only son, suffered from rickets and had a water head. He was as small as a dwarf. Rabbi Gabriel married him off when he was fifteen, but his wife became enlightened and left him. He never remarried. At twenty-nine, Shmaya was beardless as a eunuch. There was madness in his black bulging eyes.

Shmaya had decided that he could best serve God by se-cluding himself. He immersed himself in the cold ritual bath at midnight. He limited his study to the Zohar. Every few weeks he had a convulsive attack, and the only way to revive him was to put a key into his clenched fist and recite the words "Thou shalt not be afraid for the terror by night; nor for the arrow that flieth by day . . . A thousand shall fall at thy side, and ten thousand at thy right hand; but it shall not come nigh thee." The Hasidim of Rabbi Gabriel knew that Shmaya would not last long and that after his father's demise there would be no one to succeed him.

During the daytime Rabbi Gabriel managed to do his duties. He was the head of the yeshiva, and he took special care of every student. He taught them not in the casuistic method of hairsplitting arguments but with the precise inter-pretation of the ancient commentators. Rabbi Gabriel had grasped a long time ago that arguing with Satan was of no avail. One must conquer him by deeds and not allow him time for temptation. The nights became more and more difficult. The rabbi would sleep for an hour and then waken, frightened by his own lust. Lately he could not approach Menucha Alte at all. She was prey to a dozen maladies. She kept on moaning and whispering prayers. She had already prepared her shrouds, which she kept under her pillow, along with a bag of chalky earth from the Holy Land on which her head would rest in her grave. She had written her will, leaving her moth-eaten trousseau for orphan brides. But the years passed by and Menucha Alte lived. Once in Purim, after the rabbi had one glass of wine too many, he said jokingly that Menucha Alte had no strength to die—the Resurrection would have come before she managed to pass away.

Rabbi Gabriel was famous for his wit. He even kibitzed the Almighty. His adversaries considered him a mocker and half mad. Like many of those with a humorous nature, the rabbi was prone to melancholy. Once, after days of depression, he came from his room where he had locked himself in and stopped a cheder boy. He asked him, "Tell me why the

Almighty has created the world?" The boy did not answer and the rabbi pulled his ear and said, "So that fools like myself should ask questions."

One afternoon late in the summer, when Rabbi Gabriel sat in his study and looked into *The Orchard of Pomegranates*, the door opened and Avigdor the beadle entered.

"Rabbi, a female relative of yours has come to visit you. She says she is some rabbi's widow. She refuses to leave. She wants to talk to you."

"She wants, huh? You know that I don't accept women. Who is she? Most probably a schnorrer."

"She came in her own carriage with her own coachman."

The rabbi clutched at his beard with one hand and with the other he rubbed his forehead. "What is her name? How is she my relative?"

"She says that she's the rabbi's niece or some relative like that. It is very urgent."

"Let her in, but leave the door open."

The rabbi barely managed to finish his sentence when the woman crossed the threshold. She was tall, slender, dressed in a silk cape, a pleated skirt, and patent-leather shoes of which only the tips could be seen. Over her blond wig hung a black tulle shawl. In one hand she held a fancy parasol, in the other a handbag with beads and fringes. Her face seemed young, almost that of a girl. But the rabbi could see that she was not really young. She smelled of big city and worldliness. He turned his head away. *"Nu?"*

"Rabbi, I am Binele, your Aunt Temerl's daughter."

The rabbi shuddered. He had forgotten that his Aunt Temerl had a child. Temerl had lost her mind over thirty years ago. Her husband, a rich man from Galicia, placed her in a private clinic in Vienna. To be allowed to remarry, he had had to get a written permission signed by a hundred rabbis. The rabbi asked, "Your mother is alive?"

"Woe to such a life!"

Rabbi Gabriel bent his head. Years had passed and he did not remember his Aunt Temerl, who wasted away in an insane asylum. The words of the prophet Isaiah ". . . and that thou hide not thyself from thine own flesh" came to his mind. His throat and his eyes became hot. He asked, "How is your father?"

"My father passed away. It was a year only last week."

"Did he have children with his second wife?"

"I have three sisters and two brothers."

"*Nu*, the years run, it's all futile and vain," the rabbi murmured. He well knew that he should not let Binele stand, but to offer her a chair would mean giving her a chance to linger. That scatterbrain, Avigdor, had closed the door. The rabbi asked, "What happened to your late husband?"

"I have been a widow for three years. My husband was a rabbi, a scholar, and had an honorary doctorate besides. We lived in Karlsbad."

"Children?"

"We had no children."

The rabbi glanced at her. Her face was narrow, dark-skinned. Her eyes were black. She wore a string of pearls, and diamond earrings dangled from her earlobes. She resembled her mother, who had been known as a beauty. After some hesitation, the rabbi pointed to a chair. "*Nu*, sit down."

"Thank you." She put her parasol and her handbag on the rabbi's table. She spoke in a singsong. "My brothers both became doctors. One is a surgeon in Lemberg and the other a heart specialist in Franzensbad. My sisters are all married. My stepmother lives with her oldest daughter in Drohobycz. My brother-in-law is an owner of oil wells. I am the only one in the family who married a rabbi. He left three commentaries on the Talmud and a thesis about Maimonides written in German."

The rabbi of Klintow had heard about the big world—rabbis who trimmed their beards, reformed synagogues that called themselves temples, rich Jews who traveled to the spas and associated with Gentiles, yeshiva boys who became professors—but it never occurred to him that he might have any connection with such people. Now the Evil One had brought one of them to his house. The rabbi wanted to get up and open the door, but he was embarrassed to do it. He asked, "Why did you come here, to this kingdom of pauperhood?"

"Because you are my nearest relative on my mother's side. I wanted to see you."

"What is there to see? The body turns to dust and the soul is steeped in wickedness. Soon I will have to give an account before the Judgment on High."

"You, too, are afraid to give account?"

"There are no privileges in Heaven."

"You still have years of time. You look, thank God, a strong man."

The rabbi sat silent. No one had ever spoken to him like this. He rose and opened the door, but immediately the wind slammed it shut again.

Binele smiled with amusement. She searched her purse to take out a lace handkerchief, and the rabbi noticed that she had long fingers and polished nails. She said, "Don't be nervous. I'm a kosher Jewish daughter. How is your wife, the rebbetzin, God bless her?"

The rabbi told her about Menucha Alte's illnesses and Binele said, "If you had sent her to Vienna, they might have been able to cure her. Now it would be too late."

"It's always too late. Do you ever go to see your mother?"

"I go, but there is nothing to see. A dazzling beauty still, but mute as a fish. She doesn't recognize me. She stares somewhere over my head. Such sadness I've never seen in a human being except in those of our family. The anguish of generations looks out from her eyes."

"Most probably she sees the truth," the rabbi said, baffled by his own words.

"It may be. But as long as one lives one must live. When my husband left me, I had one desire: that he take me with him. He was all I could wish for—handsome, kind, wise, a philosopher. He was invited to lecture in universities. Priests and nuns came to hear him. But what the earth covers one must forget. Before his demise he called me to his bed and said, 'Binele, it is my wish that you remarry.' Those were his last words." A sob burst from Binele's throat. Her face became red, and shiny tears ran down her cheeks. She opened her purse and began to rummage for another handkerchief.

Rabbi Gabriel said, "It is not our world. What the Creator intends we shall never know."

∎

On the evening of this very day, Menucha Alte had one of her attacks. The nursing maid put a hot compress on her belly, but she continued to groan. The rabbi lay in his private bedroom across the hall. "Father in Heaven, cure her or take her away!" he cried out within himself. He knew well that one might not tell God what to do, but why should she suffer so uselessly? She was a saint, a holy victim. At the same time that the rabbi was filled with compassion for her, a malicious voice spoke: If Menucha Alte should die, he could marry Binele. The rabbi pulled his sidelocks. "Wicked lecher, in spite of your foul wishes she will live to be a hundred and twenty!"

He covered his face with his feather bed and tried to doze off, but his body felt hot. He imagined Binele cleansing herself for him in the ritual bath, standing with him under the canopy, copulating with him. "You are better than my husband," she was moaning in her passion. "You are stronger than Samson!"

"Well, I'm losing the world to come," the rabbi admonished himself. "Even Gehenna is too small a punishment for me. The demons will drag me into the desert behind the Black Mountains where Asmodeus and Lilith rule, into the abyss of defilement, into the darkness of no return."

He fell asleep and Binele stood before him naked, her nipples red as fire. She kissed him, caressed him, braided his beard and sidelocks. She bent down on all fours and commanded, "Ride on me as on Balaam's ass." The rabbi awoke with a start. Was it still night? Was it already daybreak?

The window was covered with a shutter. From his wife's room he heard her maid speak and an outcry from the sick woman. The rabbi went to her. The maid stepped aside, and Menucha Alte asked in a choked voice, "Who was that female? Why did you accept her?"

"She's Binele, my Aunt Temerl's daughter."

"What does she want. To take my place?"

"God forbid. You will soon recover."

"My end has come. Give me your hand and swear that you will send her away."

Outside, the day was breaking. The rabbi could see Menucha Alte stretching out a bony hand. His mind filled with wrath. He heard himself shout, "You have tortured me enough all these years! I refuse to swear."

He ran back to his bedroom and in the dark banged his knee and spilled the dish of the morning ablution water. He stepped with his bare foot into the puddle it made. "Let her die, the nuisance!" Rage seethed in him. He went out into the courtyard and hit his forehead against the doorpost on the wooden case of the mezuzah. In the east the sky reddened. Dew was falling. Crows croaked. The rabbi stopped at the well and filled a bucket with water. He poured it over his fingers but he did not have the courage to recite "I thank Thee." Perhaps he should throw himself into the well? He gazed into its depth and saw his face, dark and diffused. He had a desire to run and scream. It was she who brought me to these ungodly reveries by depriving me, he thought. I should have divorced her the very first year of our marriage. He suddenly remembered what a Hasid had told him speaking about his own wife: that not blood ran in her veins but tepid dishwater. The rabbi laughed and gritted his teeth. "I shall not give her an oath."

The sun emerged like a bloody head from a womb. The rabbi breathed the cool air deeply. He recalled what the Talmud said of Joseph: Joseph was about to lie with Potiphar's wife, but the image of his father revealed itself to him and prevented him. There are passions that even the saints cannot overcome without grace from on High. After a while the rabbi returned to his room. He put on his breeches, his stockings, his fringed garment, and his slippers, and he went to the study house. The oak door was closed and the rabbi knocked three times to warn the corpses, who pray there during the night, that the day had arrived. Inside, a remnant of a memorial candle glimmered in the menorah. In the study house it was still night. The rabbi stood, perplexed. Was he allowed to pray after such profane thoughts? He heard quiet steps. Shmaya slipped in, a figure without substance, a mere shadow.

"Father, Mother has . . ." He did not finish the sentence.

The rabbi lifted one eyebrow. "I know. I killed her."

After Menucha Alte's grave was filled and Shmaya recited Kaddish, his father approached him and in a loud voice said, "Mazel tov, Rabbi."

Shmaya stood before him, dazed. A murmur of protest rose from the Hasidim. Eyes bulged; beards and sidelocks shook.

His father said, "I am no longer permitted to be a leader of Jews."

Binele was at the cemetery and she tried to push her way to Rabbi Gabriel, but two beadles held her back. Later, in the time of shivah, his hangers-on attempted to convince him that allowing Shmaya to take his place would create a furor in all the rabbinical courts. People would suspect Rabbi Gabriel of having committed a mortal sin; it would also be interpreted as a victory for the enlightened ones and for the anti-Hasidim. He sat on a low stool in his stocking feet, his lapel torn, which is the sign of mourning, and a volume of the Book of Job on his knees, and he kept silent. Beila the cook told people that the rabbi had stopped eating. All he took through the day was a glass of black coffee. Again and again Binele made an effort to call on him. She even offered a bribe to the beadles, but Rabbi Gabriel had given them strict orders not to let her in. Shmaya, who observed shivah by himself in his attic room, came to his father to beg him to keep his chair. Rabbi Gabriel said to him, "Your father is a murderer."

On the Sabbath, shivah is interrupted, and the beadles prepared the usual repast in the study house for Rabbi Gabriel and his Hasidim, who had come from all sides of Poland to attend his wife's funeral. But Rabbi Gabriel refused to leave his room. He chained the door from inside, and no pleading could persuade him. Avigdor brought benediction wine, challah, fish, and meat, but the rabbi ate only a piece of challah dunked in horseradish. When it grew late and the Hasidim realized that nothing could be done, they grasped Shmaya by the collar of his robe and put him at the head of the table. They poured wine for him into a goblet and he mumbled the benediction. With shaky hands, he broke a slice of braided challah and tasted a small piece, and the Hasidim caught the crumbs that fell from it and swallowed them, since the bread had been sanctified by the new rabbi's touch. The Hasidim sang table chants, and Shmaya muttered the words. After a while he interpreted the Torah, but his hushed voice could hardly be heard.

The next day the same thing happened. The beadles who served his father now served Shmaya. He sat at the head of the table—pale, his back bent, in a fur hat too small for his head—

and it was obvious to everyone that he was overcome with grief. In his sermon he did not preach anything new but quoted sayings of his saintly grandfather, blessed be his memory, and of his father, he should live long. Some of the younger Hasidim maintained that Shmaya was greater than the father in fear of God and in his humility.

Sabbath night, after Havdalah, for the last time Binele asked to be announced to Rabbi Gabriel. When the door remained locked against her, she ordered the coachmen to harness the horses, and her carriage disappeared down the Lublin road. Since the Sabbath was over, the rabbi returned to the observance of shivah. Almost all the Hasidim who had come to Menucha Alte's funeral left the same night or the morning after.

On Monday, the court was empty. Because the rabbi had ceased lecturing in the yeshiva, many students had stopped studying and were roaming the village. Everyone in Klintow knew that Shmaya was too weak to be the head of the yeshiva. He had neither the voice nor the skill to make students understand a difficult passage in the Gemara. There was a time when there had been in the Klintow court about forty old men, disciples who stayed there all year round and ate from a common kettle. Most of them had died. The owners of inns and hostels grumbled that if Shmaya was to be the rabbi the court would lose its followers and Klintow would become a deserted town.

The seven days of mourning were over, and then the thirty days of mourning, but Rabbi Gabriel remained secluded. He seemed not to sleep; all night one could see the glow of the oil lamp through the crevices of his shutter. In the month of Elul the days became shorter, the evenings longer, gossamer webs floated through the air, cool breezes wafted from the pine forest nearby. In the study house the ram's horn was blown every morning to deceive Satan into believing that the Messiah was about to come and he should withdraw his instigations against Jews. The leaves on the few trees in Rabbi Gabriel's garden turned as yellow as saffron and kept falling all day and all night. Shmaya came to his father to complain that the yeshiva was about to disintegrate and that after the Days of Awe the last of the students would have gone. He said to his father, "Forgive me, but penitence like this is nothing but selfishness."

That night Rabbi Gabriel did not sleep a wink. He sat on the edge of his bed and pondered until daybreak. He had been waging war not only with his body but also with his soul. Both of them are no good, he mused. The body is a glutton on this earth, and the soul wants to gobble up Leviathan in Paradise. He could not forget Menucha Alte's face as he had seen it before her burial: white as chalk, with an open mouth, her nose crooked as a beak, one eye opened and glazed. Even though she had not a single tooth, her lips looked bitten and wounded. She appeared to be screaming without a voice, "Of what avail were my torments? How did I deserve all this pain?"

If this was the aim of creation, cursed be creation, Rabbi Gabriel decided. Actually, the Almighty never answered Job's questions. All He did was boast about His wisdom and His might. At dawn he fell asleep. He dreamed that he was a bridegroom being led to the wedding canopy with Menucha Alte in the synagogue yard. It was a hot summer evening. A green moon, as large as the sun and almost as bright, was shining. Girls dressed in white held wax candles, boys carried torches. Strange birds the size of eagles circled in the sky. They flapped their wings and threw silvery shadows. Everything happened at once. The musicians were playing, Hasidim were singing, the yeshiva students were discussing the Talmud. The old wedding jester, Reb Getzl, was cracking jokes and turning somersaults. At the same time, Father was reciting the benedictions. Grandmother was dancing a kosher dance with a cluster of old women. He, young Gabriel, was sitting with his new spouse partaking of the golden broth. He gazed at Menucha Alte and could not believe it was she. She was so beautiful that he was overcome with astonishment. How can such splendor exist? he wondered. She was both matter and spirit. An otherworldly radiance fell from her eyes. Even her veil and gown shone with their own light. Could she be an angel disguised as a human being? Had the redemption come and Mother Rachel descended from the Nest of the Bird where she dwells and revealed herself to him?

Rabbi Gabriel began to cry and he woke up trembling. His bed trembled with him. The sun had risen and a fiery chariot sailed in the sky from the west to the east. He had slept long, he was late reciting the Shema. He remembered the passage in the Psalms: "The heavens declare the glory of God; and the firmament showeth His handiwork . . . as a bridegroom coming out of his chamber . . . His going forth is from the end of the heaven, and his circuit unto the ends of it."

Rabbi Gabriel got up, washed his hands, dressed, and went out into the courtyard on the way to the study house. "Where else can I go?" he said to himself. "To a tavern, to a house of ill repute?" He had wakened with new vigor and with a hunger for learning. A cheder boy was walking toward him, his face white, his sidelocks disheveled. He carried a Pentateuch and a paper bag of food. Rabbi Gabriel stopped him. "Do you want to earn two groschen?" he asked.

"Yes, Rabbi."

"What should a Jew do who has lost the world to come?"

The boy seemed to ponder. "Be a Jew."

"Even though he has lost the world to come?"

"Yes."

"And study Torah?"

"Yes."

"Since he is lost, why the Torah?"

"It's good."

"It's good, eh? As good as candy?"

The boy hesitated for a moment. "Yes."

"Well, you earned the two groschen." Rabbi Gabriel put his hand into his right pocket where he kept money for charity, and gave two groschen to the boy. He bent down to him, pinched his cheek, and kissed his forehead. "You are cleverer than all of them. Go and buy yourself some sweets."

The boy grabbed the coin and began to run, his sidelocks flying, his fringed garment blowing in the wind. Rabbi Gabriel went straight to the yeshiva. He was afraid that all the students had left, but some fourteen or fifteen still remained. They had come to study at sunrise, as was the custom in Klintow. When they saw the rabbi they rose in awe. The rabbi shouted, "The boy knows the truth!"

And he began to lecture on the section where he had left off weeks ago.

There Are No Coincidences

ALTHOUGH party invitations no longer frightened me, I still found myself making careful preparations for this particular party. I got a haircut, laid out my best suit, selected a special shirt, tie, and cuff links. I had recently gone on a diet, but because I didn't want to look too thin, I discontinued it. What should I bring my hosts? Flowers? Wine? What kind of wine? Port? Sherry? Or possibly even champagne? Meeting new people was still a major undertaking.

It was scheduled for this Saturday and I decided to take a cab to the suburb where it was being held. It was early autumn and the weather had been mild, but that morning it turned cold and rainy, and as I listened to the steam hissing in my radiator, it already felt like midwinter. Trees, visible from my window, covered with foliage only yesterday, had become bare overnight. Churning clouds augured a further change in the weather. From my newspaper I learned that a hurricane which had already struck another state was on its way to New York, though it might veer out to sea. The storm left destruction in its wake. In one village an entire cottage was sheared from its foundation and blown into the ocean together with its occupants.

As I lay in bed the morning of the party, I envisioned a change also taking place in me. A loose tooth which hadn't bothered me suddenly sent a stabbing pain through my jaw. Ordinarily I'm not prone to headaches, but I awoke with a dull ache on the left side of my head. Several disturbing dreams had given me a restless night, though I could only remember them vaguely. In one dream I recalled shouting at someone and being involved in a fight. There was also something about an animal, but what it was I couldn't recollect. What did stay with me afterward was the despairing knowledge that one leads a double life—each part hermetically sealed off from the other.

Well, perhaps the mail would bring some good news. True, last week's mail was particularly light, except for a few advertisements which I threw into the wastebasket. But generally on Saturdays my mail was more abundant than on other days and I hoped today's mail would bring something interesting.

Occasionally a check arrived in payment for a piece which had been included in an anthology. I might even receive a letter from a woman. Sometimes the clipping service sent a belated review. The postman arrives about ten o'clock. Though my bedroom is some distance from the entrance door, I'm always able to hear the sound of the letters being shoved underneath.

There was no particular reason for me to get up early that Saturday morning, so I decided to stay in bed until the mail arrived. Meanwhile, I leafed through a collection of modern French poetry which was on my night table. My knowledge of French is scant, and since the selected poets were all modern, their poems seemed almost meaningless to me. From the biographical notes it was clear that the authors were all young. What were they saying? What was troubling them? I was certain that apart from my meager comprehension of the language, it was difficult for me to understand them altogether because I was of a different generation.

I thought I heard a piece of paper being slipped under the door. I listened carefully and waited for more, but that was all. Without my robe or slippers I rushed to the door, and to my disappointment, I found a single printed advertisement put out by some rug-cleaning firm. I angrily tossed the ad into the trash can thinking that a year or two ago a tree was felled in Canada to create paper for this.

Because the mail was so unsatisfactory I had to seek my little pleasure elsewhere and I went into my combination living/dining room. The bookshelves were tightly packed. On some of the shelves the books were lined up vertically, one row in front of the other, while on top of each I had stacked various journals and oversized volumes.

That morning I had no appetite, neither for reading nor for breakfast. I stood staring at the books, trying to find something that would capture my interest, but I knew in advance that it was futile. The philosophical works, especially, seemed repugnant to me. Not a single thought of theirs could be of any help to me at this time. From the library I wandered into the kitchen, where I gazed with apathy at the milk, the eggs, the cereals, and the jellies.

God in Heaven, there was a time when I dreamed of having my own apartment with a private bedroom, my own library, and a kitchen where I could prepare some tea or coffee. But now all these gifts lost their meaning, if only for a while. The person responsible for all of this was, of course, Esther. As long as she was here, everything had charm. But whose fault was it that she left? Mine, I knew. Now it was too late. But I mustn't starve myself if I wished to look good at the party. I filled a bowl with cereal, poured milk over it, and sprinkled raisins on top. In this kitchen, as in the library, were hidden treasures but one had to bite into them.

I passed the day napping and strolling in the rain. The phone only rang once and it was a wrong number. After lunch I walked twenty blocks south from the restaurant where I had eaten and then back again. On the return trip the wind waged war with my umbrella and tried by every means to rip it apart, while I was just as determined not to let it happen. Sometimes a gust of wind would swoop down from above and make the umbrella feel heavy in my hand. Another time the gust would come from below and the umbrella would try to fly away. I fantasized that I was a sea captain steering a ship through a stormy sea. When I entered the hallway of my house with my umbrella still intact, I experienced the pride of a victorious fighter. The water streamed from my umbrella as I waited for the elevator. Alone in the elevator, like a child I wrote my name on the floor with the wet umbrella tip, then erased it.

When I looked at the kitchen clock I realized that though I still had some time to rest, it would be necessary to leave for the party shortly.

The cab driver informed me in advance that he wasn't too familiar with the suburb I asked to be driven to. I suggested that he start driving anyway and ask directions along the route. He was doing me a great favor. Several times he hinted that he would expect an extra tip. "I stay away from such neighborhoods," he said with pride, intimating that those who did go there were people with lower standards than his. He seemed to regret having taken me as a fare and muttered to himself all the way. It started to thunder and lightning. The driver kept looking back at me angrily as though it were my fault that nature was acting this way. As the storm intensified, it became impossible to check our course. The roads were flooded and the cab seemed to be enveloped in flame with every streak of lightning. I could almost feel the million-volt electrical current around me. Though the windshield wipers worked furiously, there was little visibility. We could barely see the headlights of the oncoming cars. Of all things, I had forgotten to bring my umbrella, the very one for which I had waged such a campaign.

The driver finally seemed to give himself over to his destiny completely and ceased turning around to glare at me. As far as I could figure out, he had taken the wrong road. Between the two of us there arose the hostility which comes when people are forced into a dangerous situation together. The taxi sped on, away from New York, away from the party. One or two cars passed seemingly propelled by fatalistic speed. Perhaps they, too, were lost.

A garage loomed up in front of us and we headed for it. The dark face of a man appeared. Despite the fury of the elements he seemed quite at ease. My driver rolled his window down and asked for directions. The garage man, without so much as a glance at me, told him how to go. His instructions were complicated. "Make a right turn at the light, continue straight ahead, then turn right again, then left, then straight ahead again, past three lights, then a blinker, and make a sharp left." It was impossible to believe that the driver could remember it all. But he repeated the information and it was clear that he had a picture of the route in his mind. I was impressed with the patience of the man talking to him. He was wringing wet.

This party would cost me half a week's salary. I sat back, shut my eyes, and resigned myself, though I hoped I would at least arrive before the other guests departed.

2

The driver found the correct address, but the street was so narrow and full of parked cars that it was impossible for him to pull up directly in front of the house, so that I had to get out on the opposite side of the street. Another car blocked my way, and though I wasn't standing in the rain for more than a few seconds, I was thoroughly drenched. It was as if some celestial prankster had poured a tub of water over my head. In a split second, all my clothes were ruined—the pressed suit, the new shirt, the tie, the shined shoes. People were getting into the elevator but I had to stand there for a while, just to shake the water off. My eyeglasses were covered with rain and I reached into my pocket for a handkerchief to wipe them with, but it too was soaked. Standing there, I had to laugh inwardly at my wasted efforts. The cold moisture chilled my body and I felt like sneezing. That would be the final irony—to get a lung inflammation from all this.

"Well, it serves me right for wanting worldly pleasures," I reprimanded myself. I found the apartment and rang the doorbell, prepared to meet new people. The years had taught me to mask my shyness. The others were, after all, no more than human beings, each with his own weaknesses and failures. "Be nice to them and they will be nice to you," I encouraged myself.

My friend B. himself opened the door. He was coatless and looked as though he had had a few drinks too many. He squinted curiously at me, as if he didn't remember having invited me. Then his face broke out into a broad smile.

"Come in. Oh, you're all wet."

"I came here by taxi, but the few feet between . . ."

"I know, I know. Take off your jacket."

He helped me remove my jacket and left me standing there in my wet shirt. I caught a glimpse of myself in the hall mirror and saw a disheveled person, gaunt and stooped, with a wet bald pate, a wrinkled collar, and a tie which hung limply. My host impatiently grabbed my arm and forcefully shoved me into the living room, though I shuffled my feet, trying to slow down my entry, in order to repair some of the damage done by the storm. Through my wet glasses, I glimpsed a darkened room, full of silent figures. Apparently the conversation had stopped when this belated guest entered. My host introduced me, and as I walked up to each one with uncertain steps, the men rose. My name was not familiar to them. The hostess appeared from the kitchen.

It was apparent that she, too, had either forgotten about me or assumed that I wouldn't come. A chair was pointed out to me. B. asked what I would like to drink and I told him. I was hungry, but I soon saw that the meal was buffet-style. How strange that not one person said a word to me or made a remark about how wet I was. Well, this was a literary group and no attention was paid to the amenities. After a while, the hostess handed me a plate of hors d'oeuvres which I balanced on my lap while holding a highball in my hand. At least the whiskey would warm me and perhaps help me forget my embarrassment. While sipping the drink and nibbling the food on the plate, I felt like both sneezing and coughing. With the napkin I was handed, I wiped my spectacles and for the first time was able to see who was there. Literary parties are always noisy, with everyone talking at once, but here one woman was talking while the others listened. Most of the guests were middle-aged, trying to look young. The windows were hung with drapes and the storm on the other side of the wall might just as well not have existed. Here, everything was dry, warm; in fact, too warm.

Now I too began to listen to the woman who was holding forth. She seemed young, but I couldn't be certain. Her dark eyes, large and bulgy, made me feel that she was saying "I love people but demand that they respect and love me, too. When I speak, I presume they listen to me." There was an aggressiveness in her congeniality and in the soft tone of her voice. She was delivering a discourse on a study she had made at Sing Sing prison and the conditions under which the inmates had to live. Her speech was slow and monotonous, with the self-confidence of someone who knows for certain that no one would dare to interrupt. Each phrase expressed compassion for the prisoners and contempt, mixed with derision, for the administrators. I had read enough studies of this kind and was certain that she hadn't discovered anything new, but for some reason most of the group sat quietly and allowed her to carry on a long, tedious monologue.

For a while I forgot my wet clothing and became absorbed in what was going on. Where does her power lie? I wondered. Has she such a strong personality? I soon realized what it was about her that had such an effect on people. First, her location: she sat in a chair which dominated the entire room. She had selected the most strategic spot. Secondly, she had touched on a theme which addressed itself to the issues of civil rights and social justice. To ignore her would be tantamount to siding with brutality.

I noted how the people pretended interest in what she was saying, asking brief questions to which they knew the answers, making short comments intended to express sympathy for the prisoners and disdain for the wardens. There was a moment when I wanted to ask: "How about the victims of these criminals? Don't they deserve any compassion?" But I knew her reply beforehand. I recalled the saying from the Talmud, that those who pity the wicked are cruel to the just.

There was a woman sitting quietly to one side of the room and I now noticed her for the first time. Just as the speaker's location was advantageous, hers was disadvantageous. Instead of a regular chair she was seated on a stool which could topple at any moment. Her face was small, her lips thin, and her cheekbones high. Though her nose had a bump in the middle, it turned up at the tip. Her green-gold eyes were surrounded by fine lines and wrinkles. She might have been in her late thirties. One could guess that she had had a hard life. Her mouth and eyes expressed both impatience and resignation. She was the only one who didn't pretend to be interested in the speaker's harangue. On the contrary, she looked annoyed. She wore a black dress and had a thin gold chain around her neck. Her chestnut-colored hair was combed in an outmoded style. I was puzzled as to what type of person she was. Was she a writer? Was she Jewish? Her face had a quality of intelligence, but it also hinted of hysteria. I felt that this was a woman who could be keenly witty, love intensely, perhaps hate intensely. When such a person becomes enraged, she is capable of hurling dishes or throwing herself out the window. She probably made love with great passion.

What struck me most about her was that she refused to be mesmerized, like the others, by the sentimental claptrap. While smoking her cigarette she was engrossed in her own thoughts. I looked at her, thinking: I'm with you. She returned my glance, surprised, yet curious, as if she had now seen *me* for the first time. But our chairs were situated in such a way as to make talk between us impossible.

I hoped that something would transpire which would change the circumstances or that the story of Sing Sing would come to an end, but neither happened. The guests remained seated as if stuck to their chairs. Because I had arrived late, I realized the evening was as good as over. Several of the guests finally started to leave. Unquestionably, the party had been a failure. Since the "do-gooder" squelched all conversation, everyone wanted to get away from her as soon as they were able to. She stared angrily at those who dared to leave, like a Salvation Army preacher abandoned in the middle of a hymn. As she extended her hand to them in parting, her expression signified: "I forgive you, but whether the human race will, I'm not so sure."

She continued prattling, drawing out her words as unhurriedly and as full of self-assuredness as before, though her audience was dwindling. A few still nodded agreement. I glanced at my wristwatch, saw it was five minutes to eleven, and stood up. At that exact moment, the chestnut-haired woman also rose, both of us having come to a similar decision at the same time.

Our host, who had been immobilized throughout the evening by the penal injustices, shook himself out of his trance. He looked surprised to see his guests departing and tried to persuade them to remain. His wife also mumbled something about it being too early to go. Notwithstanding their pleas, the woman in the black dress and I both replied that we had a long trip and that it was late.

I hastily bid goodbye to the people I hadn't even spoken to. When I said good night to the storyteller, she raised her eyebrows and glared at me hatefully. Perhaps she knew all along that I wasn't in her power. I had been the profaner who upset the séance.

The woman in the black dress and I walked to the elevator together. We waited in silence. Gathering up my courage, I said: "Allow me to introduce myself; the merciful protector of prisoners never even permitted me to speak to anyone."

"Did you ever see such chutzpah?" she asked. "In all my life

I never lived through such a miserable evening. You're lucky you arrived late. From six o'clock on, no one was able to speak. She just sat there and droned on and on. What kind of creature is she? Who does she think she is? And why are bores like that invited to parties? Well, I'm glad to be out of that place. Never again will I cross their threshold." As she spoke these words, I knew there was a bond between us.

3

A half hour had gone by and still no cab came along. We left the street where the party had been held and a passerby indicated a taxi stand, but it was empty. The cabs that did pass were occupied. It was practically midnight and here we were stranded in a godforsaken suburb. My clothes still hadn't dried and I felt chilled. Nor did her coat seem heavy enough for a cold fall night. We found a bus stop and waited there, but it soon became apparent that no buses were in operation at this hour. In an attempt to warm myself, I raised my jacket collar. She shivered sporadically. Above us, the sky was heavy with dark clouds, laden with rain and perhaps snow.

The woman decided to overcome her pride and began to wave at passing automobiles, but one car after another sped by without stopping. We both realized the danger: the rain might start again at any moment; it was just beginning to drizzle. I could feel the sharp mist on my face. There was always the possibility of returning to the party and spending the night with our hosts, but neither of us was in the mood to impose on these people. As for myself, I would rather sleep in the street than put others in an awkward position.

It felt odd to stand here with a woman whose name I didn't know, sharing with her an unfortunate night after a miserable party. I still hoped that a cab might drive up, though I knew full well that the chances weren't too good. Where is it written that taxis must cruise around Long Island in the middle of the night? I recalled David Hume's words: The fact that the sun has risen every morning till now is no guarantee that it will rise again tomorrow. What is the law of averages altogether? Of what scientific worth are statistics? It occurred to me that there might be a hotel nearby, but I didn't dare mention this to my companion. Who knows what she might suspect me of? Actually, the only thing to do was walk, rather than to remain standing in one spot. But I noticed that she wore high-heeled shoes. I remembered reading of people who had frozen to death on cool nights. The moment comes when the body has no more resistance and the internal temperature begins to fall. At eighty degrees Fahrenheit, one is as good as gone.

"Well, that was really some party!" she said, speaking to me as well as to herself. "God knows, I didn't want to come, but they insisted. Don't laugh, but I didn't even get enough to eat."

"Neither did I."

"Why do people give parties if they can't or won't make their guests feel at home? I've stopped inviting people once and for all. I have neither the room nor the time to spend in preparation. I assumed that after a while I would no longer be asked out, but people's mills, like God's, grind slowly."

"You live alone, I assume."

"Yes, alone."

"I do too."

A taxi appeared. From a distance I could see that it was taken, but my partner raised her hand to signal it with the desperation of one whom only a miracle, or an error in the order of things, could save. The driver stared at her coldly, calling out: "Are you blind?"

"I'm afraid we're never going to get a taxi here," I said.

"What do you suggest?"

"I think we should start walking. At least we won't freeze."

"But where to? I don't even know in which direction New York lies. A cab won't pass this way," she added, raising her voice.

"It's not that late."

"I once waited for one on Fifth Avenue for over an hour. Would you like a cigarette?"

"No, thanks."

"Have one. It will warm you up some."

She handed me a cigarette and lit it with her lighter, holding it longer than was necessary, seemingly to warm my face with the flame.

Just as I inhaled the first puff, there was a flash of lightning followed by a frightful thunderclap. Judging from the brief time between the lightning and the thunder, it struck close. My new friend grabbed my arm and clung to me.

"Oh, this is terrible!"

"We have to go inside somewhere!"

"Where? The houses are all locked."

There was a building near us which had shops on the ground floor but no overhang under which to stand. We began to walk and saw a house with an awning over the entrance gate. We were protected for a while, but in a few minutes the drizzle had become a driving torrent which pummeled the awning like hailstones. As the storm gathered momentum, it wet us from all sides. We huddled against the door to protect our backs from the wind and rain. Every degree of warmth was now of utmost value. Like two stray animals, we pressed hard against one another. "If only there was a hotel somewhere," I said.

"What? Where?"

I don't know why, but I asked, "Are you in the literary field?"

After a pause, she replied, "I suppose you could call it that."

"What do you do?"

"I write children's books."

"Really? How interesting!"

"Yes. I write and also edit them. That's how I make a living."

"One has to know how to write for children," I said, to make conversation. In a way, words added warmth.

"Yes, people don't appreciate that fact. They think anyone can write for children. Every year we received hundreds of manuscripts that we send back, some from famous writers."

"You've never written for adults?" I asked, embarrassed at the urgency in my voice.

The rain had now leveled off. It was pouring steadily without intensifying.

"I've sinned in that area, too," she admitted, "but soon realized that literature for adults simply wasn't my métier. I don't have the patience. Somehow I do have the patience for children's books. It's a mystery to me in a way, since I don't especially care for children. I don't even have any. I'm divorced."

"Aha."

"At least I didn't ruin an innocent child's life."

We stood watching the rain. It began to taper off and looked as though it was coming through a sieve, straight and thin. Just as it seemed to be ending, it again increased and came down faster and with greater force. It pelted the asphalt with the arrogance of an element responsible to no one, oblivious of precedents. Steam rose from the pavement. The gushing water slithered off cars driving past. This brought to my mind a newspaper photograph I had seen during World War II—an Allied bomb had blown up a German dam. A passing car was being pursued by a wall of water. The photo was taken from an airplane in the fraction of a second before the driver was engulfed.

"Would you be so kind as to let me hold your hand?" she asked. I wanted to dry it first but there wasn't anything to use. When I gave her my hand, I felt hers was wet, too, but warmer than mine.

At that moment there was a streak of lightning, the likes of which I had never seen before. An enormous bolt lit up the sky, turning it into an otherworldly purplish red. It became day for an instant—sunset or sunrise. The thunder that followed immediately jolted the brain in my skull. We clasped each other's hand more tightly. "God in Heaven, what can we do?" the woman cried. She looked at me with fright, mixed with the hatred of someone who feels he must perish on account of another person's ill fortune.

Suddenly an old car pulled up, the kind plumbers or repairmen use, and a short man, wearing a raincoat but no hat, got out. Though he dashed under the awning, the few instants in the downpour got him drenched. He fished a key out of his pocket and in an Italian accent asked: "Are you folks waiting here for a taxi? You can wait all night."

"Do you live here?" the woman shouted. "Can you at least let us go inside for a while?"

"Come on in. I'm the night watchman here. You shouldn't be outside on a night like this."

"Oh, God Himself has sent you!"

He unlocked the door and we followed him in. I thought this must have been the way the animals had walked into

Noah's ark. Somewhere I read that Noah himself led the tame creatures, but the wild beasts came rushing in only after the flood had started. I even imagined I had once seen a picture of a lion pleading to be allowed onto the ark—a bedraggled, half-running, half-swimming beast.

For the second time in one day I found myself leaving puddles behind me in the lobby. My eyeglasses became fogged. Through the haze I heard the night watchman say: "You know what, folks. Come downstairs, I have a little room there. I'll make some tea for you and you can rest."

"You're a wonderful man," the woman said. "No one else but God could have sent you."

"Well, you just can't let people die."

We took the freight elevator to the cellar, where there were gas meters, red brick walls, and an uneven ceiling. On one side was an enormous furnace and next to it a coal bin. Trunks, folding beds, and all kinds of furniture belonging to tenants were stored in an alcove.

He ushered us into a small room which was like the dressing room of a shabby downtown theater. It contained a sofa covered with a torn spread and an armchair from which the stuffing was falling out. Spots of dried paint spattered the naked ceiling bulb. Faded photos of movie actresses as well as magazine and newspaper clippings hung from the walls. A teapot and a glass with a rusty tin spoon in it stood on a lopsided table.

I had removed my eyeglasses and could now clearly see our benefactor. He was slight, with short legs and a protruding belly. The man was no longer young and his hair was streaked with gray. His heavy-lidded eyes expressed a special Italian quality of good humor and friendliness. He seemed to be saying: "I know how you feel. We are all no more than flesh and blood." He lit the gas burner and filled the kettle with water. From a cupboard he brought tea bags, a sugar bowl, a package of crackers, and two teacups. The woman burst out laughing. I removed my jacket and hat, sat down, and said to her: "There is some good left in the world."

"Yes, I'll never forget this as long as I live!"

We drank our tea, nibbled our crackers, and talked. Here we were in a dugout below the ground, the safest spot in a storm.

The Italian had gone back upstairs to the lobby, but he promised to let us know as soon as the storm subsided.

I don't know how it began but the woman started to tell me all about her family, her ex-husband, how she had been penniless in New York and had gotten a job at the last moment. Her life, like my own, was peppered with miracles. Just as with the watchman tonight, so destiny, or whatever one calls it, had sent her a savior in every crisis: each time when the water came up to her neck, her guardian angel stood by her, as it were. "Isn't that strange? Why should fate continually play cat-and-mouse with a person? Why terrify and then make a last-minute rescue? It's simply that we explain every good coincidence as being a miracle and we blame all the adverse things on blind nature."

We talked of this and that. I asked: "How do you define co-incidence? Of all the poorly defined words, this word is the most confusing."

"Coincidence is when things happen according to physical laws, but we interpret them as good or bad. For example: had that bolt of lightning struck us, it would simply have been because the electrical explosion had taken place a few yards closer than it actually had . . ."

"How do you know there isn't some knowing force that directed the lightning?" I asked.

"How can you prove there is?"

"If there is a knowing force in one part of the universe, then the entire universe can't be ruled by blind forces."

The night watchman came to tell us that it was still pouring, and as far as he could tell, it would continue this way all night. He stood there scratching his head and winking good-naturedly. I thought that he was about to come out with a joke, but after some hesitation he went back upstairs.

"We'll give him a little something," the woman suggested.

"I have it prepared already," I said.

"Why just you? Let's give him ten dollars. Five dollars from each of us."

We smiled and chatted. I was thinking that if there could be anything between us, this cellar was the most unusual place for it. But were we ready for it? I gazed at her, looking for those qualities and characteristics which might please me, but her

face was too tense. She lacked that naïveté, those hints of exal-
tation which I am attracted to in women. I also knew that no
woman had ever been attractive to me at first. In all my relationships I had to undertake a slow process of erasing the first
impression, or at least overcoming it and correcting it. Behind
the façade of ugliness or egotism was always hidden another
face, or perhaps another façade. I tried to hasten the evalua-
tion, to strip away the outer layer and catch a glimpse of what
was beneath.

Meanwhile, I told her what little there was about myself.
That is to say, she asked the questions and I willingly answered
them. I even went so far as to mention Esther.

About two in the morning she rested her head on the back
of the sofa and said she wanted to try to get some sleep. I
made myself comfortable on the shabby chair, propping my
feet up on a trunk, neither falling asleep nor being fully awake.
I felt like someone dozing on a wagon and even imagined that
the storeroom was moving. Real dreams were interwoven with
daydreams. After years of sleeping alone, I again found myself
sleeping near someone, not someone close, but not exactly a
stranger, either. The glare of the light bulb shone through my
closed eyelids. I had a fantastic thought which had nothing to
do with my present circumstances. It occurred to me that if
there were local spirits, ghosts bound up with a house, with a
cemetery or a ruin, they would have to revolve with the earth
on its axis, circle the sun, fly along with the sun on its course in
the Milky Way, perhaps make the journey together with the
galaxy in infinite space. That would mean that spirits also have
gravity and motion and therefore also have weight and consequently mass. If this were so, they would have to be bound
by all other physical laws. Then again, if spirits are not bound
by physical laws, what keeps them on earth? Why shouldn't
they fly off to other planets or even cross the boundaries of
the cosmos?

These thoughts went through my mind again and again,
with all sorts of variations, as if they were a leitmotif of a sym-
phony. I had almost forgotten the woman who lay on the sofa,
but not really. Actually, I was fully aware of her presence. Even
the thoughts about the spirits were somehow related to her,
though I didn't know what the connection was.

I shivered and turned over. When I awoke I felt drugged, as if I had taken a sleeping pill. The woman was seated near the table, her face and hair showing signs of sleep. She smiled at me.

"You slept very soundly," she said.

"And you?"

"Perhaps for a moment. I can't even sleep under perfect circumstances."

I sat without speaking. Then I heard myself say: "I don't even know your name."

"Didn't I introduce myself to you?"

"I didn't hear your name clearly."

"My name is a very banal one."

"A name is a name."

"But mine is already too banal. Perhaps you can give me a name?"

"Unless it's my name," I said, baffled by my foolishness. That was equivalent to a proposal.

The woman was serious for a moment, then she smiled sleepily, seeming astonished, yet tolerant of such nonsense. I recognized that quality of beauty which I had been looking for.

"What's your name?" she asked. I told her my name.

"No more original than mine."

She stood up, I also got up, just as we did at the party when both of us simultaneously decided to leave. For a while we looked at each other with the choked laughter of friends who meet at some strange place unexpectedly and, in their utter confusion, forget momentarily the other one's name and how and when they ever met. Suddenly we fell into each other's arms like lovers who had been waiting impatiently for an encounter. A midnight heat emanated from her body. We kissed as she passionately cried out words that no longer sounded to me like English, but like some unknown language. I pressed her with all my strength. I heard something cracking, not knowing whether it was her girdle or my fountain pen. I became alarmed but was unable to loosen my grip. It all lasted not longer than a minute. Then we both seemed to realize how ridiculous our behavior was. Both of us moved a step apart, utterly bewildered.

"What happened to us? Are we out of our minds?" she asked.

"There are no coincidences," I said hoarsely, my voice shaking.

The woman looked at me out of the corner of her eyes. "Did fate need all this to make us act like two idiots?"

Not for the Sabbath

THAT Sabbath afternoon, the talk on the porch happened to be about teachers, tutors, and cheder boys. Our neighbor Chaya Riva complained that her grandchild got such a slap in the face from his teacher Michael that he lost a tooth. Michael had a reputation not only as an accomplished teacher but also as a big slapper and pincher. Cheder boys used to say that when he pinched, you saw the city of Krakow. He had a nickname—Scratch Me. If he felt an itch on his back, he gave his whipping stick to one of his pupils, with an order to scratch him under his shirt.

Two other women were sitting on our porch—Reitze Breindels and my Aunt Yentl, who wore a bonnet and a dress with arabesques in honor of the Sabbath. The bonnet had many beads and four ribbons—yellow, white, red, and green. I sat there and listened to the talk. Aunt Yentl began to smile and look around. She gave me a side glance. "Why do you sit among the women?" she asked. "Better go and study the *Ethics of the Fathers.*"

I understood that she was about to tell a story an eleven-year-old boy should not hear. I went behind the porch to the storage room, where we kept the Passover dishes, a barrel with torn books, and a pillowcase filled with my father's old manuscripts. The walls had wide cracks, and every word spoken on the porch could be heard. I sat on an oak mortar that was used to grind matzo meal. Through the cracks the sun reflected the colors of the rainbow in the floating dust. I heard my Aunt Yentl say, "In the little villages things are not so terrible yet. How many madmen can you find in a small town? Five or ten—not more. Besides, their crimes cannot be kept secret. But in a big city evil deeds can remain hidden for years. When I lived in Lublin, a man by the name of Reb Yissar Mandlebroit had a drygoods store that sold silk, velvet, and satin, as well as laces and accessories. His first wife died and he married a young wench, the daughter of a butcher. Her hair was the color of fire and she had the mouth of a shrew. From his first wife Reb Yissar had married children, but with this new one—her name was Dacha—he had only one, a boy named Yankele. He took after his mother in looks, with red sidelocks and blue shining eyes like little mirrors. In that family, Dacha was the boss. When an old man marries a young piece of flesh, she is the ruler.

"At cheder, Yankele had a teacher who should never have been allowed to teach. But how could people know? His name was Fivke. He was either divorced or a widower—a giant of a man, black like a gypsy. He wore a short robe and boots with high uppers, like a Russian. He wasn't from Lublin but from another region. He taught the Pentateuch, and also a little Russian and Polish. In those years, the wealthy Jews wanted their children to acquire some Gentile knowledge.

"First, let me tell you what happened to me. My former husband, blessed be his memory, was already a grandfather at the time we married, but his wife left him a young child, Chazkele, when she died, and I loved him more than I would have loved a child of my own. He called me Mama. Every day I took a bowl of hot soup and a slice of bread to the cheder for him. I went at two o'clock—recess time—when the children played in the courtyard. I sat with Chazkele on a log and fed him his lunch. He's a father now and lives far from here, but if I should meet him I'd want to kiss him all over. One day I came with my bowl of soup and the slice of bread, but the courtyard was empty. Only one little boy came out to urinate. I asked him, 'Where are all the boys?' He said, 'Today is whipping day.' I didn't understand. The door to the cheder was half open and I saw Fivke standing at a bench with a strap in his hand, calling out the boys to be whipped one after another— Berele, Schmerele, Koppele, Hershele. Each boy came over, pulled down his little pants, and was hit once or twice on his naked behind. Then he walked back to the long benches. The older boys laughed as if the whole thing was a game, but the very young ones burst out crying. That my heart did not break on the spot proved I was stronger than iron. I began to search for Chazkele among the children. The cruel teacher was so busy whipping he didn't see me. I had made up my mind that if he called Chazkele I would run over and throw the hot soup into his face and tear out his beard. However, it seemed my

Chazkele had already been whipped, because the performance ended quickly.

"I ran to my husband's store like a poisoned rat and told him what my eyes had seen, but all he said was, 'Children should be punished once in a while.' He opened the Bible and showed me the passage in the Book of Proverbs: 'He that spareth his rod hateth his son.' The child did not make any fuss. He was a good soul and said, 'Mama, it did not hurt.' Still, I insisted that my husband take Chazkele away from those malicious hands. When a wife stands up to something, a man listens. Only God knew the tears I shed."

"What wild people live in this world," Reitze Breindels remarked.

"I would have called the police and had him bound in chains and sent to Siberia," Chaya Riva said. "Such a murderer should rot in prison."

"That's easier said than done," answered Aunt Yentl. "Why didn't you have Michael Scratch Me arrested? To have a tooth knocked out is worse than being whipped."

"Yes, you are right."

"The story is only beginning," Aunt Yentl said in a singsong. "Yes, we took Chazkele out, and after the High Holidays he went to a different cheder. Not more than two or three months had passed before I heard a horrible story. The whole of Lublin was in turmoil. Fivke had his whipping day each month. Once when Dacha, Reb Yissar Mandlebroit's wife, brought lunch for her Yankele, she opened the door and saw her little treasure bent over the whipping bench being lashed by Fivke. The child was crying bitterly. Dacha did what I should have done—threw the hot soup into Fivke's face. Another person would have wiped off his mouth and kept silent. But Fivke had the nature of a Cossack. He let Yankele go, ran over to Dacha, and threw her onto the whipping bench. He had the strength of ten lions. Forgive me, but Fivke lifted her dress, tore down her bloomers, and whipped her with all his might. He used the belt from his pants, not the strap for the children. You can imagine the commotion. Dacha screamed as if he was slaughtering her. It's true that Lublin is a noisy city, but people heard her yelling, and they came to see what was

going on. Her wig fell off and her red locks showed. This slut
didn't shave her head. Some of the bystanders tried to hold
Fivke back, but whoever tried got a kick with his boot. There
happened to be only women there, and what female can fight
such a brigand? He flogged Dacha thirty-nine times, as the
beadles did in ancient days. Then he dragged her outside and
threw her into the gutter."

"Father in Heaven, where do you find such an outlaw
among Jews?" Reitze Breindels asked.

"There is no lack of filth anywhere," Chaya Riva said.

"Golden words," Aunt Yentl agreed. "If I tried to tell you
what went on in Lublin that day, you wouldn't believe your
ears. Dacha rushed home more dead than alive. Her howling
could be heard all over the street. When Reb Yissar heard what
had happened to his beloved wife, he ran to the rabbi immediately. There was talk about excommunication and black candles. Who has ever heard of a teacher thrashing a married
woman and bringing her to such disgrace? The rabbi sent his
sexton to Fivke and summoned him to a rabbinical trial, but
Fivke stood at the door of his house with a cudgel and roared,
'If you want to take me by force, try!' He spoke nasty words
about the rabbi, the elders, the whole community. Of course,
he soon had to give up the cheder. Who would send a child to
such a ruffian? Just talking about it makes me feel ants crawling
up my spine."

"Maybe he was possessed by a dybbuk?" Chaya Riva asked.

Aunt Yentl put on her brass-rimmed glasses, took them off,
and put them on her lap. She said, "Reb Yissar spoke to his
wife: 'Dachele, what can I do? Since Fivke refuses to go to the
rabbi, he will be humiliated in another way.' Dacha yelled,
'You are a coward! You're afraid of your own shadow—if you
really loved me, you would take revenge on that criminal!' Just
the same, she soon realized her husband was too old and weak
to fight a savage like Fivke. She grabbed a handful of silver
money from her strongbox and went to the place where the
toughs and the riffraff met. She called out, 'Whoever wants to
earn money, take a stick or a knife and come with me!' She
tossed copper coins and showed the silver to the rabble. They
rushed to pick up the coins, but only a few were willing to go
with her. Even rogues avoid getting mixed up in a brawl. A

boy who saw what went on ran to warn Fivke that men were out to get him. Fivke shouted, 'Let them try! I'm ready.' When the men approached, he took up an ax and challenged them. 'Come nearer and you will not walk back—they will have to carry you!' They got frightened. They could see in his eyes he was ready to chop off heads. They ran, and Dacha stood abandoned with her money. Fivke chased her with the ax. There was bedlam. Some women went to the chief of police for help, but he said, 'First let him kill her and then we will imprison him. We are not allowed to punish anyone before he commits the crime.'

"Since Fivke could not be a teacher any more and people ran from him like from a leper, he had nothing to do in Lublin. I guess you all know that there is a village called Piask not far from Lublin. In my time, the thieves of Piask were famous all over Poland. They would get up in the middle of the night, harness their horses, go to some town in their britskas, and rob the stores. A few were assigned to fight off the night watchmen. I'll make it short. Fivke went to Piask and became a teacher there. Bad as they were, the thieves wanted their boys to have some education. It wasn't easy for them to get a teacher, so they were happy when Fivke came. He took into his cheder only the children of the thieves. Sooner or later thieves are caught and put in jail, so there were always more women than men in those narrow streets. The storekeepers sold them merchandise on credit until their husbands were freed. They always paid back what they owed. Someone said that Fivke took the grass widows under his protection. He acted as a kind of healer—cupping them and applying leeches when they felt sick. He went to Lublin and came back with gifts he stole for them. My dear friends, not only did Fivke become a thief but a leader of the thieves—their rabbi. He went with them to fairs, and if there was a clash with the police Fivke was the first to fight back. As a rule, thieves don't carry guns—it's one thing to steal and another thing to shed blood—but Fivke got a pistol and became a horse thief. When peasants caught him stealing, he shot at them or set fire to their stables. In many places the villagers guarded their property all night with knives and rattles. Somehow he managed to escape them. If he was ever put on trial, he always got off. You know that judges and lawyers are on the side of the criminal. It isn't from the victims that they make a living. He was a smooth talker and disentangled himself every time. People began to tell wonders about him. Even if he was put into jail, he broke the bars in the middle of the night and ran away. Sometimes he released the other jailbirds."

"What happened then?" Chaya Riva asked.

"Wait. My throat is dry. I will bring some Sabbath fruit and prune juice."

I came out from the storage room and let Aunt Yentl treat me to a Sabbath cookie and a pear. She asked, "Where were you? Did you study the *Ethics of the Fathers*?"

I said, "I have finished this week's chapter."

"Go back to the study house," Aunt Yentl said. "Stories like these are not for you."

I returned to the storage room and Aunt Yentl continued: "Reb Yissar Mandlebroit grew old and could not longer attend to his business. Dacha, that blabbermouth, took over the whole trade. Her son, Yankele, studied with the rabbi. In the evenings, Dacha would come to our house for a chat. Whenever the talk rolled round to Fivke she would say, 'What do you think about my whipper?' This is how she referred to him. My mother, peace be with her, used to say, 'It's not worth talking about scum like him. There is fine flour and there is chaff.' But Dacha would smile and lick her lips. 'How could I have known that a teacher, a scholar could be so shameless?' She cursed him with all the curses of the book, yet at the same time she seemed to admire his prowess. When she left, my mother would say, 'If she wasn't Reb Yissar's wife I wouldn't let her through my door. She is proud that that monster abused her.' My mother forbade me to have anything to do with her.

"One day Reb Yissar died, and since Yankele was still a minor, Dacha became the guardian of the estate. At once, she dismissed her husband's employees and hired new ones. The former remained without bread, but this didn't bother her. She bought a plot of ground where the nobles lived and had a house built, with two balconies and a gable. She bedecked herself in so much jewelry she could hardly be seen. She used perfume and all kinds of powders and pastes. Although the matchmakers flooded her with matches, she held off. She insisted on seeing every candidate and talking with him. This one was not a businessman, the next was not handsome, the third was not shrewd. It is written somewhere in the Bible that when a slave becomes a king the earth trembles.

"Now hear something. Not far from Lublin there is a village called Wawolic. This village is known for celebrating Purim two days—the fourteenth and the fifteenth of the month of Adar. People living there had found remnants of a wall supposedly built before the time of Moses. This wall made the village so special that Purim for them was a great holiday. Everyone got drunk. This created a perfect opportunity for the thieves of Piask. As it is on Purim, the moon was full. Late at night when everybody was asleep, they went with their wagons and quick horses to rob the stores. They did not know that the Russian Army was carrying out maneuvers in the area. It was not long after the Polish uprising; the authorities were keeping a lookout for rebels. As the thieves were on their way, a regiment of Cossacks was riding toward them, led by a colonel. When the thieves saw them, their stomachs dropped. The Russians asked where they were going, and Fivke, who knew Russian, said they were a group of merchants going to a fair. But the colonel was no fool—he knew there was no fair in the neighborhood. He gave an order to put the thieves in chains and carry them to jail in Lublin. Fivke dared to resist, but no one can beat Cossacks who have guns and lances. He was bound like a ram and taken to prison. There were fences in Lublin who bought stolen goods, and they were waiting for the thieves to come with their loot. But when the sun rose and the wagons were not there the fences guessed what had happened and dispersed like mice. Soon the bad tidings reached the wives of the thieves in Piask. Never before had so many thieves been arrested at one time, and while there was Purim in Wawolic it was Tishah-b'Ab in Piask. As if this was not enough, one old and sickly thief could not hold up under the beatings and informed against the fences. They, too, were imprisoned. Some of them were quite rich and considered important members of the community. They were all disgraced, along with their families. When the peasants heard that Fivke was in chains, they came in large numbers to bear witness against him, and there was talk of Fivke's being hanged.

"During that time I happened to need lace for a dress and went to Dacha's store. She had stopped coming to us after my mother passed away. However, one could get the best merchandise from her. I went into the store and she was sitting behind the counter, her red hair uncovered, dressed like a countess. She pretended not to know me. I said to her, 'Dacha, you have lived to see your revenge.' With an angry look she answered, 'Revenge is not a Jewish trait,' and turned away. I wanted to ask her when she had become so steeped in Jewishness, but since she played the great lady I let her go. A clerk gave me what I wanted. Outside, I met an acquaintance and told her how high and mighty Dacha had become. She said to me, 'Yentl, have you been asleep or something? Don't you know what's going on?' She told me that Dacha had become a benefactress. She went to Piask and took bread and cheese to the wives of the thieves, and anything else they needed. She left the store for hours and got chummy with the wives of the fences. My dear, she had fallen in love with that Fivke—'my whipper,' as she called him—and was determined to save him. The woman told me she had hired the best lawyer in Lublin. I didn't know whether to laugh or cry. How could this be? Really, I'm afraid it's not right to tell a story like this on the Sabbath."

"Did she save him?" Reitze Breindels asked.

"She married him," Aunt Yentl said.

It was quiet for some time, and then Chaya Riva asked, "How did she get him out?"

Aunt Yentl put two fingers to her lips and thought it over. "The truth is that no one ever knew for sure," she said. "Such things are done stealthily. I heard that she gave a large sum to the governor, and herself in addition. You can believe anything about a bitch like that. Someone saw her enter the governor's palace dressed up to kill. She stayed maybe three hours. They certainly didn't chant psalms. The only thing I know is that the governor freed all the thieves except two, who remained in prison for some time. I was told that Dacha waited for Fivke at the gate of the jail, and when he came out she fell on him, kissed him, and cried. The hoodlums from Lublin who were present called her names and made catcalls at her.

"Yes, they married, but they waited a few months. He had shaved his beard and wore Gentile clothing. He sold his house in Piask and lived with Dacha in her new house. Yankele refused to stay with his mother and stepfather, and he moved to a yeshiva. Those who saw how Fivke became a merchant overnight didn't need to go to the theater. He knew as much about the drygoods business as I know Turkish. If Reb Yissar Mandlebroit could see what happened to his fortune, he would turn over in his grave.

"In the beginning it seemed that everything was fine between the pair. She called him Fivkele and he called her Dachele. They ate from one plate. Because they were rich they became greedy for prestige. He bought himself a pew in the synagogue at the eastern wall, and she at the grate in the women's section. The truth was that they only went to pray on High Holidays. She could not read and he said openly that he was a disbeliever. She wanted to join some charity circle, but the women would not allow it. The couple got nicknames: the Whipper and the Whippress. When it became clear to them that they would not get honors from the Jews, they began to cater to the Gentiles. The Polish squires shunned them just as had the Jews, so they turned to the Russians. When you give Ivan tasty food and plenty of vodka, he melts like wax. Officers and policemen visited the pair constantly. In the evening, they made *vetcherinkas* for the Russians—played cards with them, and got drunk. Dacha became so deeply involved in these lecherous parties that she began to neglect the store. Reb Yissar Mandlebroit's clerks were all honest, but Dacha had chosen swindlers for her assistants.

"As long as there was no competition, the store kept up. Then another drygoods store opened a half block from Dacha's store. The owner was Zelig from Bechow—a little man, a stranger in Lublin. He specialized in buying goods from bankruptcies. He did well from the very first day, and to the degree he succeeded Dacha and Fivke went down. It was like a curse from a holy man. Fivke threatened to burn the new store, but it was so close to his own that a fire would have consumed both. He could have killed Zelig or crippled him, but if Providence says no, it's no. Small and frail as this Zelig was, he was afraid of no one. He didn't walk; he ran like a weasel. He could scream louder than Fivke and Dacha together. He also bribed the *nachalniks.* He hired the clerks Dacha dismissed, and they divulged all her trade secrets to him. Zelig's wife was a quiet dove and seldom came to the store. She stayed home and bore one child after another. People expected Dacha to have children with Fivke, but no child was born. Only Yankele remained to her. He married someone in Lithuania and didn't even invite his mother to the wedding. I forgot to mention that Fivke became exceedingly fat. He got a big belly, and a red nose with the broken veins of a drunkard.

"One morning when Dacha's clerks came to open the store, they found the doors ajar. The thieves of Piask had come in the middle of the night and emptied all the shelves—the same thieves Dacha had saved from prison and whose wives Fivke once played with. When things begin to go bad, there's no limit. Fivke roared that he would murder them all, but he could do nothing. There is a hidden power in every human being and when this is gone the strong become weak and the proud humble. It is written somewhere in a holy book that each animal has its time. When the fox is king, the lion must bow to him."

"What happened then?" Chaya Riva asked.

"It's not for the Sabbath. I don't want to defile my mouth."

"Tell it, Yentl. Don't keep us in suspense."

"She became a whore. The Russians came to her. Fivke was the procurer. When the Poles learned what was going on, they set fire to her house. If there was fire insurance in those times, Dacha didn't have any. They lost their store, their home. They moved to a suburb close to the barracks, and their apartment became a whorehouse. I will tell you about their terrible end another time."

"What happened?"

"Not on the Sabbath."

"Yentl, I won't sleep the whole night." Chaya Riva raised her voice.

Aunt Yentl grimaced and she spat into a handkerchief. "He whipped her, and she died from his whipping."

"Someone saw it?"

"No one. Early one morning he came running to the burial society, crying that his wife had suddenly collapsed and died. The society women went to their house and the corpse was taken to the cleansing hut. When they put her on the cleansing board and saw her naked body, there was a hue and a cry. She was swollen and covered with welts. Women from the burial society are not softhearted; still, one of them fainted dead away."

"Wasn't Fivke arrested?"

"He hanged himself. Both of them were buried in the middle of the night behind the fence."

It became quiet. Aunt Yentl touched the tip of her bonnet. "I told you it was not for the Sabbath."

"What was the sense of it?" Reitze Breindels asked.

"No sense."

I had come out from the storage room, but Aunt Yentl didn't notice me. She began to murmur and look up to the sky. "The sun is setting," she said. "It's time to recite 'God of Abraham.'"

The Safe Deposit

SOME five years back, when Professor Uri Zalkind left New York for Miami after his wife Lotte's death, he had decided never to return to this wild city. Lotte's long sickness had broken his spirit. His health too, it seemed. Not long after he buried her, he fell sick with double pneumonia and an obstruction of the kidneys. He had been living and teaching philosophy in New York for almost thirty years, but he still felt like a stranger in America. The German Jews did not forgive him for having been raised in Poland, the son of some Galician rabbi, and speaking German with an accent. Lotte herself, who was German, called him *Ostjude* when she quarreled with him. To the Russian and Polish Jews he was a German, since, besides being married to a German, for many years he had lived in Germany. He might have made friends with American members of the faculty or with his students, but there was little interest in philosophy at the university, and in Jewish philosophy in particular. He and Lotte had no children. Through the first years they still had relatives in America, but most of the old ones had died and he never kept in touch with the younger generation. Just the same, this winter morning Dr. Uri Zalkind had taken a plane to New York—a man over eighty, small, frail, with a bent back, a little white beard, and bushy eyebrows that retained a trace of having once been red. Behind thick-lensed glasses, his eyes were gray, permanently inflamed.

It was a bad day to have come to New York. The pilot had announced that there was a blizzard in the city, with gusting winds. A dark cloud covered the area, and in the last minutes before landing at LaGuardia an ominous silence settled over the passengers. They avoided looking one another in the eye, as if ashamed beforehand of the panic that might soon break out. Whatever happens, I have rightly deserved it, Dr. Zalkind thought. His Miami Beach neighbors in the senior-citizens apartment complex had warned him that flying in such weather was suicide. And for what was he risking his life? For the manuscript of a book no one would read except possibly a few reviewers. He was glad that he carried no other luggage than his briefcase. He raised the fur collar of the long coat he had brought with him from Germany, and clutching his case in his right hand and holding on to his broad-brimmed hat with his left, he went out of the terminal to look for a taxi. From sitting three hours in one position his legs had become numb. Snow fell at an angle, dry as sand. The wind was icy. Although he had made a firm decision that morning to forget nothing, Professor Zalkind now realized that he had left his muffler and rubbers at home. He had planned to put on his woolen sweater in the plane and this he had forgotten, too. By the time a taxi finally stopped for him, he could not tell the driver the address of the bank to which he wanted to go. He remembered only that it was on Fifty-seventh Street between Eighth Avenue and Broadway.

Professor Zalkind had more than one reason for undertaking this journey. First, the editor of the university press that was to publish his book, *Philo Judaeus and the Cabala*, had called to tell him that he would be visiting New York in the next few days. According to the contract, Professor Zalkind was to have delivered the manuscript some two years ago. Because he had added a number of footnotes and made many alterations in the text, he decided he should meet with the editor personally rather than send the manuscript by mail. Second, he wanted to see Hilda, the only living cousin of his late wife. He hadn't seen her for five years, and her daughter had written to him that her mother was seriously ill. Third, Professor Zalkind had read in the Miami *Herald* that last Saturday thieves had broken into a bank in New York and by boring a hole in the steel door leading to the vault they had stolen everything they could. True, this theft had not occurred in the bank where Zalkind rented a safe-deposit box. Still, the news item, headlined "How Safe Is a Safe?," disturbed him to such a degree that he could not sleep the whole night after he read it. In his box were deposited Lotte's jewelry, his will, and a number of important letters, as well as a manuscript of essays on metaphysics he had written when he was young—a work he would never dare publish while he was alive but one he did not want to lose. In addition to the safe-deposit box, he had in the same bank a savings account of some seventeen thousand dollars, which he intended to withdraw and deposit in Miami. It was not that he needed money. He had a pension from his years of teaching at the university. He had been receiving a Social Security check each month since he became seventy-two; regularly, reparation money came from Germany, which he had escaped after Hitler came to power. But why keep his belongings in New York now that he was a resident of Florida?

Another motive—perhaps the most important—brought the old man to New York. For many years he had suffered from prostate trouble, and the doctors he consulted had all advised him to have an operation. Procrastination could be fatal, they told him. He had made up his mind to visit a urologist in New York—a physician from Germany, a refugee like himself.

After crawling in traffic for a long time, the taxi stopped at Eighth Avenue and Fifty-seventh Street. No matter how Professor Zalkind tried, he couldn't read the meter. Lately, the retinas of his eyes had begun to degenerate and he could read only with a large magnifying glass. Assuming that he would get change, he handed the driver a ten-dollar bill, but the driver complained that it was not enough. Zalkind gave him two dollars more. The blizzard was getting worse. The afternoon was as dark as dusk. The moment Zalkind opened the door of the taxi, snow hit his face like hail. He struggled against the wind until he reached Seventh Avenue. There was no sign of his bank. He continued as far east as Fifth. A new building was being constructed. Was it possible that they had torn down the bank without letting him know? In the midst of the storm, motors roared, trucks and cars honked. He wanted to ask the construction workers where the bank had moved, but in the clang and clamor no one would hear his voice. The words in the Book of Job came to his mind: "He shall return no more to his house, neither shall his place know him any more."

Now Zalkind had come to a public telephone, and somehow he got out a dime and dialed Hilda's number. He heard the voice of a stranger, and could not make out what was being said to him. Well, everything is topsy-turvy with me today, he thought. Presently it occurred to him that he had looked only on one side of the street, sure that the bank was there. Perhaps he was mistaken? He tried to cross the street, but his glasses had become opaque and he couldn't be sure of traffic-light colors. He finally made it across, and after a while he saw a bank that resembled his, though it had a different name. He entered. There was not a single customer in the place. Tellers sat idly behind the little windows. A guard in uniform approached him and Zalkind asked him if this was indeed his bank. At first the guard didn't seem to understand his accent. Then he said it was the same bank—it had merged with another one and the name had been changed.

"How did it come that you didn't let me know?"

"Notices went out to all our depositors."

"Thank you, thank you. Really, I began to think I was getting senile," Dr. Zalkind said to the guard and himself. "What about the safe-deposit boxes?"

"They are where they were."

"I have a savings account in this bank, and a lot of interest must have accumulated in the years I've been away. I want to withdraw it."

"As you wish."

Dr. Zalkind approached a counter and began to search for his bankbook. He remembered positively that he had brought it with him in one of the breast pockets of his jacket. He emptied both and found everything except his bankbook— his Social Security card, his airplane ticket, old letters, notebooks, a telephone bill, even a leaflet advertising a dancing school which had been handed to him on the street. "Am I insane?" Dr. Zalkind asked himself. "Are the demons after me? Maybe I put it into my case. But where is my case?" He glanced right and left, on the counter and under it. There was no trace of a briefcase. "I have left it in the telephone booth!" he said with a tremor in his voice. "My manuscript too!" The bank suddenly became dark, and a golden eye lit up on a black background—otherworldly, dreamily radiant, its edges jagged, a blemish in the pupil, like the eye of some cosmic embryo in the process of formation. This vision baffled him, and for some time he forgot his briefcase. He watched the mysterious eye growing both in size and in luminosity. What he saw now was not altogether new to him. As a child, he had seen similar entities—sometimes an eye, other times a fiery flower that opened its petals or a dazzling butterfly or some unearthly snake. Those apparitions always came to him at times of distress, as when he was whipped in cheder, was attacked by some vicious urchin, or was sick with fever. Perhaps those hallucinations were incompatible forms that the soul created without any pattern in the Ideas, Professor Zalkind pondered in Platonic terms. He leaned on the counter in order not to fall. I'm not going to faint, he ordered himself. His belly had become bloated and a mixture of a belch and a hiccup came from his mouth. This is my end!

Dr. Zalkind opened the outside door of the bank with difficulty, determined to find the telephone booth. He looked around, but no telephone booth was in sight. He choked from the blast of the wind. In all his anguish his brain remained playful. Is the North Pole visiting New York? Has the Ice Age returned? Is the sun being extinguished? Dr. Zalkind had often seen blind men crossing the streets of New York without a guide, waving a white stick. He could never understand where they acquired the courage for this. The wind pushed him back, blew up the skirts of his coat, tore at his hat. No, I can't go looking for the phantom of a telephone booth in this hurricane. He dragged himself back to the bank, where he searched again for his briefcase on the counters and floor. He had no copy of the manuscript, just a pile of papers written in longhand—actually, not more than notes. He saw a bench and collapsed onto it. He sat silent, ready for death, which, according to Philo, redeems the soul from the prison of the flesh, from the vagaries of the senses. Although Zalkind had read everything Philo wrote, he could never conclude from his writings whether matter was created by God or always existed—a primeval chaos, the negative principle of the Godhead. Dr. Zalkind found contradictions in Philo's philosophy and puzzles no mind could solve as long as it was chained in the errors of corporality. "Well, I may soon see the truth," he murmured. For a while he dozed and even began to dream. He woke with a start.

The guard was bending over him. "Is something wrong? Can I help?"

"Oh, I had a briefcase with me and I lost it. My bankbook was there."

"Your bankbook? You can get another one. No one can take out your money without your signature. Where did you lose it? In a taxi?"

"Perhaps."

"All you have to do is notify the bank that you lost the bankbook and after thirty days they will give you another one."

"I would like to go to the safe-deposit boxes."

"I'll take you in the elevator."

The guard helped Dr. Zalkind get up. He half led him, half pushed him to the elevator and pressed the button to the basement. There, in spite of his confusion, Professor Zalkind recognized the clerk who sat in front of the entrance to the safe-deposit boxes. His hair had turned gray, but his face remained young and ruddy. The man also recognized Zalkind. He clapped his hands and called, "Professor Zalkind, whom do I see! We already thought that . . . you were sick or something?"

"Yes, no."

"Let me get the figures on your account," the clerk said. He went into another room. Zalkind heard his name mentioned on the telephone.

"Everything is all right," the clerk said when he returned. "What you owe us is more than covered by the interest in your account." He gave Zalkind a slip to sign. It took some time. His hand shook like that of a person suffering from Parkinson's disease. The clerk stamped the slip and nodded. "You don't live in New York any more?"

"No, in Miami."

"What is your new address?"

Dr. Zalkind wanted to answer, but he had forgotten both the street and the number. The heavy door opened and he gave the slip to another clerk, who led him into the room holding the safe-deposit boxes. Zalkind's box was in the middle row. The clerk motioned with his hand. "Your key."

"My key?"

"Yes, your key, to open the box."

Only now did it occur to Dr. Zalkind that one needed a key to get into a safe-deposit box. He searched through his pockets and took out a chain of keys, but he was sure they were all from Miami. He stood there perplexed. "I'm sorry, I haven't the key to my box."

"You do have it. Give me those keys!" The man grabbed the key chain and showed Professor Zalkind one that was larger than the others. He had been carrying a key to his safe-deposit box with him all those years, not knowing what it was for. The clerk pulled out a metal box and led Zalkind into a long corridor, opened a door to a room without a window, and turned on the light. He put the box on the table and showed Zalkind a switch on the wall to use when he had finished.

After some fumbling, Zalkind managed to open the box. He sat and gaped. Time had turned him sick, defeated, but for these objects in the box it did not exist. They had lain there for years without consciousness, without any need—dead matter, unless the animists were correct in considering all substance alive. To Einstein, mass was condensed energy. Could it perhaps also be condensed spirit? Though Professor Zalkind had packed his magnifying glass in his briefcase, he recognized stacks of Lotte's love letters tied with ribbons, his diary, and his youthful manuscript with the title "Philosophical Fantasies"—a collection of essays, feuilletons, and aphorisms.

After a while he lifted out Lotte's jewelry. He never knew that she possessed so many trinkets. There were bracelets, rings, earrings, brooches, chains, a string of pearls. She had inherited all this from her mother, her grandmothers, perhaps her great-grandmothers. It was probably worth a fortune, but what would he do with money at this stage? He sat there and took stock of his life. Lotte had craved children, but he had refused to increase the misery of the human species and Jewish troubles, he had said. She wanted to travel with him. He deprived her of this, too. "What is there to see?" he would ask her. "In what way is a high mountain more significant than a low hill? How is the ocean a greater wonder than a pond?" Even though Dr. Zalkind had doubts about Philo's philosophy and was sometimes inclined toward Spinoza's pantheism or David Hume's skepticism, he had accepted Philo's disdain for the deceptions of flesh and blood. He had come to New York with the decision to take all these things back with him to Miami. Yet, how could he carry them now that he had no briefcase? And what difference did it make where they were kept?

How strange. On the way to the airport that morning, Zalkind still had some ambitions. He planned to make final corrections on his manuscripts. He toyed with the idea of looking over "Philosophical Fantasies" to see what might be done with it. He had sworn to himself to make an appointment with the urologist the very next day. Now he was overcome by fatigue and had to lean his forehead on the table. He fell asleep and found himself in a temple, with columns, vases, sculptures, marble staircases. Was this Athens? Rome? Alexandria? A tall man with a white beard, dressed in a toga and sandals, emerged. He carried a scroll. He recited a poem or a sermon. Was the language Greek? Latin? No, it was Hebrew, written by a scribe.

"Peace unto you, Philo Judaeus, my father and master," Dr. Zalkind said.

"Peace unto you, my disciple Uri, son of Yedidyah."

"Rabbi, I want to know the truth!"

"Here in the Book of Genesis is the source of all truth: 'In the beginning God created the heaven and the earth. And the earth was without form, and void; and darkness was upon the face of the deep. And the Spirit of God moved upon the face of the waters.'"

Philo intoned the words like a reader in the synagogue. Other old men entered, with white hair and white beards, wearing white robes and holding parchments. They were all there—the Stoics, the Gnostics, Plotinus. Uri had read that Philo was not well versed in the Holy Tongue. What a lie! Each word from his lips revealed secrets of the Torah. He quoted from the Talmud, the Book of Creation, the Zohar, Rabbi Moshe from Córdoba, Rabbi Isaac Luria. How could this be? Had the Messiah come? Had the Resurrection taken place? Had the earth ascended to Heaven? Had Metatron descended to the earth? The figures and statues were not of stone but living women with naked breasts and hair down to their loins. Lotte was among them. She was also Hilda. One female with two bodies? One body with two souls?

"Uri, my beloved, I have longed for you!" she cried out. "Idolators wanted to defile me, but I swore to be faithful."

In the middle of the temple there was a bed covered with rugs and pillows; a ladder was suspended alongside it. Uri was about to climb up when a stream of water burst through the gate of the temple. Had Yahweh broken his covenant and sent a flood upon the earth?

Uri Zalkind woke up with a start. He opened his eyes and saw the bank clerk shaking his shoulder. "Professor Zalkind, your briefcase has been found. A woman brought it. She opened it and on top there was your bankbook."

"I understand."

"Are you sick?" the clerk asked. He pointed to a wet spot on the floor.

It took a long while before Dr. Zalkind answered. "I'm kaput, that's all."

"It's five minutes to three. The bank will be closing."

"I will soon go."

"The woman with the briefcase is upstairs." The clerk went out, leaving the door half open.

For a minute, Dr. Zalkind sat still, numbed by his own indifference. His briefcase was found but he felt no joy. Beside the box, Lotte's jewelry shimmered, reflecting the colors of the rainbow. Suddenly Dr. Zalkind began to fill his coat pockets with the jewels. It was the spontaneous act of a cheder boy. A passage from the Pentateuch came into his mind: "Behold, I am at the point to die: and what profit shall this birthright do to me?" Zalkind even repeated Esau's words with the teacher's intonation.

The clerk came in with a woman who carried a wet mop and a pail. "Shall I call an ambulance?" he asked.

"An ambulance? No."

Zalkind followed the clerk, who motioned for the key. It was underneath Lotte's jewelry, and Zalkind had to make an effort to pull it out. The clerk took him up in the elevator, and there was the woman with his briefcase—small, darkish, in a black fur hat and a mangy coat. When she saw Zalkind, her eyes lit up.

"Professor Zalkind! I went to make a telephone call and saw your briefcase. I opened it and there with your papers was your bankbook. Since you use this bank, I thought they would know your address. And here you are." The woman spoke English with a foreign accent.

"Oh, you're an honest person. I thank you with all my heart."

"Why am I so honest? There is no cash here. If I had found a million dollars, the *Yetzer Hora* might have tempted me." She pronounced the Hebrew words as they did in Poland.

"It's terrible outside. Maybe you should take him somewhere," the guard suggested to the woman.

"Where do you live? Where is your hotel?" she asked. "I heard that you just arrived from Miami. What a time to come from Florida in your condition. You may, God forbid, catch the worst kind of cold."

"I thank you. I thank you. I have no hotel. I had planned to stay over with the cousin of my late wife, but it seems her telephone is out of order."

"I will take you to my own place for the time being. I live on 106th and Amsterdam. It is quite far from here, but if we get a taxi it won't be long. My dentist moved to this neighborhood and that is why I'm here."

One of the bank employees came over and asked, "Should I try to get a taxi for you?"

Even though it wasn't clear whom he addressed, Zalkind replied, "Yes—I really don't know how to express my gratitude."

Other clerks came over with offers of help, but Zalkind noticed that they winked at one another. The outside door opened and one of them called, "Your taxi!"

The snow had stopped, but it had got colder. The woman took Zalkind's arm and helped him into the taxi. She got in after him and said, "My name is Esther Sephardi. You can call me Esther."

"Are you a Sephardi?"

"No, a Jewish daughter from Lodz. My husband's surname was Sephardi. He was also from Lodz. He died two years ago."

"Do you have children?"

"One daughter in college. Why did you come in such a weather to New York?"

Dr. Zalkind didn't know where to begin.

"You don't need to answer," the woman said. "You live

alone, huh? No wife would allow her husband to go to New York on a day like this. You won't believe me, in frost worse than this I stood in a forest in Kazakhstan and sawed logs. That's where the Russians sent us in 1941. We had to build our own barracks. Those who couldn't make it died, and those who were destined to live lived. I took your briefcase with me to the Automat to get a cup of coffee and I looked into your papers. Is this going to be a book?"

"Perhaps."

"Are you a professor?"

"I was."

"My daughter studies philosophy. Not exactly philosophy but psychology. What does one need so much psychology for? I wanted her to study for a doctor but nowadays children do what they want, not what their mother tells them. For twenty years I was a bookkeeper in a big firm. Then I got sick and had to have a hysterectomy. Dr. Zalkind, I don't like to give you advice, but what you have should not be neglected. An uncle of mine had it and he delayed until it was too late."

"It's too late for me, too."

"How do you know? Did you have tests made?"

The taxi stopped in a half-dark street, with cars buried under piles of snow. Dr. Zalkind managed to get a few bills from his purse and gave them to Esther. "I don't see so well. Be so good—pay him and give him a tip."

The woman took Zalkind's hand and led him up three flights of stairs. Until now, Professor Zalkind had believed that his heart was in order, but something must have happened—after one flight he was short of breath. Esther opened a door and led him into a narrow corridor, and from there into a shabby living room. She said, "We used to be quite wealthy, but first my husband got sick with cancer and then I got sick. I'm working as a cashier during the day in a movie theater. Wait, let me take off your coat." She weighed it in her hands, glanced at the bulging pockets, and asked, "What do you have there—stones?"

After some haggling she took off his shirt and pants as well. He tried to resist, but she said, "When you are sick, you can't be bashful. Where is the shame? We are all made from the same dough."

She filled the bathtub with hot water and brought him clean underwear and a robe that must have been her late husband's. Then she made tea in the kitchen and warmed up soup from a can. Professor Zalkind had forgotten that he had had nothing to eat or drink since breakfast. As she served him, Esther kept on talking about her years in Lodz, in Russia, in New York. Her father had been a rich man, a partner in a textile factory, but the Poles had ruined him with their high taxes. He grew so distraught that he got consumption and died. Her mother lived a few years more and she, too, passed away. In Russia Esther became sick with typhoid fever and anemia. She worked in a factory where the pay was so low that one had to steal or starve. Her husband was taken away by the NKVD, and for years she didn't know if he had been killed in a slave-labor camp. When they finally reunited, they had to wait two years in Germany in a DP camp for visas to America. "What we went through in all those years only God the merciful knows."

For a moment, Professor Zalkind was inclined to tell her that even though God was omniscient, the well of goodness, one could not ascribe any attribute to Him. He did not provide for mankind directly but through Wisdom, called Logos by the Greeks. But there was no use discussing metaphysics with this woman.

After he had eaten, Dr. Zalkind could no longer fight off his weariness. He yawned; his eyes became watery. His head kept dropping to his chest. Esther said, "I will make you a bed on the sofa. It's not comfortable, but when you are tired you can sleep on rocks. Ask me."

"I will never be able to repay you for your kindness."

"We are all human beings."

Dr. Zalkind saw with half-closed eyes how she spread a sheet over the sofa, brought in a pillow, a blanket, pajamas. "I hope I don't wet the bed," he prayed to the powers that have the say over the body and its needs. He went into the bathroom and saw himself in a mirror for the first time that day. In one day his face had become yellow, wrinkled. Even his white beard seemed shrunken. When he returned to the living room, he remembered Hilda and asked Esther to call her. Esther learned from an answering service that Hilda had gone into a hospital the day before. "Well, everything falls to pieces," Zalkind said to himself. He noticed a salt shaker that Esther had neglected to take from the table, and while she lingered in the bathroom he put some of the salt on his palm and swallowed it, since salt retains water in the body. She returned in a house robe and slippers. She's not so young any more, he thought appraisingly, but still an attractive female; in spite of his maladies he had not lost his manhood.

The instant he lay down on the sofa he fell into a deep sleep. This is how he used to pass out as a boy on Passover night after the four goblets of wine. He awoke in the middle of the night with an urgent need to urinate. Thank God, the sheet was dry. The room was completely dark; the window shades were down. He groped like a blind man, bumping into a chest, a chair, an open door. Did it lead to the bathroom? No, he touched a headboard of a bed and could hear someone breathing. He was overcome with fear. His hostess might suspect him of dishonorable intentions. Eventually, he found the bathroom. He wanted light but he could not find the switch. On the way back, in the corridor, he accidentally touched the switch and turned on the light. He saw his briefcase propped against the wall, his coat hanging on a clothes tree. Yes, Lotte's jewelry was still there. He had fallen into honest hands. It had become cold during the night, and he put the coat on his shoulders over his pajamas and took the briefcase with him in order to place the jewelry in it. He had to smile—he looked as if he were going on a journey. I will give it to this goodhearted woman, he resolved. At least a part of it. I have no more need for worldly possessions. If some part of Lotte's mind still exists, she will forgive me. Suddenly his head became compressed with heat and he fell. He could hear his body thud against the floor. Then everything was still.

Professor Zalkind opened his eyes. He was lying on a bed with metal bars on both sides. Above the bed a small lamp glimmered. He stared in the semi-darkness, waiting for his memory to return. An ice bag rested on his forehead. His belly was bandaged and his hand touched a catheter. "Am I still alive?" he asked himself. "Or is it already the hereafter?" He felt like laughing, but he was too sore inside. In an instant everything he had gone through on this trip came back to him. Had it been today? Yesterday? Days before? It did not matter. Although he was aching, he felt a rest he had never known before—the sublime enjoyment of fearing nothing, having no wish, no worry, no resentment. This state of mind was not of this world and he listened to it. It was both astoundingly simple and beyond anything language could convey. He was granted the revelation he yearned for—the freedom to look into the innermost secret of being, to see behind the curtain of phenomena, where all questions are answered, all riddles solved. "If I could only convey the truth to those who suffer and doubt!"

A figure slid through the half-opened door like a shadow—the woman who had found the briefcase. She bent over his bed and asked, "You have wakened, huh?"

He did not answer and she said, "Thank God, the worst is over. You will soon be a new man."

The Betrayer of Israel

WHAT could be better than to stand on a balcony and be able to see all of Krochmalna Street (the part where the Jews lived) from Gnoyna to Ciepla and even farther, to Iron Street, where there were trolley cars! A day never passed, not even an hour, when something did not happen. One moment a thief was caught and then Itcha Meyer, the drunkard—the husband of Esther from the candy store—became wild and danced in the middle of the gutter. Someone got sick and an ambulance was called. A fire broke out in a house and the firemen, wearing brass hats and high rubber boots, came with their galloping horses. I stood on the balcony that summer afternoon in my long gaberdine, a velvet cap over my red hair, with two disheveled sidelocks, waiting for something more to happen. Meanwhile, I observed the stores across the street, their customers, and also the Square, which teemed with pickpockets, loose girls, and vendors running a lottery. You pulled a number from a bag, and if good luck was with you, you could win three colored pencils, or a rooster made of sugar with a comb of chocolate, or a cardboard clown that shook his arms and legs if you pulled a string. Once a Chinaman with a pigtail passed the street. In an instant it became black with people. Another time a dark-skinned man appeared in a red turban with a tassel, wearing a cloak that resembled a prayer shawl, with sandals on his bare feet. I learned later that he was a Jew from Persia, from the town of Shushan—the ancient capital where King Ahasuerus, Queen Esther, and the wicked Haman lived.

Since I was the rabbi's boy, everybody on the street knew me. When you stand on a balcony you are afraid of no one. You are like a general. When an enemy of mine passed I could spit on his cap and all he could do was shake a fist and call me names. Even the policeman didn't look so tall and mighty from above. Flies with violet bellies, bees and butterflies landed on the rail of the balcony. I tried to catch them or I just admired them. How did they manage to fly to Krochmalna Street, and where did they get their flamboyant colors? I had tried to read an article about Darwin in the Yiddish newspaper but I hardly understood it.

Suddenly a tumult broke out again. Two policemen were leading a little man, and screaming women ran after him. To my amazement, they all entered our gate. I could barely believe it: the policemen led this little man to our home, into my father's courtroom. He was accompanied by Shmuel Smetena, an unofficial lawyer, a crony of both the thieves and the police. Shmuel knew Russian and often served the Jews of the Street as an interpreter between them and the authorities. I soon discovered what had happened. That little man, Koppel Mitzner, a peddler of old clothes, was the husband of four wives. One lived on Krochmalna Street, one on Smocza Street, one on Praga, and one on Wola. It took quite a while for my father to orient himself to the situation. The senior policeman, with a golden insignia on his cap, explained that Koppel Mitzner had not married the women legally, with a license from the magistrate, but only according to Jewish law. The government could hardly prosecute him since the women had only Jewish marriage contracts, not Russian certificates. Koppel Mitzner contended that they were not his wives but his lovers. On the other hand, the officials could not allow him to break the law without punishment. So the head of the police had ordered the culprit brought to the rabbi. How strange that I, a mere boy, caught on to all these complications more quickly than my father. He was busy with his volumes of the Talmud and commentaries when Koppel, his wives, and the whole crowd of curious men and women burst into our apartment. Some of them laughed, others rebuked Koppel. My father, a small man, frail, wearing a long robe and with a velvet skull cap above his high forehead, his eyes blue, and his beard red, reluctantly put away pen and paper on his lectern. He sat down at the head of the table and asked others to be seated. Some sat on chairs, others on a long bench along the wall, which was lined to the ceiling with books. Between the windows stood the Ark of the holy scrolls with its gilded cornice, on which two lions held the tablets with the Ten Commandments between their curled tongues.

I listened to every word and observed each face. Koppel Mitzner, as small as a cheder boy, skin and bones, had a narrow

face, a long nose, and a pointed Adam's apple. On his tiny chin
grew a sparse little beard the color of straw. He wore a checked
jacket and a shirt which closed at the collar with an ornate
brass button. He had no lips, only a crevice of a mouth. He
smiled cunningly and tried to outscream the others with his
thin voice. He pretended that the whole event was nothing
but a joke or a mistake. When my father finally grasped what
Koppel had done, he asked, "How did you dare to commit a
sin like this? Don't you know that Rabbi Gershom decreed a
penalty of excommunication for polygamy?"

Koppel Mitzner signaled with his index finger for everyone
to be quiet. Then he said, "Rabbi, first of all, I didn't marry
them of my own free will. They caught me in a trap. A hundred times I told them I had a wife, but they attached themselves to me like leeches. The fact that I didn't end up in the
insane asylum on Bonifrate Street proves that I'm stronger
than iron. Second, I need not to be more pious than our patriarch Jacob. If Jacob could marry four wives, I am allowed to
have ten, perhaps even a thousand, like King Solomon. I also
happen to know that the ruling of Rabbi Gershom was made
for one thousand years, and nine hundred of those thousand
have already passed. Only one hundred years are left. I take the
punishment upon myself. You, Rabbi, will not roast in my
Gehenna."

There was an uproar of laughter. A few of the young men
applauded. My father clutched his beard. "What will happen a
hundred years from now we cannot know. For the time being
the ruling of Rabbi Gershom is valid and the one who breaks it
is a betrayer of Israel."

"Rabbi, I did not steal, I did not swindle. Rich Hasidim go
bankrupt twice a year and then travel to their rabbi on holidays
and sit at his table. When I buy something I pay cash. I don't
owe anybody a penny. I provide for four Jewish daughters and
nine good children."

His wives tried to interrupt Koppel but the police did not let
them. Shmuel Smetena translated Koppel's words into Russian. Even though I did not understand the language it occurred to me that he shortened Koppel's arguments—he
gesticulated, winked, and it seemed he did not want the Russians to understand all of Koppel's defenses. Shmuel Smetena

was tall, fat, with a red neck. He wore a corduroy jacket with gilded buttons and on his vest a watch chain made of silver rubles. The uppers of his boots shone like lacquer. I kept glancing at Koppel's wives. The one from Krochmalna Street was short, broad like a Sabbath stew pot, and she had a potato nose and a huge bosom. She seemed to be the oldest of the lot. Her wig was disheveled and as black as soot. She cried and wiped the tears with her apron. She pointed a thick finger with a broken nail at Koppel, calling him criminal, pig, murderer, lecher. She warned him that she would break his ribs.

One of the women looked as young as a girl. She wore a straw hat with a green band and carried a purse with a brass clasp. Her red cheeks were like those of the streetwalkers who stood at the gates and waited for guests. I heard her say, "He is a liar, the greatest cheat in the whole world. He has promised me the moon and the stars. Such a faker and braggart you cannot find in the whole of Warsaw. If he will not divorce me this very moment he must rot in prison. I have six brothers and each of them can make mincemeat out of him."

As she said these angry words, her eyes smiled and she showed dimples. She seemed lovely to me. She opened her purse, took out a sheet of paper, and shoved it in front of my father's face. "Here is my marriage contract."

The third woman was short, blond, older than the one with the straw hat but much younger than the one from Krochmalna Street. She said she was a cook in the Jewish hospital, where she had met Koppel Mitzner. He introduced himself to her as Morris Kelzer. He came to the hospital because he suffered from severe headaches and Dr. Frankel told him to remain two days for observation. The woman said to my father, "Now I understand why his head ached. If I had cooked up such a kasha as he did, my head would have ruptured and I would have lost my mind ten times a day."

The fourth woman had red hair, a face full of freckles, and eyes as green as gooseberries. I noticed a golden tooth on the side of her mouth. Her mother, who wore a bonnet with beads and ribbons, sat on the bench, screaming each time her daughter's name was mentioned. The latter tried to quiet her by giving her smelling salts, which are used on Yom Kippur for those who are neither strong enough to fast nor willing to break the fast. I heard the daughter say, "Mother, crying and wailing won't help. We have got into a mess and we must get out of it."

"There is a God, there is," the old woman screeched. "He waits long, but He punishes severely. He will see our shame and disgrace and pass judgment. Such an evildoer, such a whoremonger, such a beast!"

Her head fell back as if she was about to faint. The daughter rushed to the kitchen and returned with a wet towel. She rubbed the old woman's temples with it. "Mother, come to yourself. Mother, Mother, Mother!"

The old woman woke up with a start, and began to yell again. "People, I'm dying!"

"Here, swallow this." The daughter pushed a pill between her empty gums.

After a while the policemen left, ordering Koppel Mitzner to appear at police headquarters the next day, and Shmuel Smetena began to scold Koppel. "How can a man, especially a businessman, do something like this?" My father told Koppel that he must divorce the three other wives without delay and keep the original wife, the one from Krochmalna Street. Father requested that the women approach the table, and he asked them if they agreed to a divorce. But somehow they did not answer clearly. Koppel had six children with the wife from Krochmalna Street, two with the cook from the Jewish Hospital, and one with the redhead. Only with the youngest one did he have no children. By now I had learned the names of the women. The one from Krochmalna Street was called Trina Leah, the cook Gutsha, the redhead Naomi. The youngest one had a Gentile name, Pola. Usually when people came for a Din Torah—a judgment—Father made a compromise. If one litigant sued for twenty rubles and the other denied owing anything, my father's verdict would be to pay ten. But what kind of compromise could be made in this case? Father shook his head and sighed. From time to time he glanced toward his books and manuscripts. He disliked being disturbed in his studies. He nodded to me as if to say, "See where the Evil One can lead those who forsake the Torah."

After much haggling Father sent the women to the kitchen

to discuss their grievances and the financial details with my mother. She was more experienced than he in worldly matters. She had peered into the courtroom once or twice and threw Koppel a look of disdain. The women immediately rushed into the kitchen and I followed. My mother, taller than my father, lean, sickly white, with a sharp nose and large gray eyes, was, as always, reading some Hebrew morality book. She wore a white kerchief over her blond wig. I heard her say to Koppel's wives, "Divorce him. Run away from him like from the fire. I should be forgiven for my words, but what did you see in him? A debaucher!"

Gutsha the cook replied, "Rebbetzin, it's easy to divorce a man, but we have two children. It's true that what he pays for their support is a pittance but it's still better than nothing. Once we divorce, he will be as free as a bird. A child needs shoes, a little skirt, underpants. Well, and what should I tell them when they grow up? He used to come on Saturdays only, still to the girls he was Daddy. He brought them candy, a toy, a cookie. And he pretended to love them."

"Didn't you know that he had a wife?" my mother asked.

Gutsha hesitated for a while. "In the beginning I didn't know, and when I found out it was already too late. He said he didn't live with his wife, and they would be divorced any day. He dazzled me and bewitched me. He's a smooth talker, a sly fox."

"She knew, the whore, she knew!" Trina Leah called out. "When a man visits a woman on the Sabbath only, he's as kosher as pork. She's no better than he is. People like her only want to grab other women's husbands. She's a slut, an outcast." And Trina Leah spat in Gutsha's face.

Gutsha wiped off her face with a handkerchief. "She should spit blood and pus."

"Really, I cannot understand," my mother said to the women and to herself. Then she added, "Perhaps he could be ordered to pay for the children by the law of the Gentiles."

"Rebbetzin," Gutsha said, "if a man has a heart for his children, he doesn't need to be forced. This one came every week with a different excuse. He doled out the few guldens like alms. Today the policemen came to the hospital and took me away as if I were a lawbreaker. My enemies rejoiced at my downfall. I left my children with a nurse who must leave at four o'clock and then they will be alone."

"In that case, go home at once," my mother said. "Something will be done. There is still a remnant of order in the world."

"No order whatsoever. I dug my own grave. I must have been insane. I deserve all the blows I'm getting. I'm ready to die, but who will take care of my darlings? It is not their fault."

"She's as much of a mother as I'm a countess," Trina Leah hollered. "Bitch, leper, hoodlum!"

I had great compassion for Gutsha; nevertheless, I was curious about the men, and I ran back to the room where they were arguing. I heard Shmuel Smetena say, "Listen to me, Koppel. No matter what you say, the children should not be the victims. You will have to provide for them, and if not the Russians will put you into the cage for three years and no one would bat an eyelid. No lawyer would take a case like this. If you fall into a rage and stab someone, the judge may be lenient. But what you did day in and day out was not the act of a human being."

"I will pay, I will pay—don't be so holier-than-thou," Koppel said. "These are my children, and they will not have to go begging. Rabbi, if you permit me, I will swear on the holy scroll." And Koppel pointed to the Ark.

"Swear? God forbid!" Father replied. "First you have to sign a paper that you will obey my judgment and fulfill your obligations to your children. Who is me!" My father changed his tone. "How long does a man live altogether? Is it worth losing the world to come because of such evil passions? What becomes of the body after death? It's eaten up by the worms. As long as one breathes, one can still repent. In the grave there is no longer free choice."

"Rabbi, I'm ready to fast and to do penances. I have one explanation: I lost my senses. A demon or evil spirit entered me. I got entangled like a fly in a spider's web. I'm afraid people will take revenge on me and no one will enter my store any more."

"Jews have mercy," my father said. "If you repent with all your heart, no one will persecute you."

"Absolutely true," Shmuel Smetena agreed.

I left the men and went back to the kitchen. The old woman, Naomi's mother, was saying, "Rebbetzin, I didn't like him from the very beginning. I took one look at him and I said, 'Naomi, run from him like from the pest. He's not going to divorce his wife. First let him divorce her.' I said, 'then we will see.' My dear lady, we are not just people from the gutter. My late husband, Naomi's father, was a Hasid. Naomi was an honest girl. She became a seamstress to support me. But he has a quick tongue that spouts sweet words. The more he tried to please me with his flattery, the more I recognized what a serpent he was. But my daughter is a fool. If you tell her that there is a horse fair in Heaven, she wants to go up and buy a horse there. She had bad luck in addition. She was married and became a widow after three months. Her husband, a giant of a man, fell down like a tree. Woe what I have lived to see in my old age. I wish I had died a long time ago. Who needs me? I just spoil bread."

"Don't say this. When God tells us to live, we must live," my mother said.

"What for? People sneer at us. When she told me that she was pregnant from that mooncalf I grabbed her hair and . . . People, I'm dying!"

That day, all three women agreed to divorce Koppel Mitzner. The divorce proceedings were to take place in our house. Koppel signed a paper and gave my father an advance of five rubles. Father had already written down the names of the three women. The name Naomi was a good Jewish name. Gutsha was a diminutive of Gutte, which used to be Tovah. But what kind of name was Pola? My father looked the name up in a book with the title *People's Names*, but there was no Pola there. He asked me to bring Isaiah the scribe and they talked it over. Isaiah had much experience in such matters. He told my father that he drew a circle in a notebook each time he wrote a divorce paper and recently his son counted over eight hundred such circles. "According to the law," Isaiah said, "a Gentile name is acceptable in a divorce paper."

Naomi was supposed to be divorced first. The ritual ceremony was to take place on Sunday. But that Sunday neither Koppel nor his wives showed up. The news spread on

Krochmalna Street that Koppel Mitzner had vanished together with his youngest wife, Pola. He deserted the three other wives, and they would never be permitted to remarry. Where he and Pola went, no one knew, but it was believed that they had run away to Paris or to New York. "Where else," Mother said, "would charlatans like these run to?"

She gave me an angry look as if suspecting that I envied Koppel his journey, and, who knows, perhaps even his companion. "What are you doing in the kitchen?" she cried. "Go back to your book. Such depravities are not for you!"

Tanhum

TANHUM MAKOVER buttoned his gaberdine and twisted his earlocks into curls. He wiped his feet on the straw mat before the door, as he had been told to do. His prospective father-in-law, Reb Bendit Waldman, often reminded him that one could study the Torah and serve the Almighty and still not behave like an idle dreamer. Reb Bendit Waldman offered himself as an example. He was everything at once—a scholar, a fervent Hasid of the Sadgora rabbi as well as a successful lumber merchant, a chess player, and the proprietor of a water mill. There was time for everything if one wasn't lazy, Reb Bendit said—even to teach yourself Russian and Polish and glance into a newspaper. How his prospective father-in-law managed all this was beyond Tanhum. Reb Bendit never seemed to hurry. He had a friendly word for everyone, even an errand boy or servant girl. Women burdened down by a heavy spirit came to him for advice. Nor did he neglect to visit the sick or—God forbid—to escort a corpse. Tanhum often re-solved to be like his prospective father-in-law, but he simply couldn't manage it. He would grow absorbed in some sacred book and before he knew it half the day had gone by. He tried to maintain a proper appearance, but a button would loosen and dangle by a thread until it dropped off and got lost. His boots were always muddied, his shirt collars frayed. As often as he knotted the band of his breeches it always came untied again. He resolved to commit two pages of the Gemara to memory each day so that in three and a half years he might fin-ish with the Talmud, but he couldn't manage even this. He would become preoccupied with some Talmudic controversy and linger over it for weeks on end. The questions and doubts wouldn't let him rest. Certainly there was mercy in Heaven, but why did little children or even dumb animals have to suf-fer? Why did man have to end up dying, and a steer under the slaughterer's knife? Why had the miracles ceased and God's chosen people been forced to suffer exile for two thousand years? Tanhum probed in the Hasidic lore, the cabala volumes, the ancient philosophy books. The questions they raised in his mind plagued him like flies. There were mornings when Tanhum awoke with a weight in his limbs, a pain in his temples, and no urge at all to study, pray, or even perform his ablutions. Today was one of those days. He opened the Gemara and sat there for two hours without turning a page. At prayer, he couldn't seem to grasp the meaning of the words. While reciting the eighteen benedictions, he transposed the blessings. And it just so happened that today he was invited for lunch at his prospective father-in-law's.

Reb Bendit Waldman's house was constructed in such a way that one had to pass through the kitchen to get to the dining room. The kitchen was aswarm with women—Tanhum's prospective mother-in-law, her daughters-in-law, her daughters, including Tanhum's bride-to-be, Mira Fridl. Even before entering the house he heard the racket and commotion inside. The women of the house were all noisy and inclined to laughter, and often there were neighbors present. The cooking, baking, knitting, and needlepoint went on with a vengeance, and games of checkers, knucklebones, hide-and-seek, and wolf-and-goat were played. On Hanukkah they rendered chicken fat; after Succoth they made coleslaw and pickled cucumbers; in the summers they put up jam. A fire was always kept going in the stove and under a tripod. The kitchen smelled of coffee, braised meat, cinnamon, and saffron. Cakes and cookies were baked for the Sabbath and holidays, to go with the roast geese, chickens, and ducks. One day they prepared for a circumcision and another day for the ceremony of redeeming the firstborn son; now one of the family was becoming engaged, and now they all trouped off to a wedding. Tailors fitted coats, cobblers measured feet for shoes. At Reb Bendit Waldman's there was ample occasion to have a drink of cherry or sweet brandy and to nibble at an almond cookie, a babka, or a honey cake.

Reb Bendit made fun of the women of the house and their exaggerated sense of hospitality, but apparently he, too, enjoyed having his house full of people. Each time he went to Warsaw or Krakow he brought back various trinkets for the women—embroidered headkerchiefs, rings, shawls, and pins—and for the boys, pocketknives, pens, gold embossed skullcaps, and ornate phylactery bags. Apart from the usual wedding gifts—a set of the Talmud, a gold watch, a wine goblet, a spice box, a prayer shawl with silver brocade—Tanhum had already received all kinds of other presents. It wasn't mere talk when Tanhum's former fellow students at the Brisk Yeshiva said that he had fallen into a gravy pot. His bride-to-be, Mira Fridl, was considered a beauty, but Tanhum had not yet had a good look at her. How could he? During the signing of the marriage contract the women's parlor was jammed, and in the kitchen Mira Fridl was always surrounded by her sisters and sisters-in-law.

The moment Tanhum crossed the threshold he lowered his eyes. True, everyone had his destined mate; forty days before he, Tanhum, had been born it had already been decided that Mira Fridl would become his spouse. Still, he fretted that he wasn't a suitable enough son-in-law for Reb Bendit Waldman. All the members of the family were jolly, while he was reticent. He wasn't good at business or quick of tongue, not playful. He knew no games, was unable to perform stunts or do swimming tricks in the river. At twelve he already had to take free board at the homes of strangers in the towns where he was sent to study at the yeshivas. His father died when Tanhum was still a child. His mother had remarried. Tanhum's stepfather was a poor peddler and had six children from a previous marriage. From childhood on, Tanhum went around in rags. He constantly berated himself for not praying fervently enough or devoting himself sufficiently to Jewishness, and he warred eternally with evil thoughts.

This day, the tumult in the kitchen was louder than ever. Someone had apparently just told a joke or performed some antic, for the women laughed and clapped their hands. Usually when Tanhum came in, a respectful path was cleared for him, but now he had to push his way through the throng. Who knows, maybe they were making fun of him? The back of his neck felt hot and damp. He must be late, for Reb Bendit was already seated at the table, with his sons and sons-in-law, waiting for him to appear. Reb Bendit, in a flowered robe, his silver-white beard combed into two points and a silk skullcap high over his forehead, lolled grandly in his armchair at the head of the table. The men had apparently had a drink, for a carafe and glasses stood on the table, along with wafers to crunch. The company was in a joking mood. Reb Bendit's eldest son, Leibush Meir, a big, fleshy fellow with a huge potbelly and a round reddish beard circling his fat face, shook with laughter. Yoshe, a son-in-law—short and round as a barrel and with black eyes and thick lips—giggled into a handkerchief. Another son-in-law, Shlomele, the wag, jokester, and mimic, impudently imitated someone's gestures.

Reb Bendit asked Tanhum amiably, "You have a gold watch. Why aren't you on time?"

"It stopped running."

"You probably didn't wind it."

"He needs an alarm clock," Shlomele jested.

"Well, go wash your hands," and Reb Bendit pointed to the washstand.

While washing his hands Tanhum wet his sleeves. There was a towel hanging on the rack, but he stood helplessly dripping water on the floor. He often tripped, caught his clothing, and bumped into things, and he constantly had to be told where to go and what to do. There was a mirror in the dining room and Tanhum caught a glimpse of himself—a stooped figure with sunken cheeks, dark eyes below disheveled brows, a tiny beard on the tip of the chin, a pale nose, and a pointed Adam's apple. It took him a few seconds to realize that he was looking at his reflection. At the table, Reb Bendit praised the dish of groats and asked the woman who had prepared it what ingredients she had used. Leibush Meir demanded a second helping as usual. Shlomele complained that he had found only one mushroom in his portion. After the soup, the conversation turned serious. Reb Bendit had bought a tract of forest in partnership with a Zamość merchant, Reb Nathan Vengrover. The two partners had fallen out, and Reb Nathan had summoned Reb Bendit to the rabbi's the following Saturday night for a hearing. Reb Bendit complained to the company at lunch that his partner was totally lacking in common sense, a dolt, a ninny, a dunderhead. The sons and sons-in-law agreed that he was a jackass. Tanhum sat in terror. This was evil talk, slander, and who knows what else! According to the Gemara, one lost the world to come for speaking so disrespectfully of another man. Had they forgotten this or did they only pretend to forget? Tanhum wanted to warn them that they were violating the law: Thou shalt not go up and down as a talebearer among thy people. According to the Gemara, he should have stuffed up his ears with his lobes so as not to hear, but he couldn't embarrass his prospective father-in-law this way. He sank even lower in his chair. Two women now brought in the main course—a platter of beef cutlets and a tray of roast chicken floating in sauce. Tanhum grimaced. How could one eat such a repast on a weekday? Didn't they remember the destruction of the Temple?

"Tanhum, are you eating or sleeping?"

It was his intended, Mira Fridl, speaking. Tanhum came to with a start. He saw her now for the first time—of medium build, fair, with golden hair and blue eyes, wearing a red dress. She smiled at him mischievously and even winked.

"Which would you prefer—beef or chicken?"

Tanhum wanted to answer, but the words stuck in his throat. For some time already, he had felt an aversion to meat. No doubt everything here was strictly kosher, but it seemed to him that the meat smelled of blood and that he could hear the bellowing of the cow writhing beneath the slaughterer's knife.

Reb Bendit said, "Give him some of each."

Mira Fridl served a cutlet and then, with her serving spoon poised over the platter of chicken, asked, "Which would you like—the breast or a leg?"

Again Tanhum was unable to answer. Instead, Shlomele the wag said with a leer, "He lusts for both."

As Mira Fridl bent over Tanhum to put a chicken leg on his plate, her bosom touched his shoulder. She added potatoes and carrots, and Tanhum shrank away from her. He heard Shlomele snicker, and he was overcome with shame. I don't belong among them, he thought. They're making a fool of me . . . He had an urge to stand up and flee.

"Eat, Tanhum, don't dillydally," Reb Bendit said. "One must have strength for the Torah."

Tanhum put his fork into the sauce and dug out a sliver of meat, doused it in horseradish, and sprinkled it with salt to blot out the taste. He ate a slice of bread. He was intimidated by Mira Fridl. What would they talk about after the wedding? She was a rich man's daughter, accustomed to a life of luxury. Her mother had told him that a goldsmith from Lublin had fashioned jewelry for Mira Fridl. All sorts of fur coats, jackets, and capes were being sewn for her, and she would be provided with furniture, rugs, and porcelain. How could he, Tanhum, exercise control over such a pampered creature? And why would she want him for a husband? Her father had undoubtedly coerced her into it. He wanted a Talmudist for a son-in-law. Tanhum envisioned himself standing under the wedding canopy with Mira Fridl, eating the golden soup, dancing the wedding dance, and then being led off to the marriage chamber. He felt a sense of panic. None of this seemed fitting for his oppressed spirit. He began to sway and to beg the Almighty to guard him from temptations, impure thoughts, Satan's net. *Father in Heaven, save me!*

Leibush Meir burst into laugher. "What are you swaying for? It's a chicken leg, not Rashi's commentary."

Reb Nathan was expected to bring his arbitrator, Reb Feivel, to the hearing. Reb Bendit Waldman also had his own arbitrator, Reb Fishel, but nevertheless he invited Tanhum to attend the proceedings, too. He said that it would do Tanhum good to learn something about practical matters. If he turned to the rabbinate, he would have to know a little about business. It was entirely feasible that that stubborn villain, Reb Nathan, wouldn't agree to a compromise and would insist on the strict letter of the law, and Reb Bendit asked Tanhum therefore to take down the books and go over the sections that dealt with the codes of governing business partnerships. Tanhum agreed reluctantly. The entire Torah was holy, of course, but Tanhum wasn't drawn to those laws dealing with money, manipulation, interests, and swindle. In former years when he studied these subjects in the Gemara, it hadn't occurred to him that there really were Jews who reneged on written agreements, stole, swore falsely, and cheated. The idea of meeting in the flesh a person who would deny a debt, violate a trust, and grow rich from deception was too painful to contemplate. Tanhum wanted to tell Reb Bendit that he had no intention of becoming a rabbi, and that it would be hard for him now to lay aside the treatise in which he was absorbed and turn to matters that were alien to him. But how could he refuse Reb Bendit, who had raised him out of poverty, and given him his daughter for a bride? This would have enraged his future mother-in-law and turned Mira Fridl against him. It would have incited a feud and provoked evil gossip. It would have led to who knows what quarrels.

During the next few days, Tanhum didn't have enough time to get deeply into *The Breastplate of Judgment* and its many commentaries. He quickly scanned the text of Rabbi Caro and the annotations of Rabbi Moshe Isserles. He hummed and bit his lips. Obviously even in the old days there had been no lack of frauds and of rascals. Was it any wonder? Even the generation that received the Torah had its Korah, its Dathan, its Abiram. Still, how could theft be reconciled with faith? How could one whose soul had stood on Mount Sinai defile it with crime?

The Din Torah, the hearing, began on Saturday evening, and it looked as though it would last a whole week. The rabbi, Reb Efraim Engel, a patriarch of seventy and author of a book of legal opinions, told his wife to send all those who came seeking advice about other matters to the assistant rabbi. He bolted the door of his study and ordered his beadle to let only the participants enter. On the table stood the candles that had ushered out the Sabbath. The room smelled of wine, wax, and the spice box. From the way the family had described Reb Nathan Vengrover as a tough man and a speculator, Tanhum expected him to be tall, dark, and with the wild gaze of a gypsy, but in came a thin, stooped little man with a sparse beard the color of pepper, with a milky-white cataract in his left eye, and wearing a faded gaberdine, a sheepskin hat, and coarse boots. Pouches of bluish flesh dangled beneath his eyes and he had warts on his nose. Being the plaintiff, he was the first to speak. He immediately began to shout in a hoarse voice, and he kept on shouting and grunting throughout the proceedings.

Reb Bendit smoked an aromatic blend of tobacco in a pipe with an amber cover; Reb Nathan rolled cigarettes of cheap, stinking tobacco. Reb Bendit spoke deliberately and graced his words with proverbs and quotations from the saints; Reb Nathan slammed the table with his fist, yanked hairs from his beard, and called Reb Bendit a thief. He wouldn't even let his own arbitrator, Reb Feivel—who was the size of a cheder boy, with eyes as mild as a child's and a red beard that fell to his loins—get a word in edgewise. Reb Bendit recalled the details of the agreement from memory, but Reb Nathan consulted whole stackfuls of papers that were filled with row upon row of a clumsy scribble and stained with erasures and blots. He didn't sit in the chair provided for him but paced to and fro, coughed, and spat into a handkerchief. Reb Bendit was sent all kinds of refreshments and drinks from home, but Reb Nathan didn't even go near the tea that the rabbi's wife brought in. From day to day his face grew more drawn, and was gray as dust and wasted as if from consumption. From nervous tension, he chewed his fingernails and tore his own notes into shreds.

For the first two days, Tanhum was completely bewildered by what went on. The rabbi again and again implored Reb Nathan to speak to the point, not to mix up dates or inject matters that had no bearing on the subject. But it all came gushing out of Reb Nathan like water from a pump. Gradually Tanhum came to understand that his prospective father-in-law was being accused of holding back profits and falsifying accounts. Reb Nathan Vengrover maintained that Reb Bendit had bribed Prince Sapieha's steward to chop down more acres of timber than had been stipulated in the contract. Nor would Reb Bendit allow Reb Nathan and his associate near the Squire, or to get in contact with the merchants who purchased the timber, which was tied in rafts and floated down the Vistula to Danzig. Reb Bendit had allegedly announced one price to Reb Nathan, when he had in fact got a higher one from the merchants. Reb Bendit had claimed to have paid the brokers, loggers, and sawyers more than he actually did. He employed every trick and device to oust Reb Nathan from the partnership and to seize all the profits for himself. Reb Nathan pointed out that Reb Bendit had already twice gone bankrupt and subsequently settled for a third of his debts.

Reb Bendit had kept silent most of the time, awaiting his turn to speak, but finally he lost his patience. "Savage!" he shouted. "Hothead! Lunatic!"

"Usurer! Swindler! Robber!" Reb Nathan responded.

On the third day, Reb Bendit calmly began to refute Reb Nathan's charges. He proved that Reb Nathan contradicted himself, exaggerated, and didn't know a pine from an oak. How could he be allowed near the Squire when his Polish was so broken? How could he lay claim to half the income when he, Reb Bendit, had to lay out hush money to the gentry, stave off unfavorable decrees, shower assessors and marshals with gifts out of his own pocket? The more glibly Reb Bendit spoke, the more apparent it became to Tanhum that his prospective father-in-law had broken his agreement and had indeed sought to rob Reb Nathan of the profits and even part of his original investment. But how could this be? Tanhum wondered. How could Reb Bendit, a man in his sixties, a scholar, and a Hasid, commit such iniquities? What was his justification? He knew all the laws. He knew that no repentance could excuse the sin of robbery and theft unless one paid back every penny. The Day of Atonement didn't forgive such transgressions. Could a man who believed in the Creator, in reward and punishment and in immortality of the soul, risk the world to come for the sake of a few thousand gulden? Or was Reb Bendit a secret heretic?

In the closing days, Reb Bendit, his arbitrator, Reb Fishel, and Tanhum didn't go home for dinner—the maid brought them meat and soup. But Tanhum didn't touch the food. There was a gnawing in his stomach. His tongue was dry. He had a bad taste in his mouth, and he felt like vomiting. Although he fasted, his belly was bloated. A lump formed in his throat that he could neither swallow nor disgorge. He didn't weep but his eyes kept tearing over, and he saw everything as if through a mist. Tanhum reminded himself that only that past Succoth, when Reb Bendit had gone to the Sadgora rabbi, he had brought the rabbi an ivory ethrog box that was decorated with silver and embossed in gold. Inside, couched in flax, lay an ethrog from Corfu that was pocked and budding. The Hasidim knew that besides contributing generously to the community, of which he was an elder, Reb Bendit also gave the rabbi a tithe. But what was the sense of robbing one person to give to another? Did he do all this to be praised in the Sadgora study houses and be seated at the rabbi's table? Had the greed for money and honors so blinded him that he didn't know the wrongs he committed? Yes, so it seemed, for during evening prayers Reb Bendit piously washed his fingers in the basin, girdled his loins with a sash, stationed himself to pray at the eastern wall, swayed, bowed, beat his breast, and sighed. From time to time he stretched his hands up to Heaven. Several times during the arbitration he had invoked God's name.

Thursday night, when it came time to pass judgment, Reb Nathan Vengrover demanded a clear-cut decision: "No compromises! If the law says that what my partner did was right, then I don't demand even a groschen."

"According to law, Reb Bendit has to take an oath," Reb Nathan's arbitrator, Reb Feivel, asserted.

"I wouldn't swear even for a sackful of gold," Reb Bendit countered.

"In that case, pay up!"

"Not on your life!"

Both arbitrators, Reb Feivel and Reb Fishel, began to dispute the law. The rabbi drew *The Breastplate of Judgment* down from the bookcase.

Reb Bendit cast a glance at Tanhum. "Tanhum, why don't you speak up?"

Tanhum wanted to say that to appropriate another's possession was as serious an offense as swearing falsely. He also wanted to ask, "Why did you do it?" But he merely mumbled, "Since Father-in-Law signed an agreement, he must honor it."

"So you, too, turn on me, eh?"

"God forbid, but—"

"'Art thou for us or for our adversaries?'" Reb Bendit quoted from the Book of Joshua, in a dry voice.

"We don't live forever," Tanhum said haltingly.

"You go home!" Reb Bendit ordered.

Tanhum left the rabbi's study and went straight to his room at the inn. He didn't recite the Shema, or undress, but sat on the edge of his cot the whole night. When the light began to break, he packed his Sabbath gaberdine, a few shirts, socks, and books in a straw basket, and walked down Synagogue Street to the bridge that led out of town. Months went by without any news of him. They even dredged the river for his body. Reb Bendit Waldman and Reb Nathan Vengrover reached an agreement. The rabbi and the arbitrators wouldn't permit it to come to oath-taking. Mira Fridl became engaged to a youth from Lublin, the son of a sugar manufacturer. Tanhum had left all his presents behind at the inn, and the bridegroom from Lublin inherited them. One winter day, a shipping agent brought news of Tanhum: he had gone back to the Brisk Yeshiva, from which Reb Bendit originally brought him to his town. Tanhum had become a recluse. He ate no meat, drank no wine, put pebbles inside his shoes, and slept on a bench behind the stove at the study house. When a new match was proposed to him in Brisk, he responded, "My soul yearns for the Torah."

The Manuscript

W E SAT, shaded by a large umbrella, eating a late breakfast at a sidewalk café on Dizengoff Street in Tel Aviv. My guest—a woman in her late forties, with a head of freshly dyed red hair—ordered orange juice, an omelette, and black coffee. She sweetened the coffee with saccharine, which she plucked with her silvery fingernails from a tiny pillbox covered with mother-of-pearl. I had known her for about twenty-five years —first as an actress in the Warsaw Variety Theater, Kundas; then as the wife of my publisher, Morris Rashkas; and still later as the mistress of my late friend, the writer Menashe Linder. Here in Israel she had married Ehud Hadadi, a journalist ten years younger than herself. In Warsaw, her stage name was Shibtah. Shibtah, in Jewish folklore, is a she-demon who entices yeshiva boys to lechery and steals infants from young mothers who go out alone at night without a double apron— one worn front and back. Her maiden name was Kleinmintz.

In Kundas, when Shibtah sang her salacious songs and recited the monologues which Menashe Linder wrote for her, she made the "very boards burn." The reviewers admired her pretty face, her graceful figure, and her provocative movements. But Kundas did not last longer than two seasons. When Shibtah tried to play dramatic roles, she failed. During the Second World War, I heard that she died somewhere, in the ghetto or a concentration camp. But here she was, sitting across from me, dressed in a white mini-skirt and blouse, wearing large sunglasses and a wide-brimmed straw hat. Her cheeks were rouged, her brows plucked, and she wore bracelets and cameos on both wrists, and many rings on her fingers. From a distance she could have been taken for a young woman, but her neck had become flabby. She called me by a nickname she had given me when we were both young— Loshikl.

She said, "Loshikl, if someone had told me in Kazakhstan that you and I would one day be sitting together in Tel Aviv, I would have thought it a joke. But if one survives, everything is possible. Would you believe that I could stand in the woods sawing logs twelve hours a day? That is what we did, at twenty degrees below zero, hungry, and with our clothes full of lice. By the way, Hadadi would like to interview you for his newspaper."

"With pleasure. Where did he get the name Hadadi?"

"Who knows? They all give themselves names from the Haggadah. His real name is Zeinvel Zylberstein. I myself have already had a dozen names. Between 1942 and 1944, I was Nora Davidovna Stutchkov. Funny, isn't it?"

"Why did you and Menashe part?" I asked.

"Well, I knew that you would ask this question. Loshikl, our story is so strange that I sometimes don't believe it really happened. Since 1939 my life has been one long nightmare. Sometimes I wake up in the middle of the night and I don't remember who I am, what my name is, and who is lying next to me. I reach out for Ehud and he begins to grumble. *'Mah at rotzah?'* ('What do you want?') Only when I hear him talk in Hebrew do I recall that I am in the Holy Land."

"Why did you part with Menashe?"

"You really want to hear it?"

"Absolutely."

"No one knows the whole story, Loshikl. But I will tell you everything. To whom else, if not to you? In all my wanderings, not a day passed that I did not think of Menashe. I was never so devoted to anyone as I was to him—and I never will be. I would have gone through fire for him. And this is not just a phrase—I proved it with my deeds. I know that you consider me a frivolous woman. Deep in your heart, you have remained a Hasid. But the most pious woman would not have done a tenth of what I did for Menashe."

"Tell me."

"Oh, well, after you left for America, our few good years began. We knew that a terrible war was approaching and every day was a gift. Menashe read to me everything he wrote. I typed his manuscripts and brought order into his chaos. You know how disorganized he was, he never learned to number his pages. He only had one thing on his mind—women. I had given up the struggle. I said to myself, 'That's how he is and no power can change him.' Just the same, he became more and more attached to me. I had gotten myself a job as a manicurist and was supporting him. You may not believe me, but I cooked for his paramours. The older he became, the more he had to convince himself that he was still the great Don Juan. Actually, there were times when he was completely impotent. One day he was a giant and the next day he was an invalid. Why did he need all those sleazy creatures? He was nothing but a big child. So it went on until the outbreak of the war. Menashe seldom read a newspaper. He rarely turned on the radio. The war was not a complete surprise to anyone— they were digging trenches and piling up barricades on the Warsaw streets already in July. Even rabbis took shovels and dug ditches. Now that Hitler was about to invade them, the Poles forgot their scores with the Jews and we all became, God help us, one nation. Still, when the Nazis began to bombard us, we were shocked. After you left, I bought some new chairs and a sofa. Our home became a regular *bonbonnière*. Loshikl, disaster came in a matter of minutes. There was an alarm, and soon buildings were crumbling and corpses lay strewn in the gutters. We were told to go into the cellars, but the cellars were no safer than the upper stories. There were women who had sense enough to prepare food, but not I. Menashe went to his room, sat down in his chair, and said, 'I want to die.' I don't know what happened in other houses—our telephone stopped functioning immediately. Bombs exploded in front of our windows. Menashe pulled down the shades and was reading a novel by Alexandre Dumas. All his friends and admirers had vanished. There were rumors that journalists were given a special train—or perhaps special cars on a train—to flee from the city. In a time like this, it was crazy to isolate yourself, but Menashe did not stir from the house until it was announced on the radio that all physically able men should cross the Praga bridge. It was senseless to take luggage because trains were not running and how much can you carry when you go on foot? Of course, I refused to remain in Warsaw and I went with him.

"I forgot to tell you the main thing. After years of doing nothing, in 1938, Menashe suddenly developed an urge to write a novel. His muse had awakened and he wrote a book which was, in my opinion, the best thing he had ever written. I copied it for him, and when I did not like certain passages, he always changed them. It was autobiographical, but not entirely. When the newspapers learned that Menashe was writing a novel, they all wanted to start publishing it. But he had made up his mind not to publish a word until it was finished. He polished each sentence. Some chapters he rewrote three or four times. Its tentative title was *Rungs*—not a bad name since every chapter described a different phase of his life. He had finished only the first part. It would have become a trilogy.

"When it came to packing our few belongings, I asked Menashe, 'Have you packed your manuscripts?' And he said, 'Only *Rungs*. My other works will have to be read by the Nazis.' He carried two small valises and I had thrown some clothes and shoes, as much as I could carry, into a knapsack. We began to walk toward the bridge. In front of us and behind us trudged thousands of men. A woman was seldom seen. It was like a huge funeral procession—and that is what it really was. Most of them died, some from bombs, others at the hands of the Nazis after 1941, and many in Stalin's slave camps. There were optimists who took along heavy trunks. They had to abandon them even before they reached the bridge. Everyone was exhausted from hunger, fear, and lack of sleep. To lighten their loads, people threw away suits, coats, and shoes. Menashe could barely walk, but he carried both valises throughout the night. We were on the way to Bialystok because Stalin and Hitler had divided Poland and Bialystok now belonged to Russia. En route, we met journalists, writers, and those who considered themselves writers. They all carried manuscripts, and even in my despair I felt like laughing. Who needed their writings?

"If I were to tell you how we reached Bialystok, we would have to sit here until tomorrow. Menashe had already discarded one of the valises. Before he did, I opened it to make sure his manuscript wasn't there, God forbid. Menashe had fallen into such a gloom that he stopped talking altogether. He started to sprout a gray beard—he had forgotten his razor. The first thing he did when we finally stopped in a village was to shave. Some towns were already obliterated by the Nazi bombings. Others remained untouched, and life was going on as if there was no war. Strange, but a few young men—readers of Yiddish literature—wanted Menashe to lecture to them on some literary topic. This is how people are—a minute before their death, they still have all the desires of the living. One of these characters even fell in love with me and tried to seduce me. I did not know whether to laugh or cry.

"What went on in Bialystok defies description. Since the city belonged to the Soviets and the dangers of the war were over, those who survived behaved as though they had been resurrected. Soviet-Yiddish writers came from Moscow, from Kharkov, from Kiev, to greet their colleagues from Poland in the name of the party, and Communism became a most precious commodity. The few writers who really had been Communists in Poland became so high and mighty you would think they were about to go to the Kremlin to take over Stalin's job. But even those who had been anti-Communists began to pretend they had always been secret sympathizers or ardent fellow travelers. They all boasted of their proletarian origins. Everyone managed to find an uncle who was a shoemaker; a brother-in-law a coachman; or a relative who went to prison for the cause. Some suddenly discovered that their grandparents were peasants.

"Menashe was, in fact, a son of working people, but he was too proud to boast about it. The Soviet writers accepted him with a certain respect. There was talk of publishing a large anthology, and of creating a publishing company for these refugees. The editors-to-be asked Menashe if he had brought some manuscripts with him. I was there and told them about *Rungs*. Although Menashe hated it when I praised him—we had many quarrels because of this—I told them what I thought of this work. They all became intensely interested. There were special funds to subsidize such publications. It was decided that I was to bring them the manuscript the next day. They promised us a big advance and also better living quarters. Menashe did not reproach me for lauding his work this time.

"We came home, I opened the valise, and there lay a thick envelope with the inscription *Rungs*. I took out the manuscript, but I recognized neither the paper nor the typing. My dear, some beginner had given Menashe his first novel to read, and Menashe had put it into the envelope in which he had once kept his own novel. All this time, we had been carrying the scribblings of some hack.

"Even now when I speak about it, I shudder. Menashe had lost more than twenty pounds. He looked wan and sickly. I was afraid that he would go mad—but he stood there crestfallen and said, 'Well, that's that.'

"Besides the fact that he now had no manuscript to sell, there was danger that he might be suspected of having written an anti-Communist work which he was afraid to show. Bialystok teemed with informers. Although the NKVD did not yet have an address in Bialystok, a number of intellectuals had been arrested or banished from the city. Loshikl, I know you are impatient and I will give you the bare facts. I did not sleep the whole night. In the morning, I got up and said, 'Menashe, I am going to Warsaw.'

"When he heard these words, he became as pale as death, and asked, 'Have you lost your mind?' But I said, 'Warsaw is still a city. I cannot allow your work to get lost. It's not only yours, it's mine, too.' Menashe began to scream. He swore that if I went back to Warsaw, he would hang himself or cut his throat. He even struck me. The battle between us raged for two days. On the third day, I was on my way back to Warsaw. I want to tell you that many men who left Warsaw tried to return. They missed their wives, their children, their homes—if they still existed. They had heard what was going on in Stalin's paradise and they decided that they could just as well die with their dear ones. I told myself: To sacrifice one's life for a manuscript, one has to be insane. But I was seized with an obsession. The days had become colder and I took a sweater, warm underwear, and a loaf of bread. I went into a drugstore and asked for poison. The druggist—a Jew—stared at me. I told him that I had left a child in Warsaw and that I did not want to fall alive into the hands of the Nazis. He gave me some cyanide.

"I didn't travel alone. Until we reached the border, I was in the company of several men. I told them all the same lie—that I was pining away with longing for my baby—and they surrounded me with such love and care that I was embarrassed. They did not permit me to carry my bundle. They hovered over me as if I were an only daughter. We knew quite well what to expect from the Germans if we were caught, but in such situations people become fatalistic. At the same time, something within me ridiculed my undertaking. The chances of finding the manuscript in occupied Warsaw, and returning to Bialystok alive, were one in a million.

"Loshikl, I crossed the border without any incident, reached Warsaw, and found the house intact. One thing saved me—the rains and the cold had started. The nights were pitch dark. Warsaw had no electricity. The Jews had not yet been herded into a ghetto. Besides, I don't look especially Jewish. I had covered my hair with a kerchief and could easily have been taken for a peasant. Also, I avoided people. When I saw some-one from a distance, I hid and waited until he was gone. Our apartment was occupied by a family. They were sleeping in our beds and wearing our clothes. But they had not touched Menashe's manuscripts. The man was a reader of the Yiddish press and Menashe was a god to him. When I knocked on the door and told them who I was, they became frightened, think-ing that I wanted to reclaim the apartment. Their own place had been destroyed by a bomb and a child had been killed. When I told them that I had come back from Bialystok for Menashe's manuscript, they were speechless.

"I opened Menashe's drawer and there was his novel. I stayed with these people two days and they shared with me whatever food they had. The man let me have his bed—I mean my bed. I was so tired that I slept for fourteen hours. I awoke, ate something, and fell asleep again. The second evening, I was on my way back to Bialystok. I had made my way from Bia-lystok to Warsaw, and back to Bialystok, without seeing one Nazi. I did not walk all the time. Here and there a peasant offered me a ride. When one leaves the city and begins to hike through field, woods, and orchards, there are no Nazis or Communists. The sky is the same, the earth is the same, and the animals and birds are the same. The whole adventure took ten days. I regarded it as a great personal victory. First of all, I had found Menashe's work, which I carried in my blouse. Be-sides, I had proved to myself that I was not the coward I thought I was. To tell the truth, crossing the border back to Russia was not particularly risky. The Russians did not make difficulties for the refugees.

"I arrived in Bialystok in the evening. A frost had set in. I walked to our lodgings, which consisted of one room, opened the door, and lo and behold, my hero lay in bed with a woman. I knew her quite well: an atrocious poetess, ugly as an ape. A tiny kerosene lamp was burning. They had got some wood or coal because the stove was heated. They were still awake. My dear, I did not scream, I did not cry, I did not faint as they do in the theater. Both gaped at me in silence. I opened the door of the stove, took the manuscript from my blouse, and put it in the fire. I thought that Menashe might attack me, but he did not utter a word. It took a while before the manuscript caught fire. With a poker, I pushed the coals onto the paper. I stood there, watching. The fire was not in a hurry and neither was I. When *Rungs* became ashes, I walked over to the bed with the poker in hand and told the woman, 'Get out or you will soon be a corpse.'

"She did as I told her. She put on her rags and left. If she had uttered a sound, I would have killed her. When you risk your own life, other people's lives, too, are worthless.

"Menashe sat there in silence as I undressed. That night we spoke only a few words. I said, 'I burned your *Rungs*,' and he mumbled, 'Yes, I saw.' We embraced and we both knew that we were doing it for the last time. He was never so tender and strong as on that night. In the morning, I got up, packed my few things, and left. I had no more fear of the cold, the rain, the snow, the lonesomeness. I left Bialystok and that is the reason I am still alive. I came to Vilna and got a job in a soup kitchen. I saw how petty our so-called big personalities can be and how they played politics and maneuvered for a bed to sleep in or a meal to eat. In 1941, I escaped to Russia.

"Menashe, too, was there, I was told, but we never met— nor would I have wanted to. He had said in an interview that the Nazis took his book from him and that he was about to rewrite it. As far as I know, he has never rewritten anything. This really saved his life. If he had been writing and publishing, he would have been liquidated with the others. But he died anyhow."

For a long time we sat in silence. Then I said, "Shibtah, I want to ask you something, but you don't have to answer me. I am asking from sheer curiosity."

"What do you want to know?"

"Were you faithful to Menashe? I mean physically?"

She was silent. Then she said, "I could give you a Warsaw answer: 'It's none of your leprous business.' But since you are Loshikl, I will tell you the truth. No."

"Why did you do it, since you loved Menashe so much?"

"Loshikl, I don't know. Neither do I know why I burned his manuscript. He had betrayed me with scores of women and I never as much as reproached him. I had made up my mind long ago that you can love one person and sleep with someone else; but when I saw this monstrosity in our bed, the actress in me awoke for the last time and I had to do something dramatic. He could have stopped me easily; instead, he just watched me doing it."

We were both silent again. Then she said, "You should never sacrifice yourself for the person you love. Once you risk your life the way I did, then there is nothing more to give."

"In novels the young man always marries the girl he saves," I said.

She tensed but did not answer. She suddenly appeared tired, haggard, wrinkled, as if old age had caught up with her at that very moment. I did not expect her to utter another word about it, when she said, "Together with his manuscript, I burned my power to love."

The Power of Darkness

THE DOCTORS all agreed that Henia Dvosha suffered from nerves, not heart disease, but her mother, Tzeitel, the wife of Selig the tailor, confided to my mother that Henia Dvosha was making herself die because she wanted her husband, Issur Godel, to marry her sister Dunia.

When my mother heard this strange story she exclaimed, "What's going on at your house? Why should a young woman, the mother of two little children, want to die? And why would she want her husband to marry her sister, of all people? One mustn't even think such thoughts!"

As usual when she became excited, my mother's blond wig grew disheveled as if a strong wind had suddenly blown up.

I, a boy of ten, heard what Tzeitel said with astonishment, yet somehow I felt that she spoke the truth, wild as it sounded. I pretended to read a storybook but I cocked my ears to listen to the conversation.

Tzeitel, a dark, wide woman in a wide wig, a wide dress with many folds, and men's shoes, went on, "My dear friend, I'm not talking just to hear myself talk. This is a kind of madness with her. Woe is me, what I've come to in my old age. I ask but one favor of God—that He take me before He takes her."

"But what sense does it make?"

"No sense whatever. She started talking about it two years ago. She convinced herself that her sister was in love with Issur Godel, or he with her. As the saying goes—'A delusion is worse than a sickness.' Rebbetzin, I have to tell someone: Sick as she is, she's sewing a wedding dress for Dunia."

Mother suddenly noticed me listening and cried, "Get out of the kitchen and go in the other room. The kitchen is for women, not for men!"

I started to go down to the courtyard, and as I was passing the open door to Selig the tailor's shop I glanced inside. Selig was our next-door neighbor at No. 10 Krochmalna Street, and his shop was in the same apartment where he lived with his family. Selig sat at a sewing machine stitching the lining of a gaberdine. As wide as his wife was, so narrow was he. He had narrow shoulders, a narrow nose, and a narrow gray beard. His hands were narrow too, and with long fingers. His glasses, with brass rims and half lenses, were pushed up onto his narrow forehead. Across from him, before another sewing machine, sat Issur Godel, Henia Dvosha's husband. He had a tiny yellow beard ending in two points.

Selig was a men's tailor. Issur Godel made clothes for women. At that moment, he was ripping a seam. It was said that he had golden hands, and that if he had his own shop in the fancy streets he would make a fortune, but his wife didn't want to move out of her parents' apartment. When she got pains in the chest and couldn't breathe, her mother was there to take care of her. It was her mother—and occasionally her sister Dunia—who eased her with drops of valerian and rubbed her temples with vinegar when she grew faint. Dunia worked in a dress shop on Mead Street, wore fashionable clothes, and avoided the pious girls of the neighborhood. Tzeitel also watched over Henia Dvosha's two small children—Elkele and Yankele. I often went into Selig the tailor's shop. I liked to watch the machines stitch, and I collected the empty spools from the floor. Selig didn't speak like the people of Warsaw —he came from somewhere in Russia. He often discussed the Pentateuch and the Talmud with me, and he would speculate about what the saints did in Paradise and how sinners were roasted in Gehenna. Selig had been touched by Enlightenment and often sounded like a heretic. He would say to me, "Were your mother and father up in Heaven, and did they see all those things with their own eyes? Maybe there is no God? Or, if there is, maybe He's a Gentile, not a Jew?"

"God a Gentile? One mustn't say such things."

"How do you know one mustn't? Because it says so in the holy books? *People* wrote those books and people like to make up all kinds of nonsense."

"Who created the world?" I asked.

"Who created God?"

My father was a rabbi and I knew wouldn't want me to listen to such talk. I would cover my ears with my fingers when Selig began to blaspheme, and resolved to never enter his place again, but something drew me to this room where one wall was hung with gaberdines, vests, and trousers and the other with dresses and blouses. There was also a dressmaker's dummy with no head and wooden breasts and hips. This time I felt a strong urge to peek into the alcove where Henia Dvosha lay in bed.

Selig promptly struck up a conversation with me. "You don't go to cheder any more?"

"I've finished cheder. I'm studying the Gemara already."

"All by yourself? And you understand what you read?"

"If I don't, I look it up in Rashi's commentary."

"And Rashi himself understood?"

I laughed. "Rashi knew the whole Torah."

"How do you know? Did you know him personally?"

"Know him? Rashi lived hundreds of years ago."

"So how can you know what went on hundreds of years ago?"

"Everyone knows that Rashi was a great saint and a scholar."

"Who is this 'everybody'? The janitor in the courtyard doesn't know it."

Issur Godel said, "Father-in-Law, leave him alone."

"I asked him a question and I want an answer," Selig said.

Just then a small woman round as a barrel came in to be fitted for a dress. Issur Godel took her into the alcove. I saw Henia Dvosha sitting up in bed sewing a white satin dress that fell to the floor on both sides of the bed. Tzeitel hadn't lied. This was the wedding dress for Dunia.

I raced out of the shop and down the stairs. I had to think the whole matter out. Why would Henia Dvosha sew a dress for her sister to wear when she married Issur Godel after she, Henia Dvosha, died? Was this out of great love for her sister or love for her husband? I thought of the story of how Jacob worked seven years for Rachel and how her father, Laban, cheated Jacob by substituting Leah in the dark. According to Rashi, Rachel gave Leah signs so that she, Leah, wouldn't be shamed. But what kind of signs were they? I was filled with curiosity about men and women and their remarkable secrets. I was in a rush to grow up. I had begun watching girls. They mostly had the same high bosom as Selig's dummy, smaller hands and feet than men's, and hair done up in braids. Some had long, narrow necks. I knew that if I should go home and ask Mother what signs girls had and what Rachel could have given to Leah, she would only yell at me. I had to observe everything for myself and keep silent.

I stared at the passing girls, and thought I saw something like mockery in their eyes. Their glances seemed to say, "A little boy and he wants to know everything . . ."

Although the doctors assured Tzeitel that her daughter would live a long time and prescribed medicines for her nerves, Henia Dvosha grew worse from day to day. We could hear her moans in our apartment. Freitag the barber-surgeon gave her injections. Dr. Knaister ordered her taken to the hospital on Czysta Street, but Henia Dvosha protested that the sick were poisoned there and dissected after they died.

Dr. Knaister arranged a consultation of three—himself and two specialists. Two carriages pulled up before the gates of our building, each driven by a coachman in a top hat and a cloak with silver buttons. The horses had short manes and arched necks. While they waited they kept starting forward impatiently, and the coachmen had to yank on the reins to make them stand still. The consultation lasted a long time. The specialists couldn't agree, and they bickered in Polish. After they had received their twenty-five rubles, they climbed into their carriages and drove back to the rich neighborhoods where they lived and practiced.

A few days later Selig the tailor came to us in his shirtsleeves, a needle in his lapel and a thimble over the index finger of his left hand, and said to my father, "Rabbi, my daughter wants you to recite the confession with her."

My father gripped his red beard and said, "What's the hurry? With the Almighty's help, she'll live a hundred and twenty years yet."

"Not even a hundred and twenty hours," Selig replied.

Mother looked at Selig with reproof. Although he was a Jew, he spoke like a Gentile; those who came from Russia lacked the sensitivity of the Polish Jew. She began to wipe away her tears. Father rummaged in his cabinet and took out *The Ford of the Jabbok*, a book that dealt with death and mourning. He turned the pages and shook his head. Then he got up and went with Selig. This was the first time Father had been to

Selig's apartment. He never visited anyone except when called to officiate in a religious service.

He stayed there a long time, and when he came back he said, "Oh, what kind of people are these? May the Almighty guard and protect us!"

"Did you recite the confession with her?" Mother asked.

"Yes."

"Did she say anything?"

"She asked if you could marry right after shivah, the seven days of mourning, or if you had to wait until after sheloshim, the full thirty."

Mother made a face as if to spit. "She's not in her right mind."

"No."

"You'll see, she'll live years yet," Mother said.

But this prediction didn't come true. A few days later a lament was heard in the corridor. Henia Dvosha had just passed away. The front room soon filled with women. Tzeitel had already managed to cover the sewing machines and drape the mirror with a black cloth. The windows had been opened, according to Law. Issur Godel appeared among the throng of women. He was dressed in a vented gaberdine cut to the knee, a paper dickey, a stiff collar, a black tie, and a small cap. He soon was on his way to the community office to arrange for the funeral. Then Dunia walked into the courtyard wearing a straw hat decorated with flowers and a red dress and carrying a bag in ladylike fashion. Dunia and Issur Godel met on the stairs. For a moment they stood there without speaking, then they mumbled something and parted—he going down and she up. Dunia wasn't crying. Her face was pale, and her eyes expressed something like rage.

During the period of mourning, men came twice a day to pray at Selig the tailor's. Selig and Tzeitel sat on little benches in their stocking feet. Selig glanced into the Book of Job printed in Hebrew and Yiddish that he had borrowed from my father. His lapel was torn as a sign of mourning. He chatted with the men about ordinary matters. The cost of everything was rising. Thread, lisle, and lining material were all higher.

"Do people work nowadays?" Selig complained. "They play. In my time an apprentice came to work with the break of day. In the winter you started working while it was still dark. Every worker had to furnish a tallow candle at his own expense. Today the machine does everything and the worker knows only one thing—a new raise every other month. How can you have a world of such loafers?"

"Everyone runs to America!" Shmul the carpenter said.

"In America there's a panic. People are dying of hunger."

I went to pray each day at Selig the tailor's, but I never saw Issur Godel or Dunia there. Was Dunia hiding in the alcove or had she gone to work instead of observing shivah? As soon as this period of mourning was over, Issur Godel trimmed his beard, and exchanged his traditional cap for a fedora and the gaberdine for a short jacket. Dunia informed her mother that she wouldn't wear a wig after she was married.

The night before the wedding, I awoke just as the clock on the wall struck three. The window of our bedroom was covered with a blanket, but the moonlight shone in from each side. My parents were speaking softly, and their voices issued from one bed. God in Heaven, my father was lying in bed with my mother!

I held my breath and heard Mother say, "It's all their fault. They carried on in front of her. They kissed, and who knows what else. Tzeitel told me this herself. Such wickedness can cause a heart to burst."

"She should have got a divorce," Father said.

"When you love, you can't divorce."

"She spoke of her sister with such devotion," Father said.

"There are those that kiss the Angel of Death's sword," Mother replied.

I closed my eyes and pretended to be asleep. The whole world was apparently one big fraud. If my father, a rabbi who preached the Torah and piety all day, could get into bed with a female, what could you expect from an Issur Godel or a Dunia?

When I awoke the next day, Father was reciting the morning prayers. For the thousandth time he repeated the story of how the Almighty had ordered Abraham to sacrifice his son Isaac on an altar and the angel shouted down from Heaven, "Lay not thy hand upon the lad." My father wore a mask—a saint by day, a debaucher at night. I vowed to stop praying and to become a heretic.

Tzeitel mentioned to my mother that the wedding would be a quiet one. After all, the groom was a widower with two children, the family was in mourning—why make a fuss? But for some reason all the tenants of the courtyard conspired to make the wedding noisy. Presents came pouring in to the couple from all over. Someone had hired a band. I saw a barrel of beer with brass hoops being carried up the stairs, and baskets of wine. Since we were Selig's next-door neighbors, and my father would officiate at the ceremony besides, we were considered part of the family. Mother put on her holiday dress and had her wig freshly set at a hairdresser's. Tzeitel treated me to a slice of honeycake and a glass of wine. There was such a crush at Selig's apartment that there was no room for the wedding canopy, and it had to be set up in my father's study. Dunia wore the white satin wedding gown her sister had sewn for her. The other brides who had been married in our building smiled, responded to the wishes offered them in a gracious way, laughed and cried. Dunia barely said a word to anyone, and held her head high with worldly arrogance.

It was whispered about that Tzeitel had had to plead with her to get her to immerse herself in the ritual bath. Dunia had invited her own guests—girls with low-cut dresses and clean-shaven youths with thick mops of hair and broad-brimmed fedoras. Instead of shirts they wore black blouses bound with sashes. They smoked cigarettes, winked, and spoke Russian to each other. The people in our courtyard said that they were all socialists, the same as those who rebelled against the czar in 1905 and demanded a constitution. Dunia was one of them.

My mother refused to taste anything at the affair: some of the guests had brought along all kinds of food and drinks, and one could no longer be sure if everything was strictly kosher. The musicians played theater melodies, and men danced with women. Around eleven o'clock my eyes closed from weariness and Mother told me to go to bed. In the night I awoke and heard the stamping, the singing, the pagan music—polkas, mazurkas, tunes that aroused urges in me that I felt were evil even though I didn't understand what they were.

Later I woke again and heard my father quoting Ecclesiastes: "I said of laughter, It is mad, and of mirth, What doeth it?"

"They're dancing on graves," Mother whispered.

Soon after the wedding, scandals erupted at Selig's house. The newlyweds didn't want to stay in the alcove, and Issur Godel rented a ground-floor apartment on Ciepla Street. Tzeitel came weeping to my mother because her daughter had trimmed Yankele's earlocks and had removed him from cheder and enrolled him in a secular school. Nor did she maintain a kosher kitchen but bought meat at a Gentile butcher's. Issur Godel no longer called himself Issur Godel but Albert. Elkele and Yankele had been given Gentile names too—Edka and Janek.

I heard Tzeitel mention the number of the house where the newlyweds were living, and I went to see what was going on there. To the right of the gate hung a sign in Polish: ALBERT LANDAU, WOMEN'S TAILOR. Through the open window I could see Issur Godel. I hardly recognized him. He had dispensed with his beard altogether and now wore a turned-up mustache; he was bareheaded and looked young and Christian. While I was standing there, the children came home from school—Yankele in shorts and a cap with an insignia and with a knapsack on his shoulders, Elkele in a short dress and knee-high socks. I called to them, "Yankele . . . Elkele . . ." but they walked past and didn't even look at me.

Tzeitel came each day to cry anew to my mother: Henia Dvosha had come to her in a dream and shrieked that she couldn't rest in her grave. Her Yankele didn't say Kaddish for her, and she wasn't being admitted into Paradise.

Tzeitel hired a beadle to say Kaddish and study the Mishnah in her daughter's memory, but, even so, Henia Dvosha came to her mother and lamented that her shrouds had fallen off and she lay there naked; water had gathered in her grave; a wanton female had been buried beside her, a madam of a brothel, who cavorted with demons.

Father called three men to ameliorate the dream, and they stood in front of Tzeitel and intoned, "Thou hast seen a *goodly* vision! A goodly vision has thou seen! Goodly is the vision thou hast seen!"

Afterward, Father told Tzeitel that one dared not mourn the dead too long, or place too much importance in dreams. As the Gemara said, just as there could be no grain without straw, there couldn't be dreams without idle words. But Tzeitel could not contain herself. She ran to the community leaders and to the Burial Society demanding that the body be exhumed and buried elsewhere. She stopped taking care of her house, and went each day to Henia Dvosha's grave at the cemetery.

Selig's beard grew entirely white, and his face developed a network of wrinkles. His hands shook, and the people in the courtyard complained that he kept a gaberdine or a pair of trousers for weeks, and when he finally did bring them back they were either too short or too narrow or the material was ruined from pressing. Knowing that Tzeitel no longer cooked for her husband and that he lived on dry food only, Mother frequently sent things over to him. He had lost all his teeth, and when I appeared with a plate of groats, or some chicken soup or stuffed noodles, he smiled at me with his bare gums and said, "So you're bringing presents, are you? What for? It's not Purim."

"One has to eat the year round."

"Why? To fatten up for the worms?"

"A man has a soul, too," I said.

"The soul doesn't need potatoes. Besides, did you ever see a soul? There is no such thing. Stuff and nonsense."

"Then how does one live?"

"It's breathing. Electricity."

"Your wife—"

Selig interrupted me. "She's crazy!"

One evening Tzeitel confided to my mother that Henia Dvosha had taken up residence in her left ear. She sang Sabbath and holiday hymns, recited lamentations for the Destruction of the Temple, and even bewailed the sinking of the *Titanic*. "If you don't believe me, Rebbetzin, hear for yourself."

She moved her wig aside and placed her ear against Mother's.

"Do you hear?" Tzeitel asked.

"Yes. No. What's that?" Mother asked in alarm.

"It's the third week already. I kept quiet, figuring it would pass, but it grows worse from day to day."

I was so overcome by fear that I dashed from the kitchen. The word soon spread through Krochmalna Street and the surrounding streets that a dybbuk had settled in Tzeitel's ear, and that it chanted the Torah, sermonized, and crowed like a rooster. Women came to place their ears against Tzeitel's and swore that they heard the singing of Kol Nidre. Tzeitel asked my father to put his ear next to hers, but Father wouldn't consent to touch a married woman's flesh. A Warsaw nerve specialist became interested in the case—Dr. Flatau, who was famous not only in Poland but in all Europe and maybe in America, too. And an article about the case appeared in a Yiddish newspaper. The author borrowed its title from Tolstoy's play *The Power of Darkness*.

At just about that time, we moved to another courtyard in Krochmalna Street. A few weeks later, in Sarajevo, a terrorist assassinated the Austrian Archduke Ferdinand and his wife. From this one act of violence came the war, the shortages of food, the exodus of refugees from the small towns to Warsaw, and the reports in the newspapers of thousands of casualties.

People had other things to talk about than Selig the tailor and his family. After Succoth, Selig died suddenly, and a few months later Tzeitel followed him to the grave.

One day that winter, when the Germans and Russians fought at the Bzura River, and the windowpanes in our house rattled from the cannon fire and the oven stayed unheated because we could no longer afford coal, a former neighbor from No. 10, Esther Malka, paid a call on my mother. Issur Godel and Dunia, she said, were getting a divorce.

Mother asked, "Why on earth? They were supposed to be in love."

And Esther Malka replied, "Rebbetzin, they *can't* be together. They say Henia Dvosha comes each night and gets into bed between them."

"Jealous even in the grave?"

"So it seems."

Mother turned white and said words I've never forgotten: "The living die so that the dead may live."

Translated by Joseph Singer

The Bus

WHY I undertook that particular tour in 1956 is something I haven't figured out to this day—dragging around in a bus through Spain for twelve days with a group of tourists. We left from Geneva. I got on the bus around three in the afternoon and found the seats nearly all taken. The driver collected my ticket and pointed out a place next to a woman who was wearing a conspicuous black cross on her breast. Her hair was dyed red, her face was thickly rouged, the lids of her brown eyes were smeared with blue eyeshadow, and from beneath all this dye and paint emerged deep wrinkles. She had a hooked nose, lips red as a cinder, and yellowish teeth.

She began speaking to me in French, but I told her I didn't understand the language and she switched over to German. It struck me that her German wasn't that of a real German or even a Swiss. Her accent was similar to mine and she made the same mistakes. From time to time she interjected a word that sounded Yiddish. I soon found out that she was a refugee from the concentration camps. In 1946, she arrived at a DP camp near Landsberg and there by chance she struck up a friendship with a Swiss bank director from Zurich. He fell in love with her and proposed marriage but under the condition that she accept Protestantism. Her name at home had been Celina Pultusker. She was now Celina Weyerhofer.

Suddenly she began speaking to me in Polish, then went over into Yiddish. She said, "Since I don't believe in God anyway, what's the difference if it's Moses or Jesus? He wanted me to convert, so I converted a bit."

"So why do you wear a cross?"

"Not out of anything to do with religion. It was given to me by someone dying whom I'll never forget till I close my eyes."

"A man, eh?"

"What else—a woman?"

"Your husband has nothing against this?"

"I don't ask him. There he is."

Mrs. Weyerhofer pointed out a man sitting across the way.

He looked younger than she, with a fair, smooth face, blue eyes, and a straight nose. To me he appeared the typical banker—sober, amiable, his trousers neatly pressed and pulled up to preserve the crease, shoes freshly polished. He was wearing a panama hat. His manner expressed order, discipline. Across his knee lay the *Neue Zürcher Zeitung*, and I noticed it was open to the financial section. From his breast pocket he took a piece of cloth with which he polished his glasses. That done, he glanced at his gold wristwatch.

I asked Mrs. Weyerhofer why they weren't sitting together.

"Because he hates me," she said in Polish.

Her answer surprised me, but not overly so. The man glanced at me sidelong, then averted his face. He began to converse with a lady sitting in the window seat beside him. He removed his hat, revealing a shining bald pate surrounded by a ruff of pale-blond hair. "What could it have been that this Swiss saw in the person next to me?" I asked myself, but such things one could not really question.

Mrs. Weyerhofer said, "So far as I can tell, you are the only Jew on the bus. My husband doesn't like Jews. He doesn't like Gentiles, either. He has a million prejudices. Whatever I say displeases him. If he had the power, he'd kill off most of mankind and leave only his dogs and the few bankers with whom he's chummy. I'm ready to give him a divorce but he's too stingy to pay alimony. As it is, he barely gives me enough to keep alive. Yet he's highly intelligent, one of the best-read people I've ever met. He speaks six languages perfectly, but, thank God, Polish isn't one of them."

She turned toward the window and I lost my urge to talk to her further. I had slept poorly the night before, and when I leaned back I dozed off, though my mind went on thinking wakeful thoughts. I had broken up with a woman I loved—or at least desired. I had just spent three weeks alone in a hotel in Zakopane.

I was awakened by the driver. We had come to the hotel where we would eat dinner and sleep. I couldn't orient myself to the point of deciding whether we were still in Switzerland or had reached France. I didn't catch the name of the city the driver had announced. I got the key to my room. Someone had already left my suitcase there. A bit later, I went down to the dining room. All the tables were full, and I didn't want to sit with strangers.

As I stood, a boy who appeared to be fourteen or fifteen came up to me. He reminded me of prewar Poland in his short pants and high woolen stockings, his jacket with the shirt collar outside. He was a handsome youth—black hair worn in a crewcut, bright dark eyes, and unusually pale skin. He clicked his heels in military fashion and asked, "Sir, you speak English?"

"Yes."

"You are an American?"

"An American citizen."

"Perhaps you'd like to join us? I speak English. My mother speaks a little, too."

"Would your mother agree?"

"Yes. We noticed you in the bus. You were reading an American newspaper. After I graduate from what you call high school, I want to study at an American university. You aren't by chance a professor?"

"No, but I have lectured at a university a couple of times."

"Oh, I took one look at you and I knew immediately. Please, here is our table."

He led me to where his mother was sitting. She appeared to be in her mid-thirties, plump, but with a pretty face. Her black hair was combed into two buns, one at each side of her face. She was expensively dressed and wore lots of jewelry. I said hello and she smiled and replied in French.

The son addressed her in English: "Mother, the gentleman is from the United States. A professor, just as I said he would be."

"I am no professor. I was invited by a college to serve as writer-in-residence."

"Please. Sit down."

I explained to the woman that I knew no French, and she began to speak to me in a mixture of English and German. She introduced herself as Annette Metalon. The boy's name was Mark. The waiters hadn't yet managed to serve all the tables, and while we waited I told the mother and son that I was a Jew, that I wrote in Yiddish, and that I came from Poland. I always do this as soon as possible to avoid misunderstandings later. If the person I am talking to is a snob, he knows that I'm not trying to represent myself as something I'm not.

"Sir, I am also a Jew. On my father's side. My mother is Christian."

"Yes, my late husband was a Sephardi," Mrs. Metalon said. Was Yiddish a language or a dialect? she asked me. How did it differ from Hebrew? Was it written in Latin letters or in Hebrew? Who spoke the language and did it have a future? I responded to everything briefly. After some hesitation, Mrs. Metalon told me that she was an Armenian and that she lived in Ankara but that Mark was attending school in London. Her husband came from Saloniki. He was an importer and exporter of Oriental rugs and had had some other businesses as well. I noticed a ring with a huge diamond on her finger, and magnificent pearls around her neck. Finally, the waiter came over and she ordered wine and a steak. When the waiter heard I was a vegetarian he grimaced and informed me that the kitchen wasn't set up for vegetarian meals. I told him I would eat whatever I could get—potatoes, vegetables, bread, cheese. Anything he could bring me.

As soon as he had gone, the questions started about my vegetarianism: Was it on account of my health? Out of principle? Did it have anything to do with being kosher? I was accustomed to justifying myself, not only to strangers but even to people who had known me for years. When I told Mrs. Metalon that I didn't belong to any synagogue, she asked the question for which I could never find the answer—what did my Jewishness consist of?

According to the way the waiter had reacted, I assumed that I'd leave the table hungry, but he brought me a plateful of cooked vegetables and a mushroom omelette as well as fruit and cheese. Mother and son both tasted my dishes, and Mark said, "Mother, I want to become a vegetarian."

"Not as long as you're living with me," Mrs. Metalon replied.

"I don't want to remain in England, and certainly not in Turkey. I've decided to become an American," Mark said. "I like American literature, American sincerity, democracy, and the American business sense. In England there are no opportunities for anyone who wasn't born there. I want to marry an American girl. Sir, what kind of documents are needed to get a visa to the United States? I have a Turkish passport, not an English one. Would you, sir, send me an affidavit?"

"Yes, with pleasure."

"Mark, what's wrong with you? You meet a gentleman for the first time and at once you make demands of him."

"What do I demand? An affidavit is only a piece of paper and a signature. I want to study at Harvard University or at the University of Princeton. Sir, which of these two universities has the better business school?"

"I really wouldn't know."

"Oh, he has already decided everything for himself," Mrs. Metalon said. "A child of fourteen but with an old head. In that sense, he takes after his father. He always planned down to the last detail and years in advance. My husband was forty years older than I, but we had a happy life together." She took out a lace-edged handkerchief and dabbed at an invisible tear.

The bus routine required that each day passengers exchanged seats. It gave everyone a chance to sit up front. Most couples stayed together, but individuals kept changing their partners. On the third day, the driver placed me next to the banker from Zurich, who was apparently determined not to sit with his wife.

He introduced himself to me: Dr. Rudolf Weyerhofer. The bus had left Bordeaux, where we had spent the night, and was approaching the Spanish border. At first neither of us spoke; then Dr. Weyerhofer began to talk of Spain, France, the situation in Europe. He questioned me about America, and when I told him that I was a staff member of a Yiddish newspaper his talk turned to Jews and Judaism. Wasn't it odd that a people should have retained its identity through two thousand years of wandering across the countries of the world and after all that time returned to the land and language of its ancestors? The only such instance in the history of mankind. Dr. Weyerhofer told me he had read Graetz's *History of the Jews* and even something of Dubnow's. He knew the works of Martin Buber and Klausner's *Jesus of Nazareth*. But for all that, the essence of the Jew was far from clear to him. He asked about the Talmud, the Zohar, the Hasidim, and I answered as best I could. I felt certain that shortly he would begin talking about his wife.

Mrs. Weyerhofer had already managed to irritate the other passengers. Both in Lyons and in Bordeaux the bus had been forced to wait for her—for a half hour in Lyons and for over an hour in Bordeaux. The delays played havoc with the travel schedule. She had gone off shopping and had returned loaded down with bundles. From the way she had described her husband to me as a miser who begrudged her a crust of bread, I couldn't understand where she got the money to buy so many things. Both times she apologized and said that her watch had stopped, but the Swiss women claimed that she had purposely turned back the hands of her gold wristwatch. By her behavior Celina Weyerhofer humiliated not only her husband, who accused her in public of lying, but also me, for it was obvious to everyone on the bus that she, like me, was a Jew from Poland.

I no longer recall how it came about but Dr. Weyerhofer began to unburden himself to me. He said, "My wife accuses me of anti-Semitism, but what kind of anti-Semite am I if I married a Jewish woman just out of concentration camp? I want you to know that this marriage has caused me enormous difficulties. At that time many people in financial circles were infected with the Nazi poison, and I lost important connections. I was seriously considering emigrating to your America or even to South Africa, since I had practically been excommunicated from the Christian business community. How is this called by your people . . . cherem? My blessed parents were still living then and they were both devout Christians. You could write a thick book about what I went through.

"Though my wife converted, she did it in such a way that the whole thing became a farce. This woman makes enemies wherever she goes, but her worst enemy is her own mouth. She has a talent for antagonizing everyone she meets. She tried to establish a connection with the Jewish community in Zurich, but she said such shocking things and carried on so that the members would have nothing to do with her. She'd go to a rabbi and represent herself as an atheist; she'd launch a debate with him about religion and call him a hypocrite. While she accuses everyone of anti-Semitism, she herself says things about Jews you'd expect from a Goebbels. She plays the role of a rabid feminist and joins protests against the Swiss government for refusing to give women the vote, yet at the same time she castigates women in the most violent fashion.

"I noticed her talking to you when you were sitting together and I know she told you how mean I am with money. But the woman has a buying mania. She buys things that will never be used. I have a large apartment she's crowded with so much furniture, so many knickknacks and idiotic pictures that you can barely turn around. No maid will work for us. We eat in restaurants even though I hate not eating at home. I must have been mad to agree to go on this trip with her. But it looks as if we won't last out the twelve days. While I sit talking here with you, my mind is on forfeiting my money and leaving the bus before we even get to Spain. I know I shouldn't be confiding my personal problems like this, but since you are a writer maybe they can be of use to you. I tell myself that the camps and wanderings totally destroyed her nerves, but I've met other women who survived the whole Hitler hell, and they are calm, civilized, pleasant people."

"How is it that you didn't see this before?" I asked.

"Eh? A good question. I ask myself the same thing. The very fact that I'm telling you all this is a mystery to me, since we Swiss are reticent. Apparently ten years of living with this woman have altered my character. She is the one who allegedly converted, but I seem to have turned into almost a Polish Jew. I read all the Jewish news, particularly any dealing with the Jewish state. I often criticize the Jewish leaders, but not as a stranger—rather as an insider."

The bus stopped. We had come to the Spanish frontier. The driver went with our passports to the border station and lingered there a long time.

Dr. Weyerhofer began talking quietly, in almost a mumble, "I want to be truthful. One good trait she did have—she could attract a man. Sexually, she was amazingly strong. I don't believe myself that I am speaking of these things—in my circles, talk of sex is taboo. But why? Man thinks of it from cradle to grave. She has a powerful imagination, a perverse fantasy. I've had experience with women and I know. She has said things to me that drove me to frenzy. She has more stories in her than Scheherazade. Our days were cursed, but the nights were wild. She wore me out until I could no longer do my work. Is this characteristic of Jewish women in Eastern Europe? The Swiss Jewish women aren't much more interesting than the Christian."

"You know, Doctor, it is impossible to generalize."

"I have the feeling that many Jewish women in Poland are of this type. I see it in their eyes. I made a business trip to the Jewish state and even met Ben-Gurion, along with other Israeli leaders. We did business with the Bank Leumi. I have a theory that the Jewish woman of today wants to make up for all the centuries in the ghetto. Besides, the Jews are a people of imagination, even though in modern literature they haven't yet created any great works. I've read Jakob Wassermann, Stefan Zweig, Peter Altenberg, and Arthur Schnitzler, but they disappointed me. I expected something better from Jews. Are there interesting writers in Yiddish or Hebrew?"

"Interesting writers are rare among all peoples."

"Here is our driver with the passports."

We crossed the border, and an hour later the bus stopped and we went to have lunch at a Spanish restaurant.

In the entrance, Mrs. Weyerhofer came up to me and said, "You sat with my husband this morning and I know that the whole time he talked about me. I can read lips like a deaf-mute. You should know that he's a pathological liar. Not one word of truth leaves his lips."

"It so happens he praised you."

Celina Weyerhofer tensed. "What did he say?"

"That you are unusually interesting as a woman."

"Is that what he said? It can't be. He has been impotent several years, and being next to him has made me frigid. Physically and spiritually he has made me sick."

"He praised your imagination."

"Nothing is left me except my imagination. He drained my blood like a vampire. He isn't sexually normal. He is a latent homosexual—not so latent—although when I tell him this he denies it vehemently. He only wants to be with men, and when we still shared a bedroom he spent whole nights questioning me about my relationships with other men. I had to invent affairs to satisfy him. Later, he threw these imaginary sins up to me and called me filthy names. He forced me to confess that I had relations with a Nazi, even though God knows I would sooner have let them skin me alive. Maybe we can find a table together?"

"I promised to eat with some woman and her son."

"The one I saw you with yesterday in the dining room? Her son is a beauty, but she is too fat and when she gets older she'll go to pieces. Did you notice how many diamonds she wears? A jewelry store—tasteless, disgusting. In Lyons and Bordeaux none of us had a bathroom, but she got one. Since she is so rich, why does she ride in a bus? They don't give her a plain room but a suite. Is she Jewish?"

"Her late husband was a Jew."

"A widow, eh? She's probably looking for a match. The diamonds are more than likely imitations. What is she, French?"

"Armenian."

"Foolish men kill themselves and leave such bitches huge estates. Where does she live?"

"In Turkey."

"Be careful. One glance was enough to tell me this is a spider. But men are blind."

I couldn't believe it, but I began to see that Mark was trying to arrange a match between his mother and myself. Strangely, the mother played as passive a role in the situation as some old-time maiden for whom the parents were trying to find a husband. I told myself that it was all my imagination. What would a rich widow, an Armenian living in Turkey, want with a Yiddish writer? What kind of future could she see in this? True, I was an American citizen, but it wouldn't have been difficult for Mrs. Metalon to obtain a visa to America without me. I concluded that her fourteen-year-old son had hypnotized his mother—that he dominated her as his father had probably done before him. I also toyed with the notion that her husband's soul had entered into Mark and that he, the dead Sephardi, wanted his wife to marry a fellow Jew. I tried to avoid eating with the pair, but each time Mark found me and said, "Sir, my mother is waiting for you."

His words implied a command. When it was my turn to order my vegetarian dishes, Mark took over and told the waiter or waitress exactly what to bring me. He knew Spanish because his father had had a partner with whom he had conversed in Ladino. I wasn't accustomed to drinking wine with my meals, but Mark ordered it without consulting me. When we came to a city, he always managed that his mother and I were left alone to shop for bargains and souvenirs. On these occasions he warned me sternly not to spend any money on his mother, and if I had already done so he demanded to know how much and told his mother to pay me back. When I objected, he arched his brows. "Sir, we don't need gifts. A Yiddish writer can't be rich." He opened his mother's pocketbook and counted out whatever the amount had been.

Mrs. Metalon smiled sheepishly at this and added, half in jest, half in earnest, that Mark treated her as if she were his daughter. But she had obviously accepted the relationship.

Is she so weak? I wondered. Or is there some scheme behind this?

The situation struck me as particularly strange because the mother and son were together only during vacations. The rest of the year she remained in Ankara while he studied in London. As far as I could determine, Mark was dependent on his mother; when he needed something he had to ask for money.

At first, the two of them sat in the bus together, but one day after lunch Mark told me that I was to sit with his mother. He himself sat down next to Celina Weyerhofer. He had arranged all this without the driver's permission, and I doubted if he had discussed it with his mother.

I had been sitting next to a woman from Holland, and this changing of seats provoked whispering among the passengers. From that day on, I became Mrs. Metalon's partner not only in the dining room but in the bus as well. People began to wink, make remarks, leer. Much of the time I looked out of the window. We drove through regions that reminded me of the desert and the land of Israel. Peasants rode on asses. We passed an area where gypsies lived in caves. Girls balanced water jugs on their heads. Grandmothers toted bundles of wood and herbs wrapped in linen sheets over their shoulders. We passed ancient olive trees and trees that resembled umbrellas. Sheep browsed among cracked clods of earth on the half-burned plain. A horse circled a well. The sky, pale blue, radiated a fiery heat. Something Biblical hovered over the landscape. Passages of the Pentateuch flashed across my memory. It seemed to me that I was somewhere in the plains of Mamre, where presently would materialize Abraham's tent, and the angel would bring Sarah tidings that she would be blessed with a male child at the age of ninety. My head whirled with stories of Sodom, of the sacrifice of Isaac, of Ishmael and Hagar. The stacks of grain in the harvested fields brought Joseph's dreams to mind. One morning we passed a horse fair. The horses and the men stood still, congealed in silence like phantoms of a fair from a vanished time. It was hard to believe that in this very land, some fifteen years before, a civil war had raged and Stalinists had shot Trotskyites.

Barely a week had passed since our departure, but I felt that I had been wandering for months. From sitting so long in one position I was overcome with a lust that wasn't love or even sexual passion but something purely animalistic. It seemed that my partner shared the same feelings, for a special heat emanated from her. When she accidentally touched my hand, she burned me.

We sat for hours without a single word, but then we became gabby and said whatever came to our lips. We confided intimate things to one another. We yawned and went on talking half asleep. I asked her how it happened that she had married a man forty years older than herself.

She said, "I was an orphan. The Turks murdered my father, and my mother died soon after. We were rich but they stripped us of everything. I met him as an employee in his office. He had wild eyes. He took one look at me and I knew that he wanted me and was ready to marry me. He had an iron will. He also had the strength of a giant. If he hadn't smoked cigars from early morning till late at night, he would have lived to be a hundred. He could drink fifteen cups of bitter coffee a day. He exhausted me until I developed an aversion to love. When he died, I had the solace that I would be left in peace for a change. Now everything has begun to waken within me again."

"Were you a virgin when you married?" I asked in a half dream.

"Yes, a virgin."

"Did you have lovers after his death?"

"Many men wanted me, but I was raised in such a way I couldn't live with a man without marriage. In my circle in Turkey a woman can't afford to be loose. Everyone there knows what everyone else is doing. A woman has to maintain her reputation."

"What do you need with Turkey?"

"Oh, I have a house there, servants, a business."

"Here in Spain you can do what you want," I said, and regretted my words instantly.

"But I have a chaperon here," she said. "Mark watches over me. I'll tell you something that will seem crazy to you. He guards me even when he is in London and I'm in Ankara. I often feel that he sees everything I do. I sense it isn't he but his father."

"You believe this?"

"It's a fact."

I glanced backward and saw Mark gazing at me sharply as if he were trying to hypnotize me.

When we stopped for the night at a hotel, we first had to line up for the toilets, then wait for a long time for our dinner. In the rooms assigned to us, the ceilings were high, the walls thick, and there were old-fashioned washstands with basins and pitchers of water.

That night, we stopped late, which meant that dinner was not served until after ten. Once again, Mark ordered a bottle of wine. For some reason I let myself be persuaded to drink several glasses. Mark asked me if I had had a chance to bathe during the trip, and I told him that I washed every morning out of the washbasin with cold water just like the other passengers.

He glanced at his mother half questioningly, half imperatively.

After some hesitation, Mrs. Metalon said, "Come to our room. We have a bathroom."

"When?"

"Tonight. We leave at five in the morning."

"Sir, do it," Mark said. "A hot bath is healthy. In America everyone has a bathroom, be he porter or janitor. The Japanese bathe in wooden tubs, the whole family together. Come a half hour after dinner. It's not good to bathe immediately following the evening meal."

"I'll disturb both of you. You're obviously tired."

"No, sir. I never go to sleep until between one and two o'clock. I'm planning to take a walk through the city. I have to stretch my legs. From sitting all day in the bus they've become cramped and stiff. My mother goes to bed late, too."

"You're not afraid to walk alone at night in a strange city?" I asked.

"I'm not afraid of anybody. I took a course in wrestling and karate. I also take shooting lessons. It's not allowed boys my age, but I have a private teacher."

"Oh, he takes more courses than I have hairs on my head," Mrs. Metalon said. "He wants to know everything."

"In America, I'll study Yiddish," Mark announced. "I read somewhere that a million and a half people speak this language in America. I want to read you in the original. It's also good for business. America is a true democracy. There you must speak to the customer in his own language. I want my mother to come to America with me. In Turkey, no person of Armenian descent is sure of his life."

"My friends are all Turks," Mrs. Metalon protested.

"Once the pogroms start they'll stop being your friends. My mother tries to hide it from me but I know very well what they did to the Armenians in Turkey and to the Jews in Russia. I want to visit Israel. The Jews there don't bow their heads like those in Russia and Poland. They offer resistance. I want to learn Hebrew and to study at Jerusalem University."

We said goodbye and Mark wrote the number of their room on a small sheet he tore from a notebook. I went to my room for a nap. My legs wobbled as I climbed the stairs. I lay down on the bed in my clothes with the notion of resting a half hour. I closed my eyes and sank into a deep slumber. Someone woke me—it was Mark. To this day I don't know how he got into my room. Maybe I had forgotten to lock it or he had tipped the maid to let him in.

He said, "Sir, excuse me but you've slept a whole hour. You've apparently forgotten that you are coming to our room for your bath."

I assured Mark that I'd be at his door in ten minutes, and after some hesitation he left. Getting undressed and unpacking a bathrobe and slippers from my valise wasn't easy for me. I cursed the day I had decided to take this tour, but I hadn't the courage to tell Mark I wouldn't come. For all his delicacy and politeness Mark projected a kind of childish brutality.

I threw my spring coat over my bathrobe and on unsteady legs began climbing the two floors to their room. I was still half asleep, and for a moment I had the illusion that I was on board ship. When I got to the Metalons' floor, I could not find the slip of paper with the room number. I was sure that it was No. 43, but the tiny lamp on the high ceiling was concealed behind a dull shade and emitted barely any light. In the dimness I couldn't see this number. It took a long time of groping before I found it and knocked on the door.

The door opened, and to my amazement I saw Celina Weyerhofer in a nightgown, her face thickly smeared with cream. Her hair looked wet and freshly dyed. I grew so confused that I could not speak. Finally I asked, "Is this 43?"

"Yes, this is 43. To whom were you going? Oh, I understand. It seems to me that your lady with the diamonds is somewhere on this floor. I saw her son. You've made a mistake."

"Madam, I don't wish to detain you. I just want to tell you they invited me to take a bath there, that's all."

"A bath, eh? So let it be a bath. I haven't had a bath for over a week myself. What kind of tour is this that some passengers get privileges and others are discriminated against? The advertisement didn't mention anything about two classes of passengers. My dear Mr.—what is your name?—I warned you that that person would trap you, and I see this has happened sooner than I figured. Wait a minute—your bath won't run out. Since when do they call it a bath? We call it by a different name. Don't run. Because you've forgotten the number, you'll have to knock on strangers' doors and wake people. Everyone is dead tired. On this tour, before you can even lie down you have to get up again. My husband is a good sleeper. He lies down, opens some book, and two minutes later he's snoring like a lord. He carries his own alarm clock. I've stopped sleeping altogether. Literally. That's my sickness. I haven't slept for years. I told a doctor in Bern about this—he's actually a professor of medicine—and he called me a liar. The Swiss can be very coarse when they choose to be. He had studied something in a medical book or he had a theory, and because the facts didn't jibe with his theory this made me a liar. I've been watching you sitting with that woman. It looks as if you're telling her jokes from the way she keeps on laughing. My husband sat next to her one time before she monopolized you, and she told him things no decent woman would tell a stranger. I suspect she is a madam of a whorehouse in Turkey. Or something like that. No respectable woman wears so much jewelry. You can smell her perfume a mile away. I'm not even sure that this boy is her son. There seems to be some kind of unnatural relationship between them."

"Madam Weyerhofer, what are you saying?"

"I'm not just pulling things out of the air. God has cursed me with eyes that see. I say 'cursed' because this is for me a curse rather than a blessing. If you absolutely must take a bath, as you call it, do it and satisfy yourself, but be careful—such a person can easily infect you with God knows what."

Just at that moment the door across the hall opened and I saw Mrs. Metalon in a splendid nightgown and gold-colored slippers. Her hair was loose; it fell to her shoulders. She was made up, too. The women glared at each other furiously; then Mrs. Metalon said, "Where did you go? I'm in 48, not 43."

"Oh, I made a mistake. Truly, I'm completely mixed up. I'm terribly sorry—"

"Go to your bath!" Mrs. Weyerhofer said and gave me a light push. She muttered words in French I didn't understand but knew to be insulting. She slammed her own door shut.

I turned to Mrs. Metalon, who asked, "Why did you go to her, of all people? I waited and waited for you. There is no more hot water anyhow. And where has Mark vanished to? He went for a walk and hasn't come back. This night is a total loss to me. That woman—what's her name? Weyerhofer—is a troublemaker, and crazy besides. Her own husband admitted that she's emotionally disturbed."

"Madam, I've made a terrible mistake. Mark wrote down your room number for me, but while changing my clothes I lost the slip. It's all because I'm so tired—"

"Oh, will that red-haired bitch malign me before everyone on the bus now! She is a snake whose every word is venom."

"I truly don't know how to excuse myself. But—"

"Well, it's not your fault. It was Mark who cooked up this stew. The driver told me to keep it secret that we're getting a bathroom. He doesn't want to create jealousy among the passengers. Now he'll be mad at me and he'll be right. I can't continue this trip any longer. I'll get off with Mark in Madrid and take a train or plane back to the border or maybe even to Paris. Come in for a moment. I'm already compromised."

I went inside, and she took me to the bathroom to show me that the hot water was no longer running. The bathtub was made of tin. It was unusually high and long. On its outside hung a kind of pole with which to hold in and let out the water. The taps were copper. I excused myself again and Mrs. Metalon said, "You're an innocent victim. Mark is a genius, but like all geniuses he has his moods. He was a prodigy. At five he could do logarithms. He read the Bible in French and remembered all the names. He loves me and he is determined to have me meet someone. The truth is, he's seeking a father. Each time I join him during vacations he starts looking for a husband for me. He creates embarrassing complications. I don't want to marry—certainly not anyone Mark would pick out for me. But he is compulsive. He gets hysterical. I shouldn't tell you this, but I have a good reason to say it—when I do something that displeases him, he abuses me. Later he regrets it and beats his head against the wall. What can I do? I love him more than life itself. I worry about him day and night. I don't know exactly why you made such an impression on him. Maybe it's because you're a Jew, a writer, and from America. But I was born in Ankara and that's where my home is. What would I do in America? I've read a number of articles about America, and that's not the country for me. With us, servants are cheap and I have friends who advise me on financial matters. If I left Turkey, I would have to sell everything for a song. I tell you this only to point out there can never be anything between us. You would not want to live in Turkey any more than I want to live in New York. But I don't want to upset Mark and I therefore hope that for the duration of the trip you can act friendly toward me—sit with us at the table and all the rest. When the tour ends and you return home, let this be nothing more for you than an episode. He's due back soon. Tell him that you took a bath. You'll be able to have one in Madrid. We'll be spending almost two days there, and I'm told the hotel is modern. I'm sure you have someone in New York you love. Sit down awhile."

"I've just broken up with a woman."

"Broken up? Why? You didn't love her?"

"We loved each other but we couldn't stay together. This past year we argued constantly."

"Why? Why can't people live in peace? There was a great love between my husband and me, though I must admit I had to give in to him on everything. He bullied me so that I can't even say no to my own child. Oh, I'm worried. He never stayed away this long. He probably wants you to declare your love for me so that when he comes back everything will be settled between us. He is a child, a wild child. My greatest fear is that he might attempt suicide. He has threatened to." She uttered these last words in one breath.

"Why? Why?"

"For no reason. Because I dared disagree with him over some trifle. God Almighty, why am I telling you all this? Only because my heart is heavy. Say nothing about it, God forbid!"

The door opened and Mark came in. When he saw me sitting on the sofa, he asked, "Sir, did you take your bath?"

"Yes."

"It was nice, wasn't it? You look refreshed. What are you talking about with my mother?"

"Oh, this and that. I told her she's one of the prettiest women I've ever met," I said, astonished at my words.

"Yes, she is pretty, but she mustn't remain in Turkey. In the Orient, women age quickly. I once read that an actress of sixty played an eighteen-year-old girl on Broadway. Send us an affidavit and we'll come to you."

"Yes, I'll do that."

"You may kiss my mother good night."

I stood up and we kissed. My face grew moist and hot. Mark began to kiss me, too. I said good night and started down the stairs. Again it seemed to me that I was on board ship. The steps were running counter to my feet. I suddenly found myself in the lobby. In my confusion I had gone down an extra floor. It was almost dark here; the desk clerk dozed behind the desk. In a leather chair sat Mrs. Weyerhofer in a robe, legs crossed, veiled in shadow. She was smoking a cigarette.

When she saw me, she said, "Since I don't sleep anyway, I'd rather spend the night here. A bed is to sleep in or make love in, but when you can't sleep and have no one to love, a bed becomes a prison. What are you doing here? Can't you sleep, either?"

She drew the smoke in deeply and the glow of the cigarette temporarily lit up her eyes. They reflected both curiosity and malaise.

She said, "After that kind of bath, a man should be able to sleep soundly instead of wandering around like a lost soul."

Mark began telling everyone on the bus that his mother and I were engaged. He planned that when the bus came back to Geneva I should ask the American consul for visas for himself and his mother so that all three of us could fly to America together. Mrs. Metalon told him several times that this would be impossible—she had a business appointment in Ankara. I made up the lie that I had to go to Italy on literary business. But Mark argued that his mother and I could postpone our business affairs temporarily. He spoke to me as if I were already his stepfather. He enumerated his mother's financial assets. His father had arranged a trust fund for him, and he had left the remainder of his estate to his wife. According to Mark's calculations she was worth no less than two million dollars—maybe more. Mark wanted his mother to liquidate all her holdings in Turkey and transfer her money to America. He would go to America to study even before he graduated from high school. The interest on his mother's capital would allow us to live in luxury.

Mark had decided that we would settle in Washington. It

was childish and silly, but this boy cast a fear over me. I knew
that it would be hard to free myself from him. His mother had
hinted that another disappointment could drive him to actually attempt suicide. She suggested, "Maybe you'd spend some
time with me in Turkey? Turkey is an interesting country.
You'd have material to write about for your newspaper. You
could spend two or three weeks, then go back to America.
Mark wouldn't want to come along. He will gradually realize
that we're not meant for each other."

"What would I do in Turkey? No, that's impossible."

"If it's a matter of money, I'll be glad to cover the expenses.
You can even stay with me."

"No, Mrs. Metalon, it's out of the question."

"Well, something is bound to happen. What shall I do with
that boy? He's driving me crazy."

We had two days in Madrid, a day in Córdoba, and we were
on our way to Seville, where we were scheduled to stop for
two days. The tour program promised a visit to a nightclub
there. Our route was supposed to take us through Málaga,
Granada, and Valencia to Barcelona, and from there to Avi-
gnon, then back to Geneva.

In Córdoba, Mrs. Weyerhofer delayed the bus for nearly
two hours. She vanished from the hotel before our departure
and all searching failed to turn her up. On account of her, the
passengers had already missed a bullfight. Dr. Weyerhofer
pleaded with the driver to go on and leave his lunatic wife
alone in Spain as she deserved, but the driver couldn't bring
himself to abandon a woman in a strange country. When she
finally showed up loaded down with bundles and packages, Dr.
Weyerhofer slapped her twice. Her packages fell to the floor
and a vase shattered. "Nazi!" she shrieked. "Homosexual!
Sadist!" Dr. Weyerhofer said aloud so that everyone could
hear, "Well, thank God, this is the end of my martyrdom."
And he raised his hand to the sky like a pious Jew swearing a
vow.

The uproar caused an additional three-quarters of an hour
delay. When Mrs. Weyerhofer finally got into the bus, no one
would sit next to her, and the driver, who had seen us speaking
together a few times, asked me if I would, since there were no

single seats. Mark tried to seat me next to his mother and take my place, but Mrs. Metalon shouted at him to stay with her, and he gave in.

For a long while Mrs. Weyerhofer stared out the window and ignored me as if I were the one responsible for her disgrace. Then she turned to me and said, "Give me your address. I want you to be my witness in court."

"What kind of witness? If it should come to it, the court would find for him, and—if you'll excuse me—rightly so."

"Eh? Oh, I understand. Now that you're preparing to marry the Armenian heiress, you're already lining up on the side of the anti-Semites."

"Madam, your own conduct does more harm to Jews than all the anti-Semites."

"They're my enemies, mortal enemies. Your madam from Constantinople was glowing with joy when those devils humiliated me. I am again where I was—in a concentration camp. You're about to convert, I know, but I will turn back to the Jewish God. I am no longer his wife and he is no longer my husband. I'll leave him everything and flee with my life, as I did in 1945."

"Why do you keep the bus waiting in every city? This has nothing to do with Jewishness."

"It's a plot, I tell you. He organized the whole thing down to the last detail. I don't sleep the whole night, but comes morning, just as I'm catching a nap he turns back the clock. Your knocking on my door the other night—what was the name of the city?—when you were on your way to take a bath at the Turkish whore's, was also one of his tricks. It was a conspiracy to let him catch me with a lover. It's obvious. He wants to drive me out without a shirt on my back, and he has achieved his goal, the sly fox. I won't be allowed to remain in Switzerland, but who will accept me? Unless I can manage to make my way to Israel. Now I understand everything. You'll be the witness for *him*, not for me."

"I'll be a witness for no one. Don't talk nonsense."

"You obviously think I'm mad. That's his goal—to commit me to an asylum. For years he's been talking of this. He's already tried it. He keeps sending me to psychiatrists. He wanted to poison me, too. Three times he put poison in my

food and three times my instinct—or maybe it was God—gave
me a warning. By the way, I want you to know that this boy,
Mark, who wants so desperately for you to sit next to that
Turkish concubine, is not her son."

"Then who is he?"

"He is her lover, not her son. She sleeps with him."

"Were you there and saw it?"

"A chambermaid in Madrid told me. She made a mistake
and opened the door to their room in the morning and found
them in bed together. There are such sick women. One wants
a lapdog, and another a young boy. Really, you're crawling
into slime."

"I'm not crawling anywhere."

"You're taking her to America?"

"I'm not taking anyone."

"Well, I'd better keep my mouth shut." Mrs. Weyerhofer
turned away from me.

I leaned my head back against the seat and closed my eyes. I
knew well that the woman was paranoid; just the same, her last
words had given me a jolt. Who knows? What she told me
might have been the truth. Sexual perversion is the answer to
many mysteries. I was almost overcome with nausea. Yes, I
thought, she is right. I'm crawling into a quagmire.

I had but one wish now—to get off this bus as quickly as
possible. It occurred to me that for all my intimacy with Mrs.
Metalon and Mark, so far I hadn't given them my address.

I dozed, and when I opened my eyes Mark informed me
that we were in Seville. I had slept over three hours.

Despite our late start, we still had time for a fast meal. I had
sat as usual with Mrs. Metalon and Mark. Mark had ordered a
bottle of Malaga and I had drunk a good half of it. Vapors of
intoxication flowed from my stomach to my brain.

The topic of conversation at the tables was Dr. and Mrs.
Weyerhofer. All the women concluded that Dr. Weyerhofer
was a saint to put up with such a horror.

Mrs. Metalon said, "I'd like to think that this is her end.
Even a saint's patience has to burst sometime. He is a banker
and a handsome man. He won't be alone for long."

"I wouldn't want him for a father," Mark said.

Mrs. Metalon smiled and winked at me. "Why not, my son?"

"Because I want to live and study in America, not in Switzerland. Switzerland is only good for mountain climbing and skiing."

"Don't worry, there's no danger of it."

As she spoke, Mrs. Metalon did something she had never done before—she pressed her knee against mine.

Coaches waited in front of the hotel to take us to a cabaret. Candles flickered in their head lanterns, casting mysterious designs of light and shadow. I hadn't ridden in a horse-drawn carriage since leaving Warsaw. The whole evening was like a magic spell—the ride from the hotel to the cabaret with Mrs. Metalon and Mark, and later the performance. Inside the carriage, driving through the poorly lit Seville streets Mrs. Metalon held my hand. Mark sat facing us and his eyes gleamed like some night bird's. The air was balmy, dense with the scents of wine, olive oil, and gardenias. Mrs. Metalon kept on exclaiming, "What a splendid night! Look at the sky, so full of stars!"

I touched her breast, and she trembled and squeezed my knee. We were both drunk, not so much from wine as from fatigue. Again I felt the heat of her body.

When we got out of the coach Mark walked a few paces in front and Mrs. Metalon whispered, "I'd like to have another child."

"By whom?" I asked.

"Try to guess," she said.

I cannot know whether the actors and actresses and the music and the dancing were as masterly as I thought, but everything I saw and heard that evening enraptured me—the semi-Arabic music, the almost Hasidic way the dancers stamped their feet, their meaningful clicking of the castanets, their bizarre costumes. Melodies supposed to be erotic reminded me of liturgies sung on the night of Kol Nidre. Mark found an unoccupied seat close to the stage and left us alone. We began to kiss with the ardor of long-parted lovers. Between one kiss and the next, Mrs. Metalon (she had told me to call her Annette) insisted that I accompany her to Ankara. She was even ready to visit America. I had scored one of those victories I could never explain except by the fact that in the duel of love the victim is sometimes eager to surrender as the attacker is to conquer. This woman had lived alone for a number of years. She was accustomed to the embraces of an elderly man. As I thought these things, I warned myself that Mark would not allow our relationship to remain an affair.

From time to time he glanced back at us searchingly. I didn't believe Mrs. Weyerhofer's slanderous tale of mother and son, but it was obvious that Mark was capable of killing anyone he considered to be dishonoring her. The woman's words about wanting another child portended danger. However strong my urge for her body, I knew that I had no spiritual ties with her, that after a while misunderstandings, boredom, and regrets would take over. Besides, I had always been afraid of Turks. As a child, I had heard in detail of Abdul-Hamid's savageries. Later, I read about the pogroms against the Armenians. There in faraway Ankara they could easily fabricate an accusation against me, take away my American passport, and throw me in prison, from which I would not emerge alive. How strange, but when I was a boy in cheder I dreamed of lying in a Turkish prison bound with heavy ropes, and for some reason I had never forgotten this dream.

On the way back from the nightclub, both mother and son asked if I had a bathtub in my room. I told them no, and at once they invited me to bathe in their suite. Mark added that he was going to take a stroll through town. The fact that we were scheduled to stay in Seville through the following night meant that we did not have to get up early the next morning.

Mrs. Metalon and Mark had been assigned a suite of three rooms. I promised to come by and Mrs. Metalon said, "Don't be too late. The hot water may cool soon." Her words seemed to carry a symbolic meaning, as if they were out of a parable.

I went to my room, which was just under the roof. It exuded a scorching heat. The sun had lain on it all day and I switched on the ceiling lamp and stood for a long time, stupefied from the heat and the day's experiences. I had a feeling that soon flames would come shooting from all sides and the room would flare up like a paper lantern. On a brass bed lay a huge pillow and a red blanket full of stains. I needed to stretch out, but the sheet seemed dirty. I imagined I could smell the sperm that who knows how many tourists had spilled here. My bathrobe and pajamas were packed away in my valise, and I hadn't the strength to open it. Well, and what good would it do to bathe if soon afterward I had to lie down in this dirty bed?

In the coach and in the cabaret everything within me had seethed with passion. Now that I had a chance to be alone with the woman, the passion evaporated. Instead, I grew angry against this rich Turkish widow and her pampered son. I made sure that Mark wouldn't wake me. I locked the door with the heavy key and bolted it besides. I put out the light and lay down in my clothes on the sprung mattress, determined to resist all temptation.

The hotel was situated in a noisy neighborhood. Young men shouted and girls laughed wantonly. From time to time, I detected a man's cry followed by a sigh. Was it outside? In another room? Had someone been murdered here? Tortured? Who knows, remnants of the Inquisition might still linger here. I felt bites and I scratched. Sweat oozed from me but I made no effort to wipe it away. "This trip was sheer insanity," I told myself. "The whole situation is filled with menace."

I fell asleep and this time Mark did not come to wake me. By dawn it turned cold and I covered myself with the same blanket that a few hours earlier had filled me with such disgust. When I awoke, the sun was already burning. I washed myself in lukewarm water from the pitcher on the stand and wiped myself with a rusty towel. I seemed to have resolved everything in my sleep. Riding in the carriage through the city the night before, I had noticed branches of Cook's Tours and American Express. I had a return ticket to America, an American passport, and traveler's checks.

When I went down with my valise to the lobby, they told me that I had missed breakfast. The passengers had all gone off to visit churches, a Moorish palace, a museum. Thank God, I had avoided running into Mrs. Metalon and her son and having to justify myself to them. I left a tip for the bus driver with the hotel cashier and went straight to Cook's. I was afraid of complications, but they cashed my checks and sold me a train ticket to Geneva. I would lose some two hundred dollars to the bus company, but that was my fault, not theirs.

Everything went smoothly. A train was leaving soon for

Biarritz. I had booked a bedroom in a Pullman car. I got on and began correcting a manuscript as if nothing had happened.

Toward evening, I felt hungry and the conductor showed me the way to the diner. All the second-class cars were empty. I glanced into the diner. There, at a table near the door, sat Celina Weyerhofer struggling with a pullet.

We stared at each other in silence for a long while; then Mrs. Weyerhofer said, "If this is possible, then even the Messiah can come. On the other hand, I knew that we'd meet again."

"What happened?" I asked.

"My good husband simply drove me away. God knows I've had it up to here with this trip." She pointed to her throat.

She proposed that I join her, and she served as my interpreter to order a vegetarian meal. She seemed more sane and subdued than I had seen her before. She even appeared younger in her black dress. She said, "You ran away, eh? You did right. You would have been caught in a trap you would never have freed yourself from. She suited you as much as Dr. Weyerhofer suited me."

"Why did you keep the bus waiting in every city?" I asked.

She pondered. "I don't know," she said at last. "I don't know myself. Demons were after me. They misled me with their tricks."

The waiter brought my vegetables. I chewed and looked out the window as night fell over the harvested fields. The sun set, small and glowing. It rolled down quickly, like a coal from some heavenly conflagration. A nocturnal gloom hovered above the landscape, an eternity that was weary of being eternal. Good God, my father and my grandfather were right to avoid looking at women! Every encounter between a man and a woman leads to sin, disappointment, humiliation. A dread fell upon me that Mark would try to find me and exact revenge.

As if Celina had read my mind, she said, "Don't worry. She'll soon comfort herself. What was the reason for your taking this trip? Just to see Spain?"

"I wanted to forget someone who wouldn't let herself be forgotten."

"Where is she? In Europe?"

"In America."

"You can't forget anything."

We sat until late, and Mrs. Weyerhofer unfolded to me her fatalistic theory: everything was determined or fixed—every deed, every word, every thought. She herself would die shortly and no doctor or conjurer could help her. She said, "Before you came in here I fantasized that I was arranging a suicide pact with someone. After a night of pleasure, he stuck a knife in my breast."

"Why a knife, of all things?" I asked. "That's not a Jewish fantasy. I couldn't do this even to Hitler."

"If the woman wants it, it can be an act of love."

The waiter came back and mumbled something.

Mrs. Weyerhofer explained, "We're the only ones in the dining car. They want to close up."

"I'm finished," I said. "Gastronomically and otherwise."

"Don't rush," she said. "Unlike the driver of our ill-starred bus, the forces that drive us mad have all the time in the world."

Translated by Joseph Singer

THE COLLECTED STORIES

Contents

Author's Note   239

A Night in the Poorhouse   241

Escape from Civilization   253

Vanvild Kava   260

The Reencounter   268

Moon and Madness   274

Author's Note

It is difficult for me to comment on the choice of the forty-seven stories in this collection, selected from more than a hundred. Like some Oriental father with a harem full of women and children, I cherish them all.

In the process of creating them, I have become aware of the many dangers that lurk behind the writer of fiction. The worst of them are: 1. The idea that the writer must be a sociologist and a politician, adjusting himself to what are called social dialects. 2. Greed for money and quick recognition. 3. Forced originality—namely, the illusion that pretentious rhetoric, precious innovations in style, and playing with artificial symbols can express the basic and ever-changing nature of human relations, or reflect the combinations and complications of heredity and environment. These verbal pitfalls of so-called "experimental" writing have done damage even to genuine talent; they have destroyed much of modern poetry by making it obscure, esoteric, and charmless. Imagination is one thing, and the distortion of what Spinoza called "the order of things" is something else entirely. Literature can very well describe the absurd, but it should never become absurd itself.

Although the short story is not in vogue nowadays, I still believe that it constitutes the utmost challenge to the creative writer. Unlike the novel, which can absorb and even forgive lengthy digressions, flashbacks, and loose construction, the short story must aim directly at its climax. It must possess uninterrupted tension and suspense. Also, brevity is its very essence. The short story must have a definite plan; it cannot be what in literary jargon is called "a slice of life." The masters of the short story, Chekhov, Maupassant, as well as the sublime scribe of the Joseph story in the Book of Genesis, knew exactly where they were going. One can read them over and over again and never get bored. Fiction in general should never become analytic. As a matter of fact, the writer of fiction should not even try to dabble in psychology and its various isms. Genuine literature informs while it entertains. It manages to be both clear and profound. It has the magical power of merging causality with purpose, doubt with faith, the passions of the flesh with the yearnings of the soul. It is unique and general, national and universal, realistic and mystical. While it tolerates commentary by others, it should never try to explain itself. These obvious truths must be emphasized, because false criticism and pseudo-originality have created a state of literary amnesia in our generation. The zeal for messages has made many writers forget that storytelling is the raison d'être of artistic prose.

For readers who would like me to say something "more personal," I quote here a few passages (though not in the order in which they were written) from a recent memoir of mine: "My isolation from everything remained the same. I had surrendered myself to melancholy and it had taken me prisoner. I had presented Creation with an ultimatum: 'Tell me your secret, or let me perish.' I had to run away from myself. But how? And where? I dreamed of a humanism and ethics the basis of which would be a refusal to justify all the evils the Almighty has sent us and is preparing to bestow upon us in the future. At its best, art can be nothing more than a means of forgetting the human disaster for a while."

I am still working hard to make this "while" worthwhile.

I have had the good fortune to work with three highly talented and true editors, Robert Giroux, Cecil Hemley, and Rachel MacKenzie. I dedicate this collection to Rachel MacKenzie's sacred memory. She was blessed with wisdom, charm, and humility, and embued with a perfect understanding of literature—a great editor and, more than that, a great person.

I.B.S.

July 6, 1981

A Night in the Poorhouse

A T NINE in the evening the poorhouse attendant extinguished the kerosene lamp. He left burning a single tallow candle, which soon began to flicker. Outside, the frost glistened, but inside the poorhouse it was warm. The gravely ill lay in beds. The others slept on straw pallets on the floor.

Next to the oven lay Zeinvel the thief, whom peasants had crippled when they caught him stealing a horse, and Mottke the beadle, who for a long time had served as beadle to a bogus rabbi named Yontche, a cobbler who donned a Hasidic rabbi's attire and traveled through the Polish towns allegedly performing miracles. They had gone as far as Lithuania together. Yontche was subsequently caught in the act with a servant girl and fled to America. Mottke, too, tried to escape to America, but he was detained on Ellis Island and then deported because of trachoma. Later he became half blind. Both Mottke the beadle and Zeinvel the thief had lived in the poorhouse for years, although in separate rooms most of the time.

Zeinvel was tall, and as black as a gypsy, with slanted eyes, a head of black hair, and a mouth full of white teeth. Besides being lame, he suffered from consumption. As a young man he had had the reputation of being a dandy. He managed to trim his beard even in the poorhouse. Mottke was small, round like a barrel, with tufts of flax-blond hair around his scabby skull and with a yellow beard that grew on one cheek only. His eyes were always swollen and half closed. He was something of a scholar, and it was said that he and Yontche used to switch roles. One month Yontche would be the rabbi and Mottke the beadle; the next month it was the other way around.

After a while the tallow candle went out. A full moon was shining outside and its light reflected up from the snow upon the poorhouse walls. Zeinvel and Mottke never went to sleep before midnight. They chatted and told stories.

Mottke was saying, "Cold outside, eh? It's going to get even colder. Here in Poland the cold is still bearable, but when a frost comes up in Lithuania oaks burst in the forests. One thing is good there—wood is cheap. The villages are tiny, but almost all the men are learned. You meet a carpenter or a blacksmith—by day he planes a board or pounds his hammer on the anvil, but after the evening services he reads a chapter of the Mishnah to a group in the study house. They don't set much store by Hasidic rabbis. You can travel half of Lithuania without seeing a Hasid. The men avoided us, but the women used to come to us on the sly, and brought whatever they could—a chicken, a dozen eggs, a measure of buckwheat, even a garland of garlic. There's no lack of sickness anywhere, and we gave them all kinds of remedies—cow's eggs with duck milk, as well as various amulets and talismans we both invented. When we were in Lithuania, a thing happened that turned a village topsy-turvy."

"What happened?" Zeinvel asked.

"Something with a dybbuk."

"A dybbuk in Lithuania?"

"Yes, in Lithuania. I had been told that the Litvaks didn't believe in dybbuks. The Vilna Gaon didn't believe in such things, and from the Vilna Gaon to God is but one step. But what the eyes see can't be denied. The name of the village was Zabrynka. When Yontche and I got there, the ritual slaughterer invited us for the Sabbath repast. In Lithuania a Sabbath guest doesn't sleep in the poorhouse. A bed is made up for him at his host's house. The slaughterer's name was Bunem Leib, and his wife's Hiene—a name not heard in our parts. They had only one daughter, Freidke, a short girl with red hair and freckles. She was already engaged to a youth who was studying slaughtering under her father. His name was Chlavna. In Lithuania they have the queerest names. He was a handsome young man—tall, dark, well dressed. In Lithuania no one wears a satin robe on the Sabbath, unless maybe a rabbi. Nor are their earlocks as long as here in Poland. Everything with them is different. We put sugar into gefilte fish, they put pepper.

"Yontche was a glutton. The moment he entered a house, he took right to the food. I like to look around. I noticed that Freidke was madly in love with Chlavna. She never took her eyes off him. Her eyes were blue, sharp, and kind of melancholy. Why? It's in my nature that I notice things whether they concern me or not. A healthy young fellow should have an appetite, but it struck me that Chlavna hardly ate a thing. Whatever was served him, he left over—the Sabbath loaf, the soup, the meat, even the carrot stew. When Hiene served him a glass of tea, his hand trembled so that he spilled it on the tablecloth. Eh, I thought, a slaughterer's hand shouldn't tremble. That won't do.

"Yontche and I celebrated the Sabbath there, and after the Sabbath we went our way. We didn't know it then, but that winter was our last together. We hadn't had much luck in Lithuania, and Yontche acted more like a coachman than like a rabbi. Usually when I left a town I soon forgot everyone there, but I sat in the sleigh thinking about Freidke and Chlavna and I knew somehow that I'd be coming back to Zabrynka. But why? What did these strangers mean to me?

"We came to another town and there I really quarreled with Yontche, and told him that he was an outcast and that he should go to blazes. I felt so downhearted I went to a tavern. I sat down, took a shot of vodka, and someone came up to me —a little shipping agent—and said, 'You don't recognize me, but we met in Zabrynka. You are the beadle.'

"'What's happening in Zabrynka?' I asked, and he said, 'You haven't heard the news? A dybbuk has entered the slaughterer's daughter.'

"'A dybbuk?' I said. 'In Freidke?'

"And he told me this story: That Sabbath night, soon after we had left town, the butchers brought to Bunem Leib a large black bull with spiral horns, a tough beast. Since Freidke's fiancé, Chlavna, had learned the craft, with all its laws, and had already slaughtered several calves, Bunem Leib decided to let him slaughter it. When a bull is slaughtered, the butchers tie him with ropes, throw him to the ground, and hold him until he bleeds to death. But when Chlavna made the benediction and slashed the bull's throat the animal tore loose, lunged to its feet, and began to run round with such fury that he nearly brought down the slaughterhouse. He went racing across the marketplace and cracked a lamppost and overturned a wagon. All this time, the blood gushed from him as if from a tap. After a long chase, the butchers caught him and dragged him back to the slaughterhouse, already a carcass. Only then did they discover that Chlavna had vanished. Someone said that he was seen leaning over the well. Others saw him running toward the river. They searched with poles, but he wasn't found. The rabbi examined the knife Chlavna used and he found the blade jagged. The bull was declared unkosher. The butchers fell into such a rage against Bunem Leib for turning the job over to Chlavna that they shattered his windowpanes.

"That night was to Bunem Leib and to his household one long turmoil. At dawn, when he and his wife had finally dozed off, they were roused by a strange wail—not human but animal. Freidke stood naked in the center of the room bellowing like an ox. She was shaking, jerking, and lowing, as if she were the very bull her fiancé had botched. Then a terrible human voice tore itself out from her mouth. All Zabrynka came running, and it became clear that a dybbuk had entered Freidke. The dybbuk cried that he had been a man in life—an evildoer, a drunk, a lecher. When he died, his soul hadn't been allowed into Heaven but had been sentenced to be reincarnated as a bull. The Angel of Death told him that when this bull was slaughtered according to the ritual law and pious Jews ate his flesh after reciting the right benediction, he, the sinner, would be redeemed. Now that Chlavna had rendered the meat impure, the sinner's forsaken soul had entered Freidke.

"I was so taken aback by what the shipping agent told me that I left Yontche bag and baggage, grabbed my bundle, and headed back to Zabrynka. A deep snow had fallen and a bitter frost had settled in. I couldn't get a sleigh and I had to walk halfway there. The wind nearly blew me away. I was sure that my end had come and I began to say my confession."

"You fell in love with that Freidke, eh?"

"In love? You talk nonsense."

"What happened next?" Zeinvel asked.

"I came to Zabrynka in the middle of the night. The shutters were locked everywhere, but Bunem Leib's house was lit up and there were people inside. They seemed to have stayed to listen to the dybbuk instead of going to sleep. No one took notice of me when I entered. I learned later that Freidke's mother had become ill from grief and had been taken to some relative. I barely recognized Bunem Leib. He had become emaciated, yellow, and drained in the few days since I was there. Freidke stood there barefoot, half naked, with straggly red hair over her shoulders, her face as white as that of a corpse and her eyes bulging. She screamed with a voice I could never have believed could come out of a girl's tender throat. This was not a human voice but that of an ox. I heard her bellow, 'Slaughter me, Bunem Leib, slaughter me! I am the bull you caused to be *tref* and so doomed to eternal torment. You don't see them, but hordes of demons, hobgoblins, and devils are lurking right here waiting to tear me to pieces and carry me away to the wastelands behind the Dark Mountains. Neither your mezuzah nor the talismans and amulets you hung in all the corners of the house can help me. Look, if you are not completely blind: monsters with noses to their navels, with snakes instead of hair, with snouts of boars, as black as pitch, as red as fire, as green as gall! They dance and howl like the mad. Is it my fault, Bunem Leib, that you have chosen for your son-in-law a schlemiel, a mollycoddle who cannot wield a knife? He could as much be a slaughterer as you could be a wet nurse. His hands were shaking like those of a man of ninety. He was such a weakling that when he saw a drop of blood on the white of an egg he was ready to faint. A slaughterer cannot be afraid of blood. A real man doesn't run away from his bride-to-be when things go wrong. You picked a mama's boy for your daughter, a pampered little brat, a eunuch. He was more afraid of me, the bull, than I was of his knife! Slaughter me, Bunem Leib, and save me from all these vicious spirits. If not, I will catch you on my horns and gore you and carry you away to swamps from which there can never be any rescue.'

"'My daughter, what are you talking about? You are my child,' Bunem Leib said to her. 'Let this evil fiend only free you, and if Chlavna is not your destined one, I will find another spouse for you, God willing, and we will lead you to the wedding canopy. Merciful God, help me! I can't take any more of this anguish.'

"Bunem Leib was crying. But Freidke answered, 'I'm not your daughter but the bull you have given into the hands of a bungler. Take out your knife and slaughter me! Shed my blood! You, Bunem Leib, are a male, not a neuter. No ox, no cow, no sheep or rooster ever ran away from your knife. Kill me, Bunem Leib, kill me!'"

"You heard all this?" Zeinvel asked.

"May I hear the Messiah's ram's horn as clearly."

"Go on."

"It is impossible to tell it all. Toward dawn Bunem Leib became so tired and haggard that he had to go to sleep, but the town's rowdies took over the show. For them it was fun. Imagine, an only daughter, a quiet little dove, stands in the middle of the night, her breasts uncovered, her red hair wild as a witch's, and she confesses sins that make your head swim. I heard her say, 'While alive, I did everything to spite God. I shaved my beard, I ate pork on Yom Kippur, I fornicated with Gentile wenches and Jewish whores. I denied God, and I thought I would live to be a hundred and indulge in all my abominations. But suddenly I got sick with pox and saw that I was done for. Still, to my last breath I blasphemed God and served the idols. When I finally expired, the Burial Society wouldn't cleanse my body and they buried me without shrouds, at midnight, without anyone saying Kaddish. Even before the gravediggers had thrown the last spadeful of dirt over me, the Angel Dumah opened my grave, spat at me, pierced me with his fiery rod, and dragged me to the very gates of Gehenna. He tried to hurl me inside, but Satan slammed the door and shouted, "It is a disgrace to Gehenna to allow such scum to enter into it."'

"You can be the world's biggest heretic, Zeinvel, but when you see and hear a thing like this, you must admit that there is a God."

"No, you mustn't."

"Then what was all that?"

"Nerves."

"How do nerves know what goes on in the netherworld?" Mottke asked.

"The nerves know everything."

"What are they—prophets?"

"Even better than that," Zeinvel said. "Good night."

"Well, you are talking nonsense."

Zeinvel had fallen asleep and was snoring, but Mottke lay awake. He talked to himself: "Gone to sleep, eh? A dunce, a boob . . . Thinks he knows it all, but to me he's still a fool."

"Mottke, shut up."

"You're not asleep?"

"I am asleep, but I hear every word anyway. I learned this trick in jail. There, if you fall asleep for real they'll strip the shirt right off your back. What became of Freidke?"

"How should I know? I stayed there for three days, then I went my way. I haven't told you everything yet. Neighbors swore to me that Freidke had never sung before. True, a well-brought-up girl doesn't let her voice be heard, so as not to arouse us males; nevertheless, if a girl has a voice she'll sing while rocking a child, or she will join in the Sabbath chants. All of a sudden Freidke started singing droll songs in Yiddish, Polish, even in Russian. She serenaded a bride and made wedding jests, all in rhyme. She mocked the women haggling in the butcher shops, and their splashing in the ritual bath. The hoodlums made snide remarks to her, and she answered each one on his own terms. She fast-talked them so, they were left speechless. All the neighbors said the same—this wasn't Freidke but a wag, a rascal, with a tongue like a razor. His profanities left you rolling with laughter. Brother, I stood by and watched a female turn both into a bull and into a man. Nerves can't do this."

"What can do it?"

"Only God."

"There is no God."

"How did the world form?" Mottke asked.

"It grew from itself like a scab."

II

Zeinvel dozed off again, but Mottke still lay awake. The sick in the poorhouse sighed and mumbled in their sleep. Wasn't Zeinvel right, Mottke reflected. A merciful God wouldn't allow so much misery. People die like flies here. Each day the Burial Society comes with the ablution board to carry out a body.

For a while Mottke listened to a cricket chirping behind the stove. It jingled as if with little bells. It told a tale without a beginning or an end. How was it that it chirped the whole night, Mottke wondered. Don't crickets need sleep, too? Or do they sleep during the day? And what do they find to eat among the rags? It was crazy to think that this cricket had a father, a mother, a grandfather, a grandmother, and maybe children, too. I'm all befuddled, Mottke mused. I'm dead tired all day, but at night my brain works like a churn.

Sometimes during the day, when Mottke wanted to show off his erudition, he forgot everything, jumbled passages like some ignoramus. But in the middle of the night his brain opened up. He recalled whole chapters of the Scripture, sections of the Gemara, even the liturgies of Rosh Hashanah and Yom Kippur. People who had died so long ago that he no longer remembered their names materialized seemingly alive before him. He remembered names of villages in which he had stayed with Yontche. Chants of cantors and songs of Hasidim came back to his mind. Mottke had been raised in a religious home. His father had taken him along to the wonder rabbi at Turisk. As a boy, he had read Hasidic books, had even dreamed of becoming a rabbi. But his father had died of typhus, his mother had married some boor, and Mottke had slipped into the confidence game with Yontche.

Now Mottke began droning a song that he had heard in Turisk at the Sabbath meal:

> *I'll sing with praise*
> *To open the gates*
> *Of the Heavenly orchards*
> *For their sacred mates.*

Zeinvel got to coughing and sat up. "Why are you singing in the middle of the night? Are you hungry?"

"I'm not hungry."

"You've got a burr in your saddle, eh?"

"Wasted away a life for nothing," Mottke said, shocked at his own words.

"You want to become a penitent like that musician who blindfolded himself so that he couldn't look at women?"

"Too late for that."

"Yes, brother, for us it might have been too late when we were born," Zeinvel said. "That business with Freidke was all stuff and nonsense. It's all made up—the Jewish God, the Christian God. That Chlavna was a clumsy dolt and a miserable coward. Freidke, on the other hand, was putting on an act because he deserted her. Young girls hear old wives' tales, absorb every trifle, and then they mimic them.

"I had a wild female once, a Talmud teacher's daughter. Mindle was her name. She looked like a kosher virgin. I could have sworn she couldn't count to two—a pale little face, big black eyes. It all started when I met her at the pump and filled a pail of water for her. She gave me a pretty thank you and threw in a sweet smile. I was already a thief by then and I had had more women than you have hairs on your head. At that time, it wasn't easy to get a Jewish girl—not in our parts, anyway—but there was no shortage of shiksas. They don't know any pretenses. They've got Uncle Esau's blood in their veins. Well, but I saw fire in Mindle's eyes. Each time I saw her going with her pail, I ran outside with my pail. I must have pumped a hundred pails for her. I began thinking that it was a waste of time. Suddenly I hand her the pail and she slips a note into my hand. I ran so fast with my own pail that I spilled half of it. I walk into the house and I read, 'Meet me in the cemetery at midnight.'

"One line, that's all—fancy handwriting. I had tasted everything—girls, matrons, young, old—but I grew as rattled as a yeshiva boy. I was scared, too. In those days I still believed in the creatures of the night. What kind of girl would meet a fellow in the cemetery at midnight? It was said that corpses prayed in the synagogue at night and that if someone walked by they would call him inside to read from the Torah. Also, a carpenter's daughter had hanged herself in our town because some tramp made her pregnant, and it was said that she climbed out of her grave in the nights and wandered among the tombstones. Just the same, I couldn't wait for night to fall and, later, for the clock on the town hall to toll eleven-thirty. My piece of goods had figured out everything in advance. Her father, a fervent Hasid who wore two skullcaps, one in front and one in back, went to bed with the chickens. He got up before dawn to bewail the Destruction of the Temple. The mother traveled to fairs to support her older daughter, a penniless widow who lived in Krasnystaw with three children. She sold jackets that she padded herself.

"I'll cut it short. Mindle had scheduled our meeting for the end of the month, when the moon wasn't shining and when the mother was off to some fair. The night was hot and dark. The road to the cemetery led through Church Street. The Jews lived close to the marketplace. Farther along, only Gentiles lived—tiny houses and huge dogs. I walked by and they attacked me like a pack of wolves. With one dog you can manage, but with fifty you don't stand a chance. Besides, when the Gentiles hear their dogs bark, they come running outside with cudgels. I thought I was going to be martyred, but somehow I made it to the cemetery. I tapped, feeling my way like a blind man. I was still a believer then, and in my mind I donated eighteen groschen to charity. I stretched out my arms and there she was, as if she had emerged from the ground. When you're scared, all desire leaves you, but the moment I touched her she burned me like a hot coal. She whispered a secret in my ear. There was no need for talk. How can such a firebrand grow up in a pious teacher's house?"

"She satisfied you, eh?" Mottke asked.

"That's not the word," Zeinvel said. "We fell on each other and we couldn't break apart. I took it for granted she was a virgin, but that would be the day!"

"A tasty piece, eh?"

"We lay for hours among the headstones and I couldn't get enough. As hot as fire and as sharp as a dagger. Whenever I began to cool off she said something so spicy that I shuddered and the game started all over again. Where she had learned such talk in our little village I'll never know."

"How is it you didn't marry her?" Mottke asked.

"Eh? I wanted a respectable girl, not a slut. She spoke frankly: one man to her was like an appetizer. She needed many, always new ones. I'm no saint, but I wished a wife like my mother. In my trade, you've got to be ready to do time. To sit in prison and worry that your wife is running around with every bum is scant pleasure. Even as I fondled and kissed her and promised her the moon and the stars, I longed for my Malkele, may she rest in peace. I already knew her by then. She was a friend of my sister Zirel. I wasn't planning to remain a thief. I wanted to amass a stake and become a horse dealer. But man proposes and God disposes."

"That means you *do* believe in God," Mottke said.

"It only sounds this way. What is God? Who is He? No one has gone up to Heaven and come to an understanding with Him. It's all written in the Torah, but what's the Torah? Parchment and ink. Whoever holds the pen writes what pleases him. For nearly two thousand years Jews have been waiting for the Messiah, but he's in no hurry to show up."

"So the world is lawless, eh?"

"Whoever can, grabs. And whoever can't lies six feet under."

"Still, if good people didn't send us groats and soup here we would long since have been flat on our backs," Mottke said.

"They don't do it for us," Zeinvel said. "They think this will reserve them golden chairs in Paradise and large portions of the Leviathan."

"You once said yourself that you believe in fate," Mottke argued. "You said that the last time you went to steal a horse you knew in advance that you would come a cropper and that it was fated this way. Those were your very words."

"God is God and fate is fate. I had stolen a half-dozen nags within a few weeks, and the peasants had started sleeping in the stables. They stood guard with axes and rattles. My Malkele begged me: 'Zeinvel, enough!' She knelt before me and warned me to stay home. She spoke about opening a store or, if worst came to worst, of going to America. She demanded that I swear on the Pentateuch that I would begin a new life. But even as I took the holy oath I knew that it wasn't worth a pinch of snuff. It's not in me to stand in a store and weigh out two ounces of almonds or cream of tartar. I don't have the patience for such drivel. Nor was I drawn to the land of Columbus. Everyone who went there ended up pressing pants or peddling from door to door. Letters came telling of a depression in New York, of workers picking food out of garbage cans. I loved Malkele, but she wasn't Mindle. I was faithful to her, God is my witness, but to sit with her days and nights and have her chip away at me didn't appeal to me. She had miscarried twice. She was constantly bewailing her lot and mine, too. I wanted once and for all to test my luck."

"You believe in luck?"

"Yes. In good luck and bad luck."

"There is a God, there is!" Mottke said.

"And if there is, what of it? He sits in the seventh Heaven, the angels flatter Him with their hymns, and He cares as much about us as about last year's frost."

"What became of Mindle?" Mottke asked.

"Oh, her father married her off to some dummy, a son of a rich Hasid, a follower of his rabbi's. My little kitten stood with him under the canopy pure and veiled as if she had never been touched. Why she would allow herself to be used this way is a riddle to me. Such females sometimes marry a fool so that they'll have someone to dupe easily. There is a great thrill in cheating—almost as much as in stealing. But you pay for everything. She died two years later in childbirth."

"So that's how it turned out?"

"Yes. Her husband, the lummox, had gone to his rabbi's and he lingered there for months. I was doing time in the Janov jail. Later, they transferred me to Lublin. That time I was innocent. I had been falsely accused. When I finally got out, Mindle was already in the other world."

"It was surely a punishment from God," Mottke said.

"No."

It grew silent. Even the cricket had ceased its chirping. After a while Zeinvel said, "I haven't forgotten her. If there is a Gehenna, I want to lie next to her on one bed of nails."

Translated by Joseph Singer

Escape from Civilization

I BEGAN to plan my escape from civilization not long after learning the meaning of the word. But the village of Bilgoray, where I lived until I was eighteen, didn't have enough civilization to run away from. Later, when I went to Warsaw, all I could do was run back to Bilgoray. The idea took on substance only after I arrived in New York. It was here that I started to suffer from some kind of allergy—rose fever, hay fever, dust, who knows? I took pills by the bottleful, but they didn't do much good. The heat that early spring was as intense as in August. The furnished room where I lived on the West Side was stifling. I am not one to consult with doctors, but I paid a visit to Dr. Gnizdatka, whom I knew from Warsaw and who faithfully read anything that I managed to get published in the Yiddish press.

Dr. Gnizdatka inserted a speculum into my nostrils and a tongue depressor into my mouth and said, *"Paskudno."* ("Bad.")

"What should I do?"

"Move somewhere near the ocean."

"Where is the ocean?"

"Go to Sea Gate."

The moment Dr. Gnizdatka spoke the name, I realized that the time had finally come to escape from civilization, and that Sea Gate could serve the same purpose as Haiti or Madagascar. The following morning, I went to the bank and withdrew my savings of seventy-eight dollars, checked out of my room, packed all my belongings into a large cardboard suitcase, and walked to the subway. In a cafeteria on East Broadway, someone had told me that it was easy to get a furnished room in Sea Gate. I carried a few books to be my spiritual mainstay while away from civilization: the Bible, Spinoza's *Ethics*, Schopenhauer's *The World as Will and Idea*, as well as a textbook with mathematical formulas. I was then an ardent Spinozist and, according to Spinoza, one can reach immortality only if one meditates upon adequate ideas, which means mathematics.

Because of the heat in New York City, I expected Coney Island to be crowded and the beach lined with bathers. But at Stillwell Avenue, where I got off the train, it was winter. How surprising that in the hour it took me to get from Manhattan to the Island the weather had changed. The sky was overcast, a cold wind blew, and a needle-like rain had begun to fall. The Surf Avenue trolley was empty. At the entrance to Sea Gate there was actually a gate to keep the area private. Two police-men stationed there stopped me and asked who I was and what business I had in Sea Gate. I almost said, "I am running away from civilization," but I answered, "I came to rent a room."

"And you brought your baggage along?"

These interrogations in a country that is supposed to be free insulted me, and I asked, "Is that forbidden?"

One policeman whispered something to the other, and both of them laughed. I received permission to cross the frontier.

The rain intensified. I would have liked to ask someone where I could get a room, but there was no one to ask. Sea Gate looked desolate, still deeply sunk in its winter sleep. For courage I reminded myself of Sven Hedin, Nansen, Captain Scott, Amundsen, and other explorers who left the comforts of the cities to discover the mysteries of the world. The rain pounded on my cardboard suitcase like hail. Perhaps it *was* hailing. The wind tore the hat off my head, and it rolled and flew about like an imp. Suddenly through the downpour I saw a woman beckoning to me from the porch of a house. Her mouth moved, but the wind carried her voice away. She sig-naled me to come over and find protection from the wild ele-ments. I found myself facing a fancy house with a gabled roof, columns, an ornate door. I walked onto the porch, dropped my suitcase (books and manuscripts can be as heavy as stones), wiped my face with a handkerchief, and was able to see the woman more clearly: a brunette who seemed to me in her thir-ties, with an olive complexion, black eyes, and classic features. There was something European about her. Her eyebrows were thick. There was no sign of cosmetics on her face. She wore a coat and a beret that reminded me of Poland. She spoke to me in English, but when I answered her and she heard my accent she shifted to Yiddish.

"Who are you looking for? I saw you walking in the rain with that heavy suitcase, and I thought I might . . ."

I told her I had come to rent a room and she smiled, not without irony.

"Is this the way you look for a room? Carrying your luggage? Please come inside. I have a house full of rooms that are to let."

She led me into a parlor, the like of which I had seen only in the movies—Oriental rugs, gold-framed pictures, and an elaborate staircase with carvings and a red velvet bannister. Had I entered an ancient palace? The woman was saying, "Isn't that odd? I've just opened the house this minute. It's been closed for the winter. The weather turned warm and I decided perhaps it's time. As a rule, the season here begins in late May or early June."

"Why is the house closed in the winter?" I asked.

"There's no steam. It's an old building—seventy or eighty years old. It can be heated, but the system is complicated. The heat comes through here." She indicated a brass grate in the floor.

I now realized it was much colder inside than outside. There was a staleness in the air characteristic of places that have been without sun for a long time. We stood silent for a moment. Then she asked, "Are you wanting to move in immediately? The electricity isn't turned on yet and the telephone hasn't been connected. Usually boarders come to make arrangements, pay a deposit, and move in when the weather has become really warm."

"I gave up my room in the city."

The woman looked at me inquisitively and after some hesitation said, "I could swear I've seen your picture in the newspaper."

"Yes, they printed my photograph last week."

"Are you Warshawsky?"

"That's me."

"God in Heaven!"

Darkness had fallen and Esther Royskes lit a candle in a copper candlestick. We were sitting in the kitchen eating supper, like man and wife. She had already told me her whole story:

the trouble her ex-husband, a Communist poet, gave her; how she finally divorced him; and how he ran away with his lover to California and left Esther to take care of their two little girls. Two years ago, she had rented this house with the hope that she could earn a living from it, but it did not bring her enough income. People waited until after the Fourth of July and tried to get bargains. Last year, a number of her rooms remained empty.

I put my hand into my pocket, took out the seventy-eight dollars, and offered to give her a down payment, but she protested. "No, you are not going to do that!"

"Why not?"

"First, you have to see what you are taking. It is damp and dark here. You may, God forbid, get a cold. And where will you eat? I would gladly cook for you, but since you tell me you plan to become a vegetarian it may be difficult."

"I will eat in Coney Island."

"You will ruin your stomach. All you get there is hot dogs. A man who packs his valise and comes to Sea Gate without any forethought is not practical. It's a miracle that brought you to me."

"Yes, it is a miracle."

Her black eyes gazed at me half mockingly, and I knew that this was the beginning of a serious relationship. She seemed to be aware of it, too. She spoke to me of things that are usually not told to a stranger. The shadows cast on her face by the candlelight reminded me of a charcoal sketch on a canvas. She said, "Last week I was lying in bed reading your story in the paper. The girls were asleep, but I love to read at night. Who writes about ghosts nowadays, I wondered, and in a Yiddish newspaper to boot! You may not believe me but I thought that I would like to meet you. Isn't that strange?"

"Yes, strange."

"I want to tell you that there is a romantic story connected with this house. A millionaire built it for his mistress. Then Sea Gate was still a place for the rich and American aristocrats. After his death, his mistress remained here until she died. The furnishings are hers—even the library. She seemed not to have left any will, and the bank sold everything intact. For years it remained unoccupied."

"Was she beautiful?"

"Come, I will show you her portrait."

Esther picked up the candlestick. We had to pass through a number of dark rooms to get from the kitchen to the parlor. I stumbled on the thresholds and bumped into rocking chairs. I tripped over a bulge in a rug. Esther took me by the wrist. I felt the warmth of her hand. She asked me, "Are you cold?"

"No. A little."

In the flickering light of the candle, we stood and gazed at the portrait of the mistress. Her hair was arranged in a high pompadour; her low-cut dress exposed her long neck and the upper part of her breasts. Her eyes seemed alive in the semidarkness. Esther said, "Everything passes. I still find pressed flowers and leaves in her books, but there's nothing left of her."

"I'm sure her spirit roams these rooms at night."

The candlestick in Esther's hand trembled and the walls, the pictures, and the furniture shook like stage props in a theater. "Don't say that. I will be afraid to sleep!"

We looked at each other like two mind readers. I remember what I thought then: A situation that a novelist would have to build up slowly, gradually, through a number of chapters, over months or perhaps years, fate has arranged in minutes, in a few strokes. Everything was ready—the characters, the circumstances, the motivations. Well, but in a true drama one can never foresee what will happen the next instant.

The rain had stopped and we were back in the kitchen, drinking tea. I thought it was late, but when I looked at my wristwatch it showed twenty-five past eight. Esther glanced at her watch, too. We sat there for a while, silent. I could see that she was pondering something that required an immediate decision, and I knew what it was. I could almost hear a voice in her mind—perhaps it was the genius of the female species— saying, "It shouldn't come to him so easily. What does a man think when he's able to get a woman so quickly?"

Esther nodded. "The rain has stopped."

"Yes."

"Listen to me," she said. "You can have the best room in this house, and we will not haggle about money. I will be honored and happy to have you here. But it's too early for you to move in. I intended to spend the night here, but now I am going to lock up the house and go home to my children."

"Why don't you want to stay over? Because of me?" I asked, ashamed of my own words.

Esther looked at me questioningly. "Let it be so."

Then she said something that, according to the rules of female diplomacy, she should not have said: "Everything must ripen."

"Very well."

"Where will you sleep now that you've given up your room?"

"I will manage somehow."

"When do you intend to move in?"

"As quickly as possible."

"Will May 15th be too long for you to wait?"

"No, not too long."

"In that case, everything is decided."

And she looked at me with an expression of resentment. Perhaps she expected me to implore her and try to persuade her. But imploring and persuading have never been a part of my male strategy. In the few hours I spent with Esther I had become somewhat surer of myself. I figured that she was about ten years my senior. I had girded myself with the patience necessary to one prepared to give up civilization and its vanities.

Neither of us had removed our coats—it was too cold—so we didn't have to put them on. I took my suitcase, Esther her overnight bag. She blew out the candle. She said, "If you hadn't mentioned her spirit, I might have stayed."

"I'm sure that her spirit is a good one."

"Even good spirits sometimes cause mischief."

We left the house and Esther locked the door. The sky was now clear—light as from an invisible moon. Stars twinkled. The revolving beam from a nearby tower fell on one side of Esther's face. I didn't know why, but I imagined that it was the first night of Passover. I became aware that the house stood apart from other houses and was encircled by lawns. The ocean was only a block away. Because of the howling wind I couldn't hear its sounds earlier, but the winds had subsided and now I heard the waters churning, foaming, like a cosmic stew in a cosmic caldron. In the distance, a tugboat was towing three dark barges. I could barely believe that just an hour away from Manhattan one could reach such quiet.

Esther spoke haltingly. "You wanted to give me an advance before, but I refused to take it. If you are serious about the room, I will accept one, just to make sure that . . ."

"Will twenty dollars be enough?"

"Yes, enough. I ask for it only so that you won't change your mind," she said, and she laughed self-consciously.

In the night light, I counted out twenty dollars. We walked together to the gate. I recognized one of the policemen who had been on duty when I arrived. He looked at us and our suitcases knowingly, as if, like a wizard, he had guessed our secrets. He smiled and winked, and I heard him say, "Are you two going back to civilization?"

Translated by the author and Ruth Schachner Finkel

Vanvild Kava

IF a Nobel Prize existed for writing little, Vanvild Kava would have gotten it. During his lifetime he published one thin brochure and a few articles. Half of the brochure consisted of writer's names and titles of books. Just the same he was a member of the Yiddish Writers' Club in Warsaw and even belonged to the P.E.N. club.

When I acquired a guest card to the Writers' Club, Kava had already been there for many years. He was known as a strange character and the most severe critic possible. He declared such Yiddish classics as Sholom Aleichem and Peretz to be half-talents, and Mendele Mocher Sforim talentless. Sholem Asch he called a promising young man who didn't keep his promise. My brother, I. J. Singer, and my friend Aaron Zeitlin he considered barely beginners. Like a schoolteacher, Kava liked to grade achievements in numbers, and he gave them both two sevenths. I could not bargain with him about my brother, but I told him that Zeitlin was the closest thing to a master that I could think of. I compared him to such writers as Edgar Allan Poe, Lermontov, and Slowacki. But Kava's opinion of even these poets was not too high. He found faults in everyone. Kava maintained that since civilization and culture are only some five thousand years old, literature is still at the beginning of its development, actually in its infancy. It may take another five thousand years for a full-fledged literary genius to appear. I argued that every artist must start from the beginning; unlike science, art does not thrive on the information and qualities of others. But Kava replied, "Art has its mutations and selections, its own biological growth."

It seemed unbelievable that such an angry critic could exist in the Warsaw Yiddish Writers' Club. Every Friday in the book sections of the Yiddish newspapers, reviewers revealed at least half a dozen new talents. They were as lenient as Kava was strict. After he was willing to grant me .003 as my rating (quite lavish praise for a fledgling like myself), we had many conversations about literature. Kava pointed out to me that Tolstoy's

War and Peace may be quite rich and accurate in description and dialogue, but is poor in construction. Dostoevsky had a greater vision than Tolstoy, but he had only a single accomplished work—*Crime and Punishment.* Shakespeare's value was in his poetry—not as much in his sonnets as in the few poems that appear in his plays. Kava admitted that, as a primitive, Homer was readable. He called Heine a jingle writer. In his brochure he listed all the literary and scientific works that needed to be translated into Yiddish in order for it to be more than a dialect. The Yiddishists attacked him as their worst enemy, but the professional translators praised him. Some literati felt that Kava should be thrown out of the Yiddish Writers' Club, and others defended him, saying that he was too ridiculous to be taken seriously.

Fate and Kava himself did their best to make him appear as a clown. He was small, emaciated, had a crooked mouth, and lisped out of its corner. The jokers in the Writers' Club specialized in mimicking him, his extreme understatements, his use of scientific phrases, and his pedantic style of talking. To Kava, Freud was a mere dilettante and Nietzsche a would-be philosopher. The literary wags gave Kava a nickname—Diogenes.

Kava lived on pennies. His only income came from substituting for the proofreaders of the Yiddish press when they went on their summer vacations. However, the typesetters completely ignored his corrections, since he had his own concepts about grammar and syntax. He brought entire encyclopedias, lexicons, and various dictionaries to the composing room. The editors maintained that if all of Kava's corrections were to be followed up, the daily newspapers could appear only once in three months.

Needless to say, Kava was an old bachelor. What woman would have married one such as Vanvild Kava? Summer and winter he wore a faded derby, a coat down to his ankles, a stiff collar which used to be called "father murderer." I was told that in his vest pocket he kept a chronometer instead of a watch. If someone asked him what time it was, he would say, "A minute and twenty-one seconds to five." When he read proofs, he used a watchmaker's eyepiece. Kava lived in a tiny fifth-floor walk-up attic room, all the walls of which were lined with books. On his visits to the Writers' Club he ordered nothing from the buffet, not even a glass of tea. He had discovered a bazaar where he could buy stale black bread, cheese, and fruit for next to nothing. It was said that he washed his own linen and pressed it by laying it under the heavy volumes of his library. Still, there was never a stain on his clothing. He had a system of sharpening razor blades on a glass. Vanvild Kava was an ascetic—not in the name of religion, but in the name of his version of worldliness.

Suddenly one day the Writers' Club was shaken by a sensation. Kava married. And whom? A young and beautiful girl. One had to know the Yiddish Writers' Club and its passion for gossip to realize the uproar this piece of news created. At first, everyone considered it a joke. But it soon became clear that it was no joke. The proofreaders and typesetters had already published their congratulations in their newspapers. One day Kava brought his new wife to the Writers' Club at exactly the time he came every day—seventeen minutes after eleven. She seemed in her late twenties, was dressed fashionably; had dark, short hair and polished nails. She spoke both Polish and Yiddish well. All that those who were present that day in the club could do was gape. Kava ordered two glasses of coffee for himself and his beloved and some cake. When the pair left, exactly seventeen minutes after twelve, the club began to buzz with excitement. A number of explanations and theories were created on the spot. I remember only one of them—that Kava was a kind of Yiddish Rasputin, a sexual miracle worker. But this theory was immediately dismissed as sheer nonsense. Every man in the Writers' Club considered all the other male members as impotent. Kava could not be the exception.

For days and weeks the Yiddish Writers' Club was busy solving this riddle, but as quickly as a solution was found, it collapsed. Some of the writers knew that I was friendly with Kava; I had also gone up in his ratings a few fractions of a point, and they insisted that I provide them with some insight. But I was just as bewildered as the others. No one would have dared to approach Kava and ask him any personal questions. There was a pride in this little man that did not allow for intimacy.

Then something happened. A girl whose home I visited had a friend from the town of Pulava. Pulava had a large printing shop where some Yiddish books were printed. The towns-people also boasted about having a few writers and translators. This girl from Pulava was a friend of Kava's wife, and one evening they both visited my girlfriend while I was there. It was an unexpected stroke of luck. I ate supper with a person who was part of a mystery. She seemed clever and tactful, and there was nothing enigmatic about her behavior. We discussed politics, literature, the literary group in Pulava. After supper, Mrs. Kava lit a cigarette and chatted with me while the other two girls washed the dishes. I said to her, "I would like to ask you something, but don't be offended if it is too personal. You really don't have to answer me if . . ."

"I know what you want to ask me," she interrupted. "Why I married Kava. Everybody is asking me the same thing. I will tell you why. I wasn't born yesterday, I know men, but all the men I had the misfortune of meeting bored me stiff. Not one of them had an opinion of his own. They all said the usual things that young men say to girls. They repeated the editori-als in the newspapers almost verbatim and read all the books the reviewers recommended. Some of them offered to marry me, but how could I go and live with a man who made me yawn even at our first meeting? Conversation with a man is of high importance to me. Of course he must be a man, but this is not everything. Then I met Vanvild Kava and I found all the qualities in him I was looking for since I grew up—a person with knowledge and with opinions of his own. I began playing chess when I was twelve and I guess you know that Kava is a splendid chess player. He could have become a grand master if he had devoted his time to it. Of course he's older than I am, and poor, but I never looked for riches. I make a living as a teacher and don't need to be supported. I don't know what you think of his writing, but I consider him a mighty good writer. I hope that near me he will work on a regular basis and produce good works. That's all I can tell you."

Mrs. Kava's every word expressed decisiveness. It was the first time someone had spoken about Kava without laughing at him and mocking his mannerisms. I told her I knew Kava and admired his erudition and strong opinions, although they were overly extreme at times. She said to me, "He's original. Never banal. His trouble is that he writes in Yiddish. In another medium he would be highly appreciated, whether they agreed with him or not."

When I came to the Writers' Club the next day and told my cronies that I had met Kava's wife and repeated what she told me, they all looked disappointed. One of them asked, "How can you love someone like Kava?" And I gave him the usual answer: "No one has yet determined who can be loved and who cannot be."

After a while I stopped going to the house where I had met Kava's wife and Kava's visits to the Writers' Club became less frequent than in his bachelor years. The only news I heard about him was that he gave up his job as a substitute proof-reader. I began to believe that he might mellow with this woman and perhaps write something of value. I had no doubt that the man possessed high literary potential. A person who demands so much from others might also demand much of himself under the right circumstances.

But then something so peculiar occurred that I'm still puzzled by it forty years later. A year or two had passed, and my friend Aaron Zeitlin, who had become the editor of a tri-monthly magazine, offered me a position as an associate editor. We were looking for an important essay about Yiddish literature or literature in general for the first issue, and I proposed to Zeitlin that Kava write it. At first Zeitlin demurred. "Kava, of all people?" he said. "First of all, it would take him a year or two. Secondly, he will make mincemeat out of everybody. It will give us a bad name from the very beginning." But I answered, "Don't be so sure. My impression is that he has changed since he married. But even if he does tear everyone to pieces, we can always say in a footnote that we disagree with him. It might even help the magazine to come out with something totally negative."

After long haggling, I managed to persuade Zeitlin to give it a try, but he stipulated that Kava must agree to an eventual footnote of disagreement, and he must also give a definite date of delivery. I was happy that Zeitlin let himself be persuaded. Somehow I felt that Kava might surprise us.

It so happened that Kava came the next day to the Writers' Club, and when I make this proposition to him he seemed shaken. He said, "You ask me to write the leading article? I have been excommunicated from Yiddish literature for years. The name Kava was not kosher. Suddenly you choose me."

I assured Kava that both Zeitlin and I had a high opinion of him. I pleaded with him not to demand the impossible from writers and I also assured him that we would change nothing in his essay. If worst came to worst, we would add a footnote that we disagreed. That would be all.

After much hesitation Kava consented to write the essay and gave me a date of delivery. He promised that in no case would the essay be longer than fifty pages. I told Kava my premonition that this essay would be a turning point in his literary career. Kava shrugged, and said in his laconic way, "Time will tell."

The time to deliver the manuscript was close but we had not heard a word from Kava. He stopped coming to the Writers' Club altogether, and this was a sign for me that he was busy working on the essay. One day I got a telephone call from him. He asked for an extension of two weeks on the delivery of the manuscript. I asked him how the work was going and he said, "I'm afraid it may be somewhat longer than fifty pages."

"How much longer?" I asked.

"Nine and a half pages."

I knew that Zeitlin would be angry with me. Even fifty pages was too long. But I also knew that if a work is good the reader and the critics will accept any length. There was a moment when I wanted to ask Kava to let me have a fragment of his work but I decided not to show impatience. When I told Zeitlin what had happened he said, "I'm afraid Kava will bring us not fifty-nine and a half pages but fifty-nine and a half lines."

The day came and I met Kava in the Writers' Club. He brought the manuscript. It was fifty-nine and a half pages. I could see that it had many erasures as well as quotations in German, French, and even in English, which could be a problem for a printer of a Yiddish magazine. Also his lines were written so close together that the fifty-nine and a half pages in Kava's longhand might make eighty pages in print. He said, "I'm giving this to you under the condition that you don't read it here, but go home and read it by yourself. Only then can you give it to Zeitlin."

I took the manuscript and ran home as quickly as I could. I was possessed with the desire to prove to Zeitlin that I was right. The moment I entered my furnished room, I threw myself on the sofa and began to read. I read three or four pages and everything pleased me. Kava began with a characterization of literature generally, and of Yiddish fiction specifically. The style was right, the sentences short and concise. I've never enjoyed reading a manuscript as much as I did those first five pages. On page 6, Kava wrote something about a "full-blooded writer." He had put the expression in quotation marks, noting that this term is used to categorize racehorses, not to evaluate talent. It is odd that in Yiddish, of all languages, this idiom should be applied to levels of the mind.

I read further and to my astonishment saw that Kava dwelled too long on the explanation of this borrowed idiom. It is certainly a digression that could be cut, I thought, if Kava wouldn't mind. But the further I read, the more perplexed I became. Kava had written an entire essay on horses—Arabian horses, Belgian horses, racehorses, Appaloosa horses. I read names I had never heard. I literally could not believe my own eyes. "Perhaps I'm dreaming," I said to myself. I pinched my cheeks to make sure that it was not a nightmare. Vanvild Kava had done excessive research, quoted scores of books, for an article on horses, their physiology, anatomy, and behavior, their various subspecies. He even added a bibliography. "Is he mad?" I asked myself. "Was this a game of spite?" The idea that I would have to bring this manuscript to Zeitlin made me shudder. There was no question that we could never publish it. I would have to break my word of honor and give the manuscript back to Kava. In all my anguish I felt like laughing.

After long brooding, I called on Zeitlin. I will never forget his grimaces when he reached the pages where Kava began to elaborate on the expression "full-blooded." He lifted his yellowish eyebrows and never let them down until he finished. For a while his face reflected a mixture of irony and disgust. Then I saw in his eyes something like the grief of a doctor when a patient comes to complain about a head cold and it turns out to be a malignant tumor. He said to me, "What did I tell you? How could you expect anything else from Kava?"

I had no choice. I had to return the manuscript. I asked Kava why he did what he did and pleaded with him to give me some explanation. He sat there motionless and pale. Then I heard him say, "I told you I was excommunicated from Yiddish literature. Don't come to me anymore with invitations to write. I will have to live out my years without your magazine." There was a moment when I was tempted to call Mrs. Kava and tell her of my predicament, but I was sure that she knew about this essay and that she would most probably defend her husband. Over the years a distorted outlook on things may become contagious.

It was kind of Kava that he did not stop speaking to me after that incident. Neither of us ever mentioned it. For many months I got up in the middle of the night and pondered: Was this an act of masochism? Was it some form of insanity? If so, what kind? Schizophrenia? Paranoia? Premature senility? One thing was clear: Kava had put a huge amount of work and study into this useless essay. No one in the Yiddish circle had the slightest interest in horses. Young as I was, I had already come to the conclusion that there are multitudes of human actions for which there is no motivation. As a matter of fact, in fiction motivations always spoil the story.

In 1935, when I left for America, the Yiddish section of the P.E.N. club published my first novel, *Satan in Goray*. The executive board hired Kava to do the proofreading and to write a preface. I was afraid that he would find myriads of errors in my book and use the preface for some of his freakish conceptions. But he made no special difficulties in the proofreading and his preface was short and to the point. No, Kava was not insane. I had the feeling his treatise on horses was his last spree into the absurd. Just then I left for America.

Once in a while I still try to fathom what might have been the meaning of Kava's bizarre act, but I know that if there was any, it dwells there where Vanvild Kava is now—in the so-called Great Beyond.

The Reencounter

THE telephone rang and Dr. Max Greitzer woke up. On the night table the clock showed fifteen minutes to eight. "Who could be calling so early?" he murmured. He picked up the phone and a woman's voice said, "Dr. Greitzer, excuse me for calling at this hour. A woman who was once dear to you has died. Liza Nestling."

"My God!"

"The funeral is today at eleven. I thought you would want to know."

"You are right. Thank you. Thank you. Liza Nestling played a major role in my life. May I ask whom I am speaking to?"

"It doesn't matter. Liza and I became friends after you two separated. The service will be in Gutgestalt's funeral parlor. You know the address?"

"Yes, thank you."

The woman hung up.

Dr. Greitzer lay still for a while. So Liza was gone. Twelve years had passed since their breaking up. She had been his great love. Their affair lasted about fifteen years—no, not fifteen; thirteen. The last two had been filled with so many misunderstandings and complications, with so much madness, that words could not describe them. The same powers that built this love destroyed it entirely. Dr. Greitzer and Liza Nestling never met again. They never wrote to one another. From a friend of hers he learned that she was having an affair with a would-be theater director, but that was the only word he had about her. He hadn't even known that Liza was still in New York.

Dr. Greitzer was so distressed by the bad news that he didn't remember how he got dressed that morning or found his way to the funeral parlor. When he arrived, the clock across the street showed twenty-five to nine. He opened the door, and the receptionist told him that he had come too early. The service would not take place until eleven o'clock.

"Is it possible for me to see her now?" Max Greitzer asked. "I am a very close friend of hers, and . . ."

"Let me ask if she's ready." The girl disappeared behind a door.

Dr. Greitzer understood what she meant. The dead are elaborately fixed up before they are shown to their families and those who attend the funeral.

Soon the girl returned and said, "It's all right. Fourth floor, room three."

A man in a black suit took him up in the elevator and opened the door to room number 3. Liza lay in a coffin opened to her shoulders, her face covered with gauze. He recognized her only because he knew it was she. Her black hair had the dullness of dye. Her cheeks were rouged, and the wrinkles around her closed eyes were hidden under makeup. On her reddened lips there was a hint of a smile. How do they produce a smile? Max Greitzer wondered. Liza had once accused him of being a mechanical person, a robot with no emotion. The accusation was false then, but now, strangely, it seemed to be true. He was neither dejected nor frightened.

The door to the room opened and a woman with an uncanny resemblance to Liza entered. "It's her sister, Bella," Max Greitzer said to himself. Liza had often spoken about her younger sister, who lived in California, but he had never met her. He stepped aside as the woman approached the coffin. If she burst out crying, he would be nearby to comfort her. She showed no special emotion, and he decided to leave her with her sister, but it occurred to him that she might be afraid to stay alone with a corpse, even her own sister's.

After a few moments, she turned and said, "Yes, it's her."

"I expect you flew in from California," Max Greitzer said, just to say something.

"From California?"

"Your sister was once close to me. She often spoke about you. My name is Max Greitzer."

The woman stood silent and seemed to ponder his words. Then she said, "You're mistaken."

"Mistaken? You aren't her sister, Bella?"

"Don't you know that Max Greitzer died? There was an obituary in the newspapers."

Max Greitzer tried to smile. "Probably another Max Greitzer." The moment he uttered these words, he grasped the truth: he and Liza were both dead—the woman who spoke to him was not Bella but Liza herself. He now realized that if he were still alive he would be shaken with grief. Only someone on the other side of life could accept with such indifference the death of a person he had once loved. Was what he was experiencing the immortality of the soul, he wondered. If he were able, he would laugh now, but the illusion of body had vanished; he and Liza no longer had material substance. Yet they were both present. Without a voice he asked, "Is this possible?"

He heard Liza answer in her smart style, "If it is so, it must be possible." She added, "For your information, your body is lying here too."

"How did it happen? I went to sleep last night a healthy man."

"It wasn't last night and you were not healthy. A degree of amnesia seems to accompany this process. It happened to me a day ago and therefore—"

"I had a heart attack?"

"Perhaps."

"What happened to *you*?" he asked.

"With me, everything takes a long time. How did you hear about me, anyway?" she added.

"I thought I was lying in bed. Fifteen minutes to eight, the telephone rang and a woman told me about you. She refused to give her name."

"Fifteen minutes to eight, your body was already here. Do you want to go look at yourself? I've seen you. You are in number 5. They made a *krasavetz* out of you."

He hadn't heard anyone say *krasavetz* for years. It meant a beautiful man. Liza had been born in Russia and she often used this word.

"No. I'm not curious."

In the chapel it was quiet. A clean-shaven rabbi with curly hair and a gaudy tie made a speech about Liza. "She was an intellectual woman in the best sense of the word," he said. "When she came to America, she worked all day in a shop and at night she attended college, graduating with high honors.

She had bad luck and many things in her life went awry, but she remained a lady of high integrity."

"I never met that man. How could he know about me?" Liza asked.

"Your relatives hired him and gave him the information," Greitzer said.

"I hate these professional compliments."

"Who's the fellow with the gray mustache on the first bench?" Max Greitzer asked.

Liza uttered something like a laugh. "My has-been husband."

"You were married? I heard only that you had a lover."

"I tried everything, with no success whatsoever."

"Where would you like to go?" Max Greitzer asked.

"Perhaps to your service."

"Absolutely not."

"What state of being is this?" Liza asked. "I see everything. I recognize everyone. There is my Aunt Reizl. Right behind her is my Cousin Becky. I once introduced you to her."

"Yes, true."

"The chapel is half empty. From the way I acted toward others in such circumstances, it is what I deserve. I'm sure that for you the chapel will be packed. Do you want to wait and see?"

"I haven't the slightest desire to find out."

The rabbi had finished his eulogy and a cantor recited "God Full of Mercy." His chanting was more like crying and Liza said, "My own father wouldn't have gone into such lamentations."

"Paid tears."

"I've had enough of it," Liza said. "Let's go."

They floated from the funeral parlor to the street. There, six limousines were lined up behind the hearse. One of the chauffeurs was eating a banana.

"Is this what they call death?" Liza asked. "It's the same city, the same streets, the same stores. I seem the same, too."

"Yes, but without a body."

"What am I then? A soul?"

"Really, I don't know what to tell you," Max Greitzer said. "Do you feel any hunger?"

"Hunger? No."

"Thirst?"

"No. No. What do you say to all this?"

"The unbelievable, the absurd, the most vulgar superstitions are proving to be true," Max Greitzer said.

"Perhaps we will find there is even a Hell and a Paradise."

"Anything is possible at this point."

"Perhaps we will be summoned to the Court on High after the burial and asked to account for our deeds?"

"Even this can be."

"How does it come about that we are together?"

"Please, don't ask any more questions. I know as little as you."

"Does this mean that all the philosophic works you read and wrote were one big lie?"

"Worse—they were sheer nonsense."

At that moment, four pallbearers carried out the coffin holding Liza's body. A wreath lay on top, with an inscription in gold letters: "To the unforgettable Liza in loving memory."

"Whose wreath is that?" Liza asked, and she answered herself, "For this he's not stingy."

"Would you like to go with them to the cemetery?" Max Greitzer asked.

"No—what for? That phony cantor may recite a whining Kaddish after me."

"What do you want to do?"

Liza listened to herself. She wanted nothing. What a peculiar state, not to have a single wish. In all the years she could remember, her will, her yearnings, her fears, tormented her without letting up. Her dreams were full of desperation, ecstasy, wild passions. More than any other catastrophe, she dreaded the final day, when all that has been is extinguished and the darkness of the grave begins. But here she was, remembering the past, and Max Greitzer was again with her. She said to him, "I imagined that the end would be much more dramatic."

"I don't believe this is the end," he said. "Perhaps a transition between two modes of existence."

"If so, how long will it last?"

"Since time has no validity, duration has no meaning."

"Well, you've remained the same with your puzzles and paradoxes. Come, we cannot just stay here if you want to avoid seeing your mourners," Liza said. "Where should we go?"

"You lead."

Max Greitzer took her astral arm and they began to rise without purpose, without a destination. As they might have done from an airplane, they looked down at the earth and saw cities, rivers, fields, lakes—everything but human beings.

"Did you say something?" Liza asked.

And Max Greitzer answered. "Of all my disenchantments, immortality is the greatest."

Moon and Madness

OUTSIDE, a thick snow was falling. It had begun at dawn and continued all day long and into the early evening. Then a frost set in. In the Radzymin study house it was warm. A pair of beggars with ropes around their loins sat by the oven roasting potatoes. Jeremiah, an old man, was reciting psalms. He had gone blind but had managed to learn the Book of Psalms by heart. At a long table across from the Ark of the Holy Scroll sat Zalman the glazier, Levi Yitzchok, who suffered from trachoma and wore dark glasses even at night, and Meir the eunuch, a Cabalist, who was known to be sane for half the month and insane the other half, after the moon became full. The conversation turned to pity, and Zalman the glazier said:

"Of course, pity is virtuous, but too much of it can do damage. Not far from our town of Radoszyce lived a Polish squire, Count Jan Malecki, the owner of big estates. Long before the czar had decreed the serfs to be free, the Count called all his peasants to a meeting and said to them, 'The earth belongs not to me but to those who work it. You're not my slaves any more. Elect an elder and divide the grounds among yourselves.' I can see this Malecki before my eyes—a big man, fat, with a red face and with a blond mustache that reached almost to his shoulders. He had no children, but his wife, the squiress, had five sisters and two brothers. They each had many children and Malecki provided for the whole impoverished family. It is peculiar that although he freed the peasants, Malecki himself worked the fields—plowed, sowed, and harvested. He had acquired a machine to cut straw, which he mixed with hay for feeding cattle. He could stand for hours at this machine working like a hired hand, while his brothers-in-law and sisters-in-law and their brats walked around idly, dressed up as if they were going to a ball. Once, his court Jew, Zelig, asked him what was the sense of allowing the others to behave this way and Malecki answered, 'Every man should do what he wants. I like to carry the burden, so I carry it. They like to be idle, so they should be.' By the way, all of Malecki's relatives indulged in quarrels and calumny. The young ones also stole. His nephews got drunk, walked around with pistols; they went hunting in the Count's forests and sometimes aimed at one another. The girls played the piano and went to parties. The people in Radoszyce gave the Count a nickname—Jan Schmatte, which means 'rag.'

"Since he was not a rebel and never quarreled with anyone, the Russians held no grudge against him and made him the judge of Radoszyce and the whole county. He refused to take a salary. I am told that on the day he became judge the thieves held a banquet. They knew that Malecki would never put anyone in prison. And so it was. When they brought him a thief who defended himself by claiming that his boots were torn, he had a headache, he was penniless, Malecki not only let him go free but gave him a few rubles as well. He was satisfied with a promise from the accused to become honest from that day on. The thugs and pickpockets had something to laugh about.

"There was a man in Radoszyce by the name of Maciek Sokal, and they called him the Lawyer. He was as much a lawyer as I am a doctor. He could barely read. Just the same, whenever someone was on trial he would engage Sokal as a defender. Sokal himself was a swindler, a drunk, a low creature. Before he began to appear in court as a defender, he was known as Sokal the Year-Round Witness. For anyone accused of a crime, he would invent an alibi, come as a witness, and swear falsely. Sokal knew that Malecki was gullible and he taught the criminals how to fool him. Things reached such a state that thieves began to come to Radoszyce from other villages.

"Yes, it soon came out that Malecki had created a lot of trouble with his leniency. The storekeepers in Radoszyce did not sleep nights. They hired a watchman to guard their stores with a stick and a rattle, but the toughs beat him up and he lay sick in the poorhouse for weeks. They began to steal horses in the surrounding villages. When the peasants caught a thief and brought him into Radoszyce, Malecki immediately freed him. Some merchants were robbed so often that they sold their stores for a song and moved to other towns. Others left for America. The peasants began to say there was only one way out—to get rid of Malecki. But the Russians were on his side.

What did they care if Polish peasants suffered? People maintained that because of Sokal's shrewdness and Malecki's pity life had become more miserable than ever.

"Not far from Radoszyce was a hamlet by the name of Bojary. There was a rascal there named Wojtek—a drunk, a murderer, a thief, a rapist. He had no father. His mother bore him from a wandering gypsy. He began to steal when he was five years old. After some time his mother died and Wojtek became a *parobek*, a field hand for a peasant who had acquired land of his own. This Wojtek used to come to the weekly fair at Radoszyce every Thursday, and he always created a scandal. He went into a store to buy a cap or a jacket and then refused to pay for it. He got drunk in the tavern, beat up the peasants, broke windowpanes, turned over tables and benches. He was known as an arsonist. Whenever he had a fight with somebody, he set fire to his house. Everyone knew about it. But when he was arrested and brought to trial there were never any witnesses against him.

"In Bojary there also lived a peasant, Stach Skiba, and he had a daughter, Stasia—a healthy lass, a good worker, able at home and in the fields. She had no mother. Many of the boys wanted her for a wife and came to her with gifts. More than anybody else, Wojtek ran after her. But the girl said to him, 'Sausage is not for a dog.' He threatened to stab her as well as her father and any man she married. But peasants are not easily frightened. Stasia finally got betrothed to a strong peasant boy, Stefan, and he told Wojtek that if he ever said a bad word to his fiancée he would break his neck. After a while there was a wedding, and all the peasants came to Stach Skiba's hut and they ate, drank, danced. In the middle of the celebration a scream and a lament broke out. The house had caught fire on all sides. Some of those who tried to push their way out through the narrow door were trampled to death. Somebody had piled big stones at the threshold. Over twenty people perished in the flames, among them the bride and the bridegroom. Some others were so burned that they remained crippled for life.

"This time there was a witness. An eight-year-old girl had seen Wojtek put rocks at Skiba's door. Also, a Jewish merchant from Radoszyce named Naphtali Gorszkower told the police that on the day before the fire Wojtek had bought an oversize can of kerosene from him. The peasants caught Wojtek, beat him, and took him on a cart to Radoszyce. Immediately Sokal emerged and began to scold the peasants for hurting an innocent lad. The only policeman in town put Wojtek in jail, but Sokal went directly to Count Malecki and told him that drunken peasants had attacked an innocent boy and broken his ribs. Sokal also told Malecki that Naphtali Gorszkower had been persuaded to bear false witness by the elder of the village, who had bought salt, kerosene, and axle grease from Gorszkower. Sokal demanded that His Excellency order the release of Wojtek at once and punish those who had beaten him. Why Sokal worked so hard for Wojtek was not clear, though people said that the thieves of Radoszyce paid a weekly salary to Sokal for defending every knave in town.

"While Sokal lingered in the courthouse, where the Count was sitting in his official robes, with a cross hanging from a golden chain around his neck, doing official business, a mob of peasants gathered outside waiting for news. Suddenly the door opened and Sokal appeared waving a paper. Malecki had given him a signed order releasing Wojtek immediately and compensating him for the abuse. When the peasants saw Sokal with the paper, they went mad. They began to scream in vile voices and threw themselves on him. I am told that in less than a minute Sokal was torn to pieces. The coffinmaker, a neighbor of ours, later told us that there was little left of the body to put in the coffin. From the courthouse to the jail was only two steps. The enraged peasants broke down the door and dragged out Wojtek; someone quickly got a rope, and they hanged him on a lamppost. With the noose on his throat, he managed to call, 'Brothers, remember that I am an orphan.' And one of the peasants called back, 'You will soon stop being an orphan.'

"When the Jews heard what was going on, they were frightened. The storekeepers in the market immediately closed their shops and everyone hid. It could easily have happened that the peasants in their fury would attack the Jews. Naphtali Gorszkower didn't even bother to close his store. He began to run and he kept on running until he reached America. I just say so. He disappeared, and his wife was considered a deserted woman. Only, a year later a letter came from New York. But I will make it short. One of the rabble called out, 'Let's get Malecki!' And that's all the peasants needed. They tore into the courthouse and killed the Count. All this took place in a matter of minutes.

"When the governor learned what the peasants had done, he sent a commission with a hundred Cossacks to Radoszyce, and an investigation began, which lasted months. First of all, they put the thieves in chains and sent them to the prison in Radom, or perhaps it was some other town. The merchants in Radoszyce were relieved. However, the Jews still had plenty to worry about. There were some county officials who incited the commission against them, saying that the Jews were the ones who had set fire to Stach Skiba's house and pointing out that this was the reason Naphtali Gorszkower had run away. They even put Naphtali's wife in jail for a few weeks.

"What could the Cossacks do? They rode back and forth on their small horses, waving their whips. Whoever happened to pass by on the street got whipped. About a dozen peasants in Bojary were sent to Siberia without a trial. One of them was the father of the little girl who saw Wojtek put stones before Skiba's door. He was accused of making his daughter bear false witness, because he had once quarreled with Wojtek about a pig Wojtek had stolen. How can a commission help? They cannot revive the dead. All I can say is, there was a lot of grief because of Count Malecki's misplaced pity. I once read in a Yiddish commentary on the Bible that those who pity the wicked end up by being cruel to the innocent."

"It's in the Gemara," Meir the eunuch corrected him.

It was quiet in the Radzymin study house, and one could hear the wick in the lamp sucking kerosene. Old Jeremiah happened to recite the chapter of the psalms which spoke of God's mercy in slaying Sihon the King of the Amorites and Og the King of Bashan and giving their land to Israel as a patrimony. The two beggars had opened the door of the oven, and with their bare fingers shoved out the roasted potatoes. Reb Levi Yitzchok removed the black glasses from his red eyes and wiped them with the hem of his coat. Meir the eunuch touched his hairless cheeks. He threw a glance toward the window and the sky. The moon was not yet full, but one could discern the missing crescent. After a while, Levi Yitzchok put his dark glasses back on and said:

"There was no lack of crazy squires in Poland. Some lost their minds from too much drinking, others from too much luxury. That Count Malecki had perhaps heard of the Jewish law that no one should be judged for a sin without the testimony of two people who had admonished the culprit and told him of his crime's punishment before he committed it. It is said in the Mishnah that a court that pronounced a death sentence once in seventy years was called a killing court."

"What murderer is going to kill someone in the presence of two witnesses and after admonishment?" Zalman the glazier asked. "A murderer waits for a time when he won't be seen. They attack mostly at dark, when no one is there."

"God sees," Levi Yitzchok replied. "He is in no need of witnesses. He is Himself the witness, the judge, the punisher. But since you are talking about misplaced pity I have also a story to tell."

"Let's hear."

"In Kozienice there was a landowner by the name of Stanislaw Karlowski, a little man. He was called Crazy Karlowski. All his adult years he was involved in litigations with other landowners and he lost in these protracted wranglings a lot of money as well as prestige. He had inherited from both his grandparents so many cattle, so many fields and forests that he could indulge all his whims. He had a habit of standing in court and calling the judge bad names, accusing him of being ignorant and a bribetaker. His lawyers begged him to keep quiet. But when a man is crazy he won't listen to advice. The neighboring landowners knew of his temper and they constantly laid claim to some of his land, and he was always the loser. He had a wife, who was immensely rich, too. She came from a family of Polish kings. I never saw her, but I am told she was most beautiful and a harlot. Everyone knew that she had dozens of lovers. She even had love affairs with the squires who took her mad husband to court.

"In our times, duels are forbidden, but in those days the nobles were always dueling. One noble said about another that his racehorse didn't run as fast as it should and he was immediately challenged to a duel. A duel could not take place without seconds, as they were called. Their mission was to make peace between the antagonists, but actually they provoked them to more hatred, eager to see combat and bloodshed. Once, some noble called Karlowski's wife promiscuous. Immediately Karlowski challenged him to a duel. As always, the seconds poured oil on the fire. Karlowski took one pistol, his opponent took another, and they went to a clearing in a forest to shoot it out. The seconds lurked on both sides and waited to see who would kill whom. This is what the Gentiles called an affair of honor. According to the rules, both parties were supposed to shoot simultaneously. But how can you know the exact moment to pull the trigger? The other fired first and wounded Karlowski in the knee. After a duel the former enemies were obliged to forgive one another, shake hands, and sometimes even kiss. So the two men apologized to one another and went through the entire ceremony. The one who shot first rode home on his horse to celebrate his victory. Karlowski was bandaged, put into a britska, and taken home.

"Now, listen. At the time when Karlowski was engaged in the duel, his faithless wife took one of her paramours up to a balcony on a tower from which one could see far away, and both looked through field glasses to where the duel took place, all the while kissing and embracing and having their pleasure. Both expected Karlowski to be killed, and when they saw through the field glasses that he was being loaded into a britska, they thought he was already a corpse. They went down to drink wine and to be comforted. Later on, when Karlowski was brought back alive, his wife instantly fell into a swoon, but after she was revived she kissed him, pretended to cry from joy, and thanked him profusely for defending her reputation. He later recovered, but he walked with a limp.

"You haven't heard everything yet. After a while, she became tired of him altogether. She packed her fancy garments and all her jewelry, grabbed all the money she could get her hands on, and went abroad with a young lecher—perhaps to Paris or some such place. Her husband sent armed riders after her with warrants for her arrest, but the couple had already crossed the frontier and there was nothing their pursuers could do. Karlowski railed to the few friends he had that the young charlatan had seduced his innocent wife and made her leave the path of righteousness. Since he was embroiled in lawsuits up to his neck, he had not much time to brood about his disgrace. Every few months he had to sell another forest or piece of land to pay his litigants and advocates, as well as his penalties for contempt of court. He had to borrow money at high interest. He even became indebted to the Jew who managed the business of his ever-diminishing estates. Three years passed like this. One day a carriage approached Karlowski's castle, and who do you think was inside? His wife—not alone but with a small child, a bastard. The people who saw her arriving were sure Karlowski would come out with a gun or a sword and kill her. What can be worse than a wife who comes back to a husband with a child born of whoredom? But he forgave her. I wasn't there, but I am told that she fell on his throat, lamented, and swore that she had been yearning for him all the time. It was the fault of that young stallion who bewitched her, seduced her, and brought her to shame. How is it written? 'And thou hadst a whore's forehead, thou refusedst to be ashamed . . .' She ate and wiped her mouth and said, 'I have done no harm.' She kept crying and Karlowski tried to soothe her. It didn't last long, and she again became ruler of the castle. She found other sinners, or perhaps the old ones returned. Karlowski, because of his litigations, had often to go to Lublin or Warsaw. He even appealed to the synod in Petersburg, hoping to find justice there. His debts had become so huge that he was on the verge of bankruptcy. But then a hundred-year-old aunt of his died and left him a small fortune. So he paid his debts and could afford new litigations.

"Don't think that you have heard the whole story. One day another carriage came to the castle, and who do you think was there? The father of the baby. He had committed some crime for which he could go to jail. He made believe he had come to see his child, but it was only a pretext to ask its mother for money. It seems that she could not forget him. I am told that she pawned her pearls to pay his debts. If I am not mistaken, he had played with marked cards and his parents had disowned him. I think he was also ill, from drunkenness or from bawdiness. Well, and what do you think Karlowski did? He became an ardent friend of his wife's debaucher, took him into his castle, called doctors to cure him. Even the priests in the

surrounding villages condemned Karlowski and his insane behavior. However, Karlowski had a private chapel on his estate
and his own deacon, who preached that his lord behaved as a
pious Christian should, forgiving his enemy and turning the
other cheek."

"What happened then?" Zalman the glazier asked.

"What could have happened?" Levi Yitzchok said. "That
rake remained in the castle for a long time, rested, became
healthy and fat. The wife was not young enough for him any
more, and he was looking for younger prey. He soon found
some governess or stewardess who was ready to put herself at
his disposal. One day he broke open Karlowski's safe, took out
everything of value, even his mistress's jewels, and ran away
with that other woman. I think she was a distant relative of
the wife's. Karlowski himself continued with his litigations.
One day, when the judge brought a verdict against him, he became so shocked that he dropped dead. His wife tried to find
solace with her coachman or some other servant, but meanwhile creditors seized the estate and evicted her. She died
soon after."

"What happened to the illicit child?" Zalman the glazier
asked.

"I really don't know," Levi Yitzchok said. "But what ever
happens to the wicked and their seeds? As the psalmist says,
they are like chaff driven by the wind."

For a long while it was quiet again in the study house. One
of the beggars had stretched out on a bench and fallen asleep.
He was snoring, murmuring, and from time to time a
whistling came from his nostrils. The other beggar sat down to
listen to the stories. He had a little yellow beard and large eyes,
like those of a calf. He kept on nodding to every one of Levi
Yitzchok's words until he, too, dozed off. Meir the eunuch
wiped the frost off the windowpane with his palm and gazed
toward the sky, as if to make sure that the moon was not yet
completely full. He turned and said:

"What Squire Malecki was doing had nothing to do with
pity. Ecclesiastes has said, 'In the place of justice even there
was wickedness.' All these judges and lawyers need criminals,
just as a doctor needs patients. From the honest who were

wronged they will not draw any profit. As for the other squire, what was his name—Karlowski—he knew quite well what his shrew was doing, but he enjoyed letting her have her rotten ways. What does the Gemara say? 'The slave exults in disorder.' When a man sinks in the Forty-nine Gates of Defilement, his nature turns topsy-turvy. Bad becomes good, shame becomes honor. They wallow in slime and are proud of it. What was Sodom? What was the generation of the Flood? Nothing but perversity. And what happened to Rabbi Joseph della Reina? He had already managed to fetter Satan in chains and was about to bring Redemption. But he was suddenly overcome with mistaken pity and offered Satan a sniff of tobacco. This gesture of compassion for the Archfiend was incense to the idols, and all Rabbi Joseph's efforts collapsed. Immediately the Evil One freed himself from his shackles, regained his malign powers, and the Redemption was obstructed. Rabbi Joseph could have repented, because the doors of repentance are always open, but he had fallen into resignation. Since he could not bring the End of Days, he tried to bring the end of the world. Just as he had invoked holy names before, so he now turned to the names of the Evil Hosts. There is only one step from light to darkness.

"'The greater a man is, the greater is his passion,' says the Talmud. Rabbi Joseph was born with blood of fire. In those times, Spain belonged to the sons of Ishmael. Rabbi Joseph had heard that there was a caliph whose wife was the greatest beauty of all lands, and her name was Ptima. She was utterly lustful, a reincarnation of Cozbi, the daughter of Zur. Since Rabbi Joseph had thrown off the yoke of holiness and given up the goal of becoming totally righteous, he chose total guilt. He uttered a Satanic name and bade two demons bring him this Ptima. He was still living in a cave, as in the times when he was fasting and doing penance in order to bring the Messiah. It was said that he descended from Joseph the Righteous and was as graceful as his ancestor. No wonder that when he and Ptima met they indulged in all possible abominations.

"There is a proverb: 'In time one gets tired even of kreplech.' After some months Rabbi Joseph was told that the Grand Vizier's wife was even more voluptuous than Ptima. Her name was Grisha. Since he had given up the rewards of the soul, there was nothing to impede him from tasting this one, too. He bade the demons bring Grisha to him, and when they did he was overwhelmed by her carnal beauty. From then on, the evil spirits brought him both these females each night —Ptima from sunset to midnight, and after he sent Ptima back to her bed, a journey that lasted an instant, he enjoyed Grisha until dawn.

"Once when Ptima spent her hours with Rabbi Joseph, she found in the bed a cameo with the name Grisha engraved on it. She became jealous and asked Rabbi Joseph who this Grisha was. Just as Delilah coaxed Samson, Ptima pestered Rabbi Joseph so long that he finally divulged to her that she was the wife of the Grand Vizier. Ptima knew that Rabbi Joseph worked all these miracles by the force of an unholy name, and after she lulled him to sleep she began to search for this name. She found it inscribed on a piece of parchment that he kept in a little bag at his throat. Once she found the ungodly name, she had the upper hand. She bade the demons bind Rabbi Joseph with a sash and bring her the mightiest males in all the kingdoms of man.

"I wonder if you know that the Fallen Angels—as well as the descendants of Anak, who were seen by the spies Moses sent to Canaan—are still alive today. They're hiding behind the Black Mountains, or perhaps on the other side of the River Sambatyon. The Angel of Death has no dominion over them, since they are not of this world. Ptima ordered the demons to bring these giants to her. They did so, and she copulated with them in the presence of Rabbi Joseph for three days and three nights. You can imagine what anguish Rabbi Joseph suffered, but since she was in possession of the impure name, he could not free himself. The caliph searched for his wife, but she had disappeared.

"The first time Ptima told her evil messengers to bring her the Fallen Angels and the sons of Anak, she whispered the name so that Rabbi Joseph could not hear it. Before dawn on the fourth day, she had become so fatigued from her loathsome game that she ceased being careful and uttered the name out loud. Rabbi Joseph seemed to be asleep but he awoke at that moment. He had forgotten the name and was helpless, but now that he knew it he regained his power and commanded the messengers of the night to do his will instead of hers. Since both sides applied the same incantation for different purposes, they canceled each other's spell and the evil ones flew back to Mount Seir and stayed in equilibrium. Slowly Rabbi Joseph managed to unbind himself, and he clutched Ptima's throat, about to strangle her. How far is adultery from murder?

"When the cunning Ptima realized her end was near, she began to plead and speak sweet words to Rabbi Joseph and to defend herself by saying that she actually loved him, and that she surrendered to the celestial monsters only because of her jealousy. She said to him, 'What could you gain by killing me? You'll never find anyone more passionate.' When Rabbi Joseph answered that Grisha's flesh was even more gratifying than hers, Ptima said, 'Grisha is not among the living any more. I told my devils to do away with her, and they did. She was buried yesterday.' She went on, 'You let me live, and we two can conquer the world. You will conjure the most beautiful women, and I the richest men. We will put them to sleep and rob them of their diamonds, their medals, and all their possessions. You will become the king of the netherworld and I will be your loving queen. In gratitude for your mercy I will overcome my jealous nature and build a harem for you with more wives and concubines than King Solomon could ever boast of. We will revive the Queen of Sheba, Rahab the Harlot, and give loose rein to all our hearts' desires.'

"It is known that those who can persuade others are easily incited themselves. Rabbi Joseph asked her if she would consent to reviving Grisha and she replied, 'Your delight would be mine. Bring her back to life and we all three will rejoice together.' 'What would happen to your husband?' Rabbi Joseph asked, and she answered slyly, 'For your sake, I will make myself a widow.'

"Not only did Rabbi Joseph give in to aberrant pity but he made a fatal misjudgment. Those who study the Cabala know that with witchery one can accomplish anything but the resurrection of the dead. Once Rabbi Joseph and Ptima attempted to reanimate Grisha, they lost their potency. A wild laugh came down from Mount Seir. Satan and Lilith were laughing with such abandon that the blare echoed over all the deserts. Rabbi

Joseph della Reina was deprived of both the power of holiness and the power of the diabolic. He became sick with contamination. Ptima was now more than willing to return to the caliph, but he was four hundred miles away. Besides, the guards wouldn't have let her into the palace, because her beauty had vanished and she had become nothing but a sack of bones. No one would have recognized her."

"What did they do then?" Zalman the glazier asked.

"Rabbi Joseph spat on her and left her to her own devices. She became a beggar at the mosque and died soon after. Rabbi Joseph was too proud to repent and he expired in rebellion. He was reincarnated as a dog."

"I've never heard of this," Levi Yitzchok remarked.

"So you hear it now," Meir said.

"Have you read it in some book?" Levi Yitzchok asked.

"I am the book," Meir answered.

He got up and began to pace from wall to wall. He rubbed his hands one against the other. The kerosene lamp flickered. The wick wavered and smoked. The Radzymin study house became full of shadows. Zalman the glazier said, "Really, I will be afraid to walk home."

Meir the eunuch seemed to have heard his words, because he stopped, laughed, and cried out, "Don't be a fool, Reb Zalman. The moon is shining. The heavens are bright. Evil is nothing but a coil of madness."

THE IMAGE

AND OTHER STORIES

Contents

Author's Note   291

Advice   293

One Day of Happiness   302

The Bond   317

The Interview   325

The Divorce   339

Strong as Death Is Love   349

Why Heisherik Was Born   357

The Enemy   366

Remnants   375

On the Way to the Poorhouse   387

Loshikl   396

The Pocket Remembered   406

The Secret   424

A Nest Egg for Paradise   436

The Conference   459

Miracles   465

The Litigants   481

A Telephone Call on Yom Kippur   485

Strangers   497

The Mistake   504

Confused   514

The Image   535

Author's Note

In the years I have been writing I have heard many discouraging words about my themes and language. I was told that Jewishness and Yiddish were dying, the short story was out of vogue and about to disappear from the literary market. Some critics decided that the art of telling stories with a beginning, middle, and end—as Aristotle demanded—was archaic, a primitive form of fiction. I heard similar degrading opinions about the value of folklore in the literature of our times. I was living in a civilization which despised the old and worshipped the young. But somehow I never took these dire threats seriously. I belong to an old tribe and I knew that literature thrives best on ancient faith, timeless hopes, and illusions. A writer should never abandon his mother tongue and its treasure of idioms. Literature must deal with the past instead of planning the future. It must describe events, not analyze ideas; its topic is the individual, not the masses. It must be an art, not pretend to be a science. Moreover, belief in God and His Providence is the very essence of literature. It tells us that causality is nothing but a mask on the face of destiny. Man is constantly watched by powers that seem to know all his desires and complications. He has free choice, but he is also being led by a mysterious hand. Literature is the story of love and fate, a description of the mad hurricane of human passions and the struggle with them.

I'm glad to see that the short story is very much alive today. It is still the greatest challenge to the prose writer and it becomes his highest achievement if he succeeds at being both imaginative and brief. As to Yiddish, it has not yet been liquidated in the melting pot of assimilation—an omen to me that the same is in store for other minorities, their languages and cultures.

Many of the stories in this volume were published in *The New Yorker*, edited by Charles McGrath. All of them were edited by Robert Giroux, with whom I have been connected in admiration and friendship for the last twenty-five years, ever since I began publishing with Farrar, Straus and Giroux. My gratitude to them, as well as to my translators, who worked closely with me and spared no effort to give these stories the precision and clarity I hope for. The English translation is especially important to me because translations into other languages are based on the English text. In a way, this is right because, in the process of translation, I make many corrections. I always remember the saying of the Cabalists that man's mission is the correction of the mistakes he made both in this world and in former reincarnations.

I.B.S.

Advice

IN THE YEARS when I worked at a Yiddish newspaper in New York, giving advice, I heard many bizarre stories. As a rule, those who came to me were readers, not writers. But one time an advice-seeker happened to be a poet, an accountant by profession, whom I often met at meetings of the Yiddish Writers' Union, as well as at the literary cafeteria on East Broadway. His name was Morris Pintchover—a little man with yellow tufts of hair around a bald spot. He had sunken cheeks, a pointed chin, a short nose, and eyes the color of amber. Morris Pintchover dressed like an old-fashioned artist from Europe. He wore a broad-brimmed hat, a flowing tie, and spats over his shoes even in the summer. Pelerines—long capes for men— had been out of style for many years, but Morris Pintchover always wore one when he came to our literary gatherings. He had brought it from Warsaw near the beginning of the century. As he entered my office he said to me, "You are surprised, eh? I am also your reader and I'm entitled to ask your advice just like the others. Am I right?"

"Sit down. What can I tell you that you don't know yourself?"

"Oh, it is helpful to talk things over. After all, what is psychoanalysis? And why are Catholics so eager to make confessions? And what is literature? A number of great writers called their works confessions: Rousseau, Tolstoy, Gorky. I loved Strindberg's title *The Confessions of a Fool.* Actually, there is an element of foolishness in all confessions. I assume you've heard what's happened to me."

Morris Pintchover smiled sadly and showed a mouthful of yellowish teeth. I knew his case from the gossips in the Café Royal. His wife, Tamara, a poetess who could never find a publisher, had left Morris and gone to live with a man named Mark Lenchner, a well-known writer and a Communist, whose wife had tried suicide three times because of his constant betrayals. Mark Lenchner was known as a schnorrer and a cynic. Tamara was small, fat, with a high bosom. Her hair was set in

293

ringlets and dyed the color of carrots. Over her upper lip she sprouted a fuzzy female mustache. She told little anecdotes at which no one laughed but herself. For years she waged war with the editors of Yiddish newspapers and magazines, cursing them with vile oaths behind their backs. What Mark Lenchner saw in her no one could understand. In the literary cafeteria some maintained that what he saw was a nest egg of a few thousand dollars that she had managed to save by peddling her privately published books of poetry in the Café Royal and in the hotels in the Catskill Mountains. The couple had no children. I heard myself saying to Morris, "Yes, I was told something about the matter."

"You probably know that Tamara is now living with Lenchner openly, before the whole world," Morris said.

"I heard that, too."

"It has come to the point where the humorists print jokes about me in the newspapers."

"Idiots. I don't read the humor section."

"My dear friend, I know very well how people see someone like me—a schlemiel, a cuckold, a husband with horns. You know as well as I that when someone commits an injustice people make mincemeat of the victim, not of the culprit. It is not the first time that Tamara has exchanged me for some charlatan. I have been suffering and keeping silent, not because I believe that one should offer the other cheek but because I have the misfortune to love her. Love is a sickness—some kind of pathology that cannot be explained. If a man has a tumor he is stuck with it—he must even nurture it. The fact is that since Tamara left me I cannot eat or sleep. I make serious mistakes in my work, and I'm afraid I'm going to lose my few clients. I haven't written a single line since all this turmoil started. What I want to tell you may revolt you, but I hope that you have more understanding for human weakness than the kibitzers in the Café Royal. Since she left me, my love for that treacherous woman has been burning with a fire I'm afraid may consume me physically. I am somewhat interested in the occult. There are cases where people have ignited spontaneously and burned to death. Naturally, the rationalists scoff at such events, because these don't fit in with their clichés. However, if emotions can drive the blood into the face, produce constipation, diarrhea, eczema, and high blood pressure, why can't they cause fire? Am I right or not?"

"I'm ready to agree to everything," I said. "But how can I help you?"

"My friend, I don't come to you to complain, but to ask advice," Morris Pintchover said. "When you hear what I want to ask you, you will be convinced that I have completely lost my mind. But insanity is also human. The story goes like this. That Mark Lenchner, the outcast, and his wife, Necha—a saint of a woman—had an apartment for which he never paid rent, except perhaps for the month when they moved in. Don't ask me how he managed this. The owner of the building was somewhat of a Yiddishist, and a leftist to boot. He played the part of a philanthropist and a Maecenas. It was always a miserable apartment. The ceiling leaked, and when it rained Necha had to put out pails and pots on the floor. But what did Lenchner care? He was seldom there—always running around with all kinds of sluts. The situation went on for as long as the landlord lived. When he died the heirs sued Lenchner for non-payment, and now they are about to evict him with all his junky possessions. Vicious as he is, he cannot allow Necha to be thrown out into the gutter. Besides, he has his books and his manuscripts there. A few days ago I received a telephone call from Tamara. I was stunned. She has never called since she left me. I will make it short. Mark Lenchner, the rascal, proposed to her that he, Lenchner, and Necha and Tamara should all move in with me. I have a large apartment, and his idea was that all four of us should live together. He wants to be friends again, he said. He also would like to settle down finally and write his memoirs, or God knows what. I plead with you, don't look at me with so much irony. I know very well that Lenchner cannot be trusted. First he took my wife and now he tries to take my low-rent apartment—a real bargain. On the other hand, what could I lose? Since I cannot live without Tamara, let us at least be together under one roof. When a man stands before the gallows with a noose around his neck and they bring him the good tidings that the execution has been postponed, he does not ask any questions or impose conditions. Necha is a decent woman, a quiet dove. She will do as he tells her. What is your opinion?"

One eye of Morris's seemed to cry, the other laughed. I asked, "Why do you want to hear my opinion? You won't follow my advice anyhow."

"Possibly. Still, I would like to hear it just the same."

"My opinion is that a love of this sort is the worst kind of slavery. I still believe that man has free choice."

"Eh? I knew that you would say something like this. However, perhaps Spinoza was right that everything is predetermined. Perhaps the decision was made a billion years ago that Tamara, Necha, and Mark Lenchner should live together with me, no matter how preposterous and perverse the whole thing may seem to others. Perhaps free choice is exactly what Spinoza thought it to be, an illusion."

"If free choice is an illusion and everything is predetermined, why did he write his *Ethics*?" I asked. "What was the sense of preaching *amor dei intellectualis*, political freedom, and all the rest if we are nothing but mechanisms? That Spinoza was as full of contradictions as a pomegranate is full of seeds."

"And what was Kant?" Pintchover asked. "And what was Hegel? And what are all the other philosophers? You are right. Since I knew that I would be unable to listen to you, I shouldn't have come for advice. But a man in my state of mind cannot live according to logic. I'm sure you know that yearning is an excruciating pain. It is quite possible that hell is made up of yearning. The wicked don't roast on beds of nails, they sit on comfortable chairs and are tortured with yearning."

"For whom are they yearning?" I asked.

"For those whom they left on earth—everyone for his Tamara or her Lenchner. Be well and forgive me." Morris Pintchover extended to me a soft and moist hand. He smiled, winked, and said, "Thank you for your advice. Adieu."

A year or so passed and I heard that Mark Lenchner had been invited to live in the Soviet Union and that he had gone, leaving Necha behind. Stalin was still alive, but now in his interviews he maintained that Communism and capitalism could coexist. It was already known that he had liquidated most of the Yiddish writers in Russia, though the Communist Yiddish newspaper in New York assured its readers that all these accusations came from enemies of the people, the lackeys of Fascism. The Yiddish-speaking Communists still collected contributions for the nonexistent autonomous Jewish region, Birobidzhan. I was told that the writers in Moscow had arranged a grand reception for Lenchner, and that from there he had flown to Birobidzhan. This happened around the time when the Jewish doctors in the Soviet Union were accused of poisoning several Russian leaders. I had moved out of New York and had almost forgotten Morris Pintchover. I had lived in Israel, in France, in Switzerland. Someone in Tel Aviv or in Paris told me that Morris Pintchover had died, or perhaps he mentioned a similar name. When I returned to New York, years later, I no longer went to the office of my newspaper on East Broadway but sent my manuscripts by mail. I had ceased taking part in Yiddishist meetings and going to their lectures. Then one day I got a telephone call from the editor's secretary. The typesetter had lost a page of one of my articles, and I had to go down to East Broadway and fill in the missing page. I had to take three buses to get there from uptown. The third one ran between Union Square and East Broadway.

I passed a neighborhood where the population had changed —Puerto Ricans and blacks instead of the Jewish immigrants. Old buildings were being torn down. New ones went up. Here and there one could still see the walls of former apartments, with faded wallpaper or chipped paint. On one of these walls hung a picture of Sir Moses Montefiore. A wrecker's ball was knocking down walls with what seemed to be a light touch. Cranes lifted beams for new buildings. On one of the ruins stood four cats holding a mute consultation. I had a feeling that under the wreckage demons were buried— goblins and imps who had smuggled themselves to America in the time of the great immigration and had expired from the New York noise and the lack of Jewishness there.

After I corrected my manuscript in the typesetter's room I decided not to take the bus back but to walk to Union Square and go home from there by subway. I walked along Second Avenue. The literary cafeteria still existed, but the Café Royal, which had been a gathering place for writers and actors for many years, had closed and in its place was a dry cleaner's. I stopped at a window displaying a few long-forgotten Yiddish books with faded covers, as well as recordings of old Yiddish theater songs. After a while I continued up the avenue. And who walked toward me? Morris Pintchover—small, bent, shrunken, and in shabby clothes. The little hair that still remained on his skull had turned white. One could see a mere remnant of yellow in his eyebrows. He shuffled his feet as he walked, and leaned on a cane. So many of my colleagues had died in America or perished in Europe that I no longer knew who was alive and who was dead. He extended a bony hand and said, "I hope you recognize me."

"Yes."

"We haven't seen each other for years. Although we live in the same city, we have become estranged from one another. To tell the truth, New York is not a city but a whole country. Still, I was in contact with you—spiritually, I mean. I am reading you. After all, what is a writer? Only his works. I have published two books of poems—privately, of course. I doubt if you have ever seen them."

"If you'll send them to me, I'll read them. Almost no Yiddish bookstores are left anymore."

"Yes, we are in trouble, but the instinct to create remains as long as one breathes. I would have sent you my works, but I didn't know your address. When I send books to your newspaper they disappear. It seems there are still some people eager to steal a Yiddish book. This in itself is a miracle."

"Yes, true," I muttered.

"I guess that you don't remember my name. It's Morris Pintchover."

"I remember you very well. I have often thought about you," I said.

"Really? It's good to know."

I wanted to ask him about his wife, but I had forgotten her name. Besides, I had too often heard the same reply—"Died." As if Morris Pintchover could read my mind, he said, "Tamara is no more. She passed away two years ago. Got cancer and left me. In the old country there was such a thing as galloping consumption. Tamara died, I could say, from galloping cancer. One day she got sick and a few weeks later it was all over. Left this vale of tears like a saint. Perhaps it wasn't even cancer. When the doctors cannot find the correct diagnosis, they call it cancer. God sends more sicknesses to the world than the medics can name. Only yesterday I read that millions of viruses can live in one cubic centimeter of tissue. Yet they are made of many molecules. The microcosmos is even more fantastic than the macrocosmos. In the midst of all these wonders comes the Angel of Death and erases everything. May I ask where you are going?"

"Union Square," I answered.

"Are you walking there?"

"Yes, I am walking."

"May I accompany you?"

"Yes, with pleasure."

We walked, and Morris stopped every few steps. I wanted to ask him about Lenchner's wife, but I knew that sooner or later he would tell me anyway. He was talking to me and to himself: "A whole world has vanished, eh? When I was a boy the Yiddishist movement was only beginning. Our classics were all still alive—Mendele, Sholem Aleichem, Peretz. I remember quite well the Czernowitz conference. What optimism! It was like a new spring. When I came to America, New York had not one Yiddish theater but twenty. This whole neighborhood was boiling like a kettle with ideas and ideals. Now everything has changed, everything is different—people, houses, stores, styles. Some time ago I lay awake at night and it occurred to me: If there is a God and he exists eternally, how much could he have experienced in all this time? What would happen if he decided to write his memoirs? At what point would he begin? Would he go back one billion years? Ten billion years? A hundred billion years? It is eerie to think about such things—especially at night when one cannot fall asleep. Well, and who would be his publisher? He would have to publish himself, just as I do."

Morris Pintchover laughed, and showed a set of new false teeth. He said, "Perhaps you would like to walk along Avenue B. That is where I live."

"By yourself?"

"No, with Necha, Lenchner's widow."

"Aha."

"You most probably have heard that Lenchner went to Russia without her. He promised to bring her over to Stalin's paradise, but what did a promise mean to Lenchner? She received one postcard from him—not from Birobidzhan but from Moscow. The invitation had been nothing but a trap to do away with him. What they had against him I don't know. He served them faithfully. He defended all their evil deeds. To the last day in New York, he kept assuring everyone that the Yiddish writers in Russia lived in perfect bliss—Bergelson, Markish, Fefer, Charik, Kulbak. He called all of us here in America the worst names for suspecting the great benefactor Comrade Stalin. Lenchner knew quite well that he was lying, but he hoped that his brazen lies would save his skin if his comrades in Russia accused him of some deviation. Who knows what goes on in the brains of such villains? Since he knew what awaited him, why did he need to go there? There is something in Greek drama where the protagonist knows that he will fall into an abyss but is compelled by fate to choose death and cannot help himself. Perhaps you remember that I once came to you to ask your advice. Yes, Tamara and Lenchner and Necha moved into my apartment, and for a few weeks I imagined that I was happy. Yes, slavery. Our emotions are the rulers. They assail us like robbers, they mock all our resolutions. My neighbors ridiculed me and spat. Was I really happy? We delve into the worst suffering and we call it pleasure. When Lenchner left I became, so to say, the king. Tamara finally sobered up from her madness. How long can you be drunk? I forgave her. Did I have a choice? Nothing is as violent as the violence of love. My theory is that man is engaged in a clandestine love affair with the Angel of Death."

We stopped at a dilapidated building and Morris said, "Here is where I live. In this house, on the third floor. We have no elevator. I hope you don't mind climbing the stairs. Now that Tamara is in the true world, Necha has become everything to me—a wife, a sister, a mother. Of course, it is all platonic. She is a faithful reader of yours."

We went into a dark entrance and climbed the steps; at each landing Morris stopped and panted. He pointed to the left side of his chest. "The pump refuses to function," he said. "It has been doing it for eighty years. How long can it go on pumping? Enough is enough."

At the third floor Morris rang the bell of his apartment, but no one answered. He said, "Either she is not home or she doesn't hear. Wait. I have a key."

We entered a narrow corridor. Morris opened the door to the living room. It smelled of dust, medicine, and something rancid. Over a torn sofa with protruding springs hung a portrait of Lenchner—young, with curly hair, a black mustache, and shining eyes, which looked out with the arrogance and the complacency of those who have found the truth once and for all. Morris Pintchover remarked, "This is he. What Tamara saw in this faker I will never know. But she defended him to her last breath. As for Necha, she was a real martyr. But now where has she run away to? We are only two old people and she buys food as if we were ten. Three-quarters of it is thrown out. She has a kind of buying mania. How much can we eat? A piece of toast and a glass of tea is enough for us for the whole day. Thanks to God and to Social Security, we have more than enough of everything. Sit down. What can I offer you?"

"Absolutely nothing," I said.

"Nothing, eh? A man must want something."

For a long while we sat still. Then Morris Pintchover said, "You were right then. I should never have taken them in. But what would I have done now without Necha? She is the only person who really knew Tamara and witnessed our great love."

Translated by the author

One Day of Happiness

In the three rooms, except for the kitchen, the shades were drawn. For Mendel Bialer did not like the sun. Now that he was older, he spent most of his time lying down. What did he have to do? He was already drawing his pension. And besides, his feet hurt him. At night he tossed sleepless on the bed, but all day long he dozed. The summer sun was so hot that afternoon it penetrated even the shades. One fly landed on his forehead. He brushed it off, only to have it settle again on his reddish nose. Though half asleep, he was worrying. The pension from the bread mill where he had been employed for thirty-five years as a bookkeeper was not enough to live on. He was behind in his rent. Moreover, he had an unmarried girl in the house, his daughter Feigele, or Fela, as they had called her in school. Though she was twenty-four, Fela still acted like a girl of sixteen, read foolish books, did not look for work. The matchmakers had tried to find a husband for her but she was choosy, behaving as if she were the daughter of a rich man and a beauty, whereas in fact she hadn't a groschen and was ugly besides. In the middle of his dozing, Mendel grasped his gray beard and frowned, as if to ask, "What will come of all this? What is she waiting for?"

Mendel's wife, Malkah, was in the kitchen peeling potatoes. The water plopped every time she threw one into the pot. In the bedroom, Fela was writing a letter. That morning she had bought herself a gilt-edged sheet of paper, an envelope, and a new steel pen with a fine nib that wouldn't blotch. For weeks, day and night, she had been thinking out the contents of this letter. She knew every sentence by heart. It read as follows:

Highly esteemed and beloved General, God-inspired Poet:
  What I am doing now is madness or worse, but I cannot help myself. Some power stronger than I is driving me to write to you. I am almost sure you won't answer me. I am not at all certain you will even read my letter, for I know Your Excellency must receive hundreds and thousands of such letters from lost souls (ha ha!). I tell you right off that I am a Jewish girl, poor, and not beautiful (my picture is enclosed). But I love you with a burning love that I don't understand

myself. I am literally being consumed by this tragic—you may call it comic—love. I think about you all the time and at night I dream only of you. I could tell you how all this started, but I am afraid of making you impatient. I save all your pictures from newspapers and journals. I have even stolen because of you, my love—tearing the pages out of magazines in cafés. You are my whole life. I know all your sublime poems by heart. I read and reread all your books, especially those about your heroism at the front. I live only for you: to be able to hear your metal voice on the radio; to watch you in parades.

Once, in the Café Rzymianska, you looked at me. The happiness which that look gave me, the inspiration which filled my whole being, no pen can describe—only someone with your talent would be able to. I realize my letter is too long already and that I must come to the point. I know that you are not only a national hero and a great poet but also a man with a heart for those able to admire your gifts. I ask you humbly therefore to grant me half an hour of your time. If you would bestow upon me the privilege of spending a few minutes with you, it would be my secret treasure to guard and cherish until my last breath. Unfortunately, my parents have no telephone, so all I can do is give you my address. Mostly, I am home all day. As I write this letter, I am aware how small my chances are, how terribly foolish I am, and perhaps also selfish. Adieu, my great hero, poet, and ruler of my soul.

With a love that will never die,

Fela Bialer

P.S. My parents are old-fashioned and mustn't know of their daughter's craziness.

The last word written, Fela let out a sigh. She had trembled all the time she was writing, fearful of blotching the page. In high school her handwriting had been good, but since then it had deteriorated: she made the letters too large, the lines crooked. At school she had excelled also in composition and spelling, but now she often made childish mistakes. It was all the result of her nerves. She had never graduated, having failed in mathematics. At first she had hunted for an office job but had not succeeded in finding one. Finally she had taken a sales job in a toy store, but had been fired the first day for making the wrong change. Her mother nagged at her constantly, and her father called her his "crazy princess." Fela was small and dark, with broad hips, crooked legs, a hooked nose, and large, bulging black eyes. In her diary she compared herself to an overripe fruit. Her bosom hung down; her arms were fleshy and loose with fat. Other girls would have tried to reduce, but the dishes in Fela's home were all starchy—potatoes, dumplings, kasha. And besides, she had an unconquerable desire for chocolate. Moreover, she was constantly hungry, as if afflicted with a tapeworm. Sometimes at night, lying awake, she would feel her body beginning to swell up like dough. Her skin burned, her breasts tightened as if filled with milk. And though Fela was a virgin, she was sometimes afraid she might suddenly begin to give birth. She felt fluids coursing through her like saps in a plant before blooming. Her breath grew hot, her insides clutched and twisted, and during the night she constantly had to go to the toilet. Of late she had begun to suffer from a strange thirst. Her mother often exclaimed, "What is the matter with that girl? A fire is burning in her, God forbid!"

Fela's love for Adam Pacholski had bewildered her. She saw everything around her through a fog. She couldn't cross the room without stumbling into chairs, the table, the commode. When her mother gave her a glass of tea, she would let it slip through her fingers. She couldn't heat a pan of milk on the kitchen stove without forgetting it and letting it burn. None of Fela's dresses fit her anymore. Her girdle cut her flesh. Her shoes pinched. And no matter how often she combed and washed her hair, it always looked gluey and disheveled. Her menstrual periods came irregularly, sometimes late, sometimes early, with a rush of blood that terrified her. To compose that letter without one blotch or mistake had taken an effort almost beyond her powers. Thank God, it had come out clean! Here and there, she had even managed to finish a word with a flourish.

Fela read the letter through once, a second time, a third time. After much hesitation, she finally folded it, inserted it, wrote out the address on the envelope, stamped and sealed it. Her hands quivered, her knees trembled. She could hear her quick breathing. In the living room her father had fallen asleep. Fela intended to cross the room silently, on tiptoe, but the door screeched behind her and her heels hit the floor rebelliously. Her father sat up with a start.

"Why do you make so much noise, you wild creature?"

"Oh, Daddy, excuse me. I'm so awkward. I didn't mean to."

"Why do you hang around idle? Other girls your age are mothers of children already."

The tears welled up in Fela's eyes. "Is that my fault?"

A sob clutched her throat like vomit. She covered the letter so her tears wouldn't get it wet and escaped into the bathroom. There she could cry, cough, compose herself. She dried her face on sheets of newspaper, set there for toilet paper. She flushed the water and said aloud, "Father in heaven, you see the truth."

2

Events moved swiftly. On Monday, Fela sent out the letter. On Tuesday just at dark, she received a telegram. Thank God, nobody else was home! She wanted to give the messenger boy ten groschen but could find no small change and gave him half a zloty instead. Striking a match, she read: "Wait for me tomorrow at four o'clock at the corner of Marszalkowsky Boulevard and Wspolna Street." Fela couldn't contain herself and had to run to the bathroom. There, lighting the candle stub attached to a shelf, she read the telegram over and over again. In the cramped apartment this was her only place of privacy. She wanted to laugh; at the same time she felt like retching. She had never expected him to answer so quickly. She wasn't ready. She had no dress, no shoes. Her hair was neither washed nor curled. "It's a dream, a dream," a voice in her head screamed. "You're an idiot. Any minute now you'll wake up." Fela pinched her cheeks and bit her lips. She had begun to sweat profusely, with a sweetish smell like that of a horse. How can I go to him? she thought. I'm unclean. Oh, I'm going to faint!

She fought against the dizziness. Her head swirled as if she were drunk. A nauseous fluid seeped into her mouth and she spat it out. She went into the kitchen. Bending down to the faucet, she half drank, half splashed her face with cold water to revive herself. She saw a bottle of vinegar on a shelf, opened it, sniffed it, and took a sip. "Don't let me poison myself with too much happiness," Fela implored the higher powers. As a rule her parents were always there, but today they had gone to visit a sick friend. What should she do first? What could she wear? All her dresses were torn, stained, faded, too tight, and out of style. The fishbones in her corset were broken. "I won't go to him. I can't. I will disgrace myself," Fela said aloud. She needed someone to help her, but who? She had once had girl friends, but now they were either students at the university or else had husbands. After her failure at the final examinations, she and her friends had grown apart. Some girls would have had a lot of cousins nearby, but Fela's parents had long ago left the provinces. "Just don't lose your head," Fela warned herself. "If you do, you'll fall to pieces altogether."

She would have to buy a dress. At Jablkowski Brothers one could get ready-made dresses. But where would she get the money? And would she be able to find a dress to fit her figure? And how could she undress before the salesladies when her petticoat and brassiere were torn? They would spit on her. "Oh, dreams of a chopped-off head!" Fela muttered. "It's impossible. I'm lost—lost!" Her belly began to expand until it was hard as a drum; she heard the seams of her shift splitting; she hiccuped. "God in heaven, help me," Fela prayed. "You have shown me one miracle, show another!" She was silent, as if waiting to hear God answer. Suddenly she remembered she had forgotten to extinguish the candle in the bathroom. A fire might start. She ran to put it out. Walking back in the dark to the bedroom, she knocked over a chair, hurting her knee. She threw herself down on the bed with such force that something broke under her, most likely the board supporting the mattress. She lay inert. Suddenly she jumped. Where was the telegram? She found it still clutched in her fist.

Lying there, Fela worked out a plan. She would have to commit a crime, certainly, and steal the gold chain her mother wore only on Rosh Hashanah and Yom Kippur. She would never find out Fela had pawned it. Long before then, it would have been redeemed. Fela stood up, fumbled for matches, and lit the gas lamp. Opening the drawer of the clothes closet, a heavy piece of furniture which had an elaborately carved top and lion heads for knobs, she took out the wooden box in which her mother kept her jewelry. On the very top lay the gold chain with the sliding catch, an inheritance from Grandmother Yetta. Fela lifted it and was astonished at its weight.

I won't take a groschen less than two hundred zlotys, she decided.

The night was one long nightmare. Fela slept fitfully, starting awake, sinking back into sleep. She was hot one minute, cold the next. A leg throbbed, a hand twitched. Her throat burned and she went to get water; back in bed, she had to get up again immediately to go to the bathroom. Even before her eyes closed, dreams swarmed over her. She received not one telegram but a whole pile of telegrams, each with a different address, a different date, some of them signed Adam, others Pacholski, others simply General, others Poet. What kind of a game was this? Did he want to confuse her? Did it have something to do with military secrets? Fela shook and woke up. She searched for the chain behind her pillow, but it had disappeared. Had a thief been here? Had her mother discovered it missing? In her dream, Fela went on searching. She was caught, arrested, manacled, thrown into a dungeon. An old woman brought her a jug of water with a piece of black bread, but when Fela tried to drink, the liquid burned like poison.

At nine o'clock the next morning, Fela awoke. In the courtyard below, peddlers were already hawking cherries, peaches, smoked herring, fresh bagels. Through the open window came smells of pitch, fruit, garbage. Fela jumped out of bed. Nine o'clock until four o'clock—seven hours! In seven hours, she must do everything. To meet Adam Pacholski she must transform herself into an elegant lady—washed, bathed, combed, with a smile on her lips. A gift. What gift should she take? But no, it wasn't proper for a lady to bring a gentleman a gift at first meeting. Etiquette was against it. A lady must be dignified even if she has an appointment with an angel.

She heard her father scolding her from the other room, but about what she didn't know. She rushed in to him distracted. "Daddy, you know I love you. There's not a man in the world who could take your place." She caught his beard, clutched it, and kissed it as she had when she was a small child. On her way to the kitchen she heard him calling after her, "Crazy, crazy! Crazy girl." She turned around. "You may kill me, I worship you just the same." As usual, her mother began attacking her with complaints. Why had she slept so late? Why didn't she go out looking for a job? Why hadn't she washed the dishes last night? To all of which Fela answered only, "If you don't like me, find yourself another daughter. I only want you."

And she embraced her mother, kissing her cheeks, her nose, her forehead, even her wig.

"As I love God, the girl has lost her senses."

"Yes, yes, Mother. Your daughter is insane. I'm so happy I wish I could die."

"Let your enemies talk so!"

Fela ate, not knowing what, putting salt in her tea and stirring it with her fork instead of the little spoon. When she rose, she stumbled into the kitchen closet, bruising her shoulder. She stood for a while by the window. Outdoors, the sun was shining, the birds twittering. Magicians were performing in the courtyard. A man dressed like a clown swallowed flames from a torch and spun a glass of water around a hoop. A girl with cropped hair, wearing velvet breeches, lay on her back and rolled a barrel on the soles of her feet. "Oh, Mother, how wonderful it is to live," Fela babbled. "Why am I so happy? Oh, why? I'm so happy I could jump out the window!" Fela heard her mother mutter, "Either you are crazy or you're trying to make yourself crazy."

"I don't try, Mother dear, I am. Tell me the truth. Did you ever love Daddy? I mean with the kind of love that burns like fire?"

"Whom else did I love? The chimney sweep? But look, now it's all ended."

"Things will still be good, Mother dear. You'll have a lot of joy."

"When? Soon I won't need any."

3

Everything went so smoothly that Fela had to laugh. It was strange. For years she had been brooding. Now suddenly a day of action had come. She went to a pawnshop and pawned her mother's chain for a hundred and forty zlotys. She took a droshky to Marzalkowsky Boulevard, where she bought herself a new dress, hat, shoes, underwear. Passing a bathhouse,

she went in and bathed. God in heaven, it was astonishing
what could be done in seven hours if one had money. Wearing
the new dress, the color of *café au lait,* Fela was unrecognizable. The straw hat trimmed with a brown ribbon gave her a
ladylike appearance. The new shoes were tight but their high
heels and pointed toes looked elegant. The corset was con-
stricting but it made her figure firm and buoyant. The hot
bath had taken away all the itches and smells. Fela walked as if
on springs. Her heart fluttered like a bird behind her left
breast. She went into a coffeehouse and ordered a coffee.
When she paid for that, only one zloty remained out of the
hundred and forty, and that one would pay for the droshky to
take her to the meeting. Fela opened the picture magazine the
waiter had handed her and tried to read, but she couldn't understand the words; she couldn't even focus on the pictures
clearly. Well, one day of happiness is enough, she said to herself. Every few minutes she glanced at her wristwatch. It
wouldn't do to get there too early, but to be too late would
also be dangerous. She must figure the time closely so that he
would wait for her only a minute or two. Maybe the whole
thing was nothing but a joke to him. The police might have
been notified and would be waiting for her. Or he might bring
a bunch of officers to laugh at her. On the other hand, maybe
he would arrive with flowers. Anything was possible. This day
was her fate. She sat there in a daze. Suddenly she looked at
her watch again. It was late. She paid in a hurry and went
out. The day which had been so sunny was now overcast and
it looked as if it might rain. Birds flew low over the roofs,
croaking. A droshky was coming by, thank God. Fela got in
and said breathlessly, "The corner of Marszalkowsky and
Wspolna."

The coachman turned the droshky and Fela felt herself spinning together with the buildings, pavements, passersby. The
coffee had gone to her head like liquor. She was late already.
He would have to wait for her not just one minute but at least
five. Well, he's a man and I'm a lady. Let him wait. She was on
the verge of tears or laughter. What an adventure! Perhaps her
mother had discovered her chain was missing. Perhaps she had
notified the police. What if the driver asked for more than one
zloty? What would she do then?—bury herself alive!

God in heaven, now what. A long line of trolley cars had blocked the street. Fire wagons had stopped all traffic. The siren on an ambulance was screaming. Was there a fire? But where? A large crowd had collected. The driver turned his head in his oilcloth cap.

"Young lady, if you're in a rush, get out here. It's not far to Wspolna Street."

Fela handed him the zloty and got down. She almost tore her dress on the iron step. She made her way through the crowd as fast as she could and hastened toward Wspolna Street. She slipped in her high-heeled shoes and almost fell. That's all I need, to land in the mud, she thought. Adam Pacholski, out of uniform, was at the corner, a young fellow in a light suit, his blond hair cut in a brush. Could it be he? He smiled at Fela and waved a magazine. Reaching her quickly, he took her hand and deftly kissed the wrist above the glove, welcoming her as if she were an old acquaintance.

"You are late," he said. "But that is the privilege of the fair sex."

"There was a fire. The droshky couldn't get through."

"Follow me, please." He led her through a gateway and opened the glass door of the main entrance with a key. They entered a paneled elevator. As it rose, Fela, who had never been in an elevator, felt her brains rattling. She well knew that a girl should not go with a man to his apartment, but he hadn't given her a chance to say no. Her heart pounded; she couldn't utter a word. The movement made her dizzy. God in heaven, don't let me faint, she implored. Adam Pacholski opened a door into a corridor full of paintings. On a hanger hung a general's coat, a general's cap, and a sword. Flowers stood in a vase. Goldfish swam in an aquarium.

The room they went into was like a museum. Portraits of Polish heroes looked down from the walls, and there were medals, ribbons, all kinds of diplomas and citations. One wall was covered with the heads of stuffed animals, and with guns, pistols, sabers. The room smelled of leather and maleness. Adam Pacholski asked Fela to sit down and she thanked him. Opening a liquor cabinet, he poured out two glasses of a reddish liqueur. "In your letter, you wrote you were not good-looking," he said. "But you're a beauty."

"The general mocks me."

"Don't call me general. I am Adam and you are Fela." His tone was intimate. "Here's to your health." He clicked his glass against hers and smiled with that smile which was known all over Poland, perhaps all over the world. He was forty-two years old, but to Fela he looked no more than twenty-three. The liqueur was strong. A sweetness penetrated her limbs. The fumes made her nose smart and her eyes fill with tears. "You don't know how to drink," Pacholski remarked, getting a cookie for her and filling her glass up again. He glanced at his wristwatch. In another room the telephone rang; he disposed of the call quickly. "Everyone calls me," he remarked, rejoining Fela. "Such bores."

"Perhaps the general has no time?" Fela asked.

"For a good-looking woman I always have time," he answered.

Pacholski gazed into Fela's eyes and began to speak like a fortune-teller. "You are a girl who knows how to love. You remind me of the lines in Heine's poem where he speaks of the tribe of 'Those who die when they love.' What do you find in my poems? Sometimes it seems to me they are worthless. You are Jewish but different from the other Jewish girls, completely different. They are realistic, mercenary, but you are romantic, a dreamer. You live completely in your fantasy. The nobility of the ancient peoples is in you. You're an Oriental beauty. It's quite possible that one of your great-grandmothers sat in the harem of King Solomon . . . What do any of us know about the generations? We Slavs are young and have just emerged from the forests, while you belong to an old race. Perhaps that's why there can be no peace between us. Except when we love, for then all boundaries disappear. Then we want to merge, to pour, one might say, our wine into your skin. Come, I can't wait any longer. I have to kiss you."

"Pan General!"

"Say nothing. You are mine."

He got up from his chair, kissed her, and pressed open her mouth. She sank as if her knees were giving way, and he half carried her, half led her into another room. Fela tried to resist, but Pacholski became wild. He tore off her hat, threw her on the bed, struggled with her dress. She wanted to scream, but he covered her mouth with the palm of his hand. Everything happened quickly, brutally, with a violence such as she could never have conceived. He pulled the cord of the drapes and the bedroom became dark. He threw himself on her.

"You harlot! You Jewish whore!"

4

The telephone rang and kept on ringing. Pacholski, half-naked, tore himself from Fela and lifted the receiver. It was some woman and he quarreled with her, finally shouting, "Lightning, thunder, and cholera strike you!" The phone rang again, apparently the same woman, because Pacholski threw down the receiver with a bang. His underpants were stained with blood. Fela was bleeding profusely, almost as if she were hemorrhaging. There was blood on the bed, on the carpet.

"I have had many virgins but not one of them poured like you," said Pacholski.

He kissed Fela and scolded her. Soon, he told her, a representative from the General Staff was coming and he had to receive him. He took off his soiled underwear and threw it on the floor. The doorbell rang. Pacholski opened the door a crack and accepted a telegram. He went to the bathroom for some clean linen, but the phone rang and he returned without even covering his shame.

Fela wept. Pacholski yelled, "Don't wail, you softie. On the battlefield we bled a great deal more. I once lay bloody in a foxhole with crows waiting to pick out my eyes." He had torn her dress. He brought her another that was hanging in the closet, but it was too long for Fela to wear. He started to look for a needle and thread, but again the telephone rang. When he had hung up, he turned to her.

"You've got to get out of here."

"Please leave the room for a few minutes," she answered.

"You don't have to be ashamed in front of me."

"Leave, I beg you."

He went out and Fela began to straighten herself up. Her dress was both torn and stained. Her underwear was useless and she shoved it into her pocketbook. She tried to get the corset back on but couldn't. Without even knocking, Pacholski entered the room, already dressed, a lit cigarette hanging in the corner of his mouth. He screamed at her, "Don't act like a tragic heroine. You will find a husband and that's all. *Basta!*" At the word "husband," Fela let out a wail. In a voice she didn't know was hers she yelled back, "Don't drive me. I'm not a dog."

"I cannot allow the generals to find you here."

Forcefully, he got her into her corset and found a safety pin for the dress. Putting his hand into his trouser pocket, he pulled out a heap of bank notes. Fela clutched at her hair, refusing the money.

"We will meet," he said. "I love you. But now you have to go. If not, I am ruined."

"How can I go out on the street like this?"

"Take a taxi. Go to a hotel."

"They won't let me in. Let me wait at least until it's dark."

"Pilsudski himself is coming here!"

Taking her by the shoulders, he pushed her along the corridor, kissing her hand and her face while he did so. He gave her his handkerchief. Opening the door, he gave her one last push and a kiss on the neck. He called after her, "I will always remember you," and slammed the door.

Fela walked down the steps, blood dripping on the marble and on the carpet strip in the middle. Crumpling the handkerchief, she pushed it into the open wound. She cried, unable to stop. Coming out through the gate, she looked around, uncertain in which direction lay home. In the dusk, Marszalkowsky Boulevard looked hazy and the pavement appeared to slant uphill. Crowds of people were pouring out of movie houses, stores, exhibitions. Trolley bells clanged; autos honked. Newsboys screamed out headlines. God in heaven, how long will this day last! Fela started walking blindly, not knowing if she was going toward the center of the city beyond which lay home or farther away toward the suburb of Mokotow. If only I had fifteen groschen for a trolley, she thought. People stared at her, but she narrowed her eyes and kept them fixed on the pavement. It seemed to her that men called out loudly after her and that women laughed. She heard a policeman's whistle and was afraid she was about to be arrested. She reached Jerusalem Boulevard. At least she had walked in the right direction. She wanted to sit down on a bench, but all the seats were taken. Her wound ached and the handkerchief had worked its way down and was about to fall out. The safety pin had come open and was pricking her thigh. Her feet hurt in the tight shoes and she could barely keep her balance on the high heels. Suddenly she slipped and almost fell. She stood still. Her stockings were coming down. The seams in her clothing were splitting. She couldn't shut her pocketbook and the stained underwear showed on top. If only I had poison with me—if only I could die right now, right here on this spot! She moved on. She must reach home.

The night fell, thank God! The street lamps were being lit. Fela walked half blindly. The important thing was not to fall down. Finally she reached Holy Cross Street and turned toward Panska Street, where she lived. What can I tell Mother? What can I say? There will be a scandal. Fela wanted to pray to God, but for what? God himself could not help her anymore. She saw a shop with its shutters closed and sat down on the threshold. Now she saw what she had done to her feet. The skin over one heel had rubbed off and the stocking was soaked with blood. She looked for a piece of paper to insert to ease the pressure but couldn't find one. A drunk lurched toward her, leering, as if ready to fall on her. She got up quickly and hurried off. She came to Panska Street. The gas lamps were burning. Children were playing in the half darkness. Though Fela had been born here, the street looked strange to her. She came to the building where she lived, went through the courtyard, and began to climb the stairs. Nobody stopped her! A small gas lamp cast a feeble light. Fela took one step at a time. Only now did she realize how worn-out she was. Her knees shook and she had to hold on to the banister. If only she had taken the key with her so that she could let herself in and go straight to the bathroom. She would have to knock, and her mother would know everything immediately.

Miraculously, the door stood open. The hallway was dark and so was the kitchen. Had somebody broken in? But no, her mother must have gone out leaving the door open. In the living room, Fela could see her father standing at the east wall in the dark, bowing, apparently in the middle of his evening prayers. She hurried to the bathroom. Only after she had locked herself in did she realize that hiding here was no escape. She would have to come out. She must take off the strange dress, conceal the stained underwear. Her mother might return at any minute. She had probably only stepped across to a neighbor, which was why she had left the door open. Fela felt sick. Her stomach heaved and she had to urinate. The handkerchief was gone. Warm blood was wetting her inner thighs and trickling onto the floor. She had no match to light the candle stub. She stood up and vomited. Fiery wheels spun in front of her eyes. Inside her skull a light blazed. Fela stretched out her hand to grope for paper on the shelf and touched a scissors. She knew immediately what she must do: she must cut open her veins. God himself had put the instrument there for her. Fela trembled. She had always known this would be the end. She had foreseen it, though whether in a dream or while awake she didn't recall.

Fela wanted to say a prayer, to recite some Jewish words from the Bible or from the prayer her mother used to read with her when she was still a little girl, but she remembered nothing. "God have mercy on my soul," she murmured. Seated on the toilet bowl, she cut her hand at the wrist as if it were a piece of cloth. Soon she cut at a second place and then at a third. It did not really hurt. Thank God, no one will ever see me alive!

Sitting on the toilet bowl in the dark, Fela leaned her head against the wall, ready to die. She could feel the blood running from her wrist and she was bleeding below, too. She became light-headed and felt herself swooning. Bells rang in her ears. Colors flared in front of her eyes. She was still here but already somewhere else. Fear had evaporated. A bellows pumped away inside her. Something inflated and then collapsed. Something inflated and seemed to be growing—some entity not of this world. She couldn't tell if it was more like a frog, a lung, a turtle . . . A crowd was nearing from somewhere. There was a drumming that echoed like hoofbeats. Then a loud noise and an outcry sounded close by.

The door was forced open. Fela's father screamed; her mother wailed. Neighbors came running. They dragged Fela out, lifted her, carried her. Towels were wrapped about her arm and somebody ran to get a doctor. Fela lay on the sofa while above her people screamed, waved their arms, bent down to examine her. Strange men lifted her dress, uncovered her. I cannot even be ashamed, Fela thought. But I'm dying happy. I forgive him. I forgive. She opened one eye and saw a soldier entering with a bouquet of roses, red as blood. Despite her agony, Fela's spirit grinned. Is he the Angel of Death?

She heard her mother asking, "Who are you? What do you want? They're not for us."

"For Panna Fela, with compliments," said the soldier, "from the general."

Translated by the author and Elizabeth Pollet

The Bond

WE SAT in a sort of combined café and garden. It was summer, when twilight in Warsaw lasts for a long time. The sun sets, but the sky remains light, retaining an early-evening glow. Birds still chirped in the branches of the trees. White-winged insects madly circled the globes of the lamps. The sweet smell of flowers blended with the aromas of coffee, cocoa, and freshly baked pastries. An August moon loomed in the sky, and near it a bright star.

We sat in a small group—several writers, a painter, and a sculptor. Soon they all left except for one Yiddish writer, Reuven Berger, and me. Reuven had early become known as a great talent but then stopped writing altogether. We drank coffee, ate buns with jam, and discussed women. Reuven told anecdotes and smoked one cigarette after another. In a remote corner of the café someone tinkled the keys of a piano. From the fields and orchards on the other side of the Vistula scents of late summer wafted in.

Reuven Berger flicked the ashes from his cigarette into an ashtray and said, "There are cases when a man is forced to slap a woman. No matter how considerate he may be by nature, he has no alternative. You know that I have a reputation for being overly gentle to the fair sex, but the story I have in mind is so crazy and unlike me that each time I recall it I must laugh. Such a thing is only possible in life, not fiction. It is just too ridiculous to be believed."

"Enough suspense. Let me hear it," I said.

"All right. You know that from the age of fourteen I was involved with women. I loved them and they loved me. This event took place about eight years ago, perhaps ten. I lived with a woman who was terribly in love with me. With her kind, love becomes a total obsession. Her insane jealousy made a hell out of my life. Thousands of times I broke up with her and each time she came back. Her father was a pious Jew, an owner of a house. Her name was Bella. She used to move in our literary circles long before you began to come to the Writers' Club. She had studied in an exclusive Gymnasium for girls and had the manners of a well-bred lady. She was beautiful, too. But she began to drink on account of me. At that time I was still married. Bella would sit in her room alone, drink vodka from the bottle, smoke, and quarrel with me on the telephone if she could find me. I had to run from her. She grew worse from day to day. She tried suicide on several occasions.

"When she was in the midst of these fits, there were wild scenes. One thing alone could stop her delirious outbursts— slaps. I was forced to slap her repeatedly, and this immediately brought her to her senses. She would regain her composure, become logical and calm. I often drew an analogy to war. When a nation becomes destructively belligerent, there is only one way to bring it to its senses—defeat. If a pacifist heard this he would tear me to pieces, but it's true.

"Get rid of her? I did not want to leave her altogether. In my fashion I loved her. If not for these mad scenes, I could have been quite happy with her. But she was capable of tearing the dress from her body in the middle of the street or of trying to throw herself under the wheels of a streetcar. She would attack an innocent woman with whom I exchanged a word or two. On one occasion she was arrested for disturbing the peace. Her mother came to me to ask me to break up with Bella. But how does one end an affair with this type of woman? I would have had to run away to America or commit suicide myself.

"Now, I guess you know that for years I made a living from lecturing. But it had come to such a pass that I could not go anywhere without her appearing out of nowhere and rushing to see what I was up to. If I had to go to a lecture, she would follow me. I learned every trick in the art of conspiracy. I had a secret address, an unlisted phone number. Once I discovered a private detective lurking at my gate. Her father was quite rich."

Reuven paused and tried to balance a little spoon on the edge of a glass. He continued, "At this particular time, I was scheduled to lecture in Jedrzejow. It was a cold, rainy day. I was certain Bella knew nothing of my plans, but the moment I entered the train she was there. I will never know how she discovered I was taking this trip. The car was empty. I was too enraged even to scold her. We sat down in complete silence. After a while, she started, as I knew she would, with bitter reproaches and warned me not to attempt to put her out of my life. She was ranting and raving, as always. She became louder and more offensive from minute to minute and resorted to every type of threat and insult. I knew I had to slap her or there would be no lecture. I was so wrought up I didn't notice that at a stop other passengers had entered the car. She was, in fact, begging to be slapped. I gave her a smack across the face—one, two, three. It had the miraculous effect. One minute she was mad. The next minute the hysteria was gone. She smiled, became loving, coherent. Those who have never witnessed a sudden change like this could never imagine how complete it was. Bella leaned against the train window, still weeping a little and pressing my hand to her lap. I was so confused that I didn't notice that directly across from me sat a woman looking furious, ready to swallow me alive. She seemed a small-town woman—not young, not old. Perhaps in her late twenties or early thirties. She reminded me of the suffragettes one saw photographs of in illustrated magazines, or possibly of the sort of female who would help manufacture bombs to be thrown at the Tsar. She carried a library book, the jacket carefully protected by a paper cover. Once or twice she opened her mouth as if about to blast me, but she seemed to control herself. More people entered the car and momentarily I lost sight of my angry co-passenger. Bella by now was absolutely normal, again and again apologizing, kissing me and promising to behave forever and after.

"'Why did you follow me?' I asked her. 'This is a business trip, not a vacation.' She said meekly, 'Since I'm already here, allow me to stay with you the rest of the way. I'm dying to hear your lecture! You need not introduce me to anyone. I will stay away from you when we get off, and in the evening I will just come to hear your speech. I will find out when you are leaving and arrange to go back with you.' In short, she was not the same Bella but a quiet and humble lover. This change in personality always perplexed me anew. I thought, Who knows, perhaps slaps could be a cure even for some organic maladies.

In these moments, rare though they were, she regained her old allure and I fell in love with her again. However, peace never lasted longer than a few days.

"We arrived at our destination and I took my suitcase from the shelf; I said goodbye and we kissed. A committee was scheduled to meet me at the station and I didn't want them to see her. She might have created a new uproar. I got off the train and there was the welcoming committee. They were the typical provincial intelligentsia. Once they get an opportunity to attach themselves to a writer from Warsaw, they cling and do not leave him for a moment. I don't need to tell you that every one of them had ambitions to write. I was sure that each had ready a poem, a novel, or a play. What else can they do in their godforsaken villages?

"The village itself looked to me like a miniature Siberia—dreary, muddy, with small cottages and one two-story hotel, where there was a reservation for me. The rain had stopped, but the sky was boding snow, hail, a blizzard. Nowhere, not even in the open fields, is the sky so wide and so otherworldly as in these bleak villages—the kind of sky that hovers over cemeteries.

"They began with the usual amenities—'Honored to greet you,' 'How was your trip?'—and the usual quasi-literary talk, with its errors and mispronunciations. The young men escorted me to the hotel and on the way they plied me with questions: How do you write? When do you write? Where do you get your inspiration? One of them started to criticize me for not being progressive enough and for not caring about the future of the masses. In those places you have to be prepared for all this nonsense. It was almost time for the lecture and I had to ask the committee to leave me so I could change my shirt. I had practically to put them out by force.

"Thank God, they finally left me alone. I bolted the door and had started to undress when there was a knock on the door. Who could it be? A female voice called, 'Open the door. I am the one who will introduce you tonight.' I quickly put on my jacket again, opened the door, and who do you suppose was there before me? The woman who sat across from me on the train.

"I have experienced all sorts of surprises, but this surely was the biggest of them all. She, too, seemed startled. She looked at me and her eyes seemed to turn over. I asked her to come in, but she stood rooted to the spot, not believing what she saw. When she finally entered the room she began to speak. I don't remember exactly what she said; the sum of it was that she had read me and considered me one of the most romantic and gentle Yiddish writers in Poland. She had gone to visit a sick sister in a nearby town but came back a day sooner to introduce me. She was the Jedrzejow librarian and the chairman of the committee. She cried out that she had always been fascinated by the deep insight and understanding of women which my books revealed. 'God in heaven, how is it possible you are the same man I saw on the train? No, it isn't possible. Tell me I am in error,' she pleaded dramatically, with solemn face and clasped hands. She repeated, 'Is this really you? Is this true? Please tell me that I am mistaken!'

"'I am sorry, you are not mistaken,' I told her, 'but I will explain everything to you later.'

"'What? You are capable of such behavior?' she shrieked. 'If that is so, then everything is false. If that is possible, then the whole of literature is a sham and a fake and nothing but the meanest hypocrisy.'

"She kept on berating me, screaming louder and louder, until I managed to break in: 'Miss or Madam, whatever you may be, I must prepare for my lecture and I am already late. I will talk to you at the reception.'

"'So! You are throwing me out?' she squealed. 'Don't you have any decency or shame? You who should be the pacesetter, the example of our lesser people! This is prostitution, sheer prostitution!'

"Her voice rose to a more hysterical pitch, while my watch showed that any moment the committee would come to escort me to the lecture. I knew from experience that they always arrive earlier than they say. I fell into real despair. Just a short while ago, I had had to rid myself of Bella's onslaught and here I was beset by a second one. I realized that in some uncanny act of female imitation she sought to create the same scene Bella had—a tirade of threats, abuse, tears, name-calling that could go on forever. I let out a mighty shout: 'Are you leaving, or do I have to throw you out?'

" 'Throw me out!' she yelled. 'Let the whole world know what a charlatan you are! You and all writers! You and all men —one bunch of liars, cheaters, seducers, murderers! Let the whole world know what a foul game you play to deceive the honest reader—to fool us, trick us with your falsehoods and cynicism. You devil, you monster. You demon!'

"Yes, you guessed it. I rushed over to her, seized her, and started to drag her toward the door. She let out a terrible howl, tried to resist violently, and I began to slap her just as I had Bella in the train. It all happened so fast I could hardly believe it myself. I threw the door open and pushed her out. I expected to hear her bang on the door and bring the whole village to the show. For a while I was ready to catch up my valise and run for dear life, but instead there was complete silence outside the door.

"I imagined she was lying in a faint. Perhaps I had killed her. How ironic it would be if this idiotic lecture of mine ended with a murder! I opened the door, but the corridor was dark and empty. She had left. It was only then that I realized what had happened to me. My hands trembled, my legs buckled under me, and no matter how I tried I could not button my shirt collar.

"I had prepared a manuscript for that night but could not remember where I had put it. Perhaps it would be best to flee from the village after all. At that moment, I heard steps and voices. Two young men were coming for me. One of them asked, 'Was Zipporah here?' I understood that Zipporah was the librarian. My throat had constricted and I couldn't bring out a single word. The two men gathered how upset I was, and one of them helped me with my collar button. The other asked, 'Why have you strewn your manuscript on the floor?' He picked up the pages and put them together. We then walked down the steps. There was no sign of the woman anywhere. Outside, it had become dark and a wet snow was falling.

"We finally arrived at the hall, and there was quite a large audience awaiting us. The committee representative, or whatever he was, inquired as to Zipporah's whereabouts. She was not in the hall. There were those who wished to wait for her. She had worked on her introduction for weeks. Others pointed out that it was getting late. Finally, a young man appeared and planted himself before the speaker's table. I could not make out what he was saying. One word stood out sharply in his oration—'which,' a word he repeated again and again, probably because in the provinces this word denotes high language. When he finished, I started my lecture. My words resounded hollow and remote in my ringing ears—almost as if I spoke in some foreign tongue. I expected jeering to break out from the audience at any moment, but there was complete silence in the hall. After my lecture, I went on to read one of my stories, but the letters danced madly before my eyes, and the print changed color. Luckily, I knew this story almost by heart. It was about the encounter of a boy and girl on a moonlit night —as tender and romantic a story as I have ever written. My reading was interrupted by applause many times, and I began to regain control of myself. My vision cleared, and the first faces I recognized in the audience were Bella's and Zipporah's. They sat side by side in the first row, cheering me and applauding. Their eyes shone with enthusiasm. I started to laugh out loud. My audience seemed momentarily puzzled, because this was a serious story, not a humorous one. But laughter is infectious, and soon the entire crowd joined me. Never before had I made an audience laugh like that. Oh, I must laugh again . . ." Reuven giggled into his handkerchief and wiped the perspiration off his high, lined forehead. "I could write a story about it," he said, "but I have lost my appetite for the dirty scribbling profession."

"What happened to Bella?" I asked.

Reuven became serious in an instant. "She died. No, not suicide—not really. She killed herself gradually. She got jaundice. She ruined her kidneys, her liver. Everything. I will never know how she held out so long."

"And what about Zipporah?"

"She is still the librarian, as far as I know. From time to time she used to come to Warsaw, and on each visit she would call me on the telephone. She began each call with 'This is the woman you slapped.' She invariably asked for some small favor —for my opinion of a book, for a pair of complimentary tickets to a lecture, for an autograph. I would always accommodate her. She remained a friend of Bella's in all the time of her sickness. She visited her whenever she was in Warsaw. She sent her little presents for her birthday and for other occasions. Many times she asked me to lecture in the village. I just could not go there again. But I always promised. I would say to her on the telephone, 'Yes, my dear, I will come, and I swear to you by everything that is holy to me that I will not slap you this time. The opposite—I will kiss you if you will allow me.' And she would say, 'You had no choice. It was all my fault. As a matter of fact, what you did has created a kind of secret bond between us.' She has not called me for a long time. I hope she is all right."

"Was she ever married?" I asked.

Reuven shook his head. "Never. Sometimes I suspect that what happened between us was the closest contact she ever had with a man."

Translated by the author and Lester Goran

The Interview

I HAVE MET in my time a number of female rebels, but the first one engraved herself in my memory. I was only nineteen years old and I was the proofreader of the Yiddish literary magazine *Literarishe Bleter*. The editor sent me to interview an important visitor to Warsaw—an old philosopher, essayist, and aesthete, Dr. Gabriel Levantes, who had resided for the last twenty years in Berlin, where he was the co-editor of a Jewish encyclopedia. I had the opportunity to observe him a few days earlier at the Writers' Club. He was small and stooped, with shoulders too broad for his size, and his stomach stuck out like a pregnant woman's. He had a huge head of white hair. His beard and mustache were also white. Only in his bushy eyebrows were there a few black hairs. From under them peered out black, piercing eyes, like those of a porcupine. He wore a pelerine that reached to his ankles, and a plush hat with a broad brim. An article about him in a Warsaw Yiddish newspaper said that no one had ever seen him without an umbrella or without a cigar in his mouth. There were jokes about him that he even slept with the cigar between his lips.

This interview was my first effort at journalism, and I prepared for it days in advance. The night before, I could hardly sleep. About eleven o'clock in the morning I called up the Hotel Bristol, where Dr. Levantes was staying. He seemed to be hard of hearing, because I had to repeat every word three times. He roared at me, as if I were the deaf one, "Young man, be here punctually at four o'clock—not a second later."

At fifteen minutes after three I began to walk to the Hotel Bristol from my lodgings on Nowolipki Street, and I got to the hotel at twelve minutes to four. It was cold outside, and now snow began to fall as thin and prickly as needles. I walked to and fro before the entrance, so as not to arrive, God forbid, too early. My winter coat had lost its cotton batting and I was shivering. In my haste and my fear of being late, I had forgotten my scarf and my rubbers. The hotel doorman, in a uniform with gilded buttons and the epaulets of a general, looked me up and down with suspicion. Droshkies, and even some motor taxis, which in those days were still somewhat of a rarity, pulled up at the curb. The gusty winter day was short, and the street lamps were lit early. The sky reflected the violet of an abortive sunset. I continued to look at my wristwatch, which had misted over. At three minutes before four I tried to enter the hotel, but the doorman stopped me with his white-gloved hand. "Hey, you, where are you going?"

"To Dr. Levantes."

"I think a woman is visiting him."

After some hesitation, the doorman gave me permission to visit Dr. Levantes, but I had to climb four flights of stairs, since I could not take the elevator, which was reserved for more prominent visitors. The doorman told me to wipe my shoes and not to dirty the carpet on the marble steps inside.

Exactly at four o'clock, I rang the bell and Dr. Levantes opened his door. He wore a long dressing gown with a braided sash and a pair of huge slippers. I immediately saw the woman the doorman had mentioned. She sat on the sofa across from the doctor's desk and was wearing a short, knee-length skirt in the current fashion. She seemed to me in her late thirties, perhaps even forty. She had on a hat that resembled an inverted pot, and boots that came up to her broad calves. She wore no makeup, and I imagined that I saw signs of pockmarks on her high cheeks. Between the fingers of her right hand she held an extinguished cigarette.

Dr. Levantes showed me to the sofa, and he himself sat down on a plush chair so as to face both of us. On the edge of his desk I saw a slender unbound book, a brochure. I could read the title and the name of the author on the first page: *The Naked Truth*, by Machla Krumbein. Dr. Levantes lifted the booklet with his thumb and index finger, looked at it for a moment, then mincingly put it back on the desk.

He said to me, "You'll have to wait awhile for the interview. This woman came to me unannounced. She considers herself a poetess." He turned to the woman. "Where did you say you came from?"

The woman mentioned the name of some village.

"Where is this godforsaken shtetl?" Dr. Levantes asked. "My dear lady," he said angrily, "this young man is a mother's child, most likely a former yeshiva boy, just hatched from the egg, and I don't want to spoil him by quoting your kind of poetry. I can already see your approach. So holy is art that everything is kosher in its name, even a pig's knuckle boiled in tallow. Let me tell you clearly: pornography is not literature. The purpose of literature is to lift up the spirit, to bring out for the reader what is beautiful and lofty, not to tease his lowest instincts. I know that since the war there has been a new strain in literature—in Germany, France, and especially in Russia, among the Bolsheviks. They have turned everything topsy-turvy. Evil is good, ugly is beautiful, crooked is straight. We have in Berlin a certain Rilke, who carries his poems in a sack like a peddler. You cannot understand a word of what these poets write. Their slogan is 'Back to chaos,' but I'm too old for that and this young man is too young. There is in Russia a madman, a certain Mayakovsky, who wrote a poem about a cloud in pants, and they quote him with great admiration. How can a cloud wear pants if it is all vapor? It could just as well wear spats and a fur coat. Some of these so-called poets are Jews. What is the name of that crazy woman? Something like Lasker. Well, I can still understand all this taking place in Berlin or Paris—even in Petersburg, Petrograd, or whatever they named it lately. These places always teemed with futurists, Dadaists, nihilists—all kinds of other 'ists.' But how is it possible that a woman from a decent Jewish hamlet should use such abominable language? Do you try to imitate the maniacs of Sodom and Gomorrah?"

"I don't try to imitate anybody," the woman said, in a voice almost masculine. "But since every human being, without exception, thinks about sexual relations from the cradle to the grave, how can poetry ignore the subject?"

"Every human being?" Dr. Levantes cried out. "I don't think about it even one hour in a week. Neither did my great friend Professor Hermann Cohen. If the human brain were always occupied with thoughts of lechery, men today would still crouch like apes and live in caves. There is in Vienna a certain Dr. Freud, a half-charlatan and full-fledged dilettante, and he tries to persuade us we are all a band of sex fiends. He's trying to become the Newton of human behavior. He has a whole coterie of hangers-on. May I ask you a personal question?"

"Yes, Doctor, of course," the woman said.

"Do you have a husband or are you unmarried?"

"I had one."

"What happened to him?"

"We are divorced."

"May I ask you why you are divorced?"

"You can ask anything. I left him because he did not satisfy me. Before he said good evening it was already good night. He was as quick as a rabbit."

Young as I was, I grasped what she meant, and I felt flushed. I had already read Professor Forel's book about sex, and I think I had even looked into Krafft-Ebing. Dr. Levantes began to growl and cough. He took a large handkerchief from his pocket and spat into it.

The woman rose. "Dr. Levantes," she said, "there was an article about you in the newspaper, and the author called you an independent thinker. This is the reason I came to you. Now I see you have all the prejudices of the fanatics. You probably recite thanks every day to God that he did not create you a woman. Let me tell you, Doctor, you've studied many books, but I've studied life. Our village was occupied by the Austrians in the war, and they brought with them first the cholera and then a famine. Many girls and young women became smugglers. They wrapped meat around themselves, under their clothing, and smuggled it into what used to be Galicia. On the way back they smuggled tobacco and other articles, which they hid in their underwear. There were gendarmes, called *Finanzer*, who lurked at night in the woods around the frontier. When they caught one of these women they forced her to undress and did with her whatever they wanted. I can tell you, Doctor, one fact—"

"I don't want to hear it, I don't want to hear it!" Dr. Levantes screamed. "If you want to tell me that most people are still animals, I will have to agree with you, but poetry is written for better human beings, not for the rabble."

"Your better human beings are as interested in sexual matters as the rabble," the woman said. "Everything you, Doctor, call culture has to do with it. What is the theater? What do the painters paint? What do the sculptors sculpt? Breasts, bellies, behinds. Give this young man a choice between the most wonderful book and a voluptuous female and you'll see what he'll choose."

"Madam, be so good as to go your way!" Dr. Levantes shouted.

It had become so dark that the woman's face had turned into a bundle of shadows. Only her eyes sparkled in the wintry twilight. I wanted to say that I would choose the book rather than the female—perhaps to please Dr. Levantes—but my throat became dry and I began to sweat. The woman moved backward and hesitated. Suddenly she ran to me and caught my wrist so hard that I almost cried out in pain. "I will wait for you downstairs," she whispered, and kissed me behind my ear. She slammed the door with such strength that the window-panes rang.

Dr. Levantes called after her, "Whore! Harlot! Piece of dirt!" He shook, and said, gasping, "I don't recognize my Polish Jews anymore."

I had written a long list of questions for Dr. Levantes, but as soon as I asked the first he delivered a lengthy speech. He blew the smoke of his cigar directly into my face and spoke of many things at once—Spengler's *Decline of the West*, Bergson's *Creative Evolution*, the Balfour Declaration, the Bolshevik revolution, even Einstein's theory of relativity. He again and again attacked Freud. Even though steam hissed in the radiator, frost trees formed on the windowpanes. I wrote down as quickly as I could the doctor's clever words, but my brain was occupied with one thought: Would Machla Krumbein really wait for me? It was too cold for her to wait outside. As if Dr. Levantes could sense that I was thinking of her, he tried to refute her arguments. He compared the "human affects," as Spinoza called them, to a volcanic eruption. One must avoid the glowing lava, not try to swim in it. "There's only one question," he said. "Why did God or nature bestow on *Homo sapiens* such an abundance of emotions? What is their biological function? Neither Plato nor Spinoza nor Schopenhauer could really answer this."

Almost two hours had passed and Dr. Levantes was still pouring out his erudition. The room became filled with coils of cigar smoke. I imagined that the smoke came not only from the doctor's mouth and nostrils but also from his hairy ears, his beard, and even from behind his vest, as if he were burning in his interior. When I finally left, my knees had become shaky and I was dizzy. I opened the door to the street and breathed in deep the frosty air, and there was Machla Krumbein. She stood at a store window that was warmed by small gas flames to keep it from freezing over. I touched her shoulder and she started. I asked her if she had been waiting outside the entire time.

Her face was white from the cold, but her eyes lit up with the joy of a young girl. "So what?" she said. "I am accustomed both to the cold and to waiting. I smuggled things on days and nights when it was as cold as Siberia. Why did your interview last so long? Let's go somewhere. I'm a chunk of ice."

"Why didn't you wait in the lobby?"

"The doorman chased me out. He probably didn't like the way I'm dressed. One pauper snubbing another. Do you have some money with you? I'm without a penny."

She took my arm familiarly. The restaurants and coffee-houses in this rich neighborhood were not for the likes of us. We walked in the direction of Senatorska Street, and from there to the Jewish quarter. The whole time Machla continued to talk. "What kind of interview was this? Where's it going to be published? I went to the Writers' Club, but the receptionist would not let me in. If they had seen what I write, they would have hurled me out the window. What did you say your name was? I've never seen it in print anywhere. I had to publish my little book with my own money. That's why I'm bankrupt now. What do you write?"

"I want to write stories."

"Stories, huh? Will you at least tell the truth, or will you gloss over and prettify everything, as the other liars do? You look like an honest lad still, but when these scribblers take you into their establishment you'll become a cheater like them."

"What do you call the truth?"

"The naked truth. When those Austrian gendarmes told me to strip mother-naked I thought I would die from shame. But when you must do it you do it. Thank God, it was summer and not winter. They did to me what they wanted—four men, one more virile than the other. Then they spat at me and left as if nothing had happened. I lay there and wept for a long time, until it occurred to me that what had happened was not such a calamity after all. I realized then for the first time that this is what a female was created for."

"To be raped?"

"Yes."

Her words made me shudder. We came to a little coffee shop with a picture of a cow out front to indicate that it served dairy products. Even though I was not a vegetarian yet, I used to eat there frequently, because everything was cheap. We entered and took the one table that was not occupied. I had some money with me. The owner, an elderly Gentile woman, brought us buckwheat with milk, bread, herring, and coffee with chicory.

Although I was extremely bashful with women, Machla Krumbein, who looked old enough to be my mother and who spoke like a whore, made me daring. "What would have happened if the gendarmes had made you pregnant?" I asked.

"It couldn't have happened—I can't have children. I lived seven years with my husband and I remained barren. He was good for nothing, and after a few years I took lovers."

"Who were they?"

"Whomever I could get—a Jew, a Gentile, a coachman. Once I made love with a boy not long out of the cheder, about twelve years old. I had begun to read novels, and realized the writers were all brazen liars. They kept on beating around the bush and they never came to the point. They babbled without end about love. There is no love. It's all invented, a horse fair in the sky."

"I myself was mortally in love with a girl," I said. I could hardly keep myself from trembling.

"'Mortally,' huh? And what happened?"

"Nothing."

"This is how all loves end. Love is nothing but a dragged-out sickness. A man should immediately get what he wants, not be fed with a lot of sentimental twaddle. Do you have someone now?"

"Not really."

"You can have me tonight if you want. All we need is a bed."

"I board in a private apartment."

"Do you have a room to yourself?"

"I have to cross their living room. There's a girl there, and we two—"

"You are in love with her?"

"We read books together."

"What books?"

"Various subjects—biology, psychology. Lately we've been reading Flammarion."

"Who is he?"

"A French astronomer."

"Is your girl a virgin?"

"Yes, but we never talk about such things."

"Take me home," Machla Krumbein said, "and I will speak to her clearly. These kosher virgins are as afraid of me as the Devil is of incense."

"I cannot do that."

"In that case you're not a man but a lamb. I would take you to my place, but I stay with an old aunt and she has only one room and one bed. She's as pious as a rebbetzin. All night long she groans and mumbles sacred words. She doesn't let me sleep. Her husband, my Uncle Nahum, died twenty-two years ago and she's never touched another man—she's still faithful to my uncle. That's what the liars and bigots have done to women."

I wanted to answer her, but my throat was constricted. She took a brochure from her purse and said, "Here, read this. It's my book, *The Naked Truth*."

It had thirty-two pages of poems, each line not more than four or five words. In about fifteen minutes I had read it to the end. I had never before read such obscenities. I didn't know what was stronger in me, my passion or my nausea. I glanced at the author. She smiled, and showed a mouthful of broad, strong teeth. She asked, "Have you ever read such hot stuff?"

"Never."

"My father was a Cohen. In ancient days they would have sentenced me to be burned. This is how it's written in the Pentateuch."

"Yes."

"If you have ten zlotys you can take me to a cheap hotel."

"You need to show a passport. I don't have ten zlotys, and besides, I have to pay for our dinner."

"There are little hotels where they'll let you in without a passport," she said. "Perhaps you can borrow some money."

"Now? At night?"

We sat in silence. I looked around at the other tables. At each sat a young man and a girl. They were talking about the political situation in Poland, about the news from Soviet Russia, Palestine. Some of them I knew. There were Communists, members of the leftist Workers of Zion, even an anarchist—a vegetarian. Machla Krumbein smiled and winked at me. "I have an idea," she said. "Borrow some money from the girl with whom you read books. When the interview appears you'll repay her."

I knew this was nonsense, but I stood up and paid the bill. We walked together to Nowolipki Street, and came to the building where I lived. I knew that my girl, Ilka, had gone to the movies with a girl friend. I could not ask her mother for a loan, because I already owed her three months' rent. I told this to Machla Krumbein and she said, "All the powers are against us tonight. If that old idiot Levantes weren't such a zealot, we could have made love all three of us together."

"With that old man?"

"I love old men. Some of them are lustier than the young. A threesome with you and him would have been fun, but it wasn't destined."

"Do you believe in God?" I asked.

"Everything comes from him."

We stood at the gate of my building, and Machla Krumbein said, "Perhaps your girl will soon be back from the movies. Sometimes if they don't like a show these girls leave immediately. I myself stopped going to the movies—they bore me stiff. A man meets a girl and the moment he kisses her he's in love forever. The heroines are all beautiful beyond words. Those who are not beautiful don't exist at all in these inventions. The men are all immensely tall and rich and eager to marry. Lies, lies. In all literature I found only one writer who writes the truth—Strindberg. He's translated into Yiddish. What he says about us women is real. In my village they are all my blood enemies. They curse me with the vilest oaths. Why can't you take me up to your room? If you live there, you're entitled to bring in any guest you want."

"My landlady doesn't let me. Once, a girl visited me and the old woman ordered me to leave the door open."

"They are jealous, that's what they are. They are like dogs watching a stack of hay: they can't eat it themselves and they won't let others eat. How can I ever sell my book? The printer has put together five hundred copies. Would any bookstore take them from me?"

"I'm afraid no bookstore would sell them."

"That means I'm already excommunicated in Warsaw, too. The printers in Lublin refused to print it, but I found an old bachelor, and he became my publisher—anonymously, of course. I gave him what a man wants, and he turned romantic and did it all for me. He even proposed marriage to me, but I will marry the Angel of Death."

"Why do you say that? You are still young."

"Not so young."

"What do you do in that village?" I asked.

"I am a seamstress. The women won't give me any work, but the men come to me and let me take measurements for their shirts and underwear. While I take their sizes I tickle them. Oy, I must laugh."

"What's so funny?"

"Those hypocrites! A few days ago I became forty and I decided to live five years more, not a day longer. But for those five years I've promised myself to indulge all my whims. Women such as I should never get old. The warden of the burial society warned me that when I die he will bury me behind the fence, among the suicides and whores, and I told him that as far as I'm concerned he can cut me to pieces and throw me to the dogs. All they write in the holy books is balderdash. There is a God, but he never split the Red Sea. He never gave the Torah. Moses wrote it all from his head. He himself played around with a black female. When do they close the gate here?"

"They may do it soon."

The moment I uttered the words, the janitor came out from

his cubicle with his big key and with his old dog limping after him. He gave us both an ugly look and asked, "Are you two going in or out? I'm closing."

Machla Krumbein started to give me her address. She planted a kiss on my mouth. She actually bit me. The janitor slammed the gate before her, and instead of going up the dark steps I went over to the garbage bin in the courtyard and wiped my mouth with a handkerchief. In the light of a single lantern that glimmered over the entrance I saw blood.

Someone rang the bell, and the janitor went to open the gate. It was Ilka—small, with a head of cropped hair as shaggy as a sheep's. Ilka's father had died in the typhus epidemic. Her mother sold secondhand clothes in the Karcelak Place bazaar. Ilka had gone to the Gymnasium, but she flunked the final examination. Lately we had read together a book entitled *The Life of an Amoeba*. We often spoke of chromosomes, centrosomes, and cytoplasm. I sided with the vitalists and Ilka with the mechanists. We also discussed Bukharin's work about historical materialism and Otto Weininger's *Sex and Character*. When Ilka entered the courtyard and saw me standing at the garbage bin she asked, "Why are you standing out here in the dark? Did you have the interview?"

"Yes, I had it."

"What did he say?" she asked.

"He said that a girl wasn't created to read about amoebas but for a man to sleep with," I said, baffled at my own words.

Ilka seemed more astonished than I was. We both stood speechless for a while. Then I heard her say, "At least you found the courage to tell the truth. A woman is nothing for you but a lump of flesh. Is that correct?"

"Yes, correct."

"In that case we must sever all our relations."

"If you think so."

"What is the sense of our standing at the garbage bin? Let's go up."

We walked up the dark steps to the first landing and stopped. I embraced Ilka and she did not resist. I kissed her and she kissed me back. I felt her face burn. She pushed me away and said, "You're a pig, like all the other men."

"That's what I am."

"You've disappointed me bitterly."

We went up another flight and we again stopped and kissed. From behind a door I could hear a baby crying and the mother singing a dirgelike lullaby.

"What a night," Ilka said. "First a disgusting movie that turned my stomach, then your strange behavior. Sometimes I feel that death is the only way out."

"Yes, let's die together, but before we die let's give in to all our desires."

"Why do you want to die with me?" Ilka asked. "Since you don't love me."

"There is no love," I announced.

"What is there?"

"Just lust."

"You kill everything."

We knocked at our door and Ilka's mother opened it. She cried out to me, "Who bloodied your mouth?" She clapped her hands and screamed, "Yours, too, Ilka! Woe is to me and to my dismal life."

Ilka rushed into the bathroom. I ran into my room. As a rule, we used to drink tea and eat bread with jam before we went to sleep. Now I threw myself on the bed in my clothes. I could hear from the other side of the door the old woman's nagging words and Ilka's answer: "Leave me alone. Don't bore me. Be still."

The door opened abruptly, and the old woman put her head in. She had taken off her wig and covered her shaved head with a kerchief. She had already taken out her false teeth and put them in a glass of water, and her face sagged. "Be so good as to move out immediately tomorrow," she said.

"Yes, I will."

"And pay what you owe me."

"Not before my interview is published."

"You wild beast!" She spat, and slammed the door.

I extinguished the gas lamp and lay quietly in the dark. I could still hear the old woman's grumbling and her daughter's annoyed responses. I fell into a deep sleep. In the middle of the night someone nudged my shoulder. I woke up and it was Ilka. She murmured, "Here's your lump of flesh."

I stretched out my hand to pull her closer, but she resisted. I kissed her and swore love to her, and she said, "Shameless liar."

About fifty years passed, and I never heard the name Machla Krumbein, either in Warsaw or in New York, where I lived after I emigrated to America. I looked for her little book in Yiddish libraries and bibliographies, but both the writer and the book had vanished without a trace. Whenever I met someone from her region, I asked if he had ever heard of such a person and the answer was always no. I began to doubt whether this episode had ever happened. I knew from experience that certain occurrences of whose reality I was certain proved later to be nothing but dreams or fantasies. For years I used to dream I was in Siberia. I saw Siberian towns and forests. I traveled over Siberian taigas and tundras. Whenever I woke up at night I believed for a while that I really had been there, but after some pondering and consideration I realized that I couldn't have been, unless in a former reincarnation. Perhaps my meeting with Machla Krumbein was the same kind of figment.

In 1974, I was invited to speak at Oxford University, in England. The day after the lecture the librarian of the Jewish section gave me a tour of arcane Hebrew and Yiddish books and manuscripts in the Bodleian Library. I found a number of small storybooks that I had read in my childhood and that I was sure had been lost in the Holocaust. I recognized the faded covers, the typography, even the misprints in those flimsy and worn pages. Suddenly my gaze fell on a booklet that lay on a metal shelf without a library stamp, without a cover— an unbound remnant of a book which no one seemed to have catalogued. My God, I saw the name Machla Krumbein and the title *The Naked Truth*. When I lifted it, the pages crumbled between my fingers. The librarian had been called away to the telephone, and in some ten minutes I read the book again from the beginning to the end. No, it was not a dream or an illusion. There it was, with its crooked lines, provincial expressions, amateurish style. It again perplexed me, and ignited my imagination with the same uncanny power that it had in the little vegetarian restaurant on that winter night. Every poem proclaimed the erotic heat of a woman who didn't know and didn't care about any literary conventions. That village seamstress had wished that all human females would perish in some biological catastrophe and that she, Machla Krumbein, would remain the only woman in the whole world. All men would stand in rows from Spain to Vladivostok, from Alaska to the Antarctic, and she would copulate with every one of them— young and old, Chinese and Turks, Zulus and pygmies, lepers and perverts, murderers and maniacs. No, Machla Krumbein was not an idealist. She wanted all males for herself and no one else.

For some reason the librarian dallied at the telephone, and I kept reading the booklet forward and backward. I don't remember the librarian's returning or my leaving for the car that was supposed to be waiting for me. In all those years I had been convinced that Machla Krumbein and her work, if they ever really existed, had been burned in Treblinka, Majdanek, in one of the ghettos or concentration camps. But one last copy had been left for me to read and appreciate before total oblivion. Or perhaps some friendly demon, imp, or hobgoblin had restored it magically and brought it to me on this special visit from a mountain of ashes.

Translated by the author and Lester Goran

The Divorce

Many divorce cases were handled in my father's court. The court was nothing more than our living room, where my father kept his religious books and the ark for the Torah scrolls. As the rabbi's son, I never missed an opportunity to listen in on the petitioners who came for a divorce. Why should a man and a wife, often parents of children, suddenly decide to become strangers? I seldom got a satisfactory answer.

My father never began a divorce proceeding until he had attempted with all his power to make peace between the couple. He always asked the assistance of my mother, his rebbetzin. The couple often spoke to her first and then to my father. In almost every case, my father quoted the saying of the Talmud that when a man divorces his first wife even the altar of the Temple sheds tears. When I was a boy, the Holy Temple and the altar had been destroyed for about two thousand years. Just the same, in our apartment, at 10 Krochmalna Street, the Holy Temple, the altar, the priests, and sacrifices were more actual than the news in the daily Yiddish newspaper. Once, when my father spoke about the altar shedding tears, the woman who came to get a divorce cried out, "My dear Rabbi, if the altar knew how much I suffered from this tyrant it would cry day and night."

This time, the couple who came to us were not from our street but from Twarda Street. They had a store in a bazaar called Ulrich's Yard. Neither of them appeared to be over thirty. The husband wore a long gaberdine, a small cap, and an open-collared shirt with no tie. From behind his vest his fringed garment hung out. He was quite tall, with a long nose, a yellowish little beard, and barely any sidelocks. His eyes, too, appeared to me yellow. I could see that he was a decent man but not exactly a Hasid or a scholar. He said that he owned a store that sold dry-goods remnants—a bargain store. His wife seemed to be somewhat enlightened—she wore no wig, but she covered her head with a kerchief, so as not to offend the rabbi. Her shoes had high heels, and her skirt reached only to the middle of her calves and was held up at the waist by a black patent-leather belt with a brass buckle. She had large gray eyes, an angular nose, and a wide mouth. She seemed to me girlish, proud, and resentful at having to come to a rabbi's court with her private troubles.

When my father asked why they came to him, the young man said to his wife, "Since you summoned me to the rabbi, not I you, you answer first."

"Rabbi, we came to be divorced," the woman said in a clear and sure voice.

As a rule, my father avoided looking at a female, especially if she was married, to keep from falling into sinful thoughts. But now he glanced for an instant her way. With his left hand he grasped his red beard, and with his right hand he touched a large handkerchief that lay on the table. The touching of this handkerchief by the petitioners would symbolize a silent consent to my father's decree.

"Divorce?" he asked. "How long have you been married?"

"Over five years," the husband answered. "A week after Hanukkah it will be exactly six years."

"Divorce is not a small matter," my father said. "It is not to be taken lightly. The Talmud says that when a man divorces his first wife even the altar sheds tears for them."

"Rabbi, I know all this, but we can't live together," the woman said in a decisive tone.

"Do you have children?" my father asked.

"Three beautiful little girls," the husband cried out. "The oldest one is not yet four years old."

"For what reason do you want a divorce?" my father asked.

For a long while husband and wife kept silent. Then the woman cleared her throat, as if she were about to swallow the words she was going to utter: "Rabbi, he's a fool."

My father raised the brows over his blue eyes. He did not seem less astonished by this answer than I was. After a while he said, "King Solomon, the wisest of all men, deals in his Proverbs with wisdom and foolishness. According to him, only a sinner is a fool. Nothing can be more foolish than to spite God and his commandments. In the first chapter there is the saying 'The fear of the Lord is the beginning of knowledge: but fools despise wisdom.' As you see, the wicked are the fools. But your husband does not look wicked to me, God forbid."

The young man's yellowish eyes became full of laughter. "Rabbi, *she* is wicked."

"Don't say this," my father reproached him. "Anger, too, is silliness. The same King Solomon says in Ecclesiastes, 'For anger resteth in the bosom of fools.'"

"Rabbi, there are also good-natured fools," the woman said.

"No, goodness is the very essence of wisdom," my father answered.

My father quoted a few other passages from the Bible as well as from the Talmud. The young man must have been encouraged by all this indirect praise, because he said, "Rabbi, she only waits for an opportunity to call me names. The moment I open my mouth to say something she is already scolding me. She shames me before the customers. If I say it's day, she immediately says it's night. How can one dwell with a sharp-tongued person like her? She makes my life miserable. She has tortured me for so long that our being together is nothing but Gehenna."

"Did you say that you have three children?" my father asked.

"Yes, Rabbi," the husband answered. "One more beautiful than the other and all of them as sweet as sugar. Just from looking at them one's spirit is uplifted. But when a woman calls her husband ugly names and insults him in front of the children they, too, begin to lose respect. What does a child know? If their beloved mother says that Daddy is a shmegegge, they repeat it."

"This is wrong," my father said. "The Gemara says that a righteous wife cherishes her husband. In the 'Woman of Valor,' which all Jews recite on the eve of Sabbath, it is said, 'She doeth him good and not evil all the days of her life . . . She openeth her mouth with wisdom and on her tongue is the law of kindness.'"

"Rabbi, you listen only to what he has to say," the woman complained. "Why don't you listen to me?"

"I will listen to you, too," my father assured her. "It is my duty to hear both sides. Please, let me hear yours."

"Rabbi, he's a simpleton and a ne'er-do-well. He has as

much sense in his head as I have in my left shoe. When you have a store you must be able to recognize who comes to buy and who comes just to browse and examine things and make a mess. There are many such customers. They go from store to store because they have nothing else to do. When I look at one of them I know immediately that she has no intention to buy and I get rid of her quickly, but this pinhead will strike up a long conversation. When a real customer comes and has to wait and listen to their silly chatter, she loses patience and leaves. We worked out a code. I would rearrange the comb in my hair when this annoying kind of person entered, and this would serve as a sign for him not to bother with her. But somehow he never notices anything. There is a saying that women have nine measures of talk, but he has eighteen measures. A woman tells him what sort of matzoh balls she cooked on Passover three years ago, and he talks to her a whole hour about his Aunt Yachna's noodle pudding. When it comes the first of the month and I have to pay the rent, I have to borrow money from a usurer at high interest. Is this true or not?"

While the woman spoke her husband gazed at her lovingly. He even smiled at me, the rabbi's boy. I could see that he was amused by her ridicule. Even her insults seemed to please him. She is right—he is a big fool, I thought.

"Young man, I forgot to ask your name," my father asked.

"My name is Shmuel Mayer, but everybody calls me Shmelke," the man said. "Actually, I have three names— Shmuel, Mayer, and Alter. The third name I was given when I was two years old and sick with scarlet fever and—"

I had never seen my father interrupt anybody in the middle of a sentence, but this time he didn't let him finish. "Reb Shmelke, what do you have to say to your wife's complaints?"

"What is there to say? She has a polished tongue. Rabbi, she can always convince anybody that she is right. I am a simple man, not a mind reader. How can I know whether the woman comes to buy or just to browse? It is not written on anybody's forehead. At home I was taught that when a person speaks you listen. And when I am busy with someone I can't see what my wife is doing with her comb. Once, her code was that she would begin to cough. But how do you know whether she's coughing as a signal or whether she's really coughing? When the winter comes, with its snow and frost, everybody is coughing. Immediately after the Succoth holiday we get throat lozenges for our children, but they cough anyhow. The truth is that my wife—Salka is her name—was born with a bad temper. Her mother, may she rest in peace, told me that as a baby she was always crying. Some unexplained wrath burns in her. She must take it out on someone. We have three wonderful little daughters but she screams at them all the time, and when they do something that displeases her she beats them and pinches them. To beat a little child you must have the heart of a highway robber."

The door opened and my mother put in her pale face. "Young lady, be so good as to come to me in the kitchen," she said.

"The rebbetzin wants me?" Salka asked.

"Yes, you. I hope you don't mind."

"Yes, Rebbetzin. Just wait one moment. I know quite well, Rabbi, that when I leave he will say terrible things about me. But I really don't care anymore. I have to free myself from him somehow. I would rather rot in my grave than live with this blockhead." And the woman left for the kitchen.

I had a great desire to go and listen to the conversation in the kitchen, but I was afraid my mother would yell at me. Both my father and my mother had warned me not to listen in when petitioners came to our house. My father may have forgotten his warning, but my mother had a good memory.

I remained in my father's courtroom, and Shmelke said, "Rabbi, she is clever, beautiful, and charming. But she is a bitter piece. She is always frustrated, because of our struggle to make a living. A few steps from us there is another store like ours, and it teems with customers. The owners are drowning in money. The truth is that Salka's anger drives away the customers. In our business those who come to buy do a lot of haggling. No matter how cheap a price we ask, the customer always tries to bargain us down to a half. Who comes to buy remnants and secondhand material? Only those who like to get something for nothing. My competitor has a shrewd wife. She always wears a sweet smile and knows her business inside out. If I tell my wife to act friendlier to the customers she attacks me violently. Her eyes are as sharp as knives. Sometimes I think that the Angel made a mistake. She should have been born a man. One way or another, things go badly."

"Peace brings success," my father said. "If you two could live more peacefully, then . . ."

I wasn't eager to hear what could happen if the couple lived in peace, and made my way into the kitchen. I stood in a corner, hoping my mother would not notice me in the dim light of the little kerosene lamp. I had left a storybook there on a stool, and pretended to be reading as I cocked my ears. I was interested in people's talk—their expressions, their excuses for wrong deeds, and how they twisted things to suit themselves. I heard the woman say, "Rebbetzin, he is a fool, and there is no remedy for that from the apothecary. It is written somewhere that when the Messiah comes all the sick will be cured but the fools will remain fools. Why is this so, my good lady?"

"It is very simple," my mother replied. "The sick know that they are sick and they pray to God to be healed. But since a fool thinks that he is clever he never prays for help, and therefore he is doomed to remain what he is."

"Golden words. It is really as my grandmother used to say: 'Where there is Torah there is knowledge.' The moment he opens his eyes in the morning, even before he recites 'I Thank Thee,' he begins to pour out nonsense. I say to him, 'What is your rush? The day is only beginning. You will have plenty of time to make an ass of yourself.' He loves to tell me his dreams. I dream, too, but when I open my eyes it all evaporates. He remembers his dreams from beginning to end. His dreams are as silly as he is. He wakes up and says, 'I dreamed that I swallowed a saltshaker.' Only an idiot can have a dream like this. I hope I won't be punished for my words, but even his boots seem silly to me."

"His boots?" my mother asked.

"Yes, his boots. Isn't that strange? Once I looked at his feet and I thought, A foolish pair of boots. Forgive me, Rebbetzin, I now talk like a fool myself. But when you live six years with a fool it rubs off on you. On a clever man everything looks clever, even his clothing. Even when a smart man tries to be silly, somehow it all comes out smart. With a fool the very opposite is true."

"Salkele, forgive me," my mother said, "but such hatred for a man is not good, either for the soul or for the body. God forbid, you may get sick from that. It can affect your livelihood."

"You are right, Rebbetzin, a thousand times right. I don't hate him. He didn't do me any evil. I know it's not his fault, but when he starts to talk and to praise me I feel nauseated. I am ashamed to visit people with him. You know very well that a woman likes to look up to her husband, and if she looks down on him she cannot submit to him."

I decided to return to the men, eager to see Shmelke's foolish boots. He was now sitting at the table, which obscured his feet. I heard him say, "Rabbi, I am giving her everything—the apartment, the store, the merchandise. How will she be able to manage a store with three little children? But this is what she wanted. I will earn my piece of bread. I will contribute for the children as much as I am able. She wants me to come to see the children only on the Sabbath. I know beforehand that I will miss them terribly."

"Reb Shmelke, I don't know if the law is clear to you, but once you are divorced you are not allowed to stay together under one roof."

"Why not?"

"This is the law. Man and wife are accustomed to one another and the temptation is great. They may fall into sin. If she remarries, the sin would be even greater."

"Rabbi, how can I ever see the children? Every house has a roof. And in the winter one cannot take the children outside."

"Someone must be present when you come to see them. It is human nature that a man is more ashamed before other people than before God."

I put my hand into the pocket of my gaberdine and began to play with the groschen I had received as pocket money in the morning before going to cheder. I took it out, and accidentally it fell from my hand and rolled under the table. I crawled under the table and saw Shmelke's boots. In the bright light of our hanging lamp I saw that they were muddy, unusually large and clumsy, made of coarse leather, with low, broad uppers and worn-out heels. I imagined that they smelled of horse dung. Yes, these are really foolish boots, I thought.

My father bent down and asked, "Did you lose something?"

"It is my groschen. I found it already." I could barely restrain myself from laughing.

When I got up, Shmelke asked, "Where did you get the groschen? Did you find it in the street?"

"My mother gave it to me."

"What can you get for a groschen nowadays? Wait, I will give you a kopeck."

"Reb Shmelke, don't give him any money," my father said. "It is a big-city custom to give children money every day. We in Tomaszów never heard of it. When Jethro counseled his son-in-law Moses in the desert, he told him to provide from among the people men of truth, such that fear God and hate covetousness. Those who love money can be bribed easily. Many transgressions stem from the greed for money."

"Rabbi, you should have told this to my Salka. Sometimes I think that she would kill herself for a groschen. As I told you, we have a competitor and he is successful. Since it is a matter of luck, what is the sense of being envious? But she eats her heart out when she sees how well he is doing. She curses him and his wife with deadly curses. She comes home every evening sick. Rabbi, permit me to give a kopeck to the boy. This one coin will not make him covetous."

"Really, he doesn't need it."

Shmelke got up and searched long in his pockets, but he couldn't find a kopeck. Instead he took out a button, a piece of string, and a huge key—probably to the door of his store. "My Salka takes everything away from me," he said. "She cleans out my pockets. Forgive me, boy. There will be another chance."

"It doesn't matter. Thank you," I said, and I ran back to the kitchen.

I heard my mother say, "You cannot rely on maids and nannies. They are strangers. Whatever they do is for money. They don't have a mother's devotion. Every moment something can happen to a child, God forbid. It can fall, bang its head on a chair, climb up on a windowsill, get burned on the stove. There is not a day when I don't read of terrible things that happen to children when they are left to themselves."

"Rebbetzin, and what do grownups do to themselves? When I told my mother—she should intercede for us—that I was going to marry Shmelke, she said to me, 'My daughter, you are chopping off your own head.'"

The divorce took place in our home exactly four weeks later. I was there when the scribe wrote out the divorce paper with his quill and two witnesses signed their names. My father read the Shmelke out of a large volume, saying, "Listen, thou, Shmuel Mayer Alter, the son of Eliezer Moshe. Did someone force thee to give this divorce to thy wife, Sarah Salka? Say no."

"No."

"Art thou willing to give this divorce to her in thy name, in her name, and according to the divorce laws? Say yes."

"Yes."

When it came time for Shmelke to put the divorce paper into Salka's cupped hands he broke down, crying in a hoarse voice. My father said to Salka, "You are not allowed to remarry before ninety days."

And Salka said, "Of course I am about to run to the wedding canopy immediately. Who would take me except the Angel of Death?" And she, too, burst out crying. She ran to the door with her head in her hands and my mother ran after her. Salka had left her pocketbook and the divorce paper on the table. I got a lump in my throat, and for the first time I understood why the altar sheds tears when a man divorces his first wife.

I never saw either Shmelke or Salka after the divorce. But a woman neighbor of ours who knew the couple told my mother the events that followed. Shmelke had given his store to Salka, but weeks passed without anyone's buying anything. Salka was forced to sell out her stock for less than nothing and close shop. Shmelke remarried. His new wife was an old maid, and they opened another store. Just as everything Salka did failed, everything the newlyweds did succeeded. His store was always so packed with people one couldn't put a pin between them. His new wife did not consider Shmelke a fool. In comparison to her, he was a sage, our neighbor said. She was far from a beauty—small as a midget and broad as a cholent pot —but she was as good as a bright sunny day. She savored Shmelke's every word and kissed the ground he walked on. "I wish a life like hers to every decent Jewish daughter," our neighbor said.

"What about the children?" my mother asked. "Does he go to see them?"

"He sees them three times a week, perhaps every other day."

"This is not the right conduct," my mother said after some hesitation.

"Rebbetzin, he loves them more than his own life. He would kill himself for their sake."

"Why doesn't Salka remarry?" my mother asked.

"She's looking for a clever one, but why should a clever man take a shrew like her, and three children to boot?" the neighbor said. "But don't worry. Shmelke provides for them and for her nicely. He keeps bringing her gifts. I never see him in the street without packages and bundles. How does the saying go? 'A good cow lets herself be milked.'"

"Does Salka have a maid?" my mother asked. "Is there anyone present when he visits?"

"As far as I know, she has no maid. Since she has no store to attend to, she stays home and takes care of the little ones."

"It's not the right conduct," my mother repeated. "Human beings are not strong in their faith nowadays, and the Evil One is only too eager to put them to temptations."

The neighbor bit her lips and shrugged. "True, but maids are expensive, and one cannot trust them. How does the saying go? 'Everyone kindles his own fire in Gehenna.'"

The woman winked, sighed, nodded, and left our kitchen. She kissed the mezuzah twice.

Translated by the author

Strong as Death Is Love

M Y Aunt Yentl and her cronies were talking about love, and Aunt Yentl was saying, "There is such a thing as love. There is. It even existed in former times. People think that it's new. It is not true. Love is even mentioned in the Bible. Laban gave his daughter Leah to Jacob, but Jacob loved Rachel. Imagine, a saint like this. Still, he was flesh and blood. One glance at a person and you see his or her charm. The only difference is that in olden times once you liked someone you got married. Nowadays, couples get engaged but still look for others.

"Not far from Turbin there was a squire and they called him the crazy squire. Actually, all the nobles were somewhat pixilated. They lived in so much luxury that they didn't know whether they were coming or going. This squire, Jan Chwalski, was completely befuddled. He didn't speak, he screamed. He kept warning his serfs that he would whip them to death but he never laid a finger on anybody. When a peasant became sick, he sent in a doctor or at least a healer to cure him. He had a court Jew named Betzalel whom he often threatened to hang and shoot. Still, on Purim he sent him a Purim gift. When Betzalel married off his daughter, the squire sent her a wedding present. He came to the wedding and danced a Cossack dance with the Jews and made himself so ridiculous that the people almost choked from laughter. Chwalski never married because he was in love with a noblewoman who had a husband. Her name was Aliza and she was not really such a beauty as he imagined. Not bad, gentle and slender. Gentiles, as a rule, are blond but she was a brunette with black eyes and with a most charming smile. Her husband, Count Lipski, was the biggest drunkard in the whole of Poland. No one had ever seen him sober. He drank away his entire fortune. He knew that Chwalski was in love with his wife, but these things did not bother him. It was said that he used to wake up in the middle of the night and drink vodka from a pitcher through a straw. If this Aliza had been a loose woman, she could have committed the worst sins. But she was a dignified lady. She used to plead with

Chwalski not to chase after her since she was married, but Chwalski loved her too much to comply. He wrote daily love letters to her and sent them by messenger. Maybe once a year he received a reply. It always said the same thing: 'I have a husband.' On Sunday Chwalski used to go to church just to be able to gaze at her. When both of them were invited to the same ball, Aliza accepted only one dance with him. It seemed she liked him, too, but she did not want to betray her husband. The priest often beseeched Chwalski to leave Aliza in peace. But Chwalski said, 'From all the women in the whole world there is only one Aliza. All week long I live with one hope, to see her on Sunday.'

"Count Lipski, her husband, was a tall fat man with a perpetually red face and broken veins covering his nose. He drank until he burned out his lungs. The doctors forbade him to drink but he drank to the last day. A doctor in our town said, 'If a man drank as much water as Count Lipski drank spirits, he would become mortally sick.' Chwalski, on the other hand, never got drunk. He was drunk from Aliza.

"Count Lipski had the eyes of a madman. He never knew what was going on with his estate. Everything was handled by a manager who stole as much as he could, and the rest was lost through bad management. As to Aliza, she kept to herself and did not interfere with business matters. She liked to read books and to take long walks through the orchards. She never had any children. Who knows, Count Lipski might have been too drunk for anything. In his last months, he could no longer walk. The liquor had gone to his legs. He had also developed diabetes, since vodka contains a lot of sugar. One way or another he died without last rites, without confession, without a will. I was told that after his death his body blew up and became like a barrel. Almost no one from the gentry came to the funeral because he had insulted all his neighbors and blasphemed God and all the Christian saints. The hearse passed by our windows. I was still a young girl and I watched the procession. It is the custom among the Gentiles that two men lead the widow. Aliza had a brother somewhere whom I saw for the first time, and the other man was Jan Chwalski. Just as Count Lipski was tall and broad, so was Jan Chwalski small and lean, with a long yellowish mustache which reached to his chin. Aliza was dressed in black. Chwalski held on to her arm as if in fear she might run away. Love is a kind of madness.

"Lipski died, he was buried. Everyone thought that the widow would immediately marry Chwalski, but she insisted that he wait a year for the period of mourning. When Chwalski found out that he would have to wait, he raised heaven and earth. Hadn't he waited long enough? But Aliza contended that she would never marry him before a year passed. Lipski did not leave a will, and a gang of would-be heirs emerged. They came, God knows from where, and took everything away from Aliza. On the other hand, there was not much to take. Whoever could, grabbed a piece. This is how people are. They imagine that they themselves will live forever. When Chwalski heard what was going on, he took a gun and came running, ready to kill all of them. But Aliza said to him, 'You don't interfere.' And her word was holy to him. There are such people who will silently allow others to rob them. Perhaps it was gentleness or perhaps foolishness. It was known that she came from very high nobility and with some of them money has no meaning. Their main passion is their honor. One way or another, she remained with nothing. All they left her was the empty walls. Lipski had had a court Jew by the name of Yankel. But how can a Jew fight off Gentiles? He came to her and said, 'Your Excellency, they take away everything from you.' And she answered, 'They cannot take more than I possess.' She had suffered all these years with Count Lipski, but no one ever heard her complain. Some people are wolves, others are sheep. But ultimately no one takes anything with them. They brought her a document and she signed it without blinking an eye.

"Not a month had passed and a marshal of the court came with some officials and they told Aliza to move out. Neither the house nor the furniture belonged to her anymore. Again Chwalski came running, ready to defend her: a little man and yet hot-blooded. If Aliza had asked him to jump into a fire for her sake he wouldn't have hesitated for a moment. But Aliza told him to leave matters alone. He wanted to bring her to his estate but she refused to go with him as long as they were not married. To make it short, she found some wealthy peasant—a village elder. He had a little hut beside his house where he kept flax and other objects and he cleared them away for her to live in. Her husband's relatives had left her a single bed and her books. That was all she needed. She had managed to hide some of her personal jewelry, which Yankel had later sold for her, and on this she supported herself for the year. On Sabbath afternoons the tailors' and shoemakers' apprentices and the seamstresses took a walk to the village to peer into her window and see what the haughty countess was doing. She didn't even leave herself a maid. On Sunday the elder took her in his britska to church. Chwalski again and again tried to persuade her to move to his estate but she did not let herself be per-suaded. A pure soul, you should forgive the comparison, al-most a rebbetzin.

"A year passed and she became a squiress again. All the no-bility of the neighborhood came to the wedding. It is not the custom that a bride, even if she is a widow, should be dressed in mourning when she remarries. But Aliza insisted that she dress in black for the wedding. They showered her with flow-ers and gifts. The priest gave a sermon. One has never heard of peasants attending a noble wedding on their own volition. But peasants came from many villages. Since she lived in a peas-ant's hut, they considered her one on their own. She came to the wedding in the elder's britska. But from the church to Chwalski's estate she rode in a carriage drawn by eight horses and peasants dressed like dragoons rode in front. They had erected a gate hung with plants and flowers at the entrance of Chwalski's estate. A Jewish and Gentile band played a 'good night' melody for the couple. Chwalski was not especially rich, but he guarded his possessions and nobody could steal from him. It seemed that Aliza's bad luck had begun to shine. But wait a minute, I need a drink."

I brought Aunt Yentl a pitcher of water, and she murmured a blessing and drank. "Don't laugh at me," she said. "I feel like crying." And she blew her nose into her batiste handker-chief. Then she continued.

"Shortly after the wedding, Jan Chwalski gave the type of ball which was considered rare even for a king. It was a few weeks after Passover and the weather was balmy. Aliza was against it. She was quiet, proud, and no longer young. But Chwalski wanted to announce his joy to the world. He invited

hundreds of nobles, who came from faraway cities. Carriages
rolled in early in the morning and the ball lasted all day. The
stores in Turbin profited. There was a band from Zamość and
another from Lublin. For years people spoke about the ball:
the food, the wine, the dances, the music. Reb Betzalel revealed later that Chwalski was forced to sell a portion of his
forest for less than nothing to pay for all this. Of course Jews
and peasants were not invited. But many young people stood
outside and listened in, and even danced. The servants treated
them to wine and food. The next day the nobles went hunting
and killed God knows how many animals. When they left, the
estate was in shambles. Aliza had pleaded with Chwalski not to
squander his fortune, but he was insane from happiness.

"My dear people, all this good fortune lasted not longer
than a year. Suddenly one heard that Aliza was sick. What the
illness was I don't know even today. But Aliza slowly began to
waste away. Chwalski again sold a part of his estate and sent for
the biggest doctors, but no one could help her. Our own
healer, Lippe, was called in, and he heard one of the doctors
say that her blood turned to water. God forbid, when the time
comes, the Angel of Death will find a way. The sickness lingered for months, and although everyone had given up on
her, Chwalski kept bringing new doctors, professors, various
quacks. He even went to the rabbi and offered him money for
charity to light candles for Aliza's sake in the synagogue.
Nothing availed. Aliza was dying. The priest came and she
made her confession. He poured holy water on her and soon
Aliza was no more. Reb Betzalel told us that she passed away
like a saint. Who knows? There are good souls even among
them. It is written in a holy book that good Gentiles go to
Paradise.

"The way Chwalski cried and moaned and howled cannot
be described. But dead is dead. They took her to the church
and there her body stayed until the funeral. Chwalski had
bought plots for her and for himself. He grew pale and emaciated, as if he had consumption. His clothes hung on him. His
mustache became white. He walked and spoke to himself like a
madman.

"But if one has years, one lives. He tried to poison himself,
but someone forced two fingers into his mouth so that he

should vomit. Whatever was left from his fortune was lost, although Reb Betzalel tried to save as much as possible. A year or two passed and Chwalski still lived. He had a portrait of Aliza and he stared at it day and night. He spent more time at the cemetery than at home. Every day he laid flowers on her grave. He ordered a headstone with the figure of an angel carved to resemble her. He kissed the stone and spoke to it. He no longer concerned himself with business matters. Reb Betzalel had practically taken over. A number of years passed. There is a saying that what the earth covers must be forgotten. But Chwalski could not forget. The priest reproached him, saying that it is forbidden to mourn too long. Chwalski was visited by other squires and relatives who tried to cheer him up, but he could not be comforted. He also took to drink. There was no lack of beautiful women in the neighborhood, but he wouldn't even look at another female.

"Now listen to this. After Aliza was buried, Chwalski locked the bedroom and no one was allowed to enter, even the chambermaid. He also kept her boudoir locked. Every stitch of clothing—even things she simply touched—became sacred to him. He himself slept in her nanny's bedroom. The cook prepared food for him but he barely touched a thing. He became even smaller than he had been and his mustache appeared even longer. In time he dismissed all his servants. And only the nanny remained, an old woman, deaf and half blind.

"That winter was one of the coldest. The seeds in the fields froze. So much snow fell that many houses became snowed under and the people had to dig themselves out. In the midst of this cold spell, Chwalski did not miss a day at the cemetery. One day Chwalski took a spade to the cemetery, most probably to shovel the snow away from the grave and the headstone. It was strange to see a squire carrying a spade over his shoulder, but people had become accustomed to his idiosyncrasies. He often spent all day at the cemetery and sometimes late into the night. Gradually, it became warmer and the snow melted. The water flowed over the village like a river.

"One time after Passover the cemetery watchman came to the police and reported that the earth around Aliza's grave had been tampered with. There were thieves at that time who stole corpses from graves and sold them to doctors who used the bodies to perform autopsies. But those vandals only stole fresh corpses. Who would perform an autopsy on a corpse which is already decayed? In Turbin people said that Aliza rose up from the grave and roamed the city at night. When such talk begins, witnesses immediately emerge: this one saw her, that one heard her. She was standing on the bridge, she was washing linen by the river, she was knocking at someone's shutter. The rumors reached Chwalski and he only shouted, 'Idiots, I refuse to listen to such superstition.'

"*Nu*, but when an entire town talks it is not baseless. The Russian authorities ordered a few soldiers to dig under the headstone and to open the coffin.

"When Chwalski heard this, he became wild with anger, but he seemed to have forgotten that Poland was no longer independent. The Russian soldiers pushed him back, dragged out the coffin, unscrewed the lid, and the casket was found to be empty. Half the town came running together to look at the black wonder. Somebody had stolen Aliza out from the grave. You could never imagine the things that went on every day in Turbin. They ran to tell Chwalski the news, but he hollered like a madman. Reb Betzalel was still alive, but he was no longer a court Jew. For a few days the whole town was boiling like a kettle. Jews were afraid that false accusations would be brought against them. There were already those who barked that the Jews used her blood for matzohs.

"In the middle of all this a new commotion broke out in the town. It happened like this. The old woman who served the squire was cooking grits for him and lit a fire. Her hands were shaky and a piece of burning kindling-wood fell. It soon became a blaze. The old woman began to scream and peasants came to see what was going on. The firemen came running with their half-empty water barrels. Someone burst open Aliza's locked bedroom door. It gives me the creeps to talk about this. The squire lay in bed snoring—it seemed he was drunk—and next to him lay a skeleton. Yes, Chwalski himself had stolen Aliza from the grave. He yearned for her so, that one winter night he dug her up, pried open the coffin, took out her remains, and carried them home. The night was a dark one and nobody saw. He admitted to everything when the police officials took him in for a hearing. She was already decayed, he said, and he peeled off the flesh, leaving only the bones. The Russians did not believe their own ears. 'How is it possible that a person can do such a wild thing?' they asked. And he answered, 'I just could not bear the longing. Better bones than nothing. If you want to hang me, hang me, but bury me near her.'

"Nobody among the Russians knew what sort of punishment to give for such a crime. They wrote a report out to the gubernoton in Lublin. In Lublin they didn't know what to do, either, and inquired in Warsaw and from there to Petersburg. Meanwhile, they allowed Chwalski to remain free. The skeleton they buried again. Chwalski lived only one year more. He had become like a skeleton himself. They buried him with all honors right near his Aliza.

"What I mean to say is: a person gets some idea in his head and it begins to grow and take over the brain. It becomes an obsession. You can even call it a dybbuk. Both he and she were people with souls. If there is a Paradise for Gentiles, I am sure they will rest there together forever. How is it written in the Holy Book: 'Strong as death is love, cruel as the grave is jealousy.' Well, the Sabbath is over. I see three stars in the sky. A good new week to all of us."

Translated by the author

Why Heisherik Was Born

IN my first years at the Warsaw Yiddish Writers' Club, I be came known as an editor of manuscripts. Working as a proofreader for the *Literarishe Bleter*, I had published a few stories and reviews and had edited a book or two for the Kletzkin Publishing Company. They paid pennies, but I could live on pennies. I was a boarder in a private apartment where the rent was cheap, and I had no need for clothes; year in and year out, my clothes lasted. I had still not found my way as a writer, and I spent most of my time with beginners like myself.

One day, at the Writers' Club, the hostess told me that someone was asking for me. I went to the door and saw a little man with a black beard, dressed in shabby clothes and patched boots. He looked to me like a street peddler. He carried a large package tied with much-knotted string. He said this bundle was his manuscript; he had written a book. Someone had told him that I could edit Yiddish writing.

I had to persuade the hostess to let the man in. Strangers were forbidden entrance. After some hesitation, she allowed him to join me for fifteen minutes. I sat with him, and he slowly untied the knots on his package. His manuscript contained at least a thousand scrawled sheets. I could see immediately that he could neither spell nor punctuate.

He told me that he had served in the Polish Army in 1919 and 1920, in the time of the Polish-Bolshevist war. He marched with the army as far as Kiev, and then he ran back from Kiev to the Vistula, chased by the Red Army. The Reds had been about to take the whole of Poland, but at the famous battle of the Vistula, Pilsudski's army managed to stop the Bolshevist attack. The man told me that he was a pious Jew, that in all those battles he had never missed a prayer or eaten anything that wasn't kosher. Whenever his division came into a town where Jews lived, he went to the synagogue or the study-house to pray in a minyan. He also attended the ritual bath for men, even though the water was always cold.

The Christian soldiers mocked him, called him names, and played mischievous tricks on him. His decision to eat only kosher food bordered on the impossible. Sometimes he had to fast for days or live on only a dry slice of bread. He was running and starving. He had to eat with the other soldiers, and the smell of their soups and meats made him almost insane. Some of the soldiers tried to push a piece of pork into his mouth. They laid him out spread-eagled and tried to pry open his jaws to thrust strips of bacon into his mouth; but he struggled with all his might, and after a while, they let him go. A miracle happened to him. There was a Catholic priest in his company who defended him. Not one miracle but a thousand happened to him. Bullets flew over his head; near him people lost hands and legs, their lives as well, but somehow he remained alive.

"I describe it all in this volume," he said. "I want Jews to read this and to know there is a God in heaven. I went to some newspapers and publishers, and they all told me I'm in need of an editor. My spelling seems to be not quite right. I have great difficulties with the Hebrew words. I have studied in the cheder the Pentateuch with Rashi, even the beginning of Gemara, but my father—he should intercede for me—died of typhoid fever, and my mother could not pay the tuition. She became sick with consumption, and I had to peddle merchandise behind the city markets to provide for my brothers and sisters. Every day was a struggle to bring home a few groschen. From this alone, one could write a thick book. Already then the miracles began to happen to me. Later, when I became a soldier and lay in the trenches where the Angel of Death appeared constantly, I vowed that if I had the merit to survive this slaughter, I would describe all of it in a book so that people should know that Providence keeps score of all human beings each minute and each second. I kept a little book of Psalms in my bosom pocket, and by the light of the bursting shrapnel I used to recite a passage or two in the trench."

I said, "You didn't write your name on the manuscript. What's your name?"

"Heisherik. Moishe Groinam Heisherik. The Gentiles, the bigoted ones, made fun of my name, but a name is a name."

"How do you make a living?" I asked.

"I buy up tripe—entrails, liver, kidneys—in the slaughterhouses as well as in the kosher butcher shops, and I sell it to soup kitchens. This is hard work but, thank God, I have a wife with seven children, and they need to eat. In the day I have no time; but at dawn I wake up and I write. How much will you charge me to go over my manuscript?"

I knew quite well that I would have to rewrite the entire book. Not only couldn't he spell, but he had no notion of sentence structure. After three words, he put a period, an exclamation point, or dashes. For no reason, he put quotation marks around words. Some of his smearings and smudges I could never hope to decipher. The truth is, I should not have squandered my time on such works if I wanted to become a writer myself, but for some reason, I was overcome with compassion for this shlemiel who had suffered so much and had remained faithful to his Jewishness.

I offered him a rate that was cheaper than cheap, but he winced and began to bargain and haggle with me. He called the pittance that I had asked for a fortune. He began to scold me and to scream.

"You sit here in this luxurious salon without a hat, without sidelocks, your beard shaved, and you try to rob a poor writer. Where shall I get so much money? Every groschen I make comes out of the marrow of my bones. I would have to take away the last bit of food from my children to pay you such sums. God punishes for exploitation. Who do you think I am—Rothschild? I live in a single cellar room with my whole family. Every month, when I pay rent, it is a miracle, like the parting of the Red Sea."

The man's voice became louder and shriller. A few young writers stopped to listen and to mock. I became so embarrassed that I said, "In that case, I will correct your manuscript with no payment at all."

"I don't ask you to do it for nothing. I'm not a schnorrer, God forbid. When this memoir is completed, all the newspapers will compete to publish it, and I'll pay you for your efforts—but you must give me a deadline on when you'll finish it. I cannot leave the manuscript without completing arrangements. I don't have a copy. If you lose some of it, God forbid, it will be a catastrophe. You must guard it like the apple of your eye."

For a while, we remained silent. I could see that besides his piety, Heisherik had a lot of chutzpah. I knew quite well that no matter how good a job I did, no paper would publish it. The Polish-Bolshevist war was already remote. I could see from thumbing through the manuscript that there was no tension to attract a simple reader, nor were there descriptions to please a more sophisticated one. I wanted to return his manuscript immediately and tell him to find some other victim but, again, I was swept away by pity. If this creature who had suffered so much for his Jewishness could wake up at dawn and work on his manuscript for hours, why shouldn't I give him some of the time that I spent with gossipers and jokers at the Writers' Club?

I said to him, "All right, I will do what I can; but I can't give you any guarantees in the event of a fire or some other disaster. According to the Talmud, a person who undertakes to take care of someone's property without reward is not obliged to be responsible in case of theft or loss."

"What? Since it was ordained in heaven that I should write it, God will not allow any evil to happen to it—"

He was about to say more, but the doorkeeper came over and said, "Mister, your fifteen minutes are over. You must leave now."

"What is this, a police station?" Heisherik asked. "I'm a Jew and a writer, and I will not be driven out of here. I have some business with this young man."

"You have to leave right now," the woman insisted.

Heisherik argued for a while. I was in the presence of something I would term religious arrogance. The Talmud has a saying about it: "Insolence helps even in heaven." How else could this little man withstand the hunger, the cold, the mischief that the other soldiers had inflicted on him? I had taken upon myself to do a virtuous deed, and I was resolved to do it as well as I could.

Many weeks passed, but Heisherik never showed up. From time to time I tried to do some editing on the manuscript. I often had to laugh at his writing. This Jew who knew little of Jewish lore was convinced that submerging in the ritual bath on Friday was no less important than the Ten Commandments. He had often risked his life to perform some ritual that a talmudic scholar would have ignored altogether. Heisherik had actually broken the talmudic law by endangering his life for such minor rituals. He had been beaten by the corporals and the sergeants. He had been put into a military prison. He could easily have been court-martialed and shot for insubordination. While the nations had waged war with one another for their worldly ambitions, Heisherik had waged war against man's intolerance. When it came to his numerous battle descriptions, he used an identical cliché: "Blood was flowing like water." Like many of the other soldiers, Heisherik had had no idea of where he was marching and what he was fighting for. Both the Poles and their enemies, the Bolsheviks, were to him the same Gentiles whose goal it was to restrain a Jewish soldier from attending religious services on time. I edited some fifty pages, but Heisherik never appeared. He had not left me his address.

One day, when I was sitting in the lounge hall of the Writers' Club with a few young writers, discussing literature—who had talent and who did not—a young member of the club came over, his face full of laughter, and said, "Isaac, your girl friend is looking for you."

"My girl friend?"

"Yes, your girl friend—a great beauty she is. Piff-paff!"

I went to the entrance hall, and an ugly, shabby woman stood at the door. She was wrapped in a tattered shawl and wore scruffy men's shoes. In each hand she held a basket covered with rags. She said, "I'm Heisherik's wife."

When she spoke, I saw that she hadn't a tooth in her mouth.

"Yes?" I said. "What can I do for you?"

The woman immediately burst out crying, and her wrinkled face became abominably distorted.

She screeched, "My husband deserted me and left me an abandoned woman without a crumb of bread for my seven swallows. Father in heaven, what shall I do? The little ones are hungry. Woe, what happened to me! Such a misfortune, such a calamity, such an ordeal. What shall I do and where shall I go? Merciful God!"

The woman wailed and wiped her tears with her sleeves. She

put down both baskets and pinched her cheeks. The hall was full of writers, young and old, and they all came over. Some gaped; others laughed. I asked the woman, "Where did he go? How can a pious Jew do something like this?"

The woman said, "To the Holy Land."

"To the Holy Land? Do they let Jews in? You have to show a thousand pounds sterling. You also need a foreign passport and a visa," I said.

"What do I know? For weeks, he went around telling everyone he had to go to the Land of Israel. I said to him, 'Murderer, what will happen to me and your children?' But he remained stubborn. A dead saint came to him in a dream and ordered him to go there. I'm only a female and I'm not versed in books. He's a writer, a great man, and I can barely read from the prayer book; but I need to eat and my children are without bread. How can a saint tell a man to desert his wife and children? How can a writer be such a cruel beast?"

The woman howled and clapped her hands as if she were at a funeral.

I said, "I'm sorry, but what do you expect me to do?"

"You work with him—you took his money. He took away the last food from me and his infants and gave it to you."

"My dear woman, he hasn't given me a single groschen."

"He gave you, he gave you. He stuffed you with money and left us naked and starving. God Almighty, you see everything. You wait long and your punishment is severe. Give us back the money that you grabbed from him. This was not money but sweat and blood. People, have pity on us. Don't let my kittens die from hunger."

And she beat her head with both her fists.

The older writers frowned. The younger ones laughed. I said to the woman, "I swear by God and by everything holy to me that I haven't taken from your husband a single groschen."

"You took, you took. People like you overeat and let a mother with her children expire from hunger. The landlord threatens me that he will throw us and our belongings out into the gutter. We owe him three months' rent. A fire should consume him, his fever should jump as high as a roof, and then he will taste my bitterness."

The hostess took the woman by the elbow and tried to

push her out, but she would not go. Someone said, "Call the police."

"The police, huh? You call yourselves writers; bandits you are, not writers," Mrs. Heisherik howled.

I put my hand into my pocket and found a bank note there. It was ten zlotys. I gave it to the woman and said, "That's all I have; take it and never come again. I've taken nothing from your husband, and there's no reason for you to create scandals."

The woman snatched the bank note and lifted both her baskets. She uttered a long roster of curses and left, slamming the door. One should not do favors for anyone, the Evil One advised me. From now on, if anyone asks a favor of me, I will tell him to go to hell, I thought. I was hungry and had no money to eat supper that night.

The older writers shrugged their shoulders and went back to their tables, but the younger ones joshed me. One of them said, "Confess, you made her pregnant. We know, we know."

Another one said, "If she sues you, you'll have to pay alimony, like they do in America."

On the way home, I swore to myself that I would cast Heisherik's manuscript into the garbage. But somehow I could not bring myself to do it. I decided to wait until he arrived and give it back to him. However, for weeks his wife came to me at the Writers' Club—always on the same day, at the same time—and I had to hand her a ten-zloty note through the aperture in the front door. Each time she screamed that I had become rich from her husband's payments. My colleagues, the younger writers, never missed a performance.

A few months passed, and I began to believe that Heisherik's wife would remain deserted forever and I would continue to pay her "alimony" for the rest of my life. But one day Heisherik returned. I could barely recognize him. He looked sunburned and as swarthy as a gypsy. His clothes were in tatters. A part of his beard had become dirty gray. I asked him how he, a religious Jew, could have left a wife and children without any support, and he said, "I had to do it. A great yearning drew me to the Land of Israel, so great that if I didn't do it I would die. The Patriarchs—Abraham, Isaac, Jacob—and Mother Rachel came to me in my dreams. What

I went through could not be written in a thousand books. As a matter of fact, I began to add new sections to the manuscript you hold."

I told him that I would not do any further work on his manuscript, and he said, "When the editors of our newspapers read the new chapters, it will cause a tremendous sensation, and you'll be richly rewarded for all your efforts."

He sat with me for more than an hour and told me all the details of his adventurous wanderings. He had walked hundreds of miles on foot. He begged alms. He found a way to smuggle himself into the Holy Land. He slept in fields and deserts, sometimes in city gutters. He walked the length and the width of the Holy Land barefoot. He prostrated himself on all the holy graves, slept in ruins and caves. Snakes bit him. He was attacked by Bedouins and jackals. But the pleasure of breathing the sacred air healed his wounds. Sometimes weeks passed and all that he had to nurture him was water and prickly plants of the scorched earth.

I knew that he was not lying. I was especially impressed by his story of how he had burned the soles of his feet by walking on the hot sand. It had burned him like blazing coals, and he had had to tear off his shirt and wrap his blistered feet. He did all that to reach the grave of a saint whose name I had never heard. I was so touched by the man's love for the Holy Land that I promised to continue editing his book.

As far as I can remember, I never finished that work. Heisherik began to send fragments to the Yiddish newspapers, and two or three were published in some provincial magazines. The Warsaw editors scolded me for troubling them with this illiterate maniac's ravings, and I had to swear to them that I would never again burden them with such scribblings. Needless to say, I have never received a penny for my efforts.

I could finish this story here, but life added an important chapter to the Heisherik story, and I cannot avoid reciting it.

As we know, from September 1939 until the end of World War II, many families in Nazi-occupied Poland were broken up. Many men managed to escape the part of Poland that Hitler had invaded and found sanctuary in the Soviet-occupied territory. Since there was no postal service between those two regions, an illegal messenger service developed. Those messengers were called holy messengers. They not only risked their lives but also were subjected to the most savage torture when they were caught. More of them—or, perhaps, all of them—were motivated by a desire to hold the split families together, since no money in the world could have compensated them for their terrible hazard. Eventually most of them perished.

After the war, I learned that Heisherik had been one of those messengers, and he had been the most diligent of them all. He had finally been caught smuggling letters on the road from Bialystok to Warsaw and had been tortured to death. While Heisherik bothered me with his woebegone tales about the war of 1920 and, later, with his roaming, I often wondered, Why was Heisherik born? But it seems that martyrs, like soldiers, have to be trained for the mission that fate has in store for them. He could never have become a holy messenger without having gone through all the ordeals he had described in his pathetic book and had recited to me at such length. I believe that there must be, somewhere in the universe, an archive in which all human sufferings and acts of self-sacrifice are stored. There could be no divine justice if Heisherik's story did not grace God's infinite library for time eternal.

Translated by the author and Lester Goran

The Enemy

URING the Second World War a number of Yiddish writers and journalists managed to reach the United States via Cuba, Morocco, and even Shanghai—all of them refugees from Poland. I did not always follow the news about their arrival in the New York Yiddish press, so I really never knew who among my colleagues had remained alive and who had perished. One evening when I sat in the Public Library on Fifth Avenue and Forty-second Street reading *The Phantasms of the Living* by Gurney, Mayers, and Podmor, someone nudged my elbow. A little man with a high forehead and graying black hair looked at me through horn-rimmed glasses, his eyes slanted like those of a Chinese. He smiled, showing long yellow teeth. He had drawn cheeks, a short nose, a long upper lip. He wore a crumpled shirt and a tie that dangled from his collar like a ribbon. His smile expressed the sly satisfaction of a once close friend who is aware that he has not been recognized—obviously, he enjoyed my confusion. In fact, I remembered the face but could not connect it with any name. Perhaps I had become numb from the hours spent in that chair reading case histories of telepathy, clairvoyance, and the survival of the dead.

"You have forgotten me, eh?" he said. "You should be ashamed of yourself. Chaikin."

The moment he mentioned his name I remembered everything. He was a feuilletonist on a Yiddish newspaper in Warsaw. We had been friends. We had even called each other "thou," though he was twenty years older than I. "So you are alive," I said.

"If this is being alive. Have I really gotten so old?"

"You are the same shlemiel."

"Not exactly the same. You thought I was dead, didn't you? It wouldn't have taken much. Let's go out and have a glass of coffee. What are you reading? You already know English?"

"Enough to read."

"What is this thick book about?"

I told him.

"So you're still interested in this hocus-pocus?"

I got up. We walked out together, passing the Catalogue Room, and took the elevator down to the exit on Forty-second Street. There we entered a cafeteria. I wanted to buy Chaikin dinner but he assured me that he had already eaten. All he asked for was a glass of black coffee. "I hate granulated sugar," he said. "Do you think you could find me a lump of sugar I can chew on?"

It was not easy for me to make the girl behind the counter pour coffee into a glass and give me a lump of sugar for a greenhorn who missed the old ways. But I did not want Chaikin to attack America. I already had my first papers and I was about to become a citizen. I brought him his glass of black coffee and an egg cookie like the ones they used to bake in Warsaw. With fingers yellowed from tobacco Chaikin broke off a piece and tasted it. "Too sweet."

He lit a cigarette and then another, all the time talking, and it was not long before the ashtray on our table was filled with butts and ashes. He was saying, "I guess you know I was living in Rio de Janeiro the last few years. I always used to read your stories in *The Forward*. To be frank, until recently I thought of your preoccupation with superstition and miracles as an eccentricity—or perhaps a literary mannerism. But then something happened to me which I haven't been able to cope with."

"Have you seen a ghost?"

"You might say that."

"Well, what are you waiting for? There's nothing I like better than to hear such things, especially from a skeptic like you."

"Really, I'm embarrassed to talk about it. I'm willing to admit that somewhere there may be a God who mismanages this miserable world, but I never believed in your kind of hodge-podge. However, sometimes you come up against an event for which there is absolutely no rational explanation. What happened to me was pure madness. Either I was out of my mind during those days or they were one long hallucination. And yet I'm not altogether crazy. You probably know I was in

France when the war broke out. When the Vichy government was established I had a chance to escape to Casablanca. From there I went to Brazil. In Rio they have a little Yiddish newspaper, and they made me the editor. By the way, I used to reprint all your stuff. Rio is beautiful but what can you do there? I drank their bitter coffee and I scribbled my articles. The women there are another story—it must be the climate. Their demand for love is dangerous for an old bachelor. When I had a chance to leave for New York I grabbed it. I don't have to tell you that getting the visa was not easy. I sailed on an Argentine ship that took twelve days to reach New York.

"Whenever I sail on a ship I go through a crisis. I lose my way on ships and in hotels. I can never find my room. Naturally I traveled tourist class, and I shared a cabin with a Greek fellow and two Italians. That Greek was a wild man, forever mumbling to himself. I don't understand Greek, but I am sure he was cursing. Perhaps he had left a young wife and was jealous. At night when the lights were out his eyes shone like a wolf's. The two Italians seemed to be twins—both short, fat, round like barrels. They talked to each other all day long and half through the night. Every few minutes they burst out laughing. Italian is almost as foreign to me as Greek, and I tried to make myself understood in broken French. I might just as well have spoken to the wall—they ignored me completely. The sea always irritates my bladder. Ten times a night I had to urinate, and climbing down the ladder from my berth was an ordeal.

"I was afraid that in the dining room they'd make me sit with other people whose language I didn't understand. But they gave me a small table by myself near the entrance. At first I was happy. I thought I'd be able to eat in peace. But at the very beginning I took one look at my waiter and knew he was my enemy. For hating, no reason is necessary. As a rule Argentines are not especially big, but this guy was very tall, with broad shoulders, a real giant. He had the eyes of a murderer. The first time he came to my table he gave me such a mean look it made me shudder. His face contorted and his eyes bulged. I tried to speak to him in French and then German, but he only shook his head. I made a sign asking for the menu and he let me wait for it half an hour. Whatever I asked for, he laughed in my face and brought me something else. He threw down the dishes with a bang. In short, this waiter declared war on me. He was so spiteful it made me sick.

"Three times a day I was in his power, and each time he found new ways to harass me. He tried to serve me pork chops, although I always sent them back. At first I thought the man was a Nazi and wanted to hurt me because I was a Jew. But no. At a neighboring table sat a Jewish family. The woman even wore a Star of David brooch, and still he served them correctly and even chatted with them. I went to the main steward to ask for a different table, but either he did not understand me or he pretended he didn't. There were a number of Jews on the ship and I could have easily made acquaintances, but I had fallen into such a mood that I could not speak to anyone. When I finally did make an effort to approach someone, he walked away. By that time I really began to suspect that evil powers were at work against me. I could not sleep nights. Each time I dozed off I woke up with a start. My dreams were horrible, as if someone had put a curse on me. The ship had a small library, which included a number of books in French and German. They were locked in a glass case. When I asked the librarian for a book she frowned and turned away.

"I said to myself, 'Millions of Jews are being outraged and tortured in concentration camps. Why should I have it better?' For once I tried to be a Christian and answer hatred with love. It didn't help. I ordered potatoes and the waiter brought me a bowl of cold spaghetti with cheese that smelled to high heaven. I said '*Gracias,*' but that son of a dog did not answer. He looked at me with mockery and scorn. A man's eyes—even his mouth or teeth—sometimes reveal more than any language. I wasn't as much concerned about the wrongs done to me as I was consumed by curiosity. If what was happening to me was not merely a product of my imagination, I'd have to reappraise all values—return to superstitions of the most primitive ages of man. The coffee is ice cold."

"You let it get cold."

"Well, forget it."

2

Chaikin stamped out the last cigarette of his package. "If you remember, I always smoked a lot. Since that voyage I've been a chain smoker. But let me go on with the story. This trip lasted twelve days and each day was worse than the one before. I almost stopped eating altogether. At first I skipped breakfast. Then I decided that one meal a day was enough, so I came up only for supper. Every day was Yom Kippur. If only I could have found a place to be by myself. But tourist class was packed. Italian women sat all day long singing songs. In the lounge, men played cards, dominoes, and checkers, and drank huge mugs of beer. When we passed the equator it became like Gehenna. In the middle of the night I would go up to the deck and the heat would hit my face like the draft from a furnace. I had the feeling that a comet was about to collide with the earth and the ocean to boil over. The sunsets on the equator are unbelievably beautiful and frightening, too. Night falls suddenly. One moment it is day, the next is darkness. The moon is as large as the sun and as red as blood. Did you ever travel in those latitudes? I would stretch out on deck and doze just to avoid the two Italians and the Greek. One thing I had learned: to take with me from the table whatever I could: a piece of cheese, a roll, a banana. When my enemy discovered that I took food to the cabin, he fell into a rage. Once when I had taken an orange he tore it out of my hand. I was afraid he would beat me up. I really feared that he might poison me and I stopped eating cooked things altogether.

"Two days before the ship was due to land in New York, the captain's dinner took place. They decorated the dining room with paper chains, lanterns, and such frippery. When I entered the dining room that evening I barely recognized it. The passengers were dressed in fancy evening dresses, tuxedos, what have you. On the tables there were paper hats and turbans in gold and silver, trumpets, and all the tinsel made for such occasions. The menu cards, with ribbons and tassels, were larger than usual. On my table my enemy had put a fool's cap.

"I sat down, and since the table was small and I was in no mood for such nonsense, I shoved the hat on the floor. That evening I was kept waiting longer than ever. They served soups, fish, meats, compotes, and cakes, and I sat before an empty plate. The smells made my mouth water. After a good hour the waiter, in a great hurry, stuck the menu card into my hand in such a way that it cut the skin between my thumb and index finger. Then he saw the fool's cap on the floor. He picked it up and pushed it over my head so violently it knocked my glasses off. I refused to look ridiculous just to please that scoundrel, and I removed the cap. When he saw that, he screamed in Spanish and threatened me with his fist. He did not take my order at all but just brought me dry bread and a pitcher of sour wine. I was so starved that I ate the bread and drank the wine. South Americans take the captain's dinner very seriously. Every few minutes there would be the pop of a champagne bottle. The band was playing furiously. Fat old couples were dancing. Today the whole thing does not seem so great a tragedy, but then I would have given a year of my life to know why this vicious character was persecuting me. I hoped someone would see how miserably I was being treated, but no one around me seemed to care. It appeared to me that my immediate neighbors—even the Jews—were laughing at me. You know how the brain works in such situations.

"Since there was nothing more for me to eat, I returned to my cabin. Neither the Greek nor the Italians were there. I climbed the ladder to my berth and lay down with my clothes on. Outside, the sea was raging, and from the hall above I could hear music, shouts, and laughter. They were having a grand time.

"I was so tired I fell into a heavy sleep. I don't remember ever having slept so deeply. My head sank straight through the pillow. My legs became numb. Perhaps this is the way one dies. Then I awoke with a start. I felt a stabbing pain in my bladder. I had to urinate. My prostate gland is enlarged and who knows what else. My cabin mates had not returned. There was vomit all over the corridors. I attended to my needs and decided to go up on deck for some air. The planks on the deck were clean and wet, as if freshly scrubbed. The sky was overcast, the waves were high, and the ship was pitching violently. I couldn't have stayed there long, it was too cold. Still, I was determined to get a breath of fresh air and I made an effort to walk around.

"And then came the event I still can't believe really happened. I'd reached the railing at the stern of the ship and turned around. But I was not alone, as I thought. There was my waiter. I trembled. Had he been lurking in the dark waiting for me? Although I knew it was my man, he seemed to be emerging out of the mist. He was coming toward me. I tried to run away, but a jerk of the ship threw me right into his hands. I can't describe to you what I felt at that instant. When I was still a yeshiva boy I once heard a cat catch a mouse in the night. It's almost forty years away but the shriek of that mouse still follows me. The despair of everything alive cried out through that mouse. I had fallen into the paws of my enemy and I comprehended his hatred no more than the mouse comprehended that of the cat. I don't need to tell you I'm not much of a hero. Even as a youngster I avoided fights. To raise a hand against anybody was never in my nature. I expected him to lift me up and throw me into the ocean. Nevertheless, I found myself fighting back. He pushed me and I pushed him. As we grappled I began to wonder if this could possibly be my arch foe of the dining room. That one could have killed me with a blow. The one I struggled with was not the giant I feared. His arms felt like soft rubber, gelatin, down—I don't know how else to express it. He pushed almost without strength and I was actually able to shove him back. No sound came from him. Why I didn't scream for help, I don't know myself. No one could have heard me anyhow, because the ocean roared and thundered. We struggled silently and stubbornly, and the ship kept tossing from one side to the other. I slipped but somehow caught my balance. I don't know how long the duel lasted. Five minutes, ten, or perhaps longer. One thing I remember: I did not despair. I had to fight and I fought without fear. Later it occurred to me that this would be the way two bucks would fight for a doe. Nature dictates to them and they comply. But as the fighting went on I became exhausted. My shirt was drenched. Sparks flew before my eyes. Not sparks—flecks of sun. I was completely absorbed, body and soul, and there was no room for any other sensation. Suddenly I found myself near the railing. I caught the fiend or whatever he was and threw him overboard. He appeared unusually light—sponge or foam. In my panic I did not see what happened to him.

"After that, my legs buckled and I fell onto the deck. I lay there until the gray of dawn. That I did not catch pneumonia is itself a miracle. I was never really asleep, but neither was I awake. At dawn it began to rain and the rain must have revived me. I crawled back to my cabin. The Greek and the Italians were snoring like oxen. I climbed up the ladder and fell on my bed, utterly worn out. When I awoke the cabin was empty. It was one o'clock in the afternoon."

"You struggled with an astral body," I said.

"What? I knew you would say something like that. You have a name for everything. But wait, I haven't finished the story."

"What else?"

"I was still terribly weak when I got up. I went to the dining room anxious to convince myself that the whole thing had been nothing but a nightmare. What else could it have been? I could no more have lifted that bulk of a waiter than you could lift this whole cafeteria. So I dragged myself to my table and sat down. It was lunchtime. In less than a minute a waiter came over to me—not my mortal adversary but another one, short, trim, friendly. He handed me the menu and asked politely what I wanted. In my broken French and then in German I tried to find out where the other waiter was. But he seemed not to understand; anyway, he replied in Spanish. I tried sign language, but it was useless. Then I pointed to some items on the menu and he immediately brought me what I asked for. It was my first decent meal on that ship. He was my waiter from then on until we docked in New York. The other one never showed up—as if I really had thrown him into the ocean. That's the whole story."

"A bizarre story."

"What is the sense of all this? Why would he hate me so? And what is an astral body?"

I tried to explain to Chaikin what I had learned about these phenomena in the books of the occult. There is a body within our body: it has the forms and the limbs of our material body but it is of a spiritual substance, a kind of transition between the corporeal and the ghostly—an ethereal being with powers that are above the physical and physiological laws as we know them. Chaikin looked at me through his horn-rimmed glasses sharply, reproachfully, with a hint of a smile.

"There is no such thing as an astral body. I had drunk too much wine on an empty stomach. It was all a play of my fantasy."

"Then why didn't he show up again in the dining room?" I asked.

Chaikin lifted one of the cigarette stubs and began looking for his matches. "Sometimes waiters change stations. What won't sick nerves conjure up! Besides, I think I saw him a few weeks later in New York. I went into a tavern to make a telephone call and there he was, sitting at the bar—unless this, too, was a phantom."

We were silent for a long while. Then Chaikin said, "What he had against me, I'll never know."

Translated by Friedl Wyler and Herbert Lottman

Remnants

NEARLY all the members of the Yiddish Writers' Club in Warsaw, where I went in the twenties, considered themselves atheists. Free love was an accepted way of life. The younger generation was convinced that the institution of marriage was obsolete and hypocritical. Many of them had become Marxists and proclaimed something they called "Jewish worldliness."

A different kind of writer altogether was Mottele Blendower, a little man, a descendant of famous Hasidic rabbis. He had a dark, narrow face, a pointed beard, and large black eyes that expressed the gentle humility of generations. He was the author of a book about Hasidic life in Poland. One of Mottele's grandfathers had separated from his followers in his later years and had become a sort of divine recluse. After his death, his disciples destroyed his writings, because they hinted at blasphemy. Although Mottele had done away with his long gaberdine and his rabbinical hat and had cut off his sidelocks, he spoke like a rabbi, used their solemn style of language, took on their exaggerated politeness, always on the watch, God forbid, not to insult anybody. Mottele attempted to combine Yiddishist modernism with the lore of the cabala. He undertook to translate into modern Yiddish such mystical works as the Zohar, *The Book of Creation*, *The Tree of Life*, and *The Orchard of Pomegranates*. In his essays, he preached that love and sex are attributes of the godhead and that the proper use of them can be a means to penetrate the illusion of the categories of pure reason and to grasp the thing in itself and the absolute.

Some time after I met him, Mottele had fallen in love with a woman named Zina, who was known for her beauty. She was blond, tall, and the daughter of a rich Warsaw family. One year, she was elected the Queen Esther of the Yiddish literary masked ball. She had married and divorced a rich young man, a lawyer. From her parents she had inherited a large sum of money, which evaporated with inflation. Zina was a distant relative of Mottele's. They had a big, noisy wedding.

Those who knew the bride and the groom foresaw that the

match wouldn't last long. Mottele was gentle and weak, while Zina was robust. Her first husband, the lawyer, said openly that his ex-wife was a nymphomaniac. There were rumors in the Writers' Club that she had invited all her former lovers to the wedding. An intimate friend had learned that Zina confessed all her sins to Mottele, but he contended that he was not jealous about the past and that he would give her full freedom in the future. Mottele was supposed to have told her, "The roots of both of our souls are in the *sephira* of splendor, and in those spheres, sins are virtues."

One of Zina's lovers, whom she was supposed to have cared for most, was the writer Benjamin Rashkes. She told Mottele that she could never forget Rashkes. When he was forced to move from his bachelor's furnished room because he had impregnated the maid in his boardinghouse, Zina offered him a study in her new, spacious apartment. She put in a sofa, a writing table, and even a Yiddish typewriter imported from America so that Rashkes could work there whenever the Muse granted him inspiration. The trouble was that he was less and less inspired to write. He poured all his energies into so many would-be love affairs that he had no time for anything else.

There was constant talk in the Writers' Club about the triangle of Mottele, Zina, and Rashkes. Even though Rashkes promised Zina to avoid the Writers' Club and do his work, he came to the club every day and spent all the time on the telephone. Closing the door of the phone booth, he went on whispering his unending love declarations. Rashkes maintained that monogamy had destroyed eroticism. Men and women are not jealous by nature; the only thing they dislike is to be deceived. Also, they prefer the truth to come to them in small portions and as a part of the love play. Rashkes was telling his colleagues that many men enjoy sharing their wives with the right kind of lovers and that his ideas were based on his personal experience. The husbands of his paramours were all his friends and admirers, he said. They often reproached him for neglecting their wives. Rashkes claimed that he kept peace between his lovers and their husbands.

A year did not pass before the gossips in the Writers' Club had a new sensation to talk about. Zina had become seriously enamored of a known Communist leader, Leon Poznik. The

Trotsky purges had been in progress in Russia for some time, but Poznik remained an ardent Stalinist. He was the editor of two Communist magazines, one in Polish and one in Yiddish. The *Defensywa*, the Polish political police, had arrested Poznik a number of times, but they always released him. They were not interested in keeping the leftist leaders in prison too long. Poland was officially a democracy. One could not jail people on the basis of their convictions. Besides, the leaders of the *Defensywa* did not want to root out Communism in Poland and put themselves out of jobs. As for Poznik, he needed those short imprisonments to add to his prestige in the party and in the Soviet Union. He boasted about his courage during the interrogations, describing how well he lectured to the Polish Fascists about Leninism. However, the comrades called him, jokingly, the "Polish Lunacharsky"—a Communist of talk, not of deeds.

Poznik was broad-shouldered, small, and wore shoes with elevated soles and heels. His eyes, behind the horn-rimmed glasses with their thick lenses, seemed to sparkle with a light of their own. I often imagined that all the victories of world Communism shone through those glasses.

That Zina should fall in love with Poznik seemed unbelievable. He had a wife, a Communist functionary who had been sentenced to five years in prison. He bragged about his affair with an important woman in Moscow, where he was invited every few months. Besides, Zina had never shown any interest in politics. She had been at one time a disciple of the celebrated medium Kluski, who specialized in materializing spirits of the dead. It was her fascination with the occult that initially attracted her to Mottele. But who can fathom the ways of love? It became known in the Writers' Club that Zina now took part in all of Warsaw's leftist activities. The leftists published interviews with her in their magazines. She put on a leather jacket, the kind worn by the functionaries of the *Cheka*, the Soviet political prisoners. Zina had revealed to someone that the *Defensywa* had summoned her for an interrogation and that she had been kept overnight in the arrest house on Danilowiczowska Street where suspects were held. There was a saying in the Writers' Club that Communism was like influenza: everybody had to go through it sooner or later.

In the spring of 1927, Poznik and Zina left for Russia. They disappeared suddenly, without any notice to anybody in the club. I was told that not even their comrades were informed. Neither Poznik nor Zina could have acquired a foreign passport. Those who were invited to the Soviet Union had to smuggle their way across the border at the town of Nieswiez. For a long time, one heard nothing in the Writers' Club about Poznik or Zina. Then the rumor spread that Leon Poznik had been arrested in the U.S.S.R. and put into the infamous Lubyanka prison. Rashkes had received a single Yiddish postcard from Zina with an altered name—he recognized only the handwriting. She used the conspiratorial code language: "Uncle Leon is mortally sick and they put him into the Lubya hospital. The doctors give scanty hopes." She signed the card "Your despairing Aunt Charatah," which is the Hebrew word for regret. Later, it came out that in Kharkov a Yiddish magazine had published an attack on an anthology Poznik had edited two years earlier. The writer of the article, a Comrade Dameshek, had discovered in Poznik's introduction to the book traces of Trotskyism.

Not long after Poznik and Zina left, the news spread in the Writers' Club that Mottele Blendower had become a penitent —not of the modern type that compromises Jewishness with worldliness, but one who returned to extreme orthodoxy. He grew his beard and his sidelocks, exchanged his modern clothes for a long robe, and one could see his fringed garment hanging down from behind his vest. He published a letter in the Orthodox daily condemning all his former writings as heresy and poison for the soul. He forbade all the Yiddish dramatic circles to use his play and sent back his membership card to the Writers' Club. The owner of a Yiddish bookstore made it known that Mottele had bought from him all the copies of his book, spat on them, and threw them into the garbage. Rashkes had gone to Mottele's apartment to get back some of his manuscripts, but Mottele told him that he had thrown them into the stove. Mottele's marriage to Zina was annuled, and he was allowed to remarry after collecting the signatures of one hundred rabbis. It was published in the Yiddish Orthodox newspaper that Reb Mottele had married a pious Jewish daughter, a descendant of renowned rabbis, and had become the head of a yeshiva. The curious in the Writers' Club found out that his new wife was an eighteen-year-old girl who, according to the Hasidic law and custom, had shaved her head the day after the wedding and had put on a bonnet, like a rebbetzin. Mottele had changed his telephone number so that heretics and mockers could not contact him. Once, when I met him in the street, I greeted him, but he turned his head away. It was hard for me to believe that only a year ago Mottele had spoken with me about Kant, Nietzsche, Kierkegaard, and Ouspensky. Previously he had been inclined toward Zionism. Now he called the Zionists betrayers of the Jews.

One winter evening, perhaps two years later, I received a telephone call at the furnished room I rented. I could not recognize the woman's voice until she told me that she was Zina. I had never been one of her friends—I used to greet her in the Writers' Club, but we seldom spoke. Now she spoke to me as if I were an old friend. She told me that she had made her way back to Poland illegally. While in Russia, she had learned that Mottele had remarried. Here in Warsaw, she had tried to call Rashkes, but it seemed he had moved out of the room where he boarded lately. She had asked for his address in the Writers' Club but no one knew it. She expected me to know Rashke's whereabouts, but I couldn't help her. Zina's voice had changed. It sounded hoarse and old. She asked me if I could meet her in the street, at the corner of Solna and Leszno. I told her that I was afraid to be seen with her, because I might be arrested.

Zina assured me that the Polish authorities knew that she had escaped from Russia and there was no danger for me to be seen with her. She said, "My dear, I'm not the same Zina. My own mother wouldn't recognize me if she were alive. I lost everything in the Red Gehenna—my beauty, my faith in the human race. A living corpse is speaking to you."

I let myself be persuaded and went out to meet her. A mixture of snow and rain had fallen. An icy wind was blowing. At the corner of Leszno and Solna I saw Zina. I would never have known it was she. She looked emaciated and aged. Her hair had turned dark and was disheveled and stringy. She had on a gray padded jacket—the kind market vendors wore. She extended her moist hand and said, "I'm hungry and half frozen. I haven't slept for three nights. When we went to Russia, I left all my clothes in the apartment I had with Mottele. I tried to recover them, but his wife slammed the door in my face. The little money I had, I spent on telephone calls, but none of my former friends seems to be home. Where is Rashkes? Where is he hiding? They all run from me like from a leper. You won't believe it—the receptionist at the club didn't let me in. Well, I deserve it all."

Zina spoke and coughed. She spat into something that looked like a dirty napkin. She said, "My lungs are sick. I suffer from consumption or God knows what."

"What did they have against Poznik in Russia?" I asked. "He subscribed to all their lies."

"What do they have against anybody? They swallow one another like wild animals. Have pity on me and take me somewhere where it is warm."

After some hesitation, I took her to a café at 36 Leszno. The waitress frowned when she saw Zina. I ordered tomato soup for her and a glass of tea for myself. Zina had abandoned all manners. She dunked the bread in the tomato soup. She spoke loudly, and the patrons around us winced. She tilted the bowl, drank the last of the soup, and said, "I don't recognize Warsaw. I don't even recognize myself. What I went through from the day they arrested Poznik until now cannot be described. I literally lived in the streets. I hoped they would imprison me just to have a roof over my head. But when a luckless person wants something, the very opposite happens. I told them in clear words, 'You are murderers, not socialists, worse than Fascists. Your Stalin is a criminal.' They just laughed. They were even unwilling to commit me to an insane asylum. When I crossed the border on the way back to Poland, they let me go without asking for documents . . ."

Zina began to cough again. She took out the dirty napkin and blew her nose. "Don't gape at me," she said. "It's me— Zina, the ball queen of the Yiddish Writers' Club, the crowned Queen Esther. Woe to me!"

She smiled, and for a second, her face looked young and beautiful once more.

■

Years passed. I had left Warsaw and gone to the United States. The Hitler war broke out, and then the atomic bomb came, and afterward the peace. Between 1945 and 1950, we found out, more or less, who remained alive in Europe. I had heard that Poznik had died in prison in Moscow even before the war began. Others said that he had been sent to dig for gold in the north and that he died there from starvation. As far as I knew, both Mottele and Zina had perished in Poland.

In the fall of 1954, I made my first trip to Israel. There I got more details about those who had vanished in the ghettos, in the concentration camps, or in Russia. I heard gruesome facts about my own family. One day, in my Tel Aviv hotel, I was trying to read a book by the dim light that filtered through the shutters of the window. I had closed them for protection against the thin desert sand that would be carried in by the hot khamsin wind.

Someone knocked at my door. I had already become accustomed to unannounced visitors, since the telephone was seldom functioning. I opened the door and saw a little man with a white beard, dressed in a rabbinical hat, and beside him a tall woman in a wig covered with a shawl, her face golden from the khamsin sand. I looked at the couple and thought they must be a pair of schnorrers out to collect alms for some cause. I noticed that the woman carried a box in one hand and an umbrella in the other. She looked me over from head to toe and said, "Yes, it's him!"

"May I know with whom I have the honor?" I asked.

"Little honor," she answered. "My name is Zina, and this is my husband, Mottele Blendower. Don't be afraid; we didn't come from the grave to strangle you."

I should have been shocked, but since I had undertaken this journey, I had become used to the most astonishing encounters. The little man said, "A surprise, heh? Yes, we are alive. I know that I was counted among the dead. They even published my obituary here, but I'm still in this world. Zina and I met in Lublin in 1948. My other wife and my children were killed in the ghetto, and what happened to me is a story of a thousand and one nights. We came here to the Jewish state only two months ago."

"Come in. Come in. This is really a startling event," I mumbled. Zina immediately crossed the threshold, and after some hesitation, Mottele followed.

He asked, "Why do you sit in the dark? Because of the khamsin? I have experienced all kinds of storm winds, but a hot, sandy wind like this I see for the first time. The winds in Russia are always cold, even in the summer."

"Everything there is cold," Zina said. "In 1939, when the war began and the Polish radio announced that all men should cross the Praga bridge to Bialystok, I went with them—first to Bialystok and later to Vilna, which belonged to Russia. I was sure that the Communists would know my record and send me to Siberia or to the wall of the firing squad; but somehow no one paid any attention to me. What I endured in the Red paradise for the second time is not something to talk about now. I survived the siege of Leningrad and later found myself in the Caucasus Mountains, among Persian Jews. They had been there for the past two thousand years and spoke a mixture of Parsee, Hebrew, and Russian. In 1945, all the refugees attempted to return to Poland or reach the DP camps in Germany, but I said to myself, 'Since Poland is nothing more than one big cemetery, what is the rush?' But I became deadly sick with asthma. When I finally reached Warsaw, I walked among the ruins like that prophet—what was his name?—Jeremiah. I saw a young man there digging up the earth with a spade. I asked him what he was trying to find and he told me, 'Myself.' He was not exactly mad, but queer. Later, I met some of our former Communists who used to visit the Writers' Club. They had lost everything but their chutzpah. From there, I made my way to Lublin. One day, as I walked on Lewertow Street, I saw this helpless creature, my former husband. He had also managed to stay alive; isn't that funny?"

"Why are you standing?" I asked. "Sit down, both of you. I don't have any refreshments . . ."

"What? We didn't come for refreshments," Mottele said. "We came to see you. You don't look much older. We followed your work, even in Russia. In Poland, I found a book of yours. As you can see, my beard is all white. You must be wondering how we can be together again after what happened between us. The answer is that the signatures of a hundred rabbis cannot really annul the spirit of a marriage. Anyhow, our reencounter was an act of Providence. There is a lot in the Zohar about naked souls, and we two are naked souls."

"Why do you stare so at my wig?" Zina asked me. "This was Mottele's condition, that I should put on a wig and behave like a pious matron. I told him openly that I don't believe in anything anymore. But since this was his will, I gave in. What is a wig? Just some hair from a corpse. The truth is that I'm almost left without hair. I got typhoid fever while in Leningrad and became bald. I read somewhere that hair grows even on the heads of the dead in their graves. But my hair won't grow. This means that I'm worse than dead."

"Zina, don't exaggerate," Mottele said.

"What? I don't need to exaggerate. The truth is weird enough."

"Where do you two live?" I asked.

Mottele grabbed his beard. "Promise me that you won't laugh at me and I will tell you."

"I will not laugh."

"They made me a rabbi," he said.

"Nothing to laugh at. You are a son and a grandson of rabbis."

"Yes, yes, yes. We came here without a penny. The Joint Distribution Committee paid our expenses. Someone announced in the newspapers that I was alive. There are quite a number of my father's Hasidim here, and they all came to me —from Tel Aviv, from Jerusalem, from Safad, even from Haifa, though Haifa is known as a town of radicals. They began to call me rabbi immediately. 'What sort of a rabbi am I?' I said to them. 'And what about Zina?' But they answered me, 'You are a child from our school. You are the image of your saintly father.' I will make it short: I became a rabbi and she a rebbetzin right here in Tel Aviv."

"In my eyes, you are more of a rabbi than all the others," I said.

"Thank you. Jews come to me on the Sabbath, we eat at the table, and I recite Torah. What is there left to preach to them? Nothing but silence. They rented an apartment for us and they provide for us. What could I do here? I lost my strength. They offered me compensation money from Germany, but this money to me is an abomination."

For a while we were silent. Outside, the wind howled, cried, laughed, like a bevy of jackals. Zina said, "Don't be amazed that I wear makeup. I know that it does not suit a rebbetzin. But I suffer from eczema. A man can let his beard grow and cover his cheeks. Everything shows on a woman. In a wind like this, my face swells up."

We were silent again for a long while. Then Zina said, "Guess what I have in this box."

"Zinele, he's a writer," Mottele said, "not a mind reader. Tell him what is there."

"Rashkes's unfinished novel," Zina said.

"Yes, I understand."

"No, you don't. That day in September when the Warsaw radio ordered all men to run to Russia, I went over to Rashkes and tried to persuade him that we should go together. But he refused. He was as pale as death. The first day of Rosh Hashanah, he lay down on the bed and never wanted to get up again. From all his admirers, only one woman remained faithful to him—Molly Spitz, a bad writer, a psychopath."

"I knew Molly Spitz," I said. "She used to come to the Writers' Club."

"Yes, she."

"I didn't know she was Rashkes's lover," I said.

"Who wasn't his lover?" Zina asked. "He ran after all women between fifteen and eighty. When the war broke out, they all forgot him—but Molly Spitz, that monkey, remained with him. The truth is that a Nazi bomb had exploded in the house where she lived and she was homeless. I had finished with him once and for all; still, I tried to save him. I pleaded with him, but he said, 'Zinele, go wherever you want. I have lived my life and this is the end.' He told me to open a drawer, and there I found what I am carrying now. He said to me, 'Take it if you insist. The Nazis don't need my writings. Neither do the Reds. They can use these pages for cigarette paper.' These were his last words."

"You carried it for all these years?" I asked.

"Wherever I went—to Bialystok, to Vilna, to Leningrad.

This is not just a novel. This is the story of our great love. I tried to get it published in Vilna, but they had all become flatterers of Stalin. The mountain Jews in the Caucasus didn't know Yiddish. Here is his novel. I dragged it with me over all the frontiers, all the ruins. I lay with it in cold railroad stations. I took it with me to the hospital when I got typhoid fever. When I met Mottele in Lublin, I gave it to him to read and he said, 'It's a masterpiece.'"

Mottele slowly lifted up his head. "Forgive me, Zina; I never said this."

"Yes, you did. It was your idea that I should bring the novel to him," Zina said, pointing at me. "Now that we are in the Land of Israel, I want to publish it. I want you to write an introduction to it. This, too, was Mottele's idea."

Mottele shrugged. "All I said was that he knew Rashkes better than the others did."

That day I promised Zina to read the novel and write an introduction. The night after, I lay awake until three o'clock and I read the entire manuscript. I was reading and sighing. From time to time, I slapped my forehead. I had always considered Rashkes a genuine talent. But what I read that night was the worst kind of mishmash. Had he become prematurely senile? Had he forgotten the Yiddish language? The protagonist of this novel was not Zina but a man who indulged in drawn-out polemics with the Warsaw Yiddish critics in tedious pseudo-Freudian analysis, misquoting all sorts of writers, philosophers, and politicians. I never would have believed that Rashkes was capable of writing this bewildering hodgepodge if I had not recognized his handwriting. He had even forgotten how to spell. Rashkes had a reputation for being a humorist, but there was not a trace of wit in this pathetic monologue.

A few days later Mottele called me, and I told him what I thought of Rashkes's last work. He began to stammer. "I never praised it. I said one thing and she heard the opposite. If Hitler could hypnotize Germany and Stalin Russia, something is the matter with the human race altogether. Zina is sick. She was twice operated on for cancer. They cut off her left breast. I cannot tell her the truth about Rashkes. She will soon have to go to the hospital again. I myself suffer from angina pectoris. I shouldn't have visited you in that sandstorm, but she actually dragged me. What can I tell her about your introduction? Please find some excuse for declining."

"Tell her that I will send her the introduction from America."

"Yes, a good idea. There is great wisdom in delaying things. I would like to meet you alone, without her."

I made an appointment with Mottele, but a day before we were to meet, someone called me on the telephone and told me that Mottele and Zina had both been taken to the hospital. The man introduced himself as one of Mottele's Hasidim and an ardent reader of mine.

He said to me, "This may sound to you like a contradiction, huh? However, after Treblinka, one should not ask any questions."

Translated by the author and Lester Goran

On the Way to the Poorhouse

T HE INMATES of the poorhouse all wanted to get rid of her. First of all, it's a shame to share sleeping quarters with a whore. And second, she didn't even come from this area. The authorities had confined her in the Janów prison, and while there, she became paralyzed. So what is her connection with the residents of Janów? Still, the Jewish community could not throw a Jewish daughter out into the street, no matter how depraved she was. So they put a straw pallet in a corner of the general dormitory, and there she lay. She was dark-skinned, with a youthful face, black burning eyes, brows that converged over the bridge of her nose, prominent cheekbones, a pointed chin, and black hair hanging straight to her shoulders. The paupers cursed her and she replied with ten curses for one. They spat at her and she spat back, hissing like a snake: "Pox on your tongue, black in the head and green before the eyes, a behind swollen from sitting shiva . . ." Adept as she was at name-calling and profanity, she was also capable of turning on the charm and telling lewd stories about herself to the men. Even though she could not use her legs, the women of Janów were fearful she might seduce their husbands. Whenever there was an epidemic of smallpox, measles, scarlet fever, or croup, the pious matrons of the town went running to the study-house, screaming at the elders that it was all a punishment for keeping the whore in a house belonging to the community. But what could they have done with a cripple?

Her name was Tsilka, and her Yiddish had the accent of those who lived on the other side of the Vistula. The residents of the poorhouse avoided her like a leper and she ignored them, too. But when the men from the town came to visit her and brought her groats, chicken soup, or a half bottle of vodka, she smiled at them sweetly and suggestively. She wore a string of red beads around her neck. Long earrings dangled from her earlobes. She pushed the quilt down to expose the upper part of her breasts. Occasionally she let her visitors touch her sick legs. She soon had a group in town who rallied around her. The town toughs warned Zorach, the poorhouse attendant, that if he mistreated Tsilka they would break his neck. They asked her many questions about her past and she answered them, shamelessly boasting about her sins. She remembered every detail, leaving out nothing. After a while, some of those who were living at the poorhouse made peace with her, because through her they, too, got better food and even some liquor. Those who lay on straw pallets near her began to enjoy her tales. Although they wished her the black plague and eternal hell, they had to admit that her stories shortened the monotonous summer days and the long winter nights. Tsilka maintained that when she was eight years old a horse dealer enticed her into a stall and there he raped her on a pile of hay and horse dung. Later, when she became an orphan, she began to copulate with butcher boys, coachmen, and soldiers. Her town was near the Prussian border and the smugglers of contraband made love to her. Tsilka named all the towns where she was in brothels, spoke about the madams and pimps. Cossack officers preferred her to the other harlots. They danced and drank with her. A crazy squire made her bathe in a wine-filled tub and later drank from it. A rich Russian from Siberia proposed marriage to her if she would convert to the Orthodox faith. But Tsilka refused to become a Christian and to betray the God of Israel. She had no desire to marry that Ivan and bear little Ivans for him. What could he have given her that she didn't have? She wore silk shirts and underwear. She ate marzipan and roast squab.

For many years, she was fortunate. She never became pregnant, she never got the clap. Other whores who began their profession later than she rotted away in hospitals, but she remained young and beautiful. Suddenly her luck turned. In a brothel in Lublin, a girl poisoned her procurer. At the investigation, she accused Tsilka of the crime. Tsilka was charged with murder and sent to the Janów prison because the women's section of the Lublin jail was overcrowded. There she spent nine months in solitary confinement in a damp cell full of bedbugs and other vermin. The Lublin investigators had forgotten her. Her papers were misplaced somewhere. The trial never took place. They had to free her. But a few days before her release, her legs lost their power and became like wood. Tsilka bragged that the prison guards had affairs with her. In a cell next to her sat a bunch of thieves. One night they gouged out a large hole in the wall, and through this, they copulated with her. Hodel the widow, whose pallet was close to Tsilka's, began to wince, raised her fists in a fury, and shouted, "Shut your foul mouth. Your words are deadly venom."

"Sweet venom."

"God waits long and punishes well."

"For my sake, he can wait a little longer," Tsilka answered mockingly.

There was quarreling in Janów because of Tsilka. The community leaders held a meeting as to what action was to be taken. She defiled the town. Even the boys in the studyhouse discussed her. After lengthy debates that lasted until dawn, it was decided to send her to the poorhouse in Lublin. The Janów community was ready to pay for her upkeep there. Lublin is a big city and they have many like her there. The old Janów rabbi, Reb Zeinvele, admonished his congregants that one leprous sheep can contaminate the whole flock. He remarked that Satan's aides were everywhere—in the marketplace, in the tavern, in the studyhouse, even in the cemetery. The situation in Janów had come to such a pass that respectable tradesmen, fathers of children, stood for hours around Tsilka's bed listening to her obscenities. They brought her so much food and so many delicacies that she gave gifts to those who flattered her. The children in the poorhouse she treated with cookies, raisins, sunflower seeds. She no longer lay on a straw pallet but on a bed with linen. In Janów it was unheard of for a female to smoke. Tsilka asked for tobacco and cigarette paper, and she rolled her own cigarettes and blew smoke rings through her nostrils. How long can a town like Janów stand for such loose conduct? After prolonged negotiations, a letter came from the community of Lublin stating that Tsilka would be given a cot in the room where the moribund are kept. A screen was to be placed near her bed, so that the others wouldn't have to see her insolent face. Besides the expenses for her maintenance, the Lublin community asked the Janów community to pay for her burial fees in advance, even though Tsilka would be buried behind the fence. When the contents of this letter became known in Janów, the

Tsilka followers also gathered at a meeting and one, Berish the musician, who was known as a scoffer, a woman chaser, a vituperator, instigated the rabble. "The so-called upright citizens," he ranted, "are supposed to serve God, but actually they serve only themselves. They have appropriated the best of everything—the brick houses, the eastern wall in the synagogue, the stores in the marketplace, the fat women, even the best-located graves. However, the moment a shoemaker, a tailor, or a comber of pig bristles tries to raise his head, he is immediately threatened with excommunication and a bed of nails in Gehenna. We will not allow them to send Tsilka away to Lublin, where she will rot away while alive. We can take care of her here. It's true that she's a fallen woman. But who are those who fall into sin? Not the pampered daughters of the rich, may they be consumed in fire. It's our children who are fair prey to every lecher. Our daughters work as servants in the houses of the wealthy, and their sons, who are supposed to study all day long, creep into their beds at night. The mothers of these privileged boys pretend not to see. Sometimes they even encourage them." Berish spoke with such zeal and with such violent gesticulations that the crowd began to howl, to stamp their feet, and to denounce the rabbi, the elders, the leaders. One of them called out, "We have suffered long enough from these hypocrites."

"Brothers, let's go and break windows," shouted Beryl the barrelmaker. A pack of ruffians marched into the street, lifted rocks, and hurled them through the windows of the important Janów citizens. A Talmud student on his way to midnight study was beaten. A girl who came to pour out the slops was attacked and her braid cut off. From there, the rioters went into the tavern, bought a jug of vodka and a bagful of salt pretzels, and proceeded to the poorhouse. The old and the sick were already asleep, but Tsilka was awake. She had been informed about the meeting. She supported her head on two pillows, and in the darkness, her eyes glowed like those of a she-wolf. Lights were lit and drinks were passed around. Tsilka downed a full glass of the liquor, bit off a bit of salt pretzel, and began to malign the best people of Janów. Even though she knew the town only from peering through the prison bars, all the gossip and scandal had somehow reached her. The sleeping mendicants were awakened and treated to drinks. Yosele Bludgeon, who worked in the slaughterhouse, became so drunk that he tore off Tsilka's quilt, lifted her out of bed, and tried to dance with her. There was screaming, laughter, clapping of hands. The children of the poorhouse became wild, and began to jump and hop as on the day of the rejoicing of the law.

Hodel the widow went into a frenzy. "People, the world is being destroyed!"

Someone went to wake Zorach the attendant, who was also the Janów gravedigger. He tried to calm the mob, but he received a blow. He went to the rabbi. It was Reb Zeinvele's custom to wake up every night to study Torah and to write commentaries while drinking tea from the samovar. The outside door was bolted, the shutters closed. Suddenly someone banged at the shutters with a stick. Reb Zeinvele trembled. "Who's there?" he called.

"Rabbi, please open!"

The Messiah had come; the thought ran through Reb Zeinvele's mind, although he soon realized that the redemption would not begin at night. He went to unbolt the door. Zorach was panting. "Rabbi, we don't live in Janów but in Sodom," he cried.

"What happened?"

"There's lechery in the poorhouse."

The community won. A Janów salesman who delivered merchandise to Lublin paid thirty guldens to the Lublin elders, who signed a contract to keep Tsilka there until the day of her death. The Janów community was ready to send Tsilka to Lublin, but she took out a knife concealed beneath her pillow and threatened to stab anyone who tried to move her.

Berish the musician, her defender, swore that he would set fire to the houses of the community busybodies and that blood would be shed in Janów. Both sides bribed the authorities. It would have resulted in warfare if the women of the town, even those living on Bridge Street and Butcher's Alley, hadn't sided with Tsilka's enemies. Tsilka managed to instigate husbands against wives and broke up engagements. When women are determined, men lose the upper hand. Furthermore, Tsilka's pals fought among themselves and some exchanged blows. The community was now all set to execute its plan, but the coachmen's wives would not trust their husbands to take her in their wagons. Regular passengers refused to travel in her company. After much bickering, it was decided that Leibush the scabhead, who transported hides to Lublin tanneries, would take her in his cart. Leibush was already a man in his fifties and a grandfather. Other than Tsilka, he took with him a wandering beggar and two orphan sisters who went to Lublin for domestic service.

Tsilka's imprecations and knife waving were of no avail. Leibush, a small man, broad in the shoulders, with a thick red beard that began in the middle of his throat and reached his bulging eyes, stormed into the poorhouse, tore the knife out of Tsilka's hands, grabbed her like a calf destined for the slaughterhouse, and threw her among the hides. The beggar and the maids were already in the cart and Leibush headed straight toward the Lublin road. Street urchins ran alongside the wagon, screaming, "Rachav the harlot." Girls peered from behind the curtains. Tsilka poured out the most violent curses. She spat at Leibush and at the two orphans. One of them mumbled, "You should spit with blood and pus." Tsilka flung herself at the girl to scratch her eyes out. Suddenly she burst into laughter.

"I won't spit blood, but you will carry the chamber pots of your employers. All day long, you will work like an ox. At night, your mistress's precious son will force you to sleep with him and give you a belly. Later, you will be thrown out into the gutter, together with your bastard."

"You should get a boil on your behind for every decent maid there is in Lublin." Leibush spoke from the driver's seat, not turning his back.

"How do you know they are decent?" Tsilka asked. "Did you try to lie with them?"

"My own wife was a hired girl in Lublin. At the wedding, she was a kosher virgin."

"Kosher like a pig's knuckle. Greater sages than you have been tricked."

Tsilka was now pouring out vituperations. She bragged about her abominations. The two sisters, perplexed, pressed even closer to each other and remained silent. The mendicant leaned on his bag, which had been filled with food and old clothing by the charitable women of Janów. Leibush emitted a whistle, brandished his whip, and spoke inquisitively. "You have discarded your last shred of shame, haven't you?"

"Those who are ashamed don't do what I did. I wouldn't be ashamed in front of my own mother."

"Don't you have any regrets?" the beggar asked. "After all, one gets older, not younger. You see already that God has punished you."

"My profession and regret don't blend. The poorhouse is full of cripples who constantly have God on the tip of their tongues. The pious also have a taste for the flesh. I should have many good years since so many yeshiva boys were my patrons. I was even visited by an itinerant preacher who specialized in sermons about morality."

"You should live so long, if you are telling the truth," Leibush said.

"Leibush scabhead, you should have so many blisters and carbuncles for the number of times this preacher had me."

"Shut your mouth or you'll soon find your teeth in your hand," Leibush cried out. The beggar tried to quiet him.

"It doesn't pay to fall into a rage, Reb Leibush. God does not listen to a whore's swearing."

"He listens, He listens, you nasty schnorrer. If you say one more word, I'll tear out your beard, with a piece of flesh in addition."

The two sisters, twins, let out one short shriek. They came from a decent home. Both had round faces, snub noses, lips that curled upward, and high bosoms. They wore the same shawls and their hairdos were identical. Tsilka stuck her tongue out at them. "Two stuffed geese."

The night began to lower. The sun was setting; large, red, with a ribbon of cloud through the middle. The moonless night was humid; there was lightning not followed by thunder. The horse walked at a slow pace. In the darkness, one could see the glitter of glowworms, the outline of a windmill, a scarecrow, a haystack. Dogs barked in the villages. Horses spending the night in the pasture stood motionless. Once in a while, a humming could be heard, but it was difficult to know if it came from a beast or a bird of prey. After a while, the cart traveled on a road through a forest. From the thicket wafted smells of moss, wildflowers, swamp. Tsilka's talk became even more abandoned. She reviled and blasphemed. According to her, rabbis, scholars, important people had one thing on their minds only—lechery. She told of an episode with a rich young scholar who was boarding at his father-in-law's and who stayed three days and three nights in a hayloft with her. Occasionally the horse stopped for a while, pricked up its ears, as if curious to listen to these human vanities. Suddenly Tsilka cried out, "Leibush scabhead, take me down."

"What's the matter?"

"I have to go where even a king goes on foot."

Since Tsilka was paralyzed, Leibush had to carry her. He lifted her with ease, as if she were a bundle of rags, and carried her behind the bushes. One of the twins uttered a laugh and grew silent again. The beggar rummaged in his bag, pulled out an onion, bit into it, and spat it out. "By what merit does such an outcast remain alive?" he asked.

A quarter of an hour passed, perhaps more, but the two did not return. The horse kicked the ground once. The beggar remarked, "What are they doing so long?" and he answered himself, "They don't sing psalms."

Steps were heard. Leibush emerged from the thicket with Tsilka in his arms. She giggled, and one could see by the light of the stars that she was tickling him and pulling at his beard. Leibush carefully sat her in the cart. He then ordered, "Everybody else get out of the cart."

"What for?"

"I have to rearrange the hides."

The three of them alighted. Leibush jumped up onto the driver's seat, whipped the horse, and shouted, *"Heyta."*

"Where are you going? Where are you leaving us? Oy, mama!" the sisters cried out in unison.

"Thief, brigand, whoremaster! Help, people, help!" the beggar wailed hoarsely.

They tried to run after the cart, but the road led downhill. The wagon soon disappeared. Leibush had taken the beggar's bag and the baskets belonging to the girls with him. The beggar beat his breast: "Children, we are lost."

"Oy, mama!" The two girls sank down and remained sitting on the needle-covered ground.

The beggar screamed with all his might, "There is a God! There is!"

The words reverberated and resounded with the mocking echo of those who rule in the night.

All three slept in the forest. The next day they headed back toward Janów. In Zamość, Bilgoray, Frampol, and Turbin, the news spread about Leibush the hide dealer, who left a wife, children, and grandchildren and ran away with a trollop. Messengers were dispatched, but they found no trace of the pair. Some people thought that Leibush crossed the border into Galicia with her. Others were of the opinion that the two sinners went to a priest in Lublin and were converted. Yet others maintained that Tsilka was a she-demon and that she carried Leibush away into the desert of Sodom, to Mount Seir, to Asmodeus' castle, into the dominion of the netherworld.

Leibush's wife was never permitted to remarry. The mendicant swore on the Bible that he had kept sixty guldens in his bag, a dowry for his daughter, who was already past thirty. He asked the community to reimburse him for his loss.

During the winter nights, when the girls of Janów got together to pickle cucumbers, pluck feathers, or render chicken fat for Passover, they would tell the story of Tsilka the wicked and Leibush the adulterer, who vanished into regions from which no one has ever returned.

Loshikl

DUSK had fallen in the jail cell. Everyone's face was hidden in shadows. It was too dark for card playing. The guard wouldn't be bringing in the kerosene lamp for another hour yet. It was brought in late; it was allowed to burn for only half an hour and then taken out. Three prisoners, Berele Zwaniak, Yankel Dezma, and Shmuel Kluska, were sitting around, talking.

Berele Zwaniak said, "They know, they know, but they play dumb. Not all husbands are alike. One is ready to stab you if you so much as give his wife a smile or a wink. But some other sucker takes you in as a boarder and leaves you with his wife all day long and sometimes all night to boot. I knew such a couple. His name was Getzel and his wife's name was Malka. He rented an alcove in his apartment to a good pal of mine, a safecracker, Hershel Shmirer, a giant of a man. Getzel himself, a small fellow, had a little workshop two blocks away where he made paper bags. All day long he sat at his workbench and glued together the paper bags. In the evening, instead of coming home, he would grab a bite in the corner café and take off with his chums to play cards. He wouldn't get home until two o'clock in the morning, and sometimes he played till daybreak. How much could you possibly win at cards? Monday he would walk away with a ruble, Tuesday he would lose it back. But it's a kind of obsession. Something gets in your head and sticks there like a nail. Look at us. Stealing will never make you rich. But you get used to it and you think that without it you couldn't survive. It draws you like a magnet. The other day I swore to my mother by all that's holy that I would go back to shoemaking. She took a Bible out of her dresser and made me swear on it. But as soon as I walked out on the square I forgot everything I promised her. A friend of mine came along and he had a deal for me. He gave me no time to think it over. We pulled it off, slick as butter. Hard cash, not merchandise that needs to be sold through a fence on Wolowa Street. Then we dropped into Lazar's tavern and hit the bottle. But why do I tell you all this? Once you become addicted you see nothing else. At two o'clock in the morning, when Getzel, the husband, finally dragged himself home dead tired from a whole day's work and half a night's gambling, he fell into bed more dead than alive. You want to tell me that he didn't know? Card playing just came first with him."

"What would have happened if Hershel Shmirer had made her pregnant?" Shmuel Kluska asked.

"The sky wouldn't have fallen," Berele Zwaniak answered.

"What happened to them?" Yankel Dezma asked.

"It just so happened that Hershel Shmirer was caught red-handed stealing and they threw him in jail. Malka used to bring him packages to the cell."

"In love with the safe safecracker, huh?" Shmuel Kluska asked.

"A female, if you keep her happy, she latches on to you," Berele Zwaniak said.

There was in the same cell another prisoner, Itche the Blind, or Itche the Accurate. He was called Itche the Blind because he had only one eye; the other one had been gouged out many years back. The name Accurate was given to him because of his proper bearing. Itche the Blind didn't go out on the street himself anymore. He taught young punks the trade and got a percentage of every take. He was also part owner of a bordello. For almost fifteen years Itche the Blind had stayed on the loose. But he was arrested because of a run-in with a police commissar, and got entangled in a trial. He was soon supposed to be freed on bail. The guards in the jail held Itche in high esteem. He received from the outside packages of chocolate, cigarettes, even cans of sardines, to which he treated everyone.

For Itche the Blind it would have been degrading to involve himself with the petty thieves who were his cellmates. He was now stretched out on a bunk, smoking one cigarette after another. But the conversation apparently had captured his interest. From time to time he mumbled to himself. Suddenly he drew himself up to his full height, a huge man, wide-shouldered, with a shock of hair beginning to gray at the temples. He took a stride toward the others and asked, "May I say something, too?"

For a while all three thieves were speechless. Berele Zwaniak was the first to find his tongue. "Have a seat, Itche, you're like a rabbi to us."

Itche the Blind sat down.

"Have a smoke."

He offered each of the prisoners a cigarette. He took out a lighter and passed it around for them to light up. In a deep voice he said, "A rabbi, huh? We in Warsaw had only one rabbi, Chazkele, may he intercede for us. His word was gold. A day didn't go by without his hitting on some scheme. He had a mind like a trap. The chief of police himself respected him. If Chazkele hadn't become what he was, he could have been a big shot in Petersburg. I was listening to what you were saying. Men, women, whores, not-whores. Each woman has her own ways of hooking a man. In my youth I had my share of loving, I can't complain. I slowed down when I realized that one good female can satisfy a man better than five dozen tramps who are only after a pair of stockings or a mug of beer. You all are still bagel-snatchers, wet behind the ears, and what can you know? We have no Chazkele these days. No, and does anyone today remember Red Reitzele? That was what they called her. You've probably never heard of her. But there'll never be another Reitzele, either. Reitzele was a smart cookie. She had a husband, a businessman, not a crook. His name was Antshel, a real-estate broker. Those were the days when Warsaw was being built up with paved sidewalks, market-places, high buildings. The banks had a lot of money and extended credit. If you could show that you had five thousand rubles in cash, you could borrow an additional twenty or thirty thousand rubles on a mortgage. Our Jews began wheeling and dealing, and the time was ripe for a lot of brokerage business.

"Overnight, paupers became millionaires. Antshel knew how to open up doors, where and whom to offer bribes. He was a shrewd bastard. But he wasn't any good with women. For Reitzele he was barely enough for a snack, not a full meal. The likes of him have to be helped along. He wasn't one to begrudge others, like a dog on a haystack who can't eat it himself and who won't let others near it. As to Reitzele, she wasn't just a tease. When I met her I was eighteen and she a good thirty-six and maybe even a bit older. My parents had at first wanted to make a yeshiva student of me. But I didn't have a mind for the Gemara. When they saw that I would never turn out to be a scholar, they wanted me to become a tailor. However, in those days an apprentice had to spend three years in his master's house pouring out the slops and rocking the baby. It took a long time before he was allowed to sew on a button or make a buttonhole. When I found myself with my back up against the wall, I left everything and ran off to Warsaw. I found my way to Chazkele, who was the leader of all the toughs in the city. As I told you, I'm from the provinces, not from Warsaw. The Warsaw wise guys used to needle us newcomers and call us yokels or Litvak swine. In Warsaw if you were born on the other side of the city line, you're a Lithuanian. Here comes the guard with his lamp, a fire in his guts!"

A guard brought in a kerosene lamp with a blackened globe. A reddish glow spread over everyone's face. When the guard saw Itche the Blind sitting with the other inmates, he shook his head as if to say, This is beneath you.

Itche the Blind began to blink with his good eye. He spoke to the guard, "Stach, we don't need the lamp. It gives no light, only smoke."

"Mr. Itche, I'm not the boss here," the guard answered. "I'm just following orders."

"Here's a cigarette," Itche said, "but don't tell the other guards. They'll descend upon me like locusts."

"Thanks, I appreciate it."

"We're having a little chat to help us forget the stench from the can," Itche the Blind said, as if trying to excuse himself.

"Yes, I understand. I have to follow the rules. How does the saying go? 'The small fry are hanged and the big ones are thanked.'"

The guard left and Itche the Blind continued: "Chazkele talked to me for about half an hour. I told him that I couldn't find a decent night's lodging and he sent me to Red Reitzele. He said, 'Tell her Chazkele sent you and she'll open up doors for you. She likes young men, not old.' In my first half hour with him he gave me more wise counsel than the biggest lawyer could deliver in a year. If only I had listened to him, I would still have both my eyes.

"Reitzele lived on Smocza Street, in a large apartment, three rooms and a kitchen, a new building with gas and an indoor toilet. How I got the nerve first to approach Chazkele and then to go to Reitzele's is beyond me. I climbed up the painted steps, knocked, and a little woman with red hair like fire and green eyes like a cat's opened up. I stood at the threshold and she looked me up and down and inspected me as if I were to become her butler. Her teeth were sparse, but stronger than a dog's. Later on I saw her crack walnuts with those teeth. I told her that Chazkele had sent me, and a little smile lit up her face. I looked at her hands and felt a twinge of desire. Some men boast that they can tell a woman by her eyes, others claim that you can tell it all by the shape of the mouth. I can tell everything from hands. In the theater, when they want to flatter a woman, they rave about her long fingers. Nonsense! I like short fingers and short nails, too. She stood before me in a knee-length apron, a short housedress, and in slippers with pom-poms. Her knees were pointed like those of a boy. I took one look at her and knew that she'd be mine.

"Half an hour later we were kissing. We fell upon each other with thirst. She pressed her mouth to mine as if she were trying to swallow it. In bed, she asked, 'What's your name?' I told her, 'Itche,' and she said, 'I don't like Itche. I'll call you Loshikl, because you are young and strong and you jump like a colt,' and that's how it was. It lasted eight years. I would say to her, 'Reitzele, I'm an old horse already, not a colt, and she would reply, 'To me you'll always be a *loshikl* even if you're ninety.'

"That she was a good piece and that she loved men Antshel her husband knew quite well. For a couple of years he played dumb with me. Once, when he ran into me at Lazar's tavern and we had a drink, he became talkative. He said to me, 'What do you call two husbands of the same wife?' I said to him, 'Brothers-in-law,' and he said, 'That's a silly name. We're more like brothers.' He went on: 'Loshikl, now that the cat is out of the bag, what do you say to our little wife? Have you ever had anything better?' And I said, 'Never had, never will have.' He said, 'She talks the same about you. There's only one God and one Loshikl. Last year when they threw you in the slammer, she wanted to teach me your tricks, but I have no patience for such games. Jealous? How can I be jealous? She told me at the very beginning, "I'm not a rebbetzin, I like men." We are not her only ones. When she meets a man, right away she wants to try him out. If King Solomon, she says, could have a thousand wives, Reitzele can have a thousand husbands.'

"That evening, we became so close that we drank to brotherhood. Just the same, when you're in love with someone you can't be above it all. A man is not a stone, no matter how much of a front he puts up. It burns you up when you know that your beloved is sleeping around with others. But if you have no choice, you grin and bear it, as they say. You can get used to anything. You can live and love with an ulcer in your gizzard. You can dance with a toothache.

"Antshel was such a man. When Reitzele and I quarreled, he made peace between us. He wanted her to have her Loshikl.

"Yes, we all want pleasure, but what kind of pleasure is it to stretch out across someone's knee and be thrashed with a cat-o'-nine-tails till your butt swells? That's what some of my sweethearts wanted me to do to them. They would beg of me: 'Whip harder, Itchele, pull my hair! Bite my shoulder!' Reitzele had her own quirks. It started with her taking it upon herself to marry me off. I asked her, 'What good would it do you?' And she said, 'When a colt grows older he needs his own mare.' I said to her, 'What do I need my own mare for? So that she should run around with every thug while I rot in jail?' And she said, 'I have a husband and I want you to have a wife. It'll be more fun that way. We'll go to the theater together or to the circus, all four of us. We'll chat over a mug of beer.' I told her in no uncertain terms, 'It's not for me.' When she heard that, she set out to supply me with lovers. She would lie next to me on the sofa and say, 'Loshikl, I want to be your mother. I don't have any children, only one Loshikl, and I want to provide for his future. You are younger than me,' she said, 'and when I'm gone maybe you'll keep me in mind and say the Kaddish or light a candle for me.' I said, 'You're not about to croak yet, you'll outlive all of us,' and she said, 'No, Loshikl. My mother died young and my father passed away when I was a little girl of three. In our family, they barely make it to fifty.'

"I'll make it short. She wanted to set me up with some woman—if not a wife, let it be a lover. I asked her, 'What's in it for you?' And she said, 'It's interesting. It'll amuse me.' 'I could have,' she said, 'as many men as my heart desires. They still turn their heads after me in the streets as if I were a young girl, but for now, one husband and one Loshikl are enough.' Something is always nagging women on. Men go to war, or go on strike, throw bombs and get themselves banished to Siberia. A female has only one string to her bow. It's even written in the Bible.

"She wasn't just babbling," Blind Itche continued. "One day I came in for lunch and sitting there was a little female— slight, with orange-yellow hair, with a string of pearls around her neck. I saw right away that this was no ordinary piece, but well-bred, from a wealthy home. Reitzele introduced her: a doctor's wife. We had lunch and when Reitzele cooked you licked your fingers. We talked and I found out that the doctor's wife employed a cook and a maid. She had everything, but she was just about fed up with her husband, a skin doctor. He practiced at St. Lazar Hospital, and there they treat only cankers, psoriasis, lupus, what have you. All day long she didn't lay eyes on him, and when he came home in the evening, he buried himself in books and journals about people with little worms in their blood. 'He knows,' she said, 'everything. But how to satisfy a wife, that he didn't study.'

"When a woman speaks like that to a stranger, the first move is already made. After she left I asked Reitzele, 'Where did you meet this fancy lady?' And she said, 'At Lours's Café.' That's Reitzele for you. She could dress up like a countess and go to the theater, the opera, to Lazienki Gardens. She leaves Smocza Street, and right away she's a lady. The whole thing seemed crazy to me. I wanted Reitzele, not the skin doctor's wife. But Reitzele had already made up her mind. The first time it happened I couldn't believe it myself."

The jail door opened and the guard came in to retrieve the lamp. "By law, you should be asleep already," he said, "but I'll let it pass."

"We got a little involved in a conversation," Itche the Blind said. "We'll make up the sleep tomorrow."

"I know nothing. Just doing my duty," the guard said.

∎

"What's the sense in fixing up your lover with another woman?" Berele Zwaniak asked.

The cell had become dark. Only the ends of the lit cigarettes cast a glow on everyone's face. Itche the Blind paused a while. "It doesn't have to make sense," he said. "Why did Leah in the Bible present Jacob with her maid? Why are we sitting here behind bars? I could easily have had a store on Miodowa Street just like the shlemiels who came here from the provinces and made fortunes. But you begin something and you can't get out of it. Once there was a professor and he spent much time pondering lofty thoughts, until he came to the conclusion that all men are crazy. Maybe it's really so."

"I'll bet you that Reitzele got a fee from the skin doctor's wife," Berele Zwaniak said.

Itche the Blind didn't answer right away.

"I don't know," he finally said. "I didn't know then and I certainly don't know now. If she did, she was welcome to it. Why did such a cute little woman have to pay for it? Some men would have paid *her*. On the other hand, if a lady like her were to start up with one of her own kind, right away it would turn into a complicated matter. He might want her to divorce the doctor, or whatever they do in high society. For people like that checking into a hotel is dangerous. All the hotels are full of snoops. At Reitzele's, everything went smoothly. Reitzele would go out and leave us alone. She always made up some excuse. She had to go to a store or to a relative. Reitzele didn't need the money. Her husband gave her more than enough. But how does it go? People have big eyes. They are greedy for all kinds of silly thrills. The doctor's wife called herself Fania, but whether that really was her name, I don't know. She never told me where she lived, and I never asked. In those days I didn't brood about things too much. I gorged myself, guzzled it up, had my Reitzele and the other one. When I needed money, I headed toward the city markets and I always returned with a little cash. I don't know why, but women always walk around with unlocked purses. That's how it was then, that's how it is today. We talked about things making sense. Does that make any sense?"

"The reason is," Shmuel Kluska said, "that they stuff so

many gadgets into their purses they can't get them closed. My own sister does it. The buckle loosens and the purse opens by itself."

"How long did you have the doctor's wife?" Yankel Dezma asked.

"What? It didn't always go as smoothly as with Fania. One time Reitzele set me up with a queer piece. She was so besmirched with makeup that it made me sick. She spoke only Polish and refused to eat with us. If you offered her a glass of tea, she wiped the rim with a handkerchief. She started to interrogate me like a doctor: Did you ever have this? That? She'd brought a pink vial of disinfectant with her. It was all so nauseating that I began to vomit, and that was the end of that. I can see her even now, with a thick nose and a mouth like a snout. Another one wore a hat with a huge brim and a veil so heavy that you couldn't see her face. When push came to shove, she scurried off. But there were those who attracted me somehow. One was a poor girl from the provinces, a hatmaker. She worked in a store on Zabia Street. She always arrived hungry. If Reitzele gave her a bowl of soup, she asked for more. With Reitzele, it was a madness of sorts. After they left I had to report everything to her: what she said and what I said. Every little thing. She would shriek, 'Tell me more, Loshikl. Don't leave anything out.' I thought that as she got older she would cool off, but she became more and more embroiled. I had nothing to complain about really, but I was getting fed up with the whole kit and caboodle. I didn't need her meals or her lodging anymore. The cops were after me and it wasn't good for me to have a steady address. I moved to Poczajow and there I got myself younger and prettier women. Later the misfortune with my eye happened. All I did was make a joke with some jerk and the brute pounced on me with a knife. It was nothing but bad luck."

"Did you stop seeing Reitzele forever?" Berele Zwaniak asked.

"Not completely," Itche said. "Whenever we met, the fire for her was rekindled and I swore that everything would be the way it had been. But I saw her less and less. Chazkele died, and when that happened Warsaw was no longer Warsaw. As long as he lived we were his pupils. When he passed away we all became orphans. Quarrels began. Gangs formed. During the strikes in 1905, when the Reds attacked us, there was no one left to fight back. Everyone ran his own way. After Bloody Wednesday the Reds, too, scattered like mice. Many escaped to America. In the midst of it all, Reitzele died."

"Got sick, huh?" Shmuel Kluska asked.

"Who knows what she had. Her time was up. She was fifty to the day. I could sit with you three nights and tell you stories about her and it wouldn't be enough time. Children, it's getting late. Soon they'll come in to wake us."

Translated by Rena Borrow and Lester Goran

The Pocket Remembered

IN the Polish city of Plotsk there lived a man by the name of Reb Amram Zalkind, who was the court Jew for the squire, Count Bronislaw Walecki. The count was not an enemy of the Jews; he traded with them and often consulted them in business. It was the custom among the Polish squires that when they gave a ball, the court Jew made the guests merry. He disguised himself as a bear, growled, crawled on all fours, and the guests had something to laugh at and to mock. But Squire Walecki looked down on this barbaric custom. He sat Reb Amram among the other guests at a ball, and had the cook prepare vegetables in a special pot to assure the Jew that the food was kosher. The squire owned many forests in which the trees were logged and floated on rafts down the Vistula to Danzig, where German merchants bought the lumber. Reb Amram spoke Polish and German well, and the squire frequently sent him to fairs in Danzig and Leipzig. He bought all kinds of jewelry there: rings, chains, bracelets, brooches, earrings, and precious stones for the squiress, the Countess Helena Walecki, and for her daughters. Reb Amram was not a learned man, but he remembered the law that if you owe but one groschen, even to someone overseas, you must go there and repay the debt, since only the sins committed against God, not against man, are forgiven on Yom Kippur. Reb Amram could have easily become rich the way many dishonest stewards, marshals, and usurers did, but he was by nature an honest man. In handling the squire's money, he accounted for every groschen. Even Reb Amram's enemies acknowledged that in money matters he was upright. In those times, traveling salesmen wrote everything down on a small chalk board, but Amram had purchased a pen and a notebook to keep records of his accounts. His coat had two deep pockets, one for expenditures and another for income. He kept all his personal earnings in a separate leather purse. At every opportunity Squire Walecki praised his court Jew for his honesty.

In time Reb Amram became quite wealthy. Envious townspeople gossiped behind his back and hinted that he only feigned honesty but was actually cheating the squire. They maintained that a Jew who works so closely with a squire could not avoid drinking non-kosher wine or looking and lusting after the female gentry, because Alte Trina, Amram's wife, was as small as a midget and slightly hunchbacked. Reb Amram was tall, straight, with blue eyes and a blond beard. Only a few white hairs could be seen on his head and beard, even though he was approaching sixty. He had a strong singing voice, was the leader of the morning prayers on the High Holidays, and was also the blower of the shofar, the ram's horn. The young matrons in the women's section of the synagogue savored his voice. Their mothers-in-law used to reproach them, "Look into the prayer book, not at Amram."

As small and as frail as Alte Trina was, she bore Amram four sons and three daughters, and they all married well. It seemed that affluence was Reb Amram's lot. He did not, God forbid, say, "It was the might of my own hands that brought me this great wealth." He often contributed to charity. On the Sabbath or on a holiday he never returned from the synagogue without a poor guest. He gave generously to the society which married off orphaned maidens, to the watchers of the sick, toward purchasing sacred books for the studyhouse, and for redeeming innocent prisoners. Alte Trina often sent chicken soup to the sick in the poorhouse.

One summer a fair took place in Leipzig. Reb Amram Zalkind was sent there to meet with foreign merchants, to claim the debts which they owed the squire, and to negotiate down payments for new orders. Squire Walecki was marrying off his youngest daughter, the Countess Marianna, to the son of Count Zamoyski, one of the richest noblemen in Poland, and the squiress asked Reb Amram to buy for the bride-to-be a strand of pearls, a variety of gold utensils, as well as silk, velvet, fine linen, and various other costly materials. Reb Amram carefully wrote every item down in his notebook. He would be handling large sums of money and he made sure that every purchase was recorded clearly; he wanted no mistakes, God forbid, in the account. He told Alte Trina not to worry about him and not to expect him back too early, since business trips like these took much time. He said to her, "With God's help I will be back for the High Holidays."

Outside, Markel, his coachman, was waiting for him in a britska harnessed with two horses. Because he traveled so often, Reb Amram knew the prayer before embarking on a journey by heart. The maid, Reishe, brought him a basket of food, and Reb Amram rode off onto the highway which crossed the Prussian border into Leipzig. The journey was not without danger. Robbers lurked on the highways, as well as wild animals. The Poles and the Prussians constantly waged wars and minor battles. The customs officials harassed the traveling merchants, especially the Jews, who carried no swords and could not defend themselves. But, thank God, there was no mishap on this trip. They knew Reb Amram in the inns and prepared comfortable lodgings for him with strictly kosher meals. He always kept loose change—gratuities for the servants. Reb Amram had often visited Leipzig, but the city was never as full as this time. Traders had come not only from Germany and Poland but also from Russia, Italy, France—even from Spain, Portugal, and England. The inns were packed, foreign languages were heard. People could barely push their way through in the marketplace filled with covered wagons, carts, and carriages. Commodities were displayed which Reb Amram had never seen before. He was surrounded by lumber dealers and those who imported grain, flax, and hides from Poland. In addition to all the commotion, a traveling circus had come to town, with bears, lions, elephants, and horses, which were trained to dance to the sound of music. Despite high taxes and the vicious decrees imposed on them, the Jews engaged in many trades and had almost all the banks at their disposal. With letters of credit written in Hebrew or in Yiddish, they could borrow all the money they needed. The majority of Jewish bankers kept their capital in their pockets or in hollow belts strapped around their waists. The Jewish merchants lodged and ate together where everything was strictly kosher. Generally, the Gentile tradesmen got drunk toward evening, sang wild songs, and danced in the taverns with women. Leipzig attracted shady females who entertained the men. Prostitutes from all over came to the fairs. Although Reb Amram was a pious Jew, a man of the Torah, he somewhat envied the libertines who indulged all their passions. Alte Trina was always weak. Even on her clean days she had often dismissed him with various excuses: a headache, a toothache, a burning at the pit of the stomach, a chill in the bones. In her older years she became a broken shard. Reb Amram had entirely secluded himself from her, because no matter how he approached her, she immediately began to cry that he was hurting her. The evil spirit which lurks in each man and waits for him to become greedy for the pleasures of the flesh often chided Reb Amram: "Amram, you suffer needlessly. You wait for awards in the world to come, but they don't exist. What people don't grab for themselves in this world is lost forever. For almost two thousand years the Jews have anticipated the coming of their Messiah and He has still not arrived. They will go on waiting until the year 6000. There is no Paradise, no hell. The righteous do not feed on Leviathan, they don't drink the holy wine stored up for the saints, they don't wear crowns on their heads or enjoy the radiance of the Shechinah. They rot in their graves and are devoured by worms. The sinners are clever. As long as they can, they live it up." The Evil Spirit exhibited erudition: "If there was a hereafter, why is it not mentioned in the Bible? On the contrary, it is written in the Book of Ecclesiastes: 'But the dead know not any thing.' Even one of the Amorites denied the coming of the Messiah. Our ancient patriarchs—even Moses—were lecherous. Judah, whose name all Jews carry, went to a harlot."

Night fell. There was such a crush of people in the streets that Reb Amram could barely squeeze his way through. Music shrieked from taverns. The sounds of fiddles, trumpets, whistles could be heard as drummers drummed, hands clapped, feet stamped. The shouting of drunken males was mixed with salacious female laughter. From the open doors rose a heat like that from an oven and odors of wines, liquors, mead, beer, as well as from roasted chickens, geese, lamb, pork, all kinds of herbs and spices. Reb Amram had eaten a large dinner: chopped liver with onions, tripe, calves' feet, noodles with gravy, beef and horseradish, and later compote with plums and apricots. Nevertheless, the unkosher smells aroused a fresh appetite and a thirst in him. He sensed a mighty strength in his limbs. He felt he could wrench a tree out of the earth with all its roots. As he was passing an iron street lamp, a boyish need arose in him to show off and try to bend it. As he stood there contemplating his own prowess, a small woman with fiery red hair came over to him. She had green cat's eyes, a round face, and cheeks caked with rouge. She wore a short yellow dress and green high-heeled boots with black stockings. She gave him a sweet smile, revealing a full mouth of small teeth, and asked with a young voice, "Where are you from, buddy? From Poland?"

Reb Amram became so confused by her presence that for a moment he lost his tongue. Many whores had stopped him on his way, but they all spoke German, not Yiddish. He had heard that there were also Jewish whores in the big cities, but he had never encountered any. After a while he came to himself and answered, "Yes, from Poland."

"I am also from Poland," the woman said. "But I've been away for a long time."

"From where in Poland?" Reb Amram asked.

"From Piask."

"From the Piask thieves?" Reb Amram asked, and soon regretted his words. He feared she might curse him or spit at him. It was not in his nature to insult anyone. How do they say it? As long as a word is in the mouth, the mouth is the ruler; when it leaves the mouth, the word is the ruler. Thank God, the woman did not become enraged but answered him good-naturedly, "Not all Chelmites are fools and not all Piaskers are thieves. There are honest people in Piask, too."

"Forgive me, I was only joking," Reb Amram apologized.

"The truth is that there were a lot of thieves in Piask, but my father was an honest man, a tailor."

"How did you end up here?" Reb Amram asked.

The woman paused and then said, "It's a long story. I fell in love with a bear trainer—actually, not as much with him as with the bear. I was barely twelve years old, but I was already yearning to sow my wild oats. Both the bear trainer and the bear died a long time ago, but since then I have been dragging around with this circus. They pay me water on kasha so I have to earn a few extra gulden after the performance. The other women do it, too."

"Do you have a room here?" Reb Amram asked.

"I rent one for a few hours. Come."

She started to go, and Amram followed her with hesitation.

He heard the Evil Spirit say, "There is no God, there is none. Even if there were a God, He would not remember every sin in every city at every fair in every land from India to Ethiopia. This whole game of piety is not worth a sniff of tobacco."

The woman led Reb Amram into a dark alley to a structure which looked like a stable and opened a door. A wick was burning in a shard with oil. A straw mat was spread on the floor.

"This is it?" Reb Amram asked.

"Yes. Two guldens!" And saying these words, the strumpet extended one hand for the money; with the other she opened her blouse quickly and displayed two stiff breasts with fiery red nipples. With one yank she tore open the buttons of her skirt and was mother-naked except for her shoes and gartered stockings. She did something like a somersault on the straw mat. "Come!" Reb Amram was about to throw himself on her, but at that moment he heard a terrible cry, "You are losing the world to come."

Reb Amram shuddered. He recognized the voice of his father, who had died over twenty years ago. Reb Amram started running, and he beat his head against the door. He almost tripped over the threshold. The woman screamed as if possessed, but Reb Amram ran through the darkness in a state of confusion and fear, as if he were being chased by murderers. The alley was full of potholes, stones, and unharnessed wagons. He crashed into the pole of a wagon, immediately receiving a bump on his forehead. His knee was scraped. He didn't know whether he was fleeing toward the residential area of Leipzig or to the outskirts of the city. He raised his eyes and the sky was seeded with myriads of stars. One star tore away from its constellation and swept over the sky, leaving behind a luminous trace. The heavens seemed ablaze with a divine conflagration.

As Reb Amram was running, he remembered the commentary of Gemara on the Joseph story in the Book of Genesis: When Potiphar's wife grabbed Joseph by the sleeve and requested that he lie with her, Joseph was ready to fall into depravity, but his father's image appeared and helped him resist the temptation. "The dead live!" a voice screamed into Reb Amram's ears or into his mind. "There is Special Providence.

They see everything On High, every move a man is about to make, they read his mind, they weigh his deeds, they watch his steps."

Dogs barked at Reb Amram and tried to bite him, but he pushed them away with his boots, murmuring the words from the Pentateuch: "But against any of the children of Israel not even a dog will whet its tongue." Although he knew it was dangerous, he ran through the forest, where thieves and highwaymen loitered. They could have killed him there and no rooster would have crowed. He was escaping from a harlot, a demon, followed by the Angel of Death. His feet became strangely light. He skipped over fallen trees, puddles, heaps of garbage. The sweat ran over his face, cramps gnawed at his stomach, and he regurgitated a nauseating sour-sweet fluid. His belly blew up hard as a drum. In his distress it occurred to him that for the first time in his life he had forgotten to recite the afternoon prayer. He spoke aloud to the sacred soul of his demised father, thanked him for guarding him against the pitfall of lechery. He asked his father's spirit to protect him from robbers, since he was carrying the squire's money, and if he returned with empty hands, they would suspect him of theft.

Thank God, he managed to return to the city of Leipzig. Only now did he feel the pain in his forehead and in his knee. One of the dogs had bitten his leg and its teeth had torn through his pants. Reb Amram knew he was saved from many perils, those of the soul and of the body. He would have to recite the prayer for escaping danger twice and to redeem himself through much charity and many virtuous deeds. He arrived at the guesthouse where he was staying. The entrance was dark, but he heard talking and laughter from the kitchen and the chambers upstairs. What should he tell the owner of the guesthouse, the guests, his own coachman? They would see that something terrible had happened to him and ask questions. He was limping, his face was swollen, his boots were covered with horse dung and mud. He had to think up a lie quickly. Reb Amram recalled the saying from the *Ethics of the Fathers*: "One sin drags another sin after it." He stood in the darkness frightened by what had happened to him, baffled by his miraculous rescue, disgraced by his evil passions. He didn't dare to utter the name of the Lord with his defiled lips. He wasn't crying, but his eyes were burning and his cheeks were hot. He was on the verge of utter degradation and the fires of Gehenna.

2

Thank God, the trip back to Poland went without any mishap. Reb Amram brought back everything the squire and squiress had ordered, along with lumber contracts and a considerable amount of down payments. He had written down every groschen he had spent in his book. After the squire and the squiress thanked Reb Amram profusely for his diligence and good judgment in business, the squire and Reb Amram went into a separate room. Taking out heaps of golden ducats from his belt and various pockets, Reb Amram began to count the money. He had kept the bank notes and contracts in an oak box with brass fasteners and a steel lock. As always, he hoped the accounts would balance out to the last penny. But strangely, five golden ducats were missing from one account. "How is this possible?" Reb Amram asked himself. The squire, who trusted Reb Amram explicitly, dismissed the matter with a wave of the hand. He insisted that Reb Amram surely forgot to write down some small expense. When he remembered it, the account would straighten itself out. Reb Amram offered to give the squire the missing ducats from his own purse, but the squire refused to hear of it. He argued, "It doesn't pay to be so concerned over such a petty sum." The squire was familiar not only with the New Testament but also with the Old Testament, and he quoted the words Ephron said to Abraham when he bought the Cave of Machpelah from him: "What are four hundred silver shekels between you and me?"

Reb Amram promised not to worry about it, but when he went back home, his spirit remained troubled, partly from the ordeal with the lewd female and partly because of the lost ducats. He sat up half the night and made calculations. He remembered every groschen he had spent in Leipzig, even the alms he had distributed among the beggars in the marketplace. But these five ducats seemed to have slipped between his fingers. Had somebody robbed him? Did the Piask trollop steal them? He was sure she had not stood so close to him that she could put her hand into his pocket. While pondering the lost ducats, he realized he had forgotten to bring his wife, Alte Trina, a gift, as he always did when he returned from a journey. She had not mentioned a word about it, but he imagined that she greeted him less warmly than usual when he came home. He had also neglected to bring a gift to the maid.

Reb Amram awoke in the middle of the night and lay awake until daybreak. While undressing, he had discovered a knot in the sash of his pants. He often made such a knot as a reminder to pay a bill, to answer a letter, or to give money to a needy charity. It had slipped his memory when, and for what reason, he had made this particular knot. He fell asleep at dawn, and the Piask woman came to him in a dream. She stood before him naked, her red hair loose, and she was singing a song which he had once heard in a tavern:

> *Oy vey, give me tea.*
> *Tea is bitter—*
> *Give me sugar.*
> *Sugar is sweet—*
> *Give me feet.*
> *Feet are wet—*
> *Come in bed.*
> *In bed no sheet—*
> *Come in street.*
> *The street is dark—*
> *Come in park.*
> *In park no light—*
> *Hold me tight.*
> *In mud and mire*
> *Burn like fire.*

Reb Amram awoke with a start and with passion. The month of Elul was approaching, but he was wallowing in lewd fantasies. "Woe is me, I am sunk in iniquities," he mumbled. Normally Reb Amram waited impatiently for the Days of Awe to recite the morning prayers at the pulpit at the synagogue, dressed for the occasion in a white robe and a gold-embossed miter. Weeks before, he usually went over the tunes and the liturgies and practiced on the shofar, which he would blow. But now Reb Amram no longer yearned to lead the community in prayer. None other than Poorah, the Angel of Forget-fulness, must have accompanied him that fatal evening when he encountered the harlot in Leipzig. He could not even re-member the explanation he offered the people at the inn for the bump on his forehead and for his torn trousers and filthy boots. And what should he tell the squire about the missing five ducats? Although Reb Amram was prepared to repay him from his own money, the danger of being disgraced was far from over. It was possible that the coachman had already relayed the strange event to the squire. Gossip travels quickly. Reb Amram did not want to contradict himself and be la-beled a liar.

He fell asleep, and immediately the red-haired female ap-peared anew. He saw her descend the stairs of the Plotsk ritual bathhouse. She immersed herself three times, and her hair spread over the water like a red web. She began to climb out, winking at Reb Amram. "What happened?" Reb Amram asked himself. "Have I married her and she is making her ablutions? Is she cleansing herself for my sake? And where is Alte Trina? Is she, God forbid, no longer among the living?" He shuddered and awoke. "This female is one of Lilith's demons, whom she sends at night to seduce God-fearing men to pollution," Reb Amram said to himself. "I must not lead the congregation in prayer any longer. The prayers from one such as I will not reach up to heaven. They might even, perish the thought, bring evil decrees on the town—pestilence, famine, blood-shed." Reb Amram felt compelled to give the trustees of the synagogue advance notice to find a replacement.

As in the Book of Job, one evil tiding followed another. That morning after Reb Amram woke up from his troubled sleep, even before he went to pray, he heard the sound of a horse-man approaching his house. It was a messenger informing Reb Amram that the squire had sent for him. Reb Amram was shaken up. Who knows, maybe the coachman saw him with the wanton female and reported it to the squire. Even though the squire was himself guilty of adultery, he probably expected right conduct from his subordinates. "*Nu*, my seven good years are over," Reb Amram murmured to himself. He let the britska be harnessed and went to the squire. Thank God, the squire received him in a friendly way. Reb Amram began to speak about the vanished gold ducats, but the squire interrupted him.

"Don't be foolish, Amram, what are five ducats to me? I trust my entire estate to you and you make a fuss over a pittance. If it had been a matter of a thousand ducats, I would not worry. I have sent for you because I have to ask you a favor."

"The squire wants a favor from me?" Reb Amram asked in astonishment.

"Yes. A big favor. I find it distasteful to request this of you, but I have no choice. A few days ago I met with my future in-laws, Count Zamoyski and his wife, the countess. You certainly know how influential they are in Poland and what a great honor it is for my wife and me to marry off our beloved daughter to their son. The countess stems from an even higher lineage than her husband. She is a descendant of a king of Poland. As you know, we are preparing for a wedding which will not be equaled in the history of Poland. The count told me that his court Jew, Reb Nissel, who is learned in the Bible and in the Talmud and is an experienced merchant to boot, is also a talented actor. Whenever the Zamoyskis give a ball, Reb Nissel disguises himself as a bear and amuses the guests. I had told him about you and I praised you to heaven. The count mentioned in passing, 'If your Amram is as clever and as witty as my Nissel, why don't they perform together at the wedding of our children and entertain us?' I tried to explain to the count that you are of a different breed, that it is beneath your dignity to act as a comedian. I told him that I have never requested a service like this from you. But the count became adamant about the idea. He literally demanded that you perform with his court Jew. This is how the Zamoyskis are: strong-willed and adventurous. They could always have anything under the sun. No one has ever refused them anything. I will make it short. I was practically forced to promise the count that I would ask you to consent. I assure you that this will be the first and last time. I have persuaded the count to agree that Reb Nissel will perform the role of the bear and you will be the bear trainer. You can lead Reb Nissel by a rope and converse intermittently. All the high-class guests will admire your facetious dialogue. I know that you are familiar with Jewish humor and wit. It is not such a shame to play the role of a bear trainer. I promise you that if you ever need a favor from me, no matter how great, I will do it for you with pleasure."

As the squire spoke, Reb Amram felt as if a fist clutched at his heart and crushed it with a mighty force. Reb Amram knew that some court Jews performed at squires' balls and made the guests merry, but he never wanted to stoop to that level. Reb Amram realized that this request of the squire's was a punishment from heaven for dallying with the redheaded whore even for a few minutes. He felt like crying out, "Your Excellency, everything yes, but this is too much of a blow." Instead, he asked, "When will the wedding take place?"

The squire told him the date. Reb Amram quickly figured out that the wedding would fall on the first day of Succoth. While other Jews were sitting in the Succoth under the wings of the Shechinah, being hosts to the souls of such saints as Abraham, Isaac, and Jacob, Aaron, Moses, and David, he, Amram, would be leading another Jew dressed up like a bear, and making a mockery of himself and of the scholarly Reb Nissel before a band of murderers and pagans. What in essence were all these squires? How did they manage to rule the land if not by the power of the sword alone? How did they reduce all the peasants to slavery and force the people of Israel, whom God had chosen above all other nations, to become their underlings?

"What is your answer?" the squire asked with a trace of impatience.

"If I am able to, I will do it," Reb Amram answered.

"Why should you not be able to?"

"Everything is in God's hands."

For a while they were both silent. Afterward, the squire said, "I understand very well how difficult this task is for you at your age and in your position. But I am afraid of opposing this powerful family. Today they are my friends, tomorrow my bloody enemies."

"Yes, true."

"You seem tired, Reb Amram. Go home and rest."

"Yes, I will do so. Thank you, Your Excellency."

"Why does God allow people to tyrannize over one another? What does your Talmud say about this?" the squire asked.

Reb Amram thought it over. "Everything is created so that people can choose between good and evil."

"Not always," said the squire, and made a gesture which meant that the audience was over.

Returning home, Reb Amram saw Alte Trina sitting on the bench in front of the house knitting a sock. He was surprised, since she seldom sat on the bench outside at this time of the day but was usually busy in the kitchen preparing a meal. He looked at her for a while. They already had grandchildren together, but it seemed to him that only yesterday he and his wife were still young. In those years he could barely wait for her to go to the ritual bath so that he might approach her. Now she was an old woman, her face withered and wrinkled. A few white hairs had sprouted under her chin, a little female beard. With the knitting needle she scratched her earlobe, which protruded from her bonnet, and asked, "What did the squire want with you? Why did he send for you so early in the morning? I worried myself sick over your safety."

"Nothing, Alte Trina. It had to do with his daughter's wedding."

"What does he want now?"

"Oh, something about the jewelry which I had bought for her."

"How many trinkets do they need? She will be bedecked with gold and diamonds from head to toe. They forget, the fools, that people don't live forever. You look pale, Amram. This trip has exhausted you." Alte Trina changed her tone.

"No danger."

"Why did you run there so early? You hadn't even prayed."

"If the squire sends a courier, you can't keep him waiting."

"I will give you a glass of milk. This, one is allowed to drink before praying."

"No, Alte Trina. Let me first put on my prayer shawl and phylacteries."

"Amram, wait, I must have a word with you."

"What do you want?"

Alte Trina brought over a chair and made Reb Amram sit down. "Amram, maybe I shouldn't say this, but you are traveling down a crooked path. If a stranger said this, you might suspect him of being your enemy, but I am your wife, the mother of your children, and I want only the best for you. Believe me, if someone asked me to lay down my head for your sake, I would gladly do it."

"Speak clearly. What am I doing that is wrong?"

"First of all, you work too hard. A man of your age—you should live to be a hundred and twenty—doesn't need to drag himself off to fairs in distant lands. You know very well that the roads are teeming with thieves and assassins. Does it pay to risk one's health so that some shiksa can dangle her jewelry before an impudent idolator? Recently I heard that Count Zamoyski was hunting during the harvest season along with a band of noblemen. Their horses and dogs trampled and ruined hundreds of acres of fields ready for the harvest, and when the peasants pleaded with the villains not to turn God's blessings into a shambles and bring famine to the villages, they fell into such a rage that they shot off their pistols and killed a number of them. Imagine, Amram, it is their peasants, their estates, but these drunkards think they are entitled to do anything they please. People have told me that the young count set fire to stacks of wheat which had been prepared for the threshers. Your squire is planning a wedding which will cost him a fortune. He is already in debt over his head. The end will be that he will go broke. And when they get into trouble, they come to borrow from the Jew. Then if you don't give it to them willingly, they take it by force."

"For the time being, our squire is not to blame," Reb Amram said.

"This is one thing," Alte Trina went on. "Second, you had told me that, God willing, after we gave away our youngest child, we would put all business aside and devote ourselves only to Jewishness. You even mentioned going to the Holy Land."

"To the Holy Land? Old people go there, not people our age. I don't remember saying that."

"You don't remember, but I do. And God certainly remembers."

Reb Amram had a desire to scold her, as always when she interfered too much in his affairs, but he recalled the squire's humiliating proposal to him and restrained himself. He shrugged. "Alte Trina, we'll talk about this later."

"Again later?"

"Let me finish the prayers first."

Reb Amram entered the room where he kept his bookcases and prepared himself for prayer. He put on the prayer shawl and the phylacteries, wound the thongs around his arm, and began to murmur the appropriate prayers. But he was distracted by confusing thoughts and he prayed without concentration. He even overlooked certain verses. To become a buffoon for the squire's sake? Lead Reb Nissel by a rope and crack jokes? Reb Amram stood up to recite the Eighteen Benedictions, but he omitted some passages and others he repeated. He resorted to addressing God in Yiddish: "Father in heaven, I am in a terrible predicament. Save me or take me away."

Reb Amram then realized that prayer of this nature is a sin. A human being has no right to dictate to the Almighty or to admonish Him. After a while, he took off the prayer shawl and the phylacteries. A great fatigue had come over him, and he felt a weakness in his knees. He locked the door which led to the corridor, collapsed on the sofa, and fell into a deep sleep. As if the lord of dreams could scarcely wait for Reb Amram to fall asleep, he immediately brought him to Leipzig. It was again night, and he was standing with the redheaded harlot by a lamp post. Again, the Evil One cajoled him to damnation. This time Reb Amram saw Satan's fiendish image: taller than the lamp post, dark and sheer as a spiderweb, with horns like a he-goat, two holes instead of eyes, with the mouth of a frog. He whispered to Reb Amram, "Take her, the whore. Go into her. Have no fear. There is no law below, there is no judge above. And even if there were a God somewhere in the Seventh Heaven, He would not remember all the petty prohibitions, all the silly restrictions and interpretations from the times of Moses until some half-witted rabbi in a muddy village."

In his dream, Reb Amram followed the harlot, who led him into the dark hallway and opened the door of the murky shed. A wick burned in the shard with oil, a straw mat lay on the floor. The whore threw down the colorful rags and called out, "Two gulden. Come!" Reb Amram again heard his father's cry: "You are losing the world to come!" He started to run, and as he ran, he pushed his hand into his pocket and threw a handful of gold coins to the raging harlot. Reb Amram woke up instantly. The hand which threw the coins was still shaking, and his feet were scampering as if running. For a moment Reb Amram took the dream for reality. He was both in the study where he had prayed and in the shed with the whore. He fell on the floor, his teeth chattering. He lingered a while until he could fully grasp where he was. In all his anxiety Reb Amram realized that the dream had solved his riddle. In his consternation he had taken the harlot's fee from the pocket where he kept the squire's money. He had forgotten this, but the pocket, a little piece of lining fabric, had remembered and computed the balance accordingly—a silent witness that could testify against him on the Day of Judgment. Reb Amram felt like laughing and crying. If a pocket is able to remember, what about the Almighty, of whom it is said: "There is no forgetfulness before Thy Throne of Glory."

"Merciful God, have pity on me," Reb Amram called out. "My Father in Paradise, you are not dead, you live. Your sacred soul protected me in Leipzig. You hovered over me, kept a vigil during the entire journey, guarded my every step, and did not allow me to fall into the net of debauchery, to sink to the lowest abyss. There is a God, there is. There is a hereafter, there is," Reb Amram shouted in his mind to Satan the spoiler. "How could I have forgotten all this, and let myself go with a prostitute, about which King Solomon says, 'None that go unto her return again, neither take they hold of the paths of life.' God sees and the saints see and there is no death, there is none!"

Somebody knocked at the door—Alte Trina. How strange, but the moment he saw her, he also recalled the meaning of the knot in his sash: to buy for her the new edition of *Tzenah u-Reenah*, the Yiddish translation of the Pentateuch and its commentaries, since the binding of her old volume was torn and some pages had fallen out.

That day Reb Amram sent back the five gold coins to the squire by messenger. Later, he told the elders of the community that he was sick to his stomach and must see a doctor in Warsaw. In case, God forbid, he didn't recover, they would have to find another leader for the morning prayers on the

High Holidays and another man to blow the shofar. He harnessed the britska himself, took Alte Trina with him, and left only Reishe, the maid, at home. He gave her a large sum of money to cover all her expenses in case of a long absence.

Reb Amram did not come back for the High Holidays. He never returned to Plotsk. After some time his sons and daughters came to town and brought a letter from their father saying that he was giving his house and his books to preachers and talmudic scholars who came to the city. Reb Amram's sons and daughters brought additional money for Markel the coachman, for Reishe the maid, as well as a letter signed by Alte Trina which transferred ownership of her clothing and utensils to Reishe.

The wedding between Count Zamoyski's son and Walecki's daughter never came to pass. A few days before the wedding the young count went hunting in the forest, and one of the hunters mistook him for an animal and shot him dead. Walecki's daughter, the bride, fell into melancholia after this dismal event and decided to enter a cloister.

Nobody heard from Reb Amram for over two years. Some believed that he was still visiting important doctors and healers in far-off cities. Others concluded that Reb Amram and his wife were no longer among the living. One day a rabbinical messenger from Jerusalem arrived in Plotsk and brought a letter from Reb Amram. Reb Amram wrote that after many months of wanderings and tribulations he and his wife miraculously managed to arrive by ship in the Land of Israel. They found a place to live in Jerusalem. From the money which he saved and which Alte Trina had received from selling her jewelry, they now could afford to devote their old years to Jewishness. He now studied the Mishnah in the studyhouse of Rabbi Yehuda the Hasid, and recited psalms at the Wailing Wall in the corner where the Shechinah has always been present. In the month of Elul, he and Alte Trina visited the graves of Mother Rachel, Rabbi Simon son of Yochai, and other saints. They traveled to the city of Safad, and he immersed himself in the ritual bath of the holy Isaac Luria. The sky in the Land of Israel is higher than in other countries, the stars are brighter, and the air is as clear as crystal and as sweet as wine. Reb Amram asked the townspeople of Plotsk to help this messenger collect money for a yeshiva, because in heaven are kept records of every groschen contributed to charity or, God forbid, used as means of transgression. He ended the letter with the puzzling words: "A man forgets, but his pocket remembers."

Translated by Deborah Menashe

The Secret

SHE was a tiny old woman with freshly dyed black hair, a little wrinkled face, and black eyes which gleamed with a youthful zeal. She leaned on a cane, gave me a coquettish smile, and revealed a mouthful of small false teeth. Her Yiddish was rich with all the mannerisms and intonations of the Lublin region. She was saying, "I read every word you write. I never miss your advice on the radio. I've been trying to contact you for weeks, but you're impossible to reach on the telephone. Where do you run around to the whole day? Excuse me for being so familiar with you. You don't know me, but I know you like a brother."

I thanked her and offered her a seat. She handed me her cane and I stood it in a corner. The seat was too high for her, so I put a telephone book at her feet to serve as a footstool. She said, "You are looking at an old woman, but how long has it been since I've been young? In one of your articles you mentioned a poet—I have forgotten his name—who said, 'Old people die young.' Golden words. This old person who sits before you will die a young girl. The soul does not age. In a way my memory becomes younger from day to day. What happened yesterday I forget, but things which occurred sixty years ago linger before my eyes. I have an unbelievable story for you. A story like this happens once in a thousand years."

"Do you want to tell me a story, or seek advice?" I asked.

"Both. But you must be patient."

"Do me a favor and make it short," I said.

"Short, huh? How can someone make fifty or sixty years short. But I will try. I am not just a nobody. My father was a scribe. He transcribed Torah scrolls, phylacteries, mezuzahs, and we girls—we were four daughters and one son—tried to copy his script, not on parchment, but on paper. I whittled the goose-feather quills for him and lined the parchment sheets. Our mother was a learned woman and she taught us the Bible. I could sit with you seven days and seven nights and still not tell a fraction of what I lived through, but today people have no patience. I also was quick when I was young. What's the rush now? I won't be late for the grave.

"Our father, Reb Moshe the scribe, as he was called, was a saintly Jew. His father, Reb Yerucham—also a scribe—was of such piety that before he transcribed a holy name he went to the ritual bath. In certain sections of the Pentateuch, God's name is mentioned in every line, and he went from the parchment scroll to the ritual bath and back to the parchment scroll. It took him twenty years to transcribe a complete Torah scroll and weeks to write sections of the phylacteries. He and his family would have died from hunger, but our grandmother Tirtza Perl had a small store. She was married at fourteen and had seventeen children in her lifetime. I remember her being pregnant even when she was a grandmother. She and my mother always went around with bellies. Of the seventeen children my grandmother bore, eleven died. This grandmother was the type of housewife one doesn't find in our time. She worked in the store, cooked, baked, did the wash, and even chopped wood if necessary. She prepared for the Passover while carrying a child in her arms. I will never understand where these people found the strength. That was my maternal grandmother; the other grandmother died young.

"Being the oldest, I had to help my mother carry the burden of raising the younger children. There was no time to develop friendships. I was an ardent reader of literature. My brother Shmuel Chaim had secretly read Isaac Meir Dick and Mendele Mocher Sephorim, and along with older boys had subscribed to a Yiddish newspaper from Warsaw; I read it, too. Here in America I read your works and I know that you understand the human soul. I want to tell you something that I never told anyone before. I was secretly very passionate and I began to think about love very very early. I understood a great deal but I didn't want to worry my parents. We sisters read Shomer's novels. There was a maid in our town, the daughter of a watercarrier, who was impregnated by a Cossack. There were many Cossacks in the village and they often went to a nearby brothel behind the Russian cemetery. Boys went there in the dark when the moon wasn't shining. There were nights when I would lie awake and break out in a cold sweat musing about these things.

"In America people have forgotten what went on in the old country. The younger generation doesn't know how good they have it here. Every year after the Feast of Tabernacles, an epidemic spread through the town. We had a gravedigger who was nicknamed Gehenna's Beadle. When the little children began to die, he went and collected the corpses, wrapped each one in a piece of linen from a torn bedsheet or a shirt, and buried them himself. I'm sorry to say it, but he was a drunkard like all the members of the Burial Society. On the way to the cemetery he used to stop off at the tavern. Once, he left a sack of tiny bodies on a bench. There was such a hue and outcry in the town that he was dismissed.

"Both my parents died before their time, within the same year. After they passed away, the younger children, our brother Shmuel Chaim, and my three sisters scattered in all directions. One went to serve as a maid in Lublin, another married a Litvak who took her to Russia. Eventually Shmuel Chaim ended up in America. They are no longer among the living. Look at what I've become—a broken shard. I was once a pretty girl. In those times a girl had to have a dowry. My aunt Chaye Gutshe had taken responsibility for me. When people proposed a match for me, she went to examine the man. My dear writer, she married me off to a tailor—a widower who was over forty years my senior, a father and grandfather. He already had a gray beard when we stood under the wedding canopy. I thought to myself, He's a man, it's better than having nobody. I'd rather not mention his name or the town we came from. When you hear the whole story you will understand why.

"We married. He was a pious Jew, a decent man, but nothing else. I had hoped to have a child, even a few children, but a number of years passed and I did not become pregnant. With us Jews, what is a woman worth without children? The thought that I was a barren woman, or wombless, as they say, was a blow. Perhaps my husband became sterile in his old age."

"A man doesn't become sterile in his old age," I said. "He may only become impotent."

"Huh? This he was not. But he was nothing to rave about, either. He waited for me to go to the ritual bath every month and only then did he come to me. He was a men's tailor and mostly made long gaberdines. He was unusually observant. Six o'clock in the morning he went to pray. They made him a trustee in the small tailors' shul. He also led the congregation in prayer. His only worry was that my matron's wig would slip somewhat and men would see my hair and fall into sinful thoughts. His one worker was also an elderly man. I cooked for both men and carried water from the well. My life was as good as over, but I made peace with it. My husband constantly spoke of saving money. In order to live honestly, one must always have something saved for hard times. We saved what we could. I was only a spendthrift when it came to books. When a book peddler came to town I bought whatever was available in Yiddish: storybooks, a novel by Isaac Meir Dick, Solomon Ettinger, Mendele Mocher Sephorim, Sholem Aleichem, Peretz, Sholem Asch. A small Yiddish library was established in our village and I could secretly get books there. My husband spat on worldly books, calling them heretical. But reading was the only pleasure left to me. My brother Shmuel Chaim sometimes sent me books from America: Zeyfert, Shomer, Kubrin, Libin. I cannot describe the satisfaction I got from reading these books. They literally saved my life.

"Now the real story begins. Once, my husband brought home an apprentice called Motke. He was a boy of thirteen from a nearby shtetl. I say thirteen because I remember when he put on phylacteries for his bar mitzvah. The other tailors kept their apprentices like slaves. They ran errands, brought water from the pump, poured out the slop pail, and rocked babies in their cradles. These boys were given only food and a night's lodging on top of the stove. The contract was signed by the boy's father, or by a relative if he was an orphan. Many tailors cheated the boys. Months went by before they taught them to cut out a hole or sew on a button.

"Motke was an orphan and I don't remember whether my husband wrote out a contract for him or simply made a verbal agreement. My husband was honest and immediately began teaching Motke the trade. This Motke was clever and had golden hands. He grasped everything quickly, and my husband praised him to heaven. What did he look like? He was dark with black eyes, clever, with a sense of humor like none other in the world. Little jokes poured out of him. He could read and soon indulged in my books.

"My husband always protected him, warned me not to over-work the boy or take advantage of him, God forbid. Who wanted to take advantage? I cooked the meals he liked and treated him like an only son. He said that I was like a mother and my husband like a father to him. The other tailors com-plained that we pampered him, and that if other apprentices heard of the comfort he enjoyed with us, they would rebel and demand higher wages.

"Times were changing. Strikes had begun in Russia. Work-ers were beginning to revolt, carrying revolvers and throwing bombs. The Tsar had been murdered only a few years earlier. We were a little town in the hinterland, but there were already those youths who sought equality for all. They met in the woods after the Sabbath meal and organized what they called a circle. A few apprentices secretly joined the group but Motke said he would never join. How could he complain when we provided him with the best of everything? He made fun of their petitions to the government and revolutionary proclama-tions. He boasted that when he learned the trade he would himself become an employer. He wanted to be a ladies' tailor, to sew jackets and dresses for pretty girls, not gaberdines for Hasidim. He was a big talker."

"You fell in love with him, huh?" I asked.

The old woman was quiet for a long while. "One should not eat kugel with you," she said.

"Why not?"

"Because you grasp things too quickly. Yes, you are right. I saw that he looked at me constantly. Once in a while he stole a kiss. I pleaded with him not to, but he listened to me like Haman listens to the grocer. He was ready to sow his wild oats. He often behaved like a fully ripe man. I considered telling my husband, who surely would have chased him out in disgrace, but I had grown attached to him. My dear man, since you are guessing things, what's the use of trying to deny them? Yes, he became my lover."

"When did it happen? How?"

"One summer, on a Sabbath. It could never have happened in the middle of the week, since my husband worked at home.

But on Sabbath afternoons he used to go to the tailors' group to study the *Ethics of the Fathers*. Later, the congregation recited the evening prayer and ate the third meal, which consisted of stale challah and herring. Afterward they recited the Havdalah and sang valedictory songs. By the time he came home, it was already late in the evening. I used to read in bed after the Sabbath meal. That day I had fallen into a deep sleep. I opened my eyes and Motke was lying beside me in bed. I wanted to scream in alarm, but he closed my mouth with his hand like an experienced rascal. This was a devil, not an apprentice."

"Is this the whole story?" I asked.

"Just the beginning."

We sat in silence for a long while. It seemed to me the old woman's face had become younger and less wrinkled. Something of a smile appeared in her eyes. Only her head, with its black hair—dulled from the dye—trembled like an old woman's.

Then she said, "It happened and it's too late for regret now. I acted like a mother, but he treated me like a wife. At times our conduct seemed utterly sinful and ugly to me—a humiliation beyond words to me and to my parents in Paradise. He also had parents in the other world and I felt terribly degraded before them, too. I tried with all my power to drive him away, but he wouldn't hear of it. Although nobody visited us during the day on the Sabbath, still, what would I have done had the door opened and someone come in? I would have died on the spot. How I wish this had really happened, because what followed was worse than death."

"You became pregnant, huh?"

The woman's face became harsh and hostile. "God in heaven, I'm afraid of you! What are you? A mind reader?"

"I simply understand."

"Yes, it happened. But not immediately. He remained with us over two years. I had gotten so accustomed to him that I could no longer live without him. The entire week I looked forward to the Sabbath. A holy day, and I defiled it with such abominations. In the meantime, he became taller, broader, a real man. I cannot describe how good he was at tailoring, how adept at sewing on the machine which we later acquired. He helped my husband cut out material and take measurements. He held a piece of chalk in his hand and did everything with speed and precision like a master tailor. The tailors became my husband's blood enemies. It was against the rules to train an apprentice so quickly. Their notions dated back to King Sobieski's time—to keep an apprentice for three years without pay and afterward begin paying him half a ruble a month. I will make it short. The day Motke said that he was planning to leave and go to Warsaw, I knew I had lost him. For me this was a black day.

"Where was I, eh? Yes, said and done. My husband tried to talk Motke into staying with us, but with him a word was a deed. I yearned for him. The weekdays were still bearable, but when the Sabbath came I felt the pain. He promised to send a card, but it never arrived. This is what men are, egotists, young and old. Excuse me for speaking this way about your gender. It is not their fault, it's their nature. Weeks passed, months. Suddenly it dawned on me that I hadn't gotten my period, or the 'holiday,' as we called it, for some time. When this occurred, I knew I was going to become a mother and who the father was."

"How could you have known?" I asked. "You lived with two men."

"I knew. Normally I would have rejoiced at becoming a mother. My aunt always said, 'A wife without children is like a tree without fruit.' But to have a child out of wedlock, and with a young boy at that, was a sin God would not forgive and a woman, unless she is a whore, cannot bear. I seriously considered suicide, but I could not bring myself to do it. I had compassion for my husband, who became helpless after Motke left. His old age descended on him suddenly. He seemed sick to me. He had become half deaf and I had to repeat every word I said to him. He had difficulty threading a needle. His customers began to complain that their gaberdines were too long, too short, too narrow. You should excuse my frankness, but he made a pair of pants and the crotch came out too high or too low. In the middle of all this, I had to tell him the news that I was pregnant. He was a devout Jew and he took it as a gift from God, but I could see very well that he didn't feel this way. Who wants to become a father in his old age? Nobody, God forbid, suspected anything. In that time such a disgrace never happened, even among the lowest. What a crime to deliver a bastard to a husband! God in heaven, my days were hell, and at night I shook in bed as if in a fever. I begged God to let me miscarry. I had heard that if you drank vinegar or jumped off a table, a miscarriage would follow. I tried this at every opportunity, but to no avail. It was already too late. The baby was a girl. Usually people want a boy, but in this situation it's better to have a girl: she can get married and no longer carries and defiles her father's name.

"My husband lived only four years after her birth, and he loved her more than his other children. I know what you want to ask: 'How could I be sure who the father was?' From the beginning I knew, because my heart told me so. After she was born, I didn't need to rely on my heart: she looked exactly like Motke—his eyes, his ears, the shape of his mouth. I shuddered with fear that people would notice the resemblance and there would be a terrible scandal. But, thank God, no one suspected anything. Only I, the debased mother, could see the bitter truth."

"How old is your daughter?" I asked.

The woman was taken aback. "What? She is forty-five years old, but you wouldn't take her for more than thirty. A beauty, and educated as well. She is a teacher of mathematics in a high school, and they wanted to make her a professor in a college."

"When did you come to America?" I asked.

"Thirty-seven years ago, a few years before Hitler's slaughter. My brother Shmuel Chaim, or Sam as they called him here, saved me. He had become rich in America and sent me an affidavit. When I came here, he was better to me than a father."

"Is your daughter married?"

"Was. Twice. She is divorced."

"And did you marry again?"

"Yes, also twice, here in America. Both my husbands died. With one I lived only two years. With the other I lived thirteen years and he was close to ninety when he died. He left me a lot of money, but what good is money to me at this age? It is all for my daughter."

"Is that everything?"

"Wait, my dear man, this is still not the main thing I wanted to tell you. As I said, what happened to me can only happen once in a thousand years, or possibly a million."

"What happened to you?"

The old woman did not answer. Her lips quivered. She tried to speak, but she choked on the words. Finally she cried out, "My daughter lives with her father! He is her lover. They are planning to marry!"

Some time passed before the woman found her tongue. She looked at me with wrath, as if I were somehow to blame. She called out, "I alone am the cause of this abomination! Only I. Nobody else!"

"Your daughter . . ."

The old woman interrupted me. "She knew nothing and knows nothing. I had mentioned to her that we once had an apprentice, Motke, and that's all she ever knew. She came to America with me when she was still a young girl. She didn't know a word of English. I sent her to school. My brother, may he rest in peace, helped me, and she immediately took to her studies. She was the best student in her class, and it continued in this way every year. She finished high school at seventeen. She remembered my husband as her father. She had a fantastic memory, and what she couldn't remember, she asked about. She wanted to know every detail about him. Such love from a child to a father, who died somewhere in the old country before she was even five years old, always struck me as strange. Here in America children have little feeling for immigrant parents, especially if they are brought up without a father. But Sylvia—this is the American name my brother gave her, her real name is Sarah Leah—often investigated and questioned me. We had only one photograph from his Polish passport and she persuaded me to make a large portrait from it. This she framed and hung over her bed. I didn't want to talk about him too much and I didn't actually have that much to tell, but she simply exhausted me with her inquiries, year in, year out. When I remarried, she was angry with me; when I married again, she became my enemy. What could I do? In the old country I was dead. Here I came back to life. I went to night school and learned English. I went to the Yiddish theater and

later to the English theater as well. I loved my child more than
my own life, but she had waged war with me and I knew this
was a punishment from God. We had relatives, all living in
Brooklyn. I once had a job with Abraham & Straus—I became
their first saleslady. When I married the second time and gave
up my job, they made a banquet for me.

"Now about my daughter. She is clever, pretty, educated.
She resembles her father—her real father—like two drops of
water. But she had no luck with men. She was married twice
and it was wrong both times. Neither of these men wanted
children. She was dying to have a child, but it was just her bad
luck that men were always coarse to her, even brutal. My dear
man, there is a lot to tell. At times I thought that her body was
from her real father and her soul was from my first husband.
You frequently write about dybbuks, mysterious things. Can it
be that my first husband's soul entered her after his death?"

"Everything is possible."

"Ah, the world is full of secrets. I have to tell you something
which has to do with your writing. When I came to America, I
began to read the *Forward* and this opened up the world to
me. I was hospitalized twice, and my daughter had to bring
the *Forward* to me every day. She also learned to read Yiddish
and wrote an essay on Yiddish literature in college. My daughter listens to you on the radio and . . ."

"When and how did you meet Motke?" I asked.

"It happened suddenly, like all misfortunes. We were shopping for bargains on Orchard Street at the pushcarts. We
didn't find what we were looking for, but we got hungry and
went for supper on Second Avenue at Rappaport's restaurant.
After we had been sitting and eating a while, a man approached our table. He was tall, well dressed. He came over
and said, 'Ladies, excuse me, but I must ask you something.'

"'What do you want to ask?' I said. And he asked, 'Aren't
you from . . .' and he mentioned the name of our town.

"In New York we have a landsman society, a cemetery, and
all the rest of it. But for some reason I never joined. God
should not punish me, but I hid from our landsmen. Many of
my acquaintances had died and the younger generation perished with the Nazis. My two husbands here were Litvaks and
they were members of their own societies. When the man

mentioned the name of our town, I wanted to say no, but I am not a liar by nature and answered yes. My daughter became all ears. She often confronted me about avoiding my landsmen. For her it was a sign that I was trying to forget her father. The man told me he came to America many years ago and became a rich garment manufacturer here. His wife died of cancer. I will tell you something and you won't believe me. I took one look at him and at my daughter and I knew that I had fallen into a trap from which one cannot emerge."

"Why didn't you tell Sylvia that he was her father?" I asked.

"Because I knew then, and I know to this day, that she would never have forgiven me for having deceived her. It would have been her death," the old woman answered. "I fear God, but I didn't want to lose my daughter."

"Why didn't it occur to him, since she resembles him so much?" I asked.

The old woman did not answer. She lowered her head and was silent. Then she said, "Who knows if it occurred to him or not? He made it clear to me that very night that he was an atheist. When my daughter was washing her hands in the ladies' room, I made him swear to me that he would never say a word to her about what had passed between us, and he promised me. He took the whole thing lightly. He sat with us three hours and talked only about his successes in business and with women. He had a son from a previous wife. He had a house on Long Island and an apartment on West End Avenue. People knew him well in Rappaport's, they even called him to the telephone. He wouldn't let us pay for supper and left a big tip. He made a date with my daughter on the spot. When we entered the restaurant, my daughter seemed tired, pale, and old for her age. But when he drove us home to Brooklyn in his Cadillac, my daughter looked and spoke like a young girl. A mother understands such things. It was, as they say, love at first sight. She sat next to him in the front, and I sat in the back and saw how he drove the car with his left hand. His right hand he had on her lap. She turned her head to me and said out loud, 'Mama, I found my father.'

"Those were her words. She didn't know that she was speaking the truth. My heart tightened as if a fist had clamped down on it will all its strength. I thought my end had come.

But those who want to live, die, and those who want to die often live to be a hundred years."

"My dear lady, with such problems one goes to a rabbi or to a psychiatrist, not to a writer," I said. "You know yourself that I cannot help you."

"Yes, I know. But who can help me? I had one comfort: she was already too old to have children. At least she would not give birth to a bastard. But lately she began to say that she is prepared to risk everything in order to become pregnant. I have only one hope, that I will not live through the shame and the degradation."

"The world is full of illegitimate children," I said.

"Not from a father with his own daughter. People didn't commit such iniquities even in the time of the Flood," the old woman said.

She made a gesture as if to leave, and I brought her the cane. She leaned on it heavily, wobbled, and balanced herself in order not to fall.

"Come, I will lead you," I said as I held her by the shoulders.

"Please wait a minute. When I sit too long in one place, my legs get stiff," she said. "The blood no longer flows easily through my veins. My limbs are all sick, but my mind is clear. I thought that since she reads everything you write and worships you, maybe you could discourage her from this man."

"I would not be able to, nor would I want to. If God wants a kosher world, He will have to create one Himself."

"I am afraid He, too, would not know what to do in this case," the old woman said.

She smiled, and for a split second her face became young again.

Translated by Deborah Menashe

A Nest Egg for Paradise

IT ALL happened in the city of Lublin. Two brothers lived there who jointly owned a fabric shop, considered to be the finest in the province. The wealthiest landowners, and even the governor and his wife, used to shop there for their fabrics.

The older brother, Reb Mendel, had the reputation of a scholar. He was also a follower of the Hasidic master Reb Bunem of Przysucha. Because Reb Mendel was always absorbed in study and in Hasidic lore, he had little time left to devote to business. Both in his appearance and in his character Reb Mendel resembled his father, Reb Gershon of blessed memory; tall and broad, his beard and sidelocks black, his manner always gentle. The younger brother, Joel, was small, not given to learning, and a clown by nature. Joel had flaming red hair, a little red beard, and no hint of sidelocks. Whatever Joel did, he did in a hurry. He didn't walk, he ran. He spoke in a hurry, ate in a hurry, he rushed through his prayers. One minute he rose to recite the Eighteen Benedictions, the next he was done. He put on his prayer shawl and phylacteries, then promptly took them off. Because Joel had a flair for business, and because he liked to travel to all the great fairs, where he met buyers and traders from every corner of Poland and sometimes from other countries as well, Reb Mendel had drawn up a written agreement allotting sixty percent of the profits to Joel and taking the remaining forty percent himself. Basha-Meitl, Mendel's wife, fretted a good deal over her husband's agreement. Basha-Meitl had borne her husband three girls and a boy, while Lisa-Hadas, her sister-in-law, had borne Joel no children. Since the couple was childless after ten years of married life, Jewish law required Joel to divorce his wife. But Joel refused. When people asked him why he did not heed the law, Joel would answer with a joke, "I already expect a good lashing in hell. Let there be a few lashes more."

Another time he said, "If I divorced Lisa-Hadas, every widow, spinster, and divorcée would be after me to marry her. I'd never know which one to choose. Staying married is the best protection for a fellow like me."

By the time he was forty-five Reb Mendel had married off all his children. He could not provide large dowries for his daughters, but because they were pretty and well brought up, they found themselves good husbands. Basha-Meitl often complained to Reb Mendel that had he not been so immersed in Hasidic lore and practice—often spending more time in Przysucha than at home—he could have found himself more prosperous sons-in-law. But Reb Mendel would answer, "When a man reaches the world to come and is required to render accounts, the angel does not ask him how rich or poor his sons-in-law are. He asks instead, 'Did you study Torah? Was your business honorable?'"

It was the custom for Joel to send Reb Mendel his portion of the week's profits on Friday. Joel never offered to show Reb Mendel his account books and Reb Mendel never asked to see them. Although the shop had grown steadily larger and Joel had taken on additional help, and although the shelves had been stacked floor to ceiling with the finest merchandise, the earnings, it seemed, remained more or less the same. Basha-Meitl often nagged her husband to demand a precise accounting of expenses and profits. But Reb Mendel refused, saying, "If I can't trust my own brother, whom, then, can I trust? And if, God forbid, he is a swindler—what's to prevent him from falsifying the books?" And he made Basha-Meitl promise never to bring up these ugly suspicions again.

"What do they want with so much money?" Basha-Meitl would ask. "To whom will they leave their fortune?"

And Reb Mendel would answer, "With the Almighty's help, they'll live to a hundred and twenty."

As different as were the two brothers, so also were their wives. Reb Mendel's wife, Basha-Meitl, was the same age as he. A pious woman, she wore a double bonnet on her shaved head, so that when the hair on her head began to grow out again it would not be seen, God forbid, by a stranger's eye, because it is written, "A woman's hair is akin to her nakedness." Basha-Meitl fasted not only on Yom Kippur and on the Ninth of Av, as the other women did, but also on the Seventeenth of Tammuz, the Fast of Esther, and the Tenth of Tebeth, as well as the eight Fridays of the Shovavim Tat in the winter—which was only a custom and not a commanded law. Every Sabbath she read the weekly portion in the Yiddish Pentateuch, and she often read (in Yiddish translation) *The Good Heart*, *The Rod of Punishment*, *The Lamp of Light*, and *The Right Measure*. Frugal by nature, she had managed to put aside a small nest egg, so that come what may, neither she nor her husband should have to come begging, God forbid, to their children, let alone to strangers. Both she and Reb Mendel had written a will leaving one half of their savings to the children and the other half to various charities—to the poorhouse, for marrying off poor and orphaned brides, to the old-age home, and to the orphanage.

Joel's wife was ten years younger than her husband. Spared the pains of childbirth and child-rearing, she looked younger still. Lisa-Hadas indulged herself in every luxury. She did no housework at all, employing instead two maids. She had a sweet tooth and was forever nibbling cookies, cakes, strudels, sipping sweet liqueurs or cherry brandy. Instead of a bonnet she wore a wig, whose hair she combed so that it blended with her own. Lisa-Hadas was the same height as Joel, and as quick and nimble as he. She flew about on her high-heeled shoes, darting here and there like a bird. As many dresses, blouses, robes, and coats as filled her closets, she always complained of having nothing to wear and spent long hours with her tailors and seamstresses. She had a chest filled with shoes of every color and another with hats topped with silk flowers, with ostrich plumes, with wooden peaches, pomegranates, bunches of grapes. Whenever Joel traveled, he returned with a piece of jewelry for her: a necklace, a brooch, a ring, earrings. Lisa-Hadas attended the synagogue only on the High Holidays, or on those occasions when she happened to escort a bride to her wedding. Like her husband, Lisa-Hadas was forever ready with a joke. Her high-pitched laughter often ended with a squeal. When she went to the ritual bath at the end of her menstrual periods, the other wives had much to envy her for. She'd come all decked out in silk lingerie edged in exquisite lace and long stockings which reached up to her thighs. Her breasts were firm and pointed like a girl's. The younger women showered her with compliments, but the older ones acidly asked her, "What is it with you, Lisa-Hadas, not getting any older?" And

Lisa-Hadas would answer with a wink, "I have a potion which keeps whoever drinks it young till ninety."

There had been a time when Reb Mendel spent several hours in the shop ever week, so that he might not become completely estranged either from the business or from Joel. But that time had long since gone. Joel had taken on clerks to help him wait on customers and to run the shop for him when he traveled. Women's fashions and styles were constantly changing. One year dresses hung loose, the next they clung to the body. One year lapels were narrow, the next they were wide. There was no sense in paying attention to such vanity. Besides, Reb Mendel was glad to avoid running into his sister-in-law. Lisa-Hadas had become a fashion expert. She subscribed to magazines which came to her from far-off Paris—that bit of Sodom whose women were forever occupied with finding new ways to titillate men. Napoleon, who was said to have been the vicious Gog, or perhaps the Magog mentioned in the Bible, had been defeated in one of his battles and had died on some bleak and forsaken island. But still the world craved nothing better than to ape the French, to speak their language, to imitate their whims and caprices. In the larger cities pious Jews had their daughters taught to prattle in French and to play on the piano. The Enlightenment, which had begun in Germany with the heretic Moses Mendelssohn of Dessau, soon drifted over to Russia and even to Poland. In Vienna and Berlin and Budapest reform synagogues cropped up, where rabbiners delivered their sermons in German, and where an organ was played on the Sabbath and holidays. Secular writers repeated in their Hebrew magazines every blasphemous theory put forth by the philosophers. They denied the miraculous nature of the Exodus from Egypt, as well as the divinity of the Torah. Reb Mendel suspected that secretly Lisa-Hadas belonged in their camp. He did not even trust the kashruth of her household, because she let it be run by Gentile servants.

After he stopped going to the shop, Reb Mendel studied the Talmud and Hasidic books at the studyhouse in Lublin every afternoon after his nap. Lublin was a city of Hasidim. When the Seer, Rabbi Yaakov Yitzhak, was alive, Hasidim from every corner of Poland flocked to Lublin. After the Seer's death, his disciple Bunem of Przysucha had taken his place. Reb Bunem did not perform miracles, as had the Seer. Reb Bunem's way in Hasidism was the way of wisdom. He assembled around him a select circle of scholars, keen minds, young men in search of a new way in Hasidism. Reb Bunem was fluent in Polish, even in Russian. He had been a pharmacist at one time. His adversaries, the Mitnaggedim, denounced him. Even among the Hasidim there were those who thought that he was too clever, too blunt, and that some of his utterances smacked of heresy. But those who understood a thing or two could glean layer upon layer of mystery from his words.

One summer afternoon, as Reb Mendel sat alone in the studyhouse poring over the same sacred volume, the door was pushed open a crack. Reb Mendel looked up, and standing in the doorway he saw his sister-in-law, Lisa-Hadas. She was dressed in a cream-colored suit topped with a straw hat and a ribbon. In one hand she carried a handbag and in the other a white parasol like the ones carried by the wives of the rich landowners to shield themselves from the sun. So startled was Reb Mendel by her presence that he dropped the book to the floor. Something's happened to my brother was the thought that raced through his head. He stood up and said, "Do my eyes deceive me?"

"No, Mendel. It's me, your sister-in-law, Lisa-Hadas."

"What brings you here?" he asked, with a tremor in his voice.

"I looked for you at your house, but the maid told me you were here."

"What happened? Is something, God forbid, wrong with Joel?"

"Yes. Something is wrong with Joel. But don't be alarmed. He's alive."

"Taken ill, God forbid?"

"I can't talk here."

"Where, then?"

"Come home with me."

"Home, with you?"

"Yes, why not? It isn't far. I'm not a stranger to you, Mendel. I am still your brother's wife."

"Is Joel back in Lublin?"

"Joel is still in Cracow."

Lisa-Hadas spoke to Reb Mendel with a mixture of impudence and mockery, born of familiarity. Reb Mendel had never walked with a woman in public before, not even with Basha-Meitl. When once it had happened that they went somewhere together, he had walked in front and she had followed behind him. He had always been mindful of the words in the Gemara: "Better follow a lion than a woman." He had also remembered the words "Manoach was a simpleton, as it is written: 'And Manoach walked behind his wife.'"

"Can't you tell me here what has happened to my brother?" he asked.

"No."

Reb Mendel hesitated before he followed Lisa-Hadas out of the studyhouse, and then he walked half beside her and half in front. He cast furtive glances at passersby to see whether they noticed him or pointed their fingers at him.

He muttered, "What's keeping Joel in Cracow?"

"You'll soon know," Lisa-Hadas answered.

Before long they arrived at his brother's house. Reb Mendel had not been to the house in years. Lisa-Hadas had had a garden planted in front, and as he approached, Reb Mendel saw large sunflowers in bloom. She had also had a balcony added to the second story. Lisa-Hadas grabbed the large brass ring which hung on the door and knocked several times. A Gentile maid in a white apron and a starched bonnet appeared to let them in. Real squires, Reb Mendel thought to himself. An Oriental carpet covered the floor of the front foyer. Two bronze figures holding lanterns stood facing each other. Lisa-Hadas led him into a living room crowded with sofas, stuffed chairs, paintings, chandeliers, pots filled with plants such as Mendel had never seen and for which the Yiddish he spoke had no names. She showed him to a sofa upholstered in black velvet, then sat on a chair opposite him and propped her feet on an embroidered stool. She said, "Mendel, I hate to be the bearer of bad news, but your brother has become a goy."

Reb Mendel turned pale. "Not converted, God forbid?"

"I don't know. Perhaps not yet. But he's got himself a Gentile mistress."

Reb Mendel felt his mouth turn dry and his stomach tighten. For a moment he was short of breath. "How can this be? I can't believe it," he stammered.

"I found a whole stack of her letters to him. He supports her. He showers her with gifts and money. It's been going on for over five years."

"Somehow I can't bring myself to believe all this."

"I'll show you her letters. You understand Polish, don't you?"

"A little."

"When your brother and I were first married, you used to come to the shop every day, and as I remember, you spoke with the landowners and their wives in rather fluent Polish."

"*Nu.*"

For a while both sat silent. Reb Mendel glanced at his sister-in-law and wondered why he had taken in her news without a greater show of grief. He was not a whiner by nature. He had not cried even at his parents' funerals. He had often seen Jews sobbing on Yom Kippur during the Kol Nidre or on the Ninth of Av during the Lamentations, but it was not in his nature to shed tears. He always kept in mind the verse: "I stand ever ready for adversity, and my woes are always on my mind." He prepared himself for whatever might befall him. The children, God forbid, might die; he, Mendel, might suddenly be taken ill or Basha-Meitl might be taken from him, leaving him a widower. How did the saying go? "There is not a moment without its woe." And yet, that his brother, Joel, their parents' youngest born, should sink to such depths—for that he was unprepared. He heard Lisa-Hadas speaking to him: "Mendel, since we are in the midst of speaking the truth, let me confess the whole truth."

"And what is that?"

"The truth is that Joel was not honest with you. You were supposed to receive forty percent of the profits, but in all these years you've received not forty, not thirty, not even twenty percent. He is your brother while I am only an outsider— what, after all, is a sister-in-law?—but I confronted him with this I don't know how many times and his answer was always the same: you are an idler, impractical, old-fashioned, and stubborn; you don't lift a finger to help, and so on and so forth. I told him: 'Mendel could do plenty, but you drove him out of the shop, you kept things from him, you excluded him from everything.' A wife should not denounce her husband, but if he's taking up with a shiksa and makes a fool of me, I owe him nothing. Am I right or am I wrong?"

"*Nu.*"

"All these years I have been faithful to him. I could have had more lovers than I have hairs on my head. Men lose their minds over me, but I've always believed in one God and one husband. Now it's all over. He is no longer my husband and I am not his wife. Let me tell you something, Mendel. You may not believe this, but you are closer to me now than he ever was. You are honest while he is a thief. When he and I were first married, you were the accomplished merchant while he was nothing but mama's pampered little boy. I was barely fifteen then, but I remember: from the very beginning he tried to take everything over and to push you out. I know, Mendel, that you disapprove of me because I'm not one of those overly pious matrons and I like to comb my wigs in the modern way. But I've always had the greatest respect for you. Don't laugh, but even as a man I preferred you to him. When my father, may he rest in peace, used to recite the Havdalah at the close of the Sabbath, my mother would hand me the Havdalah candle and say, 'Hold it high, and you'll have a tall husband.' When I became engaged and the people gathered to draw up the marriage contract, I thought it was you I was marrying. I was a child then, not more than fourteen. But when I saw that my bridegroom was short, shorter than me, a mere boy and not a young man—my heart sank. Why am I telling you all this? Because my heart is heavy now, and because I have no children, no heirs. I want you to know, Mendel, that it is Joel's fault that we are childless, not mine. I could have had a dozen children if I had married a man instead of a barren tree."

"How can you be so sure?" Mendel asked.

"A doctor told me. An obstetrician, that's what they call themselves. He examined me head to toe. 'You, Lisa-Hadas, are a healthy female,' he said to me. Those were his very words. 'It's your husband's fault, not yours.' What shall I do, brother-in-law? What shall I do now?" Lisa-Hadas cried out in a sing-song voice.

Reb Mendel wanted to answer, but his tongue refused to obey him. A lump rose to his throat. He made an attempt to swallow the lump, then he heard his own voice saying, "For the time being do nothing. Wait until Joel returns."

"His return frightens me. I won't be able to look him straight in the eye. He'll be coming to me from the arms of that whore, from her unclean body. Mendel, what is the matter? You're as pale as a ghost. Wait, I'll get something for you."

She sprang out of her chair, ran up to a cabinet, and flung open its glass doors. She pulled out a bottle half filled with a reddish fluid and poured from it into a polished glass. In a moment she was back at his side. "Here, drink this," she said. "It's sweet liqueur, for women. Let me get you something to nibble on."

Reb Mendel held the glass tightly in his hands, but they shook so violently that it was several minutes before he could touch it to his lips. He poured the liquid into his mouth and felt a sharp burning in his tongue, his palate, his throat. Lisa-Hadas returned, carrying another glass and a plate heaped with cookies. "Drink, Mendel," she said. "I know what a shock this must be for you. I had misplaced a ring of mine, and I thought I might have hidden it in one of his drawers. I opened the drawer and saw her pack of letters bulging out from under his papers. That night I didn't sleep a wink. I lay in my bed and shivered as if in a fever. I thought of hanging myself, of taking poison."

"God forbid. You'd be committing a grave sin." Reb Mendel could hardly pronounce the words.

"How grave can it be? I considered it all very carefully. There is no God."

"What are you saying? This is blasphemy!"

"Let it be blasphemy. Don't worry, Mendel. It's I who will roast in the fires of hell, not you. Come, let me show you those brazen letters of hers."

Reb Mendel wanted to rise, but it was as if he were paralyzed. Lisa-Hadas took his hands in hers and helped him to his feet. His knees struck against hers. A shudder ran through his spine, and for a moment he was overcome by lust such as he had not known since the days of his youth. Lisa-Hadas pulled him along by both his hands, she stepping gingerly backward and he stumbling forward half-blind, shaky and trembling in a sort of drunken minuet. "Master of the Universe, help me!" a voice within him cried. Suddenly Lisa-Hadas lurched backward and fell, pulling him down to the floor. Reb Mendel had no time to grasp what was happening. He tried to tear himself away from her; he had fallen into something like a swoon—an instant of sheer drunkenness and utter helplessness. She did something to him and he could not resist. He shuddered and it was as if he had awakened from a deep sleep, from a dream, from an evil force that robbed his freedom to choose. He felt as though his body had separated itself from his soul and had committed an abomination of its own accord. So dumbfounded was Reb Mendel by what had happened to him that he could not manage to shout out his grief. He lay there on the floor consumed with one wish—never to rise again. She helped him stand up and he heard her say, "He rightly deserved it." It was the voice of a Lilith: one of those female demons sent by Asmodeus to defile yeshiva students. Verses from the Book of Proverbs crowded his head: "She eats, then wipes her mouth, saying, 'I have done no wrong . . .'" "Her feet point to the grave, her footsteps lead into the chambers of death."

Evening came, and then sudden darkness. Lisa-Hadas grasped his arm and he allowed himself to follow her like an ox to the slaughter. What was the difference anyway? Lower than the deepest abyss one couldn't sink. His knees buckled under him and his feet were unsteady. Lisa-Hadas hung on to his arm and pressed her bosom to his ribs. "Shall I have the carriage harnessed to take you home?" she asked. "First I'll have to find the groom."

"No, no."

"It's not far to your home, but it's dark outside. You could slip and fall, God forbid."

He wanted to say, "Fall still more?" but instead he said, "No, I can see."

"Basha-Meitl will wonder what's become of you," Lisa-Hadas said with a chuckle.

Reb Mendel wanted her to let him go, but for some reason

she clung to him. She said, "The darkness of Egypt is out there. I'd better go with you."

"I beg you, no."

"Mendel, forgive me."

"*Nu.*"

"We both must have been out of our minds," Lisa-Hadas blurted out to him and to the night. "Be careful."

Hesitantly she let go of his arm, and he set out on his way, unsteady like a drunk. "I've lost the world to come," a voice within him murmured. Everything happened in quick succession as in the Book of Job: "Even as one fellow was speaking, the second fellow arrived." Scarcely two hours ago Reb Mendel had been an honest, upstanding Jew. Now he was depraved, a Zimri ben Salu, a betrayer of God, a lecher. If at least a Phinehas arose to avenge the Lord of Hosts. His, Mendel's, vision had always been adequate. He could even read the small letters in Rashi. But now it was as though he had gone blind. "*Nu*, my iniquity surpasses my endurance." Words from the Gemara came rushing back to him: "May it be God's will that my death atone for my sinfulness." Someone came walking toward him, and Mendel halted. It was a young man, a Przysucha Hasid whose name was Hershel Roizkes. Recognizing Mendel in the darkness, the young man asked him, "And where might you be going at this late hour, Reb Mendel?"

Mendel didn't know what answer to give. He felt himself literally speechless.

"May I accompany you home?"

"*Nu.*"

The young Hasid took Reb Mendel's arm, the very arm that Lisa-Hadas had earlier held, and said, "The city pays some Gentile to keep the lanterns lit, yet the streets are always dark. God forbid, a person could break a leg or even his neck. In the summertime one can tolerate it, but when winter comes with its snows and frosts and the streets become slippery, a person risks his life every time he leaves his house. You're probably planning to spend Rosh Hashanah in Przysucha, Reb Mendel, eh?"

Again Reb Mendel had no answer to give. That he, Mendel, should present himself at the rebbe's in Przysucha? It was sacrilege even to mention that saint's name in the same breath with his, adulterer that he was, an outcast to his people, disgraced and polluted. But he had to answer the young Hasid's question and he murmured, "It's too early to say."

"Since you go to the rebbe every year, why not this time? Zeinvil the beadle predicts more disciples than ever this year," Hershel Roizkes said.

Despite his sorrow Reb Mendel couldn't help but smile to himself. Hershel was trying to engage him in Hasidic talk. How could he know that he, Mendel, was no longer Mendel but a villain seven times over, a man steeped in the Forty-nine Gates of Uncleanliness? And how would he, Mendel, greet Basha-Meitl when finally he arrived at his home? How would he look her in the eye?

Hershel Roizkes was speaking of Rabbi Bunem now, repeating a saying of his, quoting a witticism; but although Reb Mendel could hear his voice, he could not make out what Hershel was saying. The Torah and he, Mendel, had grown estranged, one from the other, forever. The young man spoke up: "I see, Reb Mendel, that you are a bit impatient tonight. Are you, God forbid, ill, or what?"

"I do have a touch of heartburn."

"Ah! Right away I knew that something was wrong. You shouldn't be walking the streets at this hour. It turns quite chilly in the evening and one could easily catch a cold. Go home and get into bed. Your soulmate will give you something for it. A glass of tea with honey will cure anything. Here we are, Reb Mendel, here's your house. Good night, Reb Mendel, and may you recover soon."

"Thank you, Hershel."

When Reb Mendel opened the door to his apartment, he saw Basha-Meitl standing in the middle of the room, a kerchief wrapped around her forehead. Before he had time to wish her a good evening, she began to scream, "Where have you been? Where did you run off to so late in the evening? And why are you so pale? Did something happen, God forbid? You always come home immediately after the evening prayers, and here it's already ten o'clock! The worries I've had—may they fall on our enemies' heads. The frightful disasters that came to my mind! Mendel, what is it with you? I've even developed a headache from worry."

"I lingered at the studyhouse longer than I meant to."

"Mendel, I myself went to the studyhouse to look for you. The beadle told me that you had not been there for the evening service."

Reb Mendel stood and stared at his wife, utterly stupefied. Heavenly Father, he had forgotten to recite the evening prayers! In all the years he'd been saying them, this had never happened to him before. *Nu*, apparently I'm entirely in the hands of the evil host. He saw a chair and all but collapsed into it. I'm no longer a Jew, Reb Mendel thought to himself. It's better this way. It's better if those sacred words did not pass through my unclean lips.

"Where have you been?" Basha-Meitl shrieked at him. "You're as white as a corpse!"

Reb Mendel considered how to answer his wife. Should he make up a story? What sort of story? Fabrications and lies were not in his nature. Besides, someone might have seen him with Lisa-Hadas, walking in the direction of her house. At last he said, "I was with Lisa-Hadas."

Basha-Meitl clapped her hands together. "What? Lisa-Hadas? For such a long time? Is something wrong with your brother, God forbid?"

"Yes."

"What happened? Heaven help us! Such a young man."

"He's alive, he's alive."

"What is it, then? Don't keep me in suspense!" Basha-Meitl screamed.

"Joel is having relations with a Gentile woman."

"Relations? A Gentile? I can't believe it. I can't believe it!"

"It's the truth."

"When? Where? What sort of relations?"

It occurred to Reb Mendel that he should not have spoken the word "truth." According to the Gemara, truth was the Almighty's Seal. A sinner such as he ought not to let the word cross his lips.

Man and wife talked late into the night, until finally Basha-Meitl fell asleep. Reb Mendel lay in his bed fully awake. He wanted to recite the Shema, as he did every night, but he could not bring himself to pronounce the sacred words and all the more not the Divine Name. How could a vile sinner such as he was proclaim: "In thine hand, O Lord, I entrust my soul"? He had but one request of the Almighty: to be done with this world, its lusts, its temptations. What a bizarre transition: one moment he was poring over the sacred book, and an hour later he found himself ensnared in the net of incest. "It's a fall, a punishment," Reb Mendel murmured to himself. Somewhere he had read that temptations were sent to bedevil great saints—like the Patriarch Abraham, or the Righteous Joseph—or else they were sent to the worst of sinners, putting them on the road to Sheol. Lisa-Hadas had made him drunk, just as Lot's daughter had done to Lot. Well, and how did it happen that a brother of his, a son of God-fearing Jews, should take up with a Gentile woman and shame his parents in Paradise? And why had he deceived him, his elder brother, and held back his money from him? Reb Mendel recalled the verse in the Book of Psalms: "And I, in my haste, cried out: 'All men are deceivers.'" Even a saint like King David despaired of all mankind.

Yes, King David. He, the author of the Book of Psalms, had had his own share of troubles. One of his sons, Absalom, had plotted to seize the throne from his father and had openly copulated with ten of his father's wives. Another son, Amnon, had raped his sister, Tamar. Yet another, Adonijah ben Haggith, had sought to wrest the kingdom from his brother Solomon. And that event with Bathsheba and Uriah the Hittite! Well, but all these things belonged to ancient times. What did the Gemara say? "Whoever claims that David sinned is nothing but mistaken." Every word in the Holy Book was full of secrets.

Reb Mendel himself did not know who in his brain spoke to him now: Satan or an angel of mercy? But of one thing he was sure: he needed to do penance. Even a brute like Nebuzaradan, a murderer of Jewish children—when later he regretted his deeds, heaven accepted his atonement. But how could one atone for so heinous a deed as his, Mendel's, was? For the most trivial of sins the sacred book demanded hundreds of fasts, self-flagellations, rolling the body in the snow in the winter and in thorns in the summer. An abomination such as he had committed was not even mentioned in that Holy Book at all.

Reb Mendel was too restless to remain lying down and so he sat up in bed. Basha-Meitl awoke and asked him, "Mendel, aren't you sleeping?"

"No."

"Mendel, if what Lisa-Hadas told you is true, then Joel stained the family's honor. But it is not your fault. The Patriarch Jacob also had a wicked brother: Esau."

"Yes, I know."

"Mendel, perhaps she lied. A woman like Lisa-Hadas is capable of bringing false accusations even against her own husband."

"No."

"Well, whatever happens—don't take it to heart. May God not punish me for saying this, but I never thought much of either one of them. I always told you that I had no faith in their honesty. But you ignored me, even scolded me. He stuffed his pockets with money and to you he doled out pennies. You know that is the truth."

"Go back to sleep."

"It will be a black day when word of this gets out in town."

"It's already a black day."

"When is he coming home?"

Reb Mendel didn't answer. He was reminded of the words in the Gemara: "Very good is death." That phrase had always puzzled him. The Torah was a teaching of life, not death. Only now did he understand what the words meant to say. Sometimes a man could become so hopelessly entangled that death was his only deliverance. And as if she could read his thoughts Basha-Meitl spoke: "Take care of yourself. Your life comes before everything else. Good night."

Basha-Meitl fell silent, but apparently she was not asleep. A cricket which had lived for who knew how many years behind Basha-Meitl's stove suddenly began its eternal chirping; a creature who with one haunting note could say all that it had to say night in and night out, generation after generation. In a coop near the stove slept a hen and a rooster. Basha-Meitl was raising the pair to serve as sacrifices for herself and for Mendel on the eve of Yom Kippur. Every now and then the hen clucked in its sleep. Although Basha-Meitl and Mendel possessed a clock equipped with weights and chains which chimed precisely every hour and every half hour, it was the rooster with its cock-a-doodle-doo that awoke them every morning at the break of day. A kind of envy swept over Reb Mendel for those innocent creatures. True, the Almighty had not granted them free choice, but the turmoil of breaking His commandments also didn't trouble their days. They fulfilled their mission simply and faithfully.

Although he was convinced that the night was lost to sleep, Reb Mendel finally dozed off. He slept for several hours without dreaming, or perhaps without the memory of having dreamed. When he opened his eyes the room was still dark. He awoke with a heaviness in his heart and a bitter taste in his mouth. He remembered that some dreadful event had taken place, but what it was he couldn't say. "Why am I feeling so low?" he asked himself. "Have I wronged someone—or has someone wronged me?"Basha-Meitl was sleeping now; he could hear her steady breathing. The cricket had stopped its chirping perhaps it, too, had fallen asleep. Through the window Mendel saw the heavens thickly strewn with stars. He had once heard somewhere that each star was a complete world. So many worlds had the Almighty created that every righteous man was rewarded with three hundred and ten of them. Reb Mendel shivered. All at once he remembered the disaster that had befallen him in his old age.

Days and nights passed and Reb Mendel could not sleep. He would doze off, then wake up with a start. Although the nights in Lublin were quiet, his head throbbed with noise. Sometimes he heard the wheels of a carriage clattering across the cobblestones. Another time he heard a hammer striking loudly against an anvil. "Have I become another Titus that God should send a gnat to gnaw at my brain? Am I going mad? If so, I'd rather die." Reb Mendel considered doing away with himself. But how? Should he hang himself? Drown? Take poison? Since he had already lost his share in the world to come, what was the difference what he did? In the midst of his turmoil Reb Mendel took pains to keep his condition from Basha-Meitl. But she saw it just the same and tried to comfort him. She pleaded with him: "Mendel, he is your brother, not your son. Even when a son strays from the righteous path, one mustn't torment oneself."

Reb Mendel stopped going to pray with a minyan. He could not look the other Hasidim in the eye. He could not enter a sacred place where a Holy Ark stood filled with Torah scrolls. He put on his phylacteries in his study, but he could not bring himself to recite the benediction. He did not dare to kiss the fringes of his prayer shawl. Reb Mendel knew perfectly well that a Jew was forbidden to pray for death, but what, then, was left for him to do? He planned to leave a will requesting that he be buried not among those who died virtuous but behind the fence, where suicides and other sinful Jews lay buried.

Like all other Jews, Reb Mendel used to go to the bathhouse on Fridays, but no longer. How could he undress himself and bare to other Jews that organ, the sign of God's holy covenant, which had broken the injunction against incest? And how could he pray in the Hasidim studyhouse? What if he was called upon to read from the Torah? How could he pronounce the benediction over the Torah? Basha-Meitl informed the beadle of Przysucha that Mendel was ill and that he wanted no visitors.

In order to spare Basha-Meitl grief, Reb Mendel pretended to pray in his study. Friday evenings he put on his satin gaberdine and his fur-lined hat; he recited the "Woman of Valor"; he blessed the wine—all in a hurry, without chants, without joy. He swallowed no more than two spoonfuls of the soup, touched neither the sweet stew nor the meat, barely tasted a morsel of challah. When Basha-Meitl asked why there was no singing of hymns at the Sabbath table, he said, "I don't feel like singing."

"Mendel, you've let yourself slip into melancholy. You are committing a sin."

"*Nu*, what's another sin?"

"Mendel, you frighten me."

"I won't make you suffer much longer," Reb Mendel said, against his will.

Twice a year, on Shevuoth and then again on Rosh Hasha-nah, Reb Mendel was accustomed to travel to the rebbe in Przysucha. Although he was not a wealthy man, on those occasions he hired a coach and took along a number of the poorer Hasidim, those who could not afford the expenses of the trip. He paid for their lodgings in inns along the way, as well as their stay in Przysucha. The drive itself was one long celebration. The Hasidim crooned melodies, poked fun at the Mitnaggedim, regaled each other with tales about the Rabbi of Lublin, the Maggid of Kozienice, Reb Melekh of Lizhensk, and about his brother Zusya. Reb Bunem was not an explicator of Torah, neither was he a miracle worker. He did not accept payments for advice. He did not admit women into his study, and he did not give out amulets. On weekdays he did not wear a fur hat and a satin gaberdine, or even the white coat and trousers which Rabbi Menachem Mendel of Vitebsk and Rabbi Nachum of Chernobyl had worn. Instead, he went out in boots and a cloth coat, the same as the other Hasidim. But such was his greatness that scholars from every corner of Russian Poland had flocked to him, even from far-off Galicia. His disciples—Reb Yaahov of Radzymin, Yitzhak of Worka, Mendel of Kotzk, and Itche-Meir of Warsaw—were all about the same age as he, and each addressed him by the familiar "thou." They kidded him, and he in turn kidded them. They debated with him and good-naturedly contradicted him. Because few of Reb Bunem's Hasidim were elderly—mostly they were young—Reb Mendel of Lublin occupied a special place in Przysucha.

That year Reb Mendel startled the other Przysucha Hasidim in Lublin. Instead of waiting—as he had always done—for the week before Rosh Hashanah, he rented a carriage immediately after the first of Elul and departed for Przysucha alone, unaccompanied by other Hasidim. He did not even stop to take leave of anyone. "Did he suddenly become a miser?" the younger Hasidim wondered. Was it a sudden show of arrogance? Word of his illness had spread around the town, and it was concluded that that was the reason for his abrupt departure. Those Hasidim who could not afford to travel by carriage would have to travel on foot. Why all the fuss? If the

Patriarch Jacob could hoof it all the way from Beersheba to Haran, healthy and young Hasidim could walk from Lublin to Przysucha.

It was a rare Hasid who arrived in Przysucha some three weeks before the holidays. Mendel was virtually alone. The large studyhouse was empty. Unlike other men in his position, Reb Bunem was not one to require the services of a beadle or a gabbai. Mendel opened the door to the rebbe's study and simply walked in. Reb Bunem—a tall man with a pointed black beard and flashing black eyes—stood at a lectern and scribbled with a quill on a slip of paper. Seeing Reb Mendel, the rebbe wiped off his pen on his skullcap and asked, "Am I seeing things, or is my calendar wrong?"

"No, Rebbe. Your calendar is not wrong," Reb Mendel answered.

"*Nu*, welcome, welcome."

The rebbe stretched out his hand and Mendel barely touched the tips of his fingers, so as not to defile the saint's hand with his own. Reb Bunem glanced at him and knitted his brows. He moved a stool toward Reb Mendel and sat down on the edge of a bench. "Reb Mendel, what's troubling you? You may speak openly."

"Rebbe, I've forfeited my share in the world to come," Reb Mendel blurted out.

The rebbe's eyes filled with laughter. "Forfeited, huh? Congratulations!"

"What does the rebbe mean?" Reb Mendel asked, alarmed.

"Those who pursue the world to come are engaged in a trade-off with the Almighty: 'I will observe your Torah and commandments, and you'll give me a larger portion of the Leviathan.' When a Jew forfeits his share in the world to come, he can serve the Almighty for His own sake, expecting nothing in return."

"I am not worthy of serving Him," Reb Mendel said.

"And who, then, is worthy?"

Reb Mendel hoped that the rebbe would ask what he had done, and he was prepared to make a full confession. But the rebbe did not ask him. He probably knows already, Reb Mendel thought to himself.

"Where are you staying?" Reb Bunem asked.

"I was given a bed in the inn. What more do I need?"

"Reb Mendel, take good care of yourself. The Master of the Universe has plenty of paid servants, but of those who would serve Him for nothing, He has hardly any at all."

"Rebbe, I want to do penance."

"The wish itself is penance."

Reb Mendel wanted to say something more, but Reb Bunem motioned with his hand as if to say, Enough for now. Before Mendel was out of the room, the rebbe called out to him, "Everything is permitted, except fasting!"

A fit of sobbing shook Mendel's body, and at the same time he was overcome with joy. He was not alone. The Almighty knew, and the rebbe also knew. He, Mendel, was sure to roast in the fires of all seven hells, but he also recalled a saying of the rebbe's: "Hell is for men, not for dogs." As long as there was a God and as long as there were Jews, what was the difference where one lived? Reincarnation? Let it be reincarnation. Purgatory? Let it be Purgatory. The rebbe had once said, "Among men there is justice and there is mercy. But for the Master of the Universe justice itself is mercy." Reb Mendel walked into the studyhouse. Until that moment he had carefully avoided touching a holy book. He had not even dared to kiss the mezuzah with his unclean lips. But now he felt his strength returning to him. "No, I have no use for Paradise, I have no need for a reward." He walked up to the bookshelf and pulled down the tractate of Berakhot. He sat down all alone at a long table, and he began to chant the holy words and to interpret them to himself: " 'At what time may one begin to recite the Shema in the evening? From the hour in which the priests gather to eat of their tithes.' " Rashi had inserted an explanation: " 'Priests who had become defiled and had immersed themselves in water . . .' " Yes, Reb Mendel no longer hesitated to peruse the holy letters with which the Almighty had created the universe. A sinful Jew was still a Jew. Even a convert, according to the Law, remained a Jew.

Days went by. Once again Reb Mendel was able to pray with fervor. It struck him that in all Eighteen Benedictions the prayers were written not for the individual Jew but for the Jewish people as a whole. The plural form was used throughout. How could he, Mendel, pray for himself alone, for his own body, his own lost soul? But to pray for all the Jews—that even the most wicked man on earth could do. Even the evil Balaam had been granted permission to praise the Jews and perhaps to pray for them.

Soon Reb Bunem's disciples and students from all over Poland began to gather. They were all there: Reb Mendel of Kotzk, Yaakov of Radzymin, Itche-Meir of Warsaw, Yitzhak of Worka, Mordecai Joseph of Izbica. Several of them had in the meantime themselves become rabbis, had students and followers of their own. Hasidim had also arrived from Lublin, some by horse and wagon, others on foot. Before Reb Mendel had hurried out of Lublin, it had been rumored that he was gravely ill. Some of the Hasidim had believed that he had wanted to end his days with Reb Bunem in Przysucha. Now, heaven be praised, he seemed to have come back to life. Although he had later on been given a private room at the inn, Reb Mendel had cots brought in for poor Lublin Hasidim who would otherwise have slept on a bench in the study-house, in an attic somewhere, or wherever they could find a place to put down their heads. Reb Mendel paid for their meals as well.

Yes, once again Reb Mendel became what he had always been: a Hasid among Hasidim. It was thought that after the holidays he would return to Lublin, but Succoth came and went and Reb Mendel was still in Przysucha. Somehow he learned that his brother, Joel, had converted and had gone off to live with a squire's wife. Lisa-Hadas had sold the shop without offering Basha-Meitl a share of the profits. Although according to the Law a Jew, even if he converted, remained a Jew, and although his wife could not remarry without a proper divorce, Lisa-Hadas married some "enlightened" Jew, a lawyer by profession, and the man who had helped her to perpetrate her swindle. It was rumored that the two were living in some city deep in Russia. Reb Mendel wrote to Basha-Meitl informing her that he had made up his mind to stay in Przysucha and urging her to sell the house and join him there, because a wife's place was at her husband's side.

All these events unsettled and puzzled the Jews of Lublin,

let alone the Przysucha Hasidim. That a Jew should fall in love with a Gentile and abandon Judaism was not unheard of. And besides, Joel had always been thought to be frivolous, a pleasure-seeker. For a long time it had been whispered in Lublin that he made the rounds of the big cities far too often, more often than his business required, and that he hobnobbed too closely with Gentile landowners. But that a merchant, well off as Reb Mendel had been, should forsake everything in order to sit at his rebbe's feet—that was something new. Basha-Meitl traveled to Przysucha to persuade her husband to return with her to Lublin. "Is it your fault," she pleaded with him, "if your brother strayed from the righteous path?" But Reb Mendel was adamant: "It is written: 'All Jews are responsible one for the other.' If even perfect strangers share in this responsibility, how much more so should a brother."

It took a good deal of argument before Basha-Meitl agreed to settle in Przysucha. Miraculously she had managed to save up a small nest egg. She had also inherited several good pieces of jewelry from her mother, her grandmothers, and her great-grandmothers. She rented an apartment on Synagogue Street, not far from the rebbe's studyhouse, and the couple began their new life. Reb Mendel did exactly what Reb Bunem told him to do: he served the Almighty without expecting any rewards. He rose at midnight, and he recited prayers and lamentations that had been printed in older prayer books. He prayed with fervor; he studied the Mishnah, the Gemara, other sacred texts. Although the rebbe had forbidden him to fast, Reb Mendel fasted every Monday and Thursday. From the day he had sinned, his appetite for food had diminished. He went to bed satiated and woke up feeling full. One meal in the morning, or in the evening instead, satisfied him. He no longer ate meat, except on the Sabbath. The *Reshit Chochmah* required those who committed a sin as grave as his to torture their bodies and to fast from Sabbath to Sabbath. But Reb Mendel did not want to distress his wife. The truth was that she, Basha-Meitl, was also eating less and less, even though her household duties did not diminish. Of what little money the couple possessed they gave tithes. There was a small yeshiva in Przysucha and Basha-Meitl undertook to feed several of its students, to wash their linen, to patch up their socks and shirts. Basha-Meitl did not want to arrive at the world to come without good deeds to her credit.

As for Mendel, he did not occupy himself with thoughts of the world to come. True, it was far better to sit in Paradise with a crown on one's head and to bask in the glow of the Shechinah than to wallow in thorns or to turn into a worm, or a frog, or a monster. But the pleasures of living year round in Przysucha more than made up for the torment which might be his later. A day did not go by when the rebbe did not speak a few kind words to him. Merely to gaze upon the rebbe's saintly countenance was a joy. Rabbis and scholars flocked to Przysucha from Poland, from Volhynia, and occasionally from more distant lands as well. Reb Mendel became the rebbe's gabbai, a service he preformed without pay. When Reb Bunem was consulted on matters of commerce and worldly affairs, he always called Reb Mendel in and conferred with him. Reb Bunem himself was also well versed in those matters. It was no secret that he had once been an adherent of the Enlightenment, and a pharmacist. He himself was actually a penitent.

Why dream of Paradise when Przysucha itself was Paradise? Instead of being flung into the depths of Sheol, as he deserved to be, Reb Mendel was surrounded with Torah, with wisdom, with the love and the warmth of fellow Jews. Reb Mendel never spoke of his sin to Reb Bunem, but it was clear that through the divine spirit which rested on him the rebbe knew what he, Mendel, had done. Once, on Simchas Torah, when Reb Mendel was striding behind the rebbe with the Torah scroll in his arms, Reb Bunem suddenly stopped, turned his head, and said, "Let the Mitnagged save up a nest egg for Paradise. We here in Przysucha are up to our necks in the glory of God and the radiance of the Torah right here and now."

Translated by Nili Wachtel

The Conference

THEY came together in Warsaw for a cultural conference. Actually, it was an attempt by the Party hacks to create a united front with various leftist groups. To the conference came Party members, radical Yiddishists, actors, educators, and people who always attend conferences—permanent delegates. This took place in March 1936. The organizers used every means to deceive the *Defensywa*, the Polish political police, but the police knew all about the conference.

The Party delegates came prepared with long speeches filled with doctrinal clichés. They wore thick horn-rimmed glasses, smiled shrewdly, and seemed pleased with their intellectual superiority. In the name of Yiddish culture they tried to attract to Communism some petit-bourgeois and neutral members of the intelligentsia. Every Communist was sure that Moscow would appreciate his merits; each thought that the day after the revolution he would be appointed to a high position in the proletarian government of Poland. The non-Communists seemed confused and bellicose. They had come to the conference with instructions from their factions to win all sorts of compromises and privileges. The conference was supposed to last for three days and end with a momentous banquet. The kitchen of the hotel was stocked with all kinds of provisions—fish, meat, soups, delicious pastries, and special dishes for the occasion. The management knew that no matter how much these intellectuals might haggle, they would eat in unison at the banquet tables.

Among the eighty-two delegates there were only three women, one of whom, Comrade Flora, was relatively young. She was a delegate from Lublin, part actress, reciter of poetry, singer of folk songs. Flora was small, fat, with a round face and the eyes of an owl. She tried to speak modern Yiddish, laughed loudly, garbled names. She was in possession of a few phrases which she used at every opportunity. One of these was: "Let us not scatter our progressive forces."

Almost all the male delegates developed a crush on Comrade Flora. They treated her to cigarettes and lozenges for dryness of the throat. They all attempted to arrange private meetings with her. They all wanted to confide in her. They were not understood by their wives, who were too busy with their children and households, or were too old and too frigid. Would Flora join them after the day's session? It would be nice to discuss Party matters over refreshments. Comrade Flora never said no. The first night it would be impossible; she had not slept the night before, because of work and excitement. Perhaps tomorrow . . .

At the first session the debates lasted until two in the morning. The delegates battled over various social problems, but concentrated mostly on the meaning of historical materialism. An anti-Marxist historian took three hours to prove that materialistic theory does not apply to Jewish history. Comrade Flora sat in the first row, across the floor from the dais, and the speaker did not take his eyes off her. He beat the table with his fist and screamed, "Can a materialistic point of view explain two thousand years of Jewish exile? Is it possible to use Marxist theory to explain the survival of the Hebrew language, the yearning for Zion? No, a thousand times no!" In her confusion, Flora nodded and applauded. The Communists interjected cries of "Saboteur, reactionary, liar!" The historian became hoarse. He drank one glass of water after another and wiped his glasses with his handkerchief. He attempted to support his arguments by quoting Marx, Engels, and Moses Hess, but the Communists interrupted him and mocked him. Flora soon realized that she was badly oriented. Instead of nodding agreement, she now shook her head and cried, "Comrades, let us not scatter our progressive forces."

After the historian had finished, a Communist went to the podium to answer him. He smiled cunningly, his eyes gleaming behind his glasses. He proved that the so-called historian had knowledge neither of history nor of sociology. Flora applauded and cried, "Bravo!" This speaker had already approached Flora, who had promised to meet him later. He smiled triumphantly, showing a mouth full of gold teeth. He moistened his lips with the tip of his tongue and ran his fingers through his hair. He spoke directly to Flora and watched her every movement. He asked, "What did the Jews in the ghettos eat, bread or ideas?" and Flora shrieked, "Bread! Bread!"

The second day, Flora was again the center of attention. Almost all the men flirted with her and tried to arrange a date. The moment one man began to talk to her, another broke in. The delegates openly quarreled about her, half jokingly, half seriously. They gave her hints about jobs and trips. They offered her cigarettes and cookies. They touched her naked arm with their sweaty fingers. The more daring even tried to kiss her. They all told jokes, mimicked certain delegates, and made fun of some provincial speaker. Their eyes glittered, their gorges rose and fell rapidly. Comrade Flora began to think she wouldn't be able to escape this time. Luckily, the debates became especially hot that night. The anti-Communists became highly aggressive and lashed out at Stalin's worst crimes. A number of fellow travelers began to speak like full-fledged Fascists. The Communist speaker poured scorn on every social-democratic slogan, and warned that even one step away from Stalinism would lead to reactionary darkness. One delegate shouted, "We will hang all of you from the nearest lamp post." The chairman good-naturedly reproached him from this non-parliamentary outburst. The hall reeked with the smoke of cigarettes and echoed with shouts. Foreheads became wet with perspiration, ties hung limp, pince-nez slipped from noses. Comrade Flora fanned herself with a program and cried, "Forgive me, comrades, open a window!" One of the delegates brought her a glass of seltzer water.

About one in the morning there was such pandemonium that Flora managed to steal away without being noticed. A leather manufacturer from Lublin, her lover, had taken a room adjacent to hers. Flora made sure that the delegates were unaware that she had brought her capitalist paramour with her. She locked the door, bolted it, and warned her lover to make no noise. A few minutes after he entered her room, someone knocked at the door. It was the historian.

"Miss Flora, Miss Flora, please open!" he whispered in the hallway. Flora barely managed not to burst out laughing. She lay in bed and giggled into the pillow. The manufacturer pinched her behind, calling her "harlot" and "slut" in a low voice. She bit his earlobe and whispered, "Let them knock, the shmegegges. What do you care? I'm yours."

The third morning, Flora awoke with a headache. The

manufacturer had left early to meet several traveling salesmen. Flora took an aspirin, but it did not help. She went down to the conference hall only after lunch. The conference was about to erupt again in turmoil, but slowly the delegates composed themselves because of a speech delivered by a writer who had the status of an immortal. He had come from faraway America. He was the only delegate who had not made a pass at Flora—a man in his sixties, small, broad-shouldered, with a head of gray hair, with bags under his eyes and gold-rimmed glasses. He was reading a lecture from a sheaf of papers. Like a professor he went through the whole history of Yiddishism and socialism. He spoke in a monotonous, sleepy voice. Many of the delegates yawned and dozed. Others were stealthily reading newspapers. The delegates turned to look at Flora, but she pretended she was listening to each and every word of the famous writer. After he had finished, Flora approached him and said, "Thank you for a most interesting lecture."

The immortal took off his misty glasses. "Were you really interested?"

"Immensely."

"I notice you, I notice you—we should get better acquainted."

"It would be a great honor for me!" Flora exclaimed.

Soon the conference began to fall apart again, because both camps had become extremely unyielding. But a neutral group made a last effort to patch things up, and came up with a new compromise resolution. In the banquet hall the tables were already set. In the kitchen the cooks roasted chickens and ducks and poured gravy from one pan to another, but in the conference hall the war raged on. The delegates began to insult each other personally. One delegate had his ears boxed. A Stalinist threw an inkwell at a Trotskyite. They hurled such words as "Fascist dog," "betrayer of the masses," "provocateur." But the peacemakers did not let the conference explode. This would have been a victory for the Zionists. The delegates either had to decide on common action or to part like enemies. The Communists began to give in on some points, and the opposition became softer. A three-page resolution was put together, demanding that the great powers make an end to imperialism. Greetings were sent to the comrades in China, Manchuria, and Mongolia. The United States was asked to put an end to its imperialistic greed, bloodsucking exploitation, pro-Fascism. However, the secretary who transcribed the resolution was a Communist and he altered the text. When his deception was discovered, there was an uproar of protest.

At that moment the delegates were summoned to the banquet. The waiters had to begin early; they had their union regulations. At the banquet the warring factions became friendlier. Everyone was hungry. They were given fresh rolls, carp with horseradish, vodka, wine, chicken soup with noodles, and stuffed derma. Flora sat between a Stalinist and a leader of the left labor movement. One put a hand on her knee, the other tickled her ribs. Flora drank liqueur and laughed loudly. She put a cigarette to her lips and both men lit matches in competition. Many of the delegates were angry with her for failing to make a rendezvous, but when someone proposed that she sing, there was general approval.

Flora was more than willing. She had come prepared, with a pianist. First she sang "The Day of Vengeance," and received a warm and lengthy ovation. Then she sang "On the Barricades." After a while, the delegates had had enough, but Flora had planned a long program and followed it to the end.

The last speech of the conference was made by the immortal from America. It was already after midnight. He had promised to be brief, but he became so involved in his speech that he could not finish. Just when he seemed about to come to an end, he entangled himself in a new topic. Outside, dawn was breaking in the sky. Some delegates snored, others made jokes, others winked and passed written slips to one another. Flora had to leave to rejoin her dangerously impatient manufacturer. The secretary who kept the minutes put away his pen. He yawned once and fell asleep. Only one delegate continued to write—an agent from the secret police posing as a leftist, who could not leave because he had to deliver a complete report.

The next morning, Flora slept late. When she finally went down to the conference hall, the chairs had been removed and the dais dismantled. The hall was now being prepared for a wedding. Leaning against the wall were a folded canopy, a huge bass trumpet, and a drum. Two men knelt, shellacking the floor. When Flora poked her head in, one of the workers whistled and said, "Miss, it's all over." The other said, "Comrade, come again next year, the revolution won't turn sour."

Translated by the author and Lester Goran

Miracles

I RECEIVE many telephone calls from my Yiddish readers, and often, when I place the receiver against my ear, nothing can be heard but a tense silence. Then a stammering and hesitating voice might follow which soon gains in strength. At other times, I lose patience with my caller and hang up. And sure enough, the phone rings again. On this particular occasion, the telephone rang twice, and hearing no voice, I hung up both times. The phone rang once again. After a while, I heard a stuttering voice. I am accustomed to this type of behavior. I even imagine that I can tell a person's character by his procrastination before speaking. It was a man's voice. It sounded muffled. Then the caller asked in provincial Polish-Yiddish, "Are you the writer, N.?"

I replied, "Yes, I am he—don't be embarrassed. Please feel free to speak to me."

He coughed loudly once, and then added a softer cough. "What I wish to tell you cannot all be said on the telephone. I know that you are a busy man, but—if it's possible—it is a strange tale—one of those things which the heart does not trust to the mouth, as the Talmud says—"

I set up an appointment with him. I told him what I usually say in such cases: that there is no reason for anyone to fear me; I take pleasure in listening to human experiences and one can confide in me. Immediately he became more trusting and his words more coherent.

He continued: "I have read all your writings. It is a sin to take up your time; however—"

Exactly at the appointed minute, the door opened to admit a small man with ruddy cheeks and a round gray beard. From under his yellow eyebrows peered a pair of green eyes, both piercing and gentle. Though his hair was gray, his face appeared youthful and even boyish. His head was bent and he shuffled as he walked. One shoulder seemed higher than the other. He was dressed like a modern man, yet his entire appearance was that of a Hasid from the old country. Hanging

465

loosely from his body, his jacket looked to me like a shortened caftan. After many apologies and preliminaries, he began.

"I know that you are from the Lublin region of Poland, and if so, you must have heard about the Rabbi of Mechev. You haven't? I am amazed. I am the great-grandchild of Rabbi Abraham Malach and of the Holy Jew. My grandfather was a disciple of both Rabbi Bunem and the Rabbi of Kotzk. He had a small following and was not well known. Fame was not his goal. By nature he was a man of mystery. Every summer he visited a fair in the town of Naleczow and even traveled as far as Leipzig. It was rumored that in these towns he met the Thirty-six Saints. On Mondays and Thursdays, he fasted. The disciples of Kotzk did not believe in fasting, but my grandfather had ways of his own. He died at the close of Yom Kippur, shortly after the *Ne'ila* prayer.

"Before I continue, let me tell you that I am not pious in the usual sense. I am religious in my own fashion. However, I have seen with my own eyes how a sick man immediately regained health after my paternal grandfather had touched him. Grandfather had the gift of soothsaying. He could see what was happening scores of miles away. Don't ask me how—I give you facts, not explanations. My father, Rabbi Jachiel Mayer, had the same power. My mother, peace be with her, once visited her father in the town of Zelechow in order to celebrate a family wedding. It happened on the Sabbath of Song. My father and we, the children, stayed home. We were observing the custom of tossing kasha to the birds. Suddenly my father announced, 'It's a pity that your grandfather has died. At least your mother will be able to attend the funeral.' To come to the point, my maternal grandfather died the very minute my father had uttered these words. He had collapsed in the middle of the Sabbath chants. I read somewhere that clairvoyance is hereditary. It may very well be so.

"Our family was small: two daughters and myself, the only son. After my father's demise, I was to become the Rabbi of Mechev. But first of all, my father had no following to speak of. The old Hasidim had died. The young men had gone to other rabbis or had become enlightened. Second, I myself had lost faith. The Enlightenment came about a hundred years late to Poland, but when it finally arrived, it did more in a few years than it had in an entire millennium elsewhere. In the year 1913, there were only a half-dozen so-called enlightened Jews in the whole village of Mechev. In 1918, almost all the young men had shaved off their beards and had become Zionists, Bundists, and Communists. The studyhouse was deserted. The young women turned to smuggling. Mechev was occupied by the Austrians. Girls smuggled food into Galicia and returned with bags of tobacco. A library opened in Mechev and there I began to read secular books. Truthfully, I neither wanted to be a rabbi nor was there a need for one. After my father's demise, the entire rabbinical court crumbled. Only a half-ruined studyhouse containing a few hangers-on remained. My mother had gone to live with my married sister. I sat in my father's study and learned Polish and German from dictionaries. I studied algebra from a book eighty years old. Nobody was there to supervise me. The Austrians had brought the cholera to Mechev, and almost half the villagers died. Grass sprouted in the marketplace. Because most members of the Burial Society had perished in the epidemic, the dead lay unburied for many days.

"I put aside my books and became a gravedigger. I also went from one house to another massaging the sick with alcohol. The doctor had issued strict orders against drinking unboiled water and eating raw fruit. However, I did not listen to him. Not because I wanted to commit suicide. Far from it; I cherish life, even though at times I hate it. Some inner knowledge made me sure that I would not get sick. The people of Mechev were astonished. I was perplexed by my own behavior. Already I was a full-fledged emancipated skeptic. I even neglected to put on phylacteries. I had read Spinoza's *Ethics* in Hebrew. But still, I relied on mystical powers. I also discovered that I was praying—not aloud, but silently. It was a denial of all my convictions. I somehow knew in advance who of the sick would survive and who would die. I thought of myself as being fanatical, crazy, and superstitious. Then I was not as yet familiar with what today we call parapsychology. I fully realized that secular enlightenment and the belief in miracles were contradictory. Today one might say that I suffered from conflicts and complexes. Yet at that time Freud's theories were not popular, certainly not in Mechev. After the epidemic had ceased, I was to be appointed Rabbi of Mechev by the community elders. However, I ran away to study philosophy at the University of Warsaw."

"I said that I would make it short. But I could sit with you three days and three nights and not tell you a tenth of what happened. I came to Warsaw with about fifty marks in my pocket; this was before the zloty came into use. With no formal education, I depended on what I had absorbed from some old books. Any day I would be drafted into the Polish Army. Life in the barracks would be a catastrophe for me. I am sure that I wouldn't have lasted for more than a few days; I would either have collapsed or committed suicide. But what were my chances to be rejected? It's true that I was weak, but I was not sick. Shlemiels worse than myself were taken. Maiming oneself to escape the draft, as was done in the Russian epoch, was useless. The Poles were familiar with all these tricks, and besides, the army doctors were ardent patriots. Before entering the recruiting office, I recited a prayer: 'Lord of the Universe, save me from brutal hands.' Immediately after setting foot in the hall, I was surrounded by a mob of wild peasants. They were hitting the Jewish recruits. A roughneck approached me and shouted, 'Jew, go back to Palestine.' The Jews huddled together in a corner. How can you sacrifice your life for those who spit on you? I was ordered to disrobe, and this also was an ordeal for me. In the doctor's office, two of the physicians who examined me were about to give me a clean bill of health. One doctor even said to me, 'The military will make a man out of you.' But an elderly doctor, who I believe was a colonel, disagreed: 'Why do we need such a misfit? It's a pity to waste the bread on him.' The two younger doctors tried their best to persuade the old man to change his mind, but he had the final word. I was rejected. The two young doctors looked puzzled. I would have to be blind not to see that some higher power had interceded on my behalf. But who could it have been? Perhaps my deceased father. I certainly had no merits of my own. I had committed all manner of transgressions. I even smoked on the Sabbath.

"From that time on, miracles occurred one after another. All sorts of explanations could be given for these events—coincidence, chance, and so on. But what happened to me was not in accordance with the laws of nature. I prayed and my prayers were promptly answered. I began to act spoiled, as though I was the Almighty's only child. It is written: 'Ye shall not tempt the Lord.' Still, I kept on tempting Him. It was almost impossible to get an apartment in Warsaw unless one could pay a large sum of money to both the departing tenant and the superintendent. Yet I was able to obtain a rent-controlled apartment without any additional costs. I met a beautiful girl whom I liked. At first I did not dare to ask heaven for sensual pleasures. But, sooner or later, I prayed that she would fall in love with me. On the following day, she came to me under the queerest of circumstances. She later admitted that some unknown power, which she could not resist, drew her to me. She had even heard a voice.

"I had no chance whatsoever to pass the entrance examination into the University of Warsaw. Yet I received a passing grade and was accepted. The miracles continued to occur after my admission to the university. One of the professors, who was known to be an anti-Semite, became my ardent friend. The professor lectured only once a week to a small group of graduate students. He taught Spinoza, who at that time was my beloved philosopher. I was sitting in the library browsing through Orgelbrand's *Encyclopedia*. Suddenly a hand touched my shoulder. It was he, Professor Chrabowski. He asked me, 'What are you searching for, young man?' I could understand him questioning me if he had seen me reading Spinoza or Descartes. But I happened to be glancing through an essay about Wyspianski. Professor Chrabowski was known to be an angry man and a misanthrope. He had a biting humor which could cut to the bone. Everyone feared him as though he were the Devil. But there he stood beside me, an old man of eighty years, trying to enter into conversation with a freshman. That same day, he invited me to his home. I think I was the only student in the university to be granted such an honor. And remember, I was a Jew and not even his student. He took a great liking to me. He even got me a fellowship. I was baffled by these episodes. The students spread rumors that I was a hypnotist or a warlock. Chrabowski himself mentioned that he couldn't explain why he was so gracious to me. This is only one example of hundreds."

"Why didn't you pray for a million dollars?" I asked.

"I was a fool. I was afraid to ask for too much. But actually, money was never my passion. At that time, I became interested in Kant and the so-called Marburg School. Hermann Cohen was my idol. I went to Berlin and then to Bonn. There new miracles began to occur. I didn't really know German; I brought nothing with me except a letter of recommendation from Professor Chrabowski, who was not known in Germany. I could have died from hunger and nobody would have cared. It was the time of the inflation and the despair which finally led to Nazism. As a matter of fact, Hitler had already attempted his famous *Putsch*. What could be worse than to be a poor Polish Jew, an '*Ostjude*.' Nevertheless, they made me a lector at the University of Bonn. And I was invited into homes where the sons of the best houses had no entrée. At a lecture, I met Fräulein Annelisa von Freihoff, a famous beauty and a girl of the highest nobility. What happened afterward between us, I cannot tell you. You can see I am not the most handsome of men and yet she fell in love with me in a way that was most mysterious. Please don't mock me. All of this may sound ludicrous, but I have no reason to lie. I could even show you letters to prove that what I am saying is true. Yes, Annelisa von Freihoff! To live with a shiksa is one thing, but to marry one is another. I could not forget that I am a descendant of Rabbi Abraham Malach and of the Holy Jew.

"Let me tell you that, in spite of all these events, I was at that time, and still am, an agnostic. Not as far as the existence of God and Providence is concerned, but in relation to dogma. I can't believe that each paragraph in the *Shulhan Arukh* was handed down to Moses from Mt. Sinai. However, as God created man, man's creations are also divine. I know what you are going to ask me: In that case, the works of Feuerbach and other atheists also should have a touch of divinity. Well, it is a question for which an answer does not exist in this world. If you still have a little patience, I want to continue with my story."

"Yes, tell it."

■

"You have written somewhere that every human being has a number one passion. My passion was women. It may seem funny for me to be playing the role of Don Juan. Actually, women are the passion of all shlemiels. Otto Weininger was right: the hundred percent male has no patience for the female. The hundred percent male is a warrior, not a romantic.

"I am not a sick man, but neither am I particularly healthy. Much of my time is spent in bed, and since this is my main occupation, I like to have someone with me. Of course the woman must be willing. But females in their own way can be the most unpredictable and spiteful creatures. It sometimes looks as if their only ambition is to discover a man's weaknesses. Once they succeed, they scorn their victim. I have seen giants reduced to flies in this eternal struggle. I had one weapon: prayer. I guess you read the story of Rabbi Joseph della Reina, who tried to bring the Messiah, and when his attempt failed, because he granted Satan a sniff of tobacco, he became a lecher. Through incantations, he was able to make the wife of the Grand Vizier come to him. I became a Joseph della Reina. I expressed the will to have a certain woman and almost immediately she came forth. It happened like this so many times and under such strange circumstances that rational explanations have no place here. If I did not care about your time, I could tell you many such cases. Naturally, I also had a passion number two—a career. Even though I hadn't learned German thoroughly, I became a full professor in Germany. And not really knowing philosophy, I even wrote for philosophical magazines.

"Why are you smiling? I do not lie. To know philosophy—actually the history of philosophy—one must read profusely, and for this I have no patience. Regardless of how great a philosopher is, he has only one small if inflated idea, and sometimes not even that. When I pick up one of their books, all I do is glance through the pages. This is sufficient to quench one's curiosity but not to be a professor. I was constantly in danger of exposing my ignorance. But the years passed and my reputation never suffered. When I needed to quote a particular philosopher while writing my essays, I simply opened one of his books and found the right passage. I became known as a man of erudition, while in reality I was an ignoramus. Whenever a student asked me a question involving philosophical knowledge, it just so happened that the day before while browsing through a book I had come across the answer. It may very well be that such things happen to other people who just don't pay any attention to them. Also, Providence does not like to reveal its techniques and wears the mask of causality. If one could see its work, free choice would cease. By the way, even an insight into the ways of Providence would not lead to absolute faith. The brain is constructed so that a man can simultaneously be a believer and a non-believer. The Talmud's statement that the wicked do not repent even at the gates of Gehenna is a deep psychological truth. One may roast in hell and still remain an atheist. Sometimes I suspect that even God doubts His own existence.

"In the early thirties Germany was becoming a very dangerous place for one of my kind. The only country I could escape to was France. But I didn't know French. I was a Polish citizen and a Jew to boot. There was no reason for the French consul to give me a visa. I said my prayer and went to the French consulate. I was granted a visa immediately. I arrived in Paris almost penniless. I am not thrifty and I had spent all my little earnings. I took a room in a cheap hotel and figured out that at best my money would last me four weeks. But what would I do afterward? I was not permitted to work. After all my triumphs, I remained with nothing. True, I was accustomed to miracles, but the rationalistic part of me argued, 'Better people than you have starved to death.' I knew no one in Paris. The German Embassy crawled with Nazis. I took a walk in the streets and came to the Place del l'Opéra. I saw an outdoor café and sat down at a table. I ordered an aperitif, not because I wanted it, but because I saw someone else ordering it. The waiter brought it to me, and I then sat and waited for a miracle to happen. I sat for three hours and nothing happened. I became tired and decided to go back to the hotel. Well, even manna did not fall for more than forty years. From past experience, I knew that if there was no immediate answer from On High, no answer would come. In the dramas of my life, whatever was going to happen could be seen in the first scene of the first act. I lost my way to the hotel and became exceedingly tired from walking on the boulevards of Paris. On a side street I noticed a little café with a few tables outside. I was hungry and thirsty. I sat down and a waitress came out in a dirty apron. The menu she gave me was illegible. I ordered one of the items not knowing what it was. She muttered something and went inside. After a few minutes, she returned from the kitchen and began talking to me quickly with typical French verbosity. I understood that they were out of the item that I had ordered and I decided to order something different. At a table a few steps from me sat a couple. I barely noticed them. However, it seemed that they had sensed my predicament. The lady asked me, *'Sprechen Sie Deutsch?'*

"To make it short, they were refugees from Germany, and since they knew French, they wanted to help me. I thanked them and the young woman translated the menu for me. I looked at her and I was amazed. She was a copy of Annelisa von Freihoff, only a little older. She appeared more aristocratic, even though she told me she was a Jewess. She asked if I was from Germany. Her husband moved over to my table, so finally we all sat together. He was a giant of a man, six feet or perhaps taller, handsome, an athlete with a round face, red cheeks, and brown eyes. It was summer and yet he wore spats. When he heard that I had been a professor in Bonn, he became quite excited. He had studied there and graduated as an electrical engineer. Even if his wife hadn't been wearing a ring with a huge diamond, I would have guessed that they were wealthy people. They introduced themselves: Mr. and Mrs. Eggschwinger—a strange name for Jews, but they seemed completely assimilated. The husband, Hans, told me that he owned a factory that made electrical appliances. He'd left it in the care of his cousin and planned to go with his wife to Brazil, where another cousin of his had a coffee plantation. He boasted that he had managed to bring over the greater part of his fortune from Germany. His wife Gretl smiled just as Annelisa used to smile. I asked myself, 'Is this the answer to my prayer? Did heaven send me a married woman?' After a while the pair went back to their own table and began to converse in French. I saw that he reprimanded her for something, and in response she smiled coyly, like a schoolgirl. There was a nobility in her face which cannot be expressed in words. She was blond with blue eyes, and was above average in height. She looked more Nordic than the Nordics themselves. One thing astonished me: why did a rich couple choose to dine at such a low-class restaurant? On the other hand, there are in Paris small restaurants which are famous for their cuisine and are frequented by gourmets."

"Did you fall in love with her?" I asked.

"She was the greatest love of my life."

"What did they quarrel about?"

"He was pathologically stingy. He had come with her to this restaurant because meals were a few centimes cheaper here. This was only one of his idiosyncrasies. He was also a hypochondriac and slept with her only once every three months. He took many pills and fasted one day a week. She gave me a whole list of his peculiarities; naturally, later on.

"I realized that I had stumbled into something which I couldn't cope with. Until then, the Ten Commandments had been sacred to me. But a God who helps a man steal another man's wife is like a God who helps one kill somebody. Hitler was about to take over the German government, and in his speeches he babbled about the Almighty, who would help the Nazis enslave the world. A God who helps a man commit adultery may also help the S.S. men drag the innocent into concentration camps. But the passion aroused between us was stronger than all convictions. Hans Eggschwinger was not one of those who would tolerate such doings. When he learned of our affair, he took out a revolver and placed it at my temple. He swore that he would kill both Gretl and me. He denounced me to the police and said that I was attempting to destroy his family life. I could easily have been deported. France already had an overabundance of Polish Jews. I had gotten a job as a teacher in a Talmud Torah, but according to the law a tourist was not permitted to earn money in France. Every day miracles occurred to save me, and these miracles perplexed me. I couldn't accustom myself to the idea that God could be on the side of evil. A vicious God: this is something for the Ancient Greeks or the Teutons, not for a great-grandchild of the Holy Jew. On the other hand, two Jewish philosophers believed in an amoral God—Spinoza and Shestov.

"Much took place in the years 1935–1938. Our affair turned

into a kind of sickness. We tried parting, but we could not detach ourselves from each other. Telepathy and clairvoyance were daily occurrences. When I awoke one morning, a voice commanded me to go to some exhibition. When I arrived at the destination, Gretl was there. Once we met by 'coincidence' in the strangest of circumstances, at the horse races located many kilometers from Paris. Both of us went there by taking the wrong autobus. I also became a master of conspiracy. The moment Hans left the house, I was there to take his place. Many times Hans and I would miss each other by seconds. Under such circumstances the senses become unusually sharp and all thoughts revolve around one goal. I became a lurking beast.

"And then there was always trouble with money. Though we were cautious, Gretl became pregnant and we had to pay for the abortion. Hans was so stingy that if she bought a glass of soda, he knew it. If I have something against Spinoza, it is his belittling of the passions. They are stronger than anything else in the universe.

"I still lived in the same little hotel in Belleville, a five-story walk-up full of whores and of idealists who tried to create a better world. War broke out in Spain and young Jewish men ran to defend democracy. I've long been convinced that there is a hidden Messiah in every Jew. The Jew himself is one big miracle. The hatred of the Jew is the hatred of miracles, since the Jew contradicts the laws of nature.

"One day, when I was staying home from my teaching, someone knocked on my door. I asked who it was and it seemed to me that I heard Gretl's voice. I opened the door and there stood Annelisa von Freihoff. She had married an officer who had later become a Nazi. He had come to Paris on a diplomatic mission and took his wife along with him. While her husband negotiated with the politicians, Annelisa came to visit me. How she found my address I never learned. I had nothing to offer her, not even a drink of water. She was an anti-Nazi and wanted to remain in Paris. All her plans depended on me. After I told her about my relationship with Gretl, she returned to her husband. Years later, I heard that Annelisa's husband was implicated in the plot to assassinate Hitler and was shot. Annelisa died soon after.

"In 1938, Hans Eggschwinger presented his wife with an ultimatum: either she returned to him or he would shoot all three parties involved. He swore to it on his German Bible. Neither of us had any funds. He had taken away her jewelry. She didn't even have her passport. We had to part. Hans had no business and he did only one thing—keep watch on his wife. After a while, he forced her to move with him somewhere on the French Riviera. Only a German woman would allow her husband to terrorize her to such a degree. I was now alone in Paris. It was difficult for Gretl to write to me. War was imminent. I tried to comfort myself with other women, but my yearning for Gretl did not cease for a moment. I prayed to God to help me forget her. But I must not have prayed in earnest, because I could not forget her for a minute. From time to time, she managed to write a letter, and each line exuded her passion. I understand that you are wondering what she could have seen in me. But you know the answer: love is really between the souls and not the bodies.

"Here I come to the essence of my story. I began to realize that I wished Hans dead. Until then, I had never wished death on anybody. The idea of murder made me shudder. Even as a child I was shocked when I read in Samuel II of King David's ways of getting Bathsheba and Abigail. The Jewish part of me, the *Talmud-Jude*, as the Nazis call someone like myself, could not tolerate such deeds. I can easily understand why the Hasidim looked askance at those who studied too much Bible. There is something primitive in the Bible which the Jew of the Diaspora—the real Jew—cannot swallow. I even had pity for Goliath. When I discovered my wish that Hans die, I began to pray for him. I recited a special prayer for his life, his health, and his well-being. But as I prayed for him, some tiny section of my brain—you may call it the subconscious—asked for the opposite. I stopped sleeping at night. Meanwhile, the year 1939 arrived. The Hebrew school where I taught was closed down. I had a little money, and although I knew I shouldn't, I took a trip to southern France. I deceived myself into thinking that I traveled this route to reach Palestine. But it was really Gretl I went to see. According to her last letter, she was living with her husband in Nice. However, when I arrived there, I learned that they had moved away. I asked the neighbors where the Eggschwingers had moved; nobody seemed to know. Once again I was left without any money, and again I awaited a miracle. I took a room in a fifth-class hotel and began to look at the ads in the employment section of the newspapers. Someone like myself was not needed anywhere. In my despair, I wrote a letter to the concierge of the hotel where I had stayed in Paris, asking him to forward any mail which I might have received. I could have requested the post office to do this, but I did not know my destination when I left the city. Besides, everything I do is on the spur of the moment. The concierge was lazy and a drunkard. In his house, I had seen heaps of letters which belonged to past tenants and which were never forwarded. After I mailed the letter to the concierge, a melancholy and a heaviness overcame me. In the past, whenever I was at an impasse, I prayed, but this time my lips were sealed and my thoughts turned away from prayer. I decided that my utmost desire was to die.

"A week passed, perhaps two. The little money I had was gone. I might have applied to the Jewish community for relief, but begging always revolted me. I remember it clearly: I was left with nothing but a package of crackers and half a bottle of sour wine. I owed rent on my room. I lay down on my bed and waited for death, no longer for miracles.

"Suddenly someone knocked on my door. It was a messenger with a special-delivery letter. The letter was from Paris and the address had been scrawled by my former concierge. I opened the envelope and inside I found a telegram. Hans Eggschwinger had died of pneumonia. While reading the telegram, I realized two things. First, that I was responsible for Hans's death, and second, that I would never be able to pray again."

"Where did he die?" I asked.

"In Switzerland, in St. Moritz.

"In the telegram, Gretl asked me to come to Switzerland. But I didn't have the fare. Besides, I could never have obtained a visa. The telegram had been sent on the very day I left Paris. If I had remained another hour, I would have received it there. I had no money to telegraph Gretl, but I still had a few centimes to buy postage stamps for a letter. But what could I write? As Nathan the Prophet said to David after the death of

Uriah the Hittite, 'Thou hast murdered a man and also inherited his wife.' I knew that my fate rested with the Nazi hangman. Just the same, I wrote a letter to Gretl and she sent me five hundred Swiss francs. She asked that I try to obtain a tourist visa to Switzerland. But when the people at the consulate saw my Polish passport, they refused even to talk to me. Gretl made an effort to come to France, but the Swiss government refused to guarantee her return trip. It was a time when hundreds of thousands of exiles tried to find refuge in Switzerland. All the hotels were packed. I cannot tell you all the details. Many of them I have forgotten. In 1939, Gretl's return to Switzerland was assured. She went to Paris to meet me. By this time, everything appeared to me of little importance. The powers of the universe had severed communication with me. I knew that they had even begun to spite me. There is no such thing as neutrality in heaven. I had abused a privilege and it turned into a curse. Millions of people were condemned to exile, starvation, and death, and I was one of them. Until that time I had never suffered from impotence. The opposite—I was extremely virile. The women with whom I had had relations were always amazed, because this prowess did not match my physical appearance. Hans Eggschwinger was an athlete, but at love he was weak. But that evening, en route to Paris, I was assailed by a fear of impotence. The nearer the train approached Paris, the greater my fear grew. When I stepped off the train in the morning at the Gare de l'Est and saw Gretl standing on the platform, I knew for sure that I would be at a loss with her. She had never appeared to me so beautiful and elegant as she did that morning. She wore a hat with a wide brim and a black veil. As for me, I felt ugly and shrunken. Before the train stopped, I had seen myself in the washroom mirror. I looked emaciated, wrinkled, and aged. The little hair I still had was now gray. My clothes hung on me like rags. I was terribly embarrassed, and I did something only a madman is capable of doing. I glimpsed Gretl for the last time and got lost among the crowd of passengers. I didn't want to see the disappointment in Gretl's eyes, and I was also afraid of her pity.

"The result of that sudden decision, or call it impulse, was

another year of starvation in Paris and then on to German concentration camps and all the horrors that went with them. The
little man who sits here beside you was in Dachau, Stuthoff,
and Majdanek. Even now I weigh no more than one hundred
and ten pounds. When the Americans liberated the concentration camps, I weighed exactly sixty-six pounds. The doctors
never believed that I would live. Just before the liberation,
during the last days, I had fallen into a coma. I have already
tasted death. I want to tell you now that there is nothing
sweeter. All the pleasures of this world cannot compare with
the peacefulness of death. How strange that man fears most
what brings him the greatest bliss. Apparently this fear is necessary, since without it man would not clutch at life. I want to
tell you that during the years 1941–1945 not a single miracle
happened to me. I suffered through all the tortures and ago-
nies of this period."

"When did you come to America?" I asked.

"In 1950."

"Did you marry here?"

"I'm all alone."

"Do you work?"

"I was a Hebrew teacher for some time. Now I do nothing.
I live off my compensation money. Those who had a higher
education are getting a higher allotment from the Germans. In
addition to my pension, I received an extra thousand dollars.
Somehow I manage."

"With what do you keep yourself busy all day?" I inquired.

"Nothing. Well, almost nothing. In the summer I rent a
small bungalow in the Catskills. It costs me no more than one
hundred and fifty dollars, and I stay there from June until after
Labor Day, sometimes even until the end of September. I prepare my own meals and read the newspapers. Once in a while I
pick up a book. In the winter, I do the same things in the city."

"No more love?"

"No more love."

"What happened to Gretl?"

"Gretl married the owner of the hotel in Switzerland where
she stayed. He is not Jewish."

"Do you hear from her?"

"I met her in Munich in 1948."

For a while we both were silent. Then he continued: "I didn't tell you even one thousandth of what transpired. One time I went out into the street with the intention of finding money. And on the pavement amid all the passersby I found a fifty-franc bank note. My legs had directed me to this very spot. For some time I actually supported myself this way, even though I'm nearsighted and half-blind."

"Didn't this lead you to any conclusions?" I asked.

"What conclusions? There are powers up above which play with us. Lately it occurred to me that this earth is ruled by a divine prodigy who toys with little soldiers and dolls. When he tires of them, he rips off their heads. It is even written in the Book of Psalms: 'There is that Leviathan, whom Thou hast made to play therein.'"

"A prodigy has a father."

"He may be an orphan. And besides, the father may be occupied with other worlds."

He was quiet for a while. Then he said, "You, too, are playing. This is the reason I read your works."

"How does this all tie in with your miracles?" I asked.

He grimaced, clutched his beard, wrinkled his forehead, and shook as though he were studying the Gemara. "Life, play, and miracles are identical. Death, too, is a miracle, but not a game."

"What is it?"

"The very essence of being," he answered.

Translated by the author and Judy Beeber

The Litigants

THERE was talk about lawsuits, and old Genendl, a distant relative of ours, a woman learned, as they say, in the small letters, was saying, "There are people who like this kind of legal wrangling. Even among us Jews there are those who at any opportunity will run to the rabbi for a *din torah*. In olden times, duels and trials were a madness among the Polish squires. Not far from our town there were two squires, Zbigniew Piorun and Adam Lech, small landowners, not like the Radziwills or the Zamoyskis. Piorun had a few hundred serfs. It was before the peasants were freed. He owned fields, forests, and a stable with race horses. In his younger years he was a hunter and a rider, and he used to attend all the races. There was still the Sejm in Warsaw and Piorun attended its sessions every year. It was in the constitution of Poland that when the nobles tried to vote for a certain law or impose a tax, if only one delegate vetoed it, the whole project came to nothing. This was called *vetum separatum*. They could never come to any decision. Because of this wild situation Poland was finally torn to pieces. Piorun was almost always among those who used the veto. He loved making long speeches and made mincemeat of all the programs anyone introduced. At home, every few weeks he challenged someone to a duel. He had a court Jew named Reb Getz, who was in charge of the whole estate and, among other things, of milking the cows. It was Piorun's permanent ambition to prove to Reb Getz that Jesus was the real Messiah. Once, when Piorun began a debate with Reb Getz which lasted until evening, Reb Getz said, 'Your Excellency, whoever the Messiah is or will be, he is not going to milk your cows.'

"Piorun and his wife had sons and daughters. They were all good-looking and they married into the high aristocracy. Every year he gave a ball and people of high rank came from the whole of Poland. The other squire, Adam Lech, was small and black like a gypsy, with no wife or children. He had a neglected little estate with some hundred serfs. He had no court Jew. He managed everything himself. He was an angry man, and when a peasant did something he didn't like, he whipped him with his own hands. There was an old enmity between Zbigniew Piorun and Adam Lech. Their estates had a common boundary and for many years they quarreled about a piece of land which Lech claimed as his property. Piorun had included it in his territory and had fenced it in. The dispute came to a trial, and like all trials in Poland it went on for many years. One judge issued one verdict, another judge a different verdict. Each petition had to have costly tax stamps affixed. All the clerks had to be bribed with money or gifts. Piorun could afford all this, but not Lech. How does the saying go? 'Before the fat one turns lean, the lean one dies.' Neighboring squires tried to effect a compromise. Both sides remained stubborn. In time Lech lost everything. His hair became prematurely white. From too much grief and perhaps from drinking he became emaciated as if he had consumption. Gradually he sold all his fields, his forest, and even his serfs. People expected him to die any day, but some power kept him alive. Adam Lech was supposed to have said he could not leave this world until the courts gave him back what Piorun had stolen, since the truth must come out like oil over water.

"One day both squires, Piorun and Lech, received notice from Warsaw that on a future date they had to appear before the highest tribunal, where a final verdict would be handed down. Piorun didn't care anymore about the whole business. His wife had died, his children had dispersed. He barely remembered all the details of the litigation, but since the Sejm would be convening in Warsaw, Piorun had the desire once more to set forth his veto. He had an old carriage and an old coachman by the name of Wojciech. Piorun's old-maid servant gave the squire provisions for his trip, as well as a few bottles of vodka. The carriage had traveled only a short distance when suddenly it stopped. 'Hey, Wojciech, why have you stopped?' Piorun asked, and Wojciech said, 'Adam Lech is standing in the middle of the road and doesn't let me pass.' 'What? Lech, that old corpse!' Piorun said. At once he understood why. Lech had threatened many times to shoot Piorun like a dog, and now he was about to do it. 'It's good that I haven't forgotten my pistol,' Piorun said. The sun had set and it was twilight, as Piorun began to shoot his rusty pistol. He barely saw where he was aiming. His hand trembled. Wojciech alighted from the coachman's seat and began to scream, 'Your Excellency, Adam Lech is without weapons. He is waving his empty hands.'

" 'No weapons, what kind of duel is this?' Piorun shouted.

"Why drag the story out? Lech had also received a notice to come to Warsaw, but had neither carriage nor horses and, after long brooding, had decided to ask his longtime enemy to take him to Warsaw.

"You're laughing, huh?" Genendl asked. "This is what really happened. What does a squire do who is called to a trial and has no horse and carriage? Lech came up on Piorun's carriage and began to blow and scrape, to stutter and beg Piorun to do him a favor and take him to Warsaw.

"When Piorun heard these words and saw his archenemy bend down, wrinkled, and shriveled like a skeleton, dressed in an old worn coat, with a bag on his shoulders like a beggar, he forgot all their conflicts. He began to laugh and cry, and said, 'My dear neighbor, my friend, why didn't you come to me first? By a hair I almost shot you. It is true that we were once enemies, but we are Poles, brothers of one nation, and I will not let you go to Warsaw on foot. Come in, sir, to my carriage.' The two squires seized each other and began to kiss and embrace like old chums. Piorun took out a bottle of vodka and they drank each other's health and good-humoredly drank toasts to each other's success in the trial. Then Piorun said, 'Why do I need your piece of land? To whom will I leave it? My heirs are all richer than I am. All one needs at our age is a grave.' Lech spoke in the same manner. 'The whole war between us was nothing but a mistake, a caprice, a silly ambition,' Lech said. 'Perhaps the Devil himself, who always lurks behind God's children and tries to befuddle their spirits, has corrupted us. Your Excellency, why do I need the land? I don't even have anyone to take care of my flower pots.'

"Both squires traveled together to Warsaw, talking about old times, making fun of the Polish courts, their lawyers, their accusers, the false witnesses each litigant had hired, the court language written in a Latin no one could understand. Lech said, 'My friend, I don't believe anymore that the Warsaw parasites and vampires are about to come out with a final verdict.

No litigant in Poland has ever lived long enough for a trial to be finished. The end comes to the litigants, not to the trials.'

"Adam Lech was right. In Warsaw both litigants learned that the court was far from ready to hand down a final verdict. They were asked to hire land surveyors once again to measure the land, which over the years had become overgrown with weeds and teeming with snakes, field mice, porcupines, and all kinds of vermin. These measurements were going to cost a lot of money. They were to be compared with other measurements in archives, which only God knew if they still existed. Both Piorun and Lech scolded the court officials and called them thieves, plate lickers, rats, and scavengers. Then together they went to a tavern to drink.

"There was a lot of talk about this extraordinary settlement in the corridors of the Sejm, and when both squires came to the session in the Sejm, they received an ovation from all the benches. In honor of this peacemaking, Piorun did not use his veto on this occasion. For the first time in his life, he agreed with the other lawmakers as a sign that the Poles should from then on act like a united people.

"Too late! Not long after, the Kings of Austria, Russia, and Prussia divided Poland among themselves. Piorun and Lech died, and were buried not far from each other. For many years afterward the tale of these two friendly litigants was told among the squires and landowners all over Poland."

Translated by the author and Lester Goran

A Telephone Call on Yom Kippur

I OFTEN receive telephone calls from readers who assure me that they have a true story that would shock me. Usually I get rid of such propositions with any kind of excuse: I'm about to leave town, I'm not well, I'm working on a piece with a deadline. When I do surrender to my curiosity, I'm almost always disappointed. The stories are typical recitations of treacherous husbands, unfaithful wives, ungrateful children. This time a man called who swore he had a fantastic story to tell—a piece of reality with all the elements of fantasy. After some hesitation I made an appointment with him. On the telephone his voice sounded like that of a middle-aged man, but when he came to my office I saw that he was in his seventies, tall, with a head of white hair and a wrinkled face. Only his eyes expressed youthful eagerness. He told me that in Warsaw, where he was born, he had belonged to a circle of students who considered themselves Yiddishists. In the early twenties he emigrated to America—already a grown man. Here he practiced as a dentist and a dental surgeon for over forty years. I asked him about his family and he answered, "I'm sorry, I don't have any close relatives, I've never married. In Warsaw they used to say that when an old bachelor dies he is buried without a prayer shawl, but I never had one. I've always considered myself an atheist. However, when you hear the story I'm about to tell, you will see that a full-fledged atheist has never existed. Somewhere we all believe in the supernatural. Who was it who said, 'When you scratch an unbeliever, a believer will emerge'?"

After a while my visitor began his story: "As I said, I'm not religious. This may be the reason I never wanted to marry. I doubted not only God but also women. In my youth I had affairs with a number of married women and I came to the conclusion that the saying 'Every woman has her price' is true. I'm not an anti-feminist. All I can say about women is that they are neither better nor worse than men. Our grandmothers were faithful wives because they believed in God and in the Torah, and were afraid of being roasted on a bed of nails in Gehenna. For the same reason, our grandfathers were devoted husbands.

When the fear of punishment is gone, what can restrain people from deceit? I'm an old man now, but I still have a lover. When I was young I was what they call a playboy. I was successful in my profession. I even taught orthodontics in a university. I made a lot of money; I had an office on Park Avenue and a comfortable apartment. Although I had no confidence in women, I loved them, and I am not boasting when I say that I was a success with them. What is so difficult about it?

"Yes, I had affairs—juggling a number of women simultaneously. My rule was never to take any of them too seriously. Of course I did not always succeed. There were cases in my life when my love for a woman became so intense that I was about to take her to City Hall or stand with her under the wedding canopy. But at the last moment I had the strength to say no, and still they never left me. I possess huge albums with photographs of my sweethearts, and I have boxes of love letters.

"The most important of all these women was Helena. She was from Warsaw, where she had studied in a Gymnasium—something rare for a Jewish girl in Poland in those days. We met in New York—as a matter of fact, in my office. Someone recommended me to her as a dentist. She was a beautiful woman, intelligent, well-read, and with good taste. Her husband was an optical-instrument salesman who traveled all over America and made a good living. When we began seeing one another, she had an eight-year-old daughter, Mildred. She brought her to me to be fitted for braces. Even today it is not clear to me why her husband chose a business that kept him away from home most of the time. He was sometimes absent for weeks—even months. I have always thought that traveling salesmen and sailors cannot be jealous by nature. Who knows? Perhaps they are born with an exaggerated faith in the opposite sex. Maybe they subconsciously like to share their wives with other men.

"I'm coming to the point. Yes, the husband traveled a lot and made good money. He sent his daughter to private schools. And meanwhile, a tremendous passion developed between Helena and me. We often fantasized about her leaving her husband and marrying me, but I knew that I would never do it. I had no desire to bring up another man's child, or even a child of my own. Women often reproached me, and said that

I was a cynic. Maybe I was, but what were they? Men of my disposition should remain unattached, and this is what I did. I am by nature as far from monogamy as heaven is from earth. I think it was Maupassant who said, 'Why a man should get up one morning with a decision to get married I will never understand.' He also said that he could not see why two women aren't better than one, three better than two, and ten better than three. It's possible his biographies ascribe words to him he never said. I certainly accepted his view.

"My affair with Helena went on for years, and it seemed to become stronger with time. In order not to get overly involved, I tried my best to have others on the side. Helena knew about them, and it made her bitter. Sometimes she threatened to make love to other men, but I knew it was not in her character. We had many quarrels. Whenever we separated both of us almost expired from yearning. I heard her calling me telepathically, and I answered her in the same manner. When one of us could not stand it anymore and surrendered, we fell upon each other with a thirst and an enthusiasm that almost killed us. She always said that only death could end our love. At the same time I knew that Helena never made peace with my betrayals. Her rebellion became even sharper with time; our quarrels lasted longer. We waged what they call today the battle of the sexes.

"The unavoidable happened—we parted. Mildred had already grown up and was in college. The reason for our parting was the husband's decision to move to California. Whether this had some connection with me I could never learn. It all came unexpectedly, and everything happened quickly. One day she told me that she was leaving, and a week later she was ready for the journey. They sold their furniture for next to nothing. Today people fly, but then people went by train. Helena had a phobia about flying. She once told me that her fear of flying was so great she was sure that her anxiety could cause the plane to disintegrate in midair. Helena believed in all the superstitions you write about—ghosts, premonitions, clairvoyance. I have forgotten to mention that Mildred never approved of me. She became my enemy when she grew up and understood our game.

"When Helena packed her luggage and prepared for the

trip, she insisted that her moving would be a form of suicide. I had to swear that I would come to visit her soon in California. She cried so much that I could not be angry with her. She had lost weight, and I did not like the color of her face. She had written a will, in which she asked to be cremated after death. 'I don't want to rot in the earth,' she told me. 'It is my wish that my ashes be thrown into the ocean. I don't want you to visit my grave with one of your whores.' She spoke as if she had lost her mind. I suffered terribly myself, and there were nights when I lay awake and planned to run away with her. She said that if I was ready to go with her, and if I promised to marry her after she was divorced, she would live with me even in the jungle! But where could we run? Here I had my office, my patients. I lectured in the university. I had other girl friends and was in my own way attached to them, too. Helena was not young anymore, and in my late middle age I had begun to develop a taste for young ones. The woman who is directly connected with this story was a student then, about twenty-five years old. Her name was Martha."

"Not Jewish?" I asked.

"Yes, Jewish. But wait, the story is only beginning. Helena and I parted in love and in hatred. I knew that her husband was aware of me. You cannot conceal an affair like this forever. Almost immediately after she left, wild letters began to arrive from her. She hinted, then actually stated, that she was dangerously ill and that her days were numbered. Since I considered her a hypochondriac, I didn't take her too seriously. Then, in the middle of the night, the telephone rang and it was her daughter. 'My mother is dead,' she screamed. 'Her ashes are already in the ocean. Murderer!' She abused me with the most terrible words. She wailed so that she almost burst my eardrum. She threatened to come to New York and shoot me. I tried to answer but she wouldn't let me say a word. Mildred's last words were 'To me you are already dead. You can't hide for long.' She assured me that her father, too, was out to get his revenge.

"After that night I seriously considered leaving the States—running to Europe or the Land of Israel. The Jewish state had already been proclaimed. Who knows what hysterical people can do? Still, I remained in New York, and as you can see, I am still here. What could I do? Helena was dead, and I was certainly not religious enough to say Kaddish for her. I don't need to tell you that I was shattered. I don't know how it is with others, but I can never forget anything. If you ask me, the word 'forget' should be erased from the dictionary. A day did not pass when I did not think about her. All her words, all her caresses, and all her resentment were engraved in my memory. I had told her that she was the greatest love of my life and it was true."

My visitor went on: "After some years I began to fantasize about seeing Helena's daughter again. I could not hate her forever. I said to myself that as women get older they are more likely to understand the complications of love and to forgive. In a way, I had taken part in Mildred's upbringing. When I visited I often brought her chocolate and other little gifts. I hoped I could meet her again one day. Maybe she was already married and a mother. You know what takes place in a mind that is possessed with the illusions of love. Those who love money would like to grab all the capital from all the banks, and those who love women would like the entire female sex to belong to them. As I grew older I had saved a part of my earnings, and it occurred to me to leave Mildred some money in my will. However, between thinking and doing is a far cry in my case. By nature I postpone things. It may sound like a paradox, but although I doubt God's existence I trust his providence, or call it destiny. The whole phenomenon of man is a paradox—biologically and in other ways.

"Now the real story begins. My young lover, Martha, was working then on her doctorate. She had a sister, Sheryl, ten years older, the wife of a professor of philosophy at the University of California at La Jolla. The professor, who was much older than his wife, had taken a sabbatical and gone to England. His wife, Martha's sister, was supposed to visit him at Oxford some time later. Suddenly a cable came saying that he was dead—he had been killed in a car accident. After a short visit to England the widow decided to go on a long trip to Israel. She knew that Martha and I were planning a vacation, and she persuaded us to live in her house in La Jolla during her absence. She didn't want to sublet to a stranger. Martha and I were more than willing to take care of the house. We were supposed to stay there the whole month of September and three weeks in October. The house was on a hill, and many of the windows faced the Pacific. If you have ever visited there, you know that it is one of the most beautiful places in the world—even more splendid than the Riviera. This was my first trip to California. I had never wanted to go there before, because of Helena.

"Rosh Hashanah was over and Yom Kippur was approaching. Neither Martha nor I ever celebrated the High Holidays, and it never occurred to us to look for a synagogue out there. But for some reason I always fast on Yom Kippur—perhaps just to keep some contact with my parents and with earlier generations of Jews. A day before Yom Kippur, Martha received a telegram from a cousin in New York saying that an uncle of theirs who lived in a suburb of Los Angeles had died and left his old wife alone, a women in her eighties. They had no children. The old woman was sick and helpless, and the cousin asked Martha to stay with her until the funeral. I disliked being alone on Yom Kippur, and I had hoped that no one would disturb our vacation. Martha suggested that I go with her to Los Angeles, but there was a chance that other relatives would show up and I wanted to avoid such complications. Martha prepared a pre-fast meal for me, and then she left. The death of her uncle had dampened my mood. It reminded me that the Angel of Death has jurisdiction over California, too. Everything I read in the newspapers or heard on the radio was about death, death, death . . . The professor in whose house I was staying and in whose bed I slept was dead. His portrait hung in the living room and stood on his desk. My own relatives had perished in the Holocaust. I ate the cold meal by myself, thinking about my dead parents, my brothers and sisters and their in-laws. Some of them had died a natural death, others were destroyed by the Nazis or died in exile in Russia.

"Night fell quickly. As beautiful as the sight of the Pacific is in the daytime, everything becomes gloomy and melancholy after sunset. You look out into infinite darkness. The sacred night of Yom Kippur is always connected in my mind with ancient Jewish somberness; the Kol Nidre melody and other liturgies were humming in my mind. When I was with Martha, the evenings always seemed too short, but without her the hours dragged on. A cool wind blew from the ocean, and a dense fog covered everything. I tried to read a book, but after the first few lines it began to bore me. I don't know why, but I opened one of my valises and I began to search there—for what I didn't know myself. In a side pocket I found an old notebook with addresses and telephone numbers from years back. I was overcome with a need to call someone and to wish that person a Happy New Year—an impulse on that holy night to make peace, as was the custom in Poland, with someone I had quarreled with or become estranged from. I looked over the names. Quite a number of those whose addresses I had written down were already in the other world. After poking around for some time, I found Helena's telephone number in Los Angeles. It seemed that I had never given up the idea of getting in touch with her daughter. Perhaps Mildred is still living in her mother's house, I thought. I knew that the chances of that and of the phone number's being the same were small. In America things change constantly. Nor was I sure that I really wanted to renew a relationship with someone who had called me murderer and threatened to kill me. Still, I felt an uncontrollable need to call the number, even though it is forbidden to use the telephone on Yom Kippur, when God sits on the throne of glory and signs the decrees for life and death.

"Now comes the unbelievable part, the frightful thing, which brought me here to your office. I called and someone answered. It was the voice of a woman, but not Mildred's. It was the voice of an elderly person, and she spoke in a foreign accent. God in heaven, it was Helena's voice! I realized that it could be nothing by my overwrought nerves, or else my never-extinguished love. I wanted to hang up, but my hand clung to the receiver as if from an electric shock. I heard myself uttering my name, and the voice on the other side said, 'Yes, I recognize you.' I must have been mad with fear in that moment, because I asked, 'Where are you?' And the voice replied, 'You know where.'

"I made a strong effort and threw down the receiver. My heart was beating like a hammer. It became dark before my eyes, but miraculously there was a chair nearby into which I could collapse. In a second I was soaked with perspiration. I sat there shaking and waiting for my heart to quiet down. I saw the receiver on the floor and I barely managed to lift it and hang it up. Ten minutes later when I put my fingers to my pulse it was still beating one hundred and forty times a minute. I hobbled over to the sofa and lay down. Only then did I remember that I had said the words, 'Where are you?' in Polish, *'Gdzie jestés?'* and she had answered me, *'Ty wiesz'*—'You know.' Helena came from an assimilated family and we always spoke Polish to one another, not Yiddish. But her daughter, like most children of émigrés, had no interest in the old country and didn't know a word of Polish. My heart, which had begun to subside, started hammering again. A new fear befell me—that I would have a heart attack. I lay there feeling mortally sick. 'It's an illusion,' I said to myself, 'Something is the matter with my brain.' Helena's answer, *'Ty wiesz,'* kept repeating itself in my ears. 'Could it be that I have heard a voice from the other world?' I asked myself. 'Is this an omen that I don't belong anymore to the living?' I could not remain alone in that forsaken house, but where could I go? I became cold. Martha had promised to call me when she arrived in Los Angeles, but the telephone was uncannily silent. In all my terror I decided not to mention a word of what had happened to me. Martha would be frightened to death and would rush me to a psychiatrist. I'll take this secret to my grave, I decided.

"After a long while I dragged myself into the bedroom and got into bed with my clothes and shoes on. I covered myself with whatever I could find, but I was still cold. I lay there numb and bewildered. I must have fallen asleep. The telephone on the night table rang, and I awoke in a tremor. I could hardly lift the receiver. It was Martha. She excused herself for calling so late. Her trip had taken longer than she expected, and she had found her old aunt sick and broken. None of the family, which was scattered all over the world, had appeared so far. Martha asked me how I had spent the evening and I tried to answer as calmly as possible. I recognized from her voice that she, too, was shaken by our unexpected parting. She said to me, 'This is my first direct encounter with death. It took a long time until the train reached Los Angeles, then I had to wait for a taxi. My aunt fell upon me and cried without stopping. The funeral will take place the day after tomorrow.

My uncle belonged to a *landsleit* society, and he has a plot in their cemetery. I'll come home as soon as I can. I will call you tomorrow morning.'

"My hand was trembling and I had difficulty hanging up. I stretched out again on the bed, but I did not turn off the light. For the first time since I was a child, I was afraid of the dark. If an accident had happened that night and the electricity had failed, I wouldn't be sitting with you here now. I would have been buried long ago in the Jewish cemetery in La Jolla—if there is one."

My visitor became silent and wiped his forehead with a handkerchief. His hand was shaking and I worried that something might happen to him in my office. I said to him, "Rest a while, Doctor. Shall I bring you a glass of water?"

"What? No. I'm all right."

He sat there, pale, pondering his own tale. I said, "Helena was alive, eh?"

"Yes."

"The daughter was lying?"

"With her mother's knowledge."

"Why couldn't Helena have just let you know she was finished with you?" I asked.

A frail smile appeared on my visitor's lips. "If you can lie, why tell the truth?"

He was silent again for a minute. Then I asked, "When did you learn that she was alive?"

"Not that night. I found some sleeping pills in the medicine cabinet and I swallowed at least a dozen. This threw me into a lethargy, in which I remained the whole night. I was awakened by the sun. One window in the bedroom faced east. It seemed that although I had been lying in a daze, my brain was working and seeking a solution to the riddle. If the dead want to reveal themselves, they don't need the telephone. Suddenly I grasped the truth: Helena was still living. I had become so weak that there could be no more thought of fasting. I went to the kitchen and drank a few cups of strong coffee. Only then did I find the power and the courage to ring the same number."

"Helena answered again?" I asked.

"Yes, and we spoke for over an hour. How weird it was to talk to someone whom I once loved so strongly and whom I considered dead for years. I spoke to her and shuddered. Was it true? Was I in a coma, and the whole thing one long nightmare? I won't bother you with too many details. Helena was alive, but she told me that she suffered from leukemia. Her husband had died a few years before. Mildred had married an Australian, who demanded that she convert to Christianity. She lived in Melbourne with her husband and two children. I asked Helena why she had entered upon this kind of deception, and she said, 'I wanted to chop off our affair with an ax. I knew that if you wrote to me or called, I would never get any rest. Only death could have parted us. And if not real death, then it would have to be the death that Mildred and I pretended. I knew that it was not in your nature to probe or to brood. You had others before me, and you forgot them quickly. One remarkable thing is that yesterday I thought about you all day and all evening. I wasn't just thinking. I had fallen into a sort of trance. You won't believe me, and I cannot even ask you to believe me, but when the telephone rang last night I knew it was you. I have no reason to lie to you anymore. I've reached a state where my lie will soon be the truth.'"

"Did you meet Helena later?" I asked.

"No. I wanted to, but she categorically forbade me to see her. She said, 'I want you to remember me as I was, not as I am now—a ruin. I don't even want my daughter to come to see me. She doesn't know how sick I am. It has been my fate to live all these years alone, and I intend to die alone. I hope that you will respect my wish. Don't come and don't call. If there is such a thing as life after death, we will meet in the other world.'"

"You never spoke to her again on the telephone?"

"No, but I saw her. In reality—not in dreams."

"How did this happen?"

"After that conversation I was again assailed with doubt. I could not stay alone in the house anymore. I was in fear of the coming night. To be sure that I was still there and not in my grave, I called up Martha. She cried out, 'I've been trying to call you for an hour, but the telephone was busy the whole time.' And here again is something unbelievable. Martha asked me, 'Who were you talking to for so long? Your dead lover?' She said it because she knew that Helena had lived in California. But the shudder those words brought to me I will never forget. 'Why did you say that? What was the idea?' I cried out.

" 'I'm only joking,' Martha said. 'Tell me the truth—who was on the phone that long?'

" 'It really was my dead lover,' I said.

" 'You will never know what I went through last night,' Martha said. 'It's true that my uncle is dead and my aunt's situation made me jittery. Just the same, I never knew my uncle and hardly knew my aunt. They are old people and they lived their lives. After my aunt managed to drive me crazy with crying her heart out, she went to sleep. I telephoned, as you know, and went to bed, tired from the trip and all the rest of it. I slept two hours or so. Suddenly I woke up with the feeling that someone or something had pulled my hair and whispered in my ear. I woke with a heaviness in my chest and with a terrible yearning for you. I told myself that it was silly. We have often parted for days or weeks without making much of it. Besides, I had spoken to you before I went to sleep. But I couldn't calm myself. I felt like crying, and you know I'm not a crybaby. I had a strong desire to call you again, but I didn't want to wake you. Now I hear that you, too, had a miserable night. Come and stay with me. None of the relatives has arrived yet. I have told my aunt about you. She won't make any trouble.'

"Some hours later," my visitor said, "I was sitting in the train that goes from San Diego to Los Angeles. Once there, I asked the taxi driver to pass by Helena's street on the way to Martha's. I wanted at least to see the house where she lived. Perhaps I tried to find an excuse to see her, too. I should not say it, but many things have happened in my life just because I wished them to happen. How such things occur I don't know. My theory is that causality and purpose are two faces of the same coin. If you want something very strongly, the causes and the effects begin to adjust themselves and to cooperate. The fact is that we entered her street, a little alley with old houses, and I asked the driver to stop. It was twilight already. The taxi stood there some five minutes. I was about to tell the driver to continue when I saw an old woman come out of Helena's house, and it was she. I would never have recognized her if I had seen her by chance in the street. But I am a hundred percent sure that it was her. Some trace of her former self remained. She glanced at the taxi and sharply turned away. Maybe she recognized me, too. This is the whole story."

"You never heard from her again?" I asked.

"How? No one would have written me about her death or called on the telephone, unless she herself from the hereafter—"

The last words seemed to slip from the old man's mouth of their own volition. He looked both frightened and ashamed. I heard him say, "Don't laugh at me. I'm still scared when I must make a telephone call late at night."

Translated by the author

Strangers

IT ALL happened secretly. Even Reb Eljokum's daughters
didn't know until the last minute what went on between
their father and their mother, Bleemele. Suddenly the strange
news came out: the old couple was getting a divorce. Reb
Eljokum, an old man of seventy-five, wanted to live out his last
years in the Land of Israel and to be buried on the Mount of
Olives. Bleemele simply could not leave her daughters, her
sons-in-law, her grandchildren and great-grandchildren, the
large apartment with its furniture and rugs. Husband and wife
planned the whole thing quietly. The whole fortune would go
to Bleemele: Reb Eljokum took only his personal clothing, a
few rare books which he might not find in Jerusalem, and
enough money to suffice even if he lived until ninety.

The divorce took place in our house. Reb Eljokum had a
beard as white as milk, a ruddy face and high forehead, blue
eyes below white brows. He imported tea from China and
owned some buildings. He was known as a scholar and an intimate of the Rabbi of Alexandrov. Bleemele was on her father's
side a granddaughter of the famous philanthropist Reb Samuel
Zbitkover.

Reb Eljokum had five daughters, all of them well married.
None of the girls was spoiled by modern thinking. It is true
that Reb Eljokum and his wife regretted not having a son to
recite the Kaddish after their death, but keeping the Torah and
good deeds were even better than Kaddish. Reb Eljokum supported yeshivas and each year gave a thousand rubles to the
Rabbi of Alexandrov.

As the scribe was preparing the divorce papers and the witnesses were practicing the special Hebrew script they would
have to use in signing their names, Reb Eljokum was leafing
through a Hasidic book. He wore a silk cap with a high crown
in the old Hasidic style. From time to time he took a gold
watch from his vest pocket to see what time it was. Only a few
days earlier I had heard him say to my father, "I've had enough
of business. I want to spend my last years with the Torah and
prayer. If I move to the Land of Israel now, my bones won't

have to travel underground to get there when the Messiah comes. I want to breathe holy air."

"You're a happy man, Reb Eljokum," my father said. "I hope you live to see the redemption."

"Everything is from heaven."

My father wondered why, since husband and wife had each passed the age of seventy, they needed a divorce at all. But Reb Eljokum replied, "Bleemele is younger than I am. A woman alone is helpless. If she wants to remarry I won't stand in her way."

"*Nu.*"

It was not an easy thing to leave a family, good friends, the Rabbi of Alexandrov, and to travel across the seas to a country under the domination of the Turks, but not a single sigh came out of him. Hasids of Alexandrov believed in silence. Bleemele, small, round, in a satin bonnet with ribbons and an old-fashioned cape, sat on a bench and wiped her tears with a batiste handkerchief. Her face was yellowish and looked to me as if made up of pieces of clay glued together. She shook her head, affirming a truth as old and sad as the female race. I had heard her say to my mother, "My dear lady, I wish I were dead."

"God willing, in Paradise you'll be together again," my mother comforted her.

Now in my father's study everything went according to the law. My father looked into a large volume and addressed Reb Eljokum in the second person singular. "Listen thou, Eljokum son of Eliezer Zalman. Hast thou uttered any words to negate this divorce?"

"No."

"Art thou willing to divorce thy wife, Bleema, daughter of Nathan Meir, in thy name, her name, and in the name of the Law?"

"Yes."

When my father told Bleemele to come over to the table and to cup her hands so that Reb Eljokum could place the divorce papers in them, the old woman began to collapse. My mother and another woman helped her to stay on her feet. After Reb Eljokum placed the papers in Bleemele's wrinkled hands, my father said what he always said in such cases, "You two are not permitted to remain under the same roof. If the woman wants to remarry, she must wait ninety days."

A maid and Bleemele's youngest daughter took her home in a droshky. Reb Eljokum went to the house of a former partner who was a follower of the Alexandrov Rabbi. A few days later Reb Eljokum left for the Land of Israel. I went with a few other boys of the street to watch as his luggage was loaded onto two droshkies. The rabbi came especially from Alexandrov to accompany Reb Eljokum to the train. The street was full of Hasidim. Bleemele had become ill. The daughters were angry with their father; only the sons-in-law and the male grandchildren came. The first droshky was occupied by Reb Eljokum, the rabbi, and two beadles. They were followed by a procession of droshkies packed with Hasidim. The young men sang Hasidic songs. We boys ran as far as the Vienna station.

Many weeks passed and I heard nothing of Reb Eljokum. My father remarked that he had probably arrived in the Holy Land. He had gone by train to Rumania, where he was supposed to board a ship for Jaffa. Bleemele had regained her health. I saw her often in the strictly kosher butcher shop across the street from our house. She walked with mincing steps and her maid walked behind her carrying a basket.

One day my father received a letter from Reb Eljokum. He wrote in Hebrew mixed with many Yiddish words that, praise God, he was already in Jerusalem living in the neighborhood of the Mea Sharim. He prayed every day at the Wailing Wall. He had already visited Rachel's grave and many other sacred graves. Jerusalem is filled with rabbis, scholars, Hasidim. Of course the poor suffer privation, but for money one can get everything. There are not many followers of the Alexandrov Rabbi there, but those who have come stick together.

A few weeks later we received a package from Jerusalem. It was a gift from Reb Eljokum. Inside, there was a prayer book bound in wooden covers with a carving of the Wailing Wall on the front and on the back the Cave of Machpelah. My father gave it to me. I lifted it to my nose and imagined it smelled of gopher wood, cloves, nard, myrrh, and other spices which are mentioned in the Pentateuch.

■

More time passed and I had almost forgotten Reb Eljokum. One evening I heard my father's hasty steps on the staircase—always a sign that he had heard some interesting news in the studyhouse. It was snowing outside and his red beard had turned white from the snowflakes. His velvet hat and his long robe were also trimmed with white. My mother warned him to wipe his half-shoes on the mat. In the reflection of the kerosene lamp his blue eyes seemed bluer than ever. He said, "Can you believe it? Reb Eljokum married in Jerusalem."

My mother became indignant. "That's what men are."

"He took a virgin. It looks as if he still wants a son to say Kaddish after him."

"It looks as if a young virgin is better than an old woman," my mother corrected him. Whenever she was angry her wig became disheveled by itself. I often imagined that my mother's wig was a living thing. Her sunken cheeks, usually pale from anemia, flushed. My mother had always feared that she would die prematurely and that my father would take a young woman in her place. My mother even described her. She would be small, round, with pink cheeks and a sugary smile. My mother believed that this was my father's taste. She was saying now, "I don't believe that the Holy Land was what he was looking for. That was only an excuse to divorce Bleemele. It wasn't the fear of God, only lust. Phooey."

"Since they are divorced and he has no son, what is so wrong?" my father asked. "The book says, 'In the morning sow thy seeds, and in the evening let not thy hand rest,' which the Talmud interprets as meaning that marriage may be a virtue of old age as well as youth. And . . ."

"I know what the Talmud says," my mother interrupted. "The truth is that women are faithful, attaching themselves to their husbands, but men are heartless. For over fifty years to live with a wife and their children and their children's children, and now he marries a strange wench. And why did she marry him? She's probably waiting for him to die so she can get his money."

My father shrugged his shoulders. He couldn't understand my mother's wrath, or the talk about love and an inheritance. She was too worldly for him. She read the newspapers and the impious novels which were serialized in them. In my father's sacred books love was never mentioned. As for an inheritance, according to the Mosaic Law the sons inherited, not the wife. After a while my father went to his room for his evening studies. It was not in his nature to brood about such matters.

Since the older children weren't at home, my mother spoke to me: "One is not permitted to malign anyone. Since God created men and women it must be this way. Besides, you are a man, too, and when you grow up you won't be better than the others. But this kind of hypocrisy sickens me. That Reb Eljokum acted like a saint. When I heard that he gave away most of his money to Bleemele to be able to live in the Holy Land I had a lot of respect for him. But now I've lost all my faith in him. And can you imagine what your father would do if I were to disappear? Immediately after the prescribed thirty days of mourning he'd stand under the canopy with someone else. For him I'm too skinny and too outspoken. He loves honey, but I am horseradish. I take after my father, and your father takes after his mother, who was all smiles and a do-gooder. God should forgive me for my sinful talk. If I'm fated to die . . ."

"Mother, don't speak that way!"

"What's the matter, one doesn't live forever. Once I'm buried, what do I care what he does? Do the matchmakers have any sense? They make the silliest combinations. In my case all they knew was that I was the daughter of the Bilgoray Rabbi and your father was the son of the Tomashov Rabbi. The truth is that the in-laws also didn't fit. My father was a lion and your paternal grandfather was a lamb. All day long he sat in the attic and studied the cabala. Weeks passed and he never spoke a word. If your father had more sense we wouldn't be sitting here on Krochmalna Street. Other rabbis are ambitious. They have big careers. When your father was told that he had to study Russian and be examined by the governor he exclaimed, 'Never in my life could I speak to a governor.' This is why you're wearing torn boots."

"They're not torn."

"Patched. Well, one is not allowed to speak like this. I don't have any luck in this world and I will most probably lose the world to come."

"Mommy, when I grow up I'll give you a lot of money!" I exclaimed.

My mother smiled ironically. "Where will you get so much money?"

"I'll find a treasure."

"Well, you are your father's son. Enough of that."

My mother picked up the newspaper. For a while she read the large type on the first page about Prime Minister Stolypin and the anti-Semite Purishkevich who drove the Jews from the Russian villages. Then she began to read the local news. Her eyes became sharp and sad. There were always stories about people who were run over by trams, murders, suicides, tinsmiths who fell from rooftops. There was a recurring headline, A MAN—A BEAST, which always told the same story of a janitor who came home drunk and raped his own daughter. I did not know exactly what this meant, but I understood that it was better not to ask too many questions.

One evening when my mother was reading a Hebrew book, Zelda, the wife of our neighbor Wolf the tailor, opened the door and said, "My dear lady, I have news for you."

"What happened?"

"Bleemele got married. The former wife of Reb Eljokum."

My mother's eyes were full of mockery. "Is that so? With whom?"

"With Reb Shaya Peltes from the dry-goods store. His wife died only a few months ago."

"Can it really be . . . ?"

"They were married the day before yesterday. She's already selling in his store."

"If he could do it, why not she? I don't blame her."

"In Jerusalem Reb Eljokum's new wife is pregnant. Friends of his got a letter. They might have a dozen children together."

"It wouldn't bother me."

"Oy, my dear lady, what's happening to the world? My mother became a widow at twenty-seven and she never wanted to hear about remarriage. Every time a matchmaker came to her she had one answer: 'God willing, with my husband in Paradise.'"

"There are all kinds of people."

"How can you begin to live with a stranger after being together fifty years? Reb Eljokum was such a clean man. Reb Shaya is such a dirty one. Also a miser. He took her for her money."

"At her age you can't be choosy," my mother said.

"What does she need him for? I hear that her daughters are beside themselves with grief."

The women kept on talking, shaking their heads. Zelda had begun to hint at things which I could not grasp. She slapped her mouth with closed fingers and said, "I'd better keep silent." My mother nodded. "What are husband and wife?" she asked. "Strangers. They are born strangers and die strangers."

"So who is near?" Zelda asked. "Children grow up and go their way."

My mother threw a side glance at me. "Let them go. It's not our world."

The next day after breakfast I went to Reb Shaya's dry-goods store to see Bleemele. She stood behind the counter showing spools of thread to a customer. She wore a plain weekday dress and a bonnet without ribbons. She looked as if she had always been there. She spoke to the customer through her sunken mouth. On a high stool in front of the cash drawer sat Reb Shaya, his once white beard now browned by tobacco. His skullcap was spotted and his gray coat was torn. He counted bank notes close to his myopic eyes. His eyebrows protruded like two brushes. I felt disgust for Reb Shaya, Bleemele, Reb Eljokum in Jerusalem with his pregnant wife. All grownups are liars, I thought to myself. I remembered Shaya's wife, Deborah Itta, from whom I used to buy buttons, needles, cotton. Where was she now? Did she know that Bleemele took her place? No, she didn't know. She was in Paradise. I suddenly decided that if my mother should die, God forbid, and if my father should marry that round little woman with pink cheeks, I would run away from home and become a cabalist and a recluse.

Translated by the author and Herbert R. Lottman

The Mistake

I T WAS a hot, summery Sabbath afternoon, and Aunt Yentl sat on the porch with her cronies, gossiping and telling stories. She wore her arabesque dress and her bonnet with the colored ribbons and beads. She was saying, "It's easy to say, 'I made a mistake.' But a mistake is not always a trifle. God protect us, one little mistake can ruin a life, especially of those who are proud and conceited. In our town, there was a Jew, Reb Shachne—a rich man, a learned man. He used to travel to Belz, not to the present rabbi but to his father, to ask for a blessing and offer a contribution. The rabbi himself would draw up a chair for him. Reb Shachne had a hardware store—locks, keys, nails, hammers, pliers, and other such things needed in a household or workshop. You could get goods from him that were hard to find even in the big cities. If he didn't have something in stock, he ordered it from Lublin and even from Warsaw. I was told that a tenant farmer had bought a strongbox from him with locks on it that even the most accomplished thief couldn't have picked open. Reb Shachne had in his store copper and also brass objects: mortars and pestles, chandeliers, all kinds of pots and pans. Landowners came to buy from him, and he never charged more than a fair price. Neither did he allow bargaining. I can see him now—not a tall man, of stocky build, with a red beard that fanned out from his chin. It was said about him that he was more learned than the rabbi. His wife, Lifshe, was distantly related to us.

"Lifshe bore Reb Shachne four sons and three daughters, but only two survived and the couple were left with one son and one daughter—Tevel and Gneshe, two cherished children. Tevel was known as a decent boy, willing to study and devoted to his parents. At sixteen he became a son-in-law of a rich man in Kielce, far from our region. He rarely came home for a visit. At that time there were few trains, and a journey by wagon took days. When Tevel got married, Gneshe was thirteen years old. Already she was known as a beauty; tall, with two blond braids. Girls were seldom sent to cheder, but we had one teacher who took girls into his school. His wife was a learned woman who taught the girls to pray and to write a line of Yiddish greetings. Gneshe helped her parents out in the store and spoke Polish and Russian. The Gentiles who shopped at the store would praise her beauty and refinement. There was talk that a Polish count had fallen in love with her, and had sent her a note saying that he wanted to marry her if she would convert. I wasn't there, but that's what I was told.

"Gneshe was still quite young when proposals for a match began to pour in. At Tevel's wedding, in Kielce, a wealthy woman spotted her and spoke to Lifshe openly—she wanted Gneshe for a daughter-in-law. Lifshe told her to send a matchmaker, and the woman said, 'I'll take your daughter as is. I won't bargain for a dowry.' Possibly her son had noticed the girl and had become infatuated with her. People fell in love in those days, too. Nothing came of that, but afterward our local matchmakers were always at Reb Shachne and Lifshe's door. Young as she was, Gneshe quickly showed herself to be choosy. Whoever was proposed to her she found fault with. One wasn't smart enough, another was too short, a third shuffled his feet when he walked. Lifshe would come to my mother and complain. 'I pray to the one above,' Lifshe said, 'for her to come to her senses and stop looking for perfection. Even the sun has spots.' My mother comforted her: 'Don't worry, your Gneshe won't remain an old maid.' The girl was then all of fifteen years old, but she was well formed and had a knowing look in her eyes. She liked to joke and often made fun of people. Someone said that if she lived in Warsaw she could have become a stage actress.

"When Gneshe turned sixteen and was not yet engaged, Reb Shachne also began to worry. He called his daughter into his study and had a talk with her. 'One shouldn't think too highly of oneself,' he said. 'We are all no more than flesh and blood.' Gneshe supposedly answered, 'It depends on *what* flesh and what blood. I can bear anything, but to live out my years with a fool—that I cannot abide.' Every time a match for her was proposed, Gneshe would demand to see the young man and to be allowed to speak with him. In those days this was considered scandalous. A bride was not supposed to see her intended until the wedding, when the groom lifted her veil. However, an only daughter gets her way. She could have asked for the moon.

"Now, here's a story for you. One day Gneshe had an encounter with a young man from Lublin. He was from a wealthy household and, as it turned out, quite enlightened, wearing a short caftan with a slit, a small cap, a starched collar, a necktie, polished boots. The matchmaker had brought him from Lublin just to meet Gneshe. As he passed through Zamość Street, all the girls ran to the windows to have a look. They all agreed: handsome as a prince. When Gneshe had an interview with one of her prospects, she would usually leave the door open a crack to prevent anyone from peeking through the keyhole or listening from behind the door. For an hour the two were left alone, and the whole time the sound of Gneshe's laughter was heard. He was, it seems, a joker. So much laughter was seldom heard in a Jewish household, and Reb Shachne didn't approve. He said to Lifshe, 'What's all the merriment? The Holy Temple still is in ruins and the Jews are in exile. But what do the young care about what happened in the Holy Land?' After an hour Gneshe came out to her mother in the kitchen, all radiant, and cried out, 'Mother, this one is smart, bright as the day.' Those were her words.

"I'll make it short. Right then and there the match was decided upon and a telegram was dispatched to Lublin to the groom's parents asking them to come for the signing of the engagement contract. They were well-to-do and refused to stay at Reb Shachne's but asked to be put up at a hotel. We had only one hotel in town, and it was mostly used by Gentiles, but there the groom's parents settled themselves. Reb Shachne and Lifshe threw an engagement party for their daughter almost as elaborate as a ball. A large number of guests were invited. Wine, mead, and liquor were copiously served. The groom was given a good-sized dowry and a gold watch to boot. The groom's mother was all decked out in a hat with ostrich feathers and a hoopskirt. The groom's father owned, I think, a brewery. The groom's mother presented Gneshe with a string of pearls as an engagement gift. Many young men came to the party. The groom—his name was Mully, probably derived from Shmuel—passed out cigarettes to everyone. He himself smoked a cigarette in an amber holder. He signed the engagement contract in a flowery script.

It was customary at an engagement party for the groom to debate some passage from the Talmud, but Mully rattled off jokes. Again and again, the girls and women burst into laughter. Later, Lifshe told us that after the engagement Reb Shachne said to Gneshe, 'Daughter, whatever else he is, a brooder your groom is not. But remember, my child, that the world is not a joke.' And Gneshe answered, 'What is it, then?'

"Both sides were eager to have the wedding soon. Gneshe had turned seventeen, which in those days made her almost an old maid. Mully was already twenty-one. He had just been exempted from military service and it had cost plenty to keep him out."

Aunt Yentl paused and then went on: "Since both sides agreed and there was no haggling about the dowry and the presents, there was no reason for postponing the wedding for too long a time. Yes, the wedding. Such a wedding I never saw before or after. Lifshe invited everyone. A long table for the poor was set up in Reb Shachne's yard. Everyone from the poorhouse came, and those who couldn't walk were carried in. The wedding took place on the thirty-third day in the Omer —the only day between Passover and Shavuoth on which weddings are permitted. It was a warm, sunny day. Later, there was talk that Reb Shachne had spent a fortune on the wedding and almost went bankrupt. It didn't come to that. Two bands were hired to play at the wedding. For weeks before, the tailors and seamstresses and shoemakers were up all night. The girls gathered in the evenings to dance and break in their new shoes. The hairdressers combed out who knows how many wigs. Gneshe's wedding gown had a train four lengths long. People began to grumble that such goings-on provoked the Gentiles. That's how Jews are. When times are bad they lament. When times improve, if only for a minute, they get out all their finery—and those who despise us grit their teeth. But we don't always listen to reason. Lifshe's maids weren't enough for the occasion, and she had cooks and waiters brought in from Lublin. Gneshe's mother gave her all the family chains and brooches and rings she had inherited and acquired.

"Anyone who didn't see Gneshe in her white silk gown as the veil was lowered over her face doesn't know what grandeur is. But somehow there was no joy in her eyes. The girls asked her why her face didn't glow with happiness, and Gneshe answered, 'A face is not a firefly.' That was Gneshe for you— shrewd as a fox and sharp as a razor. The wedding went on all night: the dancing and the hopping, the polkas, the mazurkas, the angry dance and the scissor dance. Two jesters outdid themselves with their mocking praises, wordplay, and witticisms, and the groom himself also threw in a joke or two. For a groom to make jokes at his wedding was unheard of, but still there was handclapping. I danced at the wedding till dawn. I was there when the bride and groom partook of the golden broth. When it was time for the seclusion of the newlyweds and just before the two mothers took the bride away, Mully must have cracked a joke, because there was a burst of laughter among those who stood nearby.

"I was quite young then, but still I thought, Enough is enough. What does the Holy Book say? 'A time to weep, and a time to laugh.' Children, I wasn't present, but my mother— may she intercede for us—told me that the day after the wedding or maybe the next day Gneshe came into Lifshe's chamber, pale as death, and said, 'Mother, I made a mistake.'

"Lifshe began to tremble, 'Daughter, what are you saying? Why?'

"And Gneshe answered, 'He is a fool.'

"Lifshe said, 'Of all things, a fool? All this time you've been telling us how brilliant he is.'

"And Gneshe cried out, 'My life is ruined.'"

"It didn't take long for the whole town to realize it. All through the seven days of benediction, Mully did nothing but clown around. He turned out to be insolent, too. He was disrespectful to Reb Shachne, to Lifshe, to the rabbi. He made fun of everyone, mimicked people. When he was served meat, he said that it was half raw or overcooked. He wanted to teach the cooks their trade. Gneshe sat there white as chalk, her eyes blazing with fury. She couldn't restrain herself any longer and spoke out: 'Mully, you are overdoing it.' Later, she told her mother, 'He has a silly smile. Where were my eyes? I must have been blind.'

"The cat was out of the bag and now everyone saw the truth. Reb Shachne was dumbfounded. He called in Gneshe and said, 'Daughter, from when I first saw him I didn't like that husband of yours, but since you were so entranced I kept quiet. What do we of the old generation know about today's world? Let me remind you, daughter, that there is such a thing as divorce among Jews. To err is human.'

"Gneshe heard him out, and answered, 'Father, there will be no divorce.'

" 'Why not?' Reb Shachne asked, and Gneshe answered, 'It was my mistake, not his. It seems I am a fool, too.'

"As was the custom. Reb Shachne had undertaken to support Mully for a number of years and to let him study as other young men who boarded with their in-laws did. But Mully was not a scholar. He was drawn to the marketplace. He stood among the shopkeepers, surrounded always by a ring of loafers, and jabbered away. He asked for the dowry money, which had been kept by his father-in-law, and went into business. He was no good at that, either. There was a toll bridge in our town, and the squire had leased it to a thickheaded youth, Leibush Cudgel. The peasants and wagon drivers who crossed the bridge had to pay two groschen each. It was considered a lowly way to earn a living. The peasants would look for ways to get out of paying. There was another bridge, at some distance, and many went across there. Leibush was dishonest; he cheated the squire, and was finally dismissed. Suddenly the news got around that Mully had taken over the toll bridge. It was a disgrace. Lifshe stopped going out in public and turned into a recluse. Reb Shachne said to the rabbi, 'I must have done something wrong to deserve such shame.' The whole thing was bizarre. When peasants looked at the young city slicker, all dressed up, they became abusive. One tried to get out of paying altogether, another said he'd pay tomorrow, later. One ruffian lashed at Mully with his whip.

"Everyone waited for the couple to divorce. But you never know what goes on inside someone else's head. All of a sudden word spread that Gneshe, in her blond wig, was sitting in the toll booth and collecting the tolls. I couldn't believe my ears, and went to see for myself. My dear people, Gneshe, already big with child, had put on a heavy vest with a deep pocket, like a market woman's, and had come out to help her husband at the toll booth. The peasants yelled at her and she yelled back. They cursed her and she cursed them. A small crowd had gathered. Some laughed and some pinched their cheeks in dismay. Someone said that a dybbuk had entered Gneshe. A woman ran to Lifshe with the bad tidings, and Lifshe said, 'I'm already dead and buried.'

"It wasn't long before she did breathe her last. Reb Shachne suffered on for another two years, but he became so emaciated that his clothes hung on him. Gneshe had already picked a fight with her parents, and had moved out of their house. She seldom came to see her mother during her illness. This was not the same Gneshe. Her eyes were always angry. Her child, a boy, was born after Lifshe's death. My mother had gone to see Lifshe when she was ill, and tried to comfort her. After all, she said, Gneshe had not killed anyone. But Lifshe said to my mother, 'This is not my daughter, it's some kind of transfiguration.' A few days before Lifshe's death, her son, Tevel, came to visit her, and he stayed until the thirty days of mourning were over. He said openly that he didn't recognize his sister.

"I forgot the most important thing. Gneshe had become a devoted wife to Mully, or so it seemed. He tried his hand at all kinds of businesses and she was always there at his side. The truth is, by himself he failed at everything. When she said buy, he bought, and when she said sell, he sold. He spouted mindless jokes and she laughed and asked to hear them again. If she, Gneshe the wise, had made a mistake, then she had to prove that it was right. It's an arrogance of sorts. She didn't let anyone say a bad word about Mully. She bore him four children. Except for the firstborn, all were girls, and they all took after their father: good-looking but silly. Gneshe bragged about how smart they were, but when she scolded them she would shriek that they were nitwits like their father. A neighbor of hers, who liked to eavesdrop at night from behind the shutters, told it to me. The children were petrified of Gneshe. If they didn't do exactly as she ordered, she'd whip them.

"Gneshe was a good businesswoman, and she soon began to

do well. It was said that Reb Shachne had left three-quarters of his fortune to charity, but it seems that Gneshe had found his will and burned it, and what remained was a previous will, in which Reb Shachne left almost everything to her. All her brother got was books, a scroll, a spice box, and other such things. There is a saying: Husband and wife sleep so long on the same pillow their heads become the same. In later years, Gneshe began to make jokes, too—not as foolish as Mully's but too many, and in the same manner. She even began to look like him—still handsome but cheap."

"I had already moved away when Mully died—struck down like a felled tree. Gneshe wailed and lamented, bought a plot for him in the most expensive part of the cemetery, even intended to have a tomb built, but the community would not allow it. A tomb is built for a holy man, not a buffoon. Gneshe denounced the head of the community to the squire and the Russian authorities. The elders of the community came close to being imprisoned. The way she carried on, you would think that for her there would always be only one God and one Mully. Nevertheless, one day Gneshe went to Kielce —supposedly to see her brother, whom she had robbed of his inheritance—and returned with a husband, a short fellow with a gray beard. His name was Reb Fishele, and he was thrice a widower. Reb Fishele was supposed to have been at one time a successful businessman and an arbitrator at rabbinical law-suits. He was called in to negotiate, he claimed, from as far away as Warsaw. Somewhere he had sons, daughters, grand-children. He talked of nothing but his own cleverness; he bab-bled and boasted. People saw immediately that Gneshe had made the same mistake all over again. He bored everyone with tales of how he had outsmarted the most learned rabbis and the shrewdest merchants. He considered himself a healer, too. He had his own remedy for every ailment. He labeled all doctors quacks.

"My dear people, everything had turned upside down. In the few months that Gneshe lived with Reb Fishele, she wasted away as if from consumption. Her hands trembled and she be-gan to walk with a cane. Reb Fishele went to the rabbi to com-plain that his wife wouldn't allow him in her bed. She openly

—in front of the maid, and even in front of strangers—called him a good-for-nothing. She tried to evict him from her house, and he summoned her to rabbinical court. She had lost all shame. It turned out that she used to beat him, too. One morning he came to synagogue with only half a beard. People asked what happened to the other half and he answered, 'My bitch tore it out.' They advised him to run for his life, and he said, 'Not without a settlement.' But she had her way after all. One day he went to hire a wagon in order to leave her. People stopped him in the marketplace, and he declared, 'She's not a human being, she is a demon. It's forbidden to live under the same roof with such evil.' The wagon drove up to Gneshe's house and from the threshold Gneshe threw out his belongings. Still, he wanted to say goodbye to her, but she shouted out to the wagon driver, 'Take him away!' "

"A vicious one, wasn't she?" said one of the women who were listening to the story.

"When you're fed up with others and yourself, you lose all dignity," Aunt Yentl answered.

"What happened then?" another woman asked.

Aunt Yentl winced. "She died in spite. Took to her bed and never rose from it. The maid would bring her food, but she barely touched it. Her son lived far away. Two of her daughters came to see how she was, but she forbade the maid to let them in. She said, 'I've had enough of fools. I want to live my last days without them.' She didn't allow the doctor in, either. She told the maid to close the shades and she lay in the dark. The women from the burial society came to her to recite the confessional with her, but she sent them away."

"She died without confessing her sins?" a woman asked.

"Without a confession and without a will," answered Aunt Yentl.

"What became of her inheritance?"

"What usually happens with an inheritance? The daughters fought over it and became enemies. The son did not attend the funeral. The burial society asked an immense sum for the plot, and the daughters refused to pay. She was buried close to the fence, among the paupers and the suicides. Only the grave-digger said Kaddish over her."

Aunt Yentl lapsed into silence. Her bonnet, with all its ribbons, shook. Its beads reflected the flames of the setting sun. Aunt Yentl raised her index finger and pronounced, "A little mistake turns into a big mistake, and a big mistake can be an open door to Gehenna, may we be spared, Father in heaven."

Translated by Rena Borrow and Lester Goran

Confused

IN THE TAXI from Kennedy airport, I dozed and mused simultaneously. I was returning to New York after a series of lectures in universities and synagogues. I had even spoken in a Catholic college for girls. I felt worn out from the steady moving around, lecturing, meeting people whose names and faces I forgot immediately, and from many sleepless nights.

In the apartment thick dust covered everything. I had left the light on in my clothes closet, shining away for the moths to eat my suits and coats. But do moths have eyes to see the light? I decided to look this up in the encyclopedia. Meanwhile, without taking off my coat or rubbers, I stretched out on the sofa and tried to rest. I hadn't turned on the lamp, but light from a tall building on West End Avenue shone into my living room. I took from my breast and trouser pockets the half-crumpled checks I had been given after each lecture. I must deposit them before they become illegible. I would soon have to turn over a good half of their total to the federal, state, and city governments. But what should I do with the rest of the money? As the years went on, I ate less and less. I had no desire for new clothes. Actually, I worked for the tax collectors.

The telephone rang, and even though I had taken an oath not to accept another lecture for this year, I heard myself saying yes to my agent for lectures as far away as San Francisco and Winnipeg. Then a woman called and she said to me in Yiddish, "You don't know me, but I know you through your books and stories. I know you are a busy man, but since I found your number in the telephone book, I can't resist the temptation of telling you how I admire you and also asking if perhaps you could meet me. Let it be just for a short while. I'm sure you get many such demands and if you refuse me I won't be insulted."

"No, I won't refuse you."

"I knew you were a man with a heart. When can I come over?"

I was silent and tried to figure things out, but without my engagement book (where was it?) any date I might give her would be wrong. I asked, "What are you? What do you do?"

"Oh, I used to be a teacher in a Yiddish school in Chicago. I'm deeply interested in psychical research. This especially has attracted me to your writing. Like you I believe that telepathy, clairvoyance, and premonitions are gifts that everyone can develop and . . ."

"May I ask how old you are?"

"Forty-two. Day before yesterday was my birthday."

"Congratulations. Where do you live?"

"Here on the West Side. I'm actually your neighbor."

Another crackpot, I thought. I am not going to bother with her. Instead, I said, "Come over right now. But I'm telling you in advance, not long. I'm just back from a lecture tour and I must go to sleep early."

"I will knock at your door in fifteen minutes. I thank you with all my being. It's not for nothing that I worship you."

There have been times I've tried to make a little order in my apartment when someone was coming to visit me, especially a woman, but now I had neither the strength for it nor the ambition. All I did was get out of my coat and rubbers and lie down again on the sofa. I closed my eyes and fell asleep immediately.

In the last few years my dreams have become strangely vivid. I dream almost exclusively about the dead. The following dream has repeated itself many times in variation: I come to visit my dead lover Ethel in Brooklyn on Ocean Avenue. It is twilight. She opens the door for me, and in the corridor I ask, "Is Leon here?" Ethel murmurs, "Yes, he's waiting for you." We enter the bedroom and Leon is already in bed. In my dream I remember that both Ethel and Leon have gone through mortal sicknesses but not that they have died. Even though the bedroom is dark, I can see Leon's face—lean, pale, with white eyebrows. He looks at me in a mixture of gratitude and reproach. I hear Ethel say, "Men, I'm yours."

The later parts of the dream I invariably forget when I waken. The dream always ends as if the Lord of Dreams decided to turn the whole adventure into a joke. Sometimes Leon starts to sing a liturgic melody that ends in cacophony. Ethel recites rhymes, like a wedding jester, in a mixture of

Yiddish, Hebrew, and Polish, and she laughs hilariously. This evening, as always, I clung to the fading images until nothing remained but the solemn beginning and the mad ending—and an urgent need to urinate. My toilet, like all the utilities in this old house, has its own caprices. Sometimes when I flush it, the water begins to pour in a stream that I cannot stop and I have to call the janitor. At other times, it does not flush at all. It only squeaks, gurgles, and whines, as if a living creature were imprisoned in the pipes. This time, my shower suddenly began to run, although I hadn't touched it. When I stood on the rim of the bathtub to shut it off, something fell out of the medicine chest—a saltshaker that I did not remember having brought in there (what for?). Inanimate objects were playing spiteful tricks on me.

2

My doorbell rang and I ran to open the door. There stood a little woman who looked younger than forty, in a shabby fur jacket and boots, a kerchief over her black hair. Her face was light, small, girlish, with high cheekbones. She wore no makeup. In her dark eyes a mixture of provincial shyness and big-city knowingness gleamed. Under her arm she held a little basket. I had a feeling that I knew her, but from where? The moment she entered, she began to tell me that she attended all my lectures in New York and even in the suburbs. She called herself my female Hasid. I helped her take off her jacket. Her figure was also girlish. She had come to America, she told me, in 1948, from a German DP camp. She lived through the war in Soviet Russia. When she entered my living room she opened the basket and took out three of my books, two in English and one in Yiddish. She said, "You have inscribed these books to me—of course you don't recognize me. Knock on wood, you look the same. Here is one of them. See for yourself."

She opened one of the books and I read on the inside cover, "To charming Pessl with friendship and with the hope to see you again." She said, "This was actually an invitation, but I was in Chicago then and in my situation it was not easy to take a trip to New York. My name is Peshe but they called me Pessl. Here in America people are ashamed of such an old-fashioned name. Even in Poland they were ashamed of such names. But to me it is a good Jewish name. My great-grandmother was called Yente Peshe. She was rich, and she gave the Rabbi of Rizin a golden goblet as a gift when I was born."

"My apartment is a mess," I said. "I hope it doesn't upset you."

"Upset me? Nothing upsets me anymore. Besides, if you need someone to clean the place up, I will do it."

"God forbid."

"Why God forbid? Here in New York I became a cleaning woman and a babysitter. In Warsaw I graduated from the Gymnasium and I even began to study at the university, but then the war broke out and I became what the Germans call 'Gleichgeschaltet.' I came to America with a sick daughter. It's a long story."

"Do you have a husband?"

"My husband perished in the Polish uprising in 1945. Don't be shocked, he was not a Jew."

"You are not upset by anything, and I'm not shocked by anything."

"Halina is almost twenty years old. She's emotionally disturbed. I have to keep her in a clinic. All my energy and almost all my earnings go into this daughter. She was brought up by her aunt, my husband's sister, while I vegetated in Russia. She never knew that she was Jewish until I came back to Warsaw after the war. The story of what I went through in Russia is too long to tell you now."

"In what way is she disturbed?"

"My sister-in-law, Stasia, is an anti-Semite, and she brought Halina up to hate Jews. I cannot tell you what a trauma it was for her to learn that her mother was Jewish. She even attacked me with her fists. In all the years that have passed since then, she has not made peace with her Jewish blood. This is not all. Days pass—sometimes weeks—and she doesn't utter a word. She's always depressed. In addition, she stopped growing. When I found her in her aunt's house in Warsaw, she was quite tall for her age, but then something happened to her and she did not develop as a child should."

"Perhaps she needs hormones."

"Oh, they tried everything, even shock treatments. With

what I earned I couldn't do much for her. But I found a lawyer who specializes in getting reparation money from the Germans and he was able to get a pension for her as well as payment for her medical treatment. My coming from Chicago to New York is also connected with her. Here I found the right clinic and a most wonderful doctor. I would like to do something for you."

"What would you like to do for me?"

"Oh, anything. I could clean your house once or twice a week. I'm even ready to wash your linen. I want to tell you that this doctor has arranged that my daughter can come home once in a while and stay with me a few days. Because of this I stopped teaching, since I never know when she may be sent home. Now my real occupation is babysitting. I can take my daughter with me when I babysit. For her it is a kind of relaxation. She hates me, but she loves children. She would never harm a child. Oh, my life is so crazy that no matter what I tell you, it is only a small part of what I'm going through. I have gotten quite a name as a babysitter. Young couples rely on me when they have to leave town. I taught in a nursery school in Warsaw and I worked for some time in the hospital for children on Slizka Street. Many couples have bars in their homes and they leave them open for me. I shouldn't tell you, but I became a drinker long before I left Russia. I wouldn't have lived through the Holocaust without alcohol. I never get drunk, only sleepy, but if a baby utters as much as a peep, I'm alert in a second. Why do I bother you with all these details? It's your own fault, you ask questions. Since I'm here, I'm going to make a little order in this house."

"Absolutely not."

"Absolutely yes."

3

I dozed on the sofa and Pessl prepared supper for me. I wanted to take her to a restaurant, but she insisted on shopping for food and on cooking.

I had to force her to take money. I was so tired that after she went to the supermarket I fell asleep. When I opened my eyes, I didn't recognize the apartment. The dust was gone. She had made order of the piles of letters, books, telegrams that had gathered in my absence. How she managed in about an hour and a half to do what had been done I could not understand. We sat at the kitchen table and we ate like an old couple. I questioned Pessl and she told me that except for her late husband, Piotr Trapinski, the one lover in Russia, she had had no other men. She had been living ten years without a man, not out of modesty, but because her daughter drained away all her strength. Besides, the men she knew in Chicago, teachers of Yiddish, never aroused any desire in her.

After supper Pessl washed the dishes. Then we lay down on the sofa. We kissed and Pessl swore that she had been in love with me from the first time she met me at that lecture in Chicago. She solemnly promised to love me not only in this world but in the world to come and in all her reincarnations as well. Such enthusiasm from a woman over forty who had been through the Hitler hell and the Stalin terror seemed to me somewhat strange, but I had experienced enough in my life not to be surprised by any human behavior. Suddenly she cried, "What time is it? I have to leave!"

"Where to?"

"Come with me. It's ten to ten."

Pessl told me in her rush that she had a babysitting job that night only a few blocks from here. It was for a woman separated from her husband because of a lover. Her husband had hired a detective to spy on her and she had to sneak away to a place where he couldn't follow her. She always left her two-year-old with Pessl. "Come with me," Pessl said. "It will be the first night of our honeymoon."

I told Pessl that I could not come and introduce myself as an assistant babysitter, but after some persuasion I agreed to come to the apartment after the owner had left. I would wait for Pessl in a nearby restaurant and telephone her to learn if the mother of the child had gone. While we were hurrying to the restaurant Pessl told me, "You can call in ten minutes or even before. She's just waiting for me. I was supposed to be there earlier and she will be angry, but who cares."

In the restaurant she stopped just long enough to write the telephone number and the number of the apartment on a napkin and ran on. I sat down at the counter, ordered a cup of coffee, and read an evening paper that someone had left on a nearby stool. After fifteen minutes I telephoned and Pessl shouted, "Come right now!"

The building had no doorman and the elevator was automatic. I went up to the fourteenth floor. Pessl was waiting for me at an open door. I entered an apartment carpeted in red from wall to wall, with wallpaper to match, and modern furniture. The living room had a television set and a bar disguised as a bookcase. A cage with a parakeet hung in the window. In the bathroom there was a picture of a boy urinating and a little girl pointing and wondering. It was all cheap, petit bourgeois. Pessl opened the sham bookcase with the names of Shakespeare, Milton, and Edgar Allan Poe on it, and she began to drink and smoke. She forced me to take a drink. She led me by the wrist to the bedroom and showed me the sleeping boy, Nicky, and his toys, among them a teddy bear almost as big as a real bear. The child had curly blond hair and flushed cheeks. He had a pacifier in his mouth.

Back in the living room we lay down on the sofa. I felt that I had known Pessl for a long time. With drinking she became cheerful, and she assured me that this was the happiest night of her life. She told me stories about her wanderings in Russia. She had been sick with typhoid fever and pneumonia. She had traveled on railroads that stopped for days in the middle of nowhere and that were so crowded one had to take care of one's needs in a chamber pot the passengers carried with them. She starved, went around in seedy clothes, smoked cigarettes made of dry oak leaves. She lived with death for years. But here she was, in a warm home, drinking cognac, smoking American cigarettes, and with whom was she? With her beloved writer. Could there be anything better? While she was saying all this, she kissed my face, my throat, even the sleeves of my jacket. I struggled with her and she cried, "When I kiss the man I love, don't you interfere."

After a while I was overcome with fatigue. Pessl, too, began to yawn. She brought a blanket and covered us. She embraced me and cuddled into me. I was lying still, about to fall asleep, when the dream of Ethel and Leon returned to me. I heard Ethel say, "Men, I'm yours."

4

I had slept long and soundly. I was awakened by a clamorous pounding, ringing, men's voices.

Pessl sat up in bewilderment. "Woe is me. Something has happened to the child!"

She ran to the bedroom, but we soon grasped that the commotion was at the door. Pessl rushed to open it. Firemen told her that there was a fire on our floor and ordered us to go down the staircase to the lobby right away. Pessl ran back to the bedroom and caught up the sleeping boy, and she shouted to me to take the cage with the parakeet. It was a miracle that we were both dressed. In the corridor we stepped over a huge hose. The air was full of smoke. The child awoke and cried. Pessl called out, "They will steal everything! Beatrice will accuse me!"

We started down the steps. In the cage the frightened parakeet jumped back and forth, trying to get out through the bars.

"Where is my watch?" I asked. I began to search in my pockets. "Where is my fountain pen?"

We walked down so many flights that I began to suspect we had gone astray in some underground labyrinth. But finally we reached the lobby, which teemed with the awakened tenants. The sofas and chairs were taken over by women and children. Men walked around in their pajamas, bathrobes, dressing gowns. Some had managed to put on slippers, but others were barefoot. Hoses were stretched across the floor. Firemen in black helmets ran to and fro, carrying axes, poles, gas masks, objects for which I had no name. Some of the apartment residents seemed angry, others laughed. I had put the cage with the parakeet on the floor and found a place on the sofa near Pessl, who rocked the little boy in her arms, trying to put him back to sleep. At the same time she spoke to me: "I knew that some calamity was bound to come. People like me are not permitted to enjoy even one good minute. My dearest, why did I have to drag you into this mess? Go home. I will find anything you have lost. You mustn't suffer because of my bad luck."

"Pessl, don't take it so tragically. They will soon put out the fire."

"If not this fire, there will be other fires. Just on the night when I could say with a full heart that I'm happy, crazy from happiness, this had to happen. *Nu*, it's a joke. Fate laughs at me and my illusions. When Beatrice comes back and sees the jumble, she will hang herself. Beatrice, Mrs. Klapperman, is the owner of the apartment. She leaves a child and runs around all night with a charlatan. She trembles over each of her trinkets. Sleep, little treasure, sleep. Mama will soon be back. Close your sweet eyes!" Suddenly she cried out, "My purse, where's my purse?" She handed me the child and screamed, "I must find my purse; everything I possess is in there. My God. Oy, my misfortune!"

I sat there holding a heavy little boy wrapped in a blanket. I saw Pessl running to the door that led to the steps. She stumbled and almost fell over one of the hoses. The child squinted and soon was crying with all his might. Women attempted to calm him. They put him on the sofa, rocked him, blew on him, called him babele, angel, sugar, but his rage only grew. He showed his teeth like a little beast. Pessl did not appear for a long time. The women began to ask who I was and in what apartment I lived. I had to admit to them that I had been visiting a babysitter. They asked me the number of the apartment, but I could remember neither the floor nor the owner's name. The women looked at one another, murmured, winked. I searched in my pockets. I had written down the number of the apartment, but the piece of paper had vanished. My God, I was stuck here with a strange child. Why, I could be accused of kidnapping. I wanted to search for Pessl, but with whom could I leave the child, who did not stop screaming?

A small woman with a head of fiery hair cut short, wearing a green nightgown and slippers of the same color, came over to me and said in a tone of surprise, "Are you living here?"

The women around me became quiet. The child ceased crying.

I said, "I was visiting a babysitter and she left to find her purse."

"You don't remember me, I see, but we had lunch together one time when you spoke to our group. I introduced you."

"A speaker?" one of the other women said.

At that moment Pessl returned. "My purse is gone! Here's

your wristwatch. I had everything with me, my money, my reading glasses, my bankbook. *Nu*, it's really a comedy."

"Maybe you left your purse at my house," I said, realizing at once that I shouldn't have said it.

"I never go out without my purse. Well, it's one of those nights."

"Firemen are not thieves," the little redheaded woman said. "You most probably left your purse somewhere else or—"

"Where is it written that firemen are not thieves?" Pessl said. "When they see a purse with money, they take it. If German officers, men who went through universities and read Goethe and Schiller, were not ashamed to tear the shirt off a poor Jew, to rob a child of its last bite of food and then cut off its head, why shouldn't some simple fireman steal a purse? Everyone grabs. They wouldn't let me into the apartment, making believe that they wanted to protect me from fire. But there is no fire in the apartment. They just destroy—"

Pessl did not manage to finish the sentence. A stout woman came over carrying two purses. "Miss, is this your purse?" she asked.

Pessl's eyes rolled. "Where did you find it?"

"It was lying right there near the wall." The woman pointed to the place where Pessl had been sitting. Pessl opened the purse, glanced inside, and closed it immediately. She said, "Somehow I came out alive from all my ordeals, but my nerves are shattered."

In all this tumult the boy had fallen asleep. A fireman called out, "Ladies and gentlemen, you can go home to sleep. Just don't break the elevator."

Everyone ran to the elevator, pushing and shoving, the little redheaded woman among them.

"Who is that redheaded creature?" Pessl asked. "I leave you alone for five minutes and you are surrounded by all kinds of pests. You know her or something?"

"She says that I had lunch with her years ago. She belonged to some ladies' auxiliary I spoke to. She was supposed to have introduced me."

"I know, I know. They look for any excuse to make acquaintances. She has the eyes of a hawk. Men work hard, get heart attacks, and these harlots have one occupation—taking men away from other women. From today on, you belong to me. I wanted to die, not once but a hundred times. But a voice inside me ordered, 'Pessl, wait!' I'm sure you don't believe in such premonitions, even though you write about them. Writers are split souls. They go on and on about love and believe only in sex. They tell stories about spirits and they themselves are the worst materialists. You probably thought that I dumped the child in your lap and ran away. Isn't that so?"

"I never knew that a child could make such a racket."

"What is a child? It has all the qualities of an adult. It is impatient to grow up and do its share of evil. I am a fool. That's what I am."

"Why do you say that?"

"What did I need the purse for since I have you? I would give away a hundred such purses for your tiniest nail. Don't look at me like that. It's all my cursed nerves. The slightest thing throws me off balance. One moment I am the happiest person in the world and then there is a fire, and to me a fire is not just a fire but the Nazi ovens. By nature I am very courageous—how could I have survived without courage? But I am also filled with fear. I had a husband and they killed him; I have a daughter and she tells me that I'm not her mother; you come to me and suddenly there is a fire. It's not an accident. Evil powers work against me. Look! There she stands, the red-haired slut. She's coming back."

The red-haired woman was approaching us. She said, "I live on the highest floor and it was impossible to enter the elevator. They push and jostle like mad. I don't intend to disturb you, I just want to tell you that meeting you under such circumstances was a surprise."

"May I introduce you?" I asked. "This is my friend Pessl. And this is—"

"I am Terry. Terry Bickman." She made a gesture to shake hands with Pessl, but Pessl backed away.

"You seem not to remember me." The redheaded woman addressed me. "You spoke to our group and afterward you took me to a vegetarian restaurant. My husband was with me then. We are divorced now."

"Yes, you refresh my memory."

"You don't live here?"

"No, I was visiting this lady and I stayed later than I realized."

"I understand. Our group would like to invite you again. I am their president now. Can you give me your address and telephone number?"

"I am in the telephone book."

"Really? That never occurred to me. Most writers have unlisted numbers."

"I don't hide from my readers."

"Good. I will be calling you. Good night."

Terry Bickman nodded to Pessl. She had barely taken three steps when Pessl said aloud, "*Nu*, am I right or wrong? She lurked there like a wolf for its victim. She wriggled like a snake. You may be sure that she will call you and you will again eat with her and who knows what else. So far as you are concerned I don't have any rights—we met today for the first time. You told me to come and I came. Just the same, let me tell you that if you are thinking of meeting this red-haired bitch, everything between us is finished. I have instincts and I received vibrations. You'll never know how far they reach."

5

After all the tenants had returned to their apartments and the elevator was empty, Pessl and I went up, together with the sleeping baby and the cage. The moment the elevator moved, Pessl slapped her forehead with the hand on which her purse hung. She had no key to the apartment. Her face became distorted. Her eyes expressed despair and a kind of masochistic triumph: her prediction of imminent disaster had come true. The corridor still smelled acrid. She handed me the baby and began to pound at the door as if she suspected that some fireman remained inside. She even took a few steps back to get a running start and lunged at the door. I told her that we must go to the superintendent and ask for a key, but she said, "Where would I find him? Besides, I doubt that he even lives in this building. The dark powers have not given up on me. They plot new catastrophes every moment."

"You wait here with the child, and I will go look for the superintendent," I proposed.

At that instant the redheaded woman appeared as if from nowhere. She wore a different housecoat and different slippers. "What's going on here?"

"Do you live on this floor?" Pessl asked her in a hostile tone.

"No, one flight higher, but I heard the banging and thought a new fire had broken out."

"They locked the door, those stupid firemen, and I have no key."

"One could get a key from the super, but he lives in the next building. He's a drunkard and never gets home before dawn. You had better come up to me. When I am awakened, the night is lost. I have a bed where no one sleeps since my divorce. I will put the baby there and we will have a cup of coffee or tea. You are invited, too, my writer. I hope your friend won't be jealous. It seems to have been destined that you pay me a visit. It will be both an honor and a pleasure to have you."

"When Beatrice Klapperman comes home and doesn't find us in the apartment, she will become hysterical," Pessl said.

"Oh, she will know that there was a fire. Leave a note on the door that you have taken the baby to Mrs. Bickman's on the top floor. She knows me, the tramp. Does she always come home this late?"

"Sometimes she comes in the morning." Pessl's eyebrows tightened and she seemed to ponder the situation. The baby began to whimper. There was no choice. We walked up one flight. I lifted the cage. The parakeet stood on his perch congealed in an avian version of Nirvana. Terry Bickman let us into an apartment similar in layout to the one where Pessl was babysitting but more elegant, with Oriental rugs, silk wallpaper, original paintings. Both women busied themselves putting the baby to bed. I walked over to the window, pulled the curtain, and looked out to the street. I could see the Hudson aglow with the lights of New York and New Jersey. Behind me there was some discussion about writing the note. Pessl had difficulty spelling in English and finally she asked Terry Bickman to write the note for her. From a drawer Terry took a golden fountain pen, a sheet of pink letter paper, and eyeglasses outlined with rhinestones. She wrote every word with a curlicue in the final letter. She gave the sheet to Pessl with a piece of Scotch tape to fasten it to Mrs. Klapperman's door. Pessl's eyes were saying, 'I understand your sly tricks, but I cannot help myself.' The moment she left, Terry Bickman gave me a knowing look. "A refugee, I take it?"

"Yes, from the Holocaust."

"Why is she so afraid? I'm not going to eat you up. How long have you known her?"

"Not long."

"I shouldn't say it, but she doesn't look to me like much of a bargain. What kind of a job is babysitting? And why does she drag you into such a situation? It certainly doesn't add to your prestige."

"I'm not looking for prestige."

"What are you looking for?"

Pessl returned. "I taped the note on the door, but if she telephones and no one answers, she will have a seizure."

"Where do they crawl around the whole night? A mother should stay home, not hang out with gigolos. What would you like to drink?" Terry asked Pessl. "I can offer you everything— even champagne. If you drink L'Chaim, you forget your miseries." She turned to me. "How about you? American writers are all drinkers, but you don't look like one to me. Would you like some cherry brandy? A screwdriver? A Bloody Mary? I have all kinds, as in Noah's ark. It's for others, not for me. When I feel wretched I bake a cake. A good book helps, too. But where do you get good books? I often go to sleep with you, I mean with your books. For each night I spend with you in bed, I would like to have a million dollars tax-free. Suddenly you appear in person, and when?—in the middle of the night, in a fire! Fate has strange ways of bringing people together. What did you say, miss, you would prefer to drink?"

"Vodka, whiskey, whatever you offer me, perhaps poison."

"On ice?"

"No ice. The ice is in my heart," Pessl said.

"Don't be so dramatic, you will drink and warm up. Since this woman runs around all night, she's in no position to complain. Do you have a family?"

"A daughter."

"I have nothing. A daughter is better than a son. A son, when he grows up and begins to play around with girls, forgets his mother. A daughter stays attached. I have a mother, she is in an institution—senile. I visit her every week. I say to her, 'I'm your daughter, Tirzah, Terry,' and she asks me, 'Are you the nurse or the doctor's wife? They don't give me to eat here. They steal everything from me.' Suddenly she starts to speak to me in Russian. I say to her, 'Mother, I don't understand you,' but she continues to talk Russian. They give her plenty to eat. She's gained twenty pounds there. Nobody steals her linen or her few dresses. I look at her and think, Is this the old age everyone wishes to reach? But what do I accomplish with my relatively young age? I'm dying to find a man, I don't sleep nights, but when I meet one and hear his silly babble, I am disgusted. I cannot go to bed with a fool." She turned to me. "What did you say you drink?"

"Do you have some Coca-Cola?"

"Anything you desire. The days pass by somehow. I go here, I go there. I go to department stores and try on dresses and fur coats I would never buy. I have stocks, and once in a while I visit my broker to see how the market is doing. But the nights are horrible. I sleep two hours and I'm through. I brood over matters that can lead only to insanity. When they knocked at my door to announce that there was a fire in the building, I was happy. A fire is better than nothing."

Terry Bickman went into the kitchen to get me a Coca-Cola. Pessl drank half a glass of whiskey. She grimaced and said, "She will take you away from me. It's been this way all my years. *Nu*, I must laugh."

6

For a whole month I was once again on a lecture tour. I traveled in so many planes, trains, and buses that everything became blurred. I gained hours and I lost hours. I was continually adjusting my watch. In almost every place, a female admirer attached herself to me and took me around in her car, invited me for breakfast the day after the lecture, and later drove me to the airport or station. For some reason they all told me their secrets. They wrote my address and telephone number in their notebooks, and in my notebook they wrote their addresses and telephone numbers. Often I had one-day love affairs with these women. We kissed when we said good-bye and I promised to write. But the moment the plane or train or bus took off, I couldn't distinguish one from the other. I arrived home in a cool evening in May, exhausted, and stretched out on the sofa. I fell asleep and awakened four hours later because the telephone was ringing. My wristwatch showed 12:35. I hesitated about whether to answer. I expected the ringing to cease, but when it continued I picked up the receiver. The voice I heard was that of a woman—a strong voice.

"This is Mrs. Bickman."

I had not the slightest idea who Mrs. Bickman was. But I did not admit that the name meant nothing to me. Instead, I said, "Yes, Mrs. Bickman."

"I have been calling for three days. This night my heart told me that you would be home. You have unwittingly thrown me into a situation where I don't know if I should laugh or cry. If I awakened you, my excuse is that I haven't been sleeping for three nights because of you."

"Because of me? How could that happen?"

"Mrs. Trapinski attempted suicide. She did it in unbelievable circumstances. Mrs. Klapperman had gone away with her lover on a vacation or on a honeymoon—call it whatever you like—and Mrs. Trapinski was supposed to remain a week with the little boy, Nicky. I want you to know that we have become quite friendly lately even though we are as different as two women can be. One thing we share, however—we are both insomniacs. The fact that you went away for so long and you didn't find it necessary to call or even to write her a card shattered her. I wanted to tell Mrs. Klapperman that to leave a baby for so long is a risk, but it's not my nature to mind other people's business. It so happened that a day after Mrs. Klapperman left, Halina came home. She found the door locked and she stayed the whole night on the stairs. How the girl found her mother the next day is a chapter in itself. I will make it short. When finally she did, she spat in her face and beat her up. She called her a leprous Jew and said that Hitler had been right. Mrs. Trapinski asked me to come to Mrs. Klapperman's apartment, so I saw what the girl had done. By the time I got there, she had disappeared. Nicky is a sweet little boy and I had fallen in love with him. But I had to leave for half an hour because a handyman was coming with a ladder to put a bulb in my hallway. When I returned to Mrs. Klapperman's, I found Mrs. Trapinski lying in the bathtub with her wrists slit. I had to call an ambulance, and the police came also. Mrs. Trapinski is in the hospital and I have had to take over as babysitter. Halina came back the next day, and believe it or not, she's also with me. I hoped that Mrs. Klapperman would call, but she hasn't, and I have no way of reaching her. This Halina is not only crazy but also full of spite. I speak to her in English, which I know she knows quite well, and she answers me in Polish. That I haven't lost my mind shows I'm stronger than iron. But I'm telling you frankly that if you do not come and rescue me from this madhouse right now, I will call the district attorney. Too much pressure can lead people to anything. Do you hear?"

"Yes, I hear. Where are you calling from?"

"From my home. As I told you, the baby and Halina are with me."

"My dear friend, I am in such a state I cannot go anywhere. I've been away a whole month. I haven't slept many nights. You must call me tomorrow morning."

"How can I believe that tomorrow morning you will not be gone again? I have done my best to defend you to Mrs. Trapinski, but I am going to tell you straight out what I think of you. Wait a minute, someone is ringing at the door. Don't hang up."

I stood with the receiver pressed to my ear, too tired to feel insulted or guilty. I have always considered that stories about amnesia have been invented by writers of filmscripts, but I was experiencing it now. Not one of all these names—Trapinski, Bickman, Halina, Klapperman—sounded familiar. I put my hand into my breast pocket, where I kept my notebook, hoping to find some clue there, but the notebook was gone. Instead, I found a special-delivery letter I had never opened. It must have come before I left on the present lecture tour. From outside I suddenly heard the sirens of fire engines. As always when I hear fire engines, I thought of the miserable situation of the victims. Instantly all the women were identified: Mrs. Bickman, the redheaded little woman; Pessl; Halina, Pessl's psychotic daughter; and Mrs. Klapperman, the mother of the

baby whom Pessl took care of. It bewildered me that I had not
recognized these names at once. I waited for a long time, but
instead of hearing Terry Bickman's voice I heard a dial tone. I
hung up and waited for the telephone to ring again, but it remained silent. I didn't have Terry Bickman's number. I must
have written it down somewhere, but to look for it would have
been hopeless. I returned to the sofa and lay there numb with
fatigue.

7

I woke up at dawn. The lights were on in both the foyer and
the living room. I remembered that someone had telephoned
me before I slept and there had been talk about a scandal, a
crisis, a suicide, but who had called me and who had committed suicide I could not recall. I put my hand into my breast
pocket, took out the special-delivery letter, and opened it. The
postmark showed that it had come from Chicago five weeks
before. A Carol Brill wrote that she was leaving her husband
and was coming to New York to look for a job. The tone was
intimate. "Don't be afraid, my dear, that I will become a burden to you," she wrote, "but since you complained to me that
you are in need of a secretary, I want to tell you, immodest as
my words may sound, that you could never get a better secretary than I am. I'm ready to accompany you on your lectures
and take care of you and your business as a friend and more
than that."

Who is Carol Brill? I asked myself. According to the letter,
she had taken me to the airport after a lecture. Like the others, she had disappeared from my memory. At the end of the
letter she asked me to answer immediately. All her plans depended on my prompt reply (underlined three times). But the
letter had been in my pocket more than five weeks. There was
no return address, only the number of a post-office box in
Chicago. I had read somewhere that all our experiences remain in the archives of our memory. With the help of will-
power, concentration, and relaxation, one can bring them back
to consciousness. But no matter how I tortured my brain, I
could not recall this particular lecture in Chicago. If only she
had had the sense to send me her photograph!

I should have undressed and gone to bed instead of lying on the sofa in my clothes, but it was too late now to bring the night back. I looked out the window onto Broadway. All the stores were closed. The only lights were in the Chock Full O'Nuts across the street, where someone was preparing the counters for customers who came early for breakfast. At the newspaper stand near the subway entrance, a short man was untying bundles of the morning newspapers. A single passerby was walking from uptown. I could not see his face. He stopped at the entrance of the Chock Full O'Nuts and the man inside gave him a sign that the place was not yet open. What would happen, I thought, if he were to take out a gun and shoot the man through the glass door? Would I volunteer to be a witness? America is a country where murderers are let out on bail and the witnesses languish in prison. I suddenly remembered that there is a sky and I lifted my eyes to it. It hovered without a moon, without stars—a part of the space that according to Newton has no limit, and even according to Einstein is not less than ten billion light-years in every direction. The light from the Chock Full O'Nuts had already traveled millions of miles since I went to the window and would continue to travel long after there was no Broadway, no New York, no people, no earth, and perhaps even no sun. What a mystery! I turned and glanced at my desk. To my amazement I noticed that Carol Brill had sent me two other letters written later. In one she expressed her astonishment that she hadn't heard from me. She said that she had a friend in New York, a woman with whom she studied at Washington University in St. Louis. She intended to live with her in the Bronx. She gave me the telephone number of this friend. The second envelope contained a photograph. The moment I saw it I remembered my lecture, the hall where I spoke, even the fact that the next morning Carol Brill had breakfast with me in the coffee shop of my hotel. She had told me then that her husband, a lawyer, was a coarse fellow and that she had never had a moment of happiness in all the nine years of their marriage. I made up my mind to answer that letter that very morning. She was young and pretty. Let her come to New York. She didn't look like the kind of a person who would become a parasite. Well, but who had telephoned me late at night? Why did the call leave me with a feeling of such uneasiness? I resolved from today on to write down in my notebook everything I did, the name of every person I met. I was not going to allow Purah, the Angel of Forgetfulness, to swallow me up.

I decided to go to the bedroom and undress. I owed a huge debt to sleep. My wristwatch showed half past five. If the telephone would leave me in peace, I could sleep another half hour. Perhaps I could take the receiver off the hook. At that second, the telephone rang. I was sure it was Carol Brill. I lifted the receiver, said hello, and heard the words "This is Terry. Terry Bickman."

The voice seemed familiar as well as the name. But I could not place her. "Yes, Terry," I said.

For a while she was silent. Then she said, "I know that it's bad to call you so early. However, I have no choice."

"Yes, I understand."

"I have woken you up, but I didn't sleep a wink—that makes the fourth night."

"Why?" I asked.

She was silent again. "You don't know who I am, do you? You sound confused."

"Yes," I said. "You are speaking to the most confused creature who has ever walked the earth."

A few days later I had a vegetarian lunch of spinach and raw mushrooms with Pessl Trapinski and her daughter, Halina, in the apartment of the red-haired woman, Terry Bickman. Mrs. Klapperman had come home from her trip with her lover and had taken her baby. Pessl had just left the hospital. She showed me the scars of her slit wrists. As far as I could see, her daughter, Halina, was not stunted in her growth, as Pessl had said. She was just short. Neither did she show any signs of morbid anti-Semitism. I couldn't believe it, but she said she would like to study Yiddish in order to read my books in the original. I had written a letter to Mrs. Carol Brill in Chicago. I told her to come to New York and become my secretary. Her friend in the Bronx answered it by calling to tell me Carol had decided to stay with her husband, since he agreed to see a psychiatrist.

I am in need of a psychiatrist myself, but since I believe

neither in Freud nor in Alder or Jung, who could be my healer? I will muddle through, one way or another. I have developed my own theory: Not all maladies must be cured. Often the sickness tastes better than the remedy. I am forty percent deaf, thirty percent blind, sixty percent senile, but I can still read my lectures, repeat my old jokes, discern a beautiful face, listen to the many secrets that women tell me on the morning after my appearance while we drink coffee and munch toast with jam. And when they kiss me before I board the plane back home or to another lecture, I kiss back and tell them all the same words: "When you happen to visit New York City, come to see me if I'm still alive."

Translated by the author

The Image

THE WOMEN came to talking about divorces, broken marriage agreements, rejected brides-to-be, and my Aunt Yentl said, "One is not allowed to shame a Jewish daughter. There is a saying, 'It is better to cut parchment than to tear paper.' You probably know what this means. Marriage agreements are written on paper, but divorces are written on parchment. It's less of a sin to divorce than to break a marriage agreement."

My mother was present, and she said, "Forgive me, Yentl, but divorce, too, is written on paper, not parchment. It's a strong kind of paper and it's written on with a goose quill and an ink called *galish*."

"This I hear for the first time," Aunt Yentl said.

"I know. In our courtroom many divorce papers have been written," my mother said.

"If you say so, it must be so, Bathsheba."

There was a neighbor woman present, Chaya Riva, and she asked, "Why is it less a sin to divorce than to break a marriage agreement?"

"Really, I don't know," Aunt Yentl said. "You tell her, Bathsheba."

My mother pondered for a while and then said, "When a couple decides to divorce they know one another—they've had many quarrels, learned about each other's faults—and it may very well be they've both made up their minds that they can't live together. But an engaged couple don't know one another. The party who wants to break the engagement does so because of money or because of gossip about the other, and this is why the one who wants to break the engagement must pay a fine of half the dowry."

"Yes, yes, yes, where there's Torah there's wisdom," Aunt Yentl said.

"Weren't you about to tell a story?" Chaya Riva asked.

Aunt Yentl rubbed her forehead, as if she had forgotten that she had a story in mind. "What? Yes. This happened in Krashnik. We lived there for a time. My grandfather was the court

Jew of the local squire, and my parents were still boarding in his house. They were boarders so long that my mother managed to have five children there. I was the youngest, and I must have been about seven years old when this event happened. Today children remain children for a long time—boys until thirteen, when they begin to put on phylacteries, and girls until twelve, when they are required to fast on Yom Kippur. In those times children ripened early. My mother, peace be with her, used to call me Old Spirit. I wanted to know everything. I listened when the adults spoke and I swallowed each word. We had a maid my age, and we could completely rely on her with soaking and salting meat, cooking, and even baking. She took care of my little brothers and sisters like a devoted mother and all she got for it was two guldens a half year. When she turned fourteen she married a shoemaker—a widower, the father of six motherless children—but this is a story in itself.

"At that time there was a small yeshiva in Krashnik—not more than a dozen students, mostly poor boys from other villages. As a rule, the head of a yeshiva is the rabbi, but our rabbi served as a judge in many litigations out of town and was often employed as an advocate for a rich businessman in Lublin. The head of the yeshiva was a talmudic scholar, Reb Pinchos. He had one son, who was already married, and two daughters. He was exceedingly poor. Reb Pinchos's wife, Greena Chasha, used to bake pretzels, and the boys would buy them from her, a groschen apiece. She also went to wealthy houses to knead dough, and sometimes even to wash linen, because to support a husband, a scholar, is a good deed and in those days Jews were still eager for good deeds. The two girls were separated by seven years. Probably some other children had died in between. The older one, Zylka, was a beauty— dark and charming, like Queen Esther. She had large black eyes and chiseled features. If one has daughters, one wants to marry them off, but girls must be given a dowry, and where could a pauper like Reb Pinchos get money for a dowry? But a miracle happened. There came from Lublin a young man, the son of a rich house, named Yakir. Why should a rich young man from a big city like Lublin be willing to study in little

Krashnik? There was talk that he had developed a passion for card games when he was very young. Cards can be a passion like any passion. It's the custom to allow children to play dreidel, and even cards, on Hanukkah. For most of the youngsters it's nothing but a diversion, but in some cases it becomes an addiction. This Yakir became so involved in cards that he began to gamble with squires and Russian officers, and they play for big money. I know of a case where a squire lost all his fortune in card games, and his wife to boot, but this is another story. Yakir caused his parents great embarrassment, and they sent him to Krashnik, where there were no Russian officers. Besides, Reb Pinchos had a reputation as a scholar and a saint. He not only taught Talmud but preached morality sermons every day.

"Yakir did not come to Krashnik like some wandering orphan. He came into the village in a carriage, like a count. There was one hotel in Krashnik, where mostly Gentiles stayed, but Yakir engaged for himself the most spacious room. He brought with him many precious possessions—for example, a music box that played 'I Thank Thee,' a magnifying glass that could light a cigarette, cuff links made from gold coins—and fancy clothes. Everybody went to look at this guest from Lublin. I'm an old woman now but, God forgive me, I've never seen in my life such a good-looking man—slim, tall, dressed like a prince. I was still a child, but when the older girls saw him they were stunned. He was clever, too. He stood in the marketplace and made jokes with everybody—men, matrons, girls, even cheder boys. There was no lack of beggars in Krashnik and he dispensed alms right and left. The yeshiva students had heard about him and they came to meet him. He was not much of a scholar, but he quoted here and there from the Bible and the Gemara. They asked him why he happened to come to Krashnik and he said, 'I owe a general ten thousand rubles and he is threatening me with a revolver.' He laughed, as if he had told a joke.

"From the market Yakir went straight to the house of Reb Pinchos and there he saw Zylka. Such men do everything grandly. He looked at the girl and immediately fell in love—as they say, head over heels. She took one look at him and it seemed the same thing happened to her. My dear people, it was an instant match. Zylka's mother, Greena Chasha, became so overwhelmed that she lost her tongue.

"Yakir asked not more and not less than that there should be a wedding right away, but Reb Pinchos would not allow this kind of nonsense. First, he began to examine the young man, and it turned out that he didn't know enough to become a yeshiva student. What he needed was a tutor. Reb Pinchos taught his pupils from large volumes with small letters. One had to be prepared for these scholarly lessons. He also told the young man that this world was not a place where everyone did as he pleased. There is a God in heaven and He gave us the Torah.

"When Yakir demanded an engagement date, Reb Pinchos said, 'You don't do such things without a matchmaker and without the knowledge of your parents.' He told the fellow in strict language never to visit his house unless he was invited. Greena Chasha was frightened that everything would be spoiled between the young pair, but she knew quite well her husband was right. Zylka became white as chalk. A great fortune had fallen into her hands and her father had plucked it out. I was not there, but there were no secrets in Krashnik. People peered into keyholes and listened behind doors. If a woman burned her grits, they spoke about it in the butcher shop. Yakir became so enamored of the girl that he hired a tutor to prepare him for the yeshiva. He paid attention and he turned out to be a diligent pupil. Neither Reb Pinchos nor his wife would allow their daughter to speak more than a few words to the young man or take a walk with him, as young people do nowadays, but Reb Pinchos invited Yakir to eat in his house on the Sabbath and on holidays, and before long it became clear that the in-laws would come from Lublin and an engagement would be signed.

"I remember Zylka from that time. It was summer and we children used to go to the forest to pick mushrooms and blueberries. We often saw her walking along on the way to the forest and sometimes in the woods. She strolled around as if she were in a dream. We had heard about love. When a tailor and a seamstress got married without a matchmaker, people said,

'Love was the matchmaker.' Among better people this kind of marriage was considered a disgrace.

"His parents soon arrived. They were not just rich—they acted like Jewish squires. They came in two carriages and took over the whole hotel. Reb Pinchos had a small house but still the engagement ceremony took place there, in the house of the bride-to-be, as was the custom. The dinner was served in the synagogue yard, and this was nothing less than a royal repast, paid for by Yakir's father."

Aunt Yentl began to cough and clear her throat. She went to the kitchen and came back with a glass of water. "Yes," she said, "the engagement party took place late in the summer, and the wedding was arranged for a Sabbath in Hanukkah. As a rule, they write into the engagement papers how much the bride will give as a dowry, but in this case the bridegroom was supposed to provide the dowry. All the time one could hear Zylka's mother murmuring, 'May no evil eye strike us, Father in heaven. People are envious. They eat us with their eyes. Such luck, such good fortune—it should not be spoiled.' The day after the engagement, Yakir's parents went home. One could see that this match was a blow for them. But what can parents do when a son is stubborn? He threatened to commit suicide if he didn't get his Zylka.

"After his parents left, Yakir returned to the yeshiva, but the other boys saw that his mind was not on learning. Yakir was allowed to see Zylka only on the Sabbath. He complained it was too long until Hanukkah. One day he let his future in-laws know that he had to go to Lublin for a week or two. My dear friends, it took him longer than a week, longer than a month, two months. He didn't even write a letter. Zylka used to go to the post office every day. They told her that if a letter came they would send it to her. Waiting for letters is a terrible ordeal. My mother once said that the wicked in Gehenna lie on their beds of nails and wait for mail.

"The summer passed, and the rain and snow began. Hanukkah was approaching, but not a word from Yakir. What Zylka went through you can't imagine. She was a solitary person by nature. She didn't have a single girl friend. People said she read her father's books. Sometimes when the yeshiva boys came to Reb Pinchos's home and discussed the Talmud, Zylka listened. She was supposed to have taught herself Hebrew. She had signed the engagement papers with a scholarly flourish. Someone in Krashnik joked that when she married she would not know how to bake a kugel.

"One winter day—outside the snow was deep—a sleigh came to Krashnik, and from it emerged a lady in a sable coat. The lady was none other than Yakir's mother. She went to the rabbi and told him that her son wanted to annul the match— he was asking for a written forgiveness paper from Zylka. His parents were ready to pay Zylka the agreed-upon fine of half the dowry. Half the dowry in this case was a sum of thousands of rubles. The rabbi sent for Reb Pinchos and gave him the bad tidings. Reb Pinchos listened and replied, 'We don't intend to drag an unwilling man to the wedding canopy. If he changed his mind, it is his privilege. A Jewish daughter should forgive when she is shamed, and we are not going to take any reward for forgiveness, God forbid.'

"The rabbi reminded Reb Pinchos that the fine had been written in black and white on the engagement papers, but Reb Pinchos said, 'There is no law that we must accept the fine. Since the young man is canceling the match, this means it was not destined. Probably the Angel decided on someone else.'

"When Greena Chasha heard the dismal news she fainted away, but Zylka took the same position as her father: if Yakir didn't want her it was unfortunate, but she would accept no payment. Yakir's mother went to Reb Pinchos, and there she stopped acting like a fancy lady and wept and bemoaned the lot of her son. He was a charlatan and had humiliated the family. He had fallen in love with the daughter of a doctor, an unbeliever who shaved his beard and didn't go to the synagogue even on Yom Kippur. The wench ran around with Russian officers. Yakir's mother pleaded with Zylka to accept the fine. She could have a large dowry and be able to find the kind of husband she deserved. Yakir's mother foresaw that her son's new madness would ruin him and them. She asked again for written forgiveness and Zylka said, 'I will give it to him but with one condition—that you take back the ring you gave me for signing the engagement agreement.' The woman did not believe her own ears. 'I gave it to you,' she said, 'and I'm not going to take it back. This is a slap in my face.' Zylka said, 'I can't keep it.' She took the ring out of a pocket in her apron. It had a huge diamond, worth a fortune.

"To make it short, the woman was forced to take back her gift, and Zylka wrote the forgiveness papers herself in Hebrew. Those who looked in through the keyhole maintained that the woman fell on her knees and begged Zylka not to return the ring, but to no avail. Zylka was supposed to have said, 'I cannot keep it. I cannot sleep at night if this ring remains in our house.'"

"A haughty princess," Chaya Riva said.

My mother remarked, "Some people are ready to disgrace themselves for a few pennies. They cheat, beg, swindle, they go bankrupt, they are always greedy to grab something for nothing. Others are so gentle they will refuse even what belongs to them. Well, she was the daughter of a scholar."

"If I were she, I would have taken everything—half the dowry and the ring. With such a treasure she could have got the best fiancé," Chaya Riva said.

"Yes, every person has her calculations," Aunt Yentl said. "She didn't want anyone else."

"What *did* she want?" Chaya Riva asked.

"Who knows? The lady from Lublin climbed into her sleigh and left—a little sleigh, with two large horses. The coachman covered her feet with the fur of a bear or some other animal. He cracked his whip and the sleigh shot off like an arrow from a bow. Krashnik had plenty to talk about. Hanukkah came and there were other weddings. Zylka's mother, Greena Chasha, had become ill. Her face was yellow. The neighbors said they heard her crying at night. It is not a small matter. First a stroke of fortune, then such a misfortune. She kept insisting that enemies had given her the evil eye. As for Zylka, she did not thrust her problems on anyone. To whom could she talk? She walked a lot and always alone. In winter, in the deepest snows, one saw her walk into the forest or toward the road that led to the watermill. People said that she could not be in her right mind. She didn't want any company. When she was spoken to, she didn't answer.

"Now, here's something. In her father's yeshiva there was a

student whose name was Illish. He was supposed to have been a prodigy. He came from the town of Kielce. He was an orphan. Why he went to a yeshiva so far from home I don't know. Since no one told him what to do, probably he had taken to the road on foot and on the way learned about the yeshiva in Krashnik. All he brought were his phylacteries. He immediately went to the yeshiva, and when Reb Pinchos examined him, he saw that the boy had the brain of a genius. He took him into the yeshiva and arranged for six patrons to feed him—each for one day of the week. On the Sabbath he ate all three meals in Reb Pinchos's house, and I think on Saturday night the valedictory meal as well.

"He was a good-looking boy, blond, with long sidelocks and blue eyes. I remember him because he ate at our house every Tuesday. The other yeshiva students were not shy. If they didn't get enough to eat they asked for more. They transacted all sorts of business between themselves: 'I give you my Thursday, you give me your Wednesday.' They knew who prepared a fat soup—a soup with gold coins, as they called it—and who prepared a lean soup. They knew which matron was stingy and which was lavish. Some women liked to question them and find out about everyone's private affairs, but my mother disliked gossip. Tuesday was a holiday for her. She cooked a sumptuous meal for Illish, but he was a small eater. He nibbled —gave a smell and a lick and he was finished. He always carried a book with him, and while he ate he looked at it. He never forgot to say 'Thank you.' A quiet boy, and bashful. When a female spoke to him he dropped his eyes. We girls loved him as if he were a brother. The matchmakers tried to arrange a match for him. Why should I deny it? My oldest sister, Zyvia, liked him. But in those days a girl would rather burst than let fall an affectionate word to a man. I was the youngest and I, too, liked him in my childish way. My sisters fought about who should serve him the meat, who the soup, and who the dessert. Yes, my mother prepared dessert for him, even though it was a weekday. She would say, 'Who knows what he gets in other houses? Let him have one good meal in the week.'

"Suddenly we heard the strange news that Illish had gone to Getzl, the matchmaker, and had sent him to Reb Pinchos with the message that he wanted to marry Zylka. He did it all secretly, but there were no secrets in Krashnik. There was an uproar in town. Our rabbi had a daughter and also two sons, but the sons had no desire to study and there was talk that Illish might marry the rabbi's daughter, Feigele, and after the rabbi's demise inherit his position. Who could have expected a quiet person like Illish to send a matchmaker to Reb Pinchos and ask for his daughter's pledge? Zylka was older than Illish. Besides, when an engagement contract is canceled, the girl is considered damaged goods. However, since Illish had no parents to take care of such matters, he had to decide for himself. I remember all this as if it happened yesterday. When the news arrived at our house all three girls cried. My mother said, 'Why are you howling? It's not Yom Kippur,' and my sister Zyvia cried out, 'If Illish marries he'll stop eating in our house on Tuesdays.' 'Nothing is forever,' my mother said. 'A boy is not born to eat at other people's tables for the rest of his life.'

"We all thought that from this dough there would be no bread. A poor boy needs his wife to bring a dowry and Zylka didn't have a penny. In the other houses where Illish ate, the women tried to dissuade him from marrying Zylka. Reb Pinchos was a pauper, his wife was sick, and Zylka was unbalanced. Why put a healthy head into a sickbed? They tried to match Illish up with other girls. He listened to everyone and answered to one. Everybody was sure that Zylka would reject him. He fit her like a square peg in a round hole. She was taller than he, and more mature. But no one really knows how a match comes to be.

"When Reb Pinchos heard that his best student, Illish, wanted his daughter, he was more than willing. He later admitted that he had wanted him for a son-in-law from the very beginning. Yakir had always displeased him. When Greena Chasha learned that Illish wanted her daughter, she became healthy again in a minute. Reb Pinchos spoke to Illish openly. He could not provide any dowry but he could keep the newlyweds in his house for some time. Greena Chasha said, 'When I cook for four it can also serve five.' Everything depended on Zylka. With a girl like this one had to be careful. Reb Pinchos spoke to her and she said she'd give him an answer. 'When?' Reb Pinchos asked, and she said, 'Tomorrow.' The next day she said yes, and they drew up a preliminary contract. They had to be cautious with her. The engagement party with Yakir had been like a ball, but the signing of the contract with Illish was attended by only a few yeshiva students. Since Illish ate in Reb Pinchos's house every Sabbath, Zylka knew him well. She was supposed to have told a neighbor, 'He never looked at me, and suddenly he wants me for his wife.' Whether she really said it or not I don't know. It was not in her nature to reveal her feelings. Perhaps her mother said it.

"There was no reason for envying the newly matched pair, but still people did envy them. Many girls in Krashnik had wanted Illish. He was considered a serious young man. Feigele, the rabbi's daughter, walked around like a chicken without a head. The fact that first Yakir and now Illish wanted Zylka meant that men desired her. 'What do they see in her?' the girls asked, but who knows what men see in a woman? They look with different eyes.

"The wedding was set for the thirty-third day in Omer. The pair didn't have long to wait. Reb Pinchos could not give his daughter a trousseau. They said in town that her mother ordered for her a single dress. Reb Pinchos did not permit Illish to eat in his house, because it was considered loose conduct to let an engaged couple see each other at the table. Illish had to find another house to dine in on the Sabbath."

Aunt Yentl paused for a moment to fix her bonnet, and then went on: "A few months passed and it was spring again. I've seen poor weddings in my life, but a pauperish wedding like Zylka's I never again experienced. Greena Chasha did not have the strength to make preparations. Zylka was supposed to have said, 'As far as I'm concerned the guests can be fed nothing better than potatoes in their skins.' She was clever in her own way, but to be too clever is not good. It was the custom in Krashnik for the wife-to-be and two of her friends to go from house to house a week before the wedding and invite women to the ceremony, but Zylka refused and people were furious. Her mother told Zylka that she had made everybody her enemy, but Reb Pinchos sided with his daughter. He said that the bride's going around to invite people was nothing but a Gentile observance.

"On the day of the wedding I went with the other girls to look in the window and see how Zylka sat in her bridal chair. It was a broken chair and Zylka was sitting on the edge of it, not in the dignified way a bride usually sits, and she looked impatient and harried. I shouldn't be punished for my words, but the whole wedding seemed like a joke. It was the custom on the night before the wedding for musicians to play a good-night melody as the bride was led into the ritual bath for her ablutions, but Reb Pinchos had no money to pay the band. The elders wanted to give him a subsidy, but he refused to take it. He took charity for the yeshiva, not alms for himself, he said. There's a saying, 'The apple doesn't fall far from the tree,' and the Krashnik wedding jester was supposed to have said, 'The apple tree is not far from the apple.' Reb Pinchos was a saintly man but overly honest. The daughter was too proud. Everything that is exaggerated does damage.

"They put up the wedding canopy in the synagogue yard, and even though few were invited, the whole town came to witness the happy event. Greena Chasha and another woman led Zylka to the canopy, but she walked too quickly and almost dragged them. Some toughs joked that the bride was in a rush. They called names after her and whistled. The rabbi recited the blessings in a hoarse voice. Illish had always been short, but that evening he appeared no taller than a cheder boy. The few guests who went to the supper reported later that they left hungry.

"Now, listen. It was a tradition in Krashnik that at dawn after a wedding a bunch of matrons dashed into the bedroom, tore away the sheet under the bride, and went outside with it to dance a kosher dance celebrating the bride's virginity. They did it this time, too, but there was no blood on the sheet. The matrons later complained that Zylka had screamed at them and scolded them. My dear people, heaven and earth conspired that no secret should remain unrevealed. Some women said that Illish was such a shlemiel he didn't know what a man should know, and others contended Zylka was not a virgin, that Yakir had skimmed off the cream. When the seven nuptial days were over, the rabbi summoned the young pair to his courtroom and began to ask questions. What was the matter and why? Illish stood there frightened and pale as a corpse and he couldn't utter a word. The rabbi had told the beadle to cover the windows, but the synagogue street was black with curious people. The rabbi continued to interrogate the pair, until the needle came out of the haystack. A man had been lying between bride and bridegroom and would not let them approach each other.

"'A man?' the rabbi cried out. 'What do you mean "a man"?' And Zylka replied, 'Yakir, his image.'

"What went on in Krashnik that day and the days and weeks thereafter one could not describe even if we sat seven days and seven nights. It was clear that it was not the real Yakir. Yakir chased around with women in Lublin, not Krashnik. It could only be a demon, but how could a demon get hold of the young pair? The rabbi told Reb Pinchos to examine the mezuzah on the door, but not a letter of the parchment had faded. Greena Chasha, the grieved mother, began to suspect that some enemy had bewitched her daughter, perhaps made a knot in her wedding dress, in the fringes of her shawl, or in the lace of her bloomers, or perhaps in a sheet or a pillowcase, but she found nothing and there was no one she could suspect.

"The rabbi and the yeshiva boys questioned Illish on whether there had really been an image lying between Zylka and him when he came to her bed, but he could not give a clear answer. He mumbled, 'Yes, no, maybe.' They looked over his phylacteries, his prayer shawl. Everything was as it should be. Zylka stopped leaving the house altogether. She lay in the dark bedroom sunk in gloom. When Illish came home for supper his mother-in-law served him his meal. Reb Pinchos did not belong to the Hasidim, but nevertheless he went to a wonder rabbi and brought home a bundle of talismans. Greena Chasha went so far in her anguish that she asked advice of an old Gentile woman, a witch, who gave her all kinds of incantations and herbs. Nothing helped. Zylka remained a virgin."

"Are you sure she was a virgin?" Chaya Riva asked.

"What else? There was no one in Krashnik with whom she could have misbehaved. There was no hiding place in Krashnik. A hundred eyes lurked in every nook."

"Were they finally divorced?" my mother asked.

Aunt Yentl did not answer right away. She said, "One day

Greena Chasha went to Zylka in the dark bedroom and said, 'My daughter, you cannot stay separated forever. There is no such thing as a Jewish cloister.' Zylka said, 'There should be. I wish there were.'

"Her mother thought this was just one of her sharp sayings, a spiteful answer. But a few hours later, when Greena Chasha came to her daughter with a glass of tea, the bedroom was empty. The mother screamed and called and went to look for her daughter, but there was no more Zylka in Krashnik—neither that day nor the days and years after. Zylka had gone to the Catholic priest and told him she wanted to give up her faith."

"She converted?" Chaya Riva asked.

"Became a nun and went into a cloister."

"When and how did they learn about it?" my mother asked.

"Not immediately, but after some time," Aunt Yentl said. "The community tried to save her, to redeem her with money, but the priest refused to hear of it. When they take captive a Jewish soul they never relinquish it."

"What happened to Yakir?" my mother asked.

"I don't know. Sinners never end up well," Aunt Yentl said. "As for Illish, he married Feigele, the rabbi's daughter, and after the rabbi's death he took his chair."

For a long while the women were silent. Then my mother said, "This image was not a demon."

"What was it?" Aunt Yentl asked, and my mother said, "A mirage, a figment of madness. You get something in your head and you cannot drive it away. It keeps on boring day and night like the gnat in the brain of the cursed Titus."

"Wasn't it a dybbuk?" Chaya Riva asked.

My mother pondered for a while, "No, Chaya Riva," she said. "A dybbuk talks, screams, howls, wails, and therefore he can be exorcised. Melancholy is silent, and therein lies its uncanny power."

Translated by the author and Lester Goran

FROM

GIFTS

Contents

Author's Introduction   553

The Trap   564

The Smuggler   576

Gifts   581

Author's Introduction

I have lived through a number of epochs in Jewish history. I was brought up in a home where the old Jewish faith burned brightly. Ours was a house of Torah and holy books. Other children had toys; I played with the volumes in my father's library. I began to write before I even knew the alphabet. I took my father's pen, dipped it in ink, and started to scribble. The Sabbath was an ordeal for me, because on that day writing is forbidden.

My father moved to Warsaw when I was still very young, and there a second epoch began for me: the age of the Enlightenment. My brother, I. J. Singer, who later wrote *The Brothers Ashkenazi*, was at that time a rationalist; it was not in his nature to hide his opinions. He spoke frankly to my parents, advancing with great clarity and precision all the arguments that the rationalists—from Spinoza to Max Nordau—had brought against religion. Though I was still a child, I listened attentively. Fortunately, my parents did not lack answers. They replied with as much skill as my brother attacked. I recall my father saying, "Well, who created the world? You? Who made the sky, the stars, the sun, the moon, man, the animals?" My brother's answer was that everything had evolved. He mentioned Darwin. "But," my mother wanted to know, "how can a creature with eyes, ears, lungs, and a brain evolve from earth and water?" My father used to say, "You can spatter ink but it won't write a letter by itself." My brother never had an answer for this; as yet none has been found.

My parents attempted to further strengthen the case for faith by constantly telling stories of imps, ghosts, and dybbuks and of the miraculous feats of famous rabbis. Some of these events they themselves had witnessed, and I knew that they were not liars. My grandfather, the Rabbi of Bilgoray, had once been visited by an old man, a fortune teller, who had been able to read the text of a closed book; whatever page my grandfather touched with his finger, the fortune teller could recite. I later used this incident in a story of mine, "The Jew of Babylon," which has not yet been translated. My mother knew of a house inhabited by a poltergeist. Indeed, I can truthfully say that by the time I was seven or eight I was already acquainted with all the strange facts that are to be found in the books of Conan Doyle, Sir Oliver Lodge, Gourney and Myers, Flammarion and Professor Rhine. In our home the most pressing questions were the eternal ones; there the cosmic riddles were not theoretical but actual. I began to read in *The Guide of the Perplexed* and *The Kuzari*, even in the Cabalistic literature, at an early age. But nevertheless, despite my studies, I remained a child and played joyfully with other children. At Cheder I astounded my fellow students with fantastic stories. I told them once that my father was a king and with such convincing detail that they believed me.

When the first World War broke out, I experienced all the social evils of the period. I saw the men on our street marching off to war, leaving behind them sobbing women and hungry children. Men from the very house I lived in were taken. In his debates with my brother, my father argued, "You keep on talking about reason and logic. What logic is there to this war? How does it happen that learned men and teachers assist in the manufacture of bombs and guns to destroy innocent people?" Again my brother had no answer. He himself was drafted. During the short time that he was a recruit, he endured every kind of humiliation. The Russian and Polish recruits accused him of murdering Jesus, poisoning wells, using Christian blood for matzohs, and spying for the Germans. In the barracks reason was bankrupt. My high-minded brother fled to Warsaw and hid in the studio of a sculptor. I used to carry food to him there.

No. The world that was revealed to me was not rational. One could as easily question the validity of reason as the existence of God. In my own spirit, there was chaos. I suffered from morbid dreams and hallucinations. I had wildly erotic fantasies. Hungry children, filthy beggars, refugees sleeping in the streets, wagons of wounded soldiers did not arouse admiration in me for human or divine reason. The spectacle of a cat pouncing on a mouse made me sick and rebellious. Neither human reason nor God's mercy seemed to be certain. I found both filled with contradictions. My brother still clung to the hope that in the end reason would be victorious. But young though I was I knew that the worship of reason was as idolatrous as bowing down to a graven image. As yet I had not read the modern philosophers, but I had come to the conclusion by myself that reason leads to antinomies when it deals with time, space, and causality; it could deal no better with these than with the *ultimate problem*, the problem of evil.

In 1917 my mother took me and one of my younger brothers to Bilgoray, which was being occupied by the Austrians. Kerensky's revolution had occurred and was regarded as the victory of reason, but soon came the October Revolution and the pogroms in the Ukraine. Bilgoray had just endured a cholera epidemic. The town had lost a third of its inhabitants. Some of my relatives had been stricken. The gruesome tales of that pestilence are still fresh in my memory.

Bilgoray had no railroad and was surrounded by forests, and there the Jewish traditions of a hundred years before were still very much alive. I had already become acquainted with the modern Hebrew and Yiddish literature. The writers of both languages were under the influence of the Enlightenment. These authors wanted the Jew to step out of his old-fashioned gaberdine and become European. Their doctrines were rationalistic, liberal, humanistic. But to me such ideas seemed already obsolete. The overthrowing of one regime and the replacing of it with another did not seem to me to be the crux of the matter. The problem was creation itself. I felt that I must achieve some sort of solution of the puzzle or perish myself.

While in Bilgoray I became acquainted with the literature of other nations. I read in translation Tolstoy, Dostoevsky, Gogol, Heine, Goethe, Flaubert, Maupassant. I read Jack London's *The Call of the Wild* and the stories of Edgar Allan Poe, all in Yiddish. It was at this time also that I first studied Spinoza's *Ethics* in a German translation. I pored over each page as though it were a part of the Talmud. Some of the axioms, definitions, and theorems I still remember by heart. I am now able to see the defects and hiatuses in Spinoza's system, but my reading of the *Ethics* had a great effect on me. My story "The Spinoza of Market Street" is rooted in this period. Later I read a history of philosophy and Hume, Kant, Schopenhauer, and Nietzsche. My childish hope was to discover the truth, and through the discovery to give sense and substance to my life. But finally my conclusion was that the power of philosophy lay in its attack upon reason, not in the building of systems. None of the systems could be taken seriously; they did not help one to manage one's life. The human intellect confronted existence, and existence stubbornly refused to be systematized. I myself was the insulted and shamed human intellect. Many times I contemplated suicide because of my intellectual impotence.

All these storms took place inside me. On the outside I was just a Chassidic boy who studied the Gemara, prayed three times a day, put on phylacteries. But the people of the town were suspicious anyway. They considered me an exotic plant. I saw with grief and sometimes envy how other boys my age made peace somehow with this world and its troubles. I lacked their humility.

At that time I began to write in Hebrew. So perturbed was my spirit that I expected my pen to at least partially express my rage. But I saw with shame that nothing issued but banal and thrashed-about phrases, similar to those I read in other books and which I criticized severely. I felt as if a devil or imp held on to my pen and inhibited it. A mysterious power did not let me reveal my inner self. After many trials I decided it was the fault of the Hebrew language. Hebrew was near to me, but it was not my mother language. While writing, I kept on searching in my memory for words and phrases from the Bible, the Mishnah, and the later literature; in addition, each Hebrew word dragged after itself a whole chain of associations. I came to the conclusion that writing in Yiddish would be easier. But I soon found that this was not so. I still had not lost my inhibitions. Satan did not allow me to express my individuality. Despite myself, I imitated Knut Hamsun, Turgenev, and even lesser writers. Every creator painfully experiences the chasm between his inner vision and its ultimate expression. This chasm is never completely bridged. We all have the conviction, perhaps illusory, that we have much more to say than appears on the paper.

I began an investigation of the techniques of literature. What, I asked myself, makes Tolstoy and Dostoevsky so great? Is it the theme, the style, or the construction? My brother,

I. J. Singer, had left Poland and gone to Russia. He was residing in Kiev, where he wrote for the Yiddish press, and had already published his story "Pearls." One day he showed up in Bilgoray to spend the day. As a writer he had "already arrived." I had sufficient character not to show him my manuscripts. I knew that I had to find my way by myself.

Some time thereafter, I went to live in Warsaw, which was then the center of Yiddish culture in Poland. It was in the early twenties. I had not yet published anything. At that time my brother was a friend of the famous Perez Markish, who was later liquidated by Stalin. Other members of his literary circle were Melechavitch, Uri Zvi Greenberg, today a famous Hebrew poet, and American Yiddish writers like Joseph Opatoshu, who came on visits to Warsaw. My brother was co-editor of the *Literarische Blatter*, and I got a job there as a proofreader. A spirit of revolution permeated the new Yiddish literature: Markish wrote in the style of Mayakovsky. But Aleksandr Blok, the Russian poet, author of the poem "Twelve," was the most beloved writer of that group. This coterie preached that classic and academic literature was bankrupt and spoke of a new time, a new period, a new style.

I was afraid to set myself against writers who were all well recognized, although I saw that their art was new in neither spirit nor style. They had merely dressed up the old clichés in red clothing. All they did was juggle words. Even a young boy like me, from the provinces, found the doctrine that the Bolshevist revolution would do away with all evil incredibly naïve. The Jewish situation in Poland was especially bad. The Polish people—the people themselves, not merely the regime—had never come to terms with the Jews. The Jews had built a separate society in Poland and had their own faith, language, holidays, and even political aspirations. We Jews were both citizens and aliens. My father, for example, could speak no Polish. I myself spoke Polish with an accent. Though my ancestors had lived in Poland for six hundred years, we were still strangers. No revolution could unite these two communities which were so profoundly separated. Communism and Zionism, the two ideals which split the Jews of Poland, were both completely alien to the Polish people. I do not mean to imply by this that I had remarkable prescience, but I saw clearly that the Jews were living on a volcano. In my bitterness I spoke about the coming catastrophe, but those around me were puffed up with optimism, rationalism, and Red dogmatism.

My brother soon freed himself of revolutionary illusions, but he nonetheless kept his belief in reason. He still thought that through evolution and progress, man would slowly see his mistakes and correct them. We had many discussions. In a sense, I had taken over the position of my parents. I tried mercilessly to destroy his humanistic optimism. I regret now that I did this, because what did I have to offer? My parents at least advocated religion. Mine was only a negative philosophy. My brother was always tolerant and deeply sympathetic to me, but I was rebellious and often insolent.

A new *Weltanschauung* which I find difficult to characterize began to develop in me. It was a kind of religious skepticism. There is a God, but He never reveals Himself; no one knows who He is or what His purpose is. There are an infinite number of universes, and even here, on this earth, powers exist of which we have no inkling, both stronger and weaker than Man. This system allowed for the possibility of angels and devils and for other beings which are and will remain forever unnamed. I had, in a curious way, combined the Ten Commandments, Humian philosophy, and the Cabalistic writing of Rabbi Moshe from Cordova and the Holy Isaac Luria, as well as the occultism of Flammarion, Sir Oliver Lodge, Sir William Crooks. This was, as one can see, a sort of kasha of mysticism, deism, and skepticism, well suited to my intellect and temperament. Instead of a concrete universe of facts, I saw a developing universe of potentialities. The thing-in-itself is pure potential. In the beginning was potentiality. What seem to be facts are really potentialities. God is the sum of all possibility. Time is the mechanism through which potentiality achieves sequence. The Cabala teaches that all worlds are created through the combination of letters. My own position was that the universe is a series of countless potentialities and combinations. I had already read Schopenhauer's *The World as Will and Idea* and so knew the Schopenhaurian view that the will is the thing-in-itself, the noumenon behind the phenomenon. But, to me, the basic substance of the world was potentiality seen as a whole.

I did not conceive of this as a philosophy for others, but

strictly for myself. Somehow or other it made sense for me, but I didn't have the means or the need to systematize it and make it understandable to others. I would say that it was more a philosophy of art than of being.

God was for me an eternal belletrist. His main attribute was creativity. God was creativity, and what He created was made of the same stuff as He and shared His desire: to create again. I quoted to myself that passage from the Midrash which says God created and destroyed many worlds before he created this one. Like my brother and myself God threw His unsuccessful works into the wastebasket. The Flood, the destruction of Sodom, the wanderings of the Jews in the desert, the wars of Joshua—these were all episodes in a divine novel, full of suspense and adventure. Yes, God was a creator, and that which He created had a passion to create. Each atom, each molecule had creative needs and possibilities. The sun, the planets, the fixed stars, the whole cosmos seethed with creativity and creative fantasies. I could feel this turmoil within myself.

I availed myself of the doctrine of *zimzum*, that wonderful notion which is so important in the Cabala of Rabbi Isaac Luria. God, Isaac Luria says, is omnipotent, but had to diminish Himself and His light so that He could create. Such shrinking is the source of creation, not only in man but also in the Godhead. The evil host makes creation possible. God could not have His infinite works without the devil. Out of suffering creativity is born. The existence of pain in the world can be compared with a writer's suffering as he describes some dreadful scene which he lives through in his imagination. As he writes the author knows that his work is only fiction produced for his and his reader's enjoyment. Each man, each animal, exists only as clay in the hands of a creator, and is itself creative. We, ourselves, are the writer, the book, and the hero. The medieval philosophers expressed a similar idea when they said that God is Himself the knower, the known, and the knowledge.

I am not seeking here to create a new philosophy. All I desire to do is to describe a state of mind. Just as an artist hopes throughout his whole life to create the great and perfect work, so does God yearn throughout all eternity to perfect His creation. God is no static perfection, as Spinoza thought, but a limitless and unsatiated will for perfection. All His worlds are nothing more than stages and experiments in a divine laboratory. When I went to the Cheder as a boy and studied "Akdamoth," the poem for Pentecost, I was amazed by the verses in the poem which said that if all skies were parchment, all men writers, all blades of grass pens, and all oceans ink, these would still be insufficient to describe the mysteries of the Torah. That parable became my credo: The skies were indeed parchment, the grasses pens, and all men in fact writers. Everything that existed wrote, painted, sculpted, and sought for creative achievement.

Since the purpose of creation was creation, creativity was also the criterion of ethics and even of sociology. There was a place only for those social systems which could advance creativity. Freedom was nothing but the freedom to create. Since creativity required leisure, and some degree of wealth, men must create a system which would furnish the requisites to experiment.

Yes, God is a writer, and we are both the heroes and the readers. A novel written by the Lord cannot endure just for one short season. As heroes of God's novel we are all immortal. A great writer's work can be understood on many levels, and this implies that our existence has more than one meaning. We exist in body. We exist as symbols, as parables, and in many other ways. When the critics praise a writer they say that his hero is three-dimensional, but God's heroes have more than three dimensions. Their dimensions are numberless.

Good novels are often translated into many languages, and so is the novel called Life. Versions of this work are read on other planets, on other galaxies of the universe.

Apropos of the critics: Like all writers, the Almighty has His critics. We know that the angels have nothing but praise for His work. Three times a day they sing: Sublime! Perfect! Great! Excellent! But there must be some angry critics too. They complain: Your novel, God, is too long, too cruel. Too little love. Too much sex. . . . They advise cutting. How can a novel be good when three quarters of it is water? They find it inconsistent, sensational, antisocial, cryptic, decadent, vulgar, pointless, melodramatic, improvised, repetitious. About one quality we all agree: God's novel has suspense. One keeps on reading it day and night. The fear of death is nothing but the fear of having to close God's book. We all want to go on with this serial forever. The belief in survival has one explanation: We refuse to have any interruptions in reading. As readers we are burning with a desire to know the events of the next chapter, and the next, and the next. We try hard to find the formula for God's best seller, but we are always wrong. The heavenly writer is full of surprises. All we can do is pray for a happy ending. . . . But according to the Cabala, God's novel will never end. The coming of the Messiah will be only the beginning of a new volume. Resurrection will bring back some characters the reader has already forgotten, but not the writer. . . . What we call death is but a temporary pause for purely literary reasons.

Suddenly my way in literature became clear to me: to transform inhibition into a method of creativity, to recognize in the inhibition a friendly power instead of a hostile one—in the terms of the Cabala, to lift up the holy sparks which had fallen from the sacred into the impure, from the World of Emanations into the unclean host. Even though I realized that this philosophy was nothing but my private concoction, I considered it valid and useful as a basis for my work. In the world of the artist, the teaching of Isaac Luria is certainly true: The shadow is often the precursor of the light; the devils and imps are temptations and challenges to further achievement. The purpose of each fall is a new rising. Each occasion for sin can become an occasion for virtue. Each passion, no matter how low, can become a ladder to ascend.

Satan in Goray, which I wrote in 1932, was a product of this state of mind. The epoch of Sabbatai Zevi was for me a rare opportunity to express these thoughts in a symbolic way. This epoch was for me a lesson in both religion and creativity: One must learn from the inhibition, discover its higher purpose; one must neither ignore it completely nor submit to it. The inhibition in the broadest sense is always an indication of new potentialities. In almost all my later works, I try to show man's urge to create, to find what is new, unique, and to overcome the disturbances and barriers in his way.

Creativity is for me a very encompassing idea. I would say that everything which gives a man pleasure is creative and what causes him pain is an inhibition in his creative desire. Like Spinoza, I am a hedonist. Like the Cabalists, I believe that the principle of male and female exists not only in the lower worlds but also in the higher ones. The universal novel of creation, like the novel of an earthly writer, is finally a love story.

The Cabalists compared the unclean host with the female, and this comparison has deep significance. A male can bring out his semen quickly and in abundance, but the female demands time, patience, and a period of ripening. She is, if you want, the inhibition, but she is also the power which transmutes intention into deed. The Cabalists saw in God a division into the masculine and the feminine, which they called the Shechinah. God Himself must have time and space for His work. In His original form He is not perfect but ripens in infinite time. God, like the Universe, is expanding. Men can serve Him by creating within their narrow worlds, in their small way, conditions which will permit creativity for all—from the bee to man, from the microbe that sours our milk to the artist. The freedom to which we aspire should not be an end in itself. Its ultimate aim must be Man's boundless creativity.

God creates continuously, and continuous creation is Man's destiny, too. God, like the artist, is free. Like the artist's His work cannot be predetermined. Laws are aesthetic and ethical and therefore bound to change. Continual change is their very essence. Beauty is their purpose. God's fantasy is their limit. God, like the artist, never knows clearly what He will do and how His work will develop. Only the intention is clear: to bring out a masterpiece and to improve it all the time. I have once called God a struggling artist. This continual aspiration is what men call suffering. In this system emotions are not passive, as in Spinoza's philosophy. God Himself is emotion. God thinks and feels. Compassion and beauty are two of His endless attributes. In my novel *The Slave*, I have expressed this notion in these words:

The summer night throbbed with joy; from all sides came music. Warm winds bore the smells of grain, fruit, and pine trees to him. Itself a Cabalistic book, the night was crowded with sacred names and symbols—mystery upon mystery. In the distance where sky and earth merged, lightning flashed, but no thunder followed. The stars looked like letters of the alphabet, vowel points, notes of music. Sparks flickered above the bare furrows. The world was a parchment scrawled with words and song. Every now and then Jacob heard a murmur in his ear as if some unseen being was whispering to him. He was surrounded by powers, some good, some evil, some cruel, some merciful, but each with its own nature and its own task to perform.

The Trap

I TRIED to write," the woman said, "but first of all I'm not a writer. Secondly, even if I were a writer I couldn't write this story. The moment I begin—and I began a number of times—my fountain pen starts to make ugly smudges on the paper. I never learned how to type. They brought me up so that I have no skill for technical things. I cannot drive a car. I cannot change a fuse. Even to find the right channel on a television set is for me a problem."

The woman who said this to me had white hair and a young face without wrinkles. I had put her crutches in a corner. She sat in my apartment in a chair which I had purchased some time ago in an antique store.

She said, "My father and mother both came from rich homes. My maternal grandfather was actually a millionaire in Germany. He lost everything in the inflation after World War I. He was lucky; he died in Berlin long before Hitler came to power. My father came from Alsace. For some reason my father always warned me not to have anything to do with Jews who come from Russia. He used to say they aren't honest and they're all communists. If he had lived to see my husband he would have been surprised. I never met as violent an adversary of communism as he was. Boris was his name. He assured me many times that Roosevelt was a hidden Bolshevik and that he had an agreement with Stalin to deliver a half of Europe to him on a silver platter and even the United States. Boris's father was a Russian, a devout Christian, and a Slavophile. His wife, Boris's mother, was Jewish. She was a Hungarian. I did not know her. She was a classic beauty and completely eccentric. In their last years husband and wife did not talk to each other. When they wanted to communicate they sent notes to each other through the maid. I'm not going to bother you with too many details. I'll come right to the point.

"I met Boris in 1938 in a hotel in Lake Placid in the Adirondacks. My father had died in Dachau, where the Nazis had sent him. From grief my mother lost her mind, and she was placed in an insane asylum. Boris was a guest in the hotel and I was a chambermaid. I had come from Germany without a penny, and this was the only job I could get. Our matchmaker was Thomas Mann's novel *Buddenbrooks*. I came to make Boris's room and there the novel lay on the table. I was in love with that work. For a while I left the bed which I was making and began to leaf through the pages. Suddenly the door opened and Boris came in. He was twelve years older than I. I was then twenty-four and he was thirty-six. I'm not going to boast to you about my good looks. What you are seeing now is a ruin. The woman who sits here before you went through five operations. In one case I actually died. I stopped breathing some hours after the operation, and the night nurse without any ceremony covered my face with a sheet. Don't laugh. Those were the happiest moments I can remember. If death is actually as blissful as those minutes were, there's no reason to fear it."

"How were you revived?" I asked.

"Oh, the night nurse suddenly decided that she'd better notify the doctor. A number of physicians ran in and brought me back to life. What a miserable life! But all the wretchedness came later. I can never tell anything in a chronological order. I have no sense of time and have no recollection for the order of events. Do me a favor and bring me a glass of water."

"Yes, of course."

I brought the woman a glass of water, and I said, "I forgot to ask you your name. Is it a secret?"

"No secret. My name is Regina Kozlov. Kozlov is my husband's surname. My maiden name is Wertheim. I will try to make my story as short as possible.

"We stood in the hotel room and we both praised Thomas Mann. Boris was tall, straight, a handsome man; perhaps too handsome. I told him that he could have been a film actor, but even then I saw something in his eyes which frightened me. They had not one color but a few colors: blue, green, and even violet. They expressed a kind of stubbornness, severity, fanaticism. Why go on? We fell in love, as they say, at first sight, and two weeks later we got married right there in Lake Placid.

"Neither he nor I had any close relatives in America. He told me he had a sister in London who was married to an English aristocrat, some sir or lord. What did I care? I was absolutely alone in the world, without means, and here I got a

husband who had received a law degree in Warsaw. He told me
that he had no patience to take a bar examination in the
United States and that he made a living from business. 'What
kind of business?' I asked him, and he said, 'Stocks and bonds.'
After the Wall Street crash most stocks fell so low they became
almost worthless, but at the end of the thirties they began to
rise. Boris had brought with him to the United States quite a
large sum of money, and in some five years he managed to
double or triple his investments. In New York he had bought a
large building for a pittance, and he sold it with a big profit.
He had an apartment in Brooklyn Heights, stocks and bonds
which may have been worth half a million dollars, and all he
needed was a wife. 'How did it happen that the girls didn't
grab you up till now?' I asked, and he said that many tried, but
he never found anyone who pleased him. He said to me, 'I'm
a serious man and to me marriage is a serious institution. I demand from a woman physical and spiritual beauty and strong
moral values. When I take one look at someone I can see all
her shortcomings, not only the actual but also the potential
ones.'

"According to his talk, I was at least an angel, if not a goddess, and he had seen all this at first sight. It's a fact that he
began to talk to me about marriage immediately in the room
which I came to clean. To make it short, one day I was a
chambermaid and a few days later I was engaged to become
Mrs. Kozlov. The hotel was full of German Jews. The announcement created quite a sensation among them. They're
not accustomed to such quick decisions. Mothers of marriage-
able daughters were bursting with envy. I must tell you a funny
episode: The first or second day he asked me if I was a virgin
and I told him yes, which was the truth. I added in a joke, 'A
virgin with a certificate.' The moment I said these words Boris
became tense and frightened. 'A certificate from whom?' he
asked. 'From a doctor? What doctor? Here in America?' I assured him again and again that I was joking. 'Certificate' is a
Yiddish expression that means one hundred percent. But I
could see that he did not have the slightest sense of humor. It
took me a long time to quiet him. I saw right away that one
could not make a joke with Boris. If there was such a thing as
a degree for humorlessness he would have gotten one *magna*

cum laude. We got married at Lake Placid by a justice of the peace, and no one took part in the ceremony but two bailiffs who served as witnesses. Boris had a sister in London, but as far as I knew he didn't inform her of our marriage. After a while we went to New York, and my entire luggage consisted of one valise. Boris lived in a small apartment in a building without an elevator: two large half-empty rooms, a kitchen, and a little room which he called his office. It may sound funny to you but he had one narrow bed, one plate, one spoon, one knife, and one glass. I asked what he did when he had company, and he said, 'No one ever comes to me.' I asked him, 'Don't you have any friends?' and he said, 'There are no friends. My only friend is my broker.' It didn't take me long to realize I had married a man who was pathologically literal. He had a book where he kept a record of every cent he spent. Once when I walked with him on the street I found a penny on the sidewalk. I gave it to him for good luck, and he later wrote down the penny as income in his book. I'm not even sure that I should call him a miser. He later bought me clothes and jewelry. He planned to buy a house, but not until I became pregnant. I would say that he was extremely serious, and the slightest hint of a joke drove him into confusion. I read some time ago that they're building robots that think. If such robots are built they'll be just like Boris: accurate, precise, practical, and pragmatic. In the short time we spent together at Lake Placid it became clear he was a silent man. He only said what he had to say. I cannot to this day say why he was so delighted with *Buddenbrooks,* a work filled with humor: perhaps because extremes attract one another. This man could have lived out his life with two words, 'yes' and 'no.' I had made a tragic mistake, but I decided to make the best of it. I wanted to be a devoted wife and later a devoted mother. We both wanted children. I hoped the children would take after my family, not his.

"It was a terribly lonesome existence from the beginning. Boris awakened every day at seven o'clock to the second. He ate the same breakfast every morning. He suffered from an ulcer and the doctor had put him on a diet, which he followed rigorously. He went to bed exactly at ten. He never changed his single bed into a double bed, waiting for the time when he'd buy a house. We were living among Jews. The war had begun. Jewish boys and girls were collecting money for Palestine, but Boris told them he was an anti-Zionist. There were also some communists on our street, and they collected money for Birobidzhan and such similar fakes. When Boris heard the word 'communists' he became wild. He screamed that Russia was ruled by murderers and vampires. He said that his only hope was that Hitler would clean up the red swamp. For a Jew to put his hopes in Hitler was a terrible thing. The neighbors all stopped greeting me. There was even a rumor that neither of us was a Jew.

"When five months passed and I did not get pregnant, Boris demanded that I visit a doctor. This was a bitter pill for me. I was always shy, and it embarrassed me to be examined by a gynecologist. I told Boris it was too early to go to doctors, and he fell into a rage. The idea that someone could see things differently from the way he did made him furious. I went to a gynecologist, and he came to the conclusion that I was a hundred percent normal. The doctor suggested that it would be quite appropriate for my husband to be examined too. I told Boris, and he immediately made an appointment. He went through a multitude of tests, and it was established that he was sterile, not I.

"It was a blow for both of us. I let it slip out that perhaps we should adopt a child. Immediately, Boris became hysterical. He screamed that never in his life would he take into his house a bastard whose parents were criminals and who would grow up to be a criminal himself. He yelled so loudly I was afraid the neighbors would come running. I kept assuring him that I wouldn't adopt anyone against his will and he needn't create scandals, but when he fell into a rage he couldn't be quieted. I must say sometimes his screams were more welcomed than his silence.

"Actually, Boris carried on long telephone conversations with his broker. Sometimes they spoke for an hour, even longer. This broker was a private consultant, not a member of a brokerage firm. In all my married years I never met him. In the five years we lived together I couldn't make Boris go with me to a theater, a movie, or a concert. He was interested in nothing but money. I must tell you all this so that you'll understand what happened later. Please be patient."

"Yes, I'm patient," I said.

We rested for a few minutes, and the woman took a lozenge and a sip of water. I asked, "What kind of a married life was this?"

The woman's eyes lit up. "It's good that you asked me," she said. "I wanted to talk about it myself. We had two exceedingly narrow beds. He never let me buy anything except food. He alone was the buyer and he always looked for bargains. No, it wasn't good between us, and it reached a stage where I thanked God when he left me alone."

"What was he? Impotent?"

"Not exactly, but he did everything in dismal silence. I had often the impression I was having an affair with a corpse."

"No caresses?"

"In the beginning some, but later he cooled off completely. He was one of those old-fashioned men who believed that the purpose of marriage was only to have children. Since we couldn't have children, sexual relations were superfluous."

"Was he perverse in some sense?" I asked.

The woman thought it over. "In a sense, yes—you'll soon hear."

"What happened?" I asked.

"The worst trauma of our lives began with a joke."

"Whose joke?" I asked.

"Mine, not his. He was not a joker. Once in a while he tried to talk to me about stocks. God shouldn't punish me, but this topic bored me stiff. Later on I thought that I should have listened to him and shown some interest in his business, but somehow I couldn't do it. The moment he began to talk about it I started to yawn. I hated his business. A man should have a profession, do something, leave the house, not sit day and night and wait for stocks to go up or down a few cents. The fact is he didn't allow me to leave the house. He kept me prisoner. When I did go out to buy food I had to tell him in advance where I was going, what I was going to spend, and how long I'd be out of the house. I can't understand to this day how I could bear all this for five years. A war was going on, the Jews in Europe were destroyed, and I rationalized that my situation was still better than to languish in a concentration camp.

"One evening we were sitting together in our living room. I read the first pages of the newspaper, and he took out the business section. Suddenly he said, 'The oils are depressed.'

"I don't know why, but I said, 'So am I.'

"I'm not sure whether I said it to myself or to him. He looked at me, astonished, sad, angry, and asked, 'Why are you depressed? What do you miss? You aren't happy with me?'

"'It's only a joke,' I said.

"'Do you regret that you married me?' he asked. 'Do you want a divorce?'

"'No, Boris, I don't want a divorce,' I said.

"'Am I not the right husband for you?' he continued. 'Am I too old for you?'

"'And what if you are too old?' I asked. 'Can you become younger? Do you want to go to Professor Voronoff and implant monkey glands into your body?' I expected him to smile. I had heard there was a professor in Europe, I think in Switzerland, who tried to make the old young. I'm not sure Professor Voronoff was still alive at the time. I said it just to hear my own voice, perhaps to hear his voice. He looked at me not only with scorn but also with a kind of regret and pity. He said, 'I couldn't let you adopt a child, but if you want to adopt a young lover I have nothing against it.'

"'Boris, I don't want to adopt anybody,' I said. 'It was just talk. It's time you weren't so literal, so serious.'

"'Well, let it be so,' he said, and he left for the room he called his office.

"I think it was the winter of 1944. Hitler was on his way down, but the Jewish misfortune had no end. Reports came that all the Jews in Europe were doomed. I never heard Boris say anything about the Jewish situation. I lived all those years with a man I never understood and who remained a stranger to me.

"A few weeks passed, I don't remember how many. The last few days Boris had left the house before breakfast and did not return for lunch, as was his custom. This was something new in our lives. One evening he came home late. I waited for him in the living room and was reading a book I had borrowed from the public library. I had left his supper in the kitchen, but he told me he'd already eaten in a restaurant. He told me a son of his sister in London, a boy of fourteen, had come from England some time ago. His sister had feared that some misfortune would happen to him in the bombardments. The boy, whose name was Douglas, was a prodigy in mathematics and physics. He was accepted here in New York at a school for prodigies. Boris had consented that the boy should live with us. 'You never told me much about your sister,' I said. 'I had the impression you two were at odds.'

" 'It's true,' he said, 'that we always disagreed. I was still a boy when she married, to a man who was good for nothing, a perfect idiot, but her son, thank God, takes after my family, the Kozlovs. You'll not need to be alone any more. I want to tell you something else,' he continued. 'I've rented an office for myself. My business is expanding. I'm drowning in paperwork. I've begun to invest in stocks for some German refugees, and Brooklyn is too far for them. My office is in Manhattan.'

"Boris never spoke for so long, especially about his family. As a rule he only reproached me, and then he didn't speak, but screamed.

"I said to him, 'Everything comes so suddenly.'

" 'Not so suddenly,' Boris said. 'I thought everything over very carefully.'

" 'Why didn't you ever mention to me that your nephew is in America?' I asked.

" 'I mention it now: He's an unusual boy. I took to him right away. He arrived here through Halifax, Nova Scotia. I'm sure you'll like him. He'll study in a special school for talented youngsters. Everything has already been arranged. Since my office is free now it can be his room. I'll buy him a bed, but until then he can sleep on the sofa. You have all the right to say no. I'm not going to force him on you.'

" 'Boris, you know very well I'll agree,' I said.

" 'He'll be here tomorrow morning,' Boris said, and went to his room.

"My first reaction when I heard the news was joy. I could not stand the loneliness anymore. God must have heard my prayers, I thought. But it soon became clear to me that Boris had contrived the whole plan in his conspiratorial manner. Men like Boris are bound by their nature to make plans way in advance and execute them precisely. They forget nothing. Even though he excoriated Stalin and called him a bloodthirsty Asian and a Genghis Khan of the twentieth century, I often thought Boris was a Stalin himself. We'll never know what people like these think. They always weave spider webs of vengeance. Did Boris bring this boy to tempt me and to be able later to sue me for infidelity? Was he connected with a lawyer? Was he in contact with another woman with a lot of money, or stocks? I could have easily saved him these sly tricks. If he had asked me for a divorce I would have given it to him without difficulties. I could still have gotten a job as a chambermaid or a saleswoman in a department store. During the war unemployment had ended. Nevertheless, I decided not to let myself be caught like an animal in a net. I intended to treat the boy from England with friendship but not to allow myself to fall into any entanglements.

"The next day Douglas came, and I'm ashamed to admit to you I fell in love with him at first sight. He was beautiful, slender, and tall for his age. Besides, he had a warmth that simply bewitched me. He called me 'Aunt,' but kissed me like a lover. He told me about his parents, and from his talk it became clear to me that his mother was a Boris in a skirt. She was a complete business-lady and had become rich from the war. She was separated from her husband, Douglas's father. The whole Kozlov family consisted of pedants and misanthropes, but Douglas seemed to have taken after his father, who came from a noble background. Douglas showed me his father's photograph. All my yearnings for a child and love, all my femininity and longings for motherhood had awakened in me. I kept reminding Douglas that he was still a child, that I could have been his mother, but he refused to listen to me.

"A day or two after Douglas's arrival Boris began to go to the office every morning, and I knew it was not accidental. There were times I wanted to ask Boris, 'What's the meaning of all this? What are you aiming at?' But I knew he would not tell me the truth. Together with the love for the boy I was assaulted by a silent fear of cold and cunning calculations. Someone had prepared a trap for me, and I was destined to fall into it."

"Did you fall into it?" I asked.

The old woman hesitated for a while. "Yes."

"Immediately?" I asked.

"Almost immediately," she said.

"How?"

"One night Boris did not come home to sleep. He had told me he was supposed to go to Boston, but I knew it was a lie. What did I have to lose? When a man goes to such lengths a woman has nothing to hope for. Boris did not come home, and Douglas without asking came into my bed. I never knew that a young boy like this could be so passionate."

"Those are supposed to be the man's strongest years." I said.

"Really? For me, it was partially curiosity and resignation. When someone spits on you you don't owe him any loyalty. Instead of spending one night in Boston Boris was gone three nights. I knew for sure he was in New York. Boston is not a center of stock speculation. When he finally called us and said that he was back in New York I told him, 'What you wanted did happen.'"

"What did he say?" I asked.

"He said that he did it all for me. I said, 'You didn't have to bring your nephew from England. You didn't have to go into such acrobatics,' but he kept on saying that he had seen that I was unhappy and he wanted to help me. I was afraid that he might try to punish Douglas. Who knows what goes on in such a crippled brain? However, when he came home that evening he was as friendly to the boy as before. He asked him many questions about school. We ate supper together, and I was surprised to see that Douglas did not show any embarrassment. Can a boy of his age be so clever and cynical? Did the two of them have an agreement? I still don't know the answer."

"How long did the whole thing last?" I asked.

"He came in the summer, and in the fall he was accepted to a college, not here in New York, but somewhere in the Middle West. He came to bid me farewell, and we spent the evening together. He told me that he would never forget me, that I'd enriched his life. He even promised he'd visit me on his winter vacation. He never smoked before, but that evening he smoked one cigarette after another. He brought me flowers and a bottle of cognac. I put the flowers into a vase and poured myself a tea glass of the drink, which I gulped down in the bathroom. He asked me about his uncle, and I told him that he would come home late, but I had to go to sleep early and that he must leave. 'Why, Auntie?' he asked, and I said, 'Because I'm tired.' 'I hoped that we would spend the night together,' he said, and I said, 'The last night one has to spend with oneself.'

"He kissed me, and I told him to leave. He hesitated for a while, and then he left. I waited for a minute or two and then I jumped out the window. We lived on the fourth floor. Thank God, I fell on the pavement and not on an innocent passerby."

"You had made the decision earlier?" I asked.

"No, but I knew all the time that this was what Boris expected and I had to comply."

"Still, you remained alive and he did not succeed," I said.

"Yes, to my regret. This is the whole story. I once heard you say on the radio that you take many of your themes from readers who come to tell you their stories, and I decided to be one of them. All I ask is that you change the names."

"What does a person think in such seconds?" I asked.

"In such seconds one doesn't think: One does what fate wants you to."

"What happened since then?"

"Nothing really. I broke my arms. I broke my legs. I broke my skull, and the doctors tried to mend me. They are still trying."

"Where's Boris?"

"I never heard from him or his nephew. I believe they both are somewhere in England."

"You're not divorced?"

"What for? No. I get reparation monies from the Germans. I need little, but every few weeks I must go to the hospital. Thank God, they don't let me become a public charge. I won't live too much longer. I came to tell you only one thing: that of all the hopes a human being can have the most splendid is death. I tasted it, and whoever tasted this ecstasy must laugh at all the other so-called pleasures. That which man fears from the cradle to the grave is the highest joy."

"Still, seldom does anyone want to speed up this kind of joy," I said.

The woman did not answer and I thought she had not heard my words, but then she said, "The anticipation is part of the joy."

Translated by the author and Lester Goran

The Smuggler

THE TELEPHONE rang, and when I answered I heard a murmuring, a stuttering and coughing. After a while a man said, "You most probably forgot about it, but you once promised to inscribe my books, I mean your books. In Philadelphia where we met you gave me your address and telephone number. Your address is the same but you've changed your telephone to a private number. I got it from your secretary but I had to promise her that I wouldn't take much of your time."

He tried to remind me of my speech that evening in Philadelphia and I realized it had happened some ten years ago. He said to me, "Are you hiding? In those days one could still find you in the telephone book. I do the same thing in my own small way. I avoid people."

"Why?" I asked.

"To explain this would take too much time and I promised not to bother you too long."

We made an appointment. He was supposed to come to my apartment late in the evening. It was in December and a heavy snow had fallen in New York. From his idiomatic Yiddish it was clear to me he must be one of those Polish refugees who emigrated to America long after the war. Those who came to America in the earlier years interspersed their Yiddish with English words. I stood at the window and looked out on Broadway. The street below was white and the sky had a violet tinge. The radiator was seething quietly and sang out a tune which reminded me of our tiled stove on Krochmalna Street and the cricket behind it and the kerosene lamp over my father's desk. From experience I knew that those who make appointments with me come earlier than the agreed time. I expected any moment to hear a ringing at the door, but half an hour passed and he did not show up. I was looking for stars in the reddish sky, but I knew in advance that I would not find one in the New York heavens. Then I heard something like a scratch at my door. I went to open it and I saw a little man behind a pushcart heaped up with books. In the cold winter my guest wore a shabby raincoat and a shirt with an open collar and a knitted cap on his head. He asked, "Your door has no bell?"

"Here's the bell button," I said.

"What? I'm half blind. It all comes with the years. We don't die at once but on the installment plan."

"Where did you get so many books of mine? Well, come in."

"I don't want to make your rug wet. I will leave the cart outside. No one will steal it."

"It doesn't matter. Come in."

I helped the man push the cart into the corridor. "I didn't know I'd brought out so many books," I said, and then I asked, "Have I really written so many books in my life?"

"They're not all yours. I also have books about you here, and various magazines and journals as well as translations."

After a while we went into the living room, and I said, "It's winter outside and you're dressed as if it were summer. Aren't you cold?"

"Cold, no. My father, he should rest in peace, used to say, 'No one wears a mask to cover one's nose. The nose doesn't get cold. A poor man is all made of nose flesh.'"

He smiled, and I saw that he had no teeth. I asked him to sit down. He looked to me like those men who live out of doors, like one of those beggars and bums one sees on the Bowery and in the hotels for the homeless. But I also saw the gentleness of his narrow face and in his eyes.

"Where do you keep all these books?" I asked. "In your apartment where you live?"

He shrugged his shoulders. "I live nowhere," he said. "In our little village in Poland there were yeshiva boys who ate every day in a different home. I sleep every night in a different house. I have here a brother-in-law, the husband of my late sister, and I sleep in his house two nights a week. I have a friend, a landsman, and I can sleep over there when there's a need. I used to live in a building in Williamsburg in Brooklyn, but the house was condemned and they wrecked it. While I was sick in the hospital thieves stole everything except my books. My landsman keeps them in his basement. I get reparation money from the Germans. After what happened to my family and my people I don't want to be settled anyplace."

"What did you do before the war?" I asked.

The man pondered for a while and smiled. "I did what you told me to do in one of your articles, to smuggle myself, to sneak by, to muddle through. I was reading you in Poland. You once wrote that human nature is such that one cannot do anything in a straight line. You always have to maneuver between the powers of wickedness and madness.

"In the time of the first World War, I was still a little boy, but my mother and sister smuggled meat from Galicia and brought back from there tobacco and other contraband. Without this we would have all starved to death. When they were caught they were beaten cruelly. There were five children in our home, an old grandmother, a cripple, and my father, who could do nothing except study Mishnah and recite psalms or the Zohar. I asked him why all these plagues descended on us and he said the same thing you said. In exile one cannot live normally. One must always steal one's way among those who have the power and carry weapons. The moment a man gets some power he becomes wicked, my father said. The one who keeps a knife stabs, the one who has a gun shoots, and the one who has a pen writes laws which are always on the side of the thieves and murderers. When I became older and I began to read worldly books I convinced myself that what my father said about the Jewish people was true about the whole human race and even about the animals. The wolves devour the sheep, the lions kill the zebras. In later years we had in our village communists who said that Comrades Lenin and Stalin would bring justice, but it soon became clear that they behaved like all the others who had power in all generations. Today a victim, tomorrow a tyrant. I read about Darwin and Malthus. These were the laws of life and I decided my father was right. After Poland became independent smuggling ceased, but as always might was right. I hadn't learned any trade, and even if I'd learned how to be a tailor or a shoemaker I hadn't the slightest desire to sit ten hours a day and sew buttons or tack heels and soles on boots. I certainly did not have the desire to get married and create new victims for the new killers. Two of my younger brothers had become communists and ended up in Stalin's prisons or the gold mines of the north. A third brother went to Israel and fell from an Arab bullet. My parents and a sister died by the Nazis. Yes, I became a smuggler, and what I smuggled was myself. My body is my contraband. My coming here to America in 1949 was, I may say, a triumph of my smuggling. The chances for me to remain alive and come to the United States were smaller than small. If you ask me what my occupation is my answer is, 'I am a Yiddish poet.' How can you know whether a person is a poet or not? If an editor needs to fill a hole in his magazine and he publishes a poem of yours, then you are a poet. If it doesn't happen then you're just a graphomaniac. I never had any luck with editors and so I belong to the second category."

"May I ask why you need autographs?" I said.

"Some little madness everyone must have. If Jack the Ripper were resurrected from his grave people would run to get his autograph, especially women. I was given an ego, a wanter, and I wage war with it. It wants to eat but I tell it to fast. It wants honors but I bring shame on it. Ego-schmego, I call it, hunger-schmunger. I do everything to spite it. It wants fresh rolls for breakfast and I give it stale bread. It likes strong coffee but I make it drink tepid water from the faucet. It still dreams about young women but it remains a virgin. Ten times a day I tell it, 'Get away from me, I need you like a hole in the head; you play the part of a friend but you're my worst enemy.' Just for spite I make it read old newspapers which I find on the floor of the subway. Thank God, I'm the stronger one, at least strong enough to make it miserable."

"Do you believe in God?" I asked.

"Yes, I do. The scientists tell us that a cosmic bomb exploded twenty billion years ago and it created all the worlds. A week does not pass when they don't discover new parts in the atom and new functions. Just the same, they maintain that it's all an accident. They've gotten a new idol which they call evolution. They ascribe more miracles to that evolution than you can find in all the books about saints in all the religions. It's good for their rapacious business. Since there is no God, no plan, no purpose, you can hit and cheat and kill with a clean conscience."

"What is your God?" I asked. "A heavenly wolf?"

"Yes, a cosmic wolf, the dictator of all dictators. It is all His work: the hungry wolf, the frightened sheep, the struggle for existence, the cancers, the heart attacks, insanity. He created them all, Hitler, Stalin, Khmelnitski, and Petlyura. It is said that He creates new angels every day. They flatter Him, sing odes to Him, and then they are liquidated, just like the old Bolsheviks."

He became quiet, and I inscribed all the adult books, all the children's books, and all his magazines. "Where did you get all this?" I asked.

"I bought it, I didn't steal it," he said. "When I can save up a few dollars I buy books, not only yours; mostly scientific ones."

"But you don't believe in the scientists," I said.

"Not in their cosmology and sociology."

"If you'd like, you can leave me some of your manuscripts," I said. "I'd be glad to read some of your poems."

My guest hesitated for a while. "What for? It's not necessary."

"I feel that you have talent," I said. "Who knows? You may be a great poet."

"No, no, not by any measurement. A man has to be something and I dabble in poetry. Thank you for the good words anyhow. Who needs poetry in our times? Not even the poets."

"There are some who need it."

"No."

My guest stretched out one hand to me and with the other began to push his wagon. I accompanied him to the door. I proposed to him again that I would like to read his works, and he said, "I thank you very much. What can poetry do? Nothing. There were quite a number of poets among the Nazis. In the day they dragged out children from their cribs and burned them and at night they wrote poems. Believe me, these two actions don't contradict one another. Absolutely not. Good night."

Translated by the author and Lester Goran

Gifts

I MET him near a bank where I cashed a check I received from a Yiddish newspaper. I was a young writer and he—I will call him Max Blendever—was known as a Zionist leader in Warsaw and a councilman in the city hall. He had quarreled with the major Zionist group and had become the head of a faction of extremists who called themselves revisionists. I recognized him from his pictures in the Yiddish press. He was of medium height, broad-shouldered, with a large head, high cheekbones, and thick eyebrows. I had noticed that politicians were inclined to let their eyebrows grow, most probably to appear more masculine or to hide their sly eyes. Max Blendever was known as a fighter. In the city council he assailed the anti-Semites violently. He had enemies not only among the Gentiles but also among the Jews who contended that he was too aggressive and did damage with his attacks.

As a rule, I would have never stopped a stranger in the street, especially not a famous man. But I had recently heard that his wife, Carola, had died in a car accident. This woman, whom I had never met, had sent me a New Year's card and a bottle of Carmel wine on the eve of Rosh Hashanah. The gift arrived at the address of the journal where I was a proofreader. It was a complete surprise to me. Was Carola Blendever a Yiddishist? Did she read me in the little magazines that never had more than a few hundred readers? As far as I knew, most of the wives of the Zionist leaders were half assimilated. I wanted to send the husband a condolence card when she passed away, but nothing ever came of it. I was one of those who considered him too arrogant. We Jews, I believed, should not forget that we are a minority in every country in the world, and should act accordingly.

But now that I encountered him face to face, I went over to him and said:

"You don't know me, but everyone knows you. My name is . . ."

"I know you, I heard of you," Max Blendever replied. He pulled out the cigar from between his lips, extended his hand to me, and shook mine vigorously. He said, "My late wife had mentioned your name once in a while. I am a politician, not a writer. Besides, I am for Hebrew, not for Yiddish, but I buy Yiddish books and journals. They are sent to me from time to time. In what direction are you walking? Perhaps you can accompany me a part of the way. You have certainly heard about the misfortune with my wife."

"Yes. I am terribly sorry. I had received a gift from her. I could not understand where she had heard about me and how I deserved it."

Max Blendever, who walked so quickly that I could barely keep up with him, suddenly stopped.

"A gift, huh? What sort of gift?"

"A bottle of Carmel wine."

Something like an angry smile appeared on his face. He measured me from head to toe. "You were not the only one," he said. "People have different passions. Some smoke opium, others take hashish. There are those whose greatest pleasure is to run in the forests and hunt bears or wolves. My Carola, may she rest in peace, had a passion for sending gifts. I was a poor boy when I married her, but she was a rich daughter. She received a handsome dowry and she spent it all on gifts."

We walked for a while in silence. Max Blendever took long strides. At Marshalkowski Street, he glanced around and said, "Now that I already began telling you about her, maybe you would like to go with me to a café? Let's drink a glass of coffee together."

"It would be an honor and a pleasure," I answered.

"What is the honor? Each of us does his own work, right or wrong. God will judge us if He exists. And if He doesn't exist, it is too bad. If you don't drink coffee, you can take a glass of tea, cocoa, or whatever you prefer. I like black coffee without cream or sugar."

We went to a café, and it was half empty in the middle of the day. A waiter came right over to our table. Max Blendever ordered black coffee for himself and tea with lemon for me. He re-lit his cigar with a lighter and said:

"Since you are a fiction writer, or plan to become one, you must be interested in people's character and their idiosyncrasies. I always knew that different types of philanthropists existed in the world. American millionaires give away fortunes for the most bizarre causes. One millionairess in Chicago, a spinster, left two million dollars to her poodle. But my Carola's passion to send gifts, often to complete strangers, was something new to me. She never told me about them, although I heard her speak about various presents. I thought this was the way rich women behaved. With them, every emotion must be expressed in concrete terms. Having had little experience with the so-called beautiful sex, I left her to her own devices. You are looking at a man who never had another woman aside from his lawful wife. For me, affairs were only a waste of time. I had the illusion that all females were more or less alike."

"If only I could have such an illusion," I said.

"Huh? My real passion was politics. It began when I was still a boy. From childhood on, I always heard Jews lamenting about their fate to live in Exile. I thought to myself: 'What can come from all this moaning and sighing? Why not do something?' And this is how I became what I am today. My father taught me that a Jew must bow his head when people abuse him and offer the other cheek. This was sheer nonsense to me. But let me return to my story. Maybe you could even write about it someday, but don't mention my name."

"I certainly wouldn't."

"Yes, my wife. I had, as they say, one God and one wife. I loved her and believe she loved me too. But her mania of sending gifts had always baffled me. Of course she also had a buying mania. You cannot give gifts without buying them first. I sometimes think that her drive to buy things was her passion number one. I could never take a walk with her. She was forever window-shopping. Once, we were walking in the vicinity of the Catholic cemetery in Powazek. We passed a store which displayed coffins and sure enough she stopped to stare at them. I asked her, 'Do you want to buy a coffin? You know that Jews don't bury their dead in coffins, at least not here in Poland.' But you could not tear her away from a store window. I tell you this to show how compulsive her buying mania was. I discovered about her obsession for gifts later. Let me make it short. Every year she sent gifts to hundreds of men, women, and children. She only waited for an excuse to celebrate some event, a holiday, a birthday, an engagement party, a wedding, a circumcision, you name it. I found a notebook where she listed countless candidates and occasions for her benefactions. She had virtually given away her entire inheritance. As you can imagine, I was often on the road—congresses, conferences, an endless number of party meetings. You know our Jewish organizations. Every party has its factions, and sooner or later every faction splits. Here in Warsaw we have a leftist politician, a certain Dr. Bruk, who has already been everything in his life: a Bundist, a communist, a member of the right Labor Zionists, the left Labor Zionists, an anarchist, a Sejmist, a Territorialist. His last party had split so many times until it became a faction of a faction of a faction. A joke is told that when his present remnant of a party decides to hold a general meeting, instead of a hall they hire a *droshky* pulled by a single horse.

"Needless to say, a man with my temperament and my big mouth has no lack of enemies. It cannot be any other way. But in the few years I began to realize that my enemies had somehow become more lenient than they used to be. Even when they attacked me, they did it, so to say, with kid gloves. Their arguments were mollified with bits of praise. Here and there they even pointed out some of my merits. 'What happened? Why have they become so charitable towards me?' I wondered. 'Do they consider me so old and far gone that I am altogether harmless? Or have my opponents grown slightly civilized in their old age?' I was too busy to ponder it. Yes, you guessed it! Carola had decided that I didn't have enough friends for her barrage of gifts and began sending presents to my enemies.

"When I found out about it I raised hell. It was the first and last time I spoke about divorce. I knew none of my enemies could ever have believed that Carola had done all this without my knowledge. They were all convinced that the wolf had become a lamb and decided to pad his career with bribery. I screamed so that our neighbors came running. My wife had entirely destroyed the little reputation I had built up in a lifetime. She had completely ruined me. How do they say it? A thousand enemies cannot do more harm to a man than a well-meaning wife can do. I say well-meaning because when my anger had subsided (how long can someone rage and break plates?) and I tried to explain to her what a catastrophe all this was for me, she swore that she could not understand why I made such a fuss. She was saying, 'What is so terrible about showing a little good will? Your enemies actually have the same goal as you: to help the Jews. It is only that their approach is different.'

"My dear young man, I don't know myself why I'm confiding all this to you. Until now, I haven't told it to anyone. After brooding over it a long time and eating my heart out, I made peace with the fact that the damage was done. What could I do? Write letters to all my adversaries explaining that my wife sent them gifts without my consent? I would only make myself ridiculous. I decided to do what I believed was my duty and that what my enemies think of me or say did not matter. I can only tell you that out of all the gifts the bottle of wine she sent to you was the most sensible. You are a young writer and have nothing to do with politics. But to send a Christmas gift to the greatest anti-Semite in Poland—Adam Nowaczynski—is absolutely an act that borders on madness."

"She did this?" I asked.

"Yes, exactly. The irony of it is that this deranged Jew-baiter wrote her an exceptionally friendly letter where he praised the Jews to Heaven. He wrote, more or less, that he maligns the Jews only because he knows how intelligent they are, what sharp minds they have developed by studying the Talmud, and how dangerous their competition is for the naïve and gullible Poles who can be outsmarted so easily. Let us find a way to utilize our respective potentials for the common good of all Polish citizens, and so on and so on. Like all demagogues, he believed his own lies."

"Giving presents is not something new in our history," I said. "When Jacob heard that his brother Esau was coming to meet him with four hundred armed ruffians, he sent a gift which would have been worth a treasure today."

"Yes. Yes. Yes. The weaker ones always try to curry favor, but it doesn't help for long," Max Blendever said. "They take what you give them, embrace you, kiss you, call you brother, and a little later they assault you again. The truth is that Carola did this not to help the Jews. It was nothing but her addiction to gifts. Freud would have interpreted it with hair-splitting casuistry, most probably with some newly discovered gift complex. He and his disciples must rationalize every sort of human peculiarity. But in what lousy book is it written that everything can be explained? My theory is that nothing can be explained."

"This is also my theory," I said. "When literature goes too far into explanations and commentaries, it becomes tedious and false."

"Yes, right," Max Blendever agreed. "Your tea has gotten cold. Should I order for you a glass of hot tea?"

"Thank you, no. Definitely not."

"Why not?" Max Blendever asked and I replied:

"This can never be explained."

Translated by Deborah Menashe

FROM

THE DEATH
OF METHUSELAH

AND OTHER STORIES

Contents

The Jew from Babylon   593

The House Friend   600

Burial at Sea   607

The Recluse   614

Disguised   622

The Accuser and the Accused   631

A Peephole in the Gate   636

The Bitter Truth   655

The Impresario   662

Logarithms   672

Runners to Nowhere   679

The Missing Line   687

The Hotel   693

Dazzled   703

Sabbath in Gehenna   711

The Last Gaze   716

The Death of Methuselah   725

Author's Note

Whenever I begin to ponder modern man and his disappointment with his own culture, my mind leads me back to the history of creation as it is described by the divine genius who wrote the Book of Genesis. The very creation of man became a disappointment to God. He had to destroy his own masterpiece, which had become corrupted. According to the Talmud and the Midrash, the corruption was all sexual. Even the animals became sexually perverted at the time of the flood, and perhaps later in Sodom and Gomorrah.

In my story "The Death of Methuselah," I explore this theme. Methuselah, the man who lived longer than any other human being, was madly in love with a she-demon I call Naahma. She and her lover Ashiel were directing a conference of perverts and sadists from all over the world. Evil had become man's greatest art, his main achievement. However, there is a spark of hope, because Methuselah's grandson Noah has undertaken the mission to save mankind from utter destruction, in his ark. This story was not planned as most of my other work was. It almost wrote itself "automatically." It told the reader and perhaps myself the story of cosmic and human art. Art must not be all rebellion and spite; it can also have the potential of building and correction. It can also in its own small way attempt to mend the mistakes of the eternal builder in whose image man was created.

All the stories in this collection were edited by my friend and redactor of many years Robert Giroux. Many thanks to him and to all the translators who have helped me prepare this, my tenth collection of stories in English.

I.B.S.

The Jew from Babylon

THE JEW from Babylon, as the miracle worker was called, traveled all night in a wagon that was taking him from Lublin to the village of Tarnigrod. The driver, a small man with broad shoulders, was silent throughout the journey. He nodded and cracked his whip at the horse, which walked slowly, step by step. The old nag would cock her ears and look back with large eyes that expressed human curiosity and reflected the light of the full moon. She seemed to wonder at their strange passenger, dressed in a velvet coat lined with fur, a fur hat on his head. She even lifted her black upper lip, which formed a sort of horse smile. The miracle worker shuddered and murmured an incantation, which made the driver realize how dangerous this passenger was.

"Giddyup, you lazy beast!"

The wagon passed plowed fields, haystacks, and a spinning windmill that emerged, disappeared, and reemerged. Its outspread arms seemed to point their way. An owl was hooting, and a shooting star tore itself away from the heavens and left a fiery wake behind. The miracle worker wrapped himself in his woolen shawl.

"Woe is me!" he groaned. "I no longer have any strength for them." He was referring to the netherworld creatures, the demons with whom he had waged war for a lifetime. Now that he had become old and frail, they had begun to take their revenge.

He had first appeared in Poland some forty-odd years ago—a tall man, lean as a stick, in a long yellow-and-white-striped robe, with the sandals and white stockings worn by Jews from Yemen and other Arabic lands. He called himself Kaddish ben Mazliach—a strange name—and maintained that he had learned the arts of clairvoyance and healing in Babylon. He could cure insomnia and madness, exorcise dybbuks, and help bridegrooms who suffered from impotence or from spells brought about by the Evil Eye. He also possessed a black mirror in which the vanished and the dead could be seen. He conducted himself as a pious Jew—on cold winter nights he even went to the unheated ritual baths, and he fasted on Mondays and Thursdays—but the rabbis and the community leaders shunned him, accusing him of being a sorcerer and a messenger of the Unclean Host. There were rumors that he had a wife of ill repute in the city of Rome, just as the False Messiah, the cursed Sabbatai Zevi, had had in his day. In whatever town he visited, pregnant women were hidden from his sight and the girls were made to wear double aprons, one in front and one behind, as a protection. Parents did not allow their children to look at him. In Lublin, where he settled in his old age after many years of wandering, he was not permitted to live in the Jewish quarter, or to enter the synagogues and study-houses, but was forced to find housing on the outskirts of the city in a broken-down hut. It pained one to look at him. His long face was brick red, and the skin was peeling. His scraggly beard pointed in all directions, as if a permanent wind blew on it. His right eye was closed, blinded by fear, it was said. His hands shook and his head bobbed like that of a newborn infant. Scholars and cabalists had warned him long ago that he was playing with fire and that the powers of evil would not let him get off easy.

In the still autumn night, Kaddish curled up on his seat in the wagon beside the long shadow that traveled with him and mumbled, "An arrow in thine eyes, Satan, Kuzu Bemuchzas, Kuzu."

Born in the Holy Land, the son of a polygamous Sephardic Jew and of his young deaf-mute wife, a Tartar and a convert to Judaism, Kaddish ben Mazliach had wandered throughout the world with his cameos and incantations. He had visited Persia, Syria, Egypt, and Morocco. He had lived in Baghdad and Bukhara. He healed not only Jews but Arabs and Turks, and although in Lublin the Polish rabbis had excommunicated him and he was treated like a leper, he remained a healer and a magician. He had saved up a bagful of diamonds and pearls, which hung hidden around his neck. He had never given up hope that in his old age he would do penance and return to the land of Israel. But luck was not always on his side. A number of times he was robbed and beaten on the road and his money stolen from him. He married several times, but the women were afraid of him and dragged him to the rabbis for a divorce, and he left them.

Just now, when his health was failing, the Evil Ones had begun to torment him and take revenge for all the times he had dominated them with his sorcery. For several years he had not been able to stay asleep through a single night. When he dozed off, he heard female laughter and the sounds of mock-wedding melodies, sung by she-demons and played on fiddles. Sometimes goblins tore at his beard and tugged at his side-locks or knocked at his windowpane. At other times they mocked him, moving his possessions from one corner to another. They tore threads from his fringed garment and prayer shawl. Naked and barefooted maidens with braids hanging to their waists sat on his bed giggling, revealing their white teeth in the darkness. They stole his gold coins—he could feel their fingers slipping into his breast pocket. They twisted their hair around his throat as if to choke him, whining and pleading with him to give himself to them so fiercely that he fainted.

"Kaddish," they said, "either way you have lost the World to Come. Surrender and become one of us."

Kaddish knew that hordes of lapiutes were waiting for his death so they could grab hold of his sinful soul and tear it to shreds. More than once when he examined the script of his mezuzah, he found that the sacred words on the parchment had been erased. His cabalistic books were eaten away by mice and moths. His phylacteries were cracked. Even though his hut on the outskirts of Lublin was heated, there was perpetual cold in the air and a cellar-like darkness in the rooms. To protect himself from theft, he hid his belongings in trunks covered with hide and reinforced with copper rings, all to no avail. No Jewish maid or housekeeper was willing to work for him. The old Gentile woman who cleaned his house hung crosses on the walls, and brought in a wild tomcat and a vicious dog. In order to avoid non-kosher food, he did the cooking himself, but the sprites and imps threw handfuls of salt in the dishes so that he could not take the food into his mouth.

Things were always the worst on the Holy Days. Toward Sabbath eve, he covered his table with a stained cloth and lit two candles in tarnished candlesticks, but they always blew out. He dreamed of creating pigeons and tapping wine from the wall, using the power of the cabala, but of late his miracles succeeded less and less. His memory had deteriorated so much that he had forgotten it was forbidden to kindle a fire on the Sabbath, and he began to smoke his pipe. The dog snarled at him and tried to bite him. Even the woman's little rabbits, kept as pets, had become insolent and crawled into his bed. It was no wonder that, whenever he was asked to perform some magic or healing or divination, he accepted no matter how far or how difficult the trip.

"I am lost anyhow. Let me at least save a single soul," he decided.

Now he was traveling to the village of Tarnigrod, to the rich Reb Falik Chaifetz, whose new home had suddenly begun to rot with fungi, and wild mushrooms were growing on his walls. Even though he was sitting up in the wagon, Kaddish was napping. His head hung low with fatigue, and he snored with a thin whistle. At dawn the sky became all aglow, and the road was obscured with a dense mist, as if they were approaching the open sea. The driver now walked cautiously beside the wagon, step by step, since people had warned him not to sit too close to the magician. Only when the mare made trouble—standing up on her hind legs and neighing— did the driver whip and scold her: "Calm down, old carcass! No horse's business!"

For a whole day Kaddish sat in Reb Falik Chaifetz's half-empty house, preparing the charms and amulets necessary for the purification of the dwelling's sickness. The rooms were damp and yellow spots covered the moist walls. Kaddish was sure that an evil spirit was hidden somewhere, perhaps in a kerchief with witch's knots, or in a cameo with unholy names, or in the hair of a mooncalf. As soon as he entered the house, he had got a whiff of the putrid smell. There was no doubt that the spirit of an enemy had lodged itself here, two-faced, unclean, and utterly vicious. Kaddish had searched in all the corners, holding a candle in his hand. He checked the chimney, the stove, and poked around between sooted cracks and nooks. He climbed the spiral stairwell to the garret and then went down to the cellar. Reb Falik accompanied him through the entire house. Kaddish set all the spiderwebs on fire, and giant spiders with white bellies slid off while his bluish lips were muttering spells. He spat on all sides where the unseen might lurk.

It was perhaps his last and most decisive battle with the Evil Ones. If they didn't surrender this time, how would they be driven away into the desert behind the black mountains forever?

Kaddish had come clandestinely to Tarnigrod. This is how it had been stipulated between him and Reb Falik Chaifetz. Nevertheless the townspeople had somehow learned of his coming. Even before his arrival, many of them gathered in front of Reb Falik's house. Women in clusters were pointing at him and whispering to one another. A few daring youths, climbing on each other's shoulders, tried to peek in between the cracks of the closed shutters. Some peasants brought their cripples, epileptics, their mad and their lame to the miracle worker. A mother carried her child ill with a seizure, its eyes rolling in their sockets. A father dragged a lunatic son, bound like an animal to a wagon. One woman brought a wench with a growth of beard on her face.

Reb Falik Chaifetz came out and admonished the crowd that no cure would come from all this. He begged them to go away, but the mob grew larger. Kaddish opened a top-floor window, stuck out a disheveled head, and pleaded, "People! I have no strength left. Don't torment me." He nevertheless received the sick and the lame all day long.

Kaddish was eager to leave town as early as possible. But suddenly the beadle came late in the evening and announced that the rabbi wanted to see him. Kaddish went with him to the rabbi's house, where the shutters were already closed for the night. The old rabbi was dressed in a black robe, his hat sat crooked on his head, and his waist was girded with a thick sash. He looked at the magician with fury, measuring him from head to toe, and asked, "Are you the infamous Kaddish ben Mazliach?"

"I am, rabbi."

"Your name, Kaddish, means holy, but you are unclean and defiled," the rabbi shouted. "Don't think that the world sleeps. You are a wizard who keeps company with the dead."

"No, rabbi."

"Don't deny it." The rabbi stamped his foot. "You conjure up demons. We will not endure this in silence."

"I know, rabbi."

"Remember, you will regret it!" the rabbi screamed, and grabbed his long pipe as if to hit Kaddish over the head. "For hundreds of years you will wander among devils and you will not even be permitted to enter hell. The world is not all chaos!"

Kaddish shuddered, attempted to answer, lost his tongue. He wanted to tell of the many people he had saved from death. He slipped his hand into a pocket where he kept letters from grateful patients, written in Hebrew, Ladino, Arabic, and even in Yiddish, but he couldn't move his fingers. He rushed out on shaky legs, hearing voices and laughter. He could not see where he was going.

He decided to return to Lublin at once, but the coachman now refused to take him back. Kaddish had no choice but to stay for the night in the empty house where he had spent the entire day. Reb Falik Chaifetz's maid brought him bedclothes, a candlestick with a thick wax candle, a kettle with hot water, bread, and a bowl of borscht.

The Jew from Babylon tried to eat, but he could not swallow. His head felt as if it were full of sand. An icy wind blew through the room, although the windows were shut. The candle flame flickered and shadows wavered in the corners, crawling like snakes. Large glossy beetles crept over the floor and a rotten stench was in the air. Kaddish lay down on his bed, fully clothed. As he napped briefly, he found himself in the cabalistic city of Sfat. His Yemenite wife knelt before him, took off his sandals, and washed his feet, drinking the water. Suddenly he was thrown out of the bed, as if an earthquake had exploded. All the lights went out. In the darkness the walls appeared to expand, and all the rooms rocked and rolled like a ship in a stormy sea. Bearded images with horns and snouts were pushing him, circling around like wolves. Bats were flying over him. Everything creaked and knocked, as if the house were about to collapse. As always, when the creatures of the night took hold of him, he opened his mouth to exorcise them, but for the first time in his life he had forgotten all the names and conjurations. His heart felt as if it had stopped and he could sense his feet turning cold. The bag which hung around his neck was torn loose, and he heard the gold coins, pearls, and diamonds pour out.

When he finally managed to get outside, Tarnigrod seemed asleep. A bloody red moon glimmered behind the skin of the clouds. Bevies of dogs who slept in the day and prowled around the butcher shops at night barked at him on all sides. He heard the steps of a multitude in a tumult behind him. A sweeping wind caught under his coat, and he was flying. Lights seemed to flare up, and he heard music, drumming, screams of laughter. He realized it was a wedding and he, Kaddish, was the bridegroom. They were dancing toward him on stilts, calling, "*Mazel tov*, Kaddish!" It was clear that the demons were marrying him off to a she-demon. Aghast, and with his last strength, he managed to exclaim, "Shaddai, destroy Satan!"

He made an effort to escape, but his knees were buckling. Long arms embraced him, picked at him from all sides, tore at him, tickled him, kneaded him and slapped him like baker's dough. He was the host of the celebration, its impure joy. They threw themselves at his throat, kissed him, fondled him, raped him. They gored him with their horns, licked him, drowned him in spit and foam. A giant female pressed him to her naked breasts, laid her entire weight over him, and pleaded, "Kaddish, don't shame me. Say, 'By this black ring I espouse thee according to the blasphemy of Satan and Asmodeus.'"

He heard with deafened ears a loud shattering of broken glass, a stamping of feet, lewd laughter, and squealing. A skeleton grandmother with geese feet danced with a braided challah in her hand and did somersaults, calling out the names of Chavriri, Briri, Ketev-Mriri. Kaddish closed his eyes and knew for the first and last time that he was one of them, married to Lilith, the Queen of the Abyss.

In the morning they found him dead, face down on a bare spot, not far from the town. His head was buried in the sand, hands and feet spread out, as if he had fallen from a great height.

Translated by Deborah Menashe

The House Friend

W ̶E WERE sitting in the Café Piccadilly, Max Stein and I, and our talk turned to married women with lovers tolerated by their husbands. "House friends" we used to call such men in the Yiddish Writers' Club. Yes, women—what else could we have talked about? Neither of us was interested in politics or business. I noticed that the men at the other tables were reading the stock and bond reports or the horse-racing results. The women were flipping through illustrated magazines with photographs of princes, princesses, murderers, adventurers, film actors. From time to time, they took out lipsticks and little mirrors and smeared their lips, which were already crimson red. Why do they do it, I asked myself. Whom do they want to impress? The men were all elderly, with gray hair on their temples. If they ever looked up from their newspapers it was to light a cigar or to rattle a spoon against a glass to signal the waiter for the bill. Max Stein, a frustrated painter, tried to make a drawing of me on a sketch pad, but without success. He said to me, "One cannot draw you. Your face changes every second. One moment you look young, another moment old. You have peculiar tics. Even your nose changes from minute to minute. What were we talking about?"

"About house friends."

"Yes, yes, yes. I say something and I lose track of it immediately. Sometimes I'm afraid that I'm getting senile. Men who tolerate house friends know exactly what's going on. They are not deceived for a minute. It is a real need. One day they get married and the next day the house friend appears on the scene. As a matter of fact, they anticipated his coming long before the wedding. These are people who are bored to death with themselves. Such men could only marry women with the same temperament and inclinations. Love is supposed to be an instinct, but what is instinct? Instinct is not blind, or what they call unconscious. The instinct knows what it wants and plans and calculates perfectly. It is often shrewd and prescient. Schopenhauer dwells constantly on the subject of blind will.

But will is far from blind—the very opposite. The intellect is blind. Give me a cigarette."

"The pack is empty," I said.

"Wait a minute." Max Stein went out to buy a pack of cigarettes. He returned and said, "It looks like rain. When I was a boy of sixteen, I was already somebody's house friend. His name was Feivl and I was still called Mottele, not Max. My parents were poor, but Feivl's father owned a dry-goods store on Gesia Street. Feivl was always loaded with money. He went out with a girl by the name of Saltcha, and I was, as it were, the house friend. Every evening they went to a delicatessen for frankfurters with mustard and a mug of beer, always insisting that I come along. I used to ask him, 'What do you need me for?' And he would answer, 'It's awkward for me when we go alone. What can you say to a girl? I ask her about her home, her parents—this, that. But right away she begins to yawn. Somehow Saltcha has got accustomed to you. When you can't come, she makes excuses not to go. She must wash her hair, she has a headache, her shoes have suddenly become too tight, she has an errand to run for her mother.'

"One place or another, we always went as a threesome. On the Sabbath, after the *cholent*, he took Saltcha to the Yiddish theater on Muranowska Street and he always bought tickets for the three of us. I used to tease him: 'Aren't you ever jealous?' And he said, 'Jealous? Why? Saltcha just loves your company. Everything you say is charming. When you are with us she is in high spirits. She's talkative, she laughs, jokes, and she is good to me, too. Without you, she gets nasty and picks on me.' Once, I asked him, 'What will happen when you get married?' And Feivl answered, 'You will have to visit us every day.'

"And so it was. Saltcha, too, came from a wealthy house. Her father gave her quite a large dowry. The wedding took place in the Vienna wedding hall, and I was the best man. I had already begun to paint, and Feivl commissioned me to paint Saltcha's portrait.

"It was fashionable even in those days for a married couple to go on a honeymoon. Feivl and Saltcha's had to be delayed, for some reason, but when at last they were settled they chose Druskieniki—a resort on the river Niemen—and you won't believe me, but man and wife insisted that I join them. When Saltcha's mother heard this, she created an uproar. 'Are you all three going crazy? People have large eyes and long tongues. They will say the worst things, and you will be the laughing-stock of the town.' Saltcha's father was too caught up in his business to be bothered. As for my parents, they couldn't care less. I had already moved out, and there were younger children to worry about. We were poorer than poor and not overly pious. Besides, who cares about the purity of a son? To make it short, Feivl and Saltcha went to Druskieniki, and I went with them. Stop smirking. What you think happened did not happen. At least not then. But I had already kissed Saltcha many times in Feivl's presence and he always encouraged me. If we met and I forgot to kiss her, Feivl would remind me. Wait, I will light a cigarette."

Max Stein lit a cigarette and continued, "There are men and women who don't know what jealousy is. They must share love, and besides, they never suspect anyone. My theory is that every human being is born with all his idiosyncrasies and caprices. Napoleon in his mother's womb was already what he would become, and so were Casanova, Rasputin, Jack the Ripper, as well as such geniuses as Shakespeare, Tolstoy—you name them. You may say that there are other factors involved —environment, education, all those phrases of the sociologists—but the way I see it, everything in man is ready-made. Why do frost designs appear on windowpanes every winter exactly like bushes and flowers swept away by a hurricane? Why are all the snowflakes hexagons? They say that the molecules always form the same pattern. But how do the molecules remember to retrace last year's pattern? I have pondered these riddles from my childhood. In all my years I continued to make my own plans, but it always happened that I became somebody's house friend. I grew so accustomed to married women that when a woman told me she was single she became *a priori* taboo. Can you understand this?"

"One can understand anything," I said.

"How do you explain it?"

"One gets conditioned."

"Is that all?"

"If you insist, I can call it a complex."

"Well, you are a cynic," Max Stein said. "At my age that isn't bad, but at your age one shouldn't be cynical. Freud was in his own way a great person. The fact that so many of his disciples are idiots isn't his fault. All disciples are idiots. What were Tolstoy's followers? What are the Marxists? What are the Hasidim who wrangle and push to pick up the holy crumbs from the rabbi's banquet? What are those would-be artists who imitate Picasso or Chagall? They're a flock of sheep, and they're always driven by a dog."

"What happened with Feivl?" I asked.

"Nothing happened. Such people live out their lives in peace and quiet. He was a bore, and after a while Saltcha became like him. They had six children and all of them took after him, not her. When you told them to sit they sat, and when you told them to lie they lay. They went to school and the Gymnasium. One of the boys studied to be a physician. Another became a lawyer. It was all perseverance."

It began to rain outside and it thundered. Night fell. The daytime patrons gathered up their newspapers and magazines and left. The waitresses took off the red tablecloths and the ashtrays and spread out white tablecloths and silverware. The café became a restaurant. Max Stein and I decided to remain for dinner. The crystal chandeliers were lit, and in their light Max Stein's face appeared yellowish and his hair white. He straightened his tie and said, "Why creep around in the rain and catch cold? We don't have wives and children. Since you want to be a writer, I have more stories for you than Scheherazade had for her sultan. I could have written them myself, but I prefer a brush, not a pen. Besides, many of these people are still alive and they would recognize themselves. I don't want any scandals. I have come to one conclusion that in life there are no rules. Beautiful women remain alone until they turn gray and wither, while ugly ones nab rich husbands and have lovers in addition. For years I was convinced that a woman could run away either from a husband or from a lover—not from both of them. But I was wrong. When I saw it happen, I realized you can never be too clever.

"The husband was a dentist and had a weakness for painting. All day long he stood at his chair and drilled teeth. In the

evening he was transformed into an artist. He wanted me to
teach him, but all he could do was imitate others. He had a
pretty little wife—Hanka, about twelve years younger than he.
For a time she was his nurse. Then she manipulated him into
getting another nurse in her place, and when I began to teach
him she, too, became my pupil. Things were easier for her
than for him. He stood on his feet all day long, while she had
a maid. Men are weaklings and women wheedle anything out
of them with a smile or a love pat. He not only loved her, he
worshiped her. Hanka this, Hanka that. He was dying to hear
me say she had talent, and I said so, for his sake. She began to
smudge one abominable canvas after another, and covered the
walls with them. She ran to all the exhibitions in the Zacheta
and the galleries and aped everybody. She read all the articles
and reviews in the newspapers and magazines and babbled the
jargon of the critics. Cubism? Let there be Cubism. Expressionism? Let there be Expressionism. All her heads came out
square, and the noses as well. Chagall painted his Jews and
deer flying in the air, and Hanka mimicked him. People of that
sort are so greedy for compliments that they beg for them
shamelessly, and if they don't get them from others they praise
themselves to the sky.

"I started up with her not because of love or passion but because Morris—this was the dentist's name—actually maneuvered us together. At every opportunity he spoke to me of
how rich the soul of an artist is and how difficult it is for an
artist to become accustomed to one person only. Such men are
not just tolerant, they push their mates to betray them. What
Feivl did out of naïveté, Morris did with deliberation. He
wanted me to sleep with his wife, and he got what he bargained for. She also wanted it, to keep pace with the other
artists who had affairs. It was the fashion with the so-called
progressive element. She attended all their meetings, marched
in their demonstrations, and ended up by running away with a
low-life fellow—a knifer, an enforcer in the porters' union.
This was something Morris and I did not expect."

"Where did she run?" I asked.

"Where did they all run?" Max Stein answered. "To the land
of socialism, to the Communist paradise. It happened suddenly, like thunder on a sunny day. Little heads can be turned

easily. She grabbed her things, left an abusive letter calling us Fascists, exploiters, imperialists, provocateurs. They ran to Nieswiez, at the Polish-Soviet frontier, and from there they smuggled themselves into Soviet Russia. The Polish guards let them cross without any difficulties. How they were accepted in Russia I learned years later. This was long before Comrade Stalin's purges and the Moscow trials, but even then they put them all into prison. While these slaves were falling on their knees kissing the socialist dust, some Chekist or soldier of the Red Army appeared and said, '*Poidyom*—let's go.' Idealism is fine, but a few months in the Lubyanka prison was the ordinary reception for an idealist. I was told that all of them were finally sent to Siberia to dig gold."

For a long while we sat quietly, and Max Stein tried to balance a fork on the edge of his plate. The fork fell, and Max Stein murmured, *"Nu."*

"What happened then?" I asked.

"What could have happened?" Max Stein said. "We were surprised and stunned, but how long can you be surprised and stunned? The first thing Morris did was rip her paintings off the walls and throw them into the garbage bin in the yard. I saw it all through the window. I expected someone to take them, but it seemed the tenants were not interested in Cubism, Expressionism, abstract art. They just stood there and gaped. There was not much time for Morris to brood. Patients had appointments and he had to see them. I heard them ask, 'Where is your wife?' and he replied, 'Out of town.' I still had a room somewhere, which I called my atelier. Since Hanka had left, there was no reason for me to remain with Morris and I told him the time had come to say goodbye. But he said to me, 'You, too, are running away? You'd better stay here.'

" 'What for?' I asked. 'To sit out the thirty days of mourning?' And he said, 'I'm not going to stay alone forever. Sooner or later, I'll find someone. I don't want to lose both of you.'

"It may sound like a joke, but I waited for Morris to get married so that I could again be his house friend. You're laughing, huh? I could laugh myself. Human life is not only tragic but also utterly comic. The room I called my atelier was small and dark. In the winter it was as cold inside as outside. I'd gone through a spiritual crisis a number of years before, and I had lost my desire to paint altogether. I certainly couldn't get a model to sit for me in that miserable hole. Morris had a comfortable home. It was light there and warm."

"Why didn't he marry his nurse?" I asked.

"This is exactly what he did," Max Stein answered. "Not immediately. It took him a few months to decide. Perhaps he tried to get a better-looking woman. Milcha, as she was called, was not a beauty. She had come from the provinces to Warsaw to study but without any means. She had taken a course in the Wszechnica, a folk university you could enter without credentials. I'll tell you something that will sound completely crazy. Because Milcha was a single girl, and not somebody's wife, I had no yen for her at all, but I knew that Morris would be forced to marry her sooner or later and so I developed an appetite for her. I started to compliment her, to praise the beauty she didn't have, and I offered to teach her a little painting. I even began to kiss her in Morris's presence. When Morris saw this, he confessed to me he had been in love with Milcha for some time. Love can be very practical, even made to order."

"How long did you stay with them?" I asked.

Max Stein thought it over. "A number of years," he said. "It's actually difficult for me to give you a precise answer. While I was with them I became a house friend at another house. I became like a yeshiva boy. I ate in one house and slept in another. You could write a book about it. I became such a specialist that when I met a couple and spoke a few words to them I could sense whether they were looking for a partner."

"People like that are all homosexuals," I said.

"What? These are just words, names," Max Stein said. "What people really are they don't know themselves. The fact is that we all are searching. No one is happy with what he has. A day after the wedding both sides begin to search, the husband as well as the wife. To me this is the naked truth."

Translated by the author and Lester Goran

Burial at Sea

THE THREE of them were sitting in a cell: Zeinvel the Slugger, Koppel the Thief, Reuven Blackjack. All afternoon they played with a deck of greasy marked cards. Nobody had money to put into the pot, so instead each one offered up his nose or an ear. The winner was entitled to pull the loser's earlobe or pinch his nose. If somebody won more than ten rubles, he could give a punch instead of a pinch. The highest bet was twenty-five rubles and a knock on the head, but it never came to that, because losing could be dangerous. Toward evening it turned dark in the cage, as the inmates referred to the prison, since the iron bars on the windows were covered with a dense wire screen, and they just talked and exchanged stories.

The subject turned to marriage, and Koppel the Thief, a man over sixty, with a narrow pockmarked face and a scar on his forehead—the relic of a knife wound—said, "Not all men are alike. Usually, a fellow of our kind will do his business with a female and then go his way. Who wants to get married? That's only for the straight ones. When you sit in this joint and your wife is free out there, she does just as she pleases. She can swear her loyalty on a Bible, bring you a package every day, kiss your feet, but you have no guarantee. For us, getting married is like a healthy man going into a sickbed. In Piask the thieves did get married, but the gang there had strict codes. If someone got nabbed by the cops, the others did everything they could for him. If his wife messed around and got pregnant by a stranger, she was done for. The father of the bastard, too, was made to regret it. I know. I lived in Piask for seven years, and it happened only once that one of their wives slipped. There was a trial and she was sentenced. She tried to talk her way out of it, but they wrapped a noose around her neck.

"Why do I tell you this? A thief, if he has any brains, doesn't rush to the wedding canopy. But strange things do happen, and sometimes they end up horribly. This didn't happen in Piask but in Warsaw—in Pociejow. Wolf the Whipper had his hangout there. Chazkele Spiegelglass was still alive. Pociejow was where all the brothels were. The streets were swarming with yokels from the provinces. Aside from Wolf's, the hangout for our crowd was a soup kitchen run by a widow, Sprintze Chodak. Sprintze kept kosher and wore a wig. She was a shrewd businesswoman. An only daughter was left to her after her husband's death. Her name was Shifra. This Shifra was the most beautiful female I have ever laid eyes on. She was clever as the day—not from schooling but from life. She spoke Polish better than the Poles and Russian like a native. And her Yiddish! A glossy tongue. You could kiss every word of hers. Her hair was red as fire, and she had the eyes of a tomcat. Her figure looked as if it had been chiseled. Whoever saw Shifra walking on a Sabbath afternoon in a tight dress, a hat with ostrich feathers, high-heeled shoes, a purse in one hand and a parasol in the other, could never forget her. Men ate her up with their eyes, but Sprintze protected her like a treasure. Before his death, husband and wife had agreed to marry her off early, and Sprintze had put away ten thousand rubles for a dowry at the Imperial Bank in Petersburg. The boys tried to trap her but to no avail. Shifra did the accounting in her mother's soup kitchen. She helped her buy food from the wholesalers. It was a pleasure to hear Shifra talk on the telephone. She bargained and she joked. I was then a young boy of twelve, but I lay awake late into the night and fantasized about her. When I finally fell asleep, she appeared in my dreams."

"Stop teasing. Get to the point," Reuven Blackjack said.

"Yeah, yeah. The point is that two rich men fell madly in love with her. One was the son of the landlord in the building where we lived—Mendele. He studied at the Gymnasium and at the Philharmonic. He always carried a fiddle in a case. When he walked through the streets, all the girls stared at him. His father, Leizer, had hired a tutor to teach Mendele the Gemara. There could have been no better match than Shifra and Mendele, but when Leizer heard that Mendele wanted Shifra for his bride he began ranting and raving and saying that he would disown him. Shifra's father had been the driver of a freight wagon. Leizer's wife said to Mendele, 'My son, your wedding will be my funeral.' But Mendele stood his ground. He answered, 'I want to marry Shifra, not her dead father.'

"The other one who fell in love with Shifra was Boris

Bundik, a practicing lawyer. He was fifteen years older than Mendele. He didn't live in Pociejow but on Graniczna Street, yet all his clients were from Pociejow. He was a big, handsome man, much taller than Mendele, and he was a friend of all the cops. It came out later that he had a wife somewhere, but in Pociejow he was considered an old bachelor. Sprintze was a client of his, and he used to go to the soup kitchen to grab a bite. They only called it a soup kitchen. It was like a regular restaurant. If she were paid for it, Sprintze could have cooked for an emperor. It became clear that Boris Bundik was coming not to eat but to steal a glance at Shifra. To sum it up, he fell in love. He wanted to marry Shifra, but she had already got tangled up with Mendele. The competition between them was fierce, and Shifra suddenly said, 'I don't know who to choose —I love both of you.'

"What I tell you now was discovered later. They discussed it for a long while, confiding secrets back and forth, until the three of them settled on a plan: since she loved both, she should marry both. It so happened that at this time Sprintze became ill with kidney stones and had to go to the hospital for an operation. Afterward she went for a month to Otwock for the fresh air. Shifra took over the entire household and business. Boris and Mendele came to Shifra and sat with her until late at night. People in Pociejow became suspicious, but Shifra was not one to let others spit into her kasha. If a drunk made a scene, she took him by the collar and threw him right into the gutter. Well, and who wanted to start up with Boris Bundik? They shuddered before his very breath.

"I will make it short. One day all three—Shifra, Mendele, and Boris Bundik—disappeared. Sprintze, who was back home now, woke up in the morning and there was no Shifra. She began screaming, frantically looking for her, but Shifra had skipped town. So had Mendele. There was an outcry in Pociejow. The police wrote out a protocol, but this was all they could do. Initially, people thought that Shifra had run off with Mendele alone. Later we heard that Boris Bundik had also vanished. The commissar from the police station was said to have sent out a missing-persons alert, but by then all three had crossed the border."

■

Koppel paused. He wiped his mouth with his sleeve and scratched the scar on his forehead.

"This is some story!" Zeinvel the Slugger said. Zeinvel was small, and round like a barrel. They called him Slugger because he had once smashed an oak table with his fist and broken all four of its legs.

"Where did they get married? In Warsaw?" Reuven Blackjack asked. Reuven Blackjack was the brains of the group. He wrote letters from jail for Koppel and Zeinvel. He had begun his career as a gambler, and he used to cheat the yokels at blackjack. Now he was serving time for forging a promissory note.

For a while all three were silent. Then Koppel continued: "Be patient. The whole truth came out months later. Yes, they were married in Warsaw. Before one rabbi, Boris Bundik played the role of Shifra's older brother and Mendele was the bridegroom. With another rabbi, Boris was the bridegroom and Mendele Shifra's younger brother. What does a rabbi know? You give him three rubles and he writes out a marriage contract. You could get married in Warsaw ten times and a rooster would not crow.

"How long can you tear your hair and curse the day you were born? Mendele's parents had six other children, and grandchildren, too. Mendele was the youngest. Sprintze cried and grew desperate, but in a soup kitchen you must be up at five in the morning and prepare huge kettles of food. Sprintze took on a maid, a cook, but you know what they say—'A stranger's hands are good only for poking fire.' Weeks passed. Months. Sprintze went to consult Max Blotnik, a wizard who claimed to be able to show missing people in a black mirror, but it was all hocus-pocus.

"One day, when Mendele's mother went with her maid to Ulrich's Bazaar, she heard someone yelling 'Mama! Mama!' She turned, and there stood Mendele, white as a corpse, in torn clothes. A tumult arose and she hollered, 'My God! Where have you been?' 'In America,' he answered. 'In America, and you are back?' she screamed, and he said, 'They deported me!'

"It turned out that the three had smuggled themselves over the border to Prussia and had gone to Hamburg. None of them had a passport, but in a foreign country you need nothing aside from money. Boris was loaded, but Mendele got only a small allowance from his father. He could hardly scrape together a hundred rubles. Shifra had her dresses and a bracelet that was supposed to be gold inset with diamonds, but when she took it to a jeweler he said it was only tin and glass beads. When Boris Bundik saw that he was the rich man and Mendele a pauper, he began to show what a pig he was. For himself and for Shifra he bought first-class tickets to New York, and for Mendele a third-class ticket. Everything would have gone smoothly except that Shifra refused to be separated from Mendele on the ship. She raised hell, but Boris got his way. He had apparently had a change of heart about the whole dirty business. Why did he need a young boy for a partner? This kind of nonsense doesn't last long. You sober up and the game is over.

"Later, Mendele told the whole story to everyone. He was lying in a hole between decks and Shifra came to visit him from the first-class cabin. They ate potatoes in their skins with brine from herring, and she slept with him on a hard bench. Boris Bundik called her back to the fancy cabin, but Shifra said, 'Since you are so mean and stingy, I don't want you for a husband. As soon as we arrive in New York, I will divorce you. I want one God and one husband.' A fight broke out between the two men, but what chance did Mendele have? Boris Bundik had the paws of a murderer. He gave Mendele one slap and he spun around three times. Boris also attacked Shifra. It all happened quickly. Mad with rage, Boris grabbed a knife and stabbed Shifra in the left breast, straight into the heart. They tried to revive her, but she died on the spot. Some of the stronger passengers ganged up on Boris. They threw him down and beat him. The captain soon found out and arrived with his crew. Some said they should stuff the murderer into a sack and throw him overboard. Others argued that this couldn't be done without a trial. A sailor brought a rope and they tied the brute up and dragged him down into the baggage hold, which teemed with rats. He was to be kept on bread and water. A ship is not allowed to carry corpses, so they wrapped Shifra in a bedsheet for a shroud and lowered her into the sea. One passenger, a religious Jew, recited the holy words and the Kaddish. Passengers of all classes came to the burial, if you can call it a burial. Mendele fell into a delirium, banging his head against the wall. He was completely covered with blood. He could not even attend the ceremony. They carried him to the infirmary, where there was a doctor and a supply of medicines, and they bandaged him up and laid him on a bunk. I know all this because I heard Mendele tell the whole story—not once but many times. When Mendele got better, one of the captain's men came to him and took him in for questioning. Mendele told everything exactly as it was and left out nothing. Both of them had loved her, and so both of them had married her. They also took Boris to a hearing, but he denied everything. According to him, he was Shifra's husband and Mendele had tried to steal away his wife.

"When the ship docked in America, the captain went to the authorities with the whole story. There is an island there called Ellis Island—the island of tears, as the passengers called it—where all the third-class passengers were held. A doctor examined each and every passenger, and if someone had weak eyes or a scab, or whatever, he was sent back. The officials on the island spoke every language—English, Yiddish, Russian, Polish, even Chinese—and they took Mendele and Boris Bundik in for another hearing. There were also witnesses. Mendele again related the entire truth, but Boris Bundik lied through his teeth to cover himself. The officials on the island were no fools. They got hold of Shifra's two wedding contracts. One was signed with Boris's name and the other with Mendele's. After some time, it was decided to deport Mendele to Hamburg and to keep Boris for sentencing in America. There a murderer is made to sit in an electric chair and they roast him to coal. Mendele was never told what happened to Boris."

"Why couldn't Mendele stay in America?" Zeinvel asked.

"Because bigamy is forbidden in America, too," Koppel answered.

"He could have argued that he was the husband and Boris the lover," Reuven Blackjack said.

Koppel laughed, and winked. "First, he didn't have your conniving little brain. Second, what good would America do him without Shifra? There he would have to press trousers. In Warsaw he had a rich father."

"Yes, true."

"What happened to him? Did he remarry?" Zeinvel asked.

"Yes, four years later," Koppel answered. "The first few months he roamed around like a man without a head. He didn't want to eat, and his mother dragged him to doctors. He wandered through the streets and talked to himself like a madman. They wrote the story up in the newspapers. Not only the Yiddish but also the Polish papers."

"Did you know his new wife?" Reuven Blackjack asked.

"Yes, I knew her. A girl from a wealthy home, but she was not Shifra."

"Did anyone hear anything about Boris Bundik?"

"Disappeared like a stone in water."

It became quiet among the prisoners, and they could hear from outside the rumbling of a tram on its rails. A spark flashed on the overhead wire, and for a moment the cell lit up with lightning.

"Love is like electricity," Zeinvel said. "It flares up for a second and is soon extinguished."

"What is the sense of marrying two men?" Reuven Blackjack asked.

"And in ancient times what was the sense of a man marrying two or four or six women?" Koppel said. "Men held the pen and they made the law as they pleased. If women ever write the laws, they will make it legal for one female to marry a dozen husbands."

"Suppose something meshugga like this ever happens. How will a man know that he is the father of his child?" Zeinvel asked.

"He won't," Reuven Blackjack said.

And the inmates burst into the hilarious laughter of those who are left with nothing to lose.

Translated by Deborah Menashe

The Recluse

THE WINTER night was long and cold. The beggars and wanderers who slept stretched out on benches in the studyhouse began to stir and wake up. One sighed, another coughed, a third one scratched his head. A memorial candle in a candelabra beside the Holy Ark cast trembling shadows over the walls and ceiling.

Footsteps were heard in the outer room and someone stamped the snow from his boots. The door opened, and a thin, pale man covered with snow entered. The beggars sat up.

"Hey, where are you coming from in the middle of the night?" one of them asked.

"I've lost my way. I was heading in the direction of Lublin on foot, but the road became completely blocked with snow and I could not continue. It is a miracle that I survived."

"In this blizzard it was more than a miracle!"

"You will have to recite the prayer of thanks on the Sabbath," another one called to him.

"You certainly must be hungry," a third beggar said.

"First I must drink."

The stranger took off his shabby coat and then another one underneath it. When he entered, his beard was white with snow, but as the snow melted, it became black again. He didn't really look like a typical beggar or a wanderer but, rather, like a merchant who had lost his way on a trip to a fair. He carried a satchel and the kind of basket used by yeshiva boys.

"What made you take to the road in such weather?" a fourth beggar asked. "You couldn't get a sleigh?"

"They didn't wait for me, and why should a horse drag me when I have my own two feet?"

"If you are hungry, I can offer you a piece of leftover meat that some good-hearted housewife gave me yesterday," said one of the beggars.

"Meat? No. Thank you."

"A slice of bread?"

"Bread, yes. But I will have to wash my hands."

"There is a washbasin in the outer room."

"Thank you. Later."

"Are you afraid that the meat is not strictly kosher?"

The stranger was silent for a while, as if he were pondering an answer. Then he said, "To me, all meat is non-kosher."

"You don't eat any meat at all?"

"No."

"What do you do on the Sabbath?"

"The Sabbath is a day of rest, not a day of meat."

"What are you? A recluse?"

"You can say so."

"*Nu*, so that's it."

The paupers began to murmur and whisper among themselves. In Lithuania, a recluse was not such a novelty, but in Poland recluses were rare. One of the beggars asked, "And wine you don't drink, either?"

"No."

"What do you do about the four cups of wine one must drink at the Passover seder?"

"These four cups I do drink."

"What else do you allow yourself?"

They all waited for a response, but the stranger was silent. He paced back and forth in the studyhouse. He warmed one hand on the hot clay oven and walked to the bookshelves. He took out a book, glanced at it, and put it back. Nobody expected him to engage in conversation, but suddenly he came over to the beggars and said, "God Almighty sends us to this world to bear our sufferings. We can never escape from them."

"Who says so? The rich indulge in pleasures and enjoy life."

"What? I was once a rich man myself," the stranger said, "and it brought me no pleasure."

"Were you sick?"

"I was as strong as iron. And I still am, thank God."

"You speak in riddles."

"My friends, I won't sleep tonight anyhow." The stranger raised his voice. "If you feel like listening, I will tell you a story. I will not drag it out but get right to the point. Maybe you can learn something from it. Unless you want to go back to sleep."

"No. Let's hear."

■

The stranger mumbled something to himself and seemed to hesitate. He again looked toward the bookshelves, as if waiting for their advice or permission. He sat down on one of the benches and began:

"I was born in the city of Radom. My father, may he rest in peace, was quite a wealthy man. I am not boasting when I say that I was a scholar as a boy and the matchmakers were after me even before I became bar mitzvah. I married an only daughter from the town of Pilitz. My father-in-law was a rich man and he took me into his business. Since my wife was an only child, his whole estate was to be mine at his demise—in a hundred and twenty years, as they say. We were childless, which was of course a misfortune, but what could we do? My father-in-law dealt in timber, and, frankly, I turned out to be a fiery merchant. I had all the other merchants in the palm of my hand. If someone had told me then that I would become what you call a recluse, I would have laughed at him. My wife— Esther was her name—did her shopping in Radom and sometimes even as far away as Warsaw, since Pilitz was a small village. She had a lot of jewelry, she kept two maids, and we feasted on roasted pigeon and marzipan on weekdays.

"When there are no children, the man of the house becomes the child. Let me tell you, I was by no means a saint. I succumbed almost entirely to worldly passions. For the sake of appearances, I studied a page of the Talmud daily, but actually I did as I pleased. Of course I ate kosher food. In what way is non-kosher food better than kosher? I especially loved what others don't hate—you understand what I mean. I am by nature a passionate man, and one female was not enough for me. My wife was prone to illness, and two weeks in the month a woman is not pure. I traveled for business, and as these things will go, I often returned home just at her impure time. This caused me a lot of grief. So whenever I met up with an appetizing female I could not resist the temptation. I knew it was a deadly sin, but I found all kinds of excuses. The Evil One plays the role of the scholar quite well. He can turn and twist matters so that it becomes a *mitzvah* to eat pork on Yom Kippur.

"One summer night I was returning home in a wagon. There happened to be two passengers—I and a woman from a village near Lublin. There would be no sense in mentioning names. The night was warm and dark. The driver just happened to be deaf. Well, the perfect setting. I struck up a conversation with her. Her husband was a pious man—an arbitrator in rabbinical lawsuits, she told me. Usually I chose a housemaid, an abandoned wife, or some waitress in an inn, though I always preferred a married woman. For some reason, this time the Evil One got more than he bargained for. 'Baruch,' he said to me, 'don't be a fool. She's ripe for the picking. Have your pleasure.' I moved closer to the woman, but she did not respond. I told her she was pretty and clever and other such compliments, and then she slowly warmed up. Why drag it out? I sinned with her that very night, right there in the wagon. The road was full of rocks and the wheels rattled over the stones. As I said, the night was pitch-dark and the driver was as deaf as a wall. While it was happening, I was astounded, and wondered why the wife of a pious man, a Jewish daughter from a respectable home, would debase herself in this way. Although at the time I felt that I was catching the greatest bargain of my life, I had some misgivings about the whole thing, and the Evil One kept comforting me: 'Was King David given permission to marry Bathsheba? He simply sent the husband, Uriah the Hittite, off to war. *Nu*, and are all the other so-called saints really so good?' The Evil One has an answer ready for everything.

"However, after two strangers meet on the road and indulge in this sort of abomination, they feel ashamed, and even estranged. I sat in one corner and she in another. After a while, my eyelids became heavy and I dozed off. In my dream I saw a man. His image was as vivid as if I were awake. He was small, with a blond beard, dressed in a velvet gaberdine, with a wide fringed garment and slippers like a rabbi's. I had never seen this man before and I knew even in the dream that he was a total stranger. I noticed that on the right side of his forehead was a tumor. He came very close to me and said, 'Baruch, what have you done? For such iniquity one loses the World to Come.'

"In the dream I asked, 'Who are you?' and he answered, 'What is the difference? The eyes see only when there is light, but the soul can also see when there is darkness.' Those were his words. I shook and awoke. I didn't know why, but his words stirred up a storm in me. I heard the woman fumbling with her purse and I asked her, 'Is you husband waiting for you at home?'

" 'Why do you want to know?' she answered.

" 'I'm just curious,' I said.

" 'Listen, mister,' she said, 'what is past is past. I don't know you and you don't know me. And that is the end of it. I will soon be at home with my husband, and you are on your way home to your wife. Let's pretend it never happened.'

"I had heard of this kind of vulgar talk from loose maids, cooks, and the like, but coming from this sort of woman it was shocking. I said nothing more. I laid my head down again and dozed off. Immediately, I saw the same man, with the blond beard, the velvet gaberdine, and the tumor on his forehead. He screamed, 'You may no longer be called Baruch. "Baruch" means blessed, but you are cursed.'

"I shivered and woke up in a cold sweat. The woman, too, must have fallen asleep. I said something to her and she didn't answer me. Just as it is written in the Book of Proverbs: She ate and wiped her mouth and said she did no wrong.

"I returned home a shattered man. I had never before felt anger toward women I had had affairs with. Why be angry? But toward this woman I felt an aversion. Something burned in me and I didn't know why. I heard someone scolding me, but I could not tell who it was and what he was saying. I began to think: If a wife like her, married to a scholarly man, is capable of betraying him so lightheartedly, then no man can really be sure of any wife. If this is so, it is the end of the world. It also occurred to me that she could have become pregnant and would then bear her husband a bastard. I could no longer rest. I began to fear that I had sunk into the Forty-nine Gates of Defilement. I looked differently at my own wife, too. Who knows? She seemed frail when she was with me, but when I went away she might suddenly rejuvenate. I could no longer find any peace, neither that night nor many nights and days after. My distrust became so wild that when the butcher came to our home and my wife bought tripe with calves' feet from him I was already suspecting the worst. I imagined that she winked at him and nodded to him. Weeks passed in this way. Usually, time heals such disturbances. But this restlessness grew worse. It was bursting my brain. I was seriously afraid that I was going mad and that I would end up in an insane asylum. For a while I thought about going to a doctor and telling him of my ordeal. I developed a terrible hatred toward my wife, while I knew deep inside me that she was a decent woman and such salacious thoughts never entered her mind for a second. One minute my love for her returned, as well as my desire to see her happy and well. Then I wished for her death and I fancied all kinds of cruel revenge. Whenever I saw her talk to a man, even if he was nothing more than the water carrier, I was sure that they were planning not only to betray me but even to kill me. To make it short, I was on the verge of madness, or perhaps even murder. My good friends, don't look at me this way. It can happen to any man if he doesn't curb the evil powers which dwell in all of us. One step away from God and one is already in the dominion of Satan and hell. You don't believe me, eh?"

"I do. I do," said one of the beggars. "In our own town a squire strangled his wife because she smiled at another squire. He tried to kill him, too, but he ran away."

"But those were Gentiles, not Jews," said another beggar. "And not a scholar of the Torah, as you seem to be."

"The Devil tempts everybody," another beggar said. "He can assail even the mind of an eighty-year-old rabbi. I heard this from a preacher in the city of Zamosc."

"True, true," the stranger said. "I didn't know it then, but I know it now. I wish I had known more of it then. My sleep would have been less tortured."

For a minute all were silent. The beggars looked at one another and shrugged their shoulders.

"Now listen to this," the stranger cried out. "One morning I went to the studyhouse and I saw a man with a blond beard, in a velvet gaberdine, and with a tumor on his forehead. He was greeted by the congregation with much respect. I asked who he was and they told me he was an arbitrator in rabbinical lawsuits from some other town. I felt as if I had been slammed over the head with a hammer. This was the man of my dream. I became white and began to shake. People came over to me and asked, 'Baruch, aren't you feeling well? What's the matter?' I clutched at my head and ran out of the study-house. I went to my wife and said, 'Esther, take over everything —all the business. Consider yourself a widow.' She thought I had lost my mind.

" 'What happened?' she asked. And I said, 'You are a good wife, but I am not worthy of being your husband.'

" 'What have you done?' she asked. I wanted to tell her the truth, but the words would not come. She was actually not well that day and I was afraid that what I would tell her might kill her. To commit adultery is one thing, but to kill your beloved wife is something else. As a matter of fact, she looked as if she might faint dead away. Since I could not tell her the truth, I had to invent a lie—that I had some trouble with my business. She tried to comfort me. 'It's only money,' she said. 'Quiet down. Your health is more important to me than all the money in the world.' I realized in those moments that to suspect the innocent can lead to the worst of crimes.

"That night I didn't sleep a wink. For a moment I wanted to ask her forgiveness for suspecting her, but then I heard the Evil One say to me, 'This other man, with whose wife you sinned, might have acted just as cowardly as you if he had had some suspicion about his wife. They are all alike: false and treacherous. Before the Temple was destroyed, when the spirit of jealousy came over a man he could lead his wife to the priest and make her drink from the water of bitterness. And if she had really betrayed him her belly would swell and her thigh would fall away. But in our time they can give in to all lecherous desires and not a cock would crow.' Immediately my hatred toward my wife returned. I felt that I had to leave her. And this is what I did. I knew that to desert a decent wife was the worst thing a man can do. But I also knew that divorce papers could be slipped into her possession and then she would still be permitted to remarry. And I did exactly this. I went to a faraway town, ordered divorce papers from a scribe, and sent them to her by messenger. I knew that staying with her would be the death both of her and of me."

"And you never went back?" one of the beggars asked.

"Never."

"You were never tempted?"

"I was tempted not once but a thousand times. But I could not do it."

"She might have been pregnant when you left her."

"I knew she wasn't."

"Do you think that what you did was right?"

"No. It was wrong, but in the years I have been wandering I have heard so many stories of treachery that my faith in human beings has ceased forever. I came to the conclusion that nothing was left for me but to become a wanderer upon the earth. More than that, I never stay longer in one place than a day or two, so as not to develop any attachments to anything or anybody."

"You are always on the run?"

"I run from nobody but myself. One of my kind should not belong to any community."

"How long are you going to stay here in this town?"

The stranger thought it over. "I have already spoken too much. I will leave at sunrise."

Translated by Deborah Menashe

Disguised

WHEN Temerl stood under the wedding canopy she surely did not know that in less than half a year she would be an abandoned wife. Temerl was the daughter of a rich man. Pinchos—or Pinchosl, as her husband was called, because he was small and slight—was a poor yeshiva student. He received a large dowry from his in-laws and was promised ten years' board. Temerl was good-looking. Why would anybody want to run away from her? But a few months after the wedding Pinchosl was gone. He stealthily packed a few garments in a bundle, took his prayer shawl and phylacteries, and left the town on foot. Even though he could have taken the entire dowry, he took only three silver guldens.

No, Pinchosl was not a thief, and neither did he chase women. He barely looked at Temerl when he lifted the veil from her face on the wedding night. Why, then, did he run off? Some people thought he was homesick for Komarov, where he had been brought up, and yearning for his mother and father. But even his parents heard nothing from him after he left his wife. Someone had seen him in Zamosc, someone else in Lublin. After that, there was no trace of him. Pinchosl had vanished.

People expressed all kinds of opinions. Maybe he had quarreled with his wife? Maybe he disliked the town where his in-laws lived? Perhaps he wanted to make an end to the Jewish Exile and return to the land of Israel? Even so, he didn't need to run away. He could have divorced Temerl, or at least sent divorce papers with a messenger. To walk out on a Jewish daughter is a grave sin, because unless she is divorced according to the laws of Moses and Israel she can never remarry.

Temerl sulked and wept. It would have been much less of a misfortune had he left her with a child. But he left her with nothing but an ache in her heart. The women questioned Temerl: "Did he come to your bed on your pure nights?" "Did he speak gently to you?" "Did you ever resist him?" From Temerl's answers it was clear that they had behaved more or less like man and wife.

As far as the family knew, the night before Pinchosl left he read a Talmudic book in the studyhouse until late. There was no sign on his face that he was preparing to do anything unusual. But in the middle of the night, as Temerl slept, he packed up and slipped away. Why? And where to? His parents and father-in-law sent messengers to look for him in the neighboring towns. The family wrote to rabbis and to community leaders across Poland. But Pinchosl had apparently managed to elude everybody.

There was only one explanation: the demons had captured him. But if the demons capture a man, he is not spotted in Zamosc and in Lublin. They drag him behind the black mountains where no people walk, no cattle tread. Some women murmured that perhaps Pinchosl harbored hatred toward Temerl. But how could anyone hate Temerl? She was a mere seventeen years old, with a silky-smooth face, dark eyes, and slender limbs, and she seemed to be utterly devoted to her husband. She had sewn an ornate prayer-shawl case for him and sent to him as a wedding gift a velvet matzoh cover embroidered with golden threads and with his name in little gems. If he dallied too long in the studyhouse, she sent her maid to call him home to lunch.

Rumors spread that a young man who looked Jewish had been seen in a procession of priests and monks at a cloister. But this certainly could not have been the learned and law-abiding Pinchosl. People often say that one cannot understand the ways of the Almighty. Yet the ways of human beings can be just as perplexing.

Two years passed. Pinchosl's parents and in-laws had searched far and wide. They inquired in every city or village where a Jew might settle. One day, Temerl surprised her parents by telling them that she had decided to go and comb the earth herself in search of her husband. Her mother, Baila, cried bitterly. How could she allow her nineteen-year-old daughter to wander over the world? Where would she go? Where would she stay? Baila was terrified that the same fate would befall Temerl as had befallen Pinchosl. But her father, Reb Shlomo Meltzer, had another viewpoint. It was not unheard of for an abandoned wife to set out in search of her husband. It had happened more than once that the wife finally found the man and got a divorce from him or else located witnesses to his death. What did Temerl have to lose? Her life was ruined either way. Reb Shlomo gave his daughter money and sent along a maid to help her in all her endeavors. The maid, a widow, was a distant relative of his.

A long journey began for Temerl. She did not travel with any specific plan. She followed all possible leads. If she was given the name of some town that the messengers might have omitted, she found a vehicle and traveled there. Wherever she went, she sought out the rabbi and the community leaders, and she visited the synagogue and the studyhouse. She searched in the marketplaces, along the side streets, in the poorhouse. She asked if anyone had seen or heard about a certain Pinchosl. People shrugged their shoulders, shook their heads. Pinchosl had no outstanding traits. He looked like an average young Hasid. When he forsook her, he had not yet begun to sprout whiskers, but by now he probably had grown a little beard. Wherever Temerl and her maid went, they heard the same refrain: "Go look for a needle in a haystack."

Months passed, and Temerl pursued her search. Traveling all over the Lublin region and farther, into the so-called Great Poland, matured her before her time. She gained the kind of knowledge that comes from staying at inns and listening to all sorts of talk. She met with other abandoned wives. Men did disappear. Once in a while, a woman, too, disappeared, but those were rare cases. Temerl learned how vast the world was and how odd people could be. Each human being had his own desires, his own calculations, and sometimes his or her own madness. In the city of Chelm, she heard, the daughter of a rich Jew had fallen in love with a pork butcher and converted to Catholicism. In Jaroslaw, a wealthy businessman divorced his wife and married a prostitute. In Lemberg, they imprisoned a charlatan who had twenty-four families in twenty-four towns and villages. Temerl also heard many tales of people who had been carried away by hobgoblins, of children captured and enslaved by gypsies, and of men who escaped to America, where, she was told, it was nighttime when it was daytime in Poland, and where people walked upside down. There was also talk about a monster who was born with a gray beard and the teeth of a wolf. But Temerl somehow felt that Pinchosl had not been seized by demons, and that neither was he lost in faraway America, across the ocean.

Temerl journeyed through all the Jewish towns. The money that her father had given her ran out, but she had her jewelry with her and was able to sell some of that. She had written to her parents, but they could not answer her, since she never stayed long enough in one place. In time, the maid became weary of roaming and she returned home. For Temerl, wandering had become a habit. In one town, she met someone who resembled Pinchosl. She alerted the community leaders, and he was taken to the rabbi and later to the ritual bath, but certain marks on his body did not coincide with Temerl's description. He did not have a black nail on the big toe of his left foot, and he did not have a wart on his neck. He denied having been born in Komarov, and swore that his name was not Pinchosl but Moshe Shmerl. He admitted that he was married and the father of children but said he had not run away from his wife. The opposite was true. His wife refused to live with him, because he could not provide for the family, and he had gone out to look for a teaching job. The rabbi and the elders believed him, and Temerl was sentenced to pay a fine of eighteen groschen for suspecting the innocent and giving a stranger a bad name.

Temerl traveled as far as the city of Kalisz, and there she was passing through a marketplace when her eyes caught sight of a woman who seemed strangely familiar. Where have I seen that face before, Temerl wondered. The woman was buying eggs from a merchant and holding a basket, into which she put the merchandise. There was nothing unusual about this, but Temerl stood there gaping and could not move from the spot. Suddenly she realized whom the woman resembled: no one else but Pinchosl! "Am I losing my mind?" Temerl asked herself in bewilderment. She remembered being fined the eighteen groschen for false accusations.

At that instant the woman glanced at Temerl and seemed to be so shaken that she dropped her basket, breaking many of the eggs. She attempted to run, but the merchant ran after her, calling that he hadn't been paid for the eggs. The woman stopped and began to look for money, but her hand was trembling and the coins fell from her purse. Temerl herself was about to faint, yet she noticed that the woman's cheeks were not smooth but fuzzy, as if she was sprouting a beard. Also, her hands were too large for those of a female. A wild thought ran through Temerl's mind: Perhaps this is Pinchosl dressed up like a woman. But why would a man want to parade around like a woman? It is forbidden by the Mosaic Law for a man to wear the garments of a woman, and vice versa.

The woman picked up the fallen coins and paid the merchant. She then began to walk away quickly. She was almost running, and Temerl ran after her, screaming and calling her back. The woman stopped short. "Why are you chasing me? What do you want?" she asked, in Pinchosl's voice.

"You are Pinchosl!" Temerl cried out.

Instead of denying it, the strange woman stood there, pale and speechless. Finally, she managed to ask—again in Pinchosl's voice—"What are you doing in Kalisz?"

"I'm looking for my husband. It is you!" Temerl exclaimed. "You left me an abandoned wife." In her dismay, Temerl began to choke and cry spasmodically.

The woman looked at her and said, "Come with me," and she pointed to a muddy alley strewn with garbage and pools of slop. There, after attempting to quiet Temerl, the strange woman admitted, "Yes, I am Pinchosl."

"Why did you run away? Why did you dress in a woman's clothes?" Temerl howled. "Are you mad, possessed by a dybbuk? What are you doing here in Kalisz and for whom were you buying eggs? Are you someone's servant or slave? Are my eyes deceiving me? Am I dreaming? Or am I bewitched? God in heaven, the terrible misfortunes that have befallen me!" Temerl began to sway and was about to collapse into a swoon. She clutched at Pinchosl's shoulder, and a horrifying shriek came out of her throat.

In fear of attracting attention and having a mob of people witness his disgrace, Pinchosl blurted out, "I know that this will shock you terribly, but I live here in Kalisz with a man."

"With a man?" Temerl gasped. "Are you fooling me? Are you joking? What do you mean with a man?"

"Yes, with a man. His name is Elkonah. We met in a yeshiva

years ago. Here we bake pretzels for yeshiva boys. This is how we earn our living, and for this I went to buy eggs. Forgive me, Temerl, but I never wanted to marry you. I was forced by my parents. That is the real truth."

"Whom did you want to marry?" Temerl asked.

"Him."

They stood motionless for a while; then Pinchosl managed to say, "I can't help it, I must confess the whole truth."

"What truth?" Temerl exclaimed. "What did you do? Have you, God forbid, forsaken your faith?"

"No, Temerl. I am still a Jew, but . . ." Pinchosl stammered and shook. He again dropped the basket, but he did not bother to pick it up. He stood before her ashamed, frightened, pale, moving his lips but unable to utter a word. Then Temerl heard him say, "I'm not a man anymore—not really, not for you . . ."

"What are you saying?" Temerl asked. "Were you sick? Did some vicious people do something to maim you? No matter what you tell me, I am still your wife and I must know!"

"No, Temerl, not this but . . ."

"Speak clearly!" Temerl, too, was trembling, and her teeth chattered.

"Temerl, come with me!" Pinchosl both ordered and pleaded.

"Where to?"

"To my house—I mean home, where we live."

"Where is your home? Who is the 'we'? Did you find another woman?"

"No, Temerl, but . . ."

"Don't lie to me! I beseech you! In the name of God. Oh, I'm afraid!"

Pinchosl started to walk ahead, and he motioned to Temerl to follow him. As they walked, Pinchosl was saying, "According to the Talmud, when a man is overcome by the evil spirit and knows of no way out he should wrap himself in black garments and go to a place where he is not known and do what his heart desires. This is what we did, Elkonah and I."

They came to another alley and to a shabby-looking house. Pinchosl urged Temerl to come inside, but she refused. He pulled her by the arm, but she stood firm. After much hesitation, she gave in. Luckily, Elkonah was not home. There was a clay oven in the house and a kneading board. The place smelled of yeast and firewood. Temerl imagined that she recognized some of Pinchosl's books in the bookcase. A ladder led up to a loft bed. Pinchosl invited her to sit down. This was no longer the modest, bashful Pinchosl she remembered but a worldly man who reminded her of the adventurers described in the storybooks she used to read before she married. Pinchosl offered her some of the pretzels he had baked and a glass of soda water. He repeatedly apologized for his sins and the suffering he had caused her and her parents. He even joked and smiled—something he had never done in former times. Temerl heard herself saying, "Since you seem to regret your sins, perhaps you could repent and return to God and even to me."

"It's too late for that," Pinchosl answered. "I can regret but not repent. Those who are trapped in our net can never escape." And he quoted the Book of Proverbs: "None who come to her return, nor do they reach the paths of life."

Shocked as Temerl was, she heard him out. She told Pinchosl that there was only one redeeming act for him, and that was to divorce her and free her as quickly as possible. Pinchosl agreed immediately, but said that the divorce could not take place in Kalisz, where he was known as Elkonah's wife. "You could have done this from the very beginning," Temerl reproached him. "And spared me all the misery I went through."

"We know that we will be punished, and we are ready for the fires of Gehenna," Pinchosl said. "Passions, too, are fires. They are Gehenna on earth, perhaps the Gate to Hell. Meanwhile, come let us have a glass of tea together."

Temerl could not believe her own eyes. Pinchosl served tea with jam for her. They were sitting and drinking like two sisters. He was saying, "My parents had hoped to have grandchildren from us, but certainly not through an outcast like me, who would be excommunicated by the Jews and hanged on the gallows by the Gentiles. But you, Temerl, will soon remarry and bring your parents all the joy they expected. I wish you good luck in advance."

"You are utterly mad, but thank you just the same," Temerl said.

That evening, when Elkonah came home—a tall, handsome man in a short coat and a silk vest, his black sidelocks curled in ringlets—he was told the whole story. While Pinchosl still spoke with the humility of a Jew, Elkonah proved to be like one of those who are referred to in the Talmud as profligates for the sake of spite. He denied the existence of God, of Providence, and the holiness of the Torah. He went so far as to suggest that Temerl should get the divorce papers from him, Elkonah, in order to save Pinchosl a costly trip.

Temerl asked Elkonah, "Have you no fear of God at all?"

He answered, "All I ask of Pinchosl is for him to come back soon and continue to bake pretzels for the yeshiva boys—some of whom I have managed to seduce." And he winked and laughed.

Some weeks later, when Baila was sitting in the kitchen with her maid, plucking goose down for a feather bed, the door opened and Temerl entered. It was snowing outside. An icy wind rattled the shutters. Baila let out a wild cry of joy and jumped up from her stool, and all the down on her apron fell off. The maid lost her tongue altogether. Even before Baila could greet and kiss her daughter, Temerl announced, "*Mazel tov!* Here are my divorce papers, written by a master scribe, signed by two kosher witnesses."

That was almost all she could tell that day and for many days, weeks, months, and even years after. The real story, with all its peculiarities, Temerl could not tell, because Pinchosl had made her swear by God, by the Pentateuch, by the lives of her father and mother, and by everything holy to her never to mention any details as long as she lived. All she could say was that she had found her husband somewhere and had got her divorce. The entire story was told to a rabbi and to the elders of the burial society many years later when Temerl lay on her deathbed and was reciting her confession, surrounded by her sons, daughters, and grandchildren, as well as friends and admirers from the region, where she lived to a ripe old age.

"There were many demands and temptations for me to

break my oath of silence," Temerl was saying, "but, thank God, I kept my lips sealed until today. Now, after all these years, I am free and ready to tell the whole story, since the place where I am going is called the World of Truth."

Temerl closed her eyes. The women of the burial society had already prepared the feather to hold under the dying woman's nostrils to see if she was still breathing. Suddenly Temerl opened her eyes and smiled, as the moribund sometimes do, and she said, "Who knows? Perhaps I will meet this madman once again in Gehenna."

Translated by Deborah Menashe

The Accuser and the Accused

THEY are both in a better world, so I can afford to tell this story. One of them, the accused, I knew from New York. There are very few mystics among the Yiddishists. Many of them are leftists or former leftists. The Yiddishist writers (almost all of them are writers, one way or another) have a social orientation. But Schikl Gorlitz, as I call him here, was interested in the cabala and also in the wisdom that comes from India. He has translated into Yiddish the *Bhagavad-Gita* and the *Dhammapada*. He worshipped Gandhi. He was planning to translate into Yiddish the Zohar, *The Tree of Life* by Rabbi Isaac Luria and *The Orchard of Pomegranates* by Rabbi Moshe of Cordova. As far as I knew, he lived alone. How he made a living I don't know to this day—certainly not from his books, which he published himself. Many of the books he gave away. Perhaps he inherited some money.

Schikl Gorlitz never came to the literary cafeteria. He was not the kind of person who complained to other people. He was small, a frail man, and it was difficult to try to guess how old he was. He could have been between fifty and seventy. There was a quietude about him and an atmosphere of spirituality, of one for whom religion, philosophy, and contemplation were the very essence of his existence.

Yes, he must have had some money, because he often made long journeys, mostly to India. Once, he brought me greetings from someone of whom I had never heard, a man famous in India. His name was Rajagopalachari, an intimate friend of Mahatma Gandhi and former Home Minister of India. Rajagopalachari had translated a story of mine, "Fire," into Tamil.

The other hero of my story, the accuser, was known as a traveling journalist. I met him in the fifties in Buenos Aires. I shall call him David Karbinsky. He traveled mostly in South America and wrote about his trips in the Yiddish press and later published his travel stories in books. He was a powerful writer and I once wrote a favorable review of his work in the *Jewish Daily Forward*. He responded with a long letter of thanks and with the usual writer's complaints about editors, critics, and even readers.

David Karbinsky was in his seventies when I met him. He was a tall man, and he looked remarkably healthy and strong for his age. His stories about the jungles where he traveled, the various tribes of Indians with whom he lived for some time, and of Jews he met in the most unlikely places enchanted me. How he covered the expenses of his trips was not known to me, because Yiddish newspapers don't compensate their writers for extensive trips like these. I knew that he had married children and perhaps they helped him financially or he had saved up funds in his younger days. In Argentina he once gave me as a gift the skin of a huge snake. I've never learned what kind of snake it was. Perhaps he told me the name when he gave me the gift, but I forgot it. The skin lay for years in my clothes closet in New York and then the cleaning maid threw it out. It was shedding too many scales. I was never a collector, and certainly not of snake skins.

May I digress? I knew a third Yiddishist traveler, a man who was looking for a territory for Yiddishists. He hoped that somewhere in Africa or South America he would find a country willing to donate a large piece of land for Yiddishists who would be eager to live out their lives with the Yiddish language. Of course, this was a sheer fantasy, because such ardent Yiddishists don't exist. There were many Zionists who at the end of the former century believed that if the Sultan of Turkey refused to give a charter for the Jews to settle in Palestine they should try to find some other territory. The fact is that the Turks did refuse and Dr. Theodor Herzl, the founder of Zionism, thought he had found a territory in Uganda. The Zionists all over the world became divided into "Zion-Zionists" and "Uganda-Zionists." It's a fact that Theodor Herzl died a Ugandist, and some of his former disciples considered him a traitor to the cause.

I mention these territorial projects because in my conversations with David Karbinsky I derived the suspicion that he, too, was looking for a territory for Jews. I really think that every Yiddishist traveler is possessed by a territory dybbuk. If there is ever a Yiddish astronaut and he lands on the planet Mars, I'm sure he will look for a territory for Yiddishists there.

Now back to the story. Who was the accuser and who was the accused?

The accuser was David Karbinsky and the accused was Schikl Gorlitz.

One day when David Karbinsky came back to Argentina from a long journey around South America he made an accusation that shook the pillars of Yiddishism. He called a press conference in Buenos Aires and he told the journalists that while he was visiting the capital of Peru, Lima, he saw a long Catholic procession on Good Friday. Hundreds of priests and nuns and other pious Catholics walked in this procession, carried crosses, icons of the saints and apostles, and sang religious liturgies. Among the priests one appeared to Karbinsky to be very familiar. He was small, somewhat bent, dressed in dark priestly garb, but Karbinsky was sure he had met him somewhere, perhaps in the literary cafeteria on East Broadway in New York. He was singing and Karbinsky was positive he had heard his voice before. Karbinsky began to follow the procession, keeping his eyes continually on the little figure of the priest, who looked to him not only familiar but like a typical East European Jew. Suddenly Karbinsky knew. The priest was Schikl Gorlitz, the translator of the *Bhagavad-Gita*, the cabalist who was about to translate the Zohar and other cabalist works into the mother language. Karbinsky called out his name, "Schikl, Schikl Gorlitz." The little priest turned his head but seemed to decide to ignore the call and continued his march. David Karbinsky could not follow the procession much longer. Thousands of onlookers filled the streets. He could not throw himself into the middle of the procession to query one of the priests about his identity. He had to let the procession pass him by, but he remained convinced that, without the slightest doubt, the frail priest with the dark eyes and the face of a yeshiva scholar was Schikl Gorlitz.

When the Yiddish journalists in Argentina heard the strange accusation they couldn't believe there was an iota of truth to it. Why should a Yiddish writer from New York play the charlatan and who ever heard that Schikl Gorlitz had made trips to South America and knew Spanish? They all said the same thing: People sometimes resemble one another. But David Karbinsky refused to rest his case. He began to do research and he learned that Schikl Gorlitz did make trips to South America. He also had translated some religious poetry from Spanish into Yiddish.

While this news was becoming public, Schikl Gorlitz was on one of his journeys. When he returned to New York and heard of the queer accusation, he denied it categorically. He was interested in Buddhism and not in Catholicism. He admitted that he had made a few trips to South America, but between making a trip and being a priest in Peru is a far cry. He said that David Karbinsky must have lost his mind, or was conspiring to ruin his reputation. But why should David Karbinsky be his enemy? They did not compete professionally. Schikl Gorlitz swore that he had not the slightest idea of what could be Karbinsky's motivation.

I want to say here that if someone with energy had undertaken to investigate the matter it would not have taken long to establish the truth. The Catholic clergy in Peru certainly knew who was who in their parishes. Also, Schikl Gorlitz couldn't have made any trips without a passport, which often bears stamps of visas and dates. Schikl Gorlitz belonged to the Peretz Verein, the union of Yiddish writers in America, and they could have clarified the situation by contacting the Peruvian clergy. But Schikl Gorlitz was not the kind of person who would insist on saving his name from the accusation of being an imposter. He suffered his disgrace in silence. True, he was accused of being a charlatan, but he most probably thought that false accusations, shame, and slanders are a part of man's karma. He denied the charges once and returned to his work. Like anyone else, rich or poor, Schikl Gorlitz might have had enemies, but he made no further effort to deny his guilt. If I'm not mistaken, he died not long after. It is quite possible that this ignoble affair may have caused his death. David Karbinsky lived two or three years longer. Schikl Gorlitz left this world as quietly as he had lived in it. If he left manuscripts, I'm sure the superintendent of the shabby rooming house threw them into the garbage together with his few other belongings. How David Karbinsky could have made such an accusation and not tried with all his means to find the truth is still a riddle to me.

Suspicion has such an uncanny power that no matter how senseless and unjust it is, it can never be completely eradicated.

I myself sometimes play with the idea that, who knows, perhaps Schikl Gorlitz was what Professor MacDougal called a multiple personality. Perhaps Schikl Gorlitz was a Yiddish writer in New York, a Buddhist in India, and a Catholic priest in Peru. Maybe he believed that there is no essential difference among these three faiths. Perhaps there was a woman (or two or three women) connected with these eerie complications. It could have been that Schikl Gorlitz was a member of a group of people whose aim it was to unite all religions into one world religion. So many impossible things have become possible in my lifetime that I've made up my mind to erase the word "impossible" from my vocabulary. I'm even capable of believing that Schikl Gorlitz and David Karbinsky have met in the heavenly spheres, where a court of justice was held and the truth came out clearly and definitely. Somewhere in the universe the truth must be stated. Of one thing I'm convinced—that here on earth justice and truth are forever and absolutely beyond our grasp.

Translated by the author and Lester Goran

A Peephole in the Gate

I WAS invited to South America by the Yiddish press. On the Argentinian boat I occupied a luxury cabin that had a Persian rug, soft chairs, a plush sofa, and a private bath, as well as a large window facing the water. The first-class passengers were outnumbered by the crew assigned to serve them. There was a special wine steward just for my table, and every time I took a sip from my glass he immediately refilled it. Luncheon and dinner meals were always accompanied by an eight-piece band. The bandleader was told that I was a Polish Jew living in America, and in my honor he often played Polish, Palestinian, and Yankee melodies. Almost all the other passengers were South Americans. In spite of all this catering I suffered from ennui. I could converse with no one and it is also difficult for me to strike up easy acquaintanceships with strangers. I had brought a chess set but couldn't find a partner, and one day I went to second class to look for one. There were only two classes.

The first class was half empty, while the second class hummed with activity. In the large lounge, men were drinking beer from mugs, others were playing cards, checkers, and dominoes. Women sat in groups and sang Spanish folk songs. Some of the faces seemed strangely wild, reminding me of animals or birds. I heard brutal voices. Women with enormous bosoms and behinds ate out of baskets and laughed with uncanny joy. A giant with mustaches that reached to his shoulders and brush-like brows told jokes in Spanish and his belly shook like bellows. The others applauded and stamped their feet. In the crowd I recognized a passenger from first class whom I had been seeing in the dining room three times a day. He sat there by himself. He always wore a tie and jacket, even for breakfast. Here he walked around in an open shirt, exposing a gray-haired chest. His face was red and he had white brows and a veined nose. I thought he was a Latin, but now, to my amazement, I saw him carrying a New York Yiddish newspaper. Approaching him, I said, "In that case let me say *sholem aleichem* to you."

His brown eyes, which had bluish bags under them, looked at me in astonishment for a while, and then he replied, "Is that so? *Aleichem sholem.*"

"What are you trying to find in second class?" I asked him.

"What are you doing here? Come, let's go out on the deck."

We went outside and sat down on two steamer chairs. The ship was approaching the equator and the weather was warm. Sailors, stripped to the waist, sat on coils of mooring rope and played with greasy cards. One sailor was painting a beam while another was sweeping up the rubbish on the deck with a long broom. The air stank of vomit and fish. I said, "The crowd here is having a much better time than we upstairs."

"Sure, that's the reason I came down here. Do you live in New York?"

"Yes, in New York."

"I lived in New York for years, but then I moved to Los Angeles. I was told it was a paradise, but the winters are cold and we have smog in addition."

"I see that you were not born in America."

"I am from Warsaw. Where are you from?"

"Also from there."

"We lived at Grzybowska, number 5."

"I went to cheder at Grzybowska, number 5," I remarked.

"At Moshe Yitzhak's?"

The moment the man mentioned this name, he became like a relative to me. The distance of the ocean and the whole foreign atmosphere vanished in one second. He told me that at home he was Shlomo Mair, but in America his name was Sam. He had left Poland over fifty years ago. "How old do you think I am?" he asked.

"I would say in the sixties."

"I will be seventy-five in November."

"You are well preserved."

"Well, I had a grandfather who lived to the age of a hundred and one. In America if you don't get a heart attack or cancer you keep on living. In the old country people died from typhoid fever or perhaps even from hunger. My father rented out flat-bottomed wagons to merchants. We had horses and stables and employed over a dozen coachmen. We lived in comfort. My father sent me to cheder and also hired a private

tutor for me. I studied a little Russian, a little Polish, and what
have you. My mother came from a better house. Her father
was a lawyer—not a lawyer like here. He didn't attend a university. He filed petitions, sometimes served as an arbiter, and
held the litigant's money in escrow. My mother wanted to
make a scholar out of me, but I was not cut out for an education. My brother, Benjamin, and I had a pigeon coop on our
roof and we used to stand there for hours chasing the pigeons
with long sticks. We also went out with girls and attended the
Yiddish theater on Muranow Place as well as the Polish one—
Nowy, Letni, the opera. On Leszno Street there was a summer
theater called the Alhambra, and there it was easy to pick up a
serving girl. All the maids got half a day off on Sundays, and
for a bar of chocolate a girl gave you everything. In those days
men were not careful. The girl got pregnant and her mistress
threw her out. There was a special clinic for such cases where
each unwed mother had to nurse her own baby for six months
as well as several foundlings. These children usually grew up
and became firemen, janitors, and sometimes policemen. What
became of the girl babies I really don't know. Respectable
women at that time hired wet nurses, and these illegitimate
mothers made a living that way. There were men whose business it was to impregnate these women, and for that they got a
bowl of soup or a slice of bread. Since you are from Warsaw
you should know these things yourself."

"I know, I know."

"Well, I had my share of the fun. I always had a pocketful of
money and with a gulden it wasn't difficult to come by. If we
wanted to, we went to the brothels in Poczajow and Tamka.
Do you care to listen to more?"

"Yes I do."

"Since you're from Warsaw, too, why don't we share a
table?"

"I would be happy to sit with you."

"I will speak to the dining-room steward. Sitting alone becomes lonely and one doesn't know what to do with oneself.
So I eat a lot and gain weight. The Latins can eat without end.
Did you notice their females? How can one get close to such a
mountain of flesh? In the States, everybody is on a diet. Here
they stuff themselves like gluttons. Do you drink beer?"

"No."

"Then I will order some for myself."

"As long as you are young," Sam continued, "you don't look into things too deeply, but when you get older you want someone to love who loves you. To pay for it is no trick. I became acquainted with a girl from Gnoyna Street. Her name was Eve—just like the Eve who gave Adam the forbidden apple and because of this all men must die. She seemed like a decent girl, with a round face, shapely legs, and a nice body. Eve was eighteen and years ago this wasn't so young anymore. My mother didn't approve of the match, because her father was poor. He worked in the kosher slaughterhouse, where his job was to skin the animals. Eve came from a large family and didn't have any dowry. But what did I need a dowry for? I knew I could make a living. An engagement party was arranged and plates were broken for good luck. I wasn't exceptionally pious so I took her to the theater on the Sabbath. During the week we used to go to a delicatessen where we ate hot frankfurters on rolls with mustard and washed them down with beer. Such crispy rolls as they baked in Warsaw are not to be gotten anywhere else; they melted in your mouth. Well, it was a real love affair. Fifty years ago an engaged couple did not behave as they do today. A girl had to remain a virgin until her wedding, but we did plenty nevertheless. This gave us a glimpse into the pleasures we would give each other after the wedding. We were already arguing about how many children we would have. I wanted six and she ten. Her father set the date for the Friday after Tisha b'Av, though this seemed like an eternity to me. It wasn't easy for a poor man to marry off a daughter, especially without a dowry. My parents gave Eve fine gifts: a gold watch, a chain, a brooch. Her father could not afford to give me anything of much value. He bought me a silver goblet for the Sabbath benediction over the wine. It was all a game to us and our love burned like fire.

"I will tell you what happened. Even talking about it now makes my blood boil. It was Saturday and we attended the theater. I still remember that they played *Chasha the Orphan*. After the play we went to Kotik's restaurant and had a big supper: fish, meat, and all the trimmings. Her father had an eleven o'clock deadline for her to be home. If she came in late he took the belt off his pants and whipped her like a small girl. I approved of his strictness. I didn't want to marry a runaround. As a matter of fact, when we became engaged, I stopped chasing the shiksas. Eve made it very plain that what I had done before was past, but now I was hers. It wasn't always easy to keep my promise. We had a maid and I used to go to her at night in the kitchen, but I had given Eve my word that I would behave. That Saturday night after we finished our meal we took a droshky from Nalewki Street to her home. It was not long after Passover. They used to close the gates in Warsaw about ten-thirty and when we got there the gate was already closed. We kissed before the gate, again and again, and then I rang the bell. The janitor's son came to open it. His name was Bolek—a mean fellow, a bully. He was often followed by a vicious dog.

"Most of the gates in Warsaw had a small peephole for the janitor to look through when someone rang the bell, because it might have been a burglar or a prowler. As a rule, when I took Eve home, it didn't occur to me to look through the peephole. What was there to see? This time I yearned for her so much that I wanted to watch her walk from the gate into the courtyard. I bent down and I almost died from shock. If there was an open grave before me I would have jumped into it. Eve was standing there kissing and hugging Bolek. I thought that I was seeing things or that I had lost my mind. They kept embracing and kissing like old lovers. This lasted for about ten minutes. I was stronger than iron or I would have had apoplexy on the spot. I won't burden you with what I went through that night. I tossed in bed as if I had a high fever. I wanted to hang myself. My mother came into my room and said, 'Shloimele, what's the matter with you?' I could not tell her about my disgrace, so I gave her some excuse. I suffered the most terrible torments until daybreak. In the morning I fell asleep, and when I awoke my mouth felt as bitter as gall. I decided that I could no longer remain in Warsaw. Many people from my neighborhood had gone to America. All one needed was passage. There were agents who got you a ticket for the ship and allowed you to pay it out in installments after finding work in America. My father had a strongbox where he kept his money. I knew where the key was hidden. When my father left for the stables and my mother went to Ulrich's Bazaar to do her shopping, I opened the strongbox and took two hundred rubles. There were many thousands there, but I wasn't a thief. I sent the first monies I earned in America back home, but this is already putting the cart before the horse.

"I went to Gnoyna Street, where Eve lived, and I walked up the stairs. Usually I went there Saturdays and Wednesdays. I found Eve standing in the kitchen frying a pancake. No one else was at home. She saw me and her face lit up. 'Shloimele,' she exclaimed, and tried to kiss me. I said, 'Don't let the pancake burn.' 'What brought you so early in the morning?' and I said, 'Someone told me that the jeweler we bought your gifts from is a swindler. The gold is not pure fourteen-karat. It's mixed with silver.' She seemed frightened, and taking the pan from the stove, she went to bring me the jewelry. I put it all into my pocket and caught her by the hair. She became pale as death. 'What are you doing?' she asked. 'I watched you through the peephole last night and saw what you did with Bolek.' She lost her tongue. I gave her one swift punch in the mouth and she began to spit out her teeth. She spat out one tooth and then a second and then a third. The best dentist couldn't have done a better job. I felt like killing her, but I am not a killer. I spat at her and left.

"My dear man, what is your name? Isaac? My dear Isaac, I didn't take leave of my father or my mother or of my brother, Benjamin—no one. I ran to the Vienna station and bought a ticket for Mlawa. I knew that there one could cross the border illegally into Prussia. The contrabandists—they were called guides—smuggled you over the border with a passport for three rubles. I had nothing with me. Not even a shirt. The guide asked me, 'Where's your bundle?' 'My bundle is here,' I said, and pointed to my heart. He understood what I meant. At night I crossed the border and early in the morning I took a train to Hamburg, where I bought a ticket for the ship to New York. I still had a nice sum left from the two hundred rubles. I also sold Eve's presents and bought myself ready-made linen, a suit, and a pair of German shoes.

"I traveled steerage, and even though I considered myself a modern man, I refused to eat non-kosher food. The truth is, I could not eat at all. Most of the passengers suffered from seasickness and vomited their guts out. You could have died from the stench. I was also sick, but it was in my head. I was afraid I would lose my mind. I now hated all women. Lifting my hands to heaven, I swore never to marry."

"Did you keep your word?"

"I have six grandchildren."

Sam asked, "Shall I continue? You want to hear more?"

"Please do."

"It's a long story but I won't drag it out. Can the story of a person's lifetime be told? In the Yiddish papers they print stories that go on for months or even for years. I read them. I love to read. To me, a writer is greater than a rabbi or a doctor. He knows everything that goes on in your soul as though he were right there. But when I travel I cannot get the papers. Someone in America saves them for me and when I come home I read the entire batch of them. Yes, I swore never to marry, but to be alone is also difficult. Years ago those who went on a ship to America became like one big family. We called ourselves ship brothers and ship sisters. Since we refused to eat non-kosher food, all we got was potatoes in their jackets and the brine of herring. In Hamburg I had spent some of the money I had with me to buy kosher salami and liverwurst, and on the ship I treated everyone. This made me a real king. The girls and women all came to me for a slice of wurst and they praised me and kissed me, but I knew it was all for the wurst. After what happened with Eve I trusted no one. Among us greenhorns there was a little young woman who was returning to America. She had gone back to Europe to bring over her aunt. They both occupied a cabin, but the old woman became seasick, so the niece spent most of her time with us, the immigrants. Her husband was a ritual slaughterer in Brownsville. What did we know about Brownsville? In Warsaw the wife of a ritual slaughterer wore a wig or a bonnet, but this woman went about with her head uncovered. She was dark, with laughing eyes. She pulled jokes out of her sleeve. Every day I gave her a large slice of salami. She nicknamed me Baby, even though I was tall and she so tiny I could have put her in my pocket. She was a big talker and clever as the dickens.

For her, things didn't have to be spelled out. One look and she knew all about you, like a gypsy. Her name was Becky. Though her real name was Breindel, in America it became Becky. I never met anyone so quick. She was everywhere and knew everything. She hopped around like a bird. Of course she could speak English. She said to me, 'Baby dear, if one woman was false to you, it isn't necessary to blame all of us.' 'How do you know that a woman was false to me?' I asked. 'Baby, it's written on your forehead,' she answered. The next day Becky invited me to her cabin. Her aunt lay there as if she were dead. Seasickness is a terrible thing. I thought that she was dying, but Becky was laughing and winking at me. She signaled me to lean toward her while she raised herself on her tiptoes. She gave me a kiss that I still remember. That the wife of a ritual slaughterer should kiss a strange man was something new to me. I said to her, 'Don't you love your husband?' and she replied, 'Yes, I do love him, but he's busy slaughtering in Brownsville and I'm here.' 'If he knew what you were doing he would slaughter you, too.' And she said, 'If people knew the truth, the world would collapse like a house of cards.' We made love right then and there. I never knew that such a small woman could have such large desires. She tired me out, not I her. All the while she kept on prattling about God. Sabbath Eve she put three candles into three potatoes, draped a shawl over her head, covered her eyes with her fingers, and blessed the candles. And so we arrived in America. On the dock a large crowd stood waiting for the new arrivals, and my piece of merchandise recognized her husband, the slaughterer. 'Listen, Baby,' she said to me, 'nothing happened between us. We are complete strangers, forget the whole thing.' I later saw her hugging the slaughterer. She kissed him and wept, and I renewed my oath never to believe a woman. Shloimele, I said to myself, it's a false world. Years later a rabbi told me that it's written in the Torah that all humans are liars."

"Not in the Torah," I said, "but in the Book of Psalms: 'I said in my haste, all men are liars.'"

"That's it. Most of the passengers were taken to Ellis Island. I was as healthy as a bear and had money, so they let me through immediately. Agents from all sorts of factories came to the ships, and the moment an immigrant landed they hired him to work. The pay was never more than three dollars a week and sometimes even less. Since I had money in my purse, I was not in a hurry to become a slave. Downtown there was a square called the Pig Market. People came there to look for work. Every tradesman carried his tools as a sign of his skill. I saw a tailor carrying the head of a sewing machine, a carpenter held a saw. This is how it is in America. In one trade there's a need for workers and in another it is slack. Everything depends on the season. Agents tried to employ me but I wanted to look around first. A young man came over and said, 'You cannot sleep in the street. Let's go and find lodgings for you.' We walked as far as Attorney Street. The streets were crowded. People ate in the street, read the papers in the street, discussed politics. Even though it was the middle of the day, a whore tried to lead us to her basement room for the price of a quarter, but we refused to go with her. It seemed that my companion was a middleman. He took me into an apartment on the third floor where boarders were lodged and introduced me to the missus. Her name was Molly. Molly is an Irish name, but it's also a Jewish name. The flat had only cold water and a toilet in the hall. If you wanted to take a bath you had to go to the barber. For two dollars a week, the landlady gave me bed and board—all three boarders in one room. Her husband was a house painter. She washed our linen for a few pennies extra. She was a decent woman who killed herself for her husband and her children, but her husband was a bum who ran around with others. Her daughter came home at two o'clock every night and necked with the boys right in front of the door. This Molly's cooking was fit for a king. How she could have given us all this for two dollars a week I still don't understand. She bought bargains from the pushcarts on Orchard Street.

"My dear man. I held out and did not marry for ten years. I'm not a philosopher, but I kept my eyes open. I thought about life and saw what went on. As long as people believed in God they were afraid of the fires in Gehenna. But our Yiddish papers wrote that there was no God and that Moses was a capitalist and a bluffer. So what was there to fear?

"When I came to America there were already cars and even a few trucks, but most of the merchandise was carried in wagons. There were troughs on many of the streets with water for the horses. I knew all about horses from Warsaw and I went into the express business. At first I drove a wagon for another man, then I bought my own express wagon and a pair of Belgian mares. I soon bought a second wagon, and the number kept growing. I had entered America with my right foot and was lucky in whatever I did. I worked sixteen hours a day but I had more than enough strength. Today I take sleeping pills. At that time I would lie down on the bare floor in my wagon, and before I knew it, I was asleep. I could sleep without interruption for ten hours. Bums used to steal into my wagons and they slept there, too. Business was good and I became rich, or what was then thought of as rich. A thousand dollars bought more than ten thousand today. I had my own apartment on Grand Street. This was considered uptown. Matchmakers were after me, but I spoke to them openly: 'Why should I marry and let another man sleep with my wife? Let the other one marry and I will sleep with his wife.' These were not just words. Do you understand me?"

"Yes, I understand."

"No, you can't be too smart. Heaven and earth have sworn that people cannot outwit fate. I already told you that I love the Yiddish theater. Can you latecomers know what the Yiddish theater meant to us? The great actors were still alive then: Adler, Tomashefsky, Madame Liptzin, and later Kessler. Most of the shopworkers could go to the theater only on Saturdays, but I, a bachelor with money, could go whenever the desire came to me—and it came to me almost every night. Today's plays are worthless. In the Yiddish plays I'm talking about there was something to see—King David, Bathsheba, the Destruction of the Temple—real history! The Jews fought the Romans and the whole battle was right before your eyes. I had plenty of women and girls to take out, but I often liked to go to the theater by myself. There was one actress, Ethel Sirota, whose name was printed in small letters, but the first time I saw her act it made my heart jump. She hasn't been onstage now for God knows how many years. She is the grandmother of my grandchildren.

"If I were to tell you how I became acquainted with her and how I took her away from her husband, I'd have to sit with you three days and three nights. How did I, a simple coachman from Warsaw, come to an American actress? But love has strange power. She later admitted to me that she often felt my gaze on her all during the show. I always bought a ticket for the first or second row. Her husband acted in the road companies. He was never engaged for the New York productions. I once saw him act in Philadelphia—a piece of wood. They had no children. Well, we fell in love. The first time I went out with her I thought I would go mad with happiness. We ate in a restaurant on Broadway and afterward went to a nightclub. There were plenty of naked women in the show but I was burning with passion for Ethel. We drank champagne and I became tipsy. 'What do you see in me?' she asked. 'My husband is ready to trade me in for the lowest yenta.' And I told her that what I saw in her could not be put into words. We kissed and each kiss was like fire. Just as they write in the novels. The very first night I proposed marriage to her. When her husband, that lughead, heard that someone else was interested in his wife, he again developed an appetite for her and a game of cat and mouse began. He finally convinced himself that it was me she wanted, not him, and he demanded money. I counted out two thousand dollars in cash. Then it was a fortune—and he divorced her. It's easier said than done. It didn't happen quite that fast. Actually it dragged out for a long time and while waiting we lived as man and wife.

"When we became close and I began to question her about her past, she swore to me that her husband was the only man she ever had. But I will give you a rule: If a woman tells you that you are her second, you can be sure you are her tenth, twentieth, or perhaps her fiftieth. It's written someplace in the Bible that snakes creeping on rocks and ships crossing the sea leave no trace. If I'm not mistaken, King Solomon said it, and you know what he was referring to. The more I queried her, the more I learned. Before she appeared in the New York theaters, she, too, acted in the road companies, and in order to get a part you had to sleep with the director or whoever was in charge. Actually it wasn't much different on Second Avenue. Without liquor Ethel kept silent, but the moment she got high she spoke freely. I jotted down a long list of her lovers, and each time I thought the list was complete, another name popped up. Meanwhile she became pregnant. I had taken her

from her husband and because of me she had left the theater—
how could I destroy her life? We quarreled and it came to
blows. Her tears could have moved a stone. I realized that this
was my fate. Eve kissed the janitor's son and Ethel sold herself
for a part. Now that she was married and pregnant, she promised to behave. But she could not give up the theater altogether. We went to see all the shows. She got the tickets for
nothing. Every cashier knew her. Once you have been part of
the Yiddish theater, you are never forgotten. Ethel gave birth
to a girl and we called her Fanny, or Feigele, after Ethel's
mother. Two years later she had twins, a boy and a girl. These
are my children.

"After her second delivery she again yearned for the theater.
Parts were offered to her, the telephone kept ringing, but I
told her in no uncertain terms that if she returned to the stage
I would leave her. Before marriage I looked upon actors as
gods, but when I learned how they conducted themselves and
how the girls had to sleep around to get parts, I stopped wor-
shipping them. On the stage you see a man dressed like a rabbi
in a satin coat and a fur hat, reciting 'Hear, O Israel,' and sac-
rificing himself for the Holy Name. Two hours later he would
be telling some aspiring wench either to go to bed with him or
forget about the theater. I had good friends and the minute
they came to my house they started to warm up to my wife.
She was pleased. Why not? But after what happened to me in
Warsaw at Eve's gate I lost my taste for such monkey business.
When one of my cronies got too close to Ethel, I grabbed him
by the collar and showed him the way out. This gave me the
reputation of being a jealous savage. Ethel lamented that I was
driving our friends away. I stopped going to the Yiddish theater and the English one didn't attract me. There they don't
act, they just recite.

"In time the express wagons were all replaced by trucks, so I
formed a trucking company. Everything would have been all
right, but my blood was poisoned already. When I wasn't
brooding about Ethel, my thoughts returned to the double-
dealing of the slaughterer's wife. At night when I lay with
Ethel I questioned her about all her lovers. She had to confess
every single detail. If she denied anything I gave her hell. In
every type of business one has to travel occasionally, but each

time I imagined that the minute I left town, Ethel's lover would be with her. I was successful with women and when I saw how other women behaved I felt that Ethel could not be different. Just as soon as you turn your back your wife is already winking at someone else. It's like a grabbag game. Things reached such a state that I had to go to a nerve doctor. Instead of giving me a prescription he made things worse. He himself was divorced from his wife and he was paying her alimony. He pointed to his sofa and said, 'If this sofa could talk, many couples would be divorced.' At night I was tormented by bad dreams and they all had to do with my suspicious nature. I would awaken in the middle of the night with an urge to strangle Ethel. I couldn't have done it, but I was overcome with rage. And when I realized that two daughters were growing up in my own house and that they would one day be as sly as the other females, I wanted to kill them, too— my own children. Do you understand such insanity? Do you consider me a murderer?"

"You are not a murderer."

"What am I?"

"A man."

They rang the gong for supper and we both went up to the first-class dining room. Sam arranged with the steward to seat us at the same table. My wine steward now served both of us. Between one course and the next there was a long wait, because every dish was cooked to order. The supper lasted two hours.

I asked Sam, "Did you stay with Ethel?"

He pushed his plate aside.

"We were divorced. I wanted to leave New York and she wouldn't live away from it. She kept on dragging me to the Yiddish theater and the Café Royale, where she met her former boyfriends. As soon as I sat down at the table with my wife we were immediately joined by some rascal who had slept with her. I could not put up with it. I may be a simple fellow, the son of a coachman, but in our home such goings-on did not exist. My mother, peace be with her, had one God and one husband. I was so overwrought I was close to killing Ethel and then committing suicide, because I was not cut out to rot in prison or go to the electric chair. Our fighting and quarreling continued for so long it turned our love sour. She became, what do you call it, frigid. She complained that when I made love to her it was painful. I went with her to the nerve doctor and he said, 'It's in her head.' We parted, then made peace, then parted again. When Ethel finally did go back to the theater, the play folded the first week. The editor, I've forgotten his name, wrote that the whole performance was one long yawn. He didn't even mention Ethel's name. These critics pay attention only to the big shots. Now it was she who demanded the divorce. I haven't fallen so low that I would force myself on anyone, so I sent her to Reno and all was finished. Of course I supported the children. She believed that once she got rid of me all the theaters would be open for her, but they kept on closing, one after another. The new generation does not know Yiddish. And why go to a theater downtown, when for forty cents you can see in your own neighborhood a Hollywood movie with music, dancing, and gorgeous girls. She lived without a man for six years and refused to speak to me when I came to see the children. She locked herself in the bedroom or left the house. Later she married a druggist, a widower with five children. New York oppressed me. She poisoned the children against their father. My older daughter, Fanny, spat at me. Today she's a doctor. The younger one was married to an actor and tried to follow in her mother's footsteps, but it didn't work out and she was divorced. As a matter of fact, she's twice divorced. I don't even know where she is. I think somewhere in the Middle West. She studied nursing. My son is a scholar, a professor in Madison, Wisconsin. Sociology. He married a Gentile girl. This boy loved me. He used to visit me in Los Angeles. He has five beautiful children, but they are not Jews. Their mother sent them to Catholic parochial school. Sundays they had to go to church. Torn away from their roots!

"I moved to Los Angeles, first because I began to suffer from colds, second because I couldn't be in the same city as Ethel. Then I had a partner in business and partners are a heartache. Either they are lazy or they are thieves, and sometimes they are both. The Hitler war began and I read in the papers what they were doing to the Jews. My parents had long since died. My father, may he rest in peace, refused to come to America because here Jews worked on the Sabbath. My brother, Benjamin, fell in the First World War. My whole family was wiped out by the Nazis. I am far from being learned, but when I read how strong, healthy murderers dragged little children out of their cribs and later played ball with their skulls, I became desperate. While still in New York I used to go to the meetings of the *landsleit* or sometimes to a protest meeting at Madison Square Garden. What the speakers said made sense. They asked for money and I contributed. Just the same, I noticed that the people took it all lightly. I could see that even the speakers themselves didn't take it too much to heart. I was told that the speakers had to be paid and they even bargained about their fee. For some reason I took it to heart more than the others. Perhaps because I lived alone and had difficulty sleeping at night. I lay awake in my bed with the newspaper, and my brain whirred like a machine. If educated people could commit such cruelties while the rest of the world played dumb, what difference is there between a man and a beast? When you live with your family you don't have time to think. A wife lies near you, you are surrounded by children. When you are alone with the four walls you begin to take score. Well, I left for California.

"How could California help me? However, I began a new business and became very busy. In Santa Barbara I became acquainted with a widow, and it looked like love. As we kissed and caressed and fondled each other, I kept thinking in my heart that she had just put her husband, the father of her children, in his grave and now she was already replacing him. All my thoughts led in one direction: there is no love, there is no loyalty. Those with whom you are close will betray you even faster than total strangers. In the beginning the widow said that she demanded nothing from me, only that I should be friendly to her. Before I turned around I was supporting her. One day she wanted a mink coat and the next day a brooch or a diamond ring. Then she insisted that I take out a quarter of a million dollars' worth of insurance, not a penny less. I told her right off that if I had to pay, I would pay those younger and more beautiful. She raised a rumpus and I sent her away. She was too clever for her own good.

"Since then I have lived alone. From time to time little affairs begin, but as soon as I make it clear to them that I don't like to mix love with money, they run as if from a fire. I gave much thought to these matters. It is true that my mother was also supported, but she gave my father children, worked in the house from morning till late at night, and was a faithful wife. When my father had to go to Zichlin or to Wengrow, he didn't have to worry that some dandy would enter his home and kiss his wife. He could have gone to America for six years and my mother would have remained loyal to him. Modern women—"

"Your father was a faithful husband," I interrupted him. "But you demand faithfulness only from others."

He pondered and looked at me inquisitively.

"Yes, this is true."

"Your Eve kissed the janitor's son and you kissed the maid in your home."

"What? I promised Eve to be true, but from time to time I had to have a female, if not—"

"Without religion there is no faithfulness."

"So what shall I do? Pray to a God who let six million Jews be killed? I don't believe in God."

"If you don't believe in God you have to live with whores."

He didn't answer for some time, and then he said, "Therefore I went away from everybody and everything."

Sam emptied his glass and the wine steward filled it at once. I also took a sip from my glass and this, too, was immediately replaced.

I asked, "Where are you running to—Buenos Aires?"

Sam pushed away his glass.

"I have nothing to do in Buenos Aires. I have nothing to do in any other country. I'm retired and have enough to live on even if I reach one hundred. I don't wish it on myself. What for? For a man like me, life is a curse. I had hoped that old age would bring me peace. I reckoned that after seventy a person stops musing about all petty things. But the head does not know how old it is. It remains young and full of the same foolishness as at twenty. I know that Eve is no longer alive. She must have perished in the Nazi slaughter. Even if she were alive she would be a tottering old woman by now. But in my mind she is still a young girl and Bolek, the janitor's son, is still a young boy and the gate is still a gate. I lie awake at night, not able to sleep a wink, and I burn up with rage at Eve. Sometimes I regret that I didn't hit her harder. I know that I would have married her if I hadn't looked through the peephole that night. Her father wanted to arrange the wedding in a hall. A carriage would have been sent for her, and Bolek would have been standing there winking and laughing."

"It may be," I said, "that if you didn't look through the peephole that evening you would never have gone to America. You and Eve and your children would all have been burned in Auschwitz or tortured to death in some other concentration camp."

"Yes, I thought about that, too. One look through a peephole and your whole life is changed. You would still have been here at this table, but not with me. Ethel wouldn't have married the druggist. She would have remained the wife of that bully. She would never have had any children. He was supposed to have been sterile. That's what the doctors told her. What does all this mean? That everything is nothing but a miserable accident."

"Perhaps God wanted you to live and therefore he made you look into the peephole."

"Now, my dear man, you talk nonsense. Why should God want me to live while millions of other people are destroyed? There is no God. There isn't any. I have no education, but I have brains in my skull, not straw. I want you to know that I have a woman on this ship." Sam suddenly changed his tone.

"In second class?"

"Yes, in second class. I told her that I am a shoemaker and that I am going to Buenos Aires because it's cheaper there and I can live on my social-security payments."

"Who is she?"

"An Italian woman. She lives in Chile. She's returning from a visit to her sister in America, where she stayed for three years and learned a little English. Four of her six children are already married. I walked around on the deck and then I sat down near her steamer chair. We began to talk. She must have been pretty in her young days. Now she's over fifty and in those countries women age faster. I asked her questions and she told me everything. Her husband is Spanish and he's a barber in Valparaiso. Her sister in New York asked her to come because she had cancer. They live on Staten Island and are not poor people. When her sister's left breast was removed the doctors promised her that everything would be all right, but later she got it in the other breast. So my woman stayed with her until she died. The people from Chile don't know what lying is. They tell you everything provided you are a stranger. She told me the whole story of her life. Before she married and after, she had men. Her husband stood in the barbershop all day long, shaving and cutting hair, while she remained at home. One day it was a neighbor, the mailman, a boy from the grocery. They all asked for it and she seldom refused. The day she arrived in America her brother-in-law immediately began to bother her. He's an electrician. Since his wife was sick he did it with her. I said to her, 'Would you do it with me?' And she answered, 'Where? I share my cabin with three other women and two of them suffer from seasickness.' I told her that I could hire an empty first-class cabin. When she heard the words 'first class,' she got frightened. I persuaded her just the same. She made herself beautiful and I took her to my cabin. You speak about God. She's very pious. In Chile she went to church every Sunday. Even on Staten Island she didn't miss church. She never eats meat on Friday, only fish. But one thing has nothing to do with the other."

"Our mothers and grandmothers did not behave this way," I said.

"How do you know?"

"You yourself said that your father could rely on your mother."

"That is what I think. One can never be sure. If I had married Eve and we had children, they wouldn't have believed that their mother fooled around with the janitor's son."

"She might have been a very faithful wife."

"It may be. But during all the years she could never have forgotten what she had done. It may even be that Bolek would have visited her in our home a few months after our wedding and threatened to divulge her secret if she didn't give herself to him. You never know what such hoodlums are capable of doing when they are in heat."

"I know very well."

"I chattered so much about myself but I never asked you what you do. By the way, what street did you live on in Warsaw?"

"On Krochmalna Street."

"That was a street of thieves."

"I'm not a thief."

"What are you?"

"A Yiddish writer."

"Really? What is your name?"

I told him my name.

I expected him to jump with surprise, because I had seen him read the newspaper to which I contribute. But he sat mute and looked at me with astonishment and sadness.

"Yes, it's you. Now that you mention it, I recognize you from the pictures. I've read every word you've ever written. I always dreamed of meeting you."

For minutes neither of us spoke. Then Sam said, "If this could happen to me on this ship, then there is a God."

Translated by the author and Ruth Schachmer Finkel

The Bitter Truth

THIS is a story of two Warsaw youths—Zeinvel and Shmerl, both of them workers in a tailor shop. Shmerl was short, chubby, and had a round face and brown eyes which expressed naïveté and goodness. He was always nibbling on candy and cookies. He often smiled and burst out laughing for no reason at all.

Zeinvel was the complete opposite: tall, thin, with sunken cheeks and narrow shoulders. His disposition was often sour and gloomy. He seasoned every morsel of food with a lot of salt and pepper and washed it down with vodka.

As they say, opposites attract. Shmerl relished Zeinvel's sharp tongue, while Zeinvel found in Shmerl an attentive listener who looked up to him with wonder. Neither one was particularly learned, although Zeinvel knew a bit of the Pentateuch and Rashi, and could explain to Shmerl the articles and jokes printed in the Yiddish newspaper.

Needless to say, Zeinvel was more temperamental and more eager for the favors of the fair sex than Shmerl. But in those times it was difficult for a poor young man to find a woman, especially one of easy virtue. His only resort was to go every week to a brothel and for a gulden or twenty kopeks satisfy his needs. Shmerl always reproached Zeinvel for this light-minded conduct. First of all, he might catch a disease, and second, it went against Shmerl's grain to buy love; he would never enter such a loathsome place. Shmerl called himself a bashful shlemiel. Still, Zeinvel tried many times to persuade him to overcome his old-fashioned modesty and accompany him.

Finally, Shmerl gave in. To summon up the courage, he stopped off at a tavern and gulped down a mug of beer. When they arrived at the house and the door was opened, Shmerl recoiled and ran away. He had gotten a glimpse of heavily made-up women dressed in glaring colors: red, green, and blue stockings attached to lace garter belts. He inhaled an offensive odor and ran away with such speed that it was a miracle he didn't trip over his own steps. Later, when they met in the soup kitchen for dinner, Zeinvel scolded him.

"Why did you run away? Nobody would have chased you."

"Shameless women like these nauseate me. Don't be angry with me, Zeinvel, I have this sort of foolish nature and I almost vomited."

"*Nu*, they are lewd, but they don't bite. And we don't marry them. For the time being, let them be of some use . . . It's better than not sleeping at night."

"You're right, Zeinvel, but I have this silly nature . . ."

"*Nu*, I won't bother you anymore."

And that's how it remained. Zeinvel continued to go to the whorehouse every week. Shmerl admitted to Zeinvel that he often envied him, but he would never again try to seek pleasure from those wanton females. He would rather perish.

When the war between Russia and Germany broke out in 1914, the two friends were separated. Zeinvel was mobilized and Shmerl got a blue card of rejection because he failed to pass the physical examination. Zeinvel promised Shmerl to send a letter from the front, but soldiers are given few chances to write or to receive letters. Zeinvel lost all contact with Shmerl. He served in the Russian Army until Kerensky's revolution took place and then deserted. Only after the Polish-Bolshevik war did Zeinvel return to Warsaw and his tailor shop. Many young men Zeinvel knew in former years had died from typhoid fever. Other simply vanished—Shmerl among them. Zeinvel tried to come back to the old routine, but he had aged and was exhausted. He had witnessed so much betrayal and depravity that he no longer trusted any woman and had given up all hope of marriage. Yet the need for a woman cannot be denied, despite all disappointments. Zeinvel had no choice but to return to houses of ill repute. He made peace with the idea that this was his fate.

One day, as Zeinvel sat eating lunch in the old soup kitchen, he heard someone speaking his name. He turned around and recognized Shmerl, who had become as round as a barrel. He was dressed like a merchant and no longer had the appearance of a tailor's apprentice. The two friends fell on each other, kissed, embraced.

Shmerl cried out, "That I have lived to see this day means there is a God! I have searched for you for years. I thought you had already gone . . ." and he pointed his finger at heaven.

"You don't look well," he went on. "You've become thinner than you were."

"And you've become wider than longer," Zeinvel said.

"Did you marry, by any chance?" Shmerl asked.

"Marry? No, I have remained a bachelor."

"*Nu*, that's why you look like this. Brother of mine, I have married and I'm happy," Shmerl said. "I don't live in Warsaw anymore, I moved to the town of Reivitz, and I'm not a tailor's apprentice. You may think I'm boasting, but I have found the best girl in all of Poland. There is no other wife like my Ruchele in the entire world. She is good, clever. She helps me in the store. What am I saying? She *is* the whole business. There are no children yet, but Ruchele is better than ten children. What are you doing, Zeinvel? Are you still going to those rotten whores on Smocza Street?"

"Do I have a choice?" Zeinvel said. "After all the wars and revolutions, there is barely a proper woman left in Warsaw. Nothing but used-up merchandise from King Sobieski's time."

"Really, I pity you, after having tasted a young and beautiful girl like my Ruchele, you just spit on this trash . . . *Oy*, this is a miracle! I would never have thought to enter this soup kitchen, but I was passing by and caught a whiff of borscht and fried onions. Something drew me in. The whole meeting was absolutely destined!"

Shmerl did not leave Zenivel's side until the next morning. He took a room for him in the guest house where he was staying, and they talked and prattled late into the night. Shmerl told Zeinvel how he had passed the war years in the provinces and met Ruchele there, and how it was love at first sight. He had been a worker long enough. From manual labor one cannot become rich. One toils a lifetime and one is left with nothing. He suggested to Zeinvel that he come to Reivitz and there he and his wife could find him a position and possibly a wife. He had told Ruchele everything about him. He had praised him so much that Ruchele became jealous. "Don't worry," Shmerl said. "Everything will be fine. She will be happy to meet you."

Zeinvel complained that his work had come to the point where it was suffocating him. He was sick and tired of the big city, the heavy scissors and irons being a burden on him, the constant grumbling of the customers. He could not find one single human being with whom he could be close. What could he make of himself here? He was prepared to travel with Shmerl to the end of the world.

Everything happened quickly. Zeinvel packed his few possessions in a valise and was ready for the trip.

They arrived in the town of Reivitz on Friday afternoon. Ruchele was working in the store, and a maid was preparing the Sabbath meal. Shmerl's house was clean, neat, and permeated with a spirit of rest which one often finds with a loving and happy couple. The maid welcomed Shmerl and his guest with a Sabbath cookie and plum pudding. Shmerl led Zeinvel to the washroom. Zeinvel dressed in his Sabbath clothing; he put on a fresh shirt and a tie, preparing to meet Shmerl's wife. He didn't need to wait long. The door opened and Ruchele came in. Zeinvel took one look at her and became as white as chalk. He knew her—she was one of the most sought-after harlots in the house he had frequented. She was known there as Rachelle. At the time, she was a young girl and was so much in demand that the men lined up for her favors. The other girls quarreled with her and constantly argued with the madam and the pimps. Rachelle was rare in the sense that she took pleasure in her debased profession. She spat fire and brimstone on so-called decent women. She laughed with insolence and with such gusto that her laughter shook the walls. She told stories she had heard in other bordellos and in prison. She was known among the guests as an insatiable whore, obsessed with men. So much so, that they had to throw her out of the brothel. Zeinvel had had her quite a number of times. Thank God, she did not recognize him. There was no doubt that this was Rachelle. She still had a scar on her cheek from being assaulted by a pimp some years ago. She had become a little more plump than before, and had grown more beautiful.

Zeinvel was so shocked that he lost his tongue altogether. He trembled and stuttered. His knees buckled and he saw sparks. He felt like running out the door, but he could not do that to Shmerl. He soon came to himself and greeted the woman as one greets the wife of a dear friend; she responded accordingly. There was not a trace of her former vulgarity.

Even her city accent had changed. She carried herself like a woman born and raised in a decent home, friendly and tactful.

He heard her say, "Any friend of Shmerl's is a friend of mine."

That Friday night they all three ate the Sabbath meal. Although Zeinvel was careful not to ask any questions, she told him that she was an orphan on both sides and had worked a few years in a chocolate factory in Warsaw. It was clear to Zeinvel that she had chosen to put an end to her vile life. But how had this come about? Did some rabbi make her repent her sins? Did she suffer some terrible sickness which shattered her? Was it her love for Shmerl? Did she experience some startling event similar to what he was going through tonight? There was no point in racking his brains over an enigma which only God or perhaps death could solve. She was receiving Zeinvel with a dignity that had apparently become her second nature.

That night Zeinvel could not sleep. The two old friends had talked half the night. The rest of the night Zeinvel tossed and turned in his bed. The most wild thoughts assailed him: Should he wake up Shmerl and tell him the truth? Should he leave stealthily and run away in the direction of Warsaw? Should he tell Rachelle that he recognized her? He hoped that Shmerl was not the victim of treachery, like so many men he knew. Shmerl, the husband of the most salacious strumpet he had ever known! At this thought Zeinvel's body became alternately hot and cold and he heard his teeth chattering. Some perverse power made him play with the idea of taking advantage of Rachelle's dilemma for his own enjoyment. "No, I would rather die than commit an abomination like that," he murmured to himself. Dawn was breaking by the time he fell asleep.

Both man and wife greeted him in the morning: she with a glass of tea, and he with a Sabbath cookie, which one is allowed to take before the morning prayer.

"What is the matter with you? You look tired and pale," Shmerl said to him. "Did you have bad dreams?"

"Did my gefilte fish upset your stomach?" Rachelle asked playfully.

And he answered her, "I haven't eaten such delightful fish since I escaped from the Bolshevik paradise."

That morning, on the way to the synagogue, Zeinvel said, "Shmerl, I want to ask you something."

"What do you want to ask?"

"What is dearer to you? The truth or your comfort?"

"I don't know what you mean. Speak simple Yiddish," Shmerl said.

"Imagine that you were given a choice to know the truth and to suffer or to remain deceived and be happy, which would you choose?"

"You are speaking strangely. What do you mean?" Shmerl said.

"Answer me."

"What's the point of truth if people suffer from it? Why are you asking me all this?"

"There was an article about it in the Warsaw newspapers and they asked the readers to express their opinions," Zeinvel said.

"The newspapers print all kinds of nonsense. Someone may tell me that tomorrow, God forbid, I will break a leg. What would I gain from knowing this beforehand?" Shmerl said. "I would rather eat my Sabbath meal in peace and let God worry about tomorrow."

"Suppose someone came and told you that you were not your father's son but a bastard, and your true father was a dog-catcher? Would you be glad to learn the truth or would this enrage you?" Zeinvel asked.

"Why would I be glad? People would rather not know such an outrageous thing."

"*Nu*, so that's how it is," Zeinvel said to himself.

"But why do you waste time with such balderdash? Old bachelors and old maids have nothing better to do with their time and they dream up impossible events," Shmerl said. "Once you are happily married and you find the right business, you won't pay attention to newspapers and their silly garble."

Zeinvel did not answer. He stayed with Shmerl until Monday. Monday morning he announced that he must return to Warsaw. All of Shmerl's protests and pleadings were to no avail. Even more than Shmerl, Ruchele seemed to insist on his remaining in Reivitz. She promised to find a fitting match for him and a lucrative business. She went so far as to offer him a partnership in their haberdashery store, since they were in need of an experienced tailor and especially an honest one. Zeinvel could hardly believe his own ears. She spoke to him with the ardor and devotion of a loving sister. She besieged him to tell her the truth: Why was he so eager to return to Warsaw? Was it because of a woman? Was he keeping a secret from his best friend? But Zeinvel knew that he could not bear to witness the deception into which Shmerl had fallen. He was also afraid that he would be unable to keep his secret forever and might eventually cause the couple's ruin. All the powers of heaven and earth seemed to conspire that he go back to Warsaw and return to his tedious job, neglected room, and bought love, and to the loneliness of one who is forced to face the bitter truth.

Translated by Deborah Menashe

The Impresario

O N MY journey to Argentina I stopped for some two weeks in Brazil. The Yiddishists were to have organized a lecture for me, but they kept postponing it. When I embarked on the boat to Santos, the sponsor had given me a large manuscript of his, apparently expecting a letter of praise. I was not in need of the lecture and neither was I willing to tell lies about his work, which I didn't like. Suddenly I had a lot of spare time on my hands.

Autumn had begun in New York, but here it was the beginning of spring. I had brought my own writings and I was working on them in my hotel room, which faced the Atlantic. Fresh breezes wafted scents of tropical plants and fruits for which I had no name in Yiddish. White sailboats rocked over the waves. They reminded me of corpses in shrouds. The sponsor of my lecture called repeatedly but I was not in a rush to respond to him. This time, after finally picking up the receiver, I heard an unfamiliar voice and the coughing and stammering of one who does not know where to begin. He was saying, "I am a devoted reader of yours. I discovered you years before anyone else. It would be a great honor for me if . . ." The man on the other end lost his tongue.

I invited him up to the room and ten minutes later he knocked at my door. I opened it and saw an emaciated man, pale, with a thin nose, sunken cheeks, and a protruding Adam's apple. He carried a little valise which I was sure was full of manuscripts. Like an experienced doctor, I made the diagnosis at first sight: He had written for years without recognition. The editors were ignorant, the publishers a bunch of money-minded fakers. Should he continue to write? I offered him a chair and he sat down, thanking me and apologizing profusely. Then I heard him say, "I have a gift for you."

"My hearty thanks," I said. Yet I heard the cynic in me saying, It's a book of poems he published himself with a dedication to his wife without whose help this work would have never been written or printed.

He took a bottle of wine and an ornate box of cookies from his valise. He mumbled something which I could not make out. My estimation of the man was completely false. He was not a poet but a professor of German and French at the University of Rio. He had deserted the Austrian Army at the time of the First World War. His father had owned an oil well in Galicia, in the region of Drohobycz. My guest's name was Alfred Reisner. He spoke an idiomatic Yiddish and had come to tell me a story and to find out why my lecture had been postponed. We became quite friendly and I said to him, "If your story is interesting, I will tell you why my lecture was postponed. But you will have to keep it a secret."

"I keep many secrets."

"Before you begin the story, may I ask you about your health? You seem frail to me, or fatigued," I said.

"What? You are mistaken, like all the others," Alfred Reisner answered. "Every time I get on a bus, passengers get up for me, even young women, as if I were a tottering old man. But I'm as strong as iron. I am in my early sixties and each day I walk between twelve and sixteen kilometers. I was never sick a day in my life. As they say, 'It should remain so for a hundred and twenty years.' However, I am not eager to live long."

"Why not?"

"You will soon know."

I called room service and ordered coffee—not the strong black coffee they drink in Brazil, but coffee with cream and sugar. We nibbled on the cookies which Alfred Reisner had brought. I heard him say, "I was afraid to call you. I have great respect for creative people. Every time I read you, I have a desire to contact you, but I never do. Why should I take up your valuable time? I hoped to meet you at the lecture here in Rio, but I knew that you would be surrounded by hordes of people. You often mention Spinoza in your stories. I imagine that he is your most beloved philosopher. Are you still a Spinozaist?"

"Not a Spinozaist, but a pantheist," I said. "Spinoza was a determinist, but I believe in free will, or *bechira*. That means . . ."

"I know what *bechira* means," Alfred Reisner said. "My father arranged for a Hebrew teacher to tutor me in the Bible and the Mishnah. When the First World War broke out and the Russians invaded Galicia, our family escaped to Vienna.

My father was religious to a degree but not at all a fanatic. He was a worldly man and knew eight languages. I was born a linguist, so to speak, myself. I entered the university of Vienna, but later I was mobilized and sent to the Italian front. As I told you, I had no desire to defend the Hapsburg empire, and so I deserted."

"Is this your story?"

"Only the beginning, if you will spare me some of your time. I hope that what I want to tell you will be of interest to you. You often write on the topic of jealousy. Have you noticed that modern fiction writers ceased writing about this subject? The critics have written with so much aversion about what they call the bedroom novel that the writers have become frightened. Jealousy has become almost an anachronism in modern literature. But I always considered jealousy a mighty human and even animal instinct and the very crux of the novel. I admired Strindberg highly and read every word he wrote. The reason for this admiration was the fact that I was, and perhaps deep in my heart still am, an extremely jealous man. When I studied in the Gymnasium it was enough that my girlfriend would smile at another student for me to cut off all relations with her. I had decided to marry a virgin; if possible, one who had never dated another man. To me a man betrayed was a mad defiled—a leper. You asked before if I was sick. The truth is that when I was twenty years of age I already looked old, sick, frail. I sometimes think that the fear of ending up a cuckold, and the knowledge that the whole male gender is at the mercy of women, wore me out. But my seeming frailty also helped me during the war. No one suspected me of being a deserter. Do you still want me to continue my story?" Alfred Reisner asked.

"Yes, I do."

"Well, it's very kind of you. At that time in Vienna I became involved with a young woman from the Russian part of Poland. She was three years younger than I. Her father and mother were unknown Yiddish actors who dragged around performing in stables and firehouses. Her name was Manya. She began to act with her parents when she was only five. They put on Goldfaden's and Letteiner's plays, and she also performed in some kitsch plays which her father had written. He spelled Noah with seven mistakes, as they say.

"At the time of the war Manya came to Vienna and tried to produce her father's plays. In Warsaw, a wealthy man impressed with her voice paid for her singing lessons. She eventually got a job in the opera chorus—no small achievement for a Jewish wench. Her father had died of typhoid fever in 1915. Her mother had become someone's housekeeper, and mistress as well.

"Even now, at sixty, Manya is still good-looking, but when I met her she was a rare beauty. I watched as she sang lascivious songs in a Yiddish theater to which Galician refugees came. It was a combination of a restaurant, a nightclub, and a hangout. If she came to visit late at night she always brought me a bag of leftovers. Once in a while I had to give her two crowns to pay for her fare. When she sang 'In the Holy Temple in a corner of the room sits the widow of Zion wrapped in gloom,' her voice enchanted me. It stirred up a storm in my soul. I fell passionately in love with her and was ready to marry her on the spot. But when Manya began to reveal her sexual past, it created a terrible crisis in me. I was so shattered that I felt like killing her as well as myself. By nineteen she had had a roster of over twenty lovers, among them her own father, he should roast in Gehenna. She also had some experience as a lesbian. She had tasted it all: sadism, masochism, exhibitionism, every possible perversion. She boasted to me about her sins, and despite my love, I developed a fierce hatred for her. I did not force her to confess, she did it willingly. She was proud of her lechery. Most of the men she had had were lowlifes, people of the underworld. In some cases she didn't even remember their names. Some of them were Poles connected with the Warsaw opera. She spoke to me and laughed as if the whole thing was nothing but a joke. This woman who sang so beautifully about the Holy Temple and the widow of Zion had not the slightest respect for Jewishness and Jewish history and no feeling for the Holy Land. Her body was nothing more than a piece of flesh for her to give away for the slightest favor, for a bit of flattery, or for the mere curiosity of tasting another male. She spat profanities like the shells of sunflower seeds. Millions of men fought on the fronts and died for their country, while Manya had one ambition: to become a cheap operetta singer and to sing out all the banalities with which the librettos are packed. And also to go to bed with those rich charlatans who boast about sleeping with actresses.

"While she confessed, she kissed and fondled me and tried to assure me that she was deeply in love with me, but I knew she spoke the same way to all the other men and would continue to do so to those who would come after me. I had fallen in love with a whore. That night I had a desire to leap from the bed and run. But that would have been pure suicide, since I was a deserter and Vienna was teeming with military police. To go home to my parents would endanger them, too."

Alfred Reisner took out a cigarette, rolled it between his fingers, and lit it with a lighter. "Yes, I wanted to run away from this lewd piece, but I did not run. She disgusted me, but as I kissed her and caressed her I was silly enough to demand that she be a woman like my mother and grandmother. She was so sure of her power over me that she refused even to promise. Instead she proposed marriage, with an agreement that both of us should be allowed to have others.

"What did she look like, you are wondering. She was not tall, but slim, with black hair and black eyes which expressed passion, insolence, mockery. She had an uncanny power of speech. We in Galicia speak Yiddish slightly mixed with German. But her Warsaw Yiddish had all the idioms and linguistic gems of your region. And they flowed from her mouth. When she cursed, the curses poured out like a stream of poison. When she became erotically excited, she used words at which a regiment of Cossacks would blush. I have met many cynics in my life, by Manya's cynicism was incomparable. I often played with the idea of writing down her salacious expressions, all her vulgar jokes, and then publishing them, but this plan of mine, like many others, was never realized.

"Everything came at once: the revolution in Russia, the pogroms in the Ukraine, the German defeat in France, the collapse of the Hapsburg empire. Poland became independent almost overnight and my parents demanded that I go back home with them. But after Vienna, Drohobycz looked like a hamlet, not a city. Besides, Manya wanted to go back to Warsaw, and that is where we went. The hooligans in Lemberg made a pogrom against the Jews. The trains were swarming with General Haller's soldiers, who cut Jewish beards. England came out with the Balfour Declaration and Zionism ceased being a dream. If you were in Warsaw at that time, you know what went on: a mixture of war, revolution, assassinations. First Pilsudski chased the Bolsheviks to Kiev. Then Trotsky chased the Polish Army to the Vistula, where a military miracle was supposed to have occurred. They wanted to make a Polish soldier out of me and send me to fight for my freshly hatched fatherland. But a 'miracle' happened to me, too. I acquired a passport with a false birth date.

"Jewish Warsaw was boiling like a kettle: Zionist demonstrators, Communist adventurers. We had arrived in Warsaw penniless, but Manya bumped into a former lover, a speculator, a would-be patron of the arts. His name was Zygmund Pelzer. When Zygmund kissed Manya, I became dizzy, and my heart was beating like a hammer. I knew that to live with this woman would be permanent hell for me. I swore a holy oath to get rid of her once and for all. Two weeks later, we got married.

"She had given me an ultimatum: Either get married or get out. She gave me three days to think it over. I convinced myself then that I was nothing but a miserable slave. I don't think I slept a wink those three nights.

"I once read an article of yours where you complained that the philosophers ignored the emotions and considered them a plague. Actually, the emotions are the very essence of our being. When Descartes said *Cogito, ergo sum*, he should have been talking about the emotions. Your Spinoza's adoration of adequate ideas is nothing but naïve rationalism.

"To make it short, we went to an unofficial rabbi and he filled out a *ketubah* and then set up a canopy. And who do you suppose gave away the bride? The same Zygmund Pelzer, her lover."

"How did you become a professor in Brazil?" I asked.

Alfred Reisner did not answer immediately. "How did it happen? Some years later, a so-called impresario, a Pole, came from South America to Warsaw. I say 'so-called' because I've never seen him practice his profession, or any other profession, for that matter. His name is Zdizislaw Romanski, a tall blond fellow and quite a charmer. He had heard Manya sing in a trashy vaudeville theater and decided that she was exactly what he was looking for. He signed her up, took her to Brazil, and I dragged after them.

"For me to learn Portuguese was easy, since I knew Latin and French. A position was open at the University of Rio for an assistant professor of German and I was hired. In time I began to teach French, too. Manya could have become rich with her voice, but the charlatan, the impresario, invaded her life and my life as well. It began on the ship to Brazil.

"Two things I have learned in my life of disgrace. First, that the whole concept of free will, free choice, and all other phrases about human freedom are sheer nonsense. Man has no more freedom than a bedbug. In this respect, Spinoza was right. However, consistent determinist that he was, he had no reason to preach ethics. The second thing I have learned is that, under certain circumstances, every human passion can reverse itself and become the very opposite of what it was. From a psychological point of view, Hegel was right: Each thesis proceeds in the direction of its antithesis. The mightiest love can become the most venomous hatred. A wild anti-Semite can become an ardent lover of the Jews or even a convert to Judaism. A miser can suddenly begin to throw all his money around. A pacifist can become a murderer. The man who sits before you lived through many metamorphoses. One time I was burning with jealousy. The mere thought that my wife could have the slightest desire for another man drove me to insanity. A few years later, I came to the point where I could lie with Manya and her lover in one bed. Please don't ask me for any details or explanations. Pleasure itself is a form of suffering. Asceticism and hedonism are actually synonymous. I know that I am not revealing anything new to you. Our religious sages knew about it in their way."

"What kind of person was this impresario?" I asked.

"A demon."

"How old was he?"

"Who knows how old a demon is? A true word never came out of his mouth—a psychopathic liar, a crazy boaster. According to him, all the beauties in Poland were his concubines,

Pilsudski and his generals were all on a first-name basis with him. In the war with the Bolsheviks he managed to perform all kinds of heroic acts and he received countless medals. As far as I could tell, he never served in the military. Neither was he descended from counts and barons. His father was nothing but a notary public in Wolhynia.

"After all I have been through, nothing astonishes me anymore. Nevertheless, whenever I have the feeling that he can no longer surprise us, he does something which baffles me completely. His physical strength was and still is extraordinary. Although he is the worst alcoholic I've known, I have never known him to be ill. According to medical theory, he should have burned out his stomach and his bowels by now. Every morning when he opens his eyes, he repeats the same joke, 'I'm going to gargle with mouthwash,' and the mouthwash is a tea glass of vodka on an empty stomach. He turned Manya into a drunkard also. He continually threatens Manya and me with suicide, or that he is going to kill both of us. He also babbles about converting to Judaism."

"Who pays the bills?" I asked.

"I do."

"Didn't he ever try to do anything?"

"Only when he was sure to fail."

"Would you call yourself a masochist?" I asked.

"As good a name as any. Yes, me, them, and the whole human race; its wars, revolutions, arts, even its religions. Humanity is nothing but a permanent rebellion against God and what Spinoza called the order of things, or nature. Man was born a slave, and with the bitterness of a slave. He has to do the opposite of what he is forced to do. He is God's eternal opposition: actually Satan."

"Do you believe that your impresario is still in love with Manya?" I asked.

Alfred Reisner seemed to shudder. "In love? Who knows what love is? The whole notion of love is vague and ambiguous. But when you are dealing with a demon, what kind of love is he capable of? He destroyed her. She calls him 'my angel of death.' She drank until she lost her voice. She has a throat disease which the doctors in Brazil cannot identify, a type of cancer. Quite often she becomes dangerously sick and we have to take her to the hospital. She gets asthma and loses the power of speech. Once, she coughed so terribly I had to rush her to the hospital, and they discovered a collapsed lung.

"It all came as a result of drinking, screaming, trying to sing without a voice, pushing the body to be young when it was ordered to be old. These two have waged a twenty-year war, a bitter war, a war of madness and mutiny. Unbelievable as it sounds, I haven't figured out in all these years what they are fighting about. You forget such things, like a nightmare. Both of them rave at the same time, she in Yiddish and he in Polish. They carry on unrelated monologues. I've often thought that if one could record their wild conversations, it would be material for a literary masterpiece. Different as we are, all three of us have one common quality: we have not the slightest knack for practical matters. When a fuse blows in our home, we sit there in the dark for hours helplessly waiting for the superintendent, who is a drunk himself and never available. We lose money, we forget dates, we are constantly in a state of utter confusion. A day doesn't pass when something doesn't break down in our caricature of a house: the electricity, the gas, the toilet, the telephone. When it rains, the water leaks right through the roof into the bedroom and we have to cover the floor with buckets. Yes, you can call us masochists. But why just the three of us? And what miserable fate keeps us together year after year after year? We have given ourselves the holiest oaths to part once and for all and put an end to this tragicomedy of an existence. We have actually run away from each other the devil knows how many times and under the most bizarre circumstances, but we always come back to the same mess, the same madness, drawn by a power for which I haven't yet found a name in any dictionary, encyclopedia, you name it. Neither Freud nor Adler nor Jung could have ever explained it by their various theories. Passion? You can call it passion, complex, insanity, or simply meshuggas. We leave and we get sick from yearning and brooding. We write desperate letters to one another and plead for peace, forgiveness, a fresh start, and other ridiculous banalities of which we make fun ourselves. We laugh and cry and spit when we meet again and we drink a toast to our mutual dybbuk. Yes, I too have learned to drink, although not as much as they. I could not afford it. I have a family to provide for, woe is me."

Alfred Reisner glanced at his wristwatch and said, "It is later than I thought. Please forgive me for taking up so much of your precious time. To whom could I tell a story like this? There are philosophers, psychologists, and even those who consider themselves writers at the university, but to confide in them would be sheer suicide. Apart from the office girl who sends my salary every month, no one knows my address. Now that I'm as good as retired, I'm as good as a corpse. Well, how about your lecture? When will it take place?"

"I'm afraid it won't," I said.

"Could you tell me the reason?"

The telephone rang and the sponsor told me that my lecture had been rescheduled. He gave me the date. I conveyed the news to my guest, and for a moment his eyes lit up.

"These are good tidings. It will be an event. We will come to hear you. All three of us."

"The Pole also?" I asked.

Alfred Reisner thought it over. "Since he is really not of this world, who knows whether he is a Pole, a Russian, or a Jew? He is a great admirer of yours. He reads you in English and in French. A little bit in Yiddish, too. Don't be afraid. He won't come to the lecture riding on a broom, with a tail and horns. When he needs to, he can be a perfect gentleman."

Translated by the author

Logarithms

THAT Sabbath afternoon the talk turned to a merchant who set fire to his store in order to obtain the insurance money. I heard Aunt Yentl say, "Well, arson is arson. It was done before him and it will be done after him. Easy money is an evil temptation. All he had to do was pour some kerosene on the merchandise and light a match. The insurance company adjusters pretend to take the merchant at his word. It's not their own money they're paying; it all comes from the banks in Petersburg. In olden times, when a merchant could not repay a debt, they took possession of his house and business or the man was imprisoned. People went to jail for such deeds. Today one can easily declare bankruptcy. At the worst, one sets a fire. If luck is on his side, he'll be released in no time or he can run off to America."

"Just the same," our neighbor Bela Zyvia said, "to risk burning a whole marketplace, and half a town to boot, one needs the heart of a murderer."

"Women, this is not a subject for the Sabbath," Aunt Yentl said.

I heard my Aunt Yentl make this statement almost every Saturday, but she frequently broke her own rule to keep the Sabbath pure and gay and told stories which had the scent of gossip. She would tap her own lips and say, "Be quiet, my mouth" or, "Don't let me sin with my own words, Father in heaven."

Aunt Yentl went to the kitchen to bring refreshments. She returned with a tray containing cherries, plums, and a drink called kvass, and said, "A man himself is his own worst enemy. A hundred enemies cannot do to a person the damage he is capable of doing to himself." She sat down, stroking the colored ribbons which hung from the top of her bonnet and the golden earrings which dangled from her earlobes, and I knew she was about to tell a story.

Aunt Yentl drank some kvass and wet her lips with the tip of her tongue. After some hesitation, she began: "True, it is not a story for the Sabbath, but there is a lesson to be learned from it. When I lived with my first husband—he should intercede for all of us—in the town of Krasnystaw, we had as a neighbor a widow from Lublin named Chaya Keila. Her husband left her with a gifted son, Yossele. He knew half the Pentateuch by heart by the age of five. He was also a mathematical wizard. His father had left him a book entitled *The Study of Algebra*, and little Yossele pored over it day and night. His mother took him from house to house to show off his remarkable talent. He had calculated how many drops of water filled the town river. He asserted that in the dense forest behind the squire's castle there were two trees with an identical number of leaves, though no one had ever counted them. People gaped in astonishment. Chaya Keila was in constant fear that the neighbors might give him the evil eye. Every two days, she took him to an old woman who knew how to exorcise malicious spirits. Before the beginning of every month, she gave the boy herbs to purge him of worms in his intestines. She had learned incantations written on parchment by the Preacher of Kozienice. Once, when Yossele became sick with fever, an old witch told the mother to dig a ditch behind the house, dress the sick boy in white linen, and make him lie in the ditch to fool the angel of death into thinking he was already buried in his shroud. When the rabbi heard about this, he sent his beadle to knock at her shutter and warn the frightened mother that this was an act of sorcery. Yes, overly protective mothers do bizarre things. The rabbi told the mother to give the boy two new names—Chaim and Alter, meaning 'life' and 'old age.' The mother called him by these two names for years, but strangers forgot them and still called him Yossele.

"I will make it short: Yossele grew up to be a genius in Torah and mathematics. At that time there was a Gentile apothecary in town who knew Latin better than most priests. Once when Chaya Keila brought Yossele to buy pills, the two conversed and suddenly the apothecary cried out to Chaya Keila, 'Congratulations, your son has already learned logarithms without a teacher.'

"I had never heard this word when his mother came running to our house with the good tidings. She repeated this difficult word so many times that I learned how to pronounce it myself. For weeks Chaya Keila spoke about nothing but logarithms—'logarithms this,' and 'logarithms that!'

"Later Yossele learned how to play chess. He could beat all the town's chess players, Jews and Gentiles alike. He played chess with the apothecary's daughter, Helena, who smoked cigarettes and was as clever as a man. He even played with the Russian chief of police and with some Polish dignitaries. A few insisted on playing for money with the boy, thus helping his widowed mother make ends meet. Every day the mother announced the boy's latest victories. The squire of the town, who was a count, presented Yossele with a chessboard and figures made of ivory, after Yossele went so far as to checkmate the magistrate himself.

"Now listen to this: There was in our town a rich Jew named Wolf Markus, a timber merchant. From the Poles impoverished by the revolution, he bought large parcels of forest and let the trees, mostly oaks, be chopped down. In order to estimate how much lumber could be made from them, one needed mathematics. When Wolf Markus heard of Yossele's knowledge, he invited him to his house and they discussed logarithms for hours with Wolf's bookkeeper. Everyone present knew mathematics and they all played chess, even Wolf's two daughters, Serele and Blumele. They all became enthusiastic about Yossele's scholarship and wisdom.

"Serele fell in love with him at first sight, as they say. He had come for an hour and conquered the world. In a small town everyone knows what's cooking in other people's pots. Chaya Keila came running to us immediately with the good tidings. But why elaborate? Wolf Markus had accumulated large dowries for his daughters and he spoke openly of his intentions. Fathers, even more than mothers, are eager to marry off their daughters. One day he spoke to Yossele of a match, and the next they wrote preliminary agreements. Two weeks later, all the relatives on both sides were invited to the engagement party. The town was boiling like a kettle. Wolf Markus went to Lublin and came back with a golden watch for Yossele. The boy was no longer his mother's son, but Wolf's. Chaya Keila laughed and cried from happiness. She almost died of fear that someone would snatch away her good fortune. I was invited to the celebration and I heard of the gifts Yossele would get—the golden watch, a silver watch, a Pentateuch in silk, a set of Mishnah bound in leather, an embroidered prayer shawl, and a fox-fur hat with thirteen tails. The one who wrote out the marriage contract had his own style, and got a percentage of everything he wrote. Chaya Keila had jewelry left from her own marriage and she gave it to the bride for signing the agreement, as was the custom. If someone had suggested she offer her head, she would not have hesitated a moment.

"It looked as if Yossele had fallen into a bed of clover, and the city reverberated with envy. Other mothers had also wanted to make brilliant matches for their daughters. Chaya Keila cursed them in advance. I heard her say, 'Was it my fault that I gave birth to a genius? It is written somewhere that the womb of a woman is like a drawer. Whatever you put in, you take out. Yossele's father, he should rest in peace, was a scholar himself. He had a great mind, and the apple does not fall far from the tree. But no one can lock people's mouths. They always search for something malicious, never for anything good.'

"I remember it all," Aunt Yentl said. "Envious people just could not stand it that a Jewish young man understood logarithms and married a rich man's daughter. It is written in the holy books that because of hatred and envy Jerusalem was destroyed. I was still a young girl then, but I was afraid that something terrible would happen to Yossele. The evil tongues went from house to house and maligned him. Even though he was a relative of mine, the evil tongues came to our house— but I am forgetting the main thing: Wolf Markus arranged for a wedding which cost him a fortune. He even brought musicians from Janok and Zamosc. Of course, he could not invite everybody, and those who were omitted burned with rage. Since Yossele had the name of a scholar, they called him up for the reading of the Torah, which was a sign of respect. And this inflamed the gossips even more.

"Now not far from Krasnystaw, in the town of Schebrshin, lived a Jew, Jacob Reifman. People considered him both a scholar and a heretic. He did not deny God, but it was said that he wrote books in German and sent them to the Maskilim —the enlightened Jews in Germany. The Hasidim and the Maskilim waged war among themselves, and the word was that

Yossele and Reifman exchanged scholarly letters and made fun of the Hasidic rabbis. A yeshiva boy in our town spread the rumor that Yossele said that those who built the Holy Temple made mistakes in measuring the columns, the sacred vessels, and the altar. Immediately there arose in town a hue and cry that Yossele considered himself cleverer than King Solomon. When Chaya Keila heard this accusation, she was ill with fear. She came running to our house, crying bitterly that her enemies were trying to tear the crown from her head.

"One Sabbath, there was pandemonium in town. When Yossele was called up as the third one to the Torah for special honors, a stranger ran up to the reading table and tried to shove him away, screaming that Yossele was an apostate and a betrayer of Israel, who should be excommunicated with the blowing of the shofar in the light of black candles. Chaya Keila had come that Saturday to the women's section of the synagogue to pray. These vicious words about her beloved son made her utter a terrible scream, and she fell to the floor with a heart seizure. They tried to revive her with Yom Kippur drops, and massaged her temples, but it was all in vain. She was carried out on the stretcher which always stood at the door of the poorhouse. This was no longer a Sabbath but a day of mourning and fasting. In the bedlam which followed, butchers, coachmen, and horse dealers rushed into the synagogue and attacked the intruder who had reviled Yossele. The readings of the Torah and the prayers were stopped immediately. The squire heard of the outburst, and a fear fell upon all the Jews. The community leaders had to send negotiators to apologize to the squire for the violence at the synagogue and pay a fine for the scandal.

"'Excommunication' is a word which creates fear even among the Gentiles. For generations such a thing never took place in Poland except when the false Messiah, Jacob Frank, converted with his wife and disciples and proclaimed in open court that the Jews used Christian blood for their matzohs. This didn't happen in my time, but I heard about it."

"But what happened to Yossele?" Bela Zyvia asked.

Aunt Yentl shook her head. "I don't like to say it on the Sabbath," she said, "but something terrible—even unbelievable."

"What was it?"

"He changed his gold coin," Aunt Yentl said.

"You mean he converted?"

"He went to the priest and married Helena, the daughter of the apothecary."

"He left his wife?" my mother asked.

"His wife, God, the Jews," Aunt Yentl answered.

"Did he divorce his wife?" my mother asked.

"The wife of a convert does not need a divorce," Aunt Yentl said.

"Yentl, you are mistaken," my mother said. "According to the law, a convert remains a Jew and his wife is considered a married woman and she needs divorce papers if she intends to remarry."

"This is the first time I've heard that," Bela Zyvia said.

"If one lives long enough, one hears many things for the first time," Aunt Yentl said. "Men look strong, but they are actually very weak."

"Well, this is the law of the Torah," my mother said. "I know of a case where one of the rebels who tried to overthrow the Czar converted while in prison. They had to bring a rabbi to the jail, and a scribe and two witnesses, and he divorced his Jewish wife according to the law of Moses and Israel while in prison. Men! What betrayers men are!"

"The Torah is like the ocean," Aunt Yentl said. "There is no bottom. Women, it's getting late. The sun is setting. We have soon to recite 'God of Abraham.'"

I turned my face to the west. The sun was setting, surrounded with glowing clouds. They reminded me of the river of fire where the wicked are punished in Gehenna. For a long while the women sat silently, with bowed heads, wiping their noses into their aprons. Then I heard Aunt Yentl reciting: "God of Abraham, Isaac, and Jacob, protect the poor people of Israel and Thine own glory. The Holy Sabbath is going away and the lovely week should come now. It should be with Torah and good deeds, riches and honor, charity and mercy. An end should come to the dark exile. The sound of Elijah's shofar should be heard and the Messiah, our redeemer, should come speedily and in our days. Amen selah."

"Amen selah," all the women answered in one voice.

"I see three stars in the sky," Aunt Yentl said. "I think one is now allowed to light a candle, but where are my matches? Every Friday when I light the candles I put away the matches, but they get lost. Old age is not a joy."

There was suddenly light. Aunt Yentl had found her matches. I looked up to the sky and saw that the moon had appeared with its face of Joshua, the son of Nun. My mother stood up and looked at me angrily, almost with contempt. Was it because I, too, was a man and might one day betray womankind as Yossele did? I had promised her many times not to come to Aunt Yentl's on the Sabbath, but her Sabbath fruit and stories were too great a temptation for me. I could not understand why I felt a great compassion arise in me for Yossele and something like a desire to know Helena, play chess with her, and learn logarithms. I remembered my brother Joshua in a quarrel saying to my father, "The other nations studied and learned, made discoveries in mathematics, physics, chemistry, astronomy, but we Jews remained stuck on a little law of an egg which was laid on a holiday." I also remembered my father answering, "This little law contains more wisdom than all the discoveries the idolaters have made since the time of Abraham."

Translated by the author and Lester Goran

Runners to Nowhere

THE TWO of us, Zeinvel Markus and I, were sitting in Rector's cafeteria on Broadway drinking coffee and eating rice pudding. The conversation turned to the period from 1939 to 1945, the Hitler war and the destruction of Warsaw. In those years I lived in the United States, but he, Zeinvel Markus, remained in Warsaw and went through all the terrors of the Second World War. In Warsaw, Zeinvel Markus had been a columnist of the kind we called a "feuilletonist." His columns, featured at the bottom of the page, were somewhat clever, a little sentimental, and used many quotations from writers and philosophers. He especially loved to quote Nietzsche. As far as I knew, Zeinvel Markus had never married. He was small and had yellowish skin and slanted eyes. He used to joke that he was a great-grandchild of Genghis Khan and the daughter of a rabbi, one of his captive concubines. Zeinvel Markus suffered from at least a dozen imaginary illnesses, among them impotence. He both complained of and boasted about this malady, at the same time hinting about his great success with German maidens. He was for many years the Berlin correspondent of a Yiddish newspaper in Warsaw. He had returned to Warsaw from Germany at the beginning of the thirties and we remained friends until I left for America.

Zeinvel Markus arrived in the United States in 1948 from Shanghai, where he had managed to live as a refugee for some time. In New York he developed a new version of impotence—a literary one. He suffered from writer's cramp in his right hand. For some reason, the editors of the Yiddish press in America had little preference for his ambiguous aphorisms and quotations from Nietzsche, Kierkegaard, Spengler, and Georg Kaiser. He also developed a sickness which seemed to me genuine—abdominal ulcers. The doctors forbade him to smoke and allowed him to drink no more than two cups of coffee a day. However, Zeinvel Markus said to me, "Without coffee my life isn't worth a pinch of tobacco. I'm not going to become an American Methuselah anyhow."

Zeinvel Markus had countless stories to tell, and I never got tired of spending time with him. He knew personally all the so-called professional Jews in the whole world. He had visited Baron Hirsch's Jewish colonies in Argentina, had gone to all the Zionist congresses, and traveled to South Africa, Australia, Ethiopia, and Persia. They translated his feuilletons in the Hebrew press in Tel Aviv. I tried many times to persuade him to write his memoirs, and as usual Zeinvel Markus answered me with a paradox: "All memoirs are full of lies, and since I can tell only the truth, how can I write my memoirs?"

That afternoon, as always when we met, we finally began to speak of love, fidelity, treachery, and Zeinvel said, "In my life I've seen at least a thousand forms of treachery, but the treachery of the two runners I never even imagined before 1939."

"Runners?" I asked. "What do you mean by runners?"

"I mean a man and a woman in the process of running," Zeinvel replied. "Wait a moment, I'm going to bring us two cups of coffee."

"I've had enough coffee already," I said.

"You will drink another. If you don't drink it, I will," Zeinvel said. "In Russia, even under the Bolsheviks, one could get a glass of hot coffee, but here in the golden land you cannot get a *hot* cup of coffee for love or money. It's not only in this cafeteria. You can't get a cup of really hot coffee even in the Waldorf-Astoria. I tried in Washington, in Chicago, in San Francisco, but to no avail. There is such a thing as collective insanity. Wait, I will be back in a moment."

I saw Zeinvel pick up an empty tray from an adjoining table and dash to the counter. Immediately he came back. "Where's my check?" he asked. "In this cafeteria if you lose your check there's only one way out for you, suicide."

"Zeinvel," I said, "you are holding the check in your hand."

"What? I'm really getting confused in America, perhaps I'm senile."

I noticed that as he went to the counter he picked up a newspaper which someone had left on a chair. He returned with two cups of coffee and an egg cookie. The newspaper was yesterday's. I touched one of the cups and said, "Zeinvel, this cup is really hot. What do you say now?"

"The cup, not the coffee," Zeinvel said. "This is an American trick: they make the dishes hot and leave the contents cold. The American does not believe in such a thing as objective truth. The judge in an American court is not interested in whether the accused is guilty or not guilty. All he cares about is whether his defense is faultless or not. This is also true of the female sex. A woman doesn't want to be beautiful, she only wants to *look* beautiful. If she wears the right makeup, then she's a beauty. When Adam and Eve discovered that they were naked, Eve immediately began to sew a fig leaf to hide it."

"Who were the runners?" I asked.

Zeinvel gave me a puzzled look, as if he didn't immediately understand my words. "Oh yes, the runners. They ran away from Hitler. It happened when the radio announced that everyone in Warsaw should hurry across the Praga Bridge and run to the part of Poland which Molotov and Ribbentrop had divided among themselves. Bombs were falling in Warsaw. Buildings had collapsed and one could see corpses protruding from the rubble. The new director, Rydz-Śmigly, Pilsudski's heir, was as much a general as I'm a Turk. All he had was an ornate cap with a shining visor. The Poles and the Jews are as far apart as the sky is from the earth but both are cursed with the same mad optimism. The Jews are sure that the Almighty, who is actually an anti-Semite, loves them more than anything else in the universe, and the Poles believe in the power of their mustaches. The Polish general staff did not possess more than brass medals and curly mustaches in those days. Their soldiers went out to fight Hitler's tanks with swords and horses, as in the times of King Sobieski. Their leaders twirled their mustaches and up until the last minute kept on assuring everybody that victory was on their side.

"I lived in a little hotel on Mylno Street. This alley was so well hidden that no one could find it, not even the letter carrier. When I heard the announcement on the radio, I took a satchel and began to run. I knew that it was beyond my strength to carry a valise in this pandemonium. I saw men running with trunks that would have been too heavy even for a camel."

Zeinvel tasted the coffee and winced. "Ice cold."

"What happened to the runners?" I asked.

"One of them you knew quite well: Feitl Porysover, the playwright. Perhaps you also knew his wife, Tsvetl."

"He had a wife?" I asked.

"It seems he married after you left for America," Zeinvel said. "As you know, Feitl had a squeaky voice, and he managed to give all his protagonists the same tone of voice. He tried to imitate Chekhov. Chekhov's heroes whisper and sigh constantly, and Feitl's chirped like the cricket behind my grandfather's stove. You remember that Feitl was small, even smaller than I am, but his wife, Tsvetl, was an aspiring actress, a giant of a woman with the voice of a man. Feitl must have promised her leading roles in his plays. He, too, got nothing but promises. Hermann, the director, assured him every year that he would produce one of his masterpieces. As to Hermann, he had a promise from a theatrical angel that he would finance his productions. It was all a chain of promises. That angel was a swindler and a bankrupt. I've forgotten his name. My memory plays hide-and-seek with me. When I need it, it's not there, and when I don't need it, it reminds me of thousands of mingy trivialities, especially at night when I cannot fall asleep.

"What was I saying? Yes, we were running. There were few women among the runners, but Tsvetl was there and also Feitl. He was carrying a valise full of plays and she carried a box full of women's garments and a huge basket of food. She ran and she ate—whole sausages, Swiss cheese, cans of sardines and herrings. She had long legs and ran quickly, but Feitl, that shlemiel, followed with his tiny steps. She ate everything herself and gave him nothing. He called after her with his shrill voice and begged her not to rush, but she played dumb. We all had to run, because any moment Nazi planes could come and destroy us with their guns.

"When we started out, everyone was laden with luggage, but in time they had to drop it. The road was full of abandoned bundles, baskets, sacks, bags. Someone told me that when Feitl realized he couldn't go much farther with his valise, he stopped and began to choose those plays he thought were his best and threw the others away. It would have been terribly comic if it hadn't been so tragic—an author having to decide in the hubbub of running where his immortality might lie. I was told that in the end he was left with only one play, the pages of which he placed in his pockets. Peasants from the villages, their wives and their children, picked up the loot, but no one was eager for Feitl's manuscripts.

"Now listen. A so-called Yiddish poet also ran among this crowd. He often appeared on the literary scene in Warsaw after you left for America. His name was Bentze Zotlmacher, a fellow from the provinces, a big boor, with the face of a boxer and a bush of hair which stood up like wires. In the Writers' Club they used to organize a lot of literary evenings in the late thirties, all for the so-called progressives. You know that there were very few proletarians among the Jews in Poland, and Jewish peasants did not exist at all. But in the poems which these scribblers wrote, all three million Jews in Poland were either workers in factories or peasants. All those writers predicted the imminent social revolution and the dictatorship of the proletariat. The last two or three years before the war, a number of Trotskyites had emerged. The Stalinists and the Trotskyites waged violent battles and called one another Fascists, enemies of the people, provocateurs, imperialists. They kept on threatening one another that when the masses rose in the streets all the traitors would be hung from lampposts. The Stalinists would hang the Trotskyites, the Trotskyites would hang the Stalinists, and both would hand the general Zionists, the right Poale Zionists, the left Poale Zionists, and, of course, all pious Jews. I remember that the president of the Yiddish Club, Dr. Gottleib, once asked in a debate, 'Where will they find so many lampposts in Warsaw?'

"Bentze had been a Stalinist first, then he became a Trotskyite. Poetry was not enough for him. He had a pair of huge paws, and when the Stalinists heckled him, he ran down from the stage and gave them mighty blows. He often got a beating himself, and went around with a bandaged head. For curiosity's sake I once listened to his recitation: the usual clichés and banalities. In that day of escaping from Warsaw, Bentze Zotlmacher proved to be the best runner of all. He carried on his back two huge rucksacks and in his hands two large valises. He seemed to have prepared himself for the task days in advance. However, since we were all running to the part of Poland that belonged to Russia, which meant to Stalin, Bentze Zotlmacher realized his dilemma: he had bet on the wrong side. The city of Bialystok, to which we were all running, was full of Russians. The Warsaw Stalinists ran in a separate group ready to take over power the moment they crossed the frontier. Someone said that Bentze would have had a better chance to remain alive among the Nazis in Warsaw than in Bialystok among his former comrades.

"Since I had taken almost no luggage, and what I had taken I abandoned even before we reached the bridge, I was unburdened and could walk quickly, almost as quickly as Bentze. I witnessed two curious events, first how Bentze while running tried to make up to the Stalinists. It didn't take him long. He switched over with shameless vulgarity. He had many packs of cigarettes and he offered cigarettes only to the Stalinists. Rarely was anyone able to take cigarettes with them in that turmoil, but Bentze was well prepared. When a Trotskyite asked him for a cigarette, he answered loudly so everyone could hear him that he didn't want to have any traffic with the Trotskyite traitors to the masses, lackeys of Rockefeller and Hearst, agents of the Fascists. I expected that the Stalinists would reject this false neophyte, but here I was mistaken. For politicians it is a natural thing that one converts to the strong side without any preliminaries. They themselves, the Stalinists, had already made similar conversions. Since Bentze spat on the Trotskyites and poured praise on Comrade Stalin, they began to treat him like one of their own. The *Homo politico* is never interested in true faith and honest intentions, only in belonging to and supporting the winning clique.

"The second brutal event was Bentze's love for Tsvetl, Feitl's wife. Bentze had left behind in Warsaw a wife and children, but now it was more expeditious for him to become close to Tsvetl. I saw them kiss and embrace while on the run. They were caressing each other like two old lovers. When she offered him some tidbit, he ate it from her hand. She seemed to have completely forgotten about Feitl, who was left kilometers behind. Laden as Bentze was with his own packs, he took Tsvetl's box and she paid him back with sausages and pretzels. It was all so obvious, and shamelessly true to the eternal laws of human conduct.

"We had come to a village—I don't remember its name—

and there was no trace of war there. It's not clear to me to this day whether it was already Stalin's part of Poland or no-man's-land. Jews came out to meet us with bread, water, milk. There was no hotel in that village and the refugees went to sleep in the studyhouse or the poorhouse. Since Bentze and Tsvetl were two of the first to get there, they both found lodgings in the house of a local Stalinist. Some hours later I saw Feitl in the studyhouse lying on a bench, barefoot, with swollen feet full of blisters. He was so confused and broken that he did not recognize me, although we had met every day in the Writers' Club. I told him who I was, and he said, 'Zeinvel, I don't belong to this world anymore.'

"I was afraid that he might die then and there, but he finally managed to make it to Bialystok, and there the Stalinists held court, judging him. I was told that he had to confess all his sins against the masses and to call himself a Fascist, a Hitler spy, and an enemy of the people. As far as I know, he escaped from Bialystok to Wilno, and there, I think, he perished at the hands of the Nazis. I had my own troubles in Bialystok. I, too, had to run away, but this, as they say, is a chapter in itself.

"About what went on in Bialystok between 1939 and 1941, one could write a whole literature. For a short time the Warsaw Stalinists became powerful. They organized their own NKVD. They dug up old Yiddish newspapers and magazines, and began an inquisition of other Yiddish writers. A young man who had been a Marxist literary critic in Warsaw had become an expert in finding traces of counter-revolution, Fascism, Trotskyism, right deviation, left deviation in poems, stories, and plays. Someone had written a poem about spring and this critic managed to find in such innocent words as 'flowers' and 'butterflies' allusions to Mussolini, Léon Blum, Trotsky, and Norman Thomas. The birds were not just simple birds but the bands of Denikin and Makhno. The flowers were nothing but symbols for the counter-revolutionists Rykov, Kamenev, and Zinoviev, who had already been purged. Bentze was one of the judges. It wasn't long before the Stalinists began to denounce one another to the authorities from Soviet Russia. It all lasted until June 1941, when the Nazis marched into Bialystok and whoever managed to remain alive had to run again."

"What happened to Bentze?" I asked. "Is he still alive?"

"Alive?" Zeinvel cried out. "Not one of those people is alive. They were all liquidated sooner or later. In 1941 I had the good luck to reach Shanghai, but someone told me that when Bentze finally got to Soviet Russia and threw himself on the ground to kiss the earth of the socialistic land, a Red Army man clutched him by his collar and arrested him. He was sent somewhere to the north to a place where the strongest man could not last longer than one year. Hundreds of thousands such as Bentze were exiled to a sure death, all in the name of a better morning and a beautiful future."

"What happened to Tsvetl?" I asked.

"What? In 1948 she managed to get to Israel. There she re-married, and then she died of cancer."

Zeinvel Markus flicked the ashes of his cigarette into a cup of cold coffee. He said, "This is what human beings are, this is their history, and I am afraid this is also their future. Meanwhile, let's have another cup of coffee."

Translated by the author and Lester Goran

The Missing Line

TOWARD evening, the large hall of the Yiddish Writers' Club in Warsaw became almost empty. At a table in a corner two unemployed proofreaders played chess. They seemed to play and doze simultaneously. Mina, the cat, had forgotten she was a literary cat written up in the newspapers and went out in the yard to hunt for a mouse or perhaps a bird. I was sitting at a table with the most important member of the club— Joshua Gottlieb, the main feuilletonist of *The Haint*. He was the president of the journalists' syndicate, a doctor of philosophy, a former student of such famous scholars as Hermann Cohen, Professor Bauch, Professor Messer Leon, Kuno Fischer. Dr. Gottlieb was tall, broad-shouldered, with a straight red neck and a potbelly. The setting sun threw a purple shine on his huge bald head. He smoked a long cigar and blew the smoke out through his nostrils. He would not have invited a beginner like myself to his table, but there was no one else available at this hour, and he liked to talk and tell stories.

Our conversation turned to the supernatural and Dr. Gottlieb was saying, "You young men are in a rush to explain everything according to your theories. For you it is theory first and facts last. If the facts don't match the theories, it is the fault of the facts. But a man of my age knows that events have a logic of their own. Above all, they are the product of causality. Your mystics feel insulted if things happen in what we call a natural way. But to me the greatest and most wonderful miracle is what Spinoza called the order of things. When I lose my glasses and then find them in a drawer which I thought I hadn't opened in two years, I know I must have put them there myself and that they were not hidden by your demons or imps. I also know that no matter how many incantations I might have recited to retrieve them, the eyeglasses would have stayed in the drawer forever. As you know, I am a great admirer of Kant, but to me causality is more than a category of pure reason. It is the very essence of creation. You may even call it the thing in itself."

"Who made causality?" I asked, just to say something.

"No one, and therein is its beauty. Let me tell you—about two years ago something happened to me which had all the earmarks of one of your miracles. I was absolutely convinced that no explanation of it was possible. Rationalist that I am, I said to myself, If this actually happened and it was not a dream, I will have to reappraise everything I learned from the first grade in Gymnasium to the universities of Bonn and Bern. But then I heard the explanation and it was as convincing and as simple as only the truth can be. As a matter of fact, I thought I would write a story about it myself. However, I don't want to compete with our literati. I guess you know that I don't have too high an opinion of fiction. It may sound like a sacrilege to you, but I find more human fallacies, more psychology, and even more entertainment in the daily press than in all your literary magazines. Does my cigar bother you?"

"Not at all."

"You certainly know—I don't need to tell you—that our typesetters on *The Haint* and in the Yiddish press generally make more errors than all the other typesetters in the whole world. Although they consider themselves ardent Yiddishists, they don't have the slightest respect for their language. I don't sleep nights because of these barbarians. Who was it who said that 99 percent of all writers die not from cancer or consumption but from misprints. Every week I read three proofs of my Friday feuilleton, but when they correct one mistake they immediately make another, and sometimes two, three, or four.

"About two years ago I happened to write an article about Kant, a *jubilieum* of a sort. When it comes to philosophic terms, our typesetters get especially rattled. Besides, the man who makes up the page layout has a tradition of losing at least one line from my feuilleton every time, and I often find it in another article, sometimes even in the news. On that day I quoted a phrase which offered a perfect target for misprints: *the transcendental unity of the apperception.* I knew our typesetters would make mincemeat out of it, but I had to use it. I read the proofs three times as usual, and miraculously the words came out correctly every time. But I uttered a little prayer for the future, just in case. That night I went to sleep as hopeful as a writer in Yiddish can afford to be.

"The papers are brought to me every morning about eight

o'clock, and Friday is always my crisis day of the week. At first everything seemed quite smooth and I hoped against hope that this time I would be spared. But no, the line with the words 'the transcendental unity of the apperception' was missing. The whole article became senseless.

"Of course I was angry and cursed all the Yiddish typesetters with the vilest oaths. After an hour of utter resentment and extreme anti-Yiddishism, I began a search for the line in the other articles and news items of our Friday issue. But this time it seemed to have been lost altogether. Somehow this was a disappointment to me. What burned me up more than anything else is that readers, even my friends in the Writers' Club, complimented me and seemed not to have noticed the missing line. I've promised myself a million times not to read *The Haint* on Friday, but you know, there is an element of masochism in each of us. In my imagination I took revenge on the typesetters, the editors, the proofreaders by shooting them, beating them, and making them memorize all my feuilletons since the year 1910.

"After a while, I decided I had suffered enough and began to read *The Moment*, our rival newspaper, to see what their feuilletonist, Mr. Helfman, had written that Friday. Of course I knew beforehand that his piece could not be anything but bad. In all twenty years of our competition, I've never read anything good by this scribbler. I don't know how you feel about him, but to me he is an abomination.

"That Friday, his concoction seemed worse than ever, so I gave up in the middle and began to read the news. I turned to an item with the title 'A Man a Beast,' the story of a janitor who came home from the tavern at night and raped his daughter. Suddenly the most impossible, unbelievable, preposterous thing happened—my missing line was right before my eyes! I knew that it must be a hallucination. However, hallucinations last no longer than a split second. Here the words lingered in black type before me: *the transcendental unity of the apperception* . . . I closed my eyes, certain that when I opened them again the mirage would have vanished, but when I did there it was—the unthinkable, the ridiculous, the absurd.

"I admit that even while disbelieving in what you call the supernatural, I often toyed with the idea that one day a phenomenon might occur which would force me to lose faith in logic and reality. But that a metal line would fly from the *Haint* composing room at 8 Chlodna Street to the *Moment* composing room at 38 Nelewski—this I certainly did not expect. My son came into the room, and I must have looked as if I had seen a ghost, because he said to me, 'Papa, what's the matter?' I don't know why, but I said to him, 'Please, go down and buy me a copy of *The Moment*.' 'But you are reading *The Moment* right now,' my boy said. I told him that I must see another copy. The boy looked at me as if to say, 'The old man is meshugga altogether,' but he went down and bought another copy.

"Sure enough, my line was there on the same page in the same item: 'He came home from the tavern and saw his daughter in bed and *the transcendental unity of the apperception . . .*' I was so baffled and distressed that I began to laugh. To be completely on the safe side, I asked my boy to read the whole item out loud. Again he gave me that look which meant 'My father is not all there,' but he read it slowly. When he came to the transposed line, he smiled and asked, 'Is this why you wanted me to buy another copy?' I didn't answer. I knew that no hallucination has ever been shared by two people."

"There are cases of collective hallucinations," I said.

"Anyhow, that Friday and Saturday I couldn't sleep and could barely eat. I decided to go on Sunday morning to speak to the manager of our printing department, my old friend, Mr. Gavza. If there is a man who cannot be fooled by abracadabra and hocus-pocus, it is he. I wanted to see the expression on his face when he saw what I saw. On the way to *The Haint* I decided it would be a good thing to find the manuscript of my feuilleton, assuming it wasn't thrown out. I asked if the copy of my article was still around, and lo and behold, they found it, and the words were there as I remembered them. I was eager to find the solution to this riddle, but I didn't want the solution to be based on some silly blunder, ludicrous misunderstanding, or lapse of memory. With my manuscript in one hand and *The Moment* in the other, I went to see Mr. Gavza. I showed him my manuscript and said, 'Please, read this paragraph.' Before I even finished my sentence he said, 'I know, I know, a line was missing in your feuilleton about Kant. I guess you want to publish a correction. Believe me, no one ever reads them.' 'No, I don't want to publish any corrections,' I said. 'What else brings you here on Sunday morning?' Gavza asked.

"I showed him the Friday *Moment* with the news item and said, 'Now read this.' Gavza shrugged, began to read, and never before have I seen an expression like that on Gavza's quiet face. He gaped at the news item, at my manuscript, at me, at the paper, again at me, and said, 'Am I seeing things? This is your missing line!'

"'Yes, my friend,' I said. 'My missing line has jumped from *The Haint* to *The Moment* a dozen streets away, over all the buildings, all the rooftops, and settled down right into their printing room, into this item. Is it possible that demons did the job? If you can explain this . . .'

"'Really, I cannot believe it,' Gavza said. 'This must be some trick, some kind of practical joke. Maybe someone glued in the line. Let me see it again.'

"'No trick and no glue,' I said. 'This line fell out of my article and appeared in *The Moment* last Friday. I have another copy of *The Moment* in my pocket.'

"'My God, how could this have happened?' Gavza asked. Again and again he compared my manuscript with the line in *The Moment*. Then I heard him say, 'If this can happen, anything can happen. Maybe demons really did steal your line from *The Haint* and carry it to *The Moment*.'

"For a long while we stood looking at each other with the painful feeling of two adults who realize that their world has turned to chaos, with logic gone and so-called reality totally bankrupt. Then Gavza burst out laughing. 'No, it wasn't demons, not even the angels. I think I know what happened,' he exclaimed.

"'Tell me quickly before I burst,' I said.

"And this was his explanation. The Jewish National Fund often publishes an appeal in both *The Haint* and *The Moment*. Sometimes they make changes to adjust the appeal for the readers of the respective newspapers. Then they don't make a matrix but carry the whole metal page by car from one newspaper to the other for adjustments. By error, my line must have been put into the metal page of the appeal. It was carried over to *The Moment* and there someone noticed the mistake, took out the line from the appeal page, and it promptly got stuck into this news item. 'The chances that such a thing should happen are not as small as one may think, considering our sort of typesetters and proofreaders,' Gavza said. 'They are the worst bunglers. No, let's not put the blame on the poor demons. No demon is as ignorant and as careless as our printers and printer's devils.'

"We had a great laugh, and in honor of that historic solution, we went and had coffee and cake. We spoke about old times and the countless absurdities published in the Yiddish press, God bless it. Especially strange were the misprints listed in the back of Yiddish books, such as: On page 69 it is printed, 'She went to see her mother in Bialystok.'—It should read: 'He had a long gray beard.' Or: On page 87 it is written, 'He had a very strong appetite.'—It should have said, 'He went to see his former wife in Vilna.' On page 379, 'They took the train to Lublin.'—It should have been, 'The chicken was not kosher.' How a typesetter can make mistakes of this kind will always be a riddle to me. Another article was written about bacteria, 'which are so small that they can be seen only with the help of a telescope.'"

Dr. Gottlieb paused, trying to revive his extinguished cigar, sucking at it violently. Then he said, "My young friend, I tell you all this just to prove to you that one should not be in a rush to decide that Mother Nature has given up her eternal laws. As far as I'm concerned, the goblins and sprites have not taken over, and the laws of nature are still valid, whether I like them or not. And when I have to convey a message to my old wife, or to my not-much-younger girlfriend, I still use the telephone, not telepathy."

Translated by the author

The Hotel

WHEN Israel Danziger retired to Miami Beach it seemed to him as if he were retiring to the other world. At the age of fifty-six he had been compelled to abandon everything he had known: the factory in New York, his houses, the office, his children, his relatives, and his friends. Hilda, his wife, bought a house with a garden on the banks of Indian Creek. It had comfortable rooms on the ground floor, a patio, a swimming pool, palms, flower beds, a gazebo, and special chairs designed to put little strain on the heart. The creek stank a bit, but there was a cool breeze from the ocean just across the street.

The water was green and glassy, like a stage decoration at the opera, with white ships skimming over its surface. Seagulls squeaked shrilly above and swooped down to catch fish. On the white sands lay half-naked women. Israel Danziger did not need binoculars to view them; he could see them behind his sunglasses. He could even hear their gabble and laughter.

He had no worries of being forgotten. They would all come down from New York in the winter to visit him—his sons, his daughters, and their in-laws. Hilda was already concerned about not having enough bedrooms and linen, and also that Israel might have too much excitement with all the visitors from the city. His doctor had prescribed complete rest.

It was September now, and Miami Beach was deserted. The hotels closed their doors, posting signs that they would reopen in December or January. In the cafeterias downtown, which only yesterday had swarmed with people, chairs were piled atop bare tables, the lights extinguished, and business at a standstill. The sun blazed, but the newspapers were full of warnings of a hurricane from some far-off island, admonishing their readers to prepare candles, water, and storm windows, although it was far from certain whether the hurricane would touch Miami. It might bypass Florida entirely and push out into the Atlantic.

The newspapers were bulky and boring. The same news items which stirred the senses in New York seemed dull and

693

meaningless here. The radio programs were vacuous and television was idiotic. Even books by well-known writers seemed flat.

Israel still had an appetite, but Hilda carefully doled out his rations. Everything he liked was forbidden—full of cholesterol —butter, eggs, milk, coffee with cream, a piece of fat meat. Instead she filled him up with cottage cheese, salads, mangoes, and orange juice, and even this was measured out to him by the ounce lest, heaven forbid, he might swallow a few extra calories.

Israel Danziger lay on a deck chair, clad only in swimming trunks and beach sandals. A fig tree cast its shadow over him; yet he still covered his bald pate with a straw cap. Without clothes, Israel Danziger wasn't Israel Danziger at all; he was just a little man, a bundle of skin and bones, with a single tuft of hair on his chest, protruding ribs, knobby knees, and arms like sticks. Despite all the suntan lotion he had smeared on himself, his skin was covered with red blotches. Too much sun had inflamed his eyes.

He got up and immersed himself in the swimming pool, splashed around for a few minutes, and then climbed out again. He couldn't swim; all he did was dip himself, as if in a *mikvah*. Some weeks ago he had actually begun to read a book, but he couldn't finish it. Every day he read the Yiddish newspaper from beginning to end, including the advertisements.

He carried with him a pad and pencil, and from time to time he would estimate how much he was worth. He added up the profits from his apartment houses in New York and the dividends earned by his stocks and bonds. And each time the result was the same. Even if he was to live to be a hundred, Israel Danziger would still have more than enough, and there'd even be plenty for his heirs. Yet he could never really believe it. How and when did he amass such a fortune? And what would he do during all the years he still was destined to live: sit in the deck chair and gaze up at the sky?

Israel Danziger wanted to smoke, but the doctor allowed him only two cigars a day, and even that might be harmful. To dull his appetite for tobacco and for food, Israel chewed unsweetened gum. He bent down, plucked a blade of grass, and studied it. Then his eyes wandered to an orange tree nearby. He wondered what he would have thought if someone in Parciewe, his hometown in Poland, had told him that one day he would own a house in America, with citrus and coconut trees on the shores of the Atlantic Ocean in a land of eternal summer. Now he had all this, but what was it worth?

Suddenly Israel Danziger tensed. He thought he heard the telephone ringing inside. A long-distance call from New York, perhaps? He got up to answer it, and realized it was just a cricket which made a noise like a bell. No one ever called him here. Who would call him? When a man liquidates his business, he's like a corpse.

Israel Danziger looked around again. The sky was pale blue, without even a cloud-puff. A single bird flew high above him. Where was it flying? The women who earlier had lain in the sand were now in the ocean. Although the sea was as smooth as a lake, they jumped up and down as if there were waves. They were fat, ugly, and broad-shouldered. There was about them a selfishness that sickens the souls of men. And for such parasites men worked, weakened their hearts, and died before their times?

Israel had also driven himself beyond his strength. The doctors had warned him. Israel spat on the ground. Hilda was supposed to be a faithful wife, but just let him close his eyes and she'd have another husband within a year, and this time she'd pick a taller man . . .

But what was he to do? Build a synagogue where no one comes to pray? Have a Torah inscribed that nobody would read? Give away money to a kibbutz and help the atheists live in free love? You couldn't even give money to charity these days. For whatever purpose you gave, the money was eaten up by secretaries, fund-raisers, and politicians. By the time it was supposed to reach the needy, there was nothing left.

In the same notebook that Israel Danziger used to total up his income lay several letters which he had received only that morning. One from a yeshiva in Brooklyn, another from a Yiddish poet who was preparing to publish his work, a third from a home for the aged which wanted to build a new wing. The letters all sang the same refrain—send us a check. But what good would come of a few additional students at the yeshiva in

Williamsburg? Who needed the poet's new verse? And why build a new wing? So that the president could arrange a banquet and take the cream off the milk? Perhaps the president was a builder himself, or else he had a son-in-law who was an architect. I know that bunch, Israel Danziger grumbled to himself. They can't bluff me.

Israel Danziger couldn't remain seated any longer. He was engulfed by an emptiness as painful as any heart attack. The force that keeps men alive was draining from him and he knew without a doubt that he was only one step away from death, from madness. He had to do something immediately. He ran inside to his bedroom, flung open the doors of his closet, put on pants, a pair of socks, a shirt, a pair of shoes, then took up his cane and went out. His car was waiting in the garage, but he didn't want to drive a car and speed without purpose over the highway. Hilda was out shopping for groceries; the house would be empty, but no one stole things here. And what did it matter if someone did try to break in? Besides, Joe the gardener was out tending the lawns, sprinkling water from a hose onto the bluish grass that had been brought here in sheets and now was spread over the sand like a carpet. Even the grass here has no roots, Israel Danziger thought. He envied Joe. At least that black man was doing something. He had a family somewhere near Miami.

What Israel Danziger was living through now was not mere boredom; it was panic. He had to act or perish. Maybe go to his broker and see how his stocks were getting along? But he'd already been there that morning for an hour. If he should take to going there twice a day, he would become a nuisance. Besides, it was now twenty minutes to three. By the time he got there, they'd be closed.

The bus station was just across the street, and a bus was pulling up. Israel Danziger ran across the road, and this very act was like a drop of medicine. He climbed on the bus and threw in the coin. He'd go to Paprov's cafeteria. There he'd buy the afternoon paper, an exact duplicate of the morning paper, drink a cup of coffee, eat a piece of cake, smoke a cigar, and, who knows, perhaps he would meet someone he knew.

The bus was half empty. The passengers all sat on the shaded side and fanned themselves, some with fans, others with folded newspapers, and still others with the flaps of pocketbooks. Only one passenger sat on the side where the sun burned, a man who was beyond caring about heat. He looked unkempt, unshaven, and dirty. Must be a drunk, Israel Danziger thought, and for the first time he understood drunkenness. He'd take a shot of whiskey, too, if he were allowed. Anything is better than this hollowness.

A passenger got off and Israel Danziger took his seat. A hot wind blew in through the open window. It tasted of the ocean, of half-melted asphalt and gasoline. Israel Danziger sat quietly. But suddenly perspiration broke out over all his body and his fresh shirt was soaked in a second. He grew more cheerful. He had reached the point where even a bus ride was an adventure.

On Lincoln Road were stores, shop windows, restaurants, banks. Newsboys were hawking papers. It was a little like a real city, almost like New York. Beneath one of the storefront awnings, Israel Danziger saw a poster advertising a big sale. The entire stock was to be sold. To Israel Danziger, Lincoln Road seemed like an oasis in the wilderness. He found himself worrying about the owners of the stores. How long would they hold out if they never saw a customer? He felt impelled to buy something, anything, to help business. It's a good deed, he told himself, better than giving to shnorrers.

The bus stopped, and Israel Danziger got off and entered the cafeteria. The revolving door, the air-conditioned chill, the bright lights burning in the middle of the day, the hubbub of customers, the clatter of dishes, the long steam tables laden with food and drink, the cashier ringing the cash register, the smell of tobacco—all this revived the spirit of Israel Danziger. He shook off his melancholy, his hypochondria and thoughts of death. With his right hand he grabbed a tray; his left hand he stuck into his rear pocket, where he had some bills and small change. He remembered his doctor's warnings, but a greater power—a power which makes the final decision—told him to go ahead. He bought a chopped-herring sandwich, a tall glass of iced coffee, and a piece of cheese cake. He lit a long cigar. He was Israel Danziger again, a living person, a businessman.

■

At another table, across from Israel Danziger, sat a little man, no taller than Danziger but stocky, broad-shouldered, with a large head and a fat neck. He wore an expensive Panama hat (at least fifty dollars, Danziger figured), and a pink, short-sleeved shirt. On one of his fingers, plump as a sausage, a diamond glittered. He was puffing a cigar and leafing through a Yiddish newspaper, breaking off pieces from an egg pretzel. He removed his hat, and his bald head shone round and smooth. There was something childlike about his roundness, his fatness, and his puckered lips. He was not smoking his cigar; he was only sucking at it, and Israel Danziger wondered who he was. Certainly he was not a native. Perhaps a New Yorker? But what was he doing here in September, unless he suffered from hay fever? And, since he was reading a Yiddish paper, Israel Danziger knew he was one of the family. He wanted to get to know the man. For a while he hesitated; it wasn't like him to approach strangers. But here in Miami you can die of boredom if you're too reserved. He got up from his chair, took the plate with the cheese cake and the coffee, and moved over to the other man's table.

"Anything new in the paper?"

The man removed the cigar from his mouth. "What should be new? Nothing. Not a thing."

"In the old days there were writers, today scribblers," said Israel Danziger, just to say something.

"It's five cents wasted."

"Well, what else can you do in Miami? It helps kill time."

"What are you doing here in this heat?"

"And what are you doing here?"

"It's my heart . . . I'm sitting around here six months already. The doctor exiled me here . . . I had to retire . . ."

"So—then we're brothers!" Israel Danziger exclaimed. "I have a heart, too, a bad heart that gives me trouble. I got rid of everything in New York, and my good wife bought me a house with fig trees, like in Palestine in the old days. I sit around and go crazy."

"Where is the house?"

Danziger told him.

"I pass it every day. I think I even saw you there once. What did you do before?"

Danziger told him.

"I myself have been in real estate for over thirty-five years," the other man said.

The two men fell into a conversation. The little man in the Panama hat said his name was Morris Sapirstone. He had an apartment on Euclid Avenue. Israel Danziger got up and bought two cups of coffee and two more egg pretzels. Then he offered him one of his cigars, and Sapirstone gave him one of his brand. After fifteen minutes they were talking as if they had known each other for years.

They had moved in the same circles in New York; both came from Poland. Sapirstone took out a wallet of alligator leather and showed Israel Danziger photographs of his wife, two daughters, two sons-in-law—one a doctor, one a lawyer—and several grandchildren. One granddaughter looked like a copy of Sapirstone. The woman was fat, like a Sabbath stew pot. Compared to her, his Hilda was a beauty. Danziger wondered how a man could live with such an ugly woman. On the other hand, he reflected, with one of her kind, you wouldn't be as lonesome as he was with Hilda. A woman like that would always have a swarm of chattering biddies around her.

Israel Danziger had never been pious, but since his heart attack and his retirement to Miami Beach he had begun to think in religious terms. Now he beheld the finger of God in his coming together with Morris Sapirstone.

"Do you play chess?" he asked.

"Chess, no. But I do play pinochle."

"Is there anybody to play with?"

"I find them."

"You're a smart man. I can't find anybody. I sit around all day long and don't see a soul."

"Why did you settle so far uptown?"

In the course of their talk Morris Sapirstone mentioned that there was a hotel for sale. It was almost a new hotel, all the way uptown. The owners had gone bankrupt, and the bank was ready to sell it for a song. All you needed was a quarter of a million in cash. Israel Danziger was far from ready for a business proposition, but he listened eagerly. Talk of money, credit, banks, and mortgages cheered him up. It was proof, somehow, that the world had not yet come to an end. Israel Danziger knew nothing at all about hotels, but he picked up bits of information from Morris Sapirstone's story. The owners of the hotel had failed because they had sought a fancy clientele and made their rates too high. The rich people had stopped coming to Miami Beach. You had to attract the middle class. One good winter season and your investment would be covered. A new element was coming to Miami—the Latin Americans who chose Florida during their summers to "cool off." Israel Danziger groped in his shirt pocket for a pencil stub. While Morris went on talking, Israel wrote figures in the margin of his newspaper with great speed. At the same time, he plied Sapirstone with questions. How many rooms in the hotel? How much can one room bring in? What about taxes? Mortgages? Personnel costs? For Israel, it was no more than a pastime, a reminder that once he, too, had been in business. He scratched his left temple with the point of the pencil.

"And what do you do if you have a bad season?"

"You have to see to it that it's good."

"How?"

"You have to advertise properly. Even in the Yiddish newspapers."

"Do they have a hall for conventions?"

An hour had passed and Israel Danziger did not know where it had gone. He clenched his cigar between his lips and turned it busily around in his mouth. New strength welled up inside him. His heart, which in recent months had alternately fluttered and hesitated, now worked as if he were a healthy man. Morris Sapirstone took a small box from his coat pocket, picked out a pill, and swallowed it with a drink of water.

"You had an attack, eh?"

"Two."

"For whom do I need a hotel? For my wife's second husband?"

Morris Sapirstone did not answer.

"How can I get to look at the hotel?" Israel Danziger asked after a while.

"Come with me."

"Do you have a car here?"

"The red Cadillac across the street."

"Ah, a nice Cadillac you got."

The two men left the cafeteria. Israel Danziger noticed that Sapirstone was using a cane. Water in his legs, he thought. An invalid and he's hunting for hotels . . . Sapirstone settled behind the steering wheel and started the engine. He gave a whack to the car behind him, but he didn't even turn around. Soon he was racing along. One hand expertly grasped the steering wheel; with the other, he worked a cigarette lighter. With a cigar clamped in his teeth, he mumbled on.

"There's no charge for looking."

"No."

"If my wife hears about this, she'll give me plenty of trouble. Before you know it, she'll tell the doctor and then they'll both eat me up alive."

"They told you to rest, eh?"

"And if they told me? One must rest *here*, in the head. But my mind doesn't rest. I lie awake at night and think about all kinds of nothings. And when you're up you get hungry. My wife went to a locksmith to find out whether she can put a lock on the refrigerator . . . All these diets make you more sick than well. How did people live in the old days? In my time there were no diets. My grandfather, he should rest in peace, used to eat up a whole plateful of onions and chicken fat as an appetizer. Then he got busy on the soup with drops of fat floating on top. Next he had a fat piece of meat. And he finished up with a shmaltz cake. Where was cholesterol then? My grandfather lived to be eighty-seven, and he died because he fell on the ice one winter. Let me tell you: someday they'll find out that cholesterol is healthy. They'll be taking cholesterol tablets just as they take vitamin pills today."

"I wish you were right."

"A man is like a Hanukkah dreidel. It gets a turn, and then it spins on by itself until it drops."

"On a smooth table, it'll spin longer."

"There aren't any smooth tables."

The car stopped. "Well, that's the hotel."

Israel Danziger took one look and saw everything in a moment. If it was true that you only had to lay down a quarter of a million, the hotel was a fantastic bargain. Everything was new. It must have cost a fortune to build. Of course it was located a little too far uptown, but the center was moving uptown now. Once, the Gentiles ran away from the Jews. Now the Jews were running away from the Jews. Across the street there was already a kosher meat market. Israel Danziger rubbed his forehead. He would have to put in a hundred and twenty-five thousand dollars as his share. He could borrow that much from the bank, giving his stocks as security. He might even be able to scrape together the cash without a loan. But should he really get involved in such headaches? It would be suicide, sheer suicide. What would Hilda say? And Dr. Cohen? They'd all be at me—Hilda, the boys, the girls, their husbands. That in itself could lead to a second attack . . .

Israel Danziger closed his eyes and for a while remained enveloped in his own darkness. Like a fortune-teller, he tried to project himself into the future and foresee what fate had in store for him. His mind became blank, dark, overcome with the numbness of sleep. He even heard himself snore. All his affairs, his entire life, hung in the balance this second. He was waiting for a command from within, a voice from his own depths . . . Better to die than to go on living like this, he mumbled finally.

"What's the matter, Mr. Danziger, did you fall asleep?" he heard Sapirstone ask.

"Eh? No."

"So come in. Let's take a look at what's going on in here."

And the two little men climbed the steps to the fourteen-story hotel.

Translated by the author

Dazzled

THE TALK turned to the subject of maids, and Aunt Genendel was saying, "Maids are not something to belittle—they can create plenty of trouble. An entire regiment of Russian soldiers was once stationed in our town, which was close to the Austrian border. There was some conflict between Russia and Austria, and the military expected a war to break out. Or perhaps the Czar anticipated a new uprising by the Poles. These Russian soldiers were under the command of a colonel and some other officers. There were barracks for the soldiers and stables for the horses. Gendarmes rode through the streets on horseback with rifles slung over their backs and swords hanging at their sides. They spread fear among the Jews. But, on the other hand, they patronized the Jewish stores, and the owners profited.

"One day we heard that a highly important nobleman named Orlov was coming from St. Petersburg—a distant member of the Czar's family, a duke. The news created excitement and confusion among the Russian officials, because a man of such high rank was almost never sent to a village as remote as ours. The quartermasters were especially concerned, because they had all taken bribes and submitted false accounts to their superiors. As a rule, the soldiers were given tasteless food, and their uniforms were not of the best quality, either. It was rumored that those who baked the bread kneaded the dough with their bare feet. The colonel immediately ordered that the soldiers be given better food and provided with decent clothing. The officials drilled the men with more rigor and warned them to say they were satisfied if the dignitary made inquiries. Instructions were given for the kitchens and kettles to be scrubbed and for the outhouses to be cleaned. Everyone had to shine his boots. A banquet was prepared for the duke, and the orchestra polished its instruments and rehearsed daily.

"Soon it was revealed that the great man was not coming for an inspection but was being exiled to our region as a punishment. He had challenged a high-ranking person to a duel and had killed him. Since putting one of the Czar's family in prison would create a scandal, they sent him to Poland for a few years.

"He arrived in an old coach drawn by two skinny horses and drove up to Lippe Reznik's inn instead of going to the quarters assigned to him. The duke looked shabby, worn-out, tired. He was short, with a little gray beard, and although he had the title of major general he was dressed like a civilian. He must have lost all his prestige in St. Petersburg. Without stripes, epaulets, and medals, the greatest lord is not more than flesh and blood. After seeing the duke, the colonel canceled his orders, and the soldiers were again given nothing but kasha and cabbage. They stopped shining their boots three times a day. The orchestra fell silent. Still, the colonel and his underlings came to pay the duke a visit at Lippe Reznik's inn. I wasn't there, but Lippe said that the duke received his guests impatiently and did not even offer them a seat. When the colonel inquired as to what His Highness needed, he answered that he needed absolutely nothing and that all he wanted was to be left in peace.

"For some reason, the duke was friendly to the Jews. One of them, a real-estate broker, suggested he buy an old wood house, and the duke took it immediately. The broker also offered him a maid. Antosha was her name—the widow of a soldier who died in the war with the Turks. She did the wash for Jewish homes and lived alone in a half-ruined hut. The truth was that she was not even fit to be a washerwoman. She once did our laundry, and everything came out so dirty that my mother had to have it redone. She couldn't iron, bleach, or prepare the wash for the mangle. An ignorant, unfortunate creature she was, but she happened to have a pretty little face for a woman of her age—blue eyes, blond hair, a chiseled nose. If I am not mistaken, she was a bastard sired by some Polish landowner. She had one good quality: she was not greedy for money. No matter what she was paid, she thanked the mistress profusely and kissed her hand. When the broker told him about Antosha, the duke asked to see her. Antosha had one dress, which she wore to church on Sundays, and one pair of shoes, which she usually carried in her hands. In these clothes, she was brought to the duke. He took one look and agreed to have her. He promised to pay her a wage excessive for a servant of such low caliber. He was quick in everything he did. Each day he walked on Lublin Street and strode so briskly that he overtook all the passersby. There was an Orthodox church near the barracks, but he never attended the services, even on Easter or on the Russian New Year. He got a reputation as a heretic and a madman. In the beginning, he used to receive a lot of mail, but he answered no one, and after a while the mailman brought him only one letter a month—the money order for his pension.

"There was a grocery store close to the duke's house. The owner, Mendel, and his wife, Baila Gitl, had become quite familiar with the duke. They provided him with everything he needed—even things that could not ordinarily be found in a grocery store, such as ink, steel pens, writing paper, wine, vodka, tobacco. Baila Gitl noticed that Antosha was ordering more food than two people could eat. On one trip, she would buy three pounds of butter and ten dozen eggs. She was keeping food so long that it became rotten and had to be thrown out. The duke complained to Baila Gitl that Antosha attracted mice and vermin into the house. Baila Gitl advised him to get rid of her and find a maid with more sense, but the duke said, 'I cannot do this to her. She might be jealous.' Apparently, he was living with this simpleton. I shouldn't sin with my words, but a man doesn't need a woman with intelligence. All he needs, you should excuse me, is a piece of flesh."

"Don't say this, Genendel!" Chaya Riva, a neighbor, cried out. "Not all men are the same."

"Huh? They are all the same," Genendel said. "There was a rabbi in Lublin who was called the Iron Head. He was a great scholar and learned in the Torah, but his wife, the rebbetzin, could not even read the prayer book. On the Sabbath and on holidays, a woman had to recite the prayers to her. All the rebbetzin could do was say 'Amen.'"

"Why didn't her husband teach her?" Chaya Riva asked.

"*Nu*, who knows? Now the real story begins. The duke tried to explain to Antosha that some food cannot be kept for weeks and months. But the peasant could not grasp this. She would sweep up the rubbish and leave it lying for days in the corner where the broom stood. Baila Gitl often saw the duke himself taking the garbage out to the rubbish pit. This Antosha was like Yussel in the Golem story. If they told him to bring water from the well, he brought so much water that it flooded the entire house. Antosha couldn't cook, either. She oversalted a dish or she forgot to salt it altogether. It got to the point where the duke would put on an apron and cook his own meal. How can a man of such high birth fall so low? He was a scholar, always reading books or writing. He was so absorbed in his own thoughts he would sometimes let the milk boil over and the meat burn.

"Baila Gitl lived in an apartment over the store, and from there she could see all the goings-on with her own eyes. She tried to teach Antosha to keep house, but it was in vain. Antosha would only say, 'Yes, yes, yes, dear mistress, I will do everything you teach me.' She wept and kissed Baila Gitl's hand, but she could never learn a thing."

"A blockhead, huh?" Chaya Riva asked.

"Silly and stubborn," Genendel answered.

"She probably gave him a lot of pleasure in bed," Chaya Riva said.

Aunt Genendel seemed embarrassed. "What can a female do more than she does? One way or another, things became worse with time. The duke began to complain to Baila Gitl that he suffered stomach pains from Antosha's cooking. A few times, Baila Gitl brought him a dish of grits or chicken broth and he ate in silence. Once, he said to her, 'On account of a foolish suspicion, I killed a friend. From sorrow and shame my wife passed away. I sinned, and here I must pay for my sin.' Later, when Baila Gitl recounted this story to her friends, she would say, 'A Gentile penitent—who has ever heard of such a thing?'

"Now listen to this. Antosha had never learned to use matches. She would light a match, forget to blow it out, then throw it right on the floor or into the garbage bucket. A few times the rubbish went up in flames. This could have started a terrible fire, but the duke happened to notice and extinguished the flames. Many times he warned Antosha that she must blow out a match before she threw it away, but each time she forgot anew. In the half-ruined hut where Antosha had lived before, there was no wooden floor, just earth, and nothing could catch fire there.

"The duke had brought books and various papers from Russia. It seemed that he was writing a book. In the evening he wrote by a kerosene lamp with a green shade. Once, late at night, when the duke was sitting and writing, he heard a scream, and when he looked up he saw that the kitchen was on fire. It was too late to try to put the flames out with a pail of water, because the entire building was burning. Antosha had thrown a lit match into the refuse and then had taken a nap. When she awoke, she saw the blaze and apparently threw herself over the flames, and her dress caught fire. The duke rushed into the kitchen, lifted Antosha in his arms, and ran outside with her. His housecoat was also ablaze. Both of them would have burned to a crisp, but there was a drainage ditch nearby, and it had rained earlier. The duke threw Antosha and himself into the ditch. Thus, Antosha remained alive, but without hair and practically without a face. The duke was also burned, but not as severely as she. He had enough strength to call for help, and Baila Gitl heard his cry and woke her husband. Had the fire gone on a bit longer, Baila Gitl's house and the store and possibly the entire street would have gone up in smoke. By the time the firemen were awakened and had come with their old hoses and half-filled barrels of water, nothing was left of the duke's property but a heap of ashes."

Aunt Genendel nodded and blew her nose. She wiped her brass-rimmed glasses with her handkerchief and went on. "The colonel had long since left town. His regiment had been transferred even closer to the Austrian border, near the river San. But the remaining soldiers had a sort of makeshift hospital, which consisted of one room with three beds, and there the duke took Antosha—a bundle of burned flesh, a sack of bones. She was neither alive nor dead. The military doctor, an old drunk, suggested they smear her with fat, but as they applied the grease her skin peeled off like an onion's. She had become as black as pitch, almost a skeleton. But as long as one breathes one is still alive. In comparison with her, the duke got off lightly, but not entirely. His beard was singed and would never grow back. Blisters covered his hands and forehead. Antosha was completely at fault, but still he worried only about her recovery. He pleaded with the doctor to save her.

The doctor said openly, 'She will not last long.' Antosha could not speak but squeaked like a mouse. She also became blind.

"Meanwhile, the news of this calamity reached St. Petersburg, and it created a commotion. People there had already forgotten about the exiled duke, but when they heard that he lay sick in some remote village in Poland and was left without a shirt on his back it aroused compassion among his former friends. The news reached the Czar (not the present Czar but his father), and he decreed that the duke should be brought back to Russia. The Czar sent a doctor and a male nurse, and asked that the governor of Lublin be notified. The event was written about in the newspapers. Reporters came and asked the townspeople a lot of questions: How did the duke live? With whom did he have dealings? This, that. The local Russians were hostile to the duke, because he had avoided them. The Poles certainly didn't have a good word to say about a Russian. But the Jews praised him. He had given charity to the poor and to the sick in the poorhouse. An entire group of officials arrived in town. The Czar had demanded that the exiled duke be sent home in style. They all knew quite well that he had a common mistress, a Polish maid who now wrangled with death, but, of course, they didn't give a hoot about her. They prepared a coach for him with eight horses. The entourage was to travel to Lublin and from there in a special railway car to St. Petersburg. But the Russians had, as they say, made their plans without the boss. The duke insisted that he could not leave without Antosha."

"He was still in love with her, huh?" Chaya Riva asked.

"Dazzled," Aunt Genendel answered.

"How can an important man care about a creature like her?" another neighbor asked.

"People in love are half insane," Genendel replied.

"What happened then?" Chaya Riva asked.

Aunt Genendel rubbed her forehead. "I forget where I was —you shouldn't have interrupted me. Yes, the officials were indignant. How could they bring her to St. Petersburg? Besides, she was at the threshold of death. They waited for her to die, but many days passed and she lived. Woe to such a life! After many arguments, the officials lost their patience. They sent a telegram to St. Petersburg saying that the defiant duke was no longer in his right mind, and the answer came back that they should leave him where he was.

"Now listen to this. The morning after the Russians left, the duke went to the Orthodox priest and asked him to marry him and Antosha. The priest couldn't believe his ears. 'Marry you? She is as good as a corpse!' he cried out. And the duke answered, 'According to the law, one is allowed to marry a person as long as he or she breathes.'

"I will not keep you much longer. The duke bought a wedding gown for Antosha and dragged the sick woman out of bed. Two soldiers carried her on a stretcher to the Orthodox church, the *tserkov*. The entire town—Jews and Gentiles both —came to stare at the bizarre wedding. People expected the bride to expire before the ceremony began, but somehow she lived. I doubt whether she knew what they were doing to her. The Polish priest contended that she was Catholic, not Orthodox, and that the Russian didn't have the right to marry her in their ritual. But the Russians were in power, not the Poles. The bells rang, the organ played, a Russian choir sang, and the groom stood there in a borrowed uniform and with a seared-off beard. Only his sword and a medal had been saved from the fire.

"Three days after the wedding, Antosha finally gave up her soul. It was a victory for the Poles that she was buried in the Polish cemetery, not in the Russian one. A few months later, the duke caught pneumonia and he, too, passed on. In his will he asked to be buried next to Antosha, but the authorities would not permit this. A dispatch came from St. Petersburg, ordering that the duke be buried with military honors. The governor of Lublin came to the funeral, the orchestra played, an old cannon was found and salutes were fired. You will not believe me, but the Jews had recited Psalms when the duke was sick. The rabbi said that in his way the duke was like a saint."

Aunt Genendel blew her nose, and wiped a tear with the edge of her shawl. "Why do I tell you all this? To show that a maid is not something to brush off with a wave of the hand. In olden times, maids were concubines to their masters. Even today, when a man is left without a wife the maid often acts as the wife. I know a story about a rabbi who fell in love with his maid and married her when he became a widower—he an old man of seventy with a white beard and she a wench of fourteen, the daughter of a water carrier."

"The town allowed this?" Chaya Riva asked.

"The elders were so furious that they exiled both of them one Friday on a cart drawn by oxen," Genendel said.

"Why by oxen?" Chaya Riva asked.

Aunt Genendel thought for a while. "Because oxen move slowly, and before this lovesick pair could reach an inhabited place the sun would have set and they would have to make the Sabbath in the middle of the road."

Translated by Deborah Menashe

Sabbath in Gehenna

ON THE Sabbath, as is known, the fires do not burn in Gehenna. The beds of nails are covered with sheets. The hooks on which the wicked males and females hang—by their tongues for gossip, their hands for theft, their breasts for lechery, their feet for running after sin—are concealed behind screens. The piles of red-hot coals and icy snow onto which transgressors are flung are invisible that day. The angels of destruction have put away their fiery rods. The sinners who remain pious even in hell (there are such) go to a little synagogue where an iniquitous cantor intones the Sabbath prayers. The freethinkers (there are many of them in Gehenna) sit on logs and converse. As is usually the case with enlightened ones, their topic is how to improve their lot, how to make a better Gehenna.

That wintry late Sabbath afternoon a sinner named Yankel Farseer was saying: "The trouble with us in hell is that we are selfish: each sinner thinks only about his own business. If he believes that he can save his behind from a few lashes by the angel Dumah, he is in seventh heaven. If we could form a united front, we would not be in need of private intercession. We would come out with demands."

When he uttered the word "demands," his mouth began to water. He choked and puffed. Yankel was a fat man with broad shoulders, a round belly, short legs. He had long hair covering his bald spot and grew a beard—not a kosher beard as the pious have in paradise, but a rebellious one, every hair of which points at revolution.

One little delinquent, who braided his long hair in a pony-tail tied with a wire he tore out of a bed of nails, asked, "What kind of demands, Comrade Yankel?"

"First, that the week in Gehenna should not last six days, but that we should have a four-day week. Second, that each villain get a six-week vacation, during which he may return to earth and break the Ten Commandments without being punished. Third, that we should not be kept away from our beloved sisters, the female sinners. We demand sex and free love. Fourth—"

"Dreams of a chopped-off head!" said Chaim Bontz, a former gangster. "The angel Dumah is not afraid of your demands and petitions. He does not even bother to read them."

"What do you propose?"

"The angels, like humans, understand only one thing—blows. We must arm ourselves. Rub out the angel Dumah, storm the court of heaven, break a few ribs among the righteous. Then we must take over paradise, Leviathan, the Wild Ox, the sanctified wine, all the other good things. Then—"

"Arm ourselves?" a petit bourgeois who had fallen into hell for swindling cried out. "Where will you get arms in hell? They don't give us a single knife or fork. The fiery coals we eat we have to pick up with our naked fingers. Besides, Gehenna does not last longer than a year except for Sabbaths and holidays. I am supposed to end my term on the day after Purim. If we begin a conspiracy now, the term may be prolonged. Do you know the punishment for conspiring against the angel Dumah?"

"This is the misfortune of us sinners," Yankel Farseer yelled out. "Everyone is only for himself. How about the wicked who will come after us? This year is not so bad yet, it has twelve months but next year will be a leap year."

"It is not my duty to worry about all the wicked in the world," replied the swindler. "I happen to be an innocent victim. All I did was forge a signature. I shed ink, not blood. Those who murder, set fire to houses and cause children to perish in the flames, those who stab and rape are not my brothers. If I were in charge here, I would keep them until the end of the six thousandth year!"

"Didn't I say that every sinner is out for himself?" Yankel Farseer spoke. "If we cannot unite, the angels can do to us as they please. In that case, why the idle talk? Let's play cards and finish out the rest of the Sabbath."

"Comrade Yankel," a sinner with eyeglasses spoke up, "may I say something?"

"Say. Talk doesn't change anything."

"My opinion is that we should concentrate mainly on culture. Before we come with maximal demands like six-week vacations with sex and free love, we must show the angels that we are sinners with spiritual goals. I propose that we publish a magazine."

"A magazine in Gehenna?"

"Yes, a magazine, and its name should be *The Gehennanik*. When you sign a petition, the angels take one look at it and they throw it away, or they blow their noses into it. But a magazine they would read. The righteous in paradise expire from boredom. They are overfed with the secrets of the Torah. They want to know what's going on in hell. They are curious about our view of the world, our way of thinking, our sex fantasies, and, most of all, they are intrigued by the fact that we are still atheists. A series of articles, 'The Atheists in Gehenna,' would become a smash hit in paradise. Of course, we would also publish a gossip column and a lot of special hell pornography. The saints would have something to enjoy and to complain about."

"Silly babble! I'm going to sleep." Chaim Bontz yawned.

"Who is going to do all this scribbling and how will this help us?" asked a sinner with a hoarse voice.

"You don't have to worry about who will do the writing," said the sinner with the eyeglasses. "We have a lot of writers here. I was a writer on earth myself. I was condemned to hell because I was supposed to be a rabble-rouser. Every Monday and Thursday, I changed my opinion. When it was profitable to preach Communism I became an ardent Communist and, likewise, I preached capitalism when that paid. They heaped accusations against me. But the fact is that I had many readers and they wrote me enthusiastic fan letters. It is true that I changed my opinions like gloves, but were my readers any more consistent? Here in hell—"

A sinner who looked young, and had long hair reaching down to his shoulders, asked, "Why publish a magazine? Why not open a theater? We have a shortage of paper here. Besides, it's so hot that the magazine will catch fire. The righteous are all half blind and don't understand our modern language and are not accustomed to our spelling. My advice is that we should organize a theatrical group."

"A theater in hell? Who's going to act? And who's going to attend? They punish us day and night."

"We will perform on Sabbaths and all holidays."

"Are there any scripts in Gehenna?"

"I have an idea for a play—a love affair between a sinner and a saint."

"What kind of love affair? The wicked and the saints never meet."

"I have thought it through thoroughly. My hero is lying on his bed of nails and screaming. He is an opera singer by profession and so wracked with pain that he breaks out into an aria. She, the saint, hears his song and falls madly in love with his voice. Then—"

"The saints in paradise are all deaf."

"This one happens not to be deaf."

"Well then, what follows?"

"To be able to meet him, she asks for permission from the angel Eshiel to dress up like a demon and to become one who dispenses lashes in Gehenna. Permission is granted, and so the two lovers meet. She is supposed to whip him, but when the angel Dumah looks away, she covers him with kisses and they soon reach a point where they cannot be one without the other."

"Melodrama of the worst kind!"

"What do you want to perform in Gehenna, *Migdal Oz* by Mosheh Chayim Luzzatto? Our sinners love action. A play like this would give the actors an opportunity to sing a song, to dance, and to make a couple of spicy jokes."

"Assuming that it works, what would the result be?"

"Theater is the best form of propaganda. It may very well be that the saints and the angels will visit our theater to see our plays. And between one act and the other, we would explain to them our point of view, our situation, and our philosophy."

"Your play is not realistic, and your plan is not realistic. Where will we perform—among the piles of coals? The saints will not come here. All day long they are busy with the secrets of the Torah and with munching Leviathan. In the evening they are afraid to leave paradise."

"What are they afraid of?"

"A couple of murderers and rapists managed to escape from Gehenna. They prowl around at night. They have already killed several saints and have tried to ravish Sarah bas Tovim."

"This is the first time I've heard this."

"Of course, as long as we don't have any magazines, no one is informed about anything. The magazine would give us news and explain—"

"Fantasies, fantasies," a sinner who had been a politician on earth called out. "Culture will not solve our problem, and neither will the theater. What we really need is a progressive political party built on democratic principles. We don't need to come out with impossible demands, Comrade Yankel. We should be satisfied with a minimum. I have heard from a very reliable source that there is a liberal group among the angels who are asking for reforms in Gehenna."

"What kind of reforms?"

"They want us to have a five-day week. Besides Saturdays and holidays, we should be given a week's vacation in the World of Illusions. Some of them would request that the nails on the beds of nails should be two millimeters shorter. I was told that there is some change in their attitude toward homosexuality, lesbianism, and certainly masturbation. We could do a lot, but we need money."

"Money?" all the sinners called out with one voice.

"Yes, money. 'And money answereth all things,' Ecclesiastes has said. If we had money we could achieve everything without revolution, without petitions, without culture. In Gehenna as everywhere else everybody has his price. You are all greenhorns. I know Gehenna from top to bottom and inside out. With money we could even—"

The politician wanted to tell his listeners what else could be accomplished with money in Gehenna, but at that instant the Sabbath ended. The fires leaped up again. The nails on the beds began to glow with heat. The punishing demons grabbed up their rods, and a lashing and a whipping and a hanging and a wailing erupted once more. The politician who had just spoken about money winked an eye at one of the other demons and they both left—where they were going no one knew. Most probably to do some unkosher Gehenna business.

Translated by the author

The Last Gaze

THE NEWS of Bessie's death came as a shock from which he knew he would not easily recover. It was fifteen months since he'd last seen her, and only now did he realize how much she meant to him. That very night he went to the funeral parlor, but the girl at the window told him, "She isn't ready. Come back tomorrow morning."

He returned home and began a chess game with himself, making the moves for both sides. He tried smoking, but the tobacco tasted bitter. Although he hadn't eaten since breakfast, he felt bloated, as if he'd consumed a heavy meal. He stretched out on the sofa, leaving the lights on, and covered himself with his overcoat.

"If there is a hereafter," he mused, "let her appear before me now. Let her face become visible in the mirror, let her voice be heard, let some sign of her presence manifest itself." The lights shone with a midnight glare. The telephone on the nightstand remained silent. The radiator hissed and gurgled its last bit of steam. He imagined that he heard the movement of the earth as it rotated on its axis. That very second, as the earth spun amid the planets and fixed stars, multitudes of people and animals were giving up their lives. At least one hundred thousand men and women lay dying; many more would die the following day, and the next, and a week hence.

He partially covered his face with his hat, like a passenger on a train, and drifted into a half-sleep. He had brooded about his relationship with Bessie for years, but he could never explain it to himself. On the surface it appeared simple enough, but behind their mutual affection hovered a kind of enmity. They could neither stay together nor remain apart. Eventually they were able to get along only in the dark.

How had they spent their last night together, he wondered. How could they have known that this was to be their final meeting? What had they said to each other? What were the last words between them? Unfortunately, this last night had blended in his memory with many other nights. Most likely he'd promised to telephone the following day, but he never called her again, nor she him. Yet during those fifteen months he had thought of her every day, perhaps every hour. More than once he had put his hand on the receiver, and was about to lift it, but the power which had the final say ordained, No. Every time his telephone rang his hope soared that it was she. Then the day came when her brother called and told him the shattering news.

The radiator had grown still. Drowsily, he tried to listen to his dreams, but there was nothing therein he could grasp. The visions changed as quickly as they do in a fever. In one dream he was in a narrow side street somewhere. It was lined with wooden shacks, with roofs like boys' caps, housing a race of dwarfs. In the middle of the alley stood a straw bed stripped of linen. He lay on this pallet and gave a tattered urchin, an occupant of one of the huts, a dollar, with the understanding that the boy was to change the bill and bring back ninety cents in silver. But the boy never returned. "He's stolen the dollar!" he berated himself, and deplored his stupidity in having trusted the youngster. And mingled with his regret was self-pity. What was he doing here in a strange bed, in this forsaken alleyway far from home, among a race of dwarfs? It all had to do with his many failures.

He woke up. The clock showed a quarter past three. He'd slept away half the night with nothing to show for it but a senseless dream. Later he showered and shaved and dressed in his finest suit. The previous day he'd sent a huge wreath of flowers to the funeral parlor. He was anxious to appear prosperous before Bessie's friends and relatives. Carefully he chose his shirt, tie, and cuff links. He prepared breakfast—not out of hunger, but to avoid a drawn appearance. He brewed strong coffee, added much sugar. Large flakes of snow were falling outside and although it was the dead of winter, a fly suddenly appeared. For a while it buzzed against the windowpane, then landed near some crystals of spilled sugar. It did not eat but seemed to ponder over them. From time to time it entangled its back feet, then straightened them out again. Finally, it landed on the brim of a saucer of leftover black coffee and gazed into it as if into an abyss. Perhaps, he had a sudden thought, the fly is Bessie.

He'd have to hurry. He wanted to see her alone, with no

one looking on. The funeral parlor was not far from his house, but he took a taxi to avoid coming in from the cold with a red nose. Soon he was standing at the little window which connected the dead to the living.

"Fourth floor," the same girl told him.

He rode up on the elevator. The funeral parlor was deserted, an emptiness that would soon be overrun by a crowd. He stopped before a door with mottled milk-glass panels, which held a card bearing Bessie's name and the hour of her funeral. It seemed to him that, in some eerie fashion, Bessie had become an official with her own office and office hours. He pushed open the door and saw her coffin with a part of its lid removed. From the ceiling a colored lamp cast a pale light, which mixed with the daylight filtering through the stained-glass windows. He was alone with Bessie.

Her face was covered by a square of gauze. She seemed almost alive, only lovelier, a perfect portrait painted by a master who wished to protect it from the dust. She seemed to smile, the smile of someone about to wake up, who savors the last few moments of stolen sleep. Her hair was combed up in a net, her throat bound in a white collar like a nun's. Did she recognize him from under her closed lids? His heart pounded like a trip-hammer and his temples pulsated. Outwardly he remained placid, but he knew that he could not endure this tension long. He did a forbidden thing, hesitantly lifting up the gauze. He imagined that Bessie was aware of his gazing at her with enchantment and trepidation. He had uncovered her face like a bridegroom at the unveiling of the bride. Then he replaced the gauze, as if she were something sacred and forbidden to be looked at. Thus as a boy he used to steal a glimpse when the kohanim blessed the congregation.

Presently he heard footsteps, and another person opened the door. Someone else wanted a private look at Bessie. In his confusion, he brushed past the newcomer, and later he could not be sure whether it had been a man or a woman.

Downstairs he was told that the services would begin in a half hour. He went out into the street to avoid meeting any of Bessie's relatives. It was too cold and he was shivering, so he went into a luncheonette and ordered coffee. He warmed his hands on the cup, took a sip, and stared into the coffee as if expecting to discover in the hot fluid the solution to the riddle.

All the old altercations with Bessie, all the friction between them had vanished, leaving in their wake the pure love that had once been theirs. If only he could have looked at her a few moments longer! He sat there, drunk with the intoxication he had known from the very beginning with her. He was falling in love with her again, and it was no longer winter but the spring of twelve years ago. The snowflakes falling outside reminded him of blossoms; a blinding stream of sunlight filtered through a split in the overcast skies.

But it was too late. One could no longer cause Bessie either good or evil. She lay there upstairs like a queen, independent of everyone, bestowing her grace equally upon all. He'd been prepared for every countermove in the chess game of love, except this. With one stroke she had checkmated him. In the wrinkles around her eyes and lips lingered an expression of triumph. He realized it only now: she had gained the upper hand completely. His heart pounded no longer but felt as if an unseen hand were squeezing it. He'd forgotten that one could lose absolutely. He hadn't reckoned with the kind of power that in one second erases everything petty and ambitious.

The clock in the coffee shop showed five minutes to eleven, and he went back to the funeral parlor. A crowd had gathered in the chapel. The coffin rested in its appointed place amid the wreaths of flowers. The electric candles were lit. All the benches were taken, save the last. Looking around, he saw unfamiliar faces. A woman sobbed with a laugh-like cry. A man honked his nose and wiped his spectacles. The women were whispering to one another, which reminded him of a women's synagogue during the Days of Awe. He sat down in an empty place. A rabbi in a tiny skullcap over a shock of freshly pomaded hair spoke with customary words, booming the biblical phrases with the usual mournful intonations: "He is the rock, His work is perfect: for all His ways are judgment: a God of truth and without iniquity, just and right is He." Afterward, the cantor chanted the prayer, "God is full of mercy." Dramatically, he switched from lulling whispers to an ear-shattering crescendo, and his chant, though obviously affected and rehearsed, tugged at the heartstrings, where grief and ceremony blend.

Afterward everyone stood up and began to file past the coffin to look at the corpse, as if for reassurance that they, the living, still possessed curiosity and strength. He did not join in this procession and went outside. The rabbi who had just concluded the eulogy was now matter-of-factly directing the cars, which had to maneuver in the narrow street to pick up mourners for the trip to the cemetery. The rabbi had forsaken his role as reverend and assumed the part of traffic expert, having cast off his solemnity like a mask.

For a while it appeared as if he, Bessie's friend, would be overlooked in the throng of mourners and bystanders, but one of the relatives spied him and directed him to a vacant seat in a limousine. He sat in the car among strangers. A man and a woman talked interminably about a lost key to her apartment, and the dire consequences of having lost it on a Sunday, when they'd been unable to locate a locksmith and had been forced to pierce the metal door with an electric drill. The relating of this incident did not exhaust the topic. The lost key became the theme of the trip. All the passengers offered up similar happenings, their own and their neighbors'.

He sat there astounded. Why had they bothered to come to the funeral at all, with so little respect for the deceased? Or was this a way to forget and ignore death while facing it? Such callousness in itself was an enigma. He pressed his face against the pane. He wanted to disassociate himself from these people. The car hurtled through the wilds of Brooklyn, through streets and avenues so strange they might as well have been in Philadelphia or Chicago. The Sunday quiet made them even uglier and more desolate than on a weekday.

They rode past a vast cemetery, a city of graves. The tombstones resembled a forest of toadstools, extending as far as the eye could see. Here and there among the crosses loomed the statue of an angel, its wings laden with snow, sorrow in its blind eyes. The living had in some mysterious fashion poured their fears and regrets into the stone and remained hollow shells themselves.

After a while, the limousine turned into the cemetery. Everything had been prepared beforehand: the open grave, the artificial grass, which did not even pretend to create an illusion. A woman cried out. Some man said Kaddish, reading the Aramaic words transliterated into English on a leaflet printed especially for such occasions. What he witnessed was not just a burial but an ancient sacrifice wherein a lot was cast to determine who should be given back to the soil on this gloomy winter day. They had to fill the grave in a hurry, before the earth froze.

As soon as the ceremony was over, the rush to depart began. Everyone spoke of one thing only—the best way to get back to the city. The matter of transportation had now become the paramount issue; men and women vied with one another in their knowledge of shortcuts, tunnels, and bridges.

He did not return to the limousine but struck out on his own, in search of a bus or subway. He had severed his relations with those who drove back in the black Cadillac with the stiff chauffeur. Someone had to acknowledge that Bessie was now lying in a casket covered with earth, while myriads of microbes were beginning to decompose her flesh and return it to the elements. Did some vestige of thought still remain in her brain? Had her spirit been entirely extinguished, and did absolute darkness alone hold sway? If that were so, Bessie hadn't even died—she had just vanished. It was actually his funeral, he thought, not hers.

He shivered and raised his collar as he trudged through snow and slush. He lifted his eyes heavenward; perhaps he would be given a sign there. Maybe the divine powers would make an exception. But the clouds overhead writhed brown as rust. The wind caught up his hat, but he recovered it at the very last second. The Lord of the Universe, or His appointees delegated to rule this insignificant planet, were apparently in no mood for revelation.

As he sloshed down the street, a hodge-podge of garages, unoccupied buildings, and empty lots, a horn sounded. He turned to see a man leaning out of a car window who said, half questioningly, "You were at the funeral. You want to go back to the city?"

"Yes."

"Get in." He got in and thanked the stranger. Only now did he take a real look at the driver, elderly but powerfully built, with broad shoulders, gray curly hair, and a red flattened face with a wide nose and thick lips clamped around a cigar. His eyes were gray and overhung by bristling brows. He wore a snappy yellowish overcoat of the kind worn by old people attempting to appear younger. His hat sat jauntily on his head, sporting a red feather in its band. Even his manner of driving accentuated his efforts to appear young: he lounged in his seat, holding the wheel negligently in one hand, with the easiness of a driver fully capable of handling any possible emergency. As he drove along, he spoke to his passenger, turning the edge of his profile carelessly in the process.

"Well, she is no longer with us," he said both to himself and to the passenger.

"Yes."

"A remarkable woman. There aren't many like her." And he pressed the car horn, barely missing a pedestrian.

For a time he maintained a morbid silence. Then he said, "I know you. That is, not personally, but Bessie told me all about you. She showed me your picture. That's how I recognized you."

"Are you a relative?"

"No, hardly that. We got to know each other about a year ago, and right off it turned, so to speak, into a friendship. She held nothing back, told me all there was to know, and I respected her for it. What's the point in bluffing? No one would expect a woman her age to be a virgin."

He abruptly braked the car for a red light. For a while neither of them spoke. Then the driver began again: "What was it that happened between you two? Why didn't you get married? —But like I say, it's all fate. There is nothing one can do to forestall destiny. I wanted her to come to some sort of a decision. I'm not rich, mind you, but she would have had a good life with me. Both my daughters are married. I'm in real estate. I build bungalows. If I wanted to, I could retire today. I offered to take her to Europe, to Israel, wherever she wanted. My sons-in-law don't need my money and you can't take it with you, so why the hell save and skimp? But she kept putting it off, putting it off.—*Hey, where do you think you're going?*" he suddenly yelled to a passerby. *"You damned bum!"*

For a time he was silent. "Do you smoke? I smoke ten cigars

a day. The doctors say it's bad for a man of my age, but one thing is sure, I won't die young anymore. And as long as I live, I want to enjoy myself. Once you're on the other side, it's already too late. Yes sir, it looked as if Bessie and I would hit it off real fine until that other party horned in—"

"The *other* party?"

"That Levy guy. She didn't tell you? I was under the impression that you'd remained friends."

"No, she didn't tell me."

"Yes, the dentist. What she saw in him I'll never know, but what do we men know about women's taste? He talks real fancy and runs to concerts at Carnegie Hall. He is also some kind of a big shot with the Zionists or whoever they are. As soon as I heard about him I warned her. She introduced us and asked my opinion. I'm the sort of guy, if I liked him, I'd have said so. I'm like that in business, too. Somebody can be my biggest competitor, but if they turn out a nice piece of work I'll be the first to admit it. But I didn't like him, so I told her, 'Do what you like, we'll still be friends.' And from that time on she started to go down. I called her a few times after that, but she didn't call me back. I took her out, too, to the theater, a restaurant. I was ready to forgive and forget, but she was proud. Too proud. She said to me, 'Sam, it's the end of me.' I said, 'Why is it the end?' She said, 'When others don't respect me I don't care, but when I lose my self-respect, then it's the finish.' What happened was, that sneaky little dentist went back to his wife because her father had died and left her a bundle. I found out that during the time he was going out with Bessie he kept a mistress, some Mrs. Rothstein, a divorcee. He is one of those guys who flit from woman to woman and think they deceive the whole world. What did she ever see in him? It wasn't love—she loved only you. But there is such a thing as ambition. Especially in women.—*Where is he going, that bum? Why do they give people like that a license?*—Yes, ambition. She was ready to marry and he, as they say, pulled the wool over her eyes. You didn't see her the last few months?"

"No."

"Well, she was crushed. Completely crushed. A good woman, a noble woman. How was it you didn't call her?"

"It just happened that way."

"I understand. I know how it is. He was at the funeral today, too, the little quack. He sat right in the first row and acted like the number-one mourner. He tried to make a speech over the body, but her brother wouldn't stand for it. Maybe you'd like to have lunch with me? I know a restaurant in this neighborhood—"

"No, thanks. But if you're hungry—"

"I'm not hungry, thank you. Even if I was, what of it? I'm too heavy as it is. The doctor ordered me to lose twenty pounds. Now how do you go about losing twenty pounds? You wouldn't think so, but I'm pushing seventy. What do I have to worry about? But her death is a great loss to me, a great loss. What about you? You live alone?"

"Yes. Alone."

"Well, as the saying goes, everyone has his own troubles. What does anyone know about anyone else? Nothing. Absolutely nothing. Less than nothing."

And he lapsed into silence. His head sank down, his back sagged, as if suddenly he felt the weight of his years. The car seemed to be hurtling downhill. Dusk descended quickly, as if a heavenly wick had been snuffed out. The sky became yellow as an old canvas. There was silence. It began to snow again—a gray snow, thick and wet, absorbing the light of day, and turning all being into primeval twilight.

Translated by Joseph Singer

The Death of Methuselah

IT WAS a sweltering hot summer day. In a wicker tent Methuselah rested, an old man way past his nine hundredth year. He was barefoot, naked, with a sash of fig leaves round his loins. He half lay, half sat on a bed of deer, goat, and oxen skins. From time to time he reached with a shriveled hand and took a drink from a jug of water. His cheeks were sunken and he was toothless. In his youth Methuselah had the reputation of a strong man. But when you pass your nine hundredth birthday, you are not what you used to be. He was emaciated, and his skin had become dark brown, parched from the sun. He had lost all his hair, even his beard and on his chest. His body was covered with boils, knots, tumors. His bones jutted out, his nose was crooked, and his ribs looked like the hoops of a barrel.

Methuselah was neither awake nor asleep. He seemed to be in a swoon from the heat and murmured to himself the murmurings of extreme old age. Still, his mind was clear. He knew quite well who he was—Methuselah, the son of Enoch, who had never died but was taken by God. His wife and many children had seen Enoch walking in the field, in the direction of the granary, when suddenly he vanished. Some said that the earth opened its mouth and swallowed him, but others maintained that the hand of God descended from heaven and brought him into the celestial heights, because Enoch was a just man who walked with the Almighty.

Methuselah hoped to pass away in the same manner. God would stretch out His divine hand and take him to Himself, to his father Enoch, and to the angels, seraphim, aralim, cherubim, sacred beasts, and other heavenly hosts. But when? He was already in his nine hundred and sixty-ninth year. As far as Methuselah knew, he was the oldest man on earth. He had heard that Naamah, a female whom he once loved, might be even older. She was supposedly the daughter of Lamech and Zillah, the sister of Tubal-Cain, who forged all implements of copper and iron. Methuselah had met Naamah many hundred years ago. Since then he had lusted after her and yearned to lie in her lap. There were rumors that she was not really Lamech's daughter but a child of one of the fallen angels who had seen how beautiful the daughters of men were and cohabited with those of their choosing. Naamah later disappeared, and there was talk that she joined a camp of demons, the daughters of Lilith, with whom Adam lay one hundred and fifty years before God had put him to sleep and formed Eve from his rib.

As he was napping, overcome by the heat, near to death, Methuselah kept brooding over Naamah. He dreamed about her at night and sometimes during the day. He could barely differentiate between dreaming and wakefulness. He would open his eyes and see images. He heard the voices of his dead brothers and sisters, sons and daughters. Methuselah had a son whom he named Lamech in memory of Naamah's father. This son gave birth to a son by the name of Noah. Of Methuselah's sons that still lived, some wandered off with flocks of sheep, donkeys, mules, horses, camels. His daughters had married men whose names he had already forgotten. Methuselah had hordes of grandchildren and great-grandchildren whom he had never met and of whom he had never heard. The earth was vast and sparsely inhabited. Many men took to hunting. They chased animals, killed them, roasted and ate their flesh, flailed their skin and made clothes and shoes with it. They learned to shoot bows and arrows and, like Tubal-Cain, could forge implements of copper and iron, and even forge gold and silver. They wore nets to catch fish in the rivers. Weapons were made, and men waged war and killed their own brothers, just as Cain killed Abel. It became known that Yahweh regretted creating man. He saw how great man's wickedness was and how every plan devised by man's mind was nothing but evil. Well, I don't really belong to the living anymore, Methuselah thought. I will soon descend into Sheol, into Dumah, the land of the shadows. Flies and gnats swarmed around him but he did not have the strength to shoo them away.

A wench entered the tent, barefoot and half naked. Methuselah did not know if she was one of his grandchildren or one of his slaves. Even if she was a slave, she still came from his seed, because all his female slaves had become his concubines. Methuselah wanted to ask the girl her name, but his throat was full of phlegm and he could not speak. She brought him a wooden bowl full of stewed dates. He held the vessel with a trembling hand and drank its sweet juices. Suddenly it occurred to him that his son Lamech had begot a son by the name of Noah. And Noah, too, had some children. "Where are they? Why did they leave me alone? Who is going to bury me after I breathe my last?"

He looked up and Naamah stood before him, mother-naked. A reddish glow from the setting sun shone over her face, breasts, and belly. Her black hair hung down to her loins. Methuselah embraced her and they kissed. She said, "Methuselah, I came to you."

"I longed for you in all these centuries," he answered.

And she said, "And I for you."

"Where have you been?" he asked.

"With my angel Ashiel, in a deep cave in the heart of the desert. I have eaten the food of heaven and drunk the wine of the gods. Demons served me and sang songs to me. They danced before me, braided my hair and Ashiel's beard. They fed me pomegranates, almond bread, dates, and honey. They played lyres for me and beat drums to please me. They lay with me and their semen filled my womb."

Naamah's words awakened lust in Methuselah and he became young and strong again. He asked, "Wasn't Ashiel jealous?"

"No, my lord. The fallen angels are all my slaves and maids. They wash my feet and drink the water."

"Why did you come to me after hundreds of years?" Methuselah asked.

"To take you with me to the city which Grandfather Cain built and named after his son," Naamah answered. She continued: "This son was the father of Irad and the grandfather of Mehujael, Methusael, and Lamech, who killed a man and a child and married Adah and my mother, Zillah. I am the daughter of a murderer and the granddaughter of a murderer and I live in a city built by a murderer. There I will take you, my beloved. Ashiel had fallen there and he brought many angels with him. You should know that Yahweh is vicious, a God of jealousy and revenge. He keeps tempting those who serve Him. The stronger their devotion is to Him, the more

He punishes them. We in Cain's city serve Satan and his wife, Lilith, with whom the father of all of us copulated. Satan and his brother Asmodeus are gods of passion, and so is their spouse, the goddess Lilith. They enjoy themselves and allow others their enjoyment. They are not faithful and they don't demand faithfulness from their mates. Yahweh's wrath is easily kindled. All pleasures are forbidden to Him, even the mere thought of them. He is always in fear that Adam's offspring might take over His domain. I have learned that He is intending to bring a flood on the earth to drown man and the animals. Blessed be my grandfather Cain, who built his city where the waters will not reach."

"How do you know all this?" Methuselah asked.

"We in Cain's city have many spies," was Naamah's reply.

"I am afraid of Yahweh and His vengeance," Methuselah said. "I have sinned a great deal in my nine hundred and sixty-nine years. I have lusted for you, Naamah, day and night."

"In Cain's city lechery is no sin," Naamah said. "The opposite: it is the highest virtue."

Methuselah wanted to say something more, but Naamah called out, "Come, fly with me to where my bed is made . . ."

Naamah spread out her arms and Methuselah soared with her. They flew in unison like two birds. All signs of illness and age had left him. He wanted to sing out and whistle in his elation. Methuselah had heard that Yahweh can work miracles only for those who served Him with all their hearts and with all their souls. But now a miracle was happening to him, the oldest of sinners.

Methuselah knew that the earth was immense and rich, yet now he could see it from on high—mountains, valleys, rivers, lakes, fields, forests, orchards, and plants of all kinds. While he, Methuselah, ate, slept and dreamed, the sons of Adam had built towns, villages, roads, bridges, houses, towers, sailboats. Naamah flew with him into Cain's city, which teemed with horsemen and pedestrians, as well as stores and workshops of all sorts. Methuselah saw many people of various races and colors: white, black, and brown. They had built temples to serve their gods. Bells were ringing. Priests sacrificed animals on altars, sprinkled blood on their corners, burned fat and incense.

Soldiers with swords hanging from their hips and spears on their backs bound captives in chains, tortured them, and killed them. Smoke rose from chimneys. Some women wore gold and silver jewelry and phallic symbols between their breasts. Naamah pointed out all the sights. Naked females stood in cages calling to shepherds and to men leading caravans to and from the deserts. Methuselah inhaled odors which were unfamiliar to him. Night had fallen and fires burned in the darkness. People in the crowds laughed, cried, danced, did somersaults. The insane shrieked with wild voices. In the desert behind the city a full moon was shining. In its light Methuselah could see an open gate into the belly of the earth. Many steps led down into an abyss. Is this Sheol or Dumah? Methuselah asked himself. Although he was pre-pared to face death, he was both afraid of it and curious. His mother had told him about the powers of the night. These powers waged war with Yahweh, rebelled against Him and His Providence. They called life death and death life. For them right was wrong and wrong right. Naamah's mother, Zillah, had told her daughter that the powers of evil were as old as *tohu* and *vohu* and the darkness which preceded Creation. These forces called themselves natives and they considered Yahweh an intruder who trespassed Satan's frontier, broke all his barriers, and defiled the world with light and life. How strange that in his late age, when Methuselah's body was about to turn to dust and his soul was bound to return to its source, he had fallen into the hands of these adversaries of God.

Naamah brought him into her chamber, and even though it was dark, he could see her bed and a huge man lying in it. It was Ashiel, a fallen angel, one of the sons of Anak, the giant men of renown. Naamah introduced Methuselah to him, saying, "Here is one of my oldest lovers," and the other asked, "Are you Methuselah? She speaks about you all the time. She craves you, not me. Even though I am a giant and you are as small as a locust."

"He is small, but he is a real man," Naamah said. "While your semen is like water and foam."

"I will go now," Ashiel said, "to the men of wisdom in our assembly."

Ashiel left, and Methuselah embraced Naamah and he came

into her. She revealed to him secrets of heaven and earth. "Your father, Enoch," she said, "became Yahweh's head of the angels, the Lord Metatron. Actually, he is nothing but His servant. Your son Lamech is among the shadows of Dumah." Naamah revealed to Methuselah that her mother, Zillah, was a harlot and she lay with all her husband's friends as well as with his enemies. She begot her, Naamah, from one of Adah's sons, Jubal, the ancestor of all who play the lyre and pipe. Naamah continued to say to Methuselah, "Let it be known to you that Yahweh's world is nothing but a madhouse. He has erred by creating man, and he commanded your grandson, Noah, to build an ark to save himself and his household and all the animals from the flood. But be sure that the flood will never come upon the earth. Here in the netherworld an assembly of wise men from all over the world is meeting. They came from Kush and from India, from Sodom and from Nineveh, from Shinar and Gomorrah. Yahweh is old and tired. He thinks He is the only God and is forever jealous of other gods, constantly in dread that His own angels might rebel against Him and take dominion of the universe. We, the demons of this generation, are young and many. Yahweh threatens to open the windows of heaven and bring the flood. But we have scholars who have discovered how to close them. In all these years when you, Methuselah, lived with your faithful wives and concubines, plowed the fields by the sweat of your brow, and attended your flocks of sheep, many men of learning sprang forth. They can split hairs, count the sand of the sea, the eyes of a fly, measure the stench of a skunk and the venom of a snake. Some of these men have learned to tame crocodiles and spiders, they can make the old young, the fools wise, and reverse the sexes. They can reach the very depths of perversion. Stay with us, Methuselah, and you will be twice as clever and ten times as virile."

Naamah kissed Methuselah and caressed him. She said, "Yahweh had only one wife, the Shekinah, and for countless years they have been separated because of His impotence and her frigidity. He has forbidden all deeds which bring pleasure to men and women, such as theft, murder, adultery. Even the sweet coveting of another man's wife He considers a crime.

But here we have turned teasing and tantalizing into the highest art. Come with me, Methuselah, and I will take you to the assembly of the wise which gathered here and you will witness their accomplishments and hear what they intend to do in the happy time to come. My lover, Ashiel, is there now and many fallen angels who became weary of the daughters of Adam and now lie one with the other. If you stay with me I will give you all my maids and many of the imps for our common delight."

Methuselah and Naamah rose and she took him through a labyrinth of many passages. They entered a temple where each scholar was speaking about his land and its people.

A sage of Sodom told the gathering that they were teaching children in Sodom the art of manslaughter, as well as the arts of arson, embezzlement, lying, robbery, treachery, the abuse of the old and the rape of the young. A glutton from Nineveh was telling how to eat the flesh of animals while they are still alive and to suck their blood in its flow. Prizes were awarded to the most accomplished thieves, robbers, forgers, liars, whores, torturers, as well as to sons and daughters who dishonored their parents and to widows who had excelled in poisoning their husbands. They had established special courses for blasphemy, profanity, and perjury. The great Nimrod himself was teaching cruelty to animals.

An old demon by the name of Shavriri was giving an oration and saying, "Yahweh is a God of the past, but we are the future. Yahweh is dying or perhaps already dead, but the serpent is alive and giving birth to countless new serpents by copulating with our queen, Lilith, and the ladies of her court. The angels in heaven have all been blinded by the curse of light, but we will bring back the primeval darkness, which is the substance of all matter."

Harsh music was being played for the assembly, and the singing was so loud it pierced Methuselah's ears. He could not tell the difference anymore between laughter and crying, the cheering of female demons and the wild cries of male hobgoblins. "I'm too old for all this revelry," Methuselah was saying, not knowing whether he spoke to himself or to Naamah. He fell on his knees and pleaded with her to take him back to his tent, to his bed, to the bliss of old age and rest. For the first time in almost a thousand years, the fear of the grave had left him. He was ready to embrace the angel of death with his sharp sword and myriad eyes.

The next morning when the servant girl brought Methuselah a bowl with date juice she found him dead. The news spread that the oldest man on earth had returned to dust. Noah soon learned that his grandfather had died, but he could not leave his wife and his three sons, Shem, Ham, and Japeth, as well as the ark which the Almighty had told him to build. God's decision to release the flood was about to take place. The windows of heaven began to open and no one could close them. All the lords of Sodom and Shinar, Nineveh and Admah were about to be swept away in the deluge. Somewhere in the depths of Dumah and Sheol a bevy of devils were hiding, Naamah among them. Methuselah knew the past quite well and he had gotten a glimpse of the future. God had taken a perilous risk when He created man and gave him dominion over all other creatures of the earth, but He was about to promise by the rainbow in the clouds never again to bring a flood and destroy all flesh. It became clear to Him that all punishment was in vain, since flesh and corruption were the same from the very beginning and always will remain the scum of creation, the very opposite of God's wisdom, mercy, and splendor. God had granted the sons of Adam an abundance of self-love, the precarious gift of reason, as well as the illusions of time and space, but no sense of purpose or justice. Man would manage somehow to crawl upon the surface of the earth, forward and backward, until God's covenant with him ended and man's name in the book of life was erased forever.

Translated by the author

UNCOLLECTED STORIES

Contents

The Bird   737

"My Adventures as an Idealist"   745

Exes   759

Between Shadows   772

Hershele and Hanele, or the Power of a Dream   775

Pity   785

The Angry Man   793

The Mathematician   799

The Building Project   808

The Painting   821

Morris and Timna   834

Two   844

Eulogy to a Shoelace   858

The Bird

MY APARTMENT overlooks one side of Central Park. I can see from my window Fifth Avenue, the City Reservoir (a silver mirror by day, copper at sunset) and the skyscrapers down to the Empire State Building. On summer nights I see the lights of the Yankee Stadium. And on the other side, of Idlewild Airport. Planes landing and taking off all the time.

My study and bedroom look out on a tiny yard, hardly big enough to put up a Sukkah there. At night you can see right into the kitchens and bedrooms of the people living opposite —all eighteen storys. There are Irish, Italians, Jews, Cubans, Puerto Ricans, Negroes, even Chinese, Japanese, and Filipinos living there. Each kitchen has the same ice-box, and almost the same pattern of linoleum on the floor. The housewives with curlers in their hair, Amazonian matriarchs, are scrubbing and mopping the floors, cooking in aluminum pots, ironing clothes with electric irons, drying their hair with electric driers. In between they glance at the serial in the magazine. I hear the radio blaring, and I catch a glimpse of the television screen in the kitchen. The menfolk come in, give their women a quick kiss, and snatch a hasty bite. I see it all, the whole eighteen storys, like a huge panorama.

I find it particularly interesting when it is raining. The rain floods the yard, and it runs like a gutter. The black asphalt looks like a deep well, mirroring the lights of the city, and the lightning flashes in the sky.

If you shout down, the echo comes back as from a chasm. When it snows the snow lies there perfectly white for a long time. Nobody treads in the snow, because nobody has any business in that small space in our civilization, which keeps climbing upward. You don't see even cats and dogs out there. These yards seem built specially for suicides.

I stand by the window, holding on so as not to lose my balance, my head tilted to the sky, which hangs like a dull metal lid glowing red with the city fires and lights, without moon or stars.

Though I have lived here in New York almost as long as I had lived previously in Warsaw, I still feel a stranger here. I am here by virtue of a visa that a kind-hearted Consul stamped into my foreign passport. My ears are full of a roar that never ceases, the underground trains, the overhead trains, the automobiles, the whirr of machinery, ambulances and fire engines rushing past, police sirens, shouting and laughing, the sound and bustle of many millions who are never silent for a moment. Sometimes I think I hear the voices of Chedar boys and Yeshiva students, and the songs of young workmen and young working girls. You can hear in this noise anything you wish.

My mind is saturated with memories of a town in ruins, of a people burned to ashes, of a language half-forgotten. There is a woman busy in the next room with whom I speak in a foreign tongue. Somewhere between the bridges, the rivers, the towering buildings, behind the countless lighted windows rising to the clouds like flaming hieroglyphics, people move about with whom I have in one way or another linked my mind-nerves, friends, relatives, dear ones, my readers—invisible threads stretch between them and me. We have our calculations. We converse through telepathy. We quarrel and are reconciled without a word. Who knows? Perhaps there wander here, in this dense atmosphere, the spirits of the dead? I have a good share already in that sphere to which we go and break off all communication. I often have a feeling that the souls watch me, silently appraising me, scoffing at my lies and my temptations. The astral body of the woman with the dark eyes rests often at twilight on a chair, or on the couch. She is silent with the silence of those whose lips are sealed.

The telephone rings in the next room; when I return I see something strange. A little bird on the window sill; not a sparrow nor a dove, but a brightly colored bird, a parakeet.

One of the neighbors must have inadvertently left the cage open, and the window open, and the bird flew out. A parakeet wouldn't know the way back. Nor could it survive long out of doors in the New York climate. Even if it could, other birds would kill it. But the bird doesn't know it is doomed. It hops about with an air of "Lost my way! Could have happened to anyone!"

I have till now protected no one from death; but I am determined not to let this small creature perish. One false move and the bird will fly out into the cold night. A long-forgotten cunning of a hunter and trapper awakens in me. I stretch out my hand from behind, to bar its way, and hold the bird by its tail. It beats its wings trying to fly, but now I have man-blocked. Against your will you will live, little bird! Your time has not come yet!

I let it go, and it flies zig-zag, to and fro, from wall to wall, corner to corner. It has banged into the furniture, against vases and other things. It has lost a few feathers. It is bewildered and frightened in this new cage to which it has blundered so unexpectedly. Then it stops still, perched on the frame of a picture. It is trembling all over with fear and exertion. A shuddering runs through its feathers. It flaps its wings in an effort to dislodge this evil visitation. Its tiny eyes, like black onyx beads set in blue, say: "See what has come upon me! Who knows what I have been trapped into!"

I telephoned the superintendent of the block of apartments. I also hung a sign in the lift that I found a parakeet; would the owner please claim it. There was no immediate response. It occurred to me that the parakeet might have come from another apartment block. Perhaps even from Fifth Avenue, from the other side of Central Park. Meanwhile I would have to feed it and look after it. And I didn't know a thing about birds.

I went into the kitchen and brought out a biscuit, and offered it to the bird. He looked at me with his bright beady eyes, but didn't budge. He seemed to say: "I know your tricks. You think that by offering me food you can lure me down and catch me." I could have chased him down with a stick, but I didn't like using force.

It was getting late, and I wanted to go to bed. I left the bird perched on the picture frame. I put a saucer of water on the table for it, and a few grains of barley. The room was warm, but I knew the central heating was turned off during the night and the radiator went cold. I told myself that even in the tropical jungles where parakeets came from there were sometimes cold nights; and there were other dangers—serpents that swallowed birds whole. I had done what I could. The rest must be left to God, who has created birds and flies and rats and all else that His Will had made, for His praise for all generations!

I went to bed, pulled the blanket over me, and switched off the light. Then I began to think about what had happened, and what had seemed in the light to be simple and natural took on in the dark a touch of the mystic. Why had the parakeet found his way just to my apartment? I remembered that a bird flying into your room through the window is regarded among the folk as a lucky sign. May be!

Perhaps the parakeet was the reincarnation of a near one. Perhaps the soul of the woman with the dark eyes sits in it, and has paid me a visit. Perhaps the bird has brought me a greeting from a being that can't get in touch otherwise with those who wander about the earth. The last dregs of sober commonsense that I possess when I am up and about were running out. I was back to the belief in demons and spirits, to say nothing of faith in God and God's Providence. What do we know about God's creatures? They may possess forces which man does not suspect.

I couldn't lie in bed any longer. I put on my dressing gown and slippers and went to have a look at the bird. I stood still for a moment in the dark, ready to hear the parakeet speak. Then I switched on the light. The bird was where I had left it, still perched on the picture frame. It hadn't touched the food or drink. It looked petrified, neither awake nor asleep, sunk in a kind of bird Nirvana. What a tiny creature it was! All feathers and down. Would weigh half an ounce in all! Yet it had everything—heart, lungs, brain, stomach, bowels, a behind. Nature had made a *multum in parvo*. How had this bird got here to me? Millions of generations of parakeets had to busy themselves for this parakeet to perch there now on the picture frame. Countless mothers laid eggs, hatched them, attracted males, sang to them.

One saw plainly that this bird thought. What were its thoughts? One thing was certain—underlying everything was submissiveness, the sacred submissiveness that leaves man as soon as he comes out from the womb and returns only when he breathes his last.

I couldn't move from the spot. Suddenly the bird began to preen itself. Its beak was busy among its feathers, wings, tail, underbody, legs. If it had a bird-bath it would surely dip in. It seemed to say: "Enough of this thinking! I must get to work now to rid myself of the dirt and vermin that attaches itself to little birds."

I stood watching for a long time, but the bird did not for a moment interrupt the process of cleansing itself. I don't know why, but it reminded me of the night of Yom Kippur, of the Priests bathing in the waters of purification. To a bird every day is Yom Kippur. A bird is a High Priest, engaged in the sacred service every day. When the morning star rises. When the face of the east lights up!

I was awakened by a song. I got out of bed, half asleep, weighed down by the dreams that crowd on me in the night. I went into the other room, and saw in the east a great sun, purple-red, just come up bathed from the sea, the ancient sun that our Father Abraham had once thought was God. It lighted up the Park like a heavenly lamp, shone on the windows of the skyscrapers, reddened the freshly-fallen snow.

Against the glow I saw my bird, with its yellow-green body, yellow-grey tail feathers, and two blue spots at the beak. That wasn't all. The Creator had put more colors and shades into robing this little bird than I have words for and my pen can describe. The yellow on the neck is a different yellow than that on the tail feathers. He has every shade of yellow—banana, saffron, lemon. He wears a coat of many colors, but wears it discreetly, not to excite the envy of his brothers. He still stood on the frame of the picture, but now he was singing a hymn of praise to the new day.

As I lack words to describe his coloring, so I lack words to describe his singing. He was doing everything at once—trilled, whistled, chirped, quavered, twittered, warbled, produced tones and semi-tones that only the ear knows what they mean. Now and again he started jabbering in a birdish slang that only King Solomon and perhaps too Ashmadai could understand. He sang as if fit for a singer by God's grace, without fee, without an audience, only for himself, purely out of the desire to thank God for the fresh beginning.

I pointed my finger to the water and the food on the table, to attract his attention. I said that singing on an empty stomach wasn't good even for a poet. I told him that God has hosts of angels singing in the celestial choir, praising Him each day, and one little bird less in the song wouldn't be noticed in

Heaven. But no scoffing and no heretical ideas of mine stopped his singing, which burst from a heart the size of a pea, out of a throat thin as a thread. This was true ecstasy. It was flaming sacred devotion. This is how the Baal Shem prayed at sunrise in the forests of Podolia. I am no Cabalist and I don't know what goes on in the heavenly spheres, but I would have sworn that angels and seraphs and cherubim were listening to this song and weaving from it crowns for the *Shechina*. Messiah himself heard this singing prayer where he sat waiting for the Redemption.

There was a ring at my door. A faint, timid ring, as though whoever it was didn't trust themselves to touch the bell, were hesitant, unwilling to intrude. It was so faint that I wondered if I had really heard it.

I went to open the door. The room was bright with sunlight. But the corridor was still dark. Here it was still night. Not yet today, but yesterday. My weariness of last night returned. My eyelids grew heavy. I stumbled against a chair. Who could it be so early?

I opened cautiously. There was a woman there, a slight little woman of about thirty, apparently still wrapped in sleep as I was, unkempt, and probably not yet dressed under her coat. I could hardly make out the face. There were so many dark shadows about. She spoke English, but with an accent, and the uncertainty of a recent arrival. She was very apologetic:

"I am sorry to disturb you so early in the morning. But I've got to go to work soon, and I wouldn't be back till late this evening. I saw the notice about the bird, when I came home last night. I didn't connect it with my bird. I don't keep my bird in a cage. I couldn't put any living thing in a prison. When I got in I found he had managed to fly out through the slightly open window, open just enough to air the room. I hadn't imagined he could have squeezed through that small opening. I didn't sleep all night. I don't know how to apologize for disturbing you now. On the other hand, why should I leave you with the burden of looking after my bird?"

"You didn't disturb me," I assured her. "I was up before you rang. I was listening to your bird singing."

"Singing?"

"Come in, and listen to him."

"I have brought the cage, to take him away in." She indicated a tall wicker cage that she had set down by the door.

"You said you don't keep your bird in a cage."

"I don't! But I give him his food in the cage. Otherwise he would make a terrible mess all over the place."

"Then come in, and take your bird."

"I hope I am not disturbing your family."

"No! My wife sleeps so that she can't be awakened. It would take much more than your coming here to waken her."

"Thank you! You are very kind. The bird is the only living thing I have in the world."

She followed me in, with the cage, which was almost as big as she was herself. A spacious dwelling for her pet. I wanted to relieve her of the load, but she wouldn't let me. In the bright daylight of the room I saw her face clearly—younger than I had thought, dark eyes, pointed chin, sunken cheeks. I had been right about her having flung on her coat over her night clothes. Her bare feet were in slippers.

She noticed my gaze and apologized for her attire. She stood regarding the bird happily. But he had stopped singing. He stared at her, in apparent recognition. He opened his beak, but made no sound.

She saw the grains of barley and the water on the table. "Thank you," she said, "for feeding him. I was afraid he would go hungry."

"You're not long in America?" I asked.

"Eight years."

"Where were you before?"

"In Germany. In the camps."

"You're Jewish?"

"Yes."

"You speak Yiddish?"

"It is my mother tongue."

"Where do you come from?"

"Kovno."

"Where were you in the Hitler years?"

"In the Ghetto. In a bunker. Then working for the Germans."

"Doing what?"

"Digging trenches, sawing timber, loading lorries."

"Your family?"

"All killed."

"What did you do before the war?"

"I was still at school. A Yiddish Secondary School."

"I am a Yiddish author," I told her, wondering at my own words, for I am not in the habit of parading myself in this way.

"What is your name?"

I told her.

"I know your work! I have read your stories. How strange!"

I looked at the tear-off calendar on my table. The date was December 16—the anniversary of the day the woman with the dark eyes died.

The Jewish World, September 1964

"My Adventures as an Idealist"

I KNOCKED on Sigmund Seltzer's bachelor-apartment door in the Hotel Warsaw, and a voice called out, "*Bitte! Entrez!* Come in!" I opened the door and saw a short, heavy-set man wearing a white suit, a Panama hat, yellow shoes, a pink shirt, and a tie with gold threads running through it. It was tacked down by a pearl stickpin. A cigar was clamped between his teeth. It was hard to tell whether he had just come in or was about to leave. A mandolin had been hung on one of the walls. Beneath it, on a table, lay several photograph albums. Placed around the room were numerous snapshots of Sigmund Seltzer with different groups of people. I thought I recognized the faces of several movie stars. He rolled his cigar artfully between thumb and forefinger and inquired: "Are you the Yiddish translator?"

"Yes."

"Well, sit down. Make yourself at home. I can't, as they say, stand formalities. You're either a friend or not, and if not, to hell with you. Would you like something to drink? Whiskey? Cognac? Sherry? Coke?"

"No, thanks."

"Something to eat?"

"I've just had lunch."

"My grandmother used to say, 'The intestine is bottomless!' Food's a necessity, and a glass of schnapps never hurt anyone. Do you know German?"

"I translated *The Magic Mountain* into Yiddish."

"What kind of mountain is that?"

"That's the title of a novel by Thomas Mann."

"I have no time for reading. Here is my book, *My Adventures as an Idealist*. It's my life story. Translate it from the German. It's been published in so many languages that now I want it to appear in my mother tongue, Yiddish. I want my parents to be proud of me. I'll send everyone in my family a copy. And I'll sell a few hundred books as well. I have a million friends. My grandmother used to say, 'Money is mud, but friends come in handy.' "

"You had a wise grandmother."

"Ninety-eight when she died. She wanted to make it to a hundred. Don't we all! I want to be Rockefeller! I want to be Greta Garbo's lover! But who can tell? If the movie they make from my book is a hit, anything can happen. The fact is I have to fly out to Hollywood this week to talk with the producer about it. How much do you want for the job? Name a figure in round numbers."

"Five hundred dollars."

"Five hundred? Okay, I won't bargain with you. In Paris I could have had it done for less, but I have to go to Hollywood. Turn the book into something worth reading. Put everything into it: a man's life, his thoughts, his soul. A book has to tug at the heartstrings. If it doesn't, it's a waste of time to read it. Do you understand me or not? In our business you can't afford to be a dope."

For a while I leafed through the book, saying nothing. Then I asked him in what language he had written it originally.

Sigmund Seltzer removed his hat. I could see now that he had a wide forehead with a jagged scar across the middle and thick, black, curly hair that glistened with pomade. I examined his features more closely. His cheeks had the blue shadow of men who look unshaven no matter how often they shave. His lips were full, and he had a broad nose with large nostrils. His dark, smiling eyes radiated congeniality. I noticed that he wore two rings on his fingers—one set with a ruby, the other with a diamond. He hesitated before replying.

"What difference does it make what language I wrote it in? I gave you the German version, and you translate from that. I hate long discussions. Either yes or no. A lot has happened in the world since the book was first published in 1932. That bastard, Hitler, took over Germany. Mussolini, that swine, gobbled up—what's the name of that place again?—oh yes, Ethiopia. Franco, that gangster, forced Fascism on Spain. You'll have to put all of that in the book so the reader will know what it's all about. Bring it up to date. Do you understand? Since the book will be in Yiddish, our struggle in Palestine, with all our strivings and hopes, should be included. I, Sigmund Seltzer, don't frighten easily. We'll tell the British to get the hell out of there. They made a Balfour Declaration, let them go back to London where they came from and leave the Jews alone. We'll know how to deal with the Arabs! Make it clear, and make it read smoothly, with class. Do you understand me?"

"Yes, I understand."

"Good. I'll give you an advance of one hundred dollars. Where is my checkbook?"

He set his cigar down on an ashtray and took a checkbook and gold fountain pen out of his breast pocket. Then he said, "Don't worry—my check is good. I've only been in America four weeks, but all the publishers are after me. *My Adventures* was sold in hundreds of thousands of copies in Europe. This pen here was presented to me in Paris at a banquet in my honor. You can't get another pen like it anywhere. The factory that made it went out of business. It's pure gold. Just take a look at the jeweler's mark. Fourteen carats! Have you ever been to Paris?"

"For a few days."

"A lively town. There's no city like it in the whole world. Once Bucharest was worth something. They called it the second Paris. But the war changed all that. Two things I love about Paris: the little rolls they bake there—brioches—and the women."

"Do you speak French?" I asked, just to make conversation.

"What language don't I speak! How much does one really have to know? A wink is enough language between a man and a woman. Just one look, and she knows exactly what you want. You call a cab and, before you know it, she's sitting next to you. Look, when you have a pocket full of francs, you can be deaf and dumb. You give the driver a little something, and he's your best friend. It's the same way in hotels and wherever you go. Here in America they say, 'Money talks.' It's true. When I come to a strange country, the first thing I do is learn how to count. Then I go into a restaurant and study the menu, because if your belly is empty, nothing else is important. The rest, my friend, comes with time. In Paris, I got to know the top writers. They gave me letters of recommendation and anything else I asked for. They posed for pictures with me. Look at this album—with the greatest! That's me, there. If someone is my friend, it's all the way. We eat together; we drink together. Money is no object. I meet their wives; they meet my relatives. I have relatives in France, too. One is a professor at the Sorbonne—the top man! All the other professors hang around him and drink in his words as if he were holy. What he says goes, and no one argues with him. A cousin of mine opened a small store in Paris a few years ago, and today he has a business that caters to the wealthiest people. He sells everything from diapers to automobiles. Rothschild is a steady customer of his. The President's wife shops there. When my family heard that I had written a book, they were really proud of me. Actually, this pen was given to me by my cousin."

Seltzer carefully drew a chair up to the table. He tested the pen point with the manicured fingernail of his left thumb, and said, "When Sigmund Seltzer gives someone a check, everything has to be perfect." He stuck out the tip of his tongue while slowly forming the letters and numbers. The script looked like hen tracks. As soon as I saw his signature, I knew the truth: This man could not have written any book in any language. It was the signature of one who barely knew the alphabet.

There was no sense in sticking to the German text. The real author of this fictitious autobiography, whom Seltzer had hired as a ghost writer, had thought up a life story that might have appealed to a German reader but never to a Yiddish one. The sentences were long, and the style turgid and full of clichés and banalities characteristic of certain types of European hack writers when they write about Jews. All the men in the book had high foreheads and long earlocks. The fathers all had white beards and were victims of pogroms. All that they required was that their children recite Kaddish and light memorial candles after their death. The young women were all dark beauties pursued by gentile millionaires. They, however, were really in love with Yeshiva boys or young Zionists.

I had to make up some other kind of drivel. I questioned Sigmund Seltzer about his origins and his youth, but for some reason he was reluctant to tell me anything. His answer to every question was the same: Just make it interesting, so that it can be turned into a radio sketch or a play. With that in mind, I gave the hero a father who was a lumber dealer in Lithuania, made the hero himself a musical prodigy, later drew him into the revolutionary movement, deposited him in a Warsaw prison, and then allowed him to escape with the aid of the jail-keeper's daughter. I didn't like this kind of work, but as a Yiddish free-lancer I had little choice. Months passed and not a word of mine appeared in the Yiddish press. My four dollars a week rent were a constant source of worry to me.

Sigmund Seltzer requested that I read him each chapter as I finished it. I was always astounded by his reaction: He seemed actually to believe the lies I was concocting about him. He would shake his head and become serious, even sad. Lost in thought, he would twist his cigar between his lips and blow smoke rings. Sometimes he would even ask me to add a few words, or elaborate on a description.

It often seemed to me that in some mysterious way I was reminding him of things he had partially forgotten. At times his round face took on the eager, yet pouting, expression of a mischievous child who was being told a story before bedtime. He would yawn, smile, rub his eyes.

Occasionally he would doze off, but only briefly, for the telephone was constantly ringing. It might be his New York agent, Seymour Katz, or someone calling from Hollywood. Once it was a woman named Sylvia, asking him where he had spent the previous night. Sigmund Seltzer reproached her, "Sylvia, darling, it's all business, business. You know you're dearest to my heart. I have one God and one Sylvia."

And he would press his middle finger into his breast as if Sylvia could see him. He hung up and said, "Cheats, every single one of them." And he relit his cigar.

Events developed rapidly and dramatically. There were times when I suspected that Sigmund Seltzer was acting out the imagined adventures of my Yiddish hero. He had given me another hundred-dollar check, but it was returned uncashed by the bank. This was bad news for me, because I was counting on the money to pay my rent. I telephoned him at his hotel and was told that he had moved out. A few weeks later I received a telegram inviting me to his wedding. He was marrying that same Sylvia. Her last name was Moscowitz.

I arrived downtown at the Hotel Delancey, a place where Orthodox weddings, bar mitzvahs, and rabbinical meetings were often held. I met the bride, her mother, her brother, and several friends. Seymour Katz, Sigmund Seltzer's agent, a tiny man holding a long cigar, was deeply engrossed in a whispered conversation with a huge rabbi who looked like a professional boxer. Sylvia, the bride, had a crooked nose like a broken beak. Her hair was dyed a carrot color and was elaborately combed in curls and ringlets. She smiled at me, and the smile was both friendly and derisive. Her yellow eyes were heavily made up. A set of porcelain teeth gleamed between bright-red lips. It was impossible to tell whether she was thirty or fifty. Her hands were wrinkled, the fingernails long, crimson, and sharp. As soon as I approached her, I was seized by a fit of sneezing.

Her mother's head was narrow at the top and ended in a broad chin. Her bosom protruded like a balcony. On her swollen, sick feet, she wore a pair of misshapen shoes trimmed with rhinestone buckles. Her stockinged legs looked like two overstuffed sausages. She apparently suffered from asthma because, as she accepted congratulations from well-wishers and thanked them, she would gulp pills and wheeze. Sigmund Seltzer, wearing a set of tails with a white boutonniere in his lapel, shouted in her ear as if she were deaf: "Mama, this is my Yiddish translator!"

It was a hot day, but Sigmund Seltzer insisted that I eat everything served at the banquet after the marriage ceremony: the chopped liver, the soup with dumplings, the roast beef with stuffed derma, and, for dessert, the egg cookies and honeycake his mother-in-law had baked herself.

Sylvia's brother, Sidney Breitman, informed me that he was in the real-estate business. At dinner he regaled us with tales of the 1929 Wall Street crash. He described the suicides and how cheap it had been to buy houses and property if one had any cash at all. He advised Sigmund not to save the money he would make in Hollywood with the sale of his book but to invest it in the construction business. He said, "Build a bungalow somewhere. The rest will take care of itself."

"My talent is in writing books," Sigmund Seltzer answered. "You can't do that in your spare time."

I was too embarrassed to tell the groom that his last check had bounced. In fact, I had even bought him a gift. He told me he and Sylvia were going away on their honeymoon. He mentioned a town and a hotel in the Catskill Mountains and said he would call me as soon as he returned to New York.

Two months passed, and I heard nothing from him. Then one day someone knocked at the door of my furnished room. Even before I had a chance to answer, Sigmund Seltzer entered, unshaven, wearing a soiled suit and a crumpled shirt, and holding in his mouth a cigar stub that was so short it was hard to see how he didn't burn his lips. The scar on his forehead looked more prominent than usual. Without rising to greet him, I asked, "What's happened to you?"

With his right hand, he brushed off his left sleeve. "It's all over."

"It didn't work out?"

"A bloodsucker."

"What did she want?"

"What do they all want? Your money."

He sat down heavily in an armchair from which the stuffing and springs protruded and said, "I came to her with an open heart, but all she cared about was my money. When we arrived at our hotel in the Catskills, I wanted to do right by her, but she sat on a chair, her legs crossed, smoking one cigarette after the other, and just wanted to stick her nose into my business. She insisted that I put all my money in her name. A bankbook is a person's best friend, she said. I met a cousin of hers in the casino the next day, and he told me the whole story. She'd already had three husbands and ruined them all. Lovers, too —a butcher and a sewing-machine salesman. She sold her body, that's all. The mother was no better. The brother was a fake. That's the long and short of it. I told her: Look, sister, this time you've got the wrong party. If you don't like it, you know what you can do."

"You're getting a divorce?"

"If she wants a divorce, let *her* get it. You have to go to Reno for a divorce here."

Not long after his marriage failed, the film deal fell through, too. The contract had been drawn up and was ready to be signed. Without warning, the producers backed out.

After Sigmund's first check had bounced, I stopped "translating" his book, and I was relieved that the agreement between us was over. But Sigmund Seltzer hadn't given up. He found a job as an insurance agent and started paying me in five- and ten-dollar bills, or whatever he could scrape together. No matter how many times I moved from one furnished room to another, he ferreted me out. Each time I would ask him how things were, and he would tell me everything. He had gone into partnership with a peddler who had a route in Staten Island. He had become part owner of a factory that manufactured women's hair nets. I don't know how, but he managed to strike up friendships with rabbis, writers, and Yiddish actors. Every time he visited me, he offered me tickets to some affair to which I didn't want to go. His clothes became more and more bedraggled, but, nevertheless, he still wore a broad-brimmed hat and fancy ties. From his overstuffed briefcase he would bring forth catalogues, photographs of famous people, letters of recommendation to publishers, rejection slips from editors. Several times he showed me pictures of women.

He would sit in my only chair—the kind always to be found in furnished rooms—smoking a cigar and listening to the new chapters I had written. I had long ago thrown away the German "original" and had half forgotten the episodes of previous chapters I had written and had given to Seltzer. All I had now was a list of names of imaginary relatives and friends from his past, which I had jotted down in a notebook.

I hoped that even Sigmund Seltzer would see how contrived and disjointed the plot was and would leave me in peace. But he found no fault with my writing. He listened eagerly to all my stories about him—his heroic deeds, his romantic adventures. He nodded his head in agreement to the many ideas I attributed to him, to the words I put in his mouth. In one episode I described him as a revolutionary leader in Kharkov; in another, as a pacifist who would rather die than fight at the front; then, in turn, as a Palestine pioneer building the Jewish homeland, and as a fighter in the defense against the Ukrainian pogroms. I had already written over two hundred pages for him, but still had received only part of the amount he had promised me. The whole affair had become a nuisance to me, but somehow my efforts to make an end to it were half-hearted. I felt I could not let this pathetic creature down. Each time he saw me he would heft the manuscript in his hand and say, "Wait, you'll see, the two of us will make a lot of money. Sigmund Seltzer isn't dead yet!"

At about this time I got a job with a newspaper and could do without the few dollars Sigmund Seltzer contributed in curled-up bills and sometimes even change. The story of his life had become so intricate, so melodramatic and contradictory, that I began to feel that I was swindling him and betraying his confidence. Again and again I decided to end this nonsense, but Sigmund Seltzer kept after me. No matter where I hid from him, he found me. Sometimes months would pass, and I would think he had disappeared for good. Then suddenly I would receive a telephone call or a telegram from him.

Years passed. I had published a few books and made somewhat of a name for myself. Nevertheless, Sigmund Seltzer still introduced me as his translator.

Sylvia had divorced Seltzer, and he had married again. He invited me to his new apartment one evening and introduced me to his wife. She looked astoundingly like the first one: the same crooked nose, the same oily smile, the same yellow eyes. She even dyed her hair the same carrot color. Other than that, she was a bit shorter and had broader hips and heavier legs. She owned a ladies'-wear shop and had raised a son from a former marriage. The second Mrs. Seltzer clasped my hand in hers and cried, "Any friend of Sigmund's is a friend of mine!"

And she made me swear a holy vow that I would come again some Friday evening for gefüllte fish and soup with dumplings, the likes of which were not to be found anywhere else in the United States.

After many excuses and broken dates, I finally did visit them one Friday evening. She kissed me and called me by my first name. She had also invited a calendar publisher, a Yiddish actor who was looking for a play, a cantor who was also a songwriter, and an owner of a kosher delicatessen store, in addition to a full household of uncles, aunts, and cousins, including a relative who was a doctor at Montefiore Hospital. They all requested that I read an excerpt from Sigmund Seltzer's manuscript, which he had had bound in leather. On the cover, engraved in gold letters, was the title, *My Adventures as an*

Idealist. Below were the words, "The Autobiography of My Own Life by Sigmund Seltzer," and, underneath, the translator's by-line.

The group crowded around me as I looked for an appropriate passage. After I finished the reading, there was applause. Sigmund Seltzer embraced me and kissed me on both cheeks in the French manner. The aunts pressed me to their bosoms. One laughed enthusiastically, a second wiped away tears. The cantor put on a skullcap, which sat like a pot lid on his thick head of hair, and sang Rosh Hashana prayers, and arias from operas. Sigmund accompanied him on the mandolin.

As I stood on the lonely subway platform at a quarter to two in the morning, half frozen, with a heavy stomach and an ache in my temples, I vowed that the very next day I would send Sigmund Seltzer a check for the money I had received from him and a letter telling him to stop plaguing me with our ridiculous opus. But somehow, as always, I didn't quite have the courage to shatter Sigmund Seltzer's grand illusion. I found myself again at work on the unbelievable manuscript.

When I reached page five hundred, I notified Sigmund Seltzer that his autobiography was completed. He still owed me money but explained that he was a little hard pressed at the present. I assured him that as long as he had no publisher I could wait.

I thought that everything between us was finished at last. However, his family and friends—rabbis, cantors, and insurance agents—arranged a banquet in his honor, and I was requested to say a few words. Sigmund Seltzer also asked me for a letter of introduction to a book publisher.

One day he informed me that he had found a publisher. The editor had corrected the manuscript and had arranged for it to be retyped. When I looked through it, I was stunned. Sigmund Seltzer had fallen into Communist hands. But the editor, after having filled the book with Communist propaganda, for some reason changed his mind in the end about publishing it.

More years passed, but Sigmund Seltzer neither succeeded in getting the book published nor would he give it up. I don't know to this day why the Communists lost interest in it.

Perhaps some higher-up in the Party found traces of Trotsky-ism in it, or some other deviation. It was the time of the purges and what was kosher one day became counterrevolutionary the next day.

I had spent two years abroad, but no sooner had I returned home than I received a telephone call from Sigmund Seltzer. He had found an editor who had deleted the Communist propaganda and translated the book from Yiddish into En-glish. He asked me to add an epilogue in which I was to de-scribe the founding of the Jewish state and the war with the Arabs, as well as the effect on the world of Franklin Delano Roosevelt's death. Sigmund Seltzer had sent copies of the manuscript to Mrs. Roosevelt, Governor Lehman of New York, Eddie Cantor, and many other personalities and had re-ceived thank-you notes from them, which to him was a sign of high recognition.

I raised my voice at him and swore that I wouldn't so much as touch the book, but he won me over again. We were sitting in a restaurant. He tugged at my sleeve, offered me the salt shaker, pushed the sugar bowl and ashtray toward me. He summoned the waiter to refill my glass of water and reminded me of the time when I didn't have a cent and his hundred dol-lars had kept me from starvation. He told me how proud his relatives were of me and how they read everything I wrote. His wife, Florence, had had a photograph of me standing with her husband enlarged. The picture hung in their bedroom. She had pasted other snapshots of me, as well as clippings, into a scrapbook. He had brought me a cigar holder as a gift.

I noticed that he was graying at the temples. He bemoaned the fact that his partner had swindled him, and complained of a kidney ailment. He mopped the perspiration from his brow with a soiled handkerchief and insisted, "What else do I have but this book? As long as I have any life in me, I'll work to see it in print."

I put aside my own work and began writing about the founding of the Israeli state, the war with the Arabs, Roose-velt's death, and even the Korean war. Sigmund Seltzer again found a publisher—one of those vanity presses that publish for a fee—to bring out the book in English. The editorial changes had been so extensive that I hardly recognized my own creation. Many pages were altogether new. Even the names of the protagonists had been changed.

The manuscript had been collecting dust in my place for some time, when one day I received a call from Sigmund Seltzer. "Is everything written up?" he wanted to know.

"More or less."

"Put in something about how women can't be trusted."

"The whole book is full of it."

"Put down that women are egotistical. A woman doesn't give a damn what happens to her husband. He works his head off for her, but as soon as he leaves the house, in comes a parasite——"

"What is this all about?"

"I'm not making it up, I assure you."

"Are you having trouble with your wife?"

Sigmund Seltzer started to cough, and his voice became hoarse and choked. "How did you know? Are people talking about it already?"

"No, I just asked."

"Let's have lunch. I have to talk to you."

We ate blintzes at a vegetarian restaurant downtown. Sigmund Seltzer swore me to secrecy. He was so disturbed that he kept sprinkling sugar on his blintzes. A coughing fit, so severe that he could barely catch his breath brought tears to his eyes. He wiped them away with his napkin. Perspiration ran down his forehead and chin and into his plate.

Yes, he, Sigmund Seltzer, had been deceived. This wolf in sheep's clothing had been coming to his home for three years —eating, drinking, pretending to be a friend—but behind his back ridiculing him, turning Florence against him. This imposter had left a wife and five children in Havana and was living here in New York with a Puerto Rican woman. He had borrowed fifty dollars from Florence and hadn't repaid so much as a penny of it. How much money the man had actually wheedled out of her, Seltzer would never know. He had discovered the truth when his so-called friend had returned to Cuba, and Florence had had a nervous breakdown. The doctors had cost him eight hundred dollars. She had had to go to a psychoanalyst, but that charlatan had not helped her. It was all wasted money.

Sigmund Seltzer began to cry. The diners at the other booths all stared at us. The waiter removed Seltzer's plate with the half-eaten blintzes.

Seltzer went to the washroom, where he remained for a long time. I stared angrily at the female patrons, having become infected with Seltzer's bitterness toward women. When he finally returned, his eyes shone with a childlike freshness. He had used the time in the washroom not only to wash his face and comb his hair, but to come to grips with himself. Apparently he had come to the conclusion that all was for the best. "Put that all down. Let the world know," he said.

"You can't put everything in one book!"

"Let it be a few pages longer. I'll pay."

It was becoming clear that the book would never be finished. Despite my reluctance to continue with it, I added a chapter about feminine treachery going back to Eve and the Garden of Eden. When I read it to Seltzer he said, "Just as if you had been in my shoes."

With the exception of the Rosh Hashana cards which he always sent, I didn't hear from Seltzer again for years. The cards were signed Florence and Sigmund Seltzer, so I knew that the couple had made up. Then one day a woman telephoned. The voice sounded vaguely familiar. She said, "This is Florence speaking."

For a moment, I didn't remember who Florence was. The woman seemed surprised. "Have you forgotten me? I'm Mrs. Seltzer."

"Oh, yes, Mrs. Seltzer."

"Sigmund is ill. He's been in the hospital three weeks. He asked me to get in touch with you."

"What's the matter with him?"

She told me that one of his kidneys had been removed, and bladder complications had developed. His heart was weakened. She was worried. "Sigmund is very sick."

I took a cab to the hospital. He was lying in a large ward in which the beds were separated from each other by linen partitions. I went up to his bed. One look at his swollen face, and I knew that he was dying. His gown was spotted with blood; from the bed hung a rubber tube leading to a urinal. For a few seconds I could hardly recognize him, but soon his face took on a familiar expression. He said to me, "Well, it will be easier to die."

"Don't talk such nonsense. You'll get well."

"What? No, my friend. I wanted you to come. First, because I wanted to say good-bye to you. After all, we've been friends all these years. You know my life backwards and forwards. You know what I've been through. Second, I want to ask you to help get my book published after my death. That's all I ask. It's all I hold dear. As for the rest of it—well, I'd better not talk."

"Where is the manuscript?"

"Right here. I didn't want to go to the hospital without my book. Florence would probably have thrown it into the garbage. I want you to promise and shake hands on it that this book will be published. I've written a will and made you— what do you call it?—yes, the executor. I want the world to know the truth."

The manuscript was lying on the night table. It had a new binding and was twice as thick now because Sigmund Seltzer had had the English translation bound in with the Yiddish original. I glanced through it. Some sentences were still familiar. I read the part where Sigmund Seltzer escaped from prison with the help of the jailkeeper's daughter. Sigmund stretched out his hand. "Give me your promise. Shake hands!"

I clasped his hand. It was cool and moist. "Do you swear?"

"Yes, I swear."

"Take the manuscript with you now. Someone's already trying to take it away."

Our eyes met in silence. His hair had become white and sparse, his forehead higher. An expression of gentleness and wisdom I had never seen before shone in his eyes. He half winked, half smiled, as if to say, I know everything that you know, and a little more in addition. He was no longer the Sigmund Seltzer I had known all these years, but a sage purified by suffering. He stared at me with a look of fatherly affection and murmured, "In the end what remains after us writers? Nothing but a bundle of paper."

Translated by Aliza Shevrin and Elizabeth Shub

The Saturday Evening Post, November 18, 1967

Exes

IN THE NEAR nineteen years they had been divorced, David Peltis often toyed with the possibility of meeting Franka somewhere, but it had not happened. The chances of its happening were slim. She had married some actor from Germany, a refugee from Hitler, who was trying to get work in Hollywood. But as far as Dr. Peltis knew, he had had no success. They lived in Los Angeles. David Peltis had remained stuck away all these years in a small college in Pennsylvania, where he taught Russian, Russian literature, and a course in Hebrew. The student, Terry, because of whom he had divorced Franka, had borne him four children—all girls. One disappointment followed another. Both of Terry's parents died within a short time. A job David Peltis was sure to get was given to someone else. Terry had grown melancholic, fat and frigid. She avoided the other professors' wives, didn't attend their parties, because she had become pathologically lazy and apathetic, and David Peltis had to go shopping at the supermarket and even cook meals. Terry became indifferent to her children.

David Peltis had failed. His book on the Russian writers Sologub and Pilniak, which a university press had published, had sold twenty copies. At the age of fifty-seven, Professor Peltis's one remaining hope was to retire at sixty-five and try to do some work on his own. But what? And for what? Thank God he had a house whose mortgage was just about paid off, and tenure. The oldest daughter, Rebecca, who had been born four months after her parents' wedding, lived with a student, a giant with a red beard and hair hanging to the shoulders. He maintained that he didn't believe in the institution of marriage. Summer and winter he went around barefoot and each morning stood ten minutes on his head. Rebecca's younger sister, Debbie (named after her grandmother Deborah Leah) was already on the pill.

Well, but that spring David Peltis's fortunes brightened somewhat. He had proposed to a publishing house in New York to compile an anthology of writers who had committed suicide and the publishers had seized upon the idea and given him a $4,000 advance. Dr. Peltis had assembled a long list. He wanted, if it was possible, to find poems or essays dealing with suicide written by these writers. Normally, Dr. Peltis taught a summer course of Russian literature at the college, but this year he elected instead to take a trip abroad. It was out of the question to consider taking Terry along. He visited France, England, Italy, and spent a week in Israel. His ticket restricted his travel abroad to forty-five days. He had come to Haifa a day before leaving to visit the Technion Institute. Since he intended to spend just one night in town, he splurged with a room in a hotel on Mt. Carmel.

Around nine the next morning as he sat in the dining room waiting for the waitress to serve him coffee—one took the food oneself from a long table arranged cafeteria style—he saw Franka. He tensed and the bite of food remained stuck in his mouth. Yes, this was Franka—the same short-trimmed red hair that she now obviously dyed, the pointy face sprinkled with freckles, the short nose, the sharp chin, the green eyes. From between her lips dangled the usual cigarette. She wore a white dress to the knees (pointed knees, not round like Terry's) and a bag dangled jauntily from the left shoulder. Only her neck had grown a touch flabby. She was standing by the entrance apparently waiting to be seated. Soon the headwaiter came up and escorted her to a table just a few steps from Peltis's. She glanced at him quickly, the kind of look one gives a stranger, then sat down in such a way that he could see her in profile. Dr. Peltis gaped at her and his breath caught.

Usually he bathed and shaved each morning, but today he had felt lazy and decided to wait until he was in Tel Aviv. He was ashamed now to let himself be seen in the shabby shirt and unpressed trousers he had thrown on in a hurry. He wanted to glance at himself in a mirror, but there was no mirror handy. After a while, Franka—if it was really she—stood up and took her plate to the buffet table. At that moment, Peltis remembered that a mirror hung in the entrance foyer. He stood up and headed there walking in sidelong, zig-zag fashion and taking care not to bump against a chair, an edge of a table, or—worst of all—a waiter. "I hope I don't get a heart attack." He spoke to a God whose existence he denied. He came out into the foyer but the mirror had vanished. Had it been taken down? But there was no trace here of a former mirror. Maybe he should run up to his room and make a quick change? Grab a fast shave? He had heard of men who had shaved in a minute and a few seconds on a bet. Putting on a fresh shirt and tie should take no more than two or three minutes. But where was the key to his room? He recalled that this morning he hadn't left the key at the front desk but had stuck it away in a trouser pocket. Yet he couldn't find it there. The end will be that I'll lose it altogether, he thought, astounded that he should be so anxious to meet his ex-wife after so many years of separation and after she had so quickly replaced him with some washed-up actor.

David Peltis tapped his left side and felt the key in his shirt pocket. The elevator door opened and David Peltis's feet raced toward it of their own volition. She would remain in the dining room at least twenty minutes, maybe longer. The doors of the elevator had already begun to close but he forced them open again. Some mischievous boy had apparently pressed all the buttons, for the elevator stopped at every floor. Such children should be punished, Peltis decided.

He got out on the eighth floor and the door to his room stood ajar. Inside, a swarthy Sephardic chambermaid had stripped the sheet from the mattress. Although he had taught Hebrew for years, in his excitement he began addressing the woman in English. At the same time he drew a lira from his pocket and handed it to her. The maid said "Todah Rabbah" (Many thanks) and promptly withdrew.

Peltis looked at himself for a moment in the mirror with the kind of objectivity one assumes when preparing to be interviewed for a job. His passport stated that he was five foot seven-and-a-half inches tall, but he had either shrunk with age, or this half inch had been a lie from the first. Most of his blond hair had fallen out and the ruff of hair around the bald skull was mixed with gray threads. He had a high forehead, sunken cheeks, a narrow nose, thin lips. A sallow cast tinged his face; only the eyes had retained their vivid blueness. In the bathroom he began to shave quickly. "A cut is all I need now!" he thought.

He flung off his shirt and pants and put on a fresh shirt and a pair of pants he had had cleaned and pressed in America and which he had put away for a special occasion. Every few seconds he glanced at his wristwatch. He had taken a tie out of his suitcase but he put it back. Let her not get the idea that he had run to change for her. He looked at himself in the mirror above the commode one last time. Thank God, there wasn't even a trace of a double chin. He looked no older than fifty—maybe even younger.

"I'm deceiving myself, deceiving myself," he mumbled. He raced from the room and back toward the elevator. He had been gone thirteen minutes. It was impossible that Franka could be through with her breakfast.

As he went into the dining room he saw her crack the shell of an egg with a knife. He came up slowly to the opposite side from where she was seated, bent toward her and in a playful manner asked: "How does the Jewish state treat you?"

He said it in Yiddish since they both came from Poland. They had often spoken Yiddish to each other during the years they had been together. Her father had been a Hebrew teacher. Franka had become a leftist in America, had even planned to settle in Russia, which had been the reason she had taken Peltis's course in Russian. At that time he had been only an instructor.

Franka didn't leap to her feet, cry out. She merely raised her head slowly and the yellow-green eyes gazed up at him without a sign of recognition or surprise. She put down the knife deliberately.

"So you don't recognize me, eh?" he asked.

"Yes, I recognize you."

Her voice had grown older—it had become the voice of a woman who no longer allows herself to be surprised.

2

David Peltis had moved over to Franka's table and a waiter brought him eggs and coffee. He didn't go to the buffet table for the other items served there—tomatoes, herring, green peppers, cheese. Franka had put several slices of Swiss cheese from her portion on his plate.

He heard her say: "We're on a tour. Our plane flies back to

America at seven in the morning day after tomorrow. We can't stay abroad more than twenty-one days."

"What kind of group is it?"

"Oh, they belong to some club or synagogue. I have no ties with them whatsoever but the travel agent got us together. Mostly old women. Several old men too."

"Is this your first time in the Jewish state?"

"Yes. With you I didn't travel. Hans is afraid to leave Los Angeles. He sits all day waiting for the phone to ring. Weeks, actually months go by and they don't call him. How he stands it I can't imagine."

"I haven't seen him in a single film."

"Oh, he gets a small role from time to time but often it's cut out later. Once he got a part in which he had to say just one word in German: '*Donnerwetter.*' Your coffee is getting cold."

David Peltis took a sip of coffee and Franka took a cigarette and lighter out of her bag. She did everything quickly and with a kind of resolution he had forgotten. She blew out the smoke.

"You're still at the same college?"

"Yes, still the same."

"Someone told me you have five daughters."

"Four."

"When we were together you trembled lest, God forbid, I bear you a daughter. That is actually the reason we had no children. I remember you saying, 'I want to sleep with others' daughters, I don't want others to sleep with my daughters.'"

"Did I say that? They're already sleeping with my daughters. At least with the two older ones."

He spoke with a tremor in his voice. He looked at her and each time was reminded of features that had slipped his memory. New lines had emerged or the old had become accentuated. It seemed to him that her cheekbones had risen, that her mouth had grown somehow crooked and that it now bore the kind of irony that comes from total disappointment and maybe too from having to do with many men.

Franka urged him several times to eat, but he had lost his appetite.

He breathed in the aroma of her cigarette smoke and said, "So you still smoke."

"More than ever."

"The more I look at you the more I see how little you've changed."

"You've forgotten. You know that I'm fifty-two years old."

"Really, you look ten years younger."

"How can I look so young? The years I spent with you were one long crisis. Continuous war. We were even about to form a suicide pact. Really, I've forgotten what caused all those storms. This is a kind of amnesia within me. I remember thousands of trifles but not the essentials. What were we fighting about?" Franka leaned her cigarette in the ashtray.

"I don't know myself. We were both crazy jealous," Peltis said.

"Eh? One is jealous when one doubts. When you know for sure that the other is betraying you, it's no longer jealousy."

"Then what is it? The word *jealousy* doesn't necessarily include doubt," Peltis heard himself intone in a professional manner.

"All I know is that we could have been happy. But when you launched the affair with your present wife we were already as good as separated. I'd like to ask if you're happy with her, but this is too banal a word even for someone like me. I'd rather say content."

"Content is banal too."

"What is not banal?"

"Actually, there are no words to adequately describe emotions," Peltis said and again it struck him funny that he was assuming such a pedantic tone.

"Perhaps the emotions themselves are banal."

"Yes, true. Spinoza maintains that all emotions are evil. What are you doing—arousing the professor in me?"

"You forget that I was your student."

"I haven't forgotten."

"How are things going with you?"

"Oh, everything with me is topsy-turvy," he replied, knowing all the while that he mustn't complain to her. He took the cold coffee and swallowed it in one gulp. He could no longer undo his mistake and he added: "If this gives you any satisfaction, I go on living only because I lack the courage to put an end to things. That's the bitter truth."

"What are you doing here?"

He began to tell her about his plan for the new book. She heard him out and from time to time took a drag on her cigarette. He was doing a thing he had always despised in other husbands—degrading his wife. He said that Terry had given up interest in spiritual matters, wouldn't read a book and had lost all urge for sex. She went around barefoot and half-naked. She gorged herself and had breasts that had swollen to the size of a wetnurse's. He added that shortly after they had married, he had entered into affairs with other women—students and wives of professors. He confessed and boasted at the same time.

Franka listened in silence. From time to time her lips twisted. She'll think me a rascal and a fool, he thought, and she'll be right. He heard himself say:

"This business of teaching students year-in, year-out, gets worse and worse. All I look forward to is the day I retire. At times I feel that I'll be forced to resign before my time. I keep away from the faculty. When people are compelled to be together for years, they become enemies. If not for the intrigues, we'd die of boredom altogether. You remember the college. Nothing has changed except that many of the old professors have died off. One time, two students committed suicide within a single week. We only have some two thousand students. The young men have huge mops of hair and wild beards. They go around in patched pants and look like bums. We have a large percentage of homosexuals and lesbians too. Maybe it only seems so to me, but never has it rained so much there as in the past two years. Summers—I teach a summer course—you get eaten alive by the mosquitoes. The winters are harsh. I've spent the whole time talking about myself. What about you?"

Franka made a gesture as if she had swallowed something.

"I've told you. Things haven't been going any better for me. Maybe worse."

"You no longer love him?"

"I'm afraid I never did."

"So what was the sense of it?"

"No sense at all. After you and I separated I tried living by myself, but I could not be alone. You can have ten lovers, but when you come home evenings there is no one there. He was living in Hollywood and I wanted to get somewhere far away. He tried to convince me that he'd make an actress out of me. Funny, eh? One good thing about him—he's always home. You burned with jealousy and accused me of all kinds of betrayals, but he doesn't know what jealousy is. I could come home three in the morning and he wouldn't even ask where I had been or with whom."

"You no longer live together?"

"He doesn't need a woman."

"Maybe he needs a man?"

"Not even that."

"A lucky guy."

"He is unhappy all the same."

"You didn't work all those years?"

"I always worked. I was actually the breadwinner."

"What did you do?"

"Oh, lots of things. I had a beauty parlor for a few years. I've got a job now too."

He wanted to ask her what kind of job, but he had already asked her too many questions. Racing to see her after changing his clothes, he had been afraid that she would insult him, be sarcastic. But she spoke with sincerity and a kind of guarded trust. The changes that he had seen in her in those first few minutes began to evaporate as if some unseen hand would have retouched the defects time had wrought. From moment to moment she grew more like the old Franka he remembered.

She said, "You didn't even ask me what I do. I have such a strange job that I'm ashamed to tell you about it."

"Are you connected with the police?" he asked, baffled by his own words. He hadn't the slightest reason for arriving at such an idea.

Franka stared at him in disbelief.

"I guessed right, eh?" he said.

"No. But why did *that* occur to you?"

"I don't know why myself."

"Oh, that's weird! No, not with the police, but with a funeral parlor."

"What do you do there?"

"I beautify the corpses. Especially the women."

3

Franka ate, sipped coffee, and from time to time took a draw on a cigarette. She said, "After I gave up my beauty parlor, I worked for someone else, but the women made me crazy with their babble. The younger ones told me all about their affairs and the older kept babbling about their sons, daughters, and grandchildren. I'd come home with my head buzzing. When I was offered my present job, I grabbed it. The dead have one great quality—they're silent."

"If I were to do something like this, I'd die ten times a day," he said, realizing how tactless he was in saying it.

"Oh, you get used to it. The dead possess a nobility that elevates you. At times when I comb a dead woman's hair, I feel as if I were combing God."

"What a strange comparison!"

"I'm not the Franka you used to know. At times I hardly recognize myself. In the East, I still retained some feeling of home. But in California no one feels at home. I used to love to walk. Remember, how we walked for miles? No one walks in Los Angeles. Either you sit home or you go racing over the freeways where you risk your life at every turn. Hans used to like to converse, but what he had to say was such nonsense and he told such lies that I didn't want to listen. Lately, he's clammed up completely. He responds to everything in a grunt."

"What actually is he?"

"Oh, I don't know. I've lived with him so many years and he's remained a total stranger. He's sick, emotionally sick. He had enormous success in Berlin. He's played leading roles under Reinhardt. For a short time only. Here, he is less than nothing and he can't forget his former glory."

"You had affairs, eh?"

Franka tensed, but she didn't answer. She began to toy with a roll. Peltis was sure she wouldn't answer him, but all of a sudden she said, "Affairs, not loves. Once I believed in love but I've suffered too many disappointments. It's not your fault alone. Even before you came into my life, things occurred that shattered my faith. It all bears on the fact that we've stopped believing in God. Why be true to someone? Why not taste everything? I saw myself in you like in a mirror, which is why everything between us turned into suspicion and hate. But to believe in a God who sits in seventh heaven and allows so much suffering and evil is something I can't do either."

"Have you found an alternative?"

"There is none. The women that I comb and make up have found a way out. It happens that I work on suicides. It's not easy, since they're often crushed and torn. Some of them have been young, pretty, rich."

David Peltis wanted to ask something further, but he was fearful that this time Franka would lose her patience. To gain time he pulled the saltcellar toward him, then pushed it away again. He tried to balance a teaspoon on the edge of his cup. He said, "Franka, the fact that we met here is nothing less than a miracle. I'm in no mood for telling lies or exaggerating, but a day hasn't gone by that I haven't thought of you. I would tell you that I never stopped loving you, but the word love is the most obscure word in the dictionary. It's as unclear as the word 'God.' All I can tell you is that I didn't forget you for a minute."

"Nor did I you."

"I want to ask you something and you can either answer me or not."

"What do you want to ask?"

"I want to know if you had someone during the time you were with me." He uttered the words in a muffled voice. He barely kept himself from trembling.

Franka's eyes reflected mockery. "Why do you want to know?"

"I don't know why. Call it curiosity or whatever you wish. It's an urge to know the truth. Sometimes it seems that this urge is the very essence of man."

Franka glanced at her pack of cigarettes.

"For the first few years I was completely faithful even though you played around with who knows how many creatures."

"Who came afterwards?" he asked and felt the pounding of his heart.

"Must you know this?"

"Yes, I must."

"Jacob Barletzsky."

"Barletzky? The hunchback?"

"Yes, he."

"Why of all people Barletzky? Well, what does it matter?"

"You ran around with others. You went off to New York and left me alone. He . . ."

Peltis began to question her almost like a prosecutor.

Franka said: "David, I don't want you to get upset. It is all past and gone. You know that Barletzky is dead."

"How long did it go on?"

"Till the next came along."

"Who was next?"

David Peltis spoke softly but his voice contained the element of a shout.

"A student."

"Who?"

"I doubt if you remember him. Leslie Micheles. He wasn't one of your students, but Barletzky's."

"A philosopher?"

"He liked to talk about Nietzsche."

"And to sleep with others' wives."

"They all want that."

David Peltis wanted to interrogate her further but he grew alarmed over the reaction her words evoked within him. His heart lurched once and he became silent. He felt his guts cramp and his stomach bloat. "It doesn't pay to die on account of such swinishness," a voice within him said. A bitter fluid filled his mouth and he spat it out into a handkerchief. He had to strain to say: "Well, that's how it is."

"Why are you so upset?" Franka asked. "You can and others can't?"

"Everyone can."

"Come, the room is empty. They probably want to clean up here."

"Wait a minute. I often regretted our parting but it seems I divorced a slut."

"And what are your others? Oh, David, you're naïve besides."

"Yes, I am."

"Come, let's go."

They headed toward the lobby. They came into the large hall to the right and he dropped into an easy chair. After some hesitation, Franka sat down alongside. A crumpled Hebrew newspaper lay on the coffee table before them and Peltis read a new item about the stock exchange in Israel. "Look what they've made of the holy tongue," he said to himself. "Maybe it isn't too late yet to become a real Jew instead of a caricature of a Jew?" went through his mind. He supplied the answer himself: "For that, you need faith." Suddenly, he was seized by an urge for Franka. In a split second his revulsion toward her had turned into passion. How is this possible? he asked himself. Unless lust and revulsion are one and the same. He studied her bosom, knees, neck, mouth. If one sinks in the slime anyway, then the deeper the better.

Franka asked: "What time is it?"

"Twenty to eleven."

"When do you have to leave for Tel Aviv?"

"I still have time."

"What are you going to do now?"

"Come up to my room."

She didn't answer. She opened her pocketbook and rummaged through her papers a moment.

"David, it won't do."

"What do you mean?"

"David, I don't want to start the whole madness all over again. We only have a few hours, at the most, till tomorrow morning."

"Till tomorrow morning you can get in a lot of nonsense."

Franka bowed her head in thought. Once more she opened her bag then closed it again. "For what? For what?" she asked him and herself. "Oh, David, what is man?"

"A pig that knows it's a pig."

"Yes, true."

"The truth is that I love you," he said, not certain if he were lying or if there was some substance in what he said.

"The truth is that I never stopped loving you," she replied. "As God is my witness."

"Don't drag God into such things."

"Why not? He created us the way we are."

"He also created Hitler," David Peltis said, frightened by his own words.

They rose with hesitation. He took her hand, which was warm and damp.

I won't be able to do anything anyway, he thought. I'm making a fool of myself all for nothing.

His urge for her had dissipated as quickly as it had come. He now saw age in her face—wrinkles around the eyes and in the forehead, everything half-covered with makeup. For a moment he had the illusion that she exuded the smell of corpse. The elevator door opened and he began to steer Franka toward it. He half-led, half-dragged her, "like a calf to slaughter," he thought.

They got into the elevator and he saw reproof in her eyes.

She said, "I'll just take a peek into your room."

"As you wish."

The elevator stopped at the eighth floor and when the door opened, the Sephardic maid stood there holding a broom and an empty pail. Although David Peltis had long since abandoned all superstitions, an empty vessel had remained a symbol of failure to him.

The maid asked, "Are you staying on? They told me you were checking out."

"The room is mine until three," he answered, and his own voice rang to him alien, as if he were hearing it from someone else.

The maid arched her brows. "Don't mess up the bed. It's no longer for your use."

Translated by Joseph Singer

Confrontation, Fall 1977

Between Shadows

A Street Scene in Old Warsaw

THE STREET was long and narrow with a few residential buildings and dominated by a huge factory, its walls brick red, its windows protected by iron grates. In the dim glow of the gas lamps inside, wheels were turning and broad leather straps rotating. The blackish windowpanes of houses that appeared to be abandoned ruins reflected the glimmer of a moon half hidden in fog. The light seemed to come both from inside and from outside. Shadows slithered over the crumbling walls like ghostly snakes.

Across the way one could see an ancient church with an ever-standing clock in its tower. On a pedestal at its locked gate a statue of the Holy Mary carried the Christ child in her arms.

Although the air was cold and damp, old women dropped to their knees and with bony fists beat their breasts in prayer. A coachman had apparently stopped off at a tavern in the neighborhood leaving an empty droshky at the curb. The scrawny mare had lowered her head and remained motionless. Her eyes—all pupil—seemed to ponder the autumn night. Something fearful and Godly looked out from them.

Near a bare tree supported by two poles loitered a young streetwalker; her cheeks heavily rouged, she wore a dingy fur coat and red high-heeled boots. Her flaxen blonde hair was combed in a bun.

Two Russian soldiers passed by and stopped; one tall, the other short, in military coats down to their ankles, their crooked swords dragging on the ground. The tall soldier appeared to haggle with her while the little one stood to the side listening like a youngster to an adult. Eventually, the tall one pulled his chum away by the elbow and they both shuffled off in their clumsy boots.

A worker came out from an alley with a bundle of firewood on his shoulders. He looked both at the prostitute and at the kneeling women, hesitated for a while and disappeared behind a corner. He might have been one of the wicked who are doomed to kindle their own fire in Gehenna.

A tall youth emerged, lanky and lean, with a childish face and wearing a cap that fell over his forehead—perhaps a high-school student who was trying to look older. Tied to a button on his coat was a small package, carefully wrapped with a red ribbon, the kind of gift a teenager would bring to his first date. He walked quickly and with determination, as if he had been late, his gaze fixed on one spot to the right. He must have imagined that he saw his girl approaching in the darkness and that he was drawing her nearer with his eyes like with two magnets. But what emerged was a short, pock-marked woman carrying a large basket with linen, the kind used by washer-women. There was a mixture of surprise and laughter on her face as if she felt that the youth mistook her for his girl. He recoiled like a fisherman who pulls a net from the water and instead of finding a fish discovers a turtle. Instantly, he turned his head away to the left. He paced from one end of the church to the other, measuring the area. Then he returned with small steps to where he was waiting before. He stopped by the droshky for a while, stroking the horse's ribs. She kicked at the gutter with one leg, which meant: "Let me think my own thoughts." He picked up a piece of discarded paper and threw it away, doodled something on his own fingernails with a pencil, grabbed a worn envelope from his bosom pocket, examined the address and shoved it back. He leaned against the fence of the church and stared upward with wide-open eyes and parted lips. He must have just realized that a sky stretched above him, scattered with clouds and stars—bright night suns that shimmer somewhere in a far off galaxy about which he had read in his science class. The moon, with the usual face of a skeleton and hollow eye sockets in its skull, had become encircled by a mother-of-pearl aura which exuded the colors of the rainbow. The longer the youth looked at it, the more he seemed to be dazzled by its celestial magic.

His girl had still not arrived and he shrugged his shoulders, ready to give up. He threw an angry glance at the prostitute as if she were to blame for his defeat. Her submissive eyes were saying, "We don't make you wait."

At this, the youth became wild with excitement. He took a

long, quick stride as if determined to run home once and for all. He tore a faded poster off the factory wall, glared at the strumpet, took up the little gift from his coat button, weighed it in his hand, as if intending to hand it over to her. He slinked sideways like a half-crazed cat sometimes does, took a few steps backwards and motioned to the whore with his finger. She had already begun to pull up the tops of the red boots over her bare knees, preparing to cross over to the frustrated youth, but just then he shuddered and drew back. His girl was standing right next to him, as if she had shot out of the ground where she might have been hiding in order to test his masculine patience. She wore a high-school uniform and a velvet beret over her cropped dark hair, and high-heeled button shoes and woolen stockings. She offered him her gloved hand, smiled and told him something in a gush of words, but the youth did not answer. He put his arm on her shoulder and turned his back on the harlot. Strange, but the mare lifted her head suddenly, as if overcome with human cruelty. The whore watched them with the pale face of an abandoned one. Her long pointed shadow spread itself before their feet. The youth grasped his girl by the arm and they rushed away, stepping over her shadow.

Translated by Deborah Menashe

Heshele and Hanele,
or the Power of a Dream

BY THE AGE of six Heshele had become known as a prodigy in Lublin and throughout the surrounding region. He played chess against the best players in Lublin and he often beat them. He could solve complex mathematical problems within minutes and in his mind. He could read and write Yiddish, Hebrew, Polish, German and French. His father, Meir Lipman, didn't send Heshele to *heder*—a rabbi and professors came to tutor him at home. Meir Lipman, the owner of a sugar factory, lived in a house with a walled garden. Heshele was an only child. His mother, Rose, the daughter of a wealthy family in Königsberg, played the piano and rode in a fancy carriage driven by a liveried coachman. She ordered her clothes from Paris.

Heshele had everything a child could want—good food, nice clothes. His father bought him all the books he asked for. Heshele was written up in newspapers in Lublin, Warsaw and even St. Petersburg. Scholars came from faraway cities to interview him and find out how he had acquired his talents but Heshele couldn't satisfy their curiosity—he had been born a prodigy.

The one thing Heshele lacked was companions. He couldn't be friends with children his age. They were afraid of his wise words and his extensive knowledge. Children like to play tag, hide-and-seek, and other such games, but Heshele (or so it was assumed) had no interest in such games. Besides no couples with young children lived in the area. The homes hereabouts were mostly inhabited by elderly squires and retired military men. There was also a church nearby and when Heshele looked out his window he often saw the nuns in their long black robes.

But even though Heshele had the mind of an adult he also had the needs of a child. He yearned for toys. He longed for someone with whom to babble childish nonsense and act silly. He liked to climb trees and turn somersaults. At times he spoke childish words to himself and told himself stories of an emperor, a princess, a cap which rendered the wearer invisible, and of an incantation that let one fly to far-off lands like a bird. Sometimes he bleated like a goat, whinnied like a horse, barked like a dog, or mimicked the clucking of hens and the chirping of crickets.

One afternoon when Heshele went out into the garden, he saw a little girl there, seemingly his own age. Heshele had black hair and dark eyes but the girl was golden-haired and blue-eyed. She wore a white pleated dress and white shoes. When Heshele saw her he grew astonished. How did she get into the garden? The garden gate was always kept locked.

He stood a moment gaping, then he asked:

"What's your name?"

The girl said: "Hanele."

"How did you get into the garden?" he asked and Hanele replied: "What's the difference? I came and I'm here."

"Where do you live? Somewhere nearby?"

"Not near and not far," the girl said.

She spoke in a childlike voice and smiled at him.

She was holding a ball and she asked: "Would you like to play ball?"

Heshele had never played any games. Somehow, he felt ashamed to play ball with a girl, but after a while he overcame his shame and said: "Yes."

They played and Hanele was apparently a skilled ballplayer. No matter how he threw the ball she always caught it. After a while she proposed that she run and that he try and catch her. Heshele was sure that he would. He knew that boys were faster than girls but Hanele was too quick for him and he couldn't catch her. When she played hide-and-seek with him, she always found him but he never found her. This amazed him to no end since there was no place to hide in the garden except behind a tree. After a while, Heshele heard Tzirel the maid's voice calling to him through the window that lunch was ready.

Heshele said to Hanele: "They're calling me in to eat."

"If they're calling you, go."

"What will you do?"

"I'll go home."

"Shall I walk you to the garden gate?"

"No, it's not necessary."

"When will you be here again?" he asked and Hanele replied: "Tomorrow at the same time."

And before he could manage to say anything else, she vanished.

"What an odd little girl!" Heshele thought. Heshele had gotten a watch from his father and when he glanced at it he was surprised to learn that he had spent three hours with Hanele.

"How could three hours go by so quickly?" he wondered.

It just so happened that neither his father nor his mother were at home. His father had gone to Cracow on business and his mother had gone to market. Tzirel had a visitor in the kitchen, another maid. She served Heshele his lunch and went right back to her guest. Soon afterwards, the professor who taught Heshele mathematics became tired and went to bed where he promptly fell into a deep sleep.

2

Heshele was used to outlandish dreams. Sometimes he even solved an algebraic or geometric problem in a dream. But tonight's dream was unlike all the others. Usually when he awoke in the mornings he immediately forgot the previous night's dream, but this time he recalled right down to the last amazing detail. He had dreamed that he was strolling in the garden. Suddenly, he saw Hanele who appeared as if out of nowhere.

She took his arm and said: "Come, let's go."

He wanted to lead her to the garden gate but she said: "It's not necessary."

She didn't walk but floated in the air and he floated beside her. They floated right through the garden wall as if it were air. They crossed meadows, fields, forests. The grasses and plants were of a rare green Heshele had never seen before. Just as rare was the blue of the sky. The birds trilled and frolicked. Hashele encountered creatures he had never known existed on earth. They talked a human language but were not parrots. They spoke words that filled his heart with rapture although he couldn't make out what they said. Suddenly, Heshele and Hanele came to a place filled with children, boys and girls. They were neither dressed nor naked but at some stage in between. This was apparently a kind of playground. Some of the children rode seesaws; others played horse, tag, hide-and-seek, or danced in circles and sang. *Who were these children? And where were their parents and nannies?* Heshele wondered. But he didn't have much time to wonder for he and Hanele were soon drawn into the play. Now a carousel went round and round and soon he was astride a horse. Now a circus passed by with giants, midgets, dancing bears and girl tightrope walkers and aerialists; soon he came to a pond where he swam together with Hanele. And as he swam, he mused: "How can this be? No one ever taught me to swim. I was always afraid of the water. . . ."

He wanted to ask Hanele about this but she was swimming ahead of him and she gestured to him to follow. On the other side of the pond stood a high pole on which hung a plaque announcing that whoever climbed it would find a prize on top. Heshele promptly began to scamper up the pole and although it had been smoothly planed, he shinnied up it as nimbly as a monkey. He soon reached the top and there in an open box lay trumpets, fiddles and harmonicas.

"What good are they to me?" Heshele asked himself. "I never studied music."

Still, he picked up a fife, stuck it in his mouth and to his amazement he began to play a melody that enchanted him with its sweetness. At the same time he heard Hanele call to him from below:

"Take something for me."

"What do you want?" he asked and she replied: "Whatever you bring will be appreciated."

He began to slide down exceedingly fast and suddenly he awoke.

Outside it was still dark. The moon shone and stars winked in the sky. The clock showed a half hour past midnight.

Heshele lay awake a long time and a feeling of yearning came over him for the girl in the dream and for the one with whom he had played the day before—they were both the same girl. Heshele had gone through all of the Scriptures with his rabbi and he knew that all dreams were mere fabrications of the mind, nevertheless he was also aware that some dreams did hold deep significance—such as the dreams of Jacob who saw the ladder which the angels climbed up to and down from heaven; the dreams of his son, Joseph, who foresaw that he would become a viceroy in Egypt; the dreams of Laban and Pharoah, and the dreams mentioned in the Book of Daniel.

Heshele resolved that when Hanele came back tomorrow, he would tell her about his dream. He wanted to ask her a number of questions such as: Where did she live? What were her parents' names? Who had taught her to play ball so well? He also wanted to know how she could have entered his garden when the gate stood locked. This time Heshele decided to wait for her by the gate and to open it for her when she knocked.

After a while he dozed off again and when he awoke in the morning, everything had become so entwined in his mind that he no longer knew what was dream and what reality. One thing was certain—he missed Hanele, and he could hardly wait till the clock tolled the hour that he could go down to meet her. He had several lessons that morning and then he went out into the garden. He came to the gate and saw that it was locked. A heavy lock hung on the inside. He searched for some kind of opening through which Hanele could have crawled through yesterday, but the wall had no openings and it was too high for even a grown man to climb over. Heshele stood there perplexed. True, a bell hung outside but would Hanele, a stranger, have rung it? And did Tzirel the maid who yesterday at that time was inside the house open the gate for her? It was all a mystery. After a while, Heshele decided to ask Tzirel for the key to the garden gate.

Tzirel asked: "What do you need the key for? No one comes to see us through the garden."

"Then how did Hanele get into the garden?" Heshele asked.

"Who is this Hanele?" Tzirel countered.

"The girl I played with in the garden yesterday."

"What girl? I didn't see any girl. Besides, if someone should come to see you, they'd come in through the house, not the garden."

Heshele wanted to answer Tzirel but he had been left speechless. He heard Tzirel say:

"No girl came to see us yesterday. Did you dream it, or what?"

3

That day Hanele didn't appear. Many days passed and the girl didn't show up again. Yes, Tzirel had apparently been right—he had dreamed the whole thing, Heshele decided. A hammock was stretched between two trees in the garden and Heshele occasionally napped there. That is what apparently happened that day—he had mistaken a dream for reality. Still, he was left with a longing for a girl about whom he had apparently dreamed twice—once during the day and once at night. Heshele the prodigy already glanced into philosophy books and he was familiar with the views held by certain philosophers that all life was merely a dream. This more-or-less was the contention of the famous Bishop Berkeley. Other philosophers before him had expressed similar opinions. Often when Heshele strolled in the garden and heard a rustle, he turned around in the hope that through some miracle Hanele had returned. Strange, but Heshele had never forgotten the melody he had played in his dream on the fife he had found on top of the pole. He would often whistle this tune and this only intensified his longing.

Time did its own and Heshele grew up both spiritually and physically. It often happens that when prodigies grow older they lose their rare talents, but thank God this didn't happen with Heshele. His mind grew ever keener and his father sent him off to study in Germany and France and at twenty-one, Heshele—now Dr. Heshel Lipman—was appointed a full professor at the University of Berne in Switzerland. He was also well-versed in the Talmud and in many other Jewish books. His parents were anxious for Heshele to marry and each time he came home for the holidays—Passover or the Days of Awe —his parents chided him good-naturedly for not finding a wife. Marriage brokers proposed matches with the prettiest and richest girls in Poland. But each time Heshele found some pretext not to marry. He said that he was too busy with his studies and that he had neither the time nor the patience for love and marriage. But the fact was that Professor Lipman loved a girl he had dreamed of when he was eight. He told himself that such a love was senseless, but love is stronger than any logic. He still dreamed often about Hanele, and in his dreams she didn't remain the girl who had come to him when he was a boy but had grown along with him. Each time he dreamed of her she appeared more mature, prettier. She spoke to him in grown-up fashion about books, far-off cities, foreign lands. She was differently dressed and wore her hair a different way yet she had remained the same. Sometimes she flew with him in the dream to that playground that he had seen on the first night after her visit, and she played grown-up games with him and with the other young men and women—tennis, croquet, and occasionally chess or checkers. Each time Heshele awoke from one of these dreams he felt this hadn't been an ordinary dream but a fragment of reality, a vision of something that sooner or later he would encounter.

In the dreams, Hanele often spoke to him and kissed him. He forgot most of what she said to him but he remembered one message: "Wait for me! Wait!"

It happened on a summer evening. Dr. Heshel Lipman was on vacation from the university and had come to Lublin to visit his parents. After they had expressed their joy over his arrival they resumed their old complaint: why wasn't he married? Heshele gave them the usual excuses—he had no time, he was still too young, he hadn't yet met the right girl, he was too busy writing a new work. After lunch he went for a walk. He strolled to the outskirts of the city and saw that a circus had come to town. In a huge clearing a number of tents had been set up with one huge tent in the center to serve as the arena. Posters featured pictures of the performers; the circus animals such as lions, bears, elephants and various monkeys and apes; the fat lady weighing eight hundred pounds; a giant who was allegedly the tallest person in the world; and midgets who were supposedly the smallest humans alive. Huge crowds of children and adults had congregated from Lublin and the nearby towns and villages. Vendors sold snacks and drinks. The performance was scheduled to begin shortly and long rows of people were lined up in front of the ticket booths.

For some reason, this place reminded Heshele of the playground he had seen in his dream. He bought a ticket and went inside the tent where benches had been set up for the public. Since he earned a good salary and his parents were affluent, the young professor bought a ticket in the front row next to the arena. The music was already playing. The trapezes where the female aerialists would perform their stunts and the high wire on which a famous tightrope artist would turn a somersault hung high in the air. There were cages for the performing animals. The air smelled of the sweets consumed by the audience and of animal odors.

The performance began and Heshele forgot that he was an adult, a doctor, a scholar. He had become a child again. In all his years Heshele had never been to a circus. He seldom went to the theater. He had been raised with the notion that all these entertainments were nothing but a waste of time. He had always concentrated on scientific matters. Even this day he was preoccupied with a mathematical problem he had been wrestling with without success for months. Even while he had been sitting down to lunch with his parents and they had been questioning him why he hadn't married and why he rejected the wealthy matches offered him, his brain had been mulling over this problem.

But now he brushed aside all these mysteries and gave himself over completely to the enjoyment of the performance. The band played familiar tunes. Girl bareback riders balanced on horses which pranced to the rhythm of the music. Male and female aerialists swung on trapezes and switched places in the air. A clown with a face painted white and a red nose performed tricks and told jokes. Bears danced. Lions climbed on top of one another to form a kind of living pyramid. Monkeys swung onto high perches. A man swallowed fire and swords. After a while, the main attraction was announced—a girl who would turn a somersault on the high wire without the usual safety net below. Failure meant a possible loss of life.

A circus is customarily noisy, but a hush now descended over the crowd as everyone held his breath. Presently, the girl appeared. Heshel Lipman glanced up at her and grew as if congealed. He recognized her at once—it was the girl of his dreams. She half walked, half slid across the high wire and at the same time she hummed a tune. God in heaven, it was the same melody he had played that night when he had dreamed about her—a melody he had never been able to put out of his mind! He sat there dumbfounded. "Maybe I'm dreaming this now?" he wondered.

But some force which can differentiate between a dream and reality told him that this was no dream. A fear fell over him lest something befall her, and he prayed to God in her behalf. He was afraid of losing the chance to meet her in person. He watched her do the somersault and end up standing on the wire. How was this possible? Where had she learned the skills to do this? He had never before seen a girl so graceful, so full of courage. "She must be mine! She and no one else!" the love within him exclaimed.

After the performance he went looking for her but she wasn't easy to find and he grew despondent. "If I don't find her, my life will be worthless," he told himself.

He came to a tent and he saw her standing there looking as if she were expecting him. He came up to her but his spirit was so disturbed he couldn't utter a word. A change seemed to come over her too when she saw him. They stood there gawking at one another, then he gathered his courage and mumbled:

"Hanele!"

"Heshele," she mumbled in return.

It was all a big miracle, but a great love is often full of miracles. Love in itself is a miracle. He gestured to her and she followed him. The night was warm and there was a full moon. They walked through fields, lawns and meadows, and spoke in the confused, disjointed words of those consumed by love and longing. Gradually they learned that they had both shared the same dreams about each other.

Hanele had been orphaned at an early age and had become a servant at the house of some distant relative who had never allowed her to play. Hanele had had the identical dream as Heshele—that she met him in a garden, played ball with him, tag and hide-and-seek, and that she went with him to that playground where thousands of children cavorted. In her dreams she had seen him grow up too.

He asked her if she knew where that playground full of children was located and she replied: "It may be a playground of dreams. Maybe all those children who never get the chance to play while awake came there to play. . . ."

Walking along and holding hands, she told him how she had become a circus performer. She had fled from that distant relative's house. There in that dream playground she got the urge to become a tightrope walker. Many young men later fell in love with her and sought to marry her but she had retained her love for the boy of her dreams. Some force told her that one day she would meet him for real.

They stopped in a rut between the cornstalks and kissed. They both knew that they would soon marry. No force on earth could ever part them again.

He said to her: "You know? It says in the Talmud that forty days before a person is born his destined mate is announced in heaven. A matchmaker merely follows the dictates of an angel in heaven."

Hanele heard him out and replied: "Our matchmaker was a dream."

Pity

WOMEN! You boys talk as if you knew all about them. But you're really nothing more than a bunch of sitting ducks. Listen to me. At my age I know that it doesn't pay to act like a Casanova. No two frails are ever the same; you have to play them by ear. They're like the wind in the fields, sometimes blowing one way, sometimes another. And there's no such thing as an expert on women. As for us, we never know what we'll do when we get the urge. Ask me. I've had my fill of them, and I'm not just boasting or running off at the mouth like you. Here in Shedletz every crumb thinks he's a Cossack, every little punk is seven feet tall. What do you know about real women? All you talk about is whores; they're a dime a dozen on every street corner in Warsaw. I lived for ten years with a high-class dame from a good family. I didn't let on to her how I made a living. I told her I was a real estate agent. She came from Kalisch and we lived in a classy section of Warsaw—far from where my boys hung out. We really fell for each other, none of your piggish small-time affairs. One look at me and she was set to go like grease. Her father owned a leather goods shop, a Hasid he was. Her brother was a Yeshiva student. But she was up-to-date, a lady. She went to dances and the theatre—actors used to come to Kalisch once in a while. Anyway, one Saturday afternoon we meet in a tea house. The moment she sets eyes on me, she's all tingles. Stop smirking, it happened twenty years ago. In those days I was a real lady-killer and so strong I could gobble up a whole goose and wash it down with twenty glasses of beer. Fifteen eggs at breakfast was nothing for me! Even now I could take on any one of you and make you cry uncle. All the skirts on Krachmalna Street and Gnoyne Street were crazy about me. I got love letters from proper virgins in the best Hasidic families. Even in Gzbibov they knew my name. If I'm lying, let me rot in this hole! Goddam those Russians bastards for sticking me here in the first place!

Well, I came to Kalisch once on a job. It didn't come through, but never mind. I'm sitting that Saturday in the tea house with some of the lads, and in she walks. Blonde like a gentile, with blue eyes. I almost drop dead. She asks for tea and twitches her bottom around. She makes eyes at me and gives me the come-on. We have a little talk. Pretty soon I leave the whole bunch behind and take her for a walk on the main street. All of Kalisch is looking at us. It doesn't help my business any, but nothing matters anymore. We hit it off—one, two, three. I kiss her and she bites my tongue. Why beat around the bush? That night she was mine. But she was a proper girl, not one of your sluts: two months later we stood under the canopy. They told her father all kinds of stories and he wouldn't come to the wedding. So what? So we did without him. It helped him as much as propping up a dead horse. We rented a two-and-a-half on Broadmilla Street and lived in style. The boys didn't even know I was married. At night I walked home or took a bus—no trolley cars then. Still, Warsaw is not Shedletz: there was talk I was carrying on with some high-class swell. But they knew I don't like people to be too nosy. I was number one in the mob then; they came to me with all their problems. Blind Itche wasn't on top yet.

A year went by, but things didn't work out. Why didn't they? All kinds of reasons. She was forever nagging me about not being home during the day. Sometimes I couldn't even come home at night. Once I was caught on a job and had to spend a few weeks cooling my heels. When she found out what I was doing, she really began to raise the devil. It was beneath her dignity, what would her family say, the whole song. To tell you the truth, I got my bellyful of her. In the beginning she was always hotter than a stove, but later she turned to ice. She had one miscarriage, a second, a third. She saw all the doctors in town and couldn't stop groaning and complaining. I love children, I'll do anything for them; I'd never beat up a kid. If she wasn't good for children, what did I need the whole show for? I told my troubles to a pal and he says: kick her out, so what, so you made a mistake. But I took pity on her. Her parents had cut her off, she had no place to go. You boys know I'm not soft. I'm no killer, true, but when the chips are down I'll use a knife like any other mug. I don't faint when the borscht flies. But for her I had—what do they call it?—compassion. The long and short of it is, I suffered but kept quiet.

You bums are all skirt-chasers. Not me. I don't run after every hot bottom I see. I like one piece at a time, but she has to be a good one. If my Kalisch lady couldn't keep me happy, what was she worth? I can have as many as I want, but I'm choosey. A woman has to set me on fire. If not, she's not worth a flick of my thumb . . . Well, a few years passed. Sometimes I came home, sometimes I didn't. But every Friday she got her money. I had plenty of luck in those days, the cops left me in peace, the commissar was slipped his. The years dragged on. She got worse, not better. She was so beautiful your eyes popped, and was always rigged out fancy. When she put on her fur piece and muff and the hat with the ostrich feather, the whole street couldn't stop looking at her. What they must have thought! But I knew it was all for show: cold fire. And she kept on bellyaching and putting on airs. Everything she did for me was a favor. No one else would dare cross me with a word, but she called me a thief and a hood. Once in a while I lost my temper and let her have it. Yet, you won't believe it, no matter how mad I got I took care not to mark her up. She was always her papa's little girl. Her father didn't want to know her, but she couldn't stop boasting about how rich he was, how many famous rabbis he knew. She would sing his Sabbath table chants and cry like a baby. She was still true to me then—but what good was her faithfulness? She was always after me with her wagging tongue; it got me down, I tell you. And she made a fool of me in front of people. If anyone else had tried that, I would have taken him apart like a herring. A filly from Kalisch and she makes my life miserable! No matter how much cash I let her have, it wasn't enough. She ran from store to store like a society frill. My place was so crowded it looked like a fence's warehouse. She even bought a dog and a parrot. The dog slept in her bed at night. Every time I want to get in, he begins to growl. When he gets sick, she runs to the doctor with him. The parrot made so much noise it nearly drove me out of my mind. Her cooking was fit only for goats. What more can I say? I suffered and bore with it—all because I was an easy touch. Another guy would have thrown her out long ago.

They say we don't know what pity is. Some joke! When she was sick I took her right to Doctor Knaster. I got her a maid too. She always took in pock-marked girls, they were so ugly you couldn't swallow a piece of bread while in the same room with them. The moment I came in the house she turned on the waterworks. Boys, I gave her my last gulden and was left without a groshen. I never thought one of us could have such pity. Goddam her! Let her guts be burned out, if she's still around and carrying on! Listen to how that harpy did me in . . .

II

She always used to say that if they put me on the inside she'd show me what a good wife could be. What do we need behind bars? Someone to visit us once in a while and send a package. Well, after they grabbed me I didn't hear a word from her, she just disappeared. My boys did what they could, they didn't let me down. But from her, not a word. I needed her packages like a hole in the head, but I was ashamed in front of the others because I told them I was married. The screws used to needle me too. Then one of my pals was sprung and I sent a message. No answer. I began to think God knows what—after all, I'm only human. In a little while there was an amnesty for all of us and they let me out. The lads had a party in one of our hangouts, and I didn't get home till the middle of the night. Guess what? That's right. I found my little bird in bed with another guy. I would have killed him then and there, but he was out the window in a second. Beat it without a stitch on his back. We lived on the first floor and it was summer. I couldn't chase him, there would have been a scene, the neighbors would have raised a stink. So I close the window and tell her, if this is the way things are I'm going to finish you off right now. I take out my gun. She turns white as a Chalah, kisses my feet and begins to cry and whine: let me live, let me live, hit me but don't shoot. She grabs my knee and winds herself around me like a snake. I bust her, I kick her, I knock her about: she won't budge. Women are not as weak as we think. I slugged as much as I could, but she wouldn't let go. She made me swear by her dead mother that I wouldn't kill her. So how do you come to do a thing like this, I ask, is this the way they behave in Kalisch? Suddenly she's soft as cream. She was alone, he helped her, gave her money, she was sick, lonesome—you know the tune they sing at times like that. Another man in my place would have crippled her for sure. But believe it or not, I'm soft-hearted by nature. I can't stand to hear anyone cry. When I pass a funeral and hear a woman screaming, "So young, and you left me alone," my eyes water. So what could I do with her? I'm not a murderer and what's the use of breaking a rib or two—it would only cost me doctor's bills. I gave her a few more belts and let her go. Some bargain she got! . . . What? Did I sleep with her that night? That's none of your damn business. Keep your mouth shut or they'll carry you out of here in a box.

Boys, we made peace. Where could I send her? Her father had passed away, her mother already had another. Would you believe I could be taken for such a ride? After a while things were quiet again, but not what they used to be. I carried a grudge inside me—here! And just about that time I met Elka. She was one of our girls, but she had class. Cheeks as red as apples. I knew her from before, but suddenly we're like Romeo and Juliet. She told me she had been eyeing me for a long time and was afraid to start up. Anyhow, this is the real thing. What can I tell you? I've had plenty of women, there was no one like Elka in all of Warsaw. A sugar cube. When you kiss her, your head flies off. When she speaks, it drives right to your heart. The other one was blonde but Elka was dark, with eyes like burning coals and a figure like Queen Esther. And what a walk! As if she's on springs. Half of Krachmalna Street was after her but she told them all where to get off. She gave up her old work and opened a legitimate corset shop. She had girls working for her and the money went into her pocket. At night in the shop the machines and tables were covered with white sheets and it was like a holiday. She walked around in a silk blouse and a lace apron. Sometimes she'd cook me a meal that was fit for Rothschild. Another time, I'd come in with a few buddies, we'd bring some meat and seeded rolls and beer. I'm no drunk, though: at one o'clock I'd tip them the high sign and they'd take off. I was so happy I forgot I had a wife! She got her money and the hell with her! She complained all right: where do you spend your time, why do you leave me alone? I covered up the best I could but women have a nose for such goings on. She was jealous and said she'd throw acid in Elka's face. I don't scare so easy. Still, I tried to smooth it over. I gave her presents, a little thing here, a little thing there. I hate scandals, that's for the low-life, the little fish.

But you know how it is with love. If it doesn't get colder, it gets hotter. Elka can't live without me and when I go home for a night I can't sleep, I miss her so much. I also stopped doing any more jobs. When you have a woman like that, you don't like to risk your neck. I had no cash but Elka slipped me a few roubles from time to time. Go, she says, buy yourself a suit or a pair of shoes. I knew then what life with a woman could be! She hints around that we should make things permanent: how long can one be a thief? She has a shop, I can buy myself a moving van or open a tavern. But what could I do with my wife—pickle her in brine?

One night Elka tells me a secret: she doesn't have the curse any more, soon we'll have a mazel tov. I was so happy I almost went dippy. All my life I've been itching for a kid. We danced for joy. But Elka keeps telling me, you have to make an end of it with her, I don't want our son to be a bastard. What should I do with her, I ask? Give her a divorce, Elka says. On Stavka Street there was a rabbi who gave divorces without any sweat. If the woman didn't want it, you pin the paper on her shawl or slip it into her pocketbook and she's done for. We didn't have any official papers anyhow, so she couldn't sue me. But here, boys, I knew how deep I was in: somehow I still had pity on her. What would she do alone? She wasn't young and beautiful any more. And just at that time she became as soft as butter, no bellyaches, no backtalk. If I'm home, good. If not, she keeps her mouth shut. She washes my feet and gives me a glass of hot tea with milk, and everything so quietly and respectfully you think she was deaf and dumb. She takes my hand and begs me: Hershel, do whatever you want, but don't break up our home. You're everything to me, my father and mother. She cried so bitterly I nearly died. I swore I would stay with her, but my heart wasn't in it. Elka saw I kept putting things off and began to get desperate. Listen to me, she says, don't think that because you filled my belly you can treat me like a rag. I'll give you three days to decide between her and me. If you want your wife, I'm taking off for America. I've thought about it a long time. I have an aunt over there. Why should I hang around in Warsaw, where every no-good bastard thinks he can put his hands on me because of the old days. I can get a customer for the shop and the machines. So give me your answer one way or the other.

Boys, if I didn't go off my noodle in those days and get carted off to the nut house, I must be made of iron! I couldn't sleep at night, I rolled around in bed as if I had malaria. I could hardly swallow a bite of food. Let them carry me out of here on a board if I'm lying to you! I knew I was killing myself: there would never be another Elka. But I felt so much pity for the other one that . . . eh, why talk about it, what's the use? I'm no lush, but I went out and really got myself tanked. One night, two nights, a whole week. During the day I would sleep the time away at a Turkish bath. I thought I was finished, I nearly lost my mind. I tortured myself, like a man digging his own grave. I stopped going to Krachmalna Street. A few weeks passed. Elka looked everywhere for me, but I hid out like a rat. I know now that my little piece of baggage from Kalisch hexed me: I've heard of those potions you can give people to drink, and that business with the black mirror. Or maybe she went to a fortune-teller, Schiller Schulnick or someone like him. I tried to go to Elka but just couldn't do it. When I started out for Krachmalna Street or Praga or Peltselvizna, I ended up somewhere else. Once I made it to the rabbi's. I wanted to talk to him about the divorce, but instead I asked him questions about soup and meat, pots and pans, whether this or that was kosher. I lost my appetite completely and grew thin as a stick. I couldn't keep my pants up. When I walked on the street, tears ran down my cheeks. I didn't know why, I only knew I couldn't do it. Perhaps her dead father had put in a good word for her in the next world. Anyway, instead of getting rid of that bargain, I managed to get rid of Elka. Why didn't I pity Elka? After all, she was a human being—and she carried my child too. But I tell you, when one of us has pity, he has it for the wrong person. We are like a blind horse who stumbles into a ditch.

Why draw it out? When I finally shook off my craziness and showed up at the shop, there was no more Elka. She sold out everything for a song and took off for America—by herself, not with a man. My boys wouldn't leave me alone: what did you do it for, they said, what was the point? But when you come to your senses, it's too late. I was so bitter I starting guzzling again to drown my troubles. With my Kalisch cutie, I suffered another year. But it was terrible. As soon as Elka left, the other one started riding her high horse again. I couldn't stand her anymore and let her have it plenty. But just then, the cops caught me on a job . . .

—Did she squeal on you, eh?

—How did you guess?

—It figured.

—Yes, she squealed. And when they locked me up she sold everything and took off with the other guy. She left me without a stitch on my back.

—Where did she go?

—Also to America.

—You don't hear anything from either of them?

—As if they sunk into the ocean.

—You don't even know whether Elka had a boy or a girl?

—I know nothing.

—Talk about suckers! You're at the head of the line!

—Sure I'm a sucker. But you'd better keep your mouth shut or I'll hit you so hard you'll see as far as Cracow.

Translated by Joel Blocker

The Angry Man

A FROST followed the snow that had been falling for three days. For the first time that winter the windowpanes of the Radzymin Study House were coated with ice. Zalman, the glazier, again said, as he did each year, that he couldn't remember such cold weather in the last sixty years. Levi Isaac's nose actually turned blue. He sat there wearing his skunk coat and galoshes, leaning his hands on the cane that was a gift from the saintly rabbi of Kozhenitz. Meir, the eunuch, at the moment in one of his sane periods, his silk hat pushed back high on his forehead, cleaned his pipe with a borrowed knitting needle. Every now and then he took a pinch of snuff and blew his nose into a red handkerchief. His eyes became moist and each time he looked as if he were about to sneeze but he didn't. He clutched his chin where a beard should have grown, and said: "One must never be angry. To be angry with people means to be angry at God. Who created us? If He had wanted the earth to be inhabited by angels, he would have filled it with angels. If He made humans flesh and blood, let them be flesh and blood. And that reminds me of something that happened in Kuzmir.

"In Kuzmir there lived a rich man called Reb Orish. My brother was married to a girl from Kuzmir and he boarded there with his father-in-law. Orish was tall, straight. He had a small black beard and angry black eyes. He owned houses and dealt in lumber. He was known as a scholar but he was also a shrewd businessman and was always complaining that people were dishonest. This one stole; that one swindled. He had a scale, and when his wife brought food home from the stores, he took the trouble to weigh it. If it were as little as half an ounce short, he would go to the merchant and rebuke him in no uncertain terms. His employees were not permitted to utter a word while they worked. He backed up his rules by quoting from the Talmud. He himself was meticulous in money matters. Especially holy to him was the passage in the Pentateuch that says:

" 'The wages of him that is hired shall not abide with thee all night until morning.'

"The story went around that once Orish had settled his accounts with a merchant who had then left for Danzig. The following day Orish checked the figures on his abacus, and discovered a mistake. He owed the man three pennies. Orish immediately ordered the horses harnessed, and sped to Danzig to pay his debt. He proved black on white that such is the law.

"Orish had no children. At the time I used to visit my brother in Kuzmir, I was considered a prodigy and my brother boasted about me in the Study House. Once Orish said to me: 'I hear that you know the *Babba Batra* by heart.' 'Yes,' I replied. He began to test me and I recited three pages. When I came to the fourth, I missed a word and Orish exclaimed: 'You rascal.' He boxed my ear and gave me a silver gulden. 'Mistakes are not permitted. If you say you know something, you must know it. If not you are committing a spiritual theft.'

"In those years a gulden was a fortune, but the box on my ear hurt. Now let me tell you what happened. There was a forest for sale near the Lithuanian border. Orish did not have enough ready cash of his own, and an agent recommended Reb Zekele Lomzer to him as a partner. Reb Zekele was well versed in the Talmud and well known for his cunning in business matters. He so managed it that he made a huge profit from this transaction, but Orish came out the loser. When Orish discovered that he had been cheated, he went to Zekele and called him thief to his face. A quarrel ensued and they came to blows.

"Zekele had a large family in Lomse, and they were all tough. He also managed the estate of the local Polish squire. He had influence wherever he turned. To make it short, there was a lawsuit with the Rabbi of Kuzmir as the judge. Reb Zekele brought with him three men to help him present his case. Reb Zekele was a small stout man with a broad white beard. In the winter he wore a sable coat and a hat to match. In the rabbi's study, Orish raved and ranted but Zekele spoke slowly, choosing his words as if they were coins. He ate continuously—cookies, crackers with jam or sardines. In the synagogue, he lingered for a long time over the Silent Prayer.

"The Rabbi of Kuzmir was a saint, but an unworldly man.

He wanted the litigants to compromise, but Orish demanded a judgment according to the letter of the law. Reb Zekele's arbitrators were of the same ilk as he. They twisted facts and argued so long that the Rabbi became confused. Orish had asked no one to plead in his behalf. He relied on himself. In the end the Rabbi's judgment was completely in Zekele's favor.

"When Orish heard the verdict, his eyes gleamed like a wolf's and he cried out: 'In that case there is no Judge and no Judgment.'

"Nevertheless he accepted the Rabbi's decision and paid Zekele to the last penny. Zekele, who suffered from diabetes, died soon afterwards, but that is another story.

"After the lawsuit Orish stopped coming to the Study House. Somehow he also stopped doing business. Getzel, the night watchman, reported that the lamp burned all night in Orish's room. He could see him pacing and murmuring to himself.

"One day three covered wagons stopped in front of Orish's house. He was moving away from Kuzmir. He stood watching the moving men load his belongings. Then the windows of the house were boarded up. His wife cried. The townspeople assembled to say goodbye but he hardly said a word to anyone. Orish had a large library of rabbinical literature and it was noticed that he did not take his books with him. Somebody asked: 'Reb Orish, for whom are you leaving your books?' 'For the mice,' he replied.

"The town was in a tumoil. It became clear that Orish had strayed from God's road. How does the saying go? Because he quarreled with the cantor, he refused to recite the Sanctification.

"What happened? Orish went to Lublin and was converted. His wife never knew until the last moment what he intended to do. When she learned the truth, she returned to Kuzmir in despair and stayed with relatives. By then he had already sold all his posessions to the gentiles. The rabbi took the tragedy so to heart that he became ill. He contemplated reversing the verdict, but Zekele was dead. How can you get anything back from a dead man?

"I forgot to mention that Orish divorced his wife by proxy.

If he hadn't done that, she could never have remarried. Such is the law. He also made her a settlement according to the terms of their marriage contract. In money matters he remained Orish."

"How could it happen that a learned man should do such a thing?" Zalman, the glazier, asked.

"Anger."

"Did his wife remarry?"

"Yes, she married a teacher."

"And then what happened?"

"For several years no one heard anything. Then his name cropped up again. In our town there lived a legal advisor called Lippe. He subscribed to a Lublin newspaper. It turned out that Orish had become rich again. He had bought up an estate and had married the widow of the late owner, a Polish noble-woman. Lippe read about him in the paper because he had again quarreled with a partner and there was a lawsuit. Orish, of course, had changed his name but at the trial the prosecutor called attention to his Jewish origin. I've forgotten most of the facts. Lippe related the whole story, but who can remember? It seems that his second wife was a witness for the prosecution. This time he not only lost the lawsuit but landed in jail.

"A year or two passed. As you know there are many hills in the vicinity of Kuzmir. And in the hills there are caves. The story goes that a hundred years ago the famous bandit Bobosh hid out there. But who is interested in caves? However, two cheder boys from Kuzmir decided to go on a hike. It was the thirty-third day after Passover, a half-holiday. As is the custom, the boys took bows and arrows, some hard boiled eggs to eat and went off into the woods. They stopped at a cave, looked in and there was a wild man with a disheveled beard, long hair, barefoot, and in tattered clothes. When he saw the boys he began to scream at them and wave his stick. The children ran back to town and reported what they had found.

"At first, nobody believed them. God knows what children can invent. But both boys swore that they were telling the truth. A group of town toughs, the butchers and the coach-man got together and went out to the cave. When they ar-rived, they too saw a half-naked man, with long tangled hair and a matted beard. At his side stood a dog. As soon as Orish spotted the men he began to shout. The dog came after them barking. But coachmen and butchers are not easily frightened. They drove the dog away and warned the man that if he did not come out of the cave, they would stone him out.

"He came out, cursing them in Polish, but it was not the Polish of a gentile. He called them dirty Jews but he looked like a Jew himself. One of the band called out: 'He looks like Orish, doesn't he?' And they suddenly realized that it was Orish. When it became clear to Orish that they knew who he was, he broke into Yiddish. 'Yes, I am Orish,' he said. 'This is my hill and my cave. Nobody can make me leave here.'

"They were all stunned speechless. Finally one of them said, 'What is the point of living in a cave?' 'There is no point to it,' he replied. 'But sometimes even what is pointless has a point.' He blasphemed, speaking half-Yiddish, half-Polish. 'There is no God,' he announced, 'And the Jews are not the chosen people.' He upbraided Christians as well. 'All are so rotten, I would rather live with animals,' he cried out.

"The men were ready to beat him up, but he pulled out a long knife from beneath his rags. Who wants to fight a wild man? They began to plead with him: 'Reb Orish, what's the use of staying here? Come back with us and be a Jew again.' Orish's reply was more abuse and profanity.

"How he managed to get food there, I still don't know. Perhaps he had some money and was able to buy supplies from the peasants. And maybe he dug up roots and wild plants from the earth. If one is wronged by the Jews one runs to the gentiles. But where does one run from the gentiles? Into the forest.

"I don't know how long Orish remained in the cave. People from the town began to visit him. The old rabbi who had ruled in favor of Zekele had died. The new rabbi went to argue with Orish. He said the same thing that the Lord said to Jeroboam. Repent. Orish came out of the cave to argue with the Rabbi. Out of perversity he showed off his erudition to prove that the Torah did not come from heaven. It was rumored that he had also insulted the priest, but I doubt that this was true.

"Frequently converts try to hide their Jewish learning, but not Orish. No one in Kuzmir had ever known that he was such a scholar. Some of the town elders tried to rebuke him; others pleaded with him not to shame his parents in paradise. It was said that his former wife sent him food and linens but he refused to accept her help. He would not even let anyone throw a bone to his dog.

"As long as it remained warm the townspeople continued to come to see Orish out of sheer curiosity. But after the Feast of Tabernacle when the rains began, they left him alone. I don't know whether he remained there through the winter or not. One day between Purim and Passover when a group of the town toughs returned to the cave, he was no longer there."

"Did he disappear for good?" Zalman, the glazier, asked.

"Like a stone in water."

"Perhaps he repented?"

"If he had, we would have heard about it. He probably drowned himself in the Vistula. However, with an Orish you can never tell. He might even have gone off to far-away America . . ."

Dusk fell and the Radzymin Study House filled with shadows. Meir, the eunuch, began to worry his naked chin as if he were searching for a hair. Levi Isaac propped the cane given to him by the saintly rabbi of Kozhenitz against the table, took off his spectacles and carefully wiped the mist from them. Zalman, the glazier, clutched the thickness of his beard which had once been grey but had turned yellowish green from his constant using of snuff and remarked:

"A body drowned in the Vistula will sooner or later rise to the surface, unless it was eaten up by the fish."

Translated by the author and Elizabeth Shub

The Mathematician

THIS STORY was told to me by Professor Solomon Rashbam's former brother-in-law, Max Pearl, my friend from the Yiddish Writers' Union. We were sitting and talking in a cafe in Warsaw when the topic turned to Solomon Rashbam, a mathematician, one of the few Jews who held the post of Professor at Warsaw University, first with the Russians and then with the Poles. Solomon Rashbam had died and I had heard many strange stories about him. Once, I even met him, a small man, stooped, with a red face, a little white beard and bulging eyes. He was considered, at least in my circle, one of the greatest mathematicians in the world, but it was also said of him that he was a complete madman. At sixty-five Solomon Rashbam divorced his wife, Max Pearl's sister, Malkah, and married a Yiddish actress. I asked Max Pearl what had caused the divorce and he said:

"When Lombroso came out with the opinion that genius and madness were related, he was attacked from all sides because he had insulted genius. In later years similar accusations were hurled at Max Nordau for his book *Paradoxes* in which he tried to prove that many of the great poets were degenerates. I'm not a scholar, only a journalist. So I cannot judge such things. But I have no doubt that my brother-in-law, Soloman Rashbam, peace be with him, was both a genius and a madman. I knew him for forty years and was connected to him for thirty years. Besides being a mathematician, he was erudite in the Talmud and the Commentaries, a linguist and a chess master; he played chess with the famous chess king, Emanuel Lasker. In our conversations, he often quoted from the Vulgate and the Septuagint by heart. Once, when we were speaking about Russian literature, he began to recite whole poems by Pushkin and Lermontov. When he found the time to study is still a riddle to me. I also heard that even as a child he was considered a genius. At the age of nine he delivered a sermon at the synagogue in his town of Plock and the rabbis praised him highly.

"But Solomon was also, he should forgive me, a maniac. My

sister Malkah was his second wife. He married his first wife in
Switzerland. She was a rich girl, the daughter of a Swiss Jew,
but after ten years they were divorced. Why they were divorced, I was never told. Solomon was not a person to let his
secrets be known. He was considered an unbeliever and a disgrace to the family, which finally severed all connections with
him. If my father were still alive and Solomon had known him,
Malkah would never have married him. But my father was
dead and Malkah had become enlightened. Her total enlightenment consisted of reading the Yiddish newspaper, *The
Friend*, every morning and of announcing to our mother that
after her wedding she would never allow her head to be shaved
as brides were accustomed to doing among the most ardent
Hassidim. Once in a while she attended a lecture by Peretz in
the Hazamir Hall. It was there that she met Rashbam. He was
at least fifteen years older than she, already a scholar of acclaim
and the young generation worshipped him. I was then still a
yeshiva boy, ten years younger than my sister, Malkah.

"I cannot describe to you the turmoil which arose in our
house when Malkah informed my mother that she was in love
with Solomon Rashbam and was going to marry him. First of
all, the word love was as unkosher as pork in our house. Secondly, Solomon Rashbam was known as an apostate. Thirdly,
he was divorced and so much older than Malkah. But my sister
had gotten the notion from reading novels that love was the
most sacred thing in all of life, and had made up her mind
consequently that Solomon Rashbam was the only man she
could love. When my mother refused to give her blessings to
the wedding she even threatened suicide. Each time I came
home from the Cheder I found the pair quarreling. Malkah
was crying, my mother was wringing her hands, and aunts and
great aunts came to intervene to no avail. The matchmakers
offered Malkah many suitable husbands but she remained
steadfast—it was Solomon or death. After a long battle my
mother surrendered, but Malkah had to swear by a Holy Scroll
that she would wear a wig and keep a strictly kosher kitchen.
The truth is that Malkah was as pious and chaste a woman as
our grandmothers. In her later years, when her own daughters
began to grow up and follow the fashion to wear short dresses
without sleeves, Malkah was scandalized.

"I guess you have heard that Solomon Rashbam, that wild man, divorced Malkah because he suspected her of betraying him with lovers—not one but a hundred. This lunacy began immediately after their marriage and as time passed worsened to the point where it became the talk of Warsaw. Malkah was in no hurry to divulge to our mother the heartbreak Solomon was causing her with his jealousy. She loved him and highly respected him. To suspect Malkah of having sinful affairs, one had to be a psychopath, too. Almost right after their marriage he began to demand an account of every minute she was away from him. Of course, at night they slept together in their bedroom. In the morning she served him breakfast. But the hours he was away from home and teaching at the university were unaccounted for. Every day he cross-examined Malkah and demanded a full report of how she spent her free time, and each time she was never able to give a precise explanation to his satisfaction. After a while, my sister had reached the state where she carried a notebook in which she jotted down the events of every minute of her day. She once showed me this ridiculous book and when I glimpsed at it I didn't know whether to laugh or cry. Solomon Rashbam had assumed that Malkah had betrayed him with the janitor of their house, the grocery man, the butcher on our street and the newspaper boy.

"For many years she was silent, too ashamed to reveal the depth of her suffering to her family. But one day she broke down. By this time, our mother was dead, so she came to cry to us, her brothers and sisters. It was the wailing of a tormented soul. Even right after she had given birth to her first daughter, Solomon suspected her of having an affair with the obstetrician or with the cheder boys who came to the delivery room to recite the Shema in return for some raisins and cookies. Explaining every second of her life to Solomon became a frightening task. For instance, when Malkah went to the seamstress to be measured for a dress, it took her an hour. You know how women are, they like to fuss about their clothes and to chatter. If Malkah wrote in her book that she had spent an hour there, Solomon would ask, 'Why did you need an hour to be measured for a dress?' He would take out a pencil and paper and calculate the minutes and seconds of how long such a process should really take. Then, when he asked for such details, she became utterly confused. He always arrived at the same conclusion, that the few minutes she couldn't give a reckoning for, she had spent with a lover. Malkah would laugh and sob, 'What lover? What do you want from my life? I have one God and one husband. For whom would I exchange you? You are the crown on my head.' She swore holy oaths of innocence, beseeching him to have mercy and to leave her in peace. But Professor Solomon Rashbam quoted episodes of female disloyalty to her from the Decameron, Casanova's memoirs, and from Paul de Coque's sexy novels.

"More than once, I tried to plead with my brother-in-law to go see the famous Dr. Flatau, one of the best psychiatrists in Poland and perhaps Europe. I advised him to confide in Dr. Flatau his miseries which he caused himself and his innocent wife. Solomon listened to me and replied, 'How can Flatau help?' Finally, he went to see the doctor, who told him the story of a patient who accused his wife of copulating with a man through a hole in the mattress while he, her husband, slept by her side in their bed, an innocent man. I once asked Solomon why he didn't hire a detective to follow Malkah but Solomon answered, 'And what guarantee would I have that she wouldn't sin with the detective?' 'Hire a female detective,' I said. And he replied, 'All these people can be bribed.'

"Solomon Rashbam's daughters were growing up and knew quite well what was going on in their home. In their presence, he accused my sister that the children weren't his. You can imagine how distressed the girls were when they heard their father saying such terrible things. Later on he gave up his professorship just to be able to guard my sister. He earned a living from the books he had written and the articles he published in magazines, but it was barely enough to keep the family from starving. Malkah almost ceased going out into the street to do shopping and to see her friends, the few she had left. Just the same, when the letter carrier brought a letter and Malkah went to the door to get it, Solomon clicked on his chronometer. When she returned with the mail he proved to her that she had tarried one minute and eight seconds longer than she should have with the postman. My sister would say to him, 'What could I have done in that one minute and the few seconds?'

And he would say, 'In a minute one can commit the worst kind of treachery.'

"There comes a time when even a martyr cannot bear his ordeal anymore. You know what the Talmud says, that if Chanania, Mishael and Azariah had been tortured, they would have surrendered and served Nebuchadnezzar. Besides, what one can bear when one is twenty-five becomes utterly unbearable at forty-five. When Malkah was forty-five Solomon was already over sixty. They had troubles with their daughters, real troubles, not imaginary ones, and of course all pointed the finger at Solomon Rashbam. The older one went to Paris to study at the Sorbonne and there I heard that she had had an affair with an adventurer from Tahiti. The other one is in a mental institution until this day."

"What is her illness?" I asked.

"Melancholy. But wait, you haven't heard the whole story.

"The moment always comes when the boil must burst. One day Malkah packed her belongings in a bundle and left home. My sisters had large families and small apartments, but my oldest brother, Zelig Mayer, had a large apartment and he took Malkah in. For her to run away from home, from the furniture she always polished, from the rugs she cherished, and from the copper pans she scrubbed until they shone like mirrors, was a catastrophe.

"About two hours after Malkah left him, the telephone began to ring in all of our homes. Solomon was demanding the return of his wife. He threatened us that for kidnapping Malkah and tolerating her misdeeds, we would all rot in prison. We all told Malkah not to approach the telephone when it rang but when no one was home she did pick up the receiver and Solomon kept her on the line for hours with his accusations. Strange that even though he asked her to return to him, he never took back his allegations. According to him she had committed adultery, God knows how many times, but he was willing to forgive her. The only thing he asked was that she confess everything and deny nothing. I'm sorry to say that Malkah has a weak character and she was ready to go back to him but we barred her from doing so. Even though Malkah had left him he still demanded a detailed report about each minute of the day and Malkah, the timid creature, kept on writing in her notebook. She somehow hoped that he would see the 'truth' of her innocence and realize what terrible damage he had done to her.

"I guess you know that Solomon later married that disgusting actress Salcha Cholewa with whom he had been having an affair. It happens that people have defects but they also have virtues, but this Salcha was completely rotten. First of all, she was a terrible actress. She played in the most vulgar comedies in cheap theatres on Smocha Street, and she was ugly to boot, with a broad nose like a duck and a quacking voice to match. In Warsaw they seldom let her on the stage, and for so many years she drifted around in the provinces where wandering actors performed in stables and granaries. Secondly, if Solomon Rashbam was looking for chastity and loyalty, he'd made a big mistake with Salcha! She slept with anyone. If she didn't have sex with the directors and the impresarios, she could never have gotten a part in any play even in the most forsaken villages.

"The news that Solomon was demanding a divorce from my sister was sudden. When Malkah heard that she was about to be divorced, she was completely shaken. Even then she still hoped that things would straighten out. But keeping a man by force was not in her character. After much resistance and hesitations, Malkah consented to give Solomon the divorce he demanded, and they went to the rabbi and were divorced. Solomon pretended that he wanted the divorce because he planned to return to Switzerland. Two weeks later we heard the bizarre news that he had married Salcha. Downtrodden as Malkah was, she began to laugh when she heard about this crazy marriage. All of Warsaw was laughing.

"Poor and ugly as Salcha was, she always had a retinue of parasites, so called admirers, or schnorrers, following her for the sheer purpose of getting a cup of tea somewhere, or a free meal. Salcha never had money, but she forever managed to find someone who would invite her over for a day or she simply invited herself. Immediately after the wedding, she started to beg in the name of Solomon Rashbam. She was Mrs. Rashbam now and she pestered all the professors and the wealthy charlatans of Warsaw for money. She ran after journalists, asking them to write articles of praise about Solomon Rashbam, inventing some kind of sickness from which he was supposed to suffer. You know, I never saw him after he divorced my sister. Perhaps he never left his apartment, where he was a prisoner of Salcha.

"Solomon never wrote on any other topic except mathematics. Now everyone heard that he was writing a book about philosophy, religion, or whatever Salcha invented. Somehow, Solomon must have known that he had fallen into a terrible quicksand from which he could never get out. His apartment became a hostel where all the dregs of Warsaw lived, ate, slept and littered. He had a large library and the books were stolen and vandalized. The humorists in the newspapers published jokes about Professor Solomon Rashbam and Salcha. I don't know how she did it but she got a pension, really for herself, from the Jewish community. Her method was to barge into a house or an institution together with a whole bunch of crackpots and to behave in such a scandalous way that one gave in to her just to get rid of her. She was always drunk and loudmouthed. Solomon had not been a professor at the university long enough to be awarded a tenure but Salcha beat down the doors of the rector's office and made such a commotion that the university allotted him a lump sum.

"And jealousy? He had no opportunity to be jealous. He didn't even have a chance to open his mouth. He lived with her for about three years and these three years were one long nightmare. When Malkah heard what that beast had done to her Solomon, she cried her eyes out. She tried to call him on the telephone but it was always busy and if someone answered, it was Salcha or one of her gang. She never allowed Solomon to approach the telephone. Malkah wrote letters to him but they probably never reached him. Salcha took over everything. I was told that she used to beat him up regularly and tear at his beard.

"Only when he finally became ill with cancer did Salcha place him in the Jewish Hospital on Czysta Street, and one could finally get to see him. However, this was no longer Solomon Rashbam but a living corpse. Malkah ran to see him bringing chicken soup and oranges, but the cancer in his throat would not let him speak, just chortle. He muttered to Malkah, 'I have made a bad calculation.' All the time he lay in the hospital, Salcha organized benefit performances in the Yiddish Theater for him. Of course, she took the money for herself or for the parasites with whom she surrounded herself.

"I guess you have heard how he died and was buried in a cemetery in the suburb of Praga, together with all the paupers and riff-raff. The community remembered his times of glory and gave him a plot in the first row.

"It turned out that Salcha had never paid any rent. The landlord was an admirer of Solomon Rashbam's. The moment Solomon died, the landlord evicted Salcha and all their belongings were thrown into the yard. There wasn't much to throw out. Her leeches had broken or sold everything.

"At the funeral, Malkah wasn't allowed to come near Solomon's hearse. When the Kaddish was said and a professor attempted to recite a eulogy, Salcha pushed him away from the grave and made a speech herself. I went to the funeral. This wasn't a sermon but a joke. Someone later wrote in a newspaper that for the first time at the cemetery Salcha had had the opportunity to really play theater in Warsaw."

"What happened to her?" I asked.

"What happens to microbes of typhus or cholera when the epidemic has run its course? They remain dormant somewhere and wait until it's time for another epidemic. Right after the Shiva, she vanished. I was told that she might be alive somewhere in South America. Malkah was relatively still young, in her best years, when Solomon died. Men wanted to marry her, but she turned everyone down, saying no one could take the place of Solomon in her heart. She cried bitterly and praised his greatness as a scholar, quoting reviews of his work in mathematics magazines. Shortly after Solomon's death, Malkah died too."

Max Pearl lit a cigarette and said, "They write a lot about those who commit suicide by hanging or shooting themselves, or jumping out of a window. But how about those who commit suicide the way Solomon Rashbam did? And of course, Malkah was as mad as her husband, a martyr in her own way, as many women are when they have the misfortune of falling in love with a madman. And why do they do it? The rabbi of Kock once said, 'There are many deep wells, but the well of madness is the deepest of them all.'"

Translated by the author and Duba Desowitz

The Building Project

WHEN a man amasses a sizeable fortune at forty and has never known failure in the bargain, then he can aim high. Nevertheless, his intimates warned that Wolf Unger was overreaching himself. He had acquired a lot in the center of town and had set about building a complex of three huge houses, each six stories high. True, the Association had promised credit, and he had obtained various sums from people who invested for high interest rates. Still, a project of this size was well calculated to swallow up hundreds of thousands of rubles, maybe more than a million. Aside from everything else, Wolf Unger had never engaged in building before; he had grown rich by buying and selling. His wife tried to dissuade him. Close friends and relatives argued: Why risk so much? Why not sit tranquilly and cut coupons? But Wolf Unger knew nothing of tranquility. Small and slight as he was, he was drawn only to large undertakings. He loved to read in the newspapers about the skyscrapers in New York, quietly planned to build railroads in Poland, dig tunnels, put up factories. Rockefeller, too, he said, had not come out of his mother's womb a full-fledged millionaire. All you needed was a bit of luck and plenty of initiative.

No one could deny that Wolf Unger had an abundant supply of the latter, and he certainly did not want for luck. How else could the son of a *shames* in Nowydwor have become a Warsaw magnate? He lived more expansively than men whose wealth was of longer standing; he drove about in a coach, occupied an apartment of eight rooms and a kitchen, entertained gentility. The girls attended an aristocratic boarding-school where Jews were, to say the least, unwelcome. Feige Golde, his wife, had changed her name to Fanny. She festooned herself with jewelry, subscribed for a box at the Warsaw opera. However, there are limits to everything. The talk in Warsaw was that this time Wolf Unger had flown too high.

It soon became apparent that Wolf Unger's legendary luck had, indeed, changed. In the course of digging for the foundation, water had been found, veritable streams of water, bubbling underground. The water had to be drained off, but the engineers were unable to agree on the proper method. Soon the City Council intervened, and there began a steady procession of inspectors and commissioners, each with his own regulations, each of whom had to be bribed. The masons suddenly organized themselves into a union and demanded higher wages. The price of lumber, steel, cement shot up. Landlords and brokers were saying that finally Wolf Unger had bitten off a chunk big enough to choke him.

As though to defy all the portents of doom, Wolf Unger now began to live more ostentatiously than ever, donating large sums for worthwhile causes, increasing the salaries of his office staff, smoking fine Havanas, frequenting exclusive restaurants and coffee-houses, buying paintings at the "Zachento" gallery. He was seen everywhere; a tiny man—skin and bones, with a pointed skull, a long nose, a narrow chin with a small goatee, and sunken cheeks. He sported a pearl in his cravat, a diamond ring, patent-leather shoes and spats even in summer, and suits of English cloth. He even appeared in a frock coat and top hat. He had veered completely away from Jewishness, and was seen drinking wine with gentiles, eating unkosher fish, and sea-creatures which are swallowed alive. He stopped speaking Yiddish, or tried to, resorting instead to a kind of pseudo-German gibberish.

"Are matters proceeding satisfactorily with you? My affairs are prospering," he was heard saying stiffly to a Jewish community official. "I whistle at all my foes," he went on, his German faltering, and then, as it failed him entirely, "May they be nine yards deep in the earth."

He blew his nose into a silk handkerchief, wrote with a gold fountain pen, carried in his vest pocket a watch which showed the time in New York and sounded the quarter-hours with a dainty melody. He was constantly searching for rare objects—things to arouse wonder. His cane, which had a gold knob, also contained an umbrella tightly coiled inside. Wolf Unger was no jeweler, yet he came often to cafés where precious stones were sold and traded, and was frequently seen examining gems through a jeweler's glass. He bought, too. It was difficult to understand how the man had so much time to spend —and so much money.

Wolf Unger had always liked to joke, but since launching his building project he seemed to ask for nothing more than to hear and tell funny stories. At the end of each story he would let out a loud cackle. Wolf Unger belittled his enemies with mockery and subtle innuendoes. In all this, everyone understood that Wolf Unger was playing a comedy. Behind the gay façade he was seeking loans, partners, and was ready to pay the most usurious premiums. It was whispered that in consummating the deal for the land, Wolf had been bamboozled.

All at once the blow descended. The Association withdrew the major portion of its credit. No one knew exactly what happened. On a summer afternoon the coach drew up in front of Wolf Unger's office. He alighted and motioned to Jan, the coachman, not to wait but to return to the house. Wolf entered his office with a haughty expression, every button in place, with a sprig of lilac in his button-hole, and called out to the staff in plain Yiddish:

"You're writing, eh? Write, write. Write me down for a good year."

They wondered. He had not used Yiddish in some time. Leon Fleder, the bookkeeper, raised his square head from his ledgers and peered tentatively at his employer from behind fogged lenses. Leon Fleder was fully aware of the true condition of Wolf's finances, knew that Wolf was putting a good face on the grim drama. The cashier, Max Bein, had in front of him a mountainous stack of bills which, for the time being, it was impossible to pay.

Leizer, the servant, had just asked, innocently, "Would the boss maybe like a glass of tea?" when, suddenly, Wolf Unger began to scream. His face was contorted, and his eyes became blood-shot. He opened a mouth full of crooked teeth and gold fillings and sent up a yowl so blood-curdling that they were all stricken with terror. He raised his cane and threw it at Leon Fleder. He ran to the desk and started ripping pages out of the ledgers. There was a heavy ash-tray on the desk and Wolf seized it and heaved it violently toward the window. Miraculously, he missed; it might have killed someone. His face grew apoplectic. Thick veins stood out on his neck and forehead. The pitch of his screams alternated between masculine and feminine. He stamped his feet and in one frenzied push swept the abacus, pens, inkwells and papers off the desk.

After a time, attempts were made to soothe him. He resisted them, fought back. He shrieked one word over and over, like one possessed, but none of them could discern what it was. The telephone began to ring. Wolf Unger lunged at the receiver and tore it off, together with the cord. The commotion must have been heard in the adjoining office; people came running in. Somebody called loudly for the Emergency Squad to be summoned. Wolf threw himself on the man, as if with deadly intent. He was seized by his arms and shoulders, pulled back, pleaded with. It became clear that Wolf Unger had lost his reason.

All at once he appeared to subdue himself, and in his normal voice said:

"What do you want, all of you? Let go of me."

"Should we call a doctor?"

"No doctor."

"What's wrong, boss?"

"I'm a pauper, that's all that's wrong."

The people who had gathered drifted away. Leon Fleder, Max Bein, and Leizer picked up the scattered papers. Wolf Unger retrieved his cane and started to leave. At the door, his head tilted forward in a gesture indicating nausea, but he regained control and descended the steps. He started to walk home. His route took him past the site of the excavation for his buildings. The foundations were already being laid. Wolf stood on the opposite curb and gaped. Scores of laborers were busily at work. They laid bricks, mixed cement, sagged under the weight of giant beams and planks. A construction foreman was scanning a roll of blueprints. Freight wagons and flatcarts came and went. The sun shone. A layer of golden dust enveloped the scene. He, Wolf, had cranked up the machine and now it ran by its own momentum. "They don't seem aware that they are building on sand," Wolf Unger murmured. "Worse than sand. On spider's webs."

He broke into laughter and the laughter turned into sobbing. The tears welled up and everything went awry, became precarious, without substance. The building project was a castle in the air, the builders devils and imps whom he had brought into being with his cupidity and his transgressions.

2

As Wolf Unger walked up the marble steps to the imposing entrance of the apartment building in which he lived, he was again overtaken by the urge to scream. He barely managed to contain it. He approached the mahogany door. On a brass plate the name "W. UNGER" was engraved in stately Latin characters. Wolf snickered. He raised one foot, attempting to kick the plate, but it was beyond his reach. He pressed the buzzer with loud, rapid jabs. The maid, a blond Polish girl in white apron and cap, came at a run. Seeing the head of the house, she stepped back deferentially. Wolf roared with laughter.

"Jadwiga, you are richer than I am!"

"Jesus and Mary, the master frightened me."

"Is my worse half at home?"

"The Madam? Yes. The young misses too. In the salon."

"Have they been eased out of school already?"

The girl crossed herself. "God forbid!"

"They'll be thrown out, never fear."

Without knocking, with his hat on and his cane in his hand, Wolf strode in and slammed the door so hard that the stippled window-panes rang. Fanny was sitting on an upholstered armchair, a large, heavy-set woman with a complexion black as a crow's, a long beak, and a wisp of beard on her double chin. From her flaring earlobes hung a pair of diamond earrings. Her eyebrows were thick, masculine. A trace of mustache sprouted on her upper lip and thin tufts of hair clung to her cheeks. The eyes, set too close, looked out with sharp malevolence, like those of a bird-of-prey. "A lump of glittering ugliness," Wolf hissed to himself. "Let her take in washing, sell horseradish in the market-place."

Across the room, Flora and Lena were slumped comfortably on a chaise longue. They were eighteen months apart, but, with their black hair arranged in bangs, their narrow noses and thin lips, they might have been twins. The eyes were different, though—Lena's black, and Flora's green as gooseberries. They wore the dark dresses and alpaca aprons of the boarding-school. Over them hung that carefree air, that consciousness of privilege, that surrounds young ladies whose only concerns are their lessons, the piano, the dancing, the balls arranged twice each semester to which are invited gentile boys from the private lycees. Wolf Unger measured them with a sidelong glance, and smiled crookedly. The daughters of the idle rich!

"Why don't you take off your hat, and put the cane away in the corridor?" Fanny demanded irritably. "This is a salon, not a coffee-house."

"This is no salon, this is a poor-house!" Wolf shot back. "Your mother peddled onions in the streets but you can't even do that. All you're fit for is to gorge yourself and eliminate."

The girls tilted their heads sharply to one side and in unison—like a pair of talking dolls—screeched:

"Papa!"

"It's over. Finished. The whole farce is over! Do you understand?" Wolf raged. "I'm wiped out, a pauper in the seventh degree. Go out into service, carry bed-pans. I'm bankrupt, a fugitive, a thief, an embezzler! I'll do time in prison, and you'll be the convict's daughters. No more fancy private schools. You'll sleep on kitchen floors. You'll empty slop-pails. Enough of pretensions. . . . Vultures! Maggots! Leeches!"

Wolf began to dance. He beat his cane on the furniture, screamed, spat. He rushed to the piano, banged his fist on the keys. The maid ran in, scared, confused. The girls jumped up. Fanny wrung her heavy, mannish hands.

"Children," she wailed, "your father is mad!"

"Yes, mad!" Wolf screamed. "I'm mad. Mass of ugliness, take off that jewelry—it isn't yours, it belongs to the creditors. We'll give them everything, the shirts off our backs, the last pot, the last spoon. We'll sew ourselves a sack and go around begging, all four of us. We'll put on rags, patches, cast-offs. We'll spend our nights in outhouses. We're panhandlers, *schnorrers*, vagrants."

"Jadwiga!" Fanny shrieked, "call the doctor at once!"

"Ox! What good can the doctor do? I'm ruined, not a groschen to my name. I lived high on other people's money, squandered the dowries of orphan girls. I'm a swindler, a crook. The police, Jadwiga, the police!"

Wolf Unger dashed to the window, tore down the drapes,

and stooped, as if preparing to jump. Fanny grabbed him by one foot, pulling off one of his trouser-legs. Jadwiga and the girls joined in the struggle to drag him from the window. The salon resounded with screams, calls for help. Neighbors rushed in, men with gleaming bald pates and women with elaborate pompadours. They all spoke to him in Polish, but Wolf cursed them in Yiddish, laughed wildly, flung himself on them with flailing fists, punctuating his curses with piercing wails of the kind sometimes heard at the funerals of the poor. He had torn off his collar and cravat, his suspenders trailed on the floor, and one foot, swathed in long underwear, protruded from his dangling trousers. The telephone rang, but nobody answered it. Wolf Unger grappled with everybody, overturning chairs, knocking down tables, smashing vases. After a while he began to chant passages of the synagogue service, to recite distorted fragments of Biblical verses and Talmudic dicta, interspersing them with obscene words, parodies, catchwords from vulgar theatrical hits. Now and then he would utter some words in faulty Polish. Flora and Lena stood together with bowed heads. Fanny, herself distraught, now turned sharply on her daughters, berating them for estranging themselves from their father, spurning Jewish ways.

Suddenly, with the agility of an acrobat, Wolf Unger leaped up to the huge, ornate candelabrum that was set into the wall, and with his hands clutching the iron brackets hung down, his feet dangling in the air. There were screams and a frenzied rush to get out of the way, as the candelabrum with its solid bronze framework and crystal prisms could maim or kill somebody. After a struggle to maintain his hold, Wolf dropped to the floor, gasping for breath.

At the height of the uproar, Dr. Spielfogel, the family physician, arrived. He was a stocky man with a heavy paunch and a white mustache. Perhaps to lend credence to his reputation for eccentricity, he wore a broad velour hat and some sort of double cape. The head of his cane resembled the antlers of a stag. He stood quietly for some moments watching guardedly as Wolf Unger played out his scene. Then, in a rasping voice, he said in Yiddish:

"Why are you making a fool of yourself, Reb Wolf? It isn't Purim, you know."

Wolf Unger threw him a withering look, his eyes darting feverishly.

"It is for me!" he shot back. "For me it's Purim, my wife is Zeresh and I am Haman. Hang me! Where is Vajezatta, my youngest son?"

And in a high-pitched monotone, like a Cheder-boy, he reeled off the familiar jingle:

> A good Purim to all,
> I walk and I fall.
> My beard is too long;
> My wife isn't strong.
> Today is Purim, tomorrow—no more;
> Give me a groschen, and show me the door.

"Come, Reb Wolf," the doctor said amiably, "we'll have a talk."

"Where do you want to drag me off to, the lunatic asylum?"

"To my private clinic. To rest."

"Your clinic costs money, and I'm penniless. I have nothing, doctor; the shirt on my back is not my own. Even the fleas are registered in my wife's name." His sides shook, but no laughter could be heard.

"Don't get upset over money, Reb Wolf. Your health is the important thing."

"If I don't, who will? My wife? She wouldn't know how to bind up a cat's tail. My daughters? Parasites! *Shikses!* Jew-haters! They regard a Jew as worse than a spider. They have sucked the marrow out of me and spat me out."

He looked around the room, as if suddenly becoming aware of his larger audience. "Look at me, neighbors, and take heed," he intoned. "Profit by my example."

The wrangling between doctor and patient continued for some time. Gradually, Wolf Unger calmed down. He pulled up his dragging trouser-leg, put on his collar and necktie, asked the strangers to leave. Only now did his daughters burst into tears. The doctor took Fanny into an adjoining room where they held a whispered conversation. When he reappeared, he said:

"Pan Unger, you will be well."

Wolf shrugged. "What do I want with health? I'm finished, doctor."

"You're still a young man," the doctor admonished. "I wish I were no older."

Fanny packed a suitcase. Leading Wolf between them, all three walked out and entered the doctor's coach which stood at the curb, surrounded by a knot of curious adults and children.

That night Wolf Unger lay in a hospital bed, and a Sister of Mercy administered drops, applied ice-packs to his head, and brought his meal. The walls there were white. The window commanded a view of the garden. Wolf Unger might have imagined he was in a hotel, but for the occasional sighs, cries and moans that seeped in from the corridor. The guests here were all gravely ill, all well-to-do. From somewhere came the sound of muffled sobbing; someone must have died.

The door opened wide and Dr. Spielfogel appeared, dressed in a white tunic that emphasized his pointed stomach. He seemed strange, stern, and addressed Wolf Unger in Polish:

"Well, how is the Pan feeling?"

"Like a dead man after the funeral."

3

Much of the time, during the first days of his stay, Wolf Unger lay in bed making calculations with a pencil and note-book he had brought. When the Sister, at the doctor's command, took them away, he tried to carry on his figuring mentally. True, he mused, he, Wolf Unger, was really a corpse—like all those other dead that inhabit the imaginary world. But he was left with a troubling uncertainty: How had he, Wolf, he who had always maintained such control over his enterprises—had all the figures instantly at his command—how had he lost his bearings so completely?

After a few days, Wolf stopped figuring. What was the difference? He was finished. Everything had been lost—his name, the children, his fortune. The creditors were cursing him. The poor brides whose dowries he had dissipated were weeping because of him. Let me assume, he said to himself, that this bed is my grave. He turned his face to the wall and dozed fitfully. He dreamt, but remembered nothing of his dreams. The doctor, the Sisters spoke to him, but their voices seemed to come from so great a distance that by the time they reached him they had tapered off into inaudibility.

His wife came to visit. She sat next to the bed dressed in black, bedecked with jewelry, and wearing a fur collar made up of little animals. He regarded her mockingly, with amused curiosity. His daughters came in, and Wolf, speaking in Yiddish, demanded:

"Come to mourn at your father's grave?"

"You will be well again, Papa," they said together.

"For what? At least, if you were boys, you would say *Kadish*."

Just as aggressively as he had formerly embraced life, Wolf Unger now bent his energies to thoughts of death. From his studies at the *Beth Midrash*, long ago, a saying from the Talmud floated into his memory: "They who are condemned to die by fire may be counted as already burned." This he paraphrased to suit his own dark outlook: "Since all are destined to die, they may be counted already dead." The dead eat. The dead trade. The dead build houses. The world is one vast burial-ground. Before the dead are lowered into their graves, they romp about briefly, play some sort of game, and this is what is called life. But who needs this game?

The Sister brought Wolf Unger his meals but he had lost all appetite. Then, too, they served him sections of dead animals. In what way is a dead fowl more appetizing than a dead man? He sipped a spoonful of chicken soup and called the Sister:

"Take this away; it was used for the corpse's ablutions."

Dr. Spielfogel called in two psychiatrists for consultation, and they diagnosed Wolf Unger's malady as melancholia. The Sister warned that unless he took himself in hand he would have to be—God forbid!—committed to a mental institution. But the food was tasteless. Dr. Spielfogel offered him a cigar and with the very first pull he was overcome by nausea. He even lost the will to perform his bodily functions and the Sisters had to resort to enemas. He virtually stopped sleeping; he lay the entire night without closing an eye. As cunningly as the clinic had been constructed to shut out noises so as to isolate each patient in an island of his own sounds, Wolf Unger heard everything. Patients died and were quietly removed. Relatives wept, but were admonished to smother their sobs. The Sisters conversed gaily in the corridor, and even giggled, but their pale faces and puffy eyes revealed an anxiety, a disillusionment that could not be masked by pretense. Dr. Spielfogel, too, played the game but Wolf Unger knew the truth, that the doctor was himself old, ill. He had admitted that he was unable to sleep without the help of pills. Once Wolf had asked him whether he believed in a world to come, and Dr. Spielfogel had answered shortly: "I don't even believe in this one."

Strange, but as soon as Wolf Unger perceived the truth, he realized that everyone else knew it too. It was only that each one had his own formula for denying it. The young try to persuade each other that there is no such thing as old age. The old pretend they are young. Relatives visiting the mortally ill wish them a speedy recovery. The hearse that drives up to the clinic gate in the evenings appears to be an ordinary coach, except that it is a little longer. Even the flies and the moths buzz and flutter as if to try to forget their approaching end. The trees outside the window, whose branches rustle and sigh in vernal rhythms, are already dotted with decaying leaves. To Wolf Unger it was the dissembling of his own family which seemed most transparent. His wife simulated devotion, but she grew heavier, and came each time adorned with new trifles. She must already be planning to remarry as soon as he was carried away. The girls brought flowers but Wolf sensed that they were really ashamed of him, that they could not endure the hospital odors, could hardly contain their impatience for the visit to end.

Summer passed with Wolf Unger scarcely aware of it. For Rash Hashanah, Fanny brought him a slice of pineapple over which to recite the *Schehechyonu*, the blessing over the New Year. He did not taste it. Yom Kippur, too, passed unnoticed. Then, during the intermediate days of Succoth, as Wolf Unger lay facing the wall lost in his morose contemplations, the door opened and Dr. Spielfogel entered.

"Pan Unger," he said cheerfully, "would you like to take a drive with me?"

"Where to? The lunatics at Bonifraten?"

"God forbid! I'll bring you back here. It's a surprise."

"What kind of surprise?"

"A pleasant one. You will ride in the coach with me."

The Sister helped Wolf Unger to dress. His shoes had shriveled somewhat, and his clothes hung loosely on his bony frame. He had become unaccustomed to walking and now he descended the steps haltingly, one at a time, supporting himself on the banister. Outside, an autumnal sun was shining but the sky was heavy with massing clouds. Wolf Unger eased himself slowly into the coach, followed by Dr. Spielfogel. The coach rolled on rubber wheels along the Warsaw thoroughfares that Wolf Unger had known so well, but already everything seemed alien—the passersby, the trolleys, the stores.

"Where are they all going?" Wolf Unger asked himself. "To their own funerals?"

All at once the coach drove into the street where Wolf Unger had begun to build. The doctor signaled the coachman to stop. Wolf Unger peered out. It took a while for him to recognize the site. The first story had already been completed, and work was under way on the second! A scaffold stood out sharply against the sky. Laborers carried pallets of bricks on their backs. The incessant trundling of vehicles mingled with the overall clanging and hammering and the animated cries of the workmen. The openings for the doors and windows formed a checkerboard of empty spaces. Over the maze of braces and beams masons crawled like acrobats, calling to each other in words that Wolf Unger could not decipher and that put him in mind of the building of the Tower of Babel.

Standing on a mound in the dust was Fanny, tall, broad-shouldered, a feather in her hat, surrounded by a group of men. She was issuing commands with the indisputable authority of possession, pointing now with her right hand, now with the left.

"What do you say to that?" Dr. Spielfogel remarked. "They are building your houses."

Wolf Unger could only stare wordlessly. How had she managed it? How had she been able to redress the deficit? Where had she obtained fresh capital? And, above all, how on earth did she know anything at all about building? She had never evinced any interest in his affairs, but never! It was all a riddle, but one which Wolf Unger felt no need to resolve. What did it matter, in any case? So another brick wall or two would stand in Warsaw. The thought occurred to him that wives only begin to live after their husbands die.

A wind blew up and a column of dust fell from the massive framework. The sun retreated behind a cloud and the light became diffused, taking on the darkening bluish cast of twilight. Through the hazy coach window and the swirling dust, everything was blurred, evanescent, half-erased, like a picture on a canvas. The scaffold seemed to Wolf Unger like a giant spider's web clotted with imprisoned insects. The voices became muted. It all seemed like a dream, or rather, as though a parable in an old morality tract had come momentarily to life. He remembered once reading about a swarm of demons in a desert, whereas in reality everything was desolate, a mirage.

He heard Dr. Spielfogel ask: "You don't marvel at all this?"

"No."

"You don't want to talk with your wife?"

"Why?"

"This is a mistake," Dr. Spielfogel said in a tired voice. "In this world it is insane to be sane."

Dr. Spielfogel leaned back and closed his eyes; it was difficult to tell whether he was awake or had dozed off. His cigar dimmed and grew to a long ash. In the front seat the driver, shoulders hunched, sat immobile. Wolf Unger reached out his hand and drew the curtain in place over the window. The horse looked back for a moment; then it turned and its head dropped with that awareness animals sometimes share with humans.

The Painting

For nearly four years I listened to scores of stories as counselor to readers of my newspaper and also to fans of the Yiddish hour over the radio. Many men and women came to me to open their hearts and confide their secrets to me. As long as I changed their names, they said, I could make use of their experiences in my writings. This particular woman telephoned me and asked me to come to her house. She spoke Polish. She said she was lame and almost blind. She lived in the Bronx on Rochambeau Avenue. I promised to visit her but kept on delaying. One day she gave me a polite ultimatum: if I did not come that week, I would never hear her fascinating story. We arranged a time. On a summer afternoon I took the "D" train to the 205th Street Station. I walked up three flights of steps—there was no elevator—and rang the doorbell. For a long time there was not the slightest sound. Then the door opened and I saw a little, old woman, supporting herself on crutches padded in red felt. She wore sunglasses. Her hair was white and arranged in a bun. I entered a living room which boasted an old-fashioned European elegance. The couch was covered in black velvet. Some pictures hung on the walls. There were many flower pots, a glass bookcase, and a piano on which stood three candlesticks. A Chinese carpet covered the floor. The woman began to talk to me in English, but soon switched to Polish. Her speech, her dress and her whole demeanor were proof that she belonged to a different class from my usual readers. She had prepared refreshments. She indicated a rocker for me to sit on. Suppressing her groans, she herself sat down with difficulty in an armchair, and rested her feet on a hassock.

"Do you live here by yourself?" I asked.

She answered in a voice that displayed a masculine firmness: "Yes. I didn't want to live in an old age home."

"Do you ever go out?"

"Only several times a year. God has blessed me with good neighbors." After a pause she said: "My husband was a painter. All the pictures in this room are his."

I took a look at them. They were all landscapes. Mounted in carved, heavy frames, the gilt peeling, they seemed to have been painted a hundred years ago. I said:

"He was an academic painter."

"That's right. And stubborn too. When we came to America in 1921, the world raged with modernistic trends in art: Expressionism, Cubism, Surrealism. But Felix, my husband, would not acknowledge the new art forms. He was still waging war on Impressionism. He was a remarkable portrait painter—in the bedroom there are some paintings he did of me and my parents. But it took him months to paint a portrait, sometimes as long as a year, and Americans don't have the patience to pose that long.

"My husband studied at the Academy of Art in Crakow. His father was a physician. He was an assimilated Jew, and many members of his family had been baptized. I am telling you all this because, unless you know the background, you won't understand my story.

"I was born in Warsaw. My father was a railroad engineer—also an assimilated Jew. But he knew Yiddish. I did not learn the Yiddish language until I came here. In the summer of 1914 my parents and I traveled to Karlsbad. My mother suffered from a liver ailment. We stayed in Paris for a while and even stopped briefly in Scotland. World War I broke out when we arrived in Vienna. As Russian citizens we were interned by the Austrians. Then my father managed to convince them that he was no Russian patriot. They released us and we settled in Crakow. The Austrians were building railroads in occupied Poland for military purposes, perhaps also to supply the local population with work. My father was especially useful to them as he spoke Polish and Yiddish. He rarely came home. My mother was a famous beauty, but my father liked women, and I am sorry to say he was not very discriminating. Once, when I was seven, I saw him kissing our peasant maid Stasha. He made me swear that I would never tell mother. She knew about his carryings-on anyway. Now that my father spent months at a time away from home, he did as he pleased.

"In Warsaw I had gone to a Polish-Russian *Gymnasium*. All subjects had to be taught in Russian, but the spirit of our education was essentially Polish. Religion was taught in school, and when the priest entered the classroom, the few of us that were Jewish left. When we came to Crakow, I was enrolled in the seventh grade of a Polish *Gymnasium*. In Warsaw you had to know Russian. Here we studied German. I became quite a linguist. Forgive me for telling my story in this haphazard way. I'll come to the point soon."

"Tell it any way you want to."

"In Crakow we lived in the same building as my husband's parents. His father was a doctor. They had a large and elegantly furnished apartment. Ours was small and modest, since we were refugees from Russia. It was unavoidable that I'd get to know Felix. I was an only child and so was he. He was a handsome youth with ruddy cheeks and blue eyes—blond, tall and slim, a real Apollo. I am now a crippled old woman, but at that time I was young and people thought me pretty. I was immensely interested in literature. That was, and has remained my passion. I couldn't survive a day without books. I eat and sleep with them beside me. What a privilege it is to have the great minds of all ages in your house! I always bless Gutenberg for inventing the printing press. Since I learned to read in Yiddish, I read your writings in the original, and believe me—"

The telephone rang. I helped the woman get up and handed her the crutches. It was the grocery store calling. I took another look at her husband's paintings and the room. It was hard to believe that this maimed woman could keep it so clean. She must be a person of strong will and used to discipline, I thought. I regretted having put off my visit so long. When she sat down again, she said:

"Well, shortly after we became close, he was drafted. He should have been in the army earlier, but he had broken his wrist. I need not tell you that our love was pure. In those days a girl from a good family hesitated a long time before she let a young man kiss her. We talked about books, poetry and art. Even when he took me to a museum my mother came along as chaperone. My black hair was braided, and I had black eyes. Now they've lost their color. And these wrinkles! Time demolishes the body, and occasionally the soul too.

"During the short period of our close relationship, I got to know his character: he was completely withdrawn. He had no friends, and sharply criticized his professors. This handsome young man was wretchedly lonely. His mother complained that he never left the house on weekends. His father scarcely spoke to him. Suddenly he was forced to go to the barracks. I realized that this would be a heavy blow for him. At first he wrote his parents and me very short letters, never more than a few lines. Then he stopped writing altogether.

"I forgot to tell you that his father was also inducted. He was given the rank of colonel. He was unusually tall, erect and stern. The few times he came home to Crakow on leave, he would enter the house and instantly open the windows, no matter how freezing it was outside. He lifted weights and did all sorts of exercises. In this respect Felix was like his father. In fact, they were like two drops of water. Perhaps that's why they couldn't get along.

"In 1919, Felix's father contracted typhus fever and died. His mother went mad and had to be institutionalized. Since she was a doctor's widow and had some funds, she was sent to a private hospital.

"After the Versailles Treaty was signed in 1919, my parents returned to Warsaw. But the town wasn't the same. Another family had moved into our apartment and our furniture had been stolen. Some months later Felix followed us. Although the Poles now governed it, Warsaw was still Russian to Felix, and he couldn't bear the atmosphere there. I forgot to tell you that he had been taken prisoner by the Russians and not released until some time after the Bolshevik Revolution in 1917. Actually he escaped. He came back a totally changed man— aged, depressed. Our love had evaporated, and to this day I don't know why I married him. Maybe because I loved no one else. My mother died in 1920, and soon after my father married a Gentile woman with three grown-up daughters.

"Between Felix's return from prison camp and our marriage and departure for America, I got to know him better. He painted but would not exhibit his pictures. Nor did he try to sell them. He had come to hate modern art, and looked upon all contemporary artists as criminals. Once when we visited a gallery he spat at a painting; there was a scuffle. You can imagine how shamed I felt. He couldn't and wouldn't control himself. He voiced all his criticisms of the new Poland and was almost jailed. He hated the Bolsheviks, in fact all Russians, with every fiber of his being. Though a Jew himself, he talked like an anti-Semite. He also turned out to be a woman hater. All in all, he was a bundle of "anti's." To marry him meant laying my healthy head on a sick pillow, as the saying goes. It is characteristic of Felix that he would not go to bed with me till we were man and wife. I was partially liberated from my strict upbringing. I had read Gabriela Zapolska and other writers like her. We had soaked up Marguerite and Dekobra, and also serious Russian authors like Alexander Blok, Mayakovsky, and Yessenin. I, for one, was enthusiastic about Chagall, and Felix and I often quarreled about him. My father had warned me that it would be suicide to marry Felix. But I couldn't leave him, nor was there anyone else to live with. I no longer recall how he obtained a visa to the United States. Even then it was hard to get one, although the open-door policy was still in effect.

"We traveled third class. The boat trip was far from comfortable. Felix was sea-sick and talked constantly of suicide. Where sex was concerned he was as odd and inhibited as in many other ways. The room had to be pitch dark, and he wouldn't let me say a single word. Sex was something dirty and sinful to him. It may seem funny for an old, crippled woman to talk about this, but it's a necessary part of my story. I myself was just the opposite. Well, that's how he was, and I couldn't change him. He looked upon all his peculiarities and eccentricities as eternal truths or divine commandments. If his taste in tea was different from somebody else's, he thought him an enemy.

"Coming to the United States was the greatest catastrophe for my husband. We had a little money when we arrived, and rented an apartment in Greenwich Village. From the very start he cursed America and everything it represented. He began planning to settle in British Columbia or Australia, although we couldn't even afford to go to Chicago. He bought paints and canvas and started on a still life. But I knew that no one would care about his glazed-looking bananas and apples.

"I had to go to work, and got a job as private nurse to the crippled old mother of a millionaire. She remembered some Polish, but preferred to speak Yiddish, and so I learned it from her. As she was nearly blind, I had to read the Yiddish paper to her—the one you write for. I learned quickly, and since then I don't think I've missed reading it a single day. I read Sholem Asch, Jonah Rosenfeld, later your brother, finally you. The Yiddish newspapers opened up new horizons for me. I found out a lot about Yiddish culture and Jewish life in the United States and also in the Soviet Union. In those days your paper was solidly socialist, at times even inclined towards communism. Dozens of articles appeared about Emma Goldman and free love. Nothing like this was printed in the American newspapers or magazines.

"Now I'll come to the point of my story. In the late twenties, the old woman I nursed died. She had promised to remember me in her will, but didn't leave me a penny. Felix was earning nothing. I tried working at a milliner's. First I was insulted, then dismissed. I looked for work in a factory, but realized the very first day that I'd rather die than go back. The heat, the stench, the coarse talk, all the vulgarity!

"My husband had always kept a rifle and a pistol in the house. He had a persecution complex and was afraid of robbers and murderers. If our plight ever became unbearable, he said, he would shoot us both. He'd bought a parrot, and would finish him off too. Then, suddenly, Wall Street crashed and the depression followed. There were no jobs at all now. We were literally starving. In the midst of all this heaven sent us an angel. What else can I call him? He was a Polish Jew who had owned an art gallery in Berlin for many years. His first name was Sigmund, actually Zaynvyl—he came from a Hassidic family in Warsaw. He was one of those perceptive people who foresaw the Nazi calamity years earlier. He had come to the conclusion that Germany would either go fascist like Italy, or communist. A number of Jews had done shabby things during the inflation of the twenties—bought up whole blocks of houses, and got involved in all sorts of financial speculations. Hitler had already made his *Putsch* and was railing against the Jews. So Sigmund emigrated to America and opened an art gallery on Third Avenue in New York City. He had a hard time of it, though he had no children to provide for. His wife got a job as a dress buyer in a department store. She was a capable but cold woman, and only interested in making money. She made up his losses in the gallery. Later on she became partner in a dress business.

"What happened was that Sigmund heard about my husband and became an immediate admirer of his. In fact, he was the only person in the whole world who appreciated Felix and even considered him a genius. He began to exhibit his paintings and do publicity for him. Not that it helped. The few times his work was shown, the critics panned it. They called it trite, old-fashioned, hackneyed—in short, 'academic.' Felix swore he'd never exhibit his paintings again and kept his oath. Yet, once in a while, Sigmund succeeded in selling a picture of his. He never took any commission; in fact, he often added money of his own. His wife disliked both Felix and me. She was jealous of me. She urged Sigmund to break off with us; if he didn't, she threatened to divorce him. But Sigmund was as stubborn as my husband."

"He had fallen in love with you, hadn't he?"

"Yes. I never believed anything like that could happen to me. But Felix and I were so totally different by nature. Weeks, sometimes months went by without his saying one nice word to me. If I asked him a question, he'd answer in a way that made further conversation impossible. I shall never know all his thoughts during all those years. Maybe he didn't think at all. His whole life had become a long and bitter silence.

"I said before that I had learned Yiddish by reading Yiddish newspapers. That's not quite true. You can't learn a language merely by reading it. I talked to Sigmund in Yiddish simply because he knew no other language properly. He had lived in Germany for years, yet his German was atrocious. Though he was born in Poland, he couldn't speak Polish. He was in business here and gave parties for American critics, but his English was full of mistakes. When I heard him ruin all these languages, I started talking Yiddish to him. It was the tongue he felt most at home in. What he looked like? He was short, thin and bald—the exact opposite of my husband. But he had one great quality: enthusiasm. If someone or something pleased him, he'd be wildly delighted. He would actually start dancing on those short legs of his, and clap his hands like a child. If anyone ever rubbed him the wrong way, he would cry and have a tantrum.

"His wife was a snob. She never forgave him for being a Polish Jew. She came from a rich family in Koenigsberg. She got to know another buyer called Alschwanger at her place of business, and was having an affair with him. Whenever one of them went to Paris, the other went along. Later they went into business together and she divorced Sigmund. They became millionaires. Now they are both dead.

"Meanwhile Sigmund had transferred his enthusiasm from my husband to me. I never imagined a man could love so ardently. He saw virtues in me that I had never dreamed of. His behavior was so bizarre that I sometimes feared he would go out of his mind. As time passed I became aware of the bitter truth: I wasn't the only woman he loved. This dwarf of a man was a real Don Juan. When I found out later about his carryings-on, I wanted to leave him. It was too late. He had awakened instincts and feelings that must have been dormant in me. After all, I too come of Polish Jewish stock. He kissed and fondled me for hours on end, and said the wildest things imaginable. When a man falls in love with another man's wife, he usually tries to belittle the husband. This was not true of Sigmund. He continued to rave about my husband's paintings. He admired us both.

"When our affair first started I resisted. The effort almost killed me. I'd been brought up to be a faithful wife. To me romance was linked with faithfulness unto death. I had told Felix that Sigmund was too attentive to me, and expected him to break off with him in spite of all he'd done for us. I was amazed to see that Felix didn't take it seriously. He listened to me and waved his hand. After a while Sigmund suggested that I go to work for him as his 'receptionist.' I thought Felix would become violent. But he agreed instantly. I decided then that he no longer needed me, and this drove me into Sigmund's arms.

"As hardly anyone ever came into Sigmund's art gallery, we were alone almost all day. You wouldn't believe this, but in all those years Felix never once 'phoned me at the gallery. Nor did he ever reproach me for coming home late. He stopped making love to me. Dead silence reigned in our house. I was sure that he knew what was going on between Sigmund and me but didn't care. Sigmund still visited us occasionally, always bringing gifts: cognac, caviar, all kinds of cakes and cheeses. If Felix had painted a new picture, he would loudly proclaim that this one would make him famous at last. Felix was a little more talkative with Sigmund. He would tell him anecdotes from his prisoner-of-war days in Russia. Roosevelt was president, and Felix became his worst enemy. He could have had work now with the WPA, but he claimed this was begging and Bolshevism, and compared Roosevelt to Stalin.

"During one of Sigmund's visits Felix said that the only man who could save the world from doom was Hitler. My limbs went ice cold. Sigmund started saying that he must be joking. He even tried to laugh, but Felix said:

"'I'm no comedian. I mean it seriously.'

"'Do you know that Hitler plans to kill all the Jews?' Sigmund asked him.

"'Yes, I know.'

"'You'd be one of them. Hitler wants to conquer the earth.'

"'Sure.'

"'And yet you agree with him?'

"'Yes.'

"Sigmund's mouth gaped in disbelief. I got up and said: 'Felix, I've taken a lot from you, but this is the end. I'm leaving you right now.'

"'Where are you going? To him?' he asked.

"'Yes.'

"'He's your lover, isn't he?'

"'Yes.'

"These moments will be etched in my memory till I die. Felix was always so serious, the image of the stern father. All of a sudden an unbelievably sweet smile spread across his face. Now he resembled his mother. Slowly he walked to the telephone and with one jerk tore the cord out of the wall. Smiling all the time, he opened a drawer and took out a pistol. I realized I was done for. I glanced at Sigmund. He was white as chalk. He mumbled: 'It's a lie, it's all a lie. We're just friends.'

"His mouth was twisted; he had become terribly ugly. I never knew a face could be so ugly. Then Felix said: 'I could finish you both off. My own life is worthless to me. But if you do as I say, I'll let you both live. You can even get married if you want to. If you don't do as I say though, you'll be dead in a minute.'

" 'What do you want me to do?' I asked.

" 'Get undressed and make love in front of me. I want to paint you. That will be my last picture.'

"Sigmund had lost his powers of speech. 'Felix,' I said, 'no one can make love at the point of a gun.'

" 'Take your clothes off, this instant! I'll count to ten: one . . .'

"Up to this point I thought I was brave. I had always said to myself that when my turn came I would die with dignity. But when you're faced with the barrel of a gun, you become a coward. I began to undress. I could see that Sigmund seemed paralyzed, and so I helped him get undressed too. He had sat down on the floor. I bent down and pulled his shoes and clothes off. His body was cold and clammy."

The old woman hid her face in her hands. She started trembling and sobbing. A clock ticked away in another room. After a while she looked up. In that short space of time her face had become unrecognizable; it was shrunken and bluish. Large sacks had sprung up under her eyes. I was afraid she might die there and then and said:

"Please compose yourself."

"Yes, I'll go to the bathroom."

I handed her the crutches. She limped, moaning to the bathroom and stayed there a long while. When she came back, I helped her into her chair. She had powdered her face and applied lipstick. She murmured: "Thank you. Forgive me."

"Did he really paint you like that?" I asked.

"I have it here. I'll show it to you. You'll be the first to see it. And the last too. I don't want it to remain behind after my death." She told me to open a drawer of her sideboard. In it was a sort of scroll packed in brown paper. I unwrapped it and found a dried up, cracked canvas, which I slowly unrolled. I expected a realistic painting, but my first impression was all smudges. It took a while before I could identify any figures. I walked to the window to see better. A naked man and woman lay face to face. They looked like two corpses in a morgue. Sigmund's head had almost no features, just a pointed skull, a daub where the eye should have been, his mouth like a hole, a twisted little neck, and two exaggeratedly large feet—all of it clear white on a black background. The woman had abnormally large hips and breasts. How strange, Felix had done a modernistic painting, in spite of himself. The limbs were painted mockingly, to emphasize the man's impotence and the woman's sexual ugliness. The canvas exuded a foul smell, the stagnant stench of something dug up from a grave. I said to the old woman:

"How long did it take him to do this?"

"I don't know. Several hours. It seemed like an eternity."

"Such a painting might cause quite a stir."

"What? No, I don't want it to survive. While he painted, the loaded pistol lay next to him. I was sure he would murder us as soon as he'd finished. Sigmund was more dead than alive. I thought he would die on the spot, but he lived in torment for another ten months. So actually Felix did kill him that day. As for me, I was destined to suffer on all these years. All my ills are the result of those hours. First I developed rheumatic pains that crippled me. Then I contracted glaucoma. I have no vision at all in my right eye. My left one is gradually going dark too."

"What happened then?"

"He went out without a word. He left behind nearly all his clothes and even the painting. He disappeared, and I thought I would never hear of him again. Three years later I was notified that he had committed suicide in California. They had found my address among his belongings. I wanted to destroy this picture right away, but some inner voice told me to wait. I wrapped it up and never looked at it again. You are the first and last person to hear this terrible story."

"Would you like to look at the picture now?" I asked.

The old woman shook her head. "No, my friend, once is enough. What was the point of such a painting? And why did he leave it here? It would have been far nobler of him to shoot us both that day. Since then I have had a great deal of time to brood about it, but I don't know to this day why he did it. I often had the urge to tell someone my story, but to whom? The people I come in contact with wouldn't have understood. When I started reading you, the thought occurred to me that you were the person I could tell. But years went by before I decided to call you. I don't know what happened to Felix in those three years, nor why he took his life. I committed a sin against him and regret it but, as God is my witness, he drove me to it. He did not say a single word to us the entire time we lay there naked that cold spring day. I begged and pleaded with him to end the nightmare, but he would not answer."

"Shall I put the painting back?" I asked.

"No, I want to destroy it, but don't know how. In my old home we had a furnace. There's no such thing in this building. And I can't throw it into the garbage can. After all, it's tied in with three lives." She was silent. Then she asked:

"Do you really believe in life after death?"

"Sometimes."

"I wish I could. All these lonely years I've tried to talk to Sigmund, or to the part of him that maybe lingers on when the body is no longer here. But I've had no sign. The dead are silent; that's why death is such an enigma. And God is silent too. Perhaps man is the only one in the universe that talks . . . Do you have an incinerator in your building?"

"Yes."

"Do me a favor: take the painting and throw it in. Forgive me for imposing on you, but I can't ask anyone else. And—I know one can't forbid a writer to tell a story if he's intrigued by it. But if you write it up, please change the names."

"Yes, of course I shall."

"How do you explain what's happened to me?"

"There is no explanation. If twenty-six letters can yield as many books as can fill the void between the earth and the sun, how many combinations are possible with countless genes?"

"Yes, that's true. Felix was a product of heredity. Sometimes when he talked to me I could hear his father's voice."

I said goodbye to the old woman. She kissed me with cold lips. I went home intending to throw the picture into the incinerator, but I still haven't done so. It's in one of my drawers and I look at it occasionally. Each time I discover something new in it.

The woman has since died. I've tried calling her, but her number has been disconnected. Her name no longer appears in the telephone directory. There is probably nothing left of her except this accursed canvas, these faded colors painted by a perverse hand to take revenge on itself, on the world, on love. Sometimes, when I am in despair, I take out the old piece of canvas and look at it. I can see it decaying. I hear it rustling. I smell its rot. Eye-sockets grin and mouth cavities sneer at me. On this evil canvas death is alive.

Translated by Shulamith Charney

Morris and Timna

M Y GOOD FRIEND, Morris Kalushiner, the Yiddish poet and proofreader on the newspaper where I was a staff member, died as quietly as he had lived. The funeral was held in mid-week in some forsaken section of Brooklyn, and was attended by no more than a half-score mourners including his few relations. He had left a will designating that he be cremated. Among the ten present was a man I was sure I had once known—even been close to—but I had been overcome by an amnesia and under no circumstances could I recall who he was. His hair was white, but I was sure that it had been black or brown when I had known him. His face was quite youthful, his tall figure erect. He was elegantly dressed. Was he an actor who had once played a lover on the Yiddish stage? My grief over Morris Kalushiner's demise grew mixed with a feeling of shame over my deteriorating memory. After the ceremony, the stranger came over, took my hand, and pressed it with a strength of a young man and said:

"So, our Morris is no more. . . ."

The voice rang familiar; I had undoubtedly heard it many times before. I stood still and the other regarded me with a half-perplexed, half-regretful stare.

"I'm afraid you don't recognize me," he said.

"That's the bitter truth," I admitted.

"Nathan. Nathan Komarov. Remember me?"

The words came like a slap in my face. Nathan Komarov had been a friend of mine, a playwright with whom I had once even tried to write a comedy.

After a while, I said, "Morris's death disconcerted me so, I wouldn't have recognized my own father."

"Well, the years do their part, too," he said. "As you see, I've gone completely white. You're lucky—you have no hair. Come, let's have a cup of coffee."

As I glanced at Nathan Komarov once again, this time it appeared that he hadn't changed much. Some twenty years before, Nathan Komarov had stopped writing plays for the

Yiddish theater and had gone into business with a brother. He had moved away from New York. Someone had told me that he had married a millionaire's widow who was a lot older than he, a grandmother of grown children. He had—as they say—slammed the door behind him. He was no longer seen at the Café Royal nor at Yiddishist affairs. Incredibly enough, an impeccably dressed chauffeur opened a Cadillac door for us. We got in and Nathan Komarov told the chauffeur to drive us to the Russian Tea Room.

He said, "I've wanted to phone or write you I don't know how many times, but it never went beyond that. But I do read some of your scribblings. You're my contact with the past. I did, however, keep in touch with Morris. You have enough friends without me, but he lived out his final years virtually alone. He even came to my house in Westchester a few times. My wife simply idolized him. She is already ashes too."

"I'm sorry. When did it happen?" I asked.

"About a year and a half ago. She was everything to me—wife, mother, sister. Well, but that's how it is, that's how your God wants it, the one with Whom you wage a private war. I've never had any dealings with Him because I've always known that He doesn't exist."

I was in no mood to get into a discussion. We sat silently while Nathan smoked a cigarette. It was already past the lunch hour, and the Russian Tea Room was half-empty. We ate blintzes and drank coffee. Nathan Komarov began talking about Morris Kalushiner.

"He suffered his life away. Decided once and for all to have nothing to do with doctors. He might still be alive today if he had agreed to an operation. On the other hand, what would he have gained? This world of ours is a nightmare. Morris knew this and he actually committed suicide, but gradually, in installments. He flung back to God all His gifts—health, career, love, sex, everything, everything. A few years ago you said in an interview that the essence of religion is a protest against the higher powers. Morris embodied the protest of life against the divine violence, the divine indifference, the divine amorality. It's my theory that the Jew has borne this kind of protest throughout his whole history, yet at the same time he is a hedonist. When hedonism and protest come together, the result is madness. The last time we ate blintzes was at the Café Royal. It was also after a funeral. Remember?"

"No," I said.

Nathan Komarov quoted a verse from a poet, "Old people die young."

Abruptly, he asked, "Do you know about Morris's platonic affair with the granddaughter of an English lord?"

"A granddaughter of a lord?" I questioned.

"In that case, if you don't remember it, he wasn't as close to you as he was to me," Nathan Komarov said.

"I know he corresponded with some woman in England and that he sent her presents, but he never told me that she was of the aristocracy."

"For years he didn't know it himself. I've forgotten her last name already, I only remember her first—Timna. That, as you know, is a biblical name. Why her father chose this name for her, I actually don't know. Maybe he opened his Bible and happened upon it. The lord's son died young and left a half-crazy son and this Timna. On the only trip Morris made to Europe since coming to America, he spent a week in England. It must have been in '36. He flew from Glasgow to London and opposite him sat two women—a young one and an older one. He heard the old one call the other: Timna. As you know, our Morris was, for all his asceticism, an incurable romantic and he fell desperately in love with this young woman. Or maybe he fell in love with her name. Another in his place would have tried to strike up an acquaintance but Morris was too shy for something like this. After he came back to America this Timna preyed on his mind to such a degree that he wrote her in care of the airline asking them to forward the letter to a passenger whose first name was Timna and who had taken the Glasgow-to-London flight on this and this date. You know, after all, what an eager correspondent Morris was. Although I don't believe in miracles, I must admit that the fact that the airline officials bothered to trace the list of passengers to forward the letter to this Timna represents a kind of miracle. This was undoubtedly a letter full of admiration for her beauty or whatever it was Morris saw in her, because it led to a correspondence between them that lasted until his end. I know this because the last time I called Morris I asked him if he had heard from Timna and he told me that he had just received a letter from her. I'm sure that he left hundreds of letters from her lying around somewhere. This Timna must already be in her late fifties, but when I met her in 1949 she was still young and almost pretty."

"You met her?" I asked.

"Yes, I met her."

"Where? In England?"

"No, right here in New York."

"Well, that *is* a surprise."

"You'll really be surprised after you've heard the whole story."

"I thought Morris had no secrets from me," I said.

"I'll order some more coffee."

We drank coffee and Nathan Komarov asked: "What did Morris tell you about this Timna?"

"Not much. I knew he was corresponding with some woman in England, but he never told me her name. Actually, he corresponded with women in half the world. It was my impression that she considered herself a medium or something of that sort," I said.

"Perhaps, it had to do with that too. In her letters to Morris she never mentioned her background. It seemed her father had already lost his fortune. He was an impoverished aristocrat and after he died, there was nothing left. Timna had to move in with some grand-aunt in the country. The grand-aunt was a rich old woman, half-deaf and half-blind, and Timna read sentimental novels and occult magazines to her, cooked for her, and literally attended her like a servant. Of course, Timna remained an old maid. Unless I'm mistaken the aunt is still alive or she just recently died. She had to be a hundred years old. I don't know why, but for some reason I became intrigued by this lengthy correspondence between two people who had never exchanged a word and of whom only one, Morris, had caught a brief glimpse of the other. Morris wasn't content to merely write—he promptly began to send presents. He considered me something of a worldly person, and he always consulted with me on what to buy her. I'm sure you know that Morris spent half his earnings on presents. I've forgotten the main thing—Timna surely doesn't know what's happened to Morris and she is probably waiting for his letter right now. I'll have to get in touch with her. Maybe he left manuscripts too, although in recent years he had stopped writing poetry.

"Before I tell you the whole story I want to say—you probably know this yourself—that in addition to Morris's countless other idiosyncracies he was also afflicted with an aversion to being photographed. As far as I know, the only photograph that exists of him is the one on his passport when he went to Europe. In his own fashion, Morris was vain. He couldn't accept his shortness, the fact that his back was stooped—he considered himself a hunchback. The truth is that in his own way, he wasn't bad-looking. He had unusually handsome eyes with long eyelashes like a girl's. His nose had been broken by some hooligan while he was a boy in Poland, but his mouth was interesting in my opinion and he wouldn't have been ugly if he hadn't had such a dislike of dentists. For a time, Morris would show me the letters he received from this Timna and in each one she asked again that he send her a photograph of himself. But he never did. I remember that in one letter she wrote: 'Even if, God forbid, you only have one eye or nose, believe me you'd be just as dear to me as if you had three eyes or two noses!' I was annoyed with Morris that he didn't oblige her.

"I wanted to take him to a photographer who could make an Apollo out of him, but he argued: 'What for? So that she should come to me later and see the truth?' Timna sent him several photos of herself. She was pretty although not a beauty.

"Thus, the few years preceding the war went by and then—the war years came. Timna often reiterated that she wanted to come to America to see Morris, but her aunt was literally helpless and Timna had no one to stay with her. She asked Morris to come to England but, as you know, first he began to suffer from Parkinson's disease or whatever it was, and later he stopped leaving his apartment altogether. This one too was destined to remain a love affair in name only, just like all his other loves.

"Now listen to this. In 1949 I got a call from Morris and as he started talking I sensed that some catastrophe had befallen him. He stuttered, gasped, and literally choked on every word.

I was frightened. I thought he had suffered a heart attack or
who knows what. After all this, it turned out that Timna was
coming to New York. Not permanently—just for a short visit.
Some relative or a former girl friend had turned up in San
Francisco and another relative in England had agreed to look
after the old woman for a few weeks. The main thing was—
Timna was coming. I said to him: 'So why are you so upset?
This is liable to be a turn for the better in your life.'

"But he said, 'Nathan, I'll have to flee New York and you
know how hard this would be for me.' 'Why flee?' I asked and
he said: 'I never want to show myself to her. I'll go someplace
and hide even if I know this will mean my life!'

"I never imagined that Morris—the stoic and fatalist—
would go so crazy. I'll cut it short—he wanted nothing more
or less but that I should impersonate him, and pose as Morris
Kalushiner to Timna! He said: 'I wouldn't care what happened. You can even sleep with her. You've got to save me!'

"I said: 'What do you need me for? If you don't want to see
her, take a room in a hotel here in New York so it would
appear you've gone out of town.'

"But Morris said: 'This would be too bitter a disappointment for her. She's actually coming here on my account.'

"I want to tell you something. Until that time, I had had no
inkling that Morris was inclined toward homosexuality. But his
remark that I could make love to her aroused my suspicions
that he was a latent homosexual. This explained many of the
questions that had bothered me concerning him. He sounded
so desperate I was afraid he'd get a real heart attack. At that
time I was still a bachelor although I already knew Mary, my
wife-to-be, and after lengthy discussion I agreed to do as he
asked. Morris actually said that he would commit suicide if I
didn't help him. Such a blend of hysteria, egotism, and who
knows what other madness could exist only in Morris. I must
tell you that I was no less frightened by the whole thing than
he. I'm no actor and was afraid that at our very first meeting
she would sense that I was deceiving her. Besides, such behavior is unethical and against all my convictions. There was still
another complication. At that time I was already in love with
Mary even though my enemies and even my friends are all
convinced that I married her for her money. Mary would

phone me daily and often not once but many times. I couldn't tell her what I was proposing to do since this would have caused a terrible row. I never imagined that Morris—who never asked a favor of anyone but always gave and did favors for others—should demand such a sacrifice from me. I was completely frightened of getting involved in such a mess of lies.

"One of the worst complications consisted of the fact that Timna knew Morris's address and could easily locate his telephone number since he was listed in the directory. Morris, therefore, had to move out of his place and I had to move in for the duration of her visit. Actually, we could have exchanged rooms, but what would Mary say if she phoned and Morris answered? Or if she kept on calling and no one answered? I had to help Morris move to a hotel to give Mary an excuse as to why I was moving into Morris's place. I told her that my ceiling was leaking and that it would take a week to fix it. During all this time I kept pointing out to Morris how foolishly he was behaving and how much better it would be for all concerned if he got up the courage to meet Timna as himself. But he was adamant. Then I realized the incredible power of a neurosis. Morris himself conceded that he was acting irrationally. But he swore to me that some force stronger than he was holding him by the throat and making him do what he did.

"After a while, everything was settled. You know Morris's place. He had thousands of books and a collection of newspapers and magazines dating back to the year he came to America. He wouldn't allow his place to be painted. Every few years the superintendent would come and announce that according to the lease he was obliged to let them paint his apartment, and Morris had to bribe him to forget all about it. Books were stacked against every wall from floor to ceiling.

"A day before Timna's arrival, Morris got a cable asking him to meet her at the airport. I had to put aside all my work to pick her up. I carried a photograph of her in my breast pocket. As it happens in such cases, the plane was two hours late. When I finally saw her I was irritated to the point of hostility. When I introduced myself to her, she shook her head and asked, 'You are Morris Kalushiner?'

" 'Yes, that's me,' I said.

" 'I pictured you altogether different, entirely so . . . ' she said.

" 'How?' I asked and she said: 'Older and not so tall. Why didn't you send your picture?'

"I gathered that she was disappointed. I had been expecting that she would fall into my arms but I had apparently infected her with my indifference and my irritation."

For a moment we were both silent, then Nathan Komarov said: "Wait. I'll get a pack of cigarettes."

We drank more coffee and nibbled along on cheesecake and between one sip and another, Nathan Komarov puffed on a cigarette. He said:

"In the cab, we slowly warmed toward each other. I questioned her and she hesitantly told me about her lineage. A lord's granddaughter, she said. Every Jew comes from rabbis and it seems that every Englishman has a lord somewhere among his ancestors. If you went back far enough, it might even turn out that every Jew stemmed from some lord and perhaps every Englishman had a rabbi for an ancestor."

"What did Timna look like?" I asked.

"I've got a photograph that we took together lying around somewhere. I know what you're after. No, I didn't sleep with her. First of all, she wasn't what you would call my type. Too thin, too tall, too civilized. My women were all short and a trifle plump. We talked a blue streak and babbled all kind of nonsense. It seems to me that Timna knew Shakespeare and a good half of all of English literature by heart. She was forever quoting poets, and not only the English but French, German and even Chinese. Who wants to go to bed with an encyclopedia?

"But wait, you haven't heard the whole story. She had a reservation in a hotel on the East Side and I took her there. Then we had lunch. Morris had me swear a holy vow to give him an accounting of all my expenditures, but I knew that he didn't have a penny. After I had finished questioning her, she politely questioned me. Being almost as familiar with Morris's biography as my own, I told her that I came from Kalushin to America at the beginning of the 1920's, and that I was a proofreader and copyreader for a Yiddish newspaper. She already knew all this from Morris's letters but it still took me a long time to explain to her that Yiddish wasn't Hebrew and that a Yiddish newspaper didn't necessarily have to be religious. That there can be such a creature as a worldly Jew is a notion the gentile brain can under no circumstances accept. Yes, I also had to play the vegetarian and as she ordered roast chicken I had to be content with a plate of vegetables. She kept raising her watery blue eyes and looking at me with surprise and suspicion. It was obvious that both my face and my manner of speaking denied the mental image she had formed of Morris Kalushiner.

"She said: 'Morris, I still can't understand why you would never send me your picture. I asked you for it so many times. I started to believe you must be some kind of monster. Actually you almost look English.'

"I knew that I was about to commit a folly, but I said: 'I'm sorry to disappoint you but I have a friend, a Yiddish writer, who might sooner fit your mental concept of me.' I quickly made up some name and began to describe Morris to her. She grew instantly intrigued. She said to me: 'Can you introduce me to this friend of yours?'

"'Maybe,' I replied, 'if he is in New York. Sometimes he goes out of town to lecture.'

"'Is he married?' she asked and I said: 'No, he's an old bachelor. He lives somewhere in a hotel.'

"Since I could play Morris's part, I thought, why couldn't he play the part of some other person? I was convinced Morris was dying to meet her, but was too shy to identify himself with what he had written in all his letters."

"What happened? Did you bring them together?" I asked.

"No, I did not."

"Why not?"

"After lunch, I telephoned Morris at the hotel and gave him a full account, but when I proposed my idea to him he grew terribly nervous and began to shout: 'No, no! Don't you dare!'

"I had to tell her that my friend was out of town. I could see that Timna was making every effort to warm up to me just as I was trying—since I was playing the role anyhow—to do likewise, but some force prevented it. I had a fleeting feeling that a part of Morris—his soul or his astral body, call it what you will—wouldn't permit it.

"I took her back to the hotel after lunch and she invited me into her room, but I made up some excuse and left. The next day, I met her for lunch again. We talked so long into the afternoon that it became time for dinner. The following day, she left for California to see a friend.

"I called Morris to tell him that Timna had left New York. He demanded a detailed story of our time together. 'What did you eat for lunch? What were the subjects of your conversation? Did you go to her room?' he asked. I knew what information he wanted. I could have fooled him and told him we had enjoyed a passionate affair. But no. First of all, I didn't want to feed Morris any lies. Secondly, after a while their correspondence was bound to be resumed and her letters would have refuted any lies I might have told him."

"She never married?" I asked.

"Never."

For a long time we sat there in silence, each preoccupied with his own thoughts. Then I asked:

"Did she stop in New York again on her way back from San Francisco?"

"No, she flew home over Canada," Nathan said.

"Did Morris ever show you her letters after she went back to England?"

"Yes, a few."

"Then you didn't kill their love?"

"No. At first the letters were somewhat disjointed and full of insinuations about her astonishment or disappointment with me. But gradually everything returned to normal."

"What would have been if Morris hadn't hidden from her and met her for real?" I asked.

"Everything would have probably come out the same."

"Now someone will have to let her know that Morris died," I said. "Unless of course you go to England and carry on where Morris supposedly left off and begin the whole affair all over again."

Translated by the author and Duba Desowitz

Two

AFTER the taxi driver had been promised $25 plus a five dollar tip he became silent. The two passengers were silent, too.

David Melnitz crammed his frail shape into a corner of the cab. He was dozing lightly, but every once in a while he opened one eye and looked through the window. The summer night had a blackness which nothing could lighten. Street lamps, headlights, lit-up windows made the darkness even denser. For a moment the air smelled to him of forests and in the next of gasoline, oil, melting asphalt and something American which the European nose can never identify. The taxi went over a bridge, through a tunnel and past a garish restaurant with richly covered tables, waiters in frock coats, men in tuxedos and women in evening dresses. Then it vanished like a mirage and the taxi rolled by a mountain of broken automobiles riding on top of one another in a kind of ruinous bacchanal. For a time the taxi stopped—David Melnitz saw police cars, a blazing light, an ambulance. Men were trying to pull a victim from under an overturned truck. Then the taxi continued.

On the left side, Dora crouched. It was hard to tell if she was asleep or just sinking into torpor. As she got into the taxi, she had said to David: "I am going to my own funeral," and since then, Melnitz hadn't heard a word from her. He wondered if she had already taken some of her sleeping pills or she had changed her mind altogether. After all, it was *her* plan.

They came to a colony of bungalows with a neon sign over the office. The taxi stopped at the door, and Melnitz handed the driver three ten dollar bills. The driver said nothing. Grim as the circumstances were, Melnitz became annoyed at the driver for not showing even the minimum of civility. "This country is falling to pieces," he said to himself. Aloud he said: "Dora, we're here."

Dora started. He took her by the wrist and helped her out. She dragged her feet and only now he noticed that she was wearing dark glasses. After the taxi rolled away, Melnitz said to her: "Don't make a scene. If you've changed your mind, tell me openly."

"I didn't change my mind." Her voice was hoarse, almost mannish.

"Wait. I'll be back soon." He left her not far from the office. She remained standing, bent like a rag doll ready to collapse. Her handbag, hanging from her wrist, almost touched the ground. "Well, she's an actress to the very end." He went to the office and paid for the room. A girl with a man's shirt and cut-off blue jeans on her naked legs took them to the bungalow. The girl opened the door and lit a single, naked bulb. The room was unpainted and had a beamed roof but no ceiling. It contained a broad bed, a clothes rack and a toilet. "The shower is outside," the girl said.

Then she went back to the office. Melnitz put down his satchel.

"Take off the dark glasses."

Dora said nothing.

"What do you need the sunglasses for? It's dark in here anyhow."

Dora sat down on the edge of the bed, with her head in her hands. He said, "It was all your idea. You always talked as if life had no value for you. I don't insist you keep your word. We can stay here tonight and tomorrow you can go wherever you want. I may stay here, but it has nothing to do with you."

"Everything will happen as said," Dora mumbled.

Melnitz went into the toilet and dallied there a few minutes. He came out and said: "This night was supposed to be a holiday for us, not Tishahb'ov. Take off the glasses. I want to see your eyes."

"Leave me alone."

He opened his satchel and took out a bottle of cognac, two glasses and a box of cookies. There was no table, so he placed them on a chair. Through the screen window he could see cars passing, and a bit of glowing sky, without moon and without stars. "This colony is a brothel where everyone must bring his own whore," he thought. He asked: "Do you want a drink?"

Without taking her hands from her face, she nodded.

He filled two glasses. Usually when they drank, they clinked glasses and said L'chaim. But now these words would have been a mockery. Dora took her left hand from her face, lifted the glass and poured the drink into her mouth with the expertise of a drunk. David sipped his slowly. He never had much desire for liquor. He felt a harshness in his nose and his throat burned. He had to chase it down with a cookie. He heard Dora say: "More." He gave her a second glass and then a third. He could never understand how such a skinny girl could pour so much alcohol into herself. She opened up her pocketbook, took out a cigarette and lit it. She was sitting up straight and her face had become somewhat more animated.

"Now," he insisted, "take off those miserable glasses."

"No."

"Well, if that's the way you want it. What are we going to do now?" he asked, ashamed of his own question. According to their plan, they were to spend the night making love, but it was clear to him that Dora would sabotage even that. "I'll be completely passive," he decided. For a while he rummaged in his open satchel where he had his passport, a pair of pajamas, two bank books which together accounted for about $1500 and an envelope with the inscription: To Whom It May Concern. Where were the pills? He found them. He put his hand absently into his breast pocket and pulled out a prescription that had never been filled and his Blue Cross card, which entitled him to three weeks in Mt. Sinai Hospital, where Dr. Beller had already arranged a semi-private room for him. All this was unnecessary now. He no longer needed doctors, documents, nurses or money. He had forgotten what day of the week it was. All he remembered was that it was the middle of August because that was when he began to suffer from hayfever.

"I wonder why I'm not sneezing," he thought, and at that moment, he felt an itching in his nose and sneezed three times.

He glanced at the bed. Dora had taken off her shoes and stretched out in her stocking feet, flat, small, thin, her hair half black, half blond from the time she had dyed it, her face narrow and white with sunken cheeks and a pointed chin. She was still wearing her sunglasses. He had almost forgotten the expression in her eyes. He stood for a while, musing to himself. Fear?—no. Desire?—no again. "I shouldn't have dragged her into all of this," he reproached himself. Aloud he said: "You can get undressed if you want."

Dora did not reply.
"I'll put out the light."
"Give me another glass."

2

Melnitz turned off the light, undressed and put on his pajamas. Dora remained in her dress and stockings. She didn't answer when he spoke to her. He nudged her from under the
sheet. It was obvious that her silence was calculated: she was
trying to wreck their plan without admitting that she had
changed her mind. He was certainly not going to remind her
of her passionate statements about their dying together and
being buried beside one another. He had bought two plots
from the Prashker Society—one for himself and one for her,
but he knew now that she was not going to be his neighbor
there.

Somewhere in his mind, he was laughing. For all his skepticism, he still believed in people and their talk. But who had
asked her to make all these promises? They lay silently, she
with her face toward the wall, he facing her back on the other
side of the bed. He put his hand on her hip for an instant and
then took it away. The pills and a glass of water were on the
night table where he had put them, but he would have to send
her away before he swallowed them. He had reached the point
at which no human behavior, no matter how contradictory,
surprised him. After Maydanek and Stuthoff, nothing could
astound him. He had seen a former Yiddish teacher become a
kapo and serve the Nazis. In the ghetto he had seen Jewish
women going to a nightclub, dressed in silk and velvet stepping over people who were dying of starvation. He witnessed
a Nazi whipping a girl to death in the presence of her mother.
Dora had been through the same things, and although their
experiences were similar, they could never really communicate
with each other when they talked about them. He could never
make out how she had survived, and she still wondered how
he got out alive. She had sworn holy oaths that she had never
given herself to the murderers, but he was far from convinced.
He heard himself say: "Dora, darling, I have no complaints.
This is my last night with you. Let's not lie around like angry

honeymooners. Talk to me. That's all I ask. Tomorrow, you'll go your way and I'll go mine."

She didn't answer, and for a while it seemed that she wouldn't speak at all. Then she said in a clear, unsleepy voice: "What should I talk about?"

"First of all, turn to me. Let's not part like strangers."

Again she waited, and then turned slowly. The springs of the mattress vibrated.

"Dora, you shouldn't think that I ever believed your promises, even for a minute." He spoke with the painful feeling that he was not saying what he wanted to say. "You're thirteen years younger than I, and thank God, you're not sick. I want you to live and if possible, be happy. Don't interrupt me. I know in advance what you want to say. You owe me nothing—absolutely nothing. What I have is cancer, not a tumor. I couldn't even get through this operation and if I did, it would only prolong the process a few months. You know this as well as I do. Your life is just beginning, and if there is a God, and one can pray to Him, you can be sure that I'll——"

"Shut up."

"Alright."

"I came here to die with you, so don't try to change my mind."

"The way you sat in the taxi, I thought——"

"I have a terrible headache. It took everything I had not to scream."

"I think I have some aspirin in my satchel," he said, realizing how wild and funny and idiotic his words sounded. He also knew that no matter what else they said tonight it would sound ridiculous, melodramatic and unnatural. Language is for the living, not for the dead. He asked: "Shall I give you something?"

"No, nothing."

"Shall I put on the light?"

"No. No."

"I'll bring out the bottle."

He rolled out of bed. By this time, he was used to the darkness. From outside, a dim light shone into the room. He got back into bed and reached her the bottle. She drank straight from it and it sounded like gargling. When she passed the bottle on to him, it was lighter in his hand. He took a draught, but he couldn't get drunk and he didn't intend to. He put the unfinished bottle on the floor. Vapors of alcohol passed from his stomach to his brain. He was neither intoxicated nor sober. Could one drink himself to death? Dora was still silent, but it seemed to him she was coming around and was getting ready to talk. He felt a rush of love for her: she had come here to die with him. He wanted to embrace her and kiss her but a bashfulness that often goes together with the deepest intimacy held him back. It had gotten colder and he was about to cover himself, but he delayed it. A single mosquito buzzed. Somewhere, in a third or fourth bungalow, a radio was playing and he heard the muffled music. If only it could always be night and the bed could be their grave! Dora said: "Come cover me."

They lay down and he covered her with the sheet and blanket. He put his arms around her and she clung to him as she had in the old days, at the beginning of their relationship: his arm around her neck, her knee between his. How many times did they lie like this, in hotels, bungalows, furnished rooms, in her house and in his! But everything had conspired to make this night the last: his tumor (or whatever it was), his quitting his job at the Bialik school, his wife's refusal to divorce him, Dora's mother's heart attack, Dora's quarrel with Sylvia and the liquidation of their shop. All of this could not be mere chance. Both of them had lost one job after another. They became estranged from their relatives and friends. It was eerie, but he had foreseen their coming here tonight—perhaps he had dreamed about it. He had envisioned the bungalow, its coolness, the broad bed, the hard pillow and the window that let in a bit of shimmering light. Even a rationalist like Spinoza had believed in the theoretical possibility of predicting life with the same exactness as charting eclipses of the sun, except that he hadn't realized that causality and teleology are two sides of one coin.

As he kissed Dora's neck, he took stock of his life. God? The mortality of the soul? Hell? If the world was a product of God's justice, then he, Melnitz, was ready to roast on a bed of coals. His acceptance of death was somehow connected with the hope of revelation. If there is a soul, and a hereafter, he wanted to know what they were like. It was strange to think that all this could be reached with a few pills.

It had started to rain. There was lightning and thunder. For a second, the bungalow lit up and he saw his jacket, his trousers, the bottle of cognac, Dora's shoes.

"Aren't you hot in that dress?" he asked.

"Hot? No."

"Why didn't you bring a nightgown with you?"

"What for?"

Yes, what for? He had imagined that in this last night with Dora he would devote himself to his passion for her body, indulge all his whims, shake off all his (and her) inhibitions. But it seemed that it was not to be. He remembered the Yiddish expression "I made my calculations without the Boss." Apparently, sex and suicide make strange bedfellows. He heard himself say: "I have one request before it's all over."

"What kind of request?"

"Let's not die with lies. Let's tell each other the entire truth, no matter how ugly." His words sounded overly solemn to him. He realized that he was preparing for their mutual confession all this time. He didn't want to die deceived or even a deceiver. Dora stiffened and moved away from him slightly. For a long time she said nothing, and he suspected that she had fallen asleep. Then she said: "Very well."

"Let's swear that we tell each other everything."

"Swear by what?"

3

They haggled, each demanding that the other confess first. He was afraid that she would change her mind about confessing if he made his revelations first, but then he gave in. They had to go through this. It was the culmination of his plans—perhaps the only reason for his bringing her here. He was giving his tongue permission to divulge all his secrets: he didn't intend to censor himself.

"I had other women while we were together," he said, with a kind of choked solemnity.

"Who? How many?"

He was silent while he counted them in his mind. According to his calculation (made days or weeks before) there had been seven, but now he remembered only five. Two had vanished from his memory. Perhaps he already was entering the amnesia that he intended to make total. He said: "It's strange, but I've forgotten."

"How many do you remember?" She moved even further away from him.

He was suddenly frightened, although he knew there was nothing to be afraid of. The worst she could do was refuse to confess.

"About one you certainly know—my wife."

"Who are the others?"

"You know about two others. I was with them before you and while we were together. Bella and Esther."

"All this time?"

"With Bella just for a year. With Esther it dragged on until not long ago."

"How long?"

"Until about half a year ago."

Even though she had moved to the other side of the bed, he could hear her heavy breathing. He thought he could feel the beat of her heart.

"Who else?" Dora's voice became rasping.

"A woman from Lublin."

"Who is she?"

"A middle-aged woman. Her husband left for Russia in 1939 and she stayed with her daughter in a village near Krasnistaw. A peasant hid them. The daughter was shot by the Nazis. She was denounced by a *Szmalcownik*. Her mother came here after 1945. I knew her when I was a teacher in Lublin."

"What happened to her husband?"

"He died in Jambul of dysentery."

"And she never re-married?"

"She has a second husband. A simple man. A furrier."

"Is he a refugee too."

"When did this happen?"

Melnitz had to think, unwilling to lie even about a date.

"A few months after we met. Do you remember an evening when I went to a lecture at the Labor Temple and you refused to go with me? I met her there."

"I remember it very well. My mother was in the hospital."

"I don't remember that."

"Who were the others?"

He told her and she asked him short, dry questions, apparently restraining her anger. He now had recalled one of the two he had forgotten, but the other had left his mind a blank. He began to doubt if there had been a number seven, as he referred to her. Of those he remembered the first he had met in a cafeteria on Broadway and the second was the mother of one of his pupils. They were all middle-aged refugees, either verging on poverty or complete paupers. The one he met in a cafeteria was a divorcée. She worked in a pocketbook shop and had a thirteen year old daughter who studied in a yeshiva in Brooklyn. These weren't love adventures, but continuations of what went on in the ghettoes, and later, after 1945, when people were smuggled across borders, searching for relatives in ruined cities and wandering from camp to camp. While he answered Dora's questions he kept on searching for some lead to his lost number seven—who had been erased from his memory leaving him numb and baffled. How could this have happened? "I can't die until I remember who she is." Dora had not yet made any comments and he knew from her clipped sentences and the way she kept away from him that what he told her had turned her into an enemy. He imagined he heard her grit her teeth. She might even try to kill him.

"Who was the seventh?"

"Really, I don't know."

"In that case, maybe there were ten others you've forgotten."

"No, not more than seven."

"Who was she?"

"Wait—it'll come to me."

He lay quietly, thoughtless, as if clearing a space in his brain for recollection. But minutes passed, and the cell that contained this adventure remained locked. "Really," he said, "there's some block in my mind. As soon as it comes to me I'll tell you. I swear."

"Very well. I'll wait."

"Tell me about you," he said, and he felt himself shudder. She didn't answer. He could almost hear her fighting with herself. Then she said, "Well, there was one."

His heart stopped for an instant.

"Who?"

"Dr. Salkind." The word hit him with a physical blow on his temple. He could barely speak: "Why?"

"Oh, just because. He was chasing after me. Besides, I knew you weren't faithful."

"How did you know?"

"I knew. I was only with him a few times."

"Why only a few times?"

"He didn't interest me, either physically or spiritually. Actually, he disgusted me."

"That didn't stop you from sleeping with him."

"Yes . . . I'm sorry." Silence followed. Salkind was the one who tried to persuade Dora to be psychoanalyzed. He had wanted to send her to a colleague of his, but she refused. Now Melnitz tried to recollect when Dora began her visits to Salkind. Did it happen this year? No, last year. Melnitz couldn't keep his teeth from chattering. At that instant he discovered who his seventh lover was: Florence, his English teacher. They had spent one miserable night together—a failure in every way; it was one of those nights when all of a man's illusions collapse. What he was feeling now was not hurt, but shame for his own conduct, for Dora's, for modern man. It didn't even pay to die. He rolled off the bed and went into the toilet, banging his knee on the chair, groping as if blind. He found the toilet and even before he could put the light on he began to vomit. He retched again and again. Fiery patterns flew in front of his eyes and bells rang in his ears, just as when he got sick as a boy. He recognized the designs, the colors, the sparks, the changing of the shapes. The whole dreamy web seemed to have been lurking in his optic nerves waiting to appear with full exactness. The smell of today's and yesterday's meals floated up to him: the cinnamon of the cookies and the aroma of the cognac. "She's unclean. Unclean," a voice called in him. He didn't know himself if it was piety or hypocrisy. "We're not Jews anymore, we're Nazis." He was about to return to bed, but his stomach lurched again. "When did I gorge so much?" He felt he was spitting out his innards. He groaned. His knees buckled. A terrible stench came out from the bowl and Melnitz realized it could not only be physical. Matter could never stink like that. He heard Dora's voice say: "What's wrong. Can I help you?"

"You can't help me," he called back, and began to retch again. He slammed the door. He tried to flush, but the chain broke.

4

They lay in bed. "Now I don't mind dying," Dora said to him. "You're such a cheat that nothing matters anymore."

"What about you? You're nothing but a whore!"

"I did it because I knew you were fooling around. In spite of all your reassurances and oaths."

"Only yesterday you swore you were faithful," he said.

"Compared to you, I was fidelity itself!"

"Wait, it'll all end tonight. We won't leave here alive. They'll carry us out."

She fell into silence. "If I could at least take my mother with me," she said half to herself and half to him.

"It's too late for that. You have no right to kill your mother. She's a decent Jewish woman."

"Who cares about rights? If everyone is so ugly, there are no rights."

"There still may be a God."

"What kind of God?"

"A heavenly Hitler."

"Yes, that's what he is. I want a cigarette."

To get out of bed, she had to crawl over him. She was look-ing for her pocketbook. She lit a match and in the pale light he saw her barefoot, her hair rumpled, a crooked smile on her half opened lips. Instead of getting back into bed, she sat on a chair. As she pulled on the cigarette, her face glowed. He saw the glint in her eyes.

"I don't want you to be buried near me, Dora. You should be buried next to Dr. Salkind."

"Dr. Salkind is not about to die." She gave a snorting laugh.

"I don't want to have your defiled body near mine."

"In that case, I'll leave a letter that they cremate me."

"Yes, you do that."

"You speak like some kind of saint," she said after a pause. "You are the worst liar and hypocrite. You keep on babbling about God, but you act like a devil. You never loved me."

"I did love you, to my regret. You said yourself that a man could love more than one woman, but if you could lie around with that schlemiel Salkind, you don't know what love is."

"If I don't know now, I never will."

"You don't even regret it."

"No, not now."

"I never hated anybody as I hate you," he said, with the feeling that he had already spoken these words, a long time ago. "Get out of here. Keep a four cubits distance from me!" he shouted, suddenly recognizing his father's voice. It was his voice, his tone, the same words his father had used years ago to rebuke him for cutting off his sidelocks and shortening his gabardine. Dora moved as if to get up. The chair squeaked under her.

"Where am I supposed to go in the middle of the night?" She took a last puff of her cigarette and threw it down on the linoleum. Melnitz watched the cigarette glow, then dim on the floor. A cigarette and it doesn't know it's a cigarette. Dying, without knowing that it's dying, Melnitz mused. Even if Spinoza was right and thought is one of the attributes of substance, what would a cigarette think? Unless each atom and molecule thinks by itself. Or maybe the earth has a brain in its center made up of molten metals—gold, iron, nickel, uranium. But it was too late for such nonsense. Aloud he said: "Did you do it in the daytime or at night?"

"The first time during the day."

"Where, in his office?"

"Yes."

"And there were patients in the waiting room?"

"There were no patients."

Melnitz felt like vomiting again. "What about the other times?"

"We went to a hotel."

"Where was I?"

"Probably with one of your whores."

"Cursed be the day I met you!" Again, it was not his language, his style. His father entered him like a dybbuk.

"Shut up. You're making a fool of yourself." She said quietly and matter-of-factly, "For you to preach morality is like Al Capone becoming a rabbi."

"Now it's even a disgrace to die," he said, almost apologetically.

"No one's forcing you."

"I'm going to gluttonize and sleep around until this cancer finishes me."

"You have no cancer. You'll go on swindling and deceiving until you're eighty."

He did not answer. He listened to his own body. He literally felt the growth in his stomach: heavy and bloated, the way, he imagined, a woman would feel if her baby died in her womb. He was pregnant with death. He could hear Dr. Beller's warning: "It has to be cut before it spreads." But how had it begun? Did he, Melnitz, subconsciously desire death? "I'm sinking in slime," he said to himself. He remembered a scene he had witnessed in a camp: a young Jew spat at a Nazi, and the Nazi buried him in excrement. Like that young fellow, he was perishing in filth. But why should that young man have had to suffer, and how could God, if He existed, ever rectify such evil? No Messiah, no angels, no paradise could compensate for the hours it took this young Jew to strangle in offal. The past is stronger than God; it is the law that even *He* has to obey. Who said it? Not even the Omnipotent can erase what has happened already.

"Come over here, you stinking carcass."

"Are you talking to me?" Dora asked.

"Who else? Come, you filth, you faithful servant of the God of Wrath," Melnitz called, surprised at his own words. There was an element of parody in them.

"What are you ranting about?"

"Oh, never mind."

"Wait. I'm going to smoke another cigarette."

"How many Nazis did you whore around with?"

She lit her cigarette and a whiff of smoke reached Melnitz. After a while, she crushed it out and went to him as if his terrible words were a code and a signal for her. She fell into his arms and he clung to her both with passion and disgust. All their inhibitions left them momentarily. They wrestled with each other, scolding one another and caressing with forgiving vengeance.

"I don't want to die," Dora moaned. "I want to kill all your females first. I'll take them all with me. I'll tear them all to pieces."

"And I'll murder that Dr. Salkind."

"Yes, do. He meant nothing to me. He didn't even satisfy me, that creep."

They fell back into their old familiar love chatter: half crazy fantasies, incoherent exclamations, promises of eternal love, dying together, being buried together, loving after the Resurrection—overtaken by that short-lived pathos which almost has an existence of its own and is degrading even while it lasts. They raved and grew silent. He closed his eyes and fell asleep. He opened them and it was still dark. "What an unending night," he wondered. "A wintry summer night." He poked Dora and she awoke—if she had not been shamming sleep.

"If you want to die, now's the time."

"I don't want to die." She hugged him tightly and wrapped her legs around him. Her hair tickled his face. Only now did he realize the strong scent of cognac on her breath. She half sighed, half giggled, in the way he once imagined Lilith the she-demon, whom Satan sends out at night to entice Yeshiva boys to sin.

"What happened to the pills?" he asked.

"I threw them down the drain."

"All of them?"

"Yes, my beloved. All of them."

Translated by the author and Laurie Colwin

Eulogy to a Shoelace

WHILE sitting on a park bench I noticed that my left shoelace was untied. When I bent down to fasten it, it tore. Part of the lace remained in my hand and part in my shoe.

How did this happen? Just this morning I tied both laces and they seemed strong and sound. Or didn't I see any difference between the lace in my left shoe and the lace in my right? Did I tug it too energetically or was the lace already threadbare without my noticing it? If so, why did it only happen to the left lace? Did it overexert itself? Was it more exposed to pressure, friction, moisture? Was it due to my negligence? I will never know. One doesn't pay attention to his shoe ties from day to day, nor study their history or guard their hygiene. Even if one did he would most probably not be able to foresee the exact time of demise of a shoelace.

I had no choice but to remove the torn remnants of the shoelace. While doing so I recited a eulogy to it. "Shoelace," I said, "you have faithfully kept my left shoe closed. You have worked with your last bit of strength to perform the function for which you were made. Now you are no longer a shoelace, but a part of the earth, of the cosmos. Your molecules will slowly separate, uniting with other molecules. There's even a chance they might disintegrate into different collections of atoms. You may become part of a plant, a creature, a mineral. Your shoe-tying epoch is finished, but somewhere in the history of the universe, where all things are recorded, your performance will be listed. Somewhere in God's bookkeeping, notice will be taken that you have been a shoe tie at such and such a time, kept such and such a shoe closed and then your function was finished, as all things sooner or later are. There are no eternal shoe ties. Only the elements of which shoe ties are made are eternal. And if they're not eternal, they are most probably part of some substance or matter that is eternal.

Actually you never stopped being the universe. While you kept my shoe together you were energy, matter, spirit. You turned, with the earth around its axis. You circled round the sun. You moved in unison with it, in some unknown direction in the milky way, and with it you participated in the movements of other galaxies. All the laws of the universe are your laws. All its missions are your missions. You were both a shoe tie and the cosmos, playing for a time the part of a shoelace. It isn't necessary to mourn for you, shoelace. You are not in need of my eulogy. The eulogy which I am reciting is really not for you but for myself, a part of the universe which was doomed to be selfish, cowardly and ignorant for a given number of years and for a reason which only God knows."

Translated by the author and Ruth Schachner Finkel

CHRONOLOGY

NOTE ON THE TEXTS

NOTES

Chronology

1904   Yitskhok Zynger (Isaac Singer) is born in Leoncin, a Polish village northeast of Warsaw (then part of the Russian Empire), the third surviving child of Basheve Zylberman and Pinkhos Menakhem Zynger. (Although his Polish passport issued in the 1930s and other sources give his birthdate as July 14, 1904, Singer told his biographer Paul Kresh that he was "born in the third week of the month of Heshvan on the Jewish calendar—which is roughly equivalent to the month of November." Father is a Hasidic rabbi from a family of distinguished rabbis, though because of his refusal to take Russian language examinations he was not certified to perform rabbinical duties by the Russian government, which limited his opportunities. Mother was the daughter of the rabbi of Biłgoraj, a town in the province of Lublin; her family were *misnagdim*, opponents of Hasidism. The couple were married in Biłgoraj in 1889. Their first child, Hinde Esther, was born in 1891, and son Israel Joshua was born in 1893. Two other young daughters died on the same day during an outbreak of scarlet fever. After making a meager living as an itinerant preacher, Singer's father was invited to serve as a rabbi in Leoncin, and the family moved there in 1897.)

1906   Brother Moishe is born.

1907   Hard times in Leoncin and increasing tensions with the local community cause Singer's father to look for a position elsewhere. He becomes head of the yeshiva in Radzymin and moves the family there, where he also acts as unofficial secretary to the local rabbi. Singer begins to attend *cheder* (religious primary school).

1908–14   The family moves to Warsaw, where father presides over a rabbinical court in the family's home at 10 Krochmalna Street, an unheated three-room apartment on the second floor. ("Krochmalna Street in Warsaw was always full of people," Singer later wrote, "and they all seemed to be screaming.") Most of the residents are poor, and some are involved in petty crime or prostitution. Family's income consists mostly of donations from those settling their affairs through the court as well as fees from private Talmud lessons given by Singer's father. Singer attends a series of *cheders* but much of his religious instruction is provided by his parents at home. Serves as messenger and collector of donations for his father. Develops friendship with a girl his age named Shosha. Browses with fascination through the books of the Kabbalah in his father's library, although he is told not to read them. Reads tales of Edgar Allan Poe and Arthur Conan Doyle as well as novels by popular Yiddish writers, such as the pseudonymous "Shomer," and detective stories featuring a hero named Max Shpitzkopf; writes stories with Shpitzkopf as a character. Brother Israel Joshua, who is drawn to secular literature and ideas and rejecting his parents' desire that he become a rabbi, has heated arguments with the family and moves out of the house at the age of 18. Sister Hinde Esther's relationship with parents grows contentious, and she consents to an arranged marriage with diamond cutter Abraham Kreitman, moving to Antwerp with him following their wedding in Berlin in 1912; after their son Moishe (later known as Morris Kreitman and Maurice Carr) is born the next year, the family sends money from Warsaw because Abraham is unemployed. Early in 1914, family moves to a larger apartment in the building next door. After the outbreak of World War I, Israel Joshua adopts an assumed name to avoid conscription into the Russian army. Singer visits him several times in the studio of a sculptor named Ostrzego. The Kreitmans flee Belgium and settle in London.

1915–16   Singer goes to Bresler's lending library for the first of many visits, borrowing books on philosophy in Yiddish and Hebrew and reading them with enthusiasm. German troops occupy Warsaw in August 1915, causing prolonged hardship and deprivation. With the city under German control, Israel Joshua comes out of hiding and resumes living with the family. Brother Moishe falls ill with typhus and the apartment is disinfected; Singer and his mother are ordered to a hospital and confined to separate quarters for more than a week.

1917–20   In summer 1917, Singer moves with mother and Moishe to Biłgoraj, where, he would later write, "the kind of Jewish behavior and customs I witnessed were those pre-

served from a much earlier time." The village, which is
occupied by Austrian troops, had recently lost many inhabitants in a cholera epidemic. Singer's father remains in
Warsaw briefly before departing for Radzymin, where he
again works for the town's rabbi. Singer is bar-mitzvahed.
Meets eight-year-old cousin Esther, with whom he develops an intense bond. Contracts typhus and spends several
months convalescing. Israel Joshua, now in Kiev, publishes stories and works as a proofreader for a Yiddish
newspaper; he marries Genia Kupfershtock in 1918. Father
comes to Biłgoraj in summer 1918 hoping to secure a rabbinical position there; his bid is unsuccessful, and the
family must rely on charity. Independent Polish republic
is declared in November 1918, and Polish troops advance
into Ukrainian Galicia and take Lemberg (L'viv); there
are widespread pogroms throughout Poland and Galicia.
During his four-year stay in Biłgoraj Singer continues his
Talmud studies while also reading widely in philosophy
(particularly Spinoza), popular science, and modern literature, including Strindberg, Tolstoy, Turgenev, Flaubert,
London, and Maupassant, complementing earlier reading
of Sforim, Sholem Aleichem, Peretz, Asch, Bergelson,
and Dostoevsky. He studies Polish, German, Esperanto,
and modern Hebrew, in which he writes sketches and
poems. One of his Hebrew poems is published in a local
newspaper, prompting threats to revoke the family's charitable stipend. ("I had to promise to recant my apostasy,"
Singer wrote in 1963, "and return to 'real' learning—to
Judaism, the Talmud.") Singer teaches Hebrew in private
homes to young men and women. Father accepts rabbinical position in nearby Dzikow and moves there in 1920.
Israel Joshua, Genia, and their infant son Yasha move to
Moscow.

1921–22   Singer goes to Warsaw to attend a rabbinical seminary in
1921 but is unhappy, poor, and often hungry. Returns to
Biłgoraj, giving Hebrew lessons there and in a nearby village. Continues intensive study of Spinoza's *Ethics* and
reads Kant's *Prolegomena* and Hamsun's *Hunger*. Goes to
live with parents and Moishe in Dzikow; now extremely
pious, Moishe lends Singer the works of Rabbi Nachman
of Bratslav. Israel Joshua returns to Warsaw with wife and
son and publishes his first collection of short stories the
following year; the couple's son Joseph is born in 1922.

1923–25   Accepting a job as proofreader arranged through his
brother, Singer moves back to Warsaw, living free in the
apartment of editor and poet Melekh Ravitch (the pen
name of Zekhariah Bergner). Begins frequenting the Warsaw PEN Yiddish Writers' Club, attending lectures and
often taking meals there. Reads about psychic research
and spiritualism. Lives alone in an unheated room he rents
during the winter of 1923–24. Meets writer Aaron Zeitlin,
who will become a lifelong friend. Looking for a new place
to live, he meets an older woman (called "Gina Halbstark"
in his memoirs) who becomes his mistress; they live together for several months. After reporting for conscription, receives deferment from the army. Despite Gina's
protests, he moves to rented room in the home of an
elderly doctor and his wife while continuing to see her
occasionally. Israel Joshua contributes regularly to New
York Yiddish newspaper *Forverts* (*Jewish Daily Forward*)
at the invitation of editor-in-chief Abraham Cahan. In
December 1924, Singer publishes his first review, using for
the only time the pseudonym "Yitskhok Tsvi," in *Literarishe bleter* (*Literary Pages*), magazine recently founded
by Israel Joshua, Melekh Ravitch, and two other writers;
he also works as proofreader for the magazine. Using the
pseudonym "Tse," publishes his first short story, "Oyf der
elter" ("In Old Age"), in *Literarishe bleter* in June 1925;
the story wins first prize in a competition sponsored by
the magazine. In Hebrew newspaper *Ha-yom* (*Today*),
where he occasionally works as a proofreader, Singer publishes Hebrew story "Nerot" ("Candles") and signs it
"Yitskhok Bashevis," pen name under which most of his
short stories in Yiddish will be published. "Be-hatser shel
nokhrim" ("In a Gentile Courtyard") appears in *Ha-yom*
in October, the second and final story he publishes in
Hebrew.

1926–27   Singer contributes stories "A dorfs-kabren" ("A Village
Gravedigger") and "Eyniklekh" ("Grandchildren") to
PEN Writers' Club publication. Is now involved with mistress Runia Shapira, a rabbi's daughter who has become a
devoted Communist; according to Singer's memoirs,
other mistresses during his adult years in Warsaw include
women referred to by pseudonyms such as "Marila," a
servant girl, and "Sabina," who works in a library. General Józef Piłsudski leads a coup against the Polish gov-

ernment in May 1926. In the summer, Hinde Esther and her son visit Warsaw for three months. Diagnosed as having weak lungs, Singer is rejected for military service in the Polish army. Continues to publish stories in *Literarishe bleter*. Around this time considers leaving Poland, and the Palestine Bureau in Warsaw issues him a certificate of immigration that contains a marriage requirement; meets woman known in his memoirs as "Stefa Janovsky," who seeks to marry Singer, then divorce him when reunited with a lover in Palestine. Their joint immigration is canceled when she discovers her lover is already married and, after proposing that Singer go through with the marriage, she becomes engaged to a prosperous Warsaw businessman instead. ("Stefa" will translate the only story of his to appear in Polish during his Warsaw years.)

1928   In April, Singer publishes story "Oyfn oylem-hatoye" ("In the World of Chaos"), about a wandering corpse. His translations of Norwegian novelist Knut Hamsun's *Pan* and *Landstrykere* (*Wayfarers*) are brought out by the publisher Boris Kletskin, the first of Singer's published translations to be signed; during his Warsaw years Singer also adapts popular German novels for the Yiddish newspaper *Radio*.

1929   Singer's father dies in Dzikow. Runia gives birth to Singer's son Israel. Three novels translated by Singer are published in Yiddish: Hamsun's *Viktoria*, D'Annunzio's *Il piacere* (*Pleasure*), and Danish writer Karin Michäelis's *Mette Trap og hendes Unger* (*Mette Trap and Her Children*); his translation of Stefan Zweig's 1921 biography of Romain Rolland appears as well. Hinde Esther returns to Poland alone with plans to stay permanently; after ten months, in which she translates Dickens (*A Christmas Carol*) and Shaw (*The Intelligent Woman's Guide to Socialism and Capitalism*) into Yiddish to help support herself, she returns to England.

1930   Boris Kletskin publishes Singer's Yiddish translations of Remarque's *All Quiet on the Western Front* and Mann's *The Magic Mountain*.

1931   Israel Joshua begins writing *Yoshe Kalb*, novel about a 19th-century Galician mystic based on a Hasidic folk tale; he reads sections of the manuscript to Singer, who also helps with research. Singer's translation of Remarque's *The Way Back* is published by Boris Kletskin.

1932   With Aaron Zetlin, Singer founds, edits, and helps finance magazine *Globus*, publishing stories "Der yid fun Bovl" ("The Jew from Babylon") and "A zokn: a khronik" ("An Old Man: A Chronicle") in its second and fourth numbers. His translations of Moshe Smilansky's Hebrew stories are published as *Araber: Folkstimlekhe geshikhtn* (*Arabs: Stories of the People*). Singer is arrested briefly during an investigation into Runia's activities. On the recommendation of his brother, Paris newspaper *Parizer haynt* (*Paris Today*) asks Singer to write about show trials of anti-Piłsudski opposition leaders; Singer attends proceedings but does not pursue assignment. Israel Joshua is invited to New York to supervise the stage adaptation of *Yoshe Kalb*, and travels there in the fall with wife and son Joseph (son Yasha dies suddenly of pneumonia just before the trip); the family remains permanently in New York, where he works for *Forverts*. Singer begins writing historical novel *Der sotn in Goray* (*Satan in Goray*), set in the 17th century against backdrop of pogroms and religious fervor caused by the false messiah Sabbatai Zevi.

1933–34   *Der sotn in Goray* is serialized in *Globus* from January through September 1933. Singer's articles appear in *Parizer haynt* and the Warsaw daily *Ekspres* (*Express*).

1935   Israel Joshua writes that *Forverts* has accepted Singer's 1925 story "Oyf der elter" ("In Old Age") for publication and encloses payment from the newspaper. As the first volume in a series issued by the Warsaw Yiddish PEN Club, *Der sotn in Goray* is published in book form with an introduction by Aaron Zeitlin. Assisted by his brother, Singer plans move to the United States. Separates from Runia, who soon immigrates to the Soviet Union with their son Israel. Travels by train from Warsaw through Germany en route to Paris, where he spends several days, staying in the Belleville section of the city. He is greeted by members of the city's Yiddish Writers' Club and attends a performance of *Yoshe Kalb*. Sails from Cherbourg on the *Champlain* and on May 1 arrives in New York, where he is met at the dock by Israel Joshua and the journalist and translator Zygmunt Salkin. In June his sketch "Reyzele: A kharakter-portrait fun varshever lebn"

("Reyzele: A Character-Portrait of Warsaw Life") is published in *Forverts*. In September, unfinished autobiographical novel *Varshe 1914–18* (*Warsaw 1914–18*) begins serialization in Warsaw daily *Dos naye vort* (*The New Word*). Lives near Israel Joshua in Sea Gate, gated community not far from Coney Island in Brooklyn; becomes romantically involved with the landlady (called "Nesha" in his memoirs) of a boarding house where he rents a room. Buys typewriter with Hebrew characters that he will use for decades. With the help of the *Forverts* staff who write to American immigration authorities on his behalf, obtains an extension of his visa. Takes long walks, a habit that will continue for the rest of his life. Writes Aaron Zeitlin and expresses regret that he has immigrated to America rather than Palestine. *Der zindiker meshiekh* (*The Sinning Messiah*), novel about 18th-century heretical mystic Jacob Frank who believed himself to be Sabbatai Zevi reincarnated, begins five-month run in *Forverts*; it is also serialized in newspapers in Paris and Warsaw.

1936   Singer moves briefly to a rooming house on East 19th Street in Manhattan, then lives for a time in Croton-on-Hudson, N.Y., and in Sheepshead Bay in Brooklyn. Contributes numerous reviews, sketches and stories as a freelance writer to *Forverts*; story "Oyf an alter shif" ("On an Old Ship") is published in anthology edited by noted Yiddish writers Joseph Opatoshu and H. Leyvick. Israel Joshua's epic novel *Di brider Ashkenazi* (*The Brothers Ashkenazi*) is published in Yiddish and in English translation to critical acclaim. Sister Hinde Esther's novel *Der sheydim-tants* (*The Devil's Dance*, translated into English as *Deborah*) is published in Warsaw.

1937   Singer contributes a few stories and sketches to *Forverts* early in the year, then stops writing fiction for several years. In the summer, meets Alma Haimann Wassermann, a recent immigrant from Germany, while both are vacationing on a farm in the Catskills; she is married, has two children, and does not speak Yiddish. Denounced as a Zionist, Runia is expelled from the Soviet Union and flees with son Israel to Istanbul.

1938   After eight months in Turkey, Runia and Israel immigrate to Palestine, settling in Tel Aviv. At the invitation of Zygmunt Salkin, Singer spends the summer at the Grine

Felder (Green Fields) arts colony in the Catskills, directing rehearsals of an English-language production of I. L.
Peretz's *At Night in the Old Marketplace*; the play is not
produced. Singer's translation from German into Yiddish
of Leon Glaser's *From Moscow to Jerusalem (The Moral
Perishes): The Autobiography of a Revolutionary* is published. First work of Singer's in English translation, an excerpt from *Satan in Goray* entitled "Hail the Messiah!,"
appears in the anthology *Jewish Short Stories of To-day*,
edited by Hinde Esther's son Morris and published by
Faber and Faber in London; the collection also includes
stories by Israel Joshua and Hinde Esther, as well as
Morris Kreitman himself (writing under pseudonym
Martin Lea).

1939   Singer resumes contributing to *Forverts* after a two-year
hiatus in April when he begins writing a long-running
column under the pen name Yitskhok Varshavski (i.e.,
"from Warsaw"); these short articles range from human-
interest stories ("What Studies Have Uncovered About
Talented Children") to summaries of current and historical events ("English Jews Fought as Heroes, Died as Martyrs in York Pogrom") to general philosophical and social
observations ("Can a Person Change?"; "Shyness—A
Plague Affecting Large and Small, Rich and Poor"; "Why
Men and Women Divorce—No Rules But the Cases Are
Interesting"). Also begins to review books regularly for
magazine *Di tsukunft* (*The Future*). Meets journalist Simon Weber. After the Germans invade Poland Singer
loses contact with his mother and brother Moishe. Israel
Joshua becomes an American citizen. Aaron Zeitlin immigrates to the United States. Alma Wassermann and her
husband divorce.

1940   Singer and Alma are married in a civil ceremony on February 14 at Brooklyn City Hall. The couple move into a
small apartment on Ocean Avenue in Brooklyn. Alma begins working as a salesperson in the women's fashion department of the Arnold Constable department store, the
first of several department-store jobs. Runia and Israel
move to Jerusalem; their contact with Singer is sporadic,
as it has been since 1935.

1941   The Singers move to Manhattan, renting an apartment on
West 103rd Street. Singer publishes more than 45 "Var-

shavski" articles in *Forverts*; during World War II his columns include war news and commentary.

1942–43 Singer becomes a salaried member of the *Forverts* staff. Moves with Alma to a small apartment on Central Park West. Returns to writing fiction and composes several stories narrated by the Devil or by a demon (later published in English as "The Destruction of Kreshev," "From the Diary of One Not Born," "Zeidlus the Pope," and "Two Corpses Go Dancing"). Along with revised version of 1932 story "Der yid fun Bovl," these stories are collected with *Der sotn in Goray* and published in book form by New York Yiddish publishing house Farlag Matones in 1943. The book sells about 1,000 copies and Singer collects $90 in royalties. Begins to sign some of his *Forverts* articles "D. Segal." Becomes an American citizen in 1943. Publishes overview of Yiddish literature in Poland as well as long essay about the problems of Yiddish literature in America. ("Words, like people, sometimes endure a severe disorientation when they emigrate, and often they remain forever helpless and not quite themselves. This is precisely what happened to Yiddish in America.") Israel Joshua's novel *Di mishpohe Karnovski* (*The Family Carnovsky*) and Hinde Esther's novel *Briliantn* (*Diamonds*) are published.

1944 Israel Joshua dies of a heart attack on February 10. Singer publishes story "Der Spinozist" ("The Spinozan," later translated as "The Spinoza of Market Street") in *Di tsukunft*. Begins researching, plotting, and taking notes for realist novel *Di familye Mushkat* (*The Family Moskat*).

1945 Publishes stories "Gimpl tam" ("Gimpel the Fool"), "Di kleyne shusterlekh" ("The Little Shoemakers"), and "Der Katlen" ("The Wife Killer") in Yiddish periodicals. Some time after the war's end, is told that his mother and brother Moishe were deported to Kazakhstan during the Soviet occupation of eastern Poland in 1939–41 and froze to death while building log huts. In the fall, has exchange of letters with Runia in which they discuss the legal status of their son: although they appear never to have been married, Runia requests a divorce so as to legitimize Israel; Singer refuses and proposes to legally adopt him, an offer rejected by Runia. In November, *Di familye Mushkat* begins more than two years of serialization in *Forverts*. The novel is also performed in Yiddish as a serial on New York radio station WEVD.

1946–47   Farlag Matones publishes *Fun a velt vos iz nishto mer* (*From a World That Is No More*), Israel Joshua's memoir of his childhood in Leoncin, in 1946. Many of Singer's "Varshavski" columns in *Forverts* discuss the works of philosophers such as Aristotle, Plotinus, and Spinoza. With Alma, Singer sails to Europe in late summer 1947. Visits England, where he sees his sister Hinde Esther for the last time. Travels to France and makes the first of many visits to Switzerland. Publishes travel sketches in *Forverts*.

1948   Serialization of *Di familye Mushkat* in *Forverts* ends in May; Singer will continue to submit radio scripts based on his stories and memoirs to be performed on WEVD. With Alma, travels to Miami Beach during the winter, the first of many Florida visits.

1949   When English translation by Abraham Gross and Nancy Gross of *The Family Moskat* is submitted to Alfred A. Knopf for publication, editor Herbert Weinstock suggests numerous cuts that Singer refuses to make, prompting a rift about the final shape of the book; Knopf writes to Singer, "I agree heartily with everyone that this book is likely to have a very poor chance indeed with the American bookseller if it is not substantially cut." Though continuing to resent the publisher's interference, Singer eventually cuts more than 100 pages and alters the novel's ending. In December, novel *Der feter fun Amerike* (*The Uncle from America*) begins 15-month serialization.

1950   In January, Singer travels to Miami. Reviews a recently issued thesaurus of Yiddish and the Kinsey report on male sexual behavior for *Forverts*. In October, Knopf publishes *The Family Moskat*, which is dedicated to Israel Joshua: "To me he was not only the older brother, but a spiritual father and master as well." For the first time, name appears as "Isaac Bashevis Singer," which is how he will sign his works in English. The Yiddish version is brought out in book form by Morris S. Sklarsky, and a Hebrew translation is published in Israel. Hinde Esther's collection of short stories *Yikhes* (*Lineage*, later translated as *Blitz and Other Stories*) is published in England.

1951–53   Singer travels to Florida and Cuba early in 1951 and returns to Florida the following winter. His many "Varshavski" and "Segal" columns for *Forverts* include "The Tragedy of Knut Hamsun," "My Spanish Neighbors," and "America Ignores Yiddish Culture." Works on long historical novel *Der hoyf* (later translated into English in two separate volumes, *The Manor* and *The Estate*), which is serialized in *Forverts*. Jacob Sloan works on translation of *Der sotn in Goray* into English. Eliezer Greenberg reads "Gimpl tam" ("Gimpel the Fool") to critic Irving Howe; at Howe's request, Saul Bellow does a translation that is published in *Partisan Review* in May 1953. After reading the story, Cecil Hemley, publisher who had cofounded the Noonday Press in 1951, meets with Jacob Sloan and then Singer himself and arranges to publish *Satan in Goray*; Singer is also introduced to Hemley's wife, Elaine Gottlieb, who will serve as one of his translators. *Der sotn in Goray* is published in Hebrew in Tel Aviv in 1953.

1954   *A Treasury of Yiddish Stories*, edited by Irving Howe and Eliezer Greenberg, includes "Gimpel the Fool" and the first English publication of "The Little Shoemakers." *Partisan Review* publishes "From the Diary of One Not Born" and includes "Gimpel the Fool" in its anthology *More Stories in the Modern Manner*. Hinde Esther Kreitman dies in England and her body is cremated.

1955   In February, son Israel (who has taken the name Israel Zamir) travels to New York on behalf of his kibbutz and sees Singer for the first time in 20 years. Memoir of Warsaw childhood *In mayn foter's bes-din shtub* (*In My Father's Court*) is serialized in *Forverts* from February to September (published in 1954 as *Mayn tatn's bes-din shtub*). Singer travels to Israel for the first of many visits. Publishes stories about his maternal grandfather's rabbinical court in Biłgoraj in *Forverts*. Story "The Wife Killer" published in English in first issue of the American Zionist quarterly *Midstream*. Noonday Press publishes *Satan in Goray* in the fall.

1956   Serialized memoir *Der shrayber-klub* (*The Writers' Club*) runs in *Forverts* from January to December.

1957   In February the story "Fire," first work of Singer's to be published in English in more than a year, appears in

Commentary, which also includes "The Gentleman from Cracow" in its September number. Novel *Shotns baym Hodson* (*Shadows on the Hudson*) is serialized in *Forverts*. Israel Zamir returns to Israel after two-year stay in New York. *Gimpel the Fool and Other Stories* is published by Noonday in November; reviewing the collection, Anzia Yezierska calls Singer "the last of the great Yiddish fiction writers." In December, eight episodes from *Mayn tatn's bes-din shtub*, including "To the Land of Israel" and "The Suicide," are dramatized by the Folksbiene (People's Theater) at the Radin Theatre on New York City's Lower East Side.

1958–60   *Satan in Goray* and *Gimpel the Fool and Other Stories* are published in England in 1958 by Peter Owen. Singer receives $1,500 grant from the National Institute of Arts and Letters in 1959. *Die kuntsmakher fun Lublin* (*The Magician of Lublin*) is serialized in *Forverts*; Elaine Gottlieb and Joseph Singer's English version is published by Noonday in June 1960. Singer and Alma move to an apartment on West 72nd Street. He reviews Tennessee Williams' *Period of Adjustment* and Sean O'Casey's *The Plough and the Stars* for *Forverts*. Novel *Der knecht* (*The Slave*) begins six-month run in *Forverts* in October 1960.

1961   The appearance of Singer's stories in mass-circulation American magazines such as *Mademoiselle*, *Esquire*, and *GQ* exposes his work to a wider audience in the United States. By now Singer has established a method of supervising his translations by working closely with collaborators (many of whom do not know Yiddish, Joseph Singer and Mirra Ginsburg being notable exceptions); his numerous collaborators and translators during his career include Ruth Schachner Finkel, Evelyn Torton Beck, Herbert Lottman, Rosanna Gerber, Elizabeth Shub, Aliza Shevrin, and many others. Reviews production of Ionesco's *Rhinoceros* starring Eli Wallach and Zero Mostel for *Forverts*, as well as Tagore's *King of the Dark Chamber*, Neil Simon's *Come Blow Your Horn*, Ester Kaufman's *A Worm in Horseradish*, the musical *Show Boat*, and Frederic Knott's *Write Me a Murder*. Farrar, Straus & Cudahy (which has acquired Noonday Press) publishes story collection *The Spinoza of Market Street* in October. Cecil Hemley and Singer work on English version of *The Slave*. Lila Karpf, director of the subsidiary rights department at Farrar, Straus & Cudahy, begins serving as Singer's unofficial literary agent.

1962   *The Spinoza of Market Street* earns Singer the first of several National Book Award nominations. On June 11, Farrar, Straus & Cudahy publishes English version of *The Slave*, which is praised by Ted Hughes and Susan Sontag, among others. Singer reads Bruno Schulz and admires his work. Reviews Tennessee Williams' *The Night of the Iguana* and other plays for *Forverts*. Roth-Kershner Productions buys film rights to *The Magician of Lublin*. "Yentl the Yeshiva Boy," English translation of story "Yentl der yehive-boher" (which will be published in Yiddish the following year), is published in *Commentary*. French translation of *Satan in Goray* is published in Paris; *The Spinoza of Market Street* is brought out in England by Secker and Warburg.

1963   Novel *A shif keyn Amerike* (*A Ship to America*) begins nine-month serialization in *Forverts* in January. Singer reviews for *Forverts* Tennessee Williams' *The Milk Train Doesn't Stop Here Anymore*, Eugene O'Neill's *Strange Interlude*, Edward Albee's adaptation of Carson McCullers' *The Ballad of the Sad Café*, and many other plays. Story collection *Gimpl tam un anderer dertseylungen* (*Gimpel the Fool and Other Stories*) is published. Spanish translation of *Satan in Goray* is published in Buenos Aires. Autobiographical narrative *Fun der alter un nayer heym* (*From the Old and the New Home*) begins two years of serialization in *Forverts*. Extensive interview with Joel Blocker and Richard Elman is featured in November issue of *Commentary*; as Singer's fame grows, he gives many more interviews for English-language magazines and newspapers, through which his views on Judaism, philosophy, spirituality, politics, and literature become widely known.

1964   A *Forverts* column, "Knape tsvey yor a vegetaryer" ("Almost Two Years a Vegetarian"), suggests that Singer became a vegetarian in 1962, an impression he will reinforce in later writings and statements in interviews (other evidence of his own and others records his vegetarian habits as far back as the 1920s). "A Sacrifice," chapter from *In My Father's Court,* is the first of several stories Singer publishes in *Harper's*; his fiction appears in *Vogue* and *The*

Saturday Evening Post as well as smaller publications (*American Judaism*, *Hadassah Magazine*) aimed primarily at a Jewish audience. National Institute of Arts and Letters elects Singer as a member. He writes an appreciation of Sholem Aleichem for *The New York Times* in September. Farrar, Straus & Giroux publishes *Short Friday and Other Stories*.

1965   The Singers move to the Belnord apartment house on the corner of Broadway and 86th Street. *The Family Moskat* is restored to print when it is published by Farrar, Straus & Giroux. Singer contributes an introduction to a new edition of Israel Joshua's *Yoshe Kalb*, published by Harper & Row, and reviews Martin Buber's *Daniel* for *Commentary*. Hebrew translation of *The Slave* published in Israel; German translation published in Hamburg. Singer is nominated for the International Publishers' Prize (also known as the Prix Formenter) and wins a prize for Best Foreign Book in France. In response to a request from *Harper's* to discuss the profession of writing, submits article discussing his royalties and financial situation, acknowledging that his "main source of income is still derived from my journalistic work for the *Jewish Daily Forward*."

1966   After a hiatus in writing about theater for *Forverts*, Singer reviews Sartre's *The Condemned of Altona*, Bellow's *Under the Weather*, and Yiddish musical *The Poor Millionaire*, starring Leo Fuchs. In February, Modern Library issues *Selected Short Stories of Isaac Bashevis Singer*, edited by Irving Howe. *Sonim, di geshikhte fun a liebe* (*Enemies, A Love Story*) appears in serial form from February to August in *Forverts*. Essay "Once on Second Avenue There Lived a Yiddish Theater" is printed in *The New York Times*. On May 2, Farrar, Straus & Giroux publishes *In My Father's Court*, abridged version of *Mayn tatn's besdin shtub*; later that month, *Forverts* publishes "Di geshikhte fun Mazel un Shlimazel" ("The Story of Mazel and Shlimazel"), the first of the many children's stories that become an increasingly important part of Singer's literary output in his later years. Collection of children's stories in English translation, *Zlateh the Goat and Other Stories*, is published in October by Harper & Row with illustrations by Maurice Sendak. Singer serves as writer-in-residence at Oberlin College, the first of several such academic appointments. Gives interview on NBC television program *The Eternal Light*, produced by the Jewish Theological Seminary. In an article about recent Nobel Prize recipient S. Y. Agnon published in *Commentary* in December, Edmund Wilson recommends Singer for a Nobel Prize. Ballet inspired by story "The Gentleman from Cracow" is performed by the Sophie Maslow Company at Madison Square Garden.

1967   Story "Hene fayer" ("Henne Fire") published in *Forverts* on January 6; the following week *Der sertifikat (The Certificate)*, autobiographical novel based on Singer's attempt to immigrate to Palestine with "Stefa Janovsky," begins five-month serialization. *The Manor*, first part of *Der hoyf* in English translation by Elaine Gottlieb and Joseph Singer, is published by Farrar, Straus & Giroux. Children's books *The Fearsome Inn* and *Mazel and Shlimazel; or, The Milk of a Lioness* are published by Scribner's and Farrar, Straus & Giroux, respectively. In October, story "Powers" is published in *Harper's* in which Singer shares translation credits with Dorothea Straus; the wife of publisher Robert Straus, she has been acquainted with Singer for several years and will help translate many stories in the late 1960s and early 1970s. Singer contributes introduction to new edition of Hamsun's *Hunger*. Receives Italian literary award, the Bancarella Prize. Profile of Alma, "The Novelist's Working Wife," runs in *The New York Times*. When "The Slaughterer" is published in *The New Yorker* on November 25, the magazine breaks long policy of refusing to print translations, eventually reserving the option of first serial publication for the English versions of Singer's stories; Singer will have a close working relationship with Rachel MacKenzie, his editor at the magazine. For the first time, *Playboy* publishes Singer stories; the third of these, "The Lecture," in its December number, wins the magazine's annual fiction award.

1968   Story "Di kafeterye" ("The Cafeteria") is published in *Di tsukunft*'s March–April issue. *The Séance and Other Stories*, dedicated to the memory of Singer's sister Hinde Esther (with her name erroneously printed as "Minda Esther"), is published by Farrar, Straus & Giroux, which also brings out children's book *When Shlemiel Went to Warsaw and Other Stories*. Barbra Streisand acquires film rights for "Yentl the Yeshiva Boy." Collection of short stories in German translation, including "Gimpel the Fool," "Taibele and Her Demon," and "The Spinoza of Market Street," is published in Hamburg.

1969   Publication of *The Estate* (translation of latter half of *Der hoyf*) and memoir for children *A Day of Pleasure: Stories of a Boy Growing Up in Warsaw*, much of which is adapted from *In My Father's Court*. In the summer, Singer leaves New York for more than three months, visiting France and Israel. Meets novelist and short-story writer Laurie Colwin, who will soon become one of his translators. "Envy; or, Yiddish in America," Cynthia Ozick's long story inspired by Singer and the resentment other Yiddish writers feel about his success, is published in *Commentary* in November. Singer's essay "I See the Child as the Last Refuge" published in *The New York Times*.

1970   Profile of Singer in *The New York Times* reports that his annual income now "comfortably exceeds" $100,000. Although he signs some of his short stories with the "Varshavski" pseudonym, he effectively ceases to write the regular column for *Forverts* that had run continuously under pseudonyms since 1939. Israel Zamir publishes account of his reunion with Singer in 1955 in Tel Aviv newspaper *Al ha-Mishmar*. After a trial run in East Hampton, N.Y., Robert Brustein's Yale Repertory Theater stages *Two Saints* in the fall, pairing dramatic adaptations of "Gimpel the Fool" and Flaubert's "St. Julian the Hospitaler." *A Day of Pleasure* receives the National Book Award in the children's literature category. Singer receives Creative Arts Awards Medal from Brandeis University. Farrar, Straus & Giroux brings out *A Friend of Kafka and Other Stories* as well as the children's books *Elijah the Slave* and *Joseph and Koza; or, The Sacrifice to the Vistula*.

1971   From now on, Singer signs his writings in Yiddish as "Bashevis" or "Bashevis Singer." In August, novel *Der fartribener zun* (*The Exiled Son*) begins six-month serialization in *Forverts*. Farrar, Straus & Giroux's *An Isaac Bashevis Singer Reader* collects stories, *The Magician of Lublin*, and four additional translated chapters of *In My Father's Court*. Children's works *Alone in the Wild Forest* and *The Topsy-Turvy Emperor of China* are published. Singer publishes essay "Hasidism and Its Origins" in the book *Tully Filmus: Selected Drawings*. Folksbiene revives

David Licht's stage adaptation of *Mayn tatn's bes-din shtub* in November, and it runs for several months.

1972   Robert Lescher becomes Singer's agent. Farrar, Straus & Giroux publishes *Enemies, A Love Story* and children's book *The Wicked City*. Photographer and filmmaker Bruce Davidson, who lives in Singer's apartment building, completes half-hour film *Isaac Singer's Nightmare and Mrs. Pupko's Beard*, a free adaptation of story "The Beard"; it wins first prize for fiction at the American Film Festival and is shown on public television in December, paired with a film about Marc Chagall.

1973   Yale Repertory Theater produces dramatization of short story "The Mirror"; while in New Haven to attend a performance, Singer does a radio interview with Irving Howe. *New York* magazine profile "The Cafeteria" is illustrated with Bruce Davidson's photographs of Singer in the Garden Cafeteria on the Lower East Side. Visiting Miami Beach for the first time in several years, Singer buys a condominium apartment at 9511 Collins Avenue in the Surfside neighborhood. Farrar, Straus & Giroux publishes *A Crown of Feathers and Other Stories* and children's book *The Fools of Chelm and Their History*. Crown Publishers issues *The Hasidim*, book of photographs with introduction and essay by Singer.

1974   *A Crown of Feathers* shares National Book Award for fiction with Thomas Pynchon's *Gravity's Rainbow*. The novels *Neshome ekspeditsyes* (*Soul Expeditions*, later translated as *Shosha*) and *Der bal-tshuve* (*The Penitent*) are serialized in *Forverts*. In April, Yale Repertory produces *Shlemiel the First*, based on portions of *The Fools of Chelm*. Children's book *Why Noah Chose the Dove* is published. Chelsea Theater Center's production of *Yentl*, adaptation of "Yentl the Yeshiva Boy" by Leah Napolin and Singer, directed by Robert Kalfin, opens on December 21 at the Brooklyn Academy of Music.

1975   Brooklyn performances of *Yentl* end January 12. *Passions and Other Stories* is published by Farrar, Straus & Giroux. In July Singer receives an honorary degree from the Hebrew University in Jerusalem; while there, *The Jerusalem Post* publishes an unflattering article about him by nephew Maurice Carr, who calls him "an escape artist, the sex-Houdini" and claims Singer had seen a "cherished mistress" while visiting Israel in 1969. In September, he is awarded the S. Y. Agnon Gold Medal by the American Friends of the Hebrew University. Receives honorary doctorate from Texas Christian University (one of his eight honorary degrees). Serves as writer-in-residence at Bard College, where he meets Dvorah Menashe (later Telushkin), who begins to drive him to speaking engagements and act as personal secretary; she translates many of Singer's works and becomes a close friend and companion. After a week of previews, *Yentl*, starring Tovah Feldshuh and John Shea, opens on Broadway at the Eugene O'Neill Theater on October 23, running for more than five months and then touring nationally.

1976   Children's book *Naftali the Storyteller and His Horse, Sus* is published by Farrar, Straus & Giroux; memoir *A Little Boy in Search of God* is brought out by Doubleday. In September, Singer meets Richard Burgin, who will conduct approximately 50 interviews over the next two years, excerpts from which will be published in *The New York Times* in 1978 and in *Conversations with Isaac Bashevis Singer* (1986). Philip Roth visits Singer in November to discuss Bruno Schulz for an interview published in *The New York Times Book Review* the following year. *Yarme un Keyle* (*Yarme and Keyle*), novel about the Warsaw underworld set just before World War I, begins ten-month serialization in *Forverts* in December.

1977–78   During the winter Singer is hospitalized in Florida for treatment of a prostate condition. Stage adaptation of story *Teibele and Her Demon* by Eve Friedman and Singer is performed at the Guthrie Theater in Minneapolis, starring F. Murray Abraham and Laura Esterman. *Shosha* is published by Farrar, Straus & Giroux in July 1978. Singer reviews Bruno Schulz's *Sanatorium Under the Sign of the Hourglass* for *The New York Times*. Shooting begins in West Germany for film of *The Magician of Lublin*, adapted and directed by Israeli filmmaker Menahem Golan and starring Alan Arkin. Memoir *A Young Man in Search of Love* is published by Doubleday. Collection *he-Mafteah: sipurim* (*The Key: Stories*), translated by Israel Zamir, is published in Tel Aviv in 1978. On October 5, 1978, Singer is awarded the Nobel Prize in Literature. Rents a hotel room so he can work on his acceptance speech without distraction; the publicity and fame of the award cause him to remove his name from the phone book. Travels to Stockholm with Alma, Simon Weber (now editor of *Forverts*), Roger and Dorothea Straus, and Israel Zamir. His acceptance speech, delivered on December 8, is in English but includes a sentence in Yiddish. *Forverts* dedicates Chanukah issue to Singer, including a diary of the Stockholm trip written by Weber.

1979   First full-length biography, Paul Kresh's *Isaac Bashevis Singer: The Magician of West 86th Street*, is published. English and Yiddish versions of Singer's Nobel lecture are published by Farrar, Straus & Giroux, as well as the story collection *Old Love*. Israel Zamir's Hebrew translation of *Enemies, A Love Story* is published in Tel Aviv. Menahem Golan's *The Magician of Lublin* is shown at the Venice Film Festival but its scheduled screening at the Cairo Film Festival is canceled by Egyptian censors; the film opens in New York on November 9 and is met with unfavorable reviews. David Schiff's opera *Gimpel the Fool*, sung in Yiddish with English narration, premieres at the 92nd Street Y in New York and is revived the following year in a longer and slightly revised version. *Teibele and Her Demon* is performed in Washington, D.C., then makes its Broadway premiere at the Brooks Atkinson Theater in December.

1980   *Teibele and Her Demon* closes in January after 25 performances. Novel *Der kenig fun di felder* (*The King of the Fields*) is serialized for more than ten months beginning in February. Having long maintained he would never return to Poland, Singer declines offer from Polish literary group to attend a conference in Warsaw. Contributes a forward to Aaron Zeitlin's posthumous collection *Literarishe un filosofishe eseyen* (*Literary and Philosophical Essays*). Book of stories in Russian translation, including "Gimpel the Fool" and "Teibele and Her Demon," is published in Tel Aviv. Two children's books are published by Farrar, Straus & Giroux: *The Power of Light: Eight Stories for Hanukkah* and *The Reaches of Heaven: A Story of the Baal Shem Tov*.

1981   Autobiographical novel *Farloyrene neshomes* (*Lost Souls*, posthumously translated as *Meshugah*) is serialized in *Forverts* beginning in April. *Lost in America*, sequel to *A Young Man in Search of Love*, is published by Doubleday.

1982   "Di mishpohe: Materyal far an oytobiografye" ("The
        Family: Material for an Autobiography") runs in *Forverts*
        from February to August, then resumes in October for
        five months. *The Collected Stories of Isaac Bashevis Singer*
        is published by Farrar, Straus & Giroux, as well as chil-
        dren's book *The Golem*.

1983   Yehuga Moralis's musical version of "Gimpel the Fool" is
        performed in Israel. When novel *The Penitent* is pub-
        lished, it receives mixed reviews. Polish translations based
        on the English versions of *The Magician of Lublin* and
        The Estate, as well as a collection of short stories, are pub-
        lished in Warsaw. After being out of print for decades,
        Hinde Esther's *Deborah* is published in England by
        Virago Press; when asked about the revival of interest in
        his sister's work, Singer chooses not to comment. *Yentl*,
        musical film directed by Barbra Streisand and starring
        Streisand, Mandy Patinkin, and Amy Irving, opens No-
        vember 18.

1984   *Yentl* is a commercial success but Singer is deeply un-
        happy about the adaptation of his story and publishes an
        essay (cast as an interview with himself) criticizing the
        film in *The New York Times* in January. Amrak Nowak's
        television film *The Cafeteria*, based on Singer's story, is
        shown on PBS as part of the "American Playhouse" series
        on February 21. In October, *A Play for the Devil*, based
        on story "The Unseen," is performed in Yiddish by the
        Folksbiene; *Shlemiel the First* opens at the Jewish Reper-
        tory Theater in New York. Autobiographical books *A Lit-
        tle Boy in Search of God*, *A Young Man in Search of Love*,
        and *Lost in America* are collected with introduction "The
        Beginning" as *Love and Exile*, published by Doubleday.
        Stories for Children is published by Farrar, Straus &
        Giroux.

1985   Farrar, Straus & Giroux brings out *The Image and Other
        Stories*. *Der ver aheim* (*The Way Home*), is serialized in
        Forverts. Singer teaches weekly creative writing class with
        Lester Goran at the University of Miami.

1986   *Conversations with Isaac Bashevis Singer*, edited by
        Richard Burgin, published by Farrar, Straus & Giroux.
        On June 23 Singer receives the Handel Medallion, cul-
        tural prize awarded by the City of New York. Story col-
        lection *Gifts* is published by the Jewish Publication Society.

Dvorah Menashe works with Singer to collect his early work in a series called "Early Steps in Literature" to be published in *Forverts*, but the project founders. Amrak Nowak's film *Isaac in America: A Journey with Isaac Bashevis Singer* is screened at the New York Film Festival in September. Paul Mazursky acquires film rights to *Enemies, A Love Story* and begins working on adaptation with screenwriter Roger L. Simon. In November, the Israeli ministry of education bans several of Singer's works from religious schools because "his values do not conform to the values of the religious public."

1987–90   *Isaac in America* is nominated for an Academy Award and wins the Sundance Film Festival's Grand Jury Prize for a documentary. *The Death of Methuselah and Other Stories* and novel *The King of the Fields* are published by Farrar, Straus & Giroux in 1988. Singer's health is now failing, and the Singers live full time in Surfside. Ronald Sanders, writer and former editor of *Midstream*, is named his official biographer (plans for other biographies, by Khone Shemruk, Leonard Wolf, and Janet Hadda, will be announced; only Hadda's is completed). The American Academy and Institute of Arts and Letters awards Singer its Gold Medal. Paul Mazursky travels to Florida to meet with Singer. *Enemies, A Love Story*, starring Ron Silver, Angelica Houston, and Lena Olin, opens in December 1989; Huston and Olin are both nominated for Academy Awards. Singer is elected to the American Academy of Arts in 1990, the first author to write in a language other than English to be so honored.

1991   Biographer Ronald Sanders dies in January. *My Love Affair with Miami Beach,* book of photographs by Richard Nagler with a short essay by Singer and an interview, is published. Farrar, Straus & Giroux publishes *Scum* in a translation by Rosaline Dukalsky Schwartz. Singer dies on July 24 in his apartment in Surfside, Florida. He is buried at the Beth-El cemetery in Paramus, New Jersey.

Note on the Texts

This volume contains the 65 short stories by Isaac Bashevis Singer in English translations published for the first time in book form in *Old Love* (1979), *The Collected Stories* (1982), *The Image and Other Stories* (1985), *Gifts* (1985), and *The Death of Methuselah and Other Stories* (1988). It also contains, as the introduction to *Gifts*, a version of a lecture that Singer had delivered often since the early 1960s. The texts of these works are taken from their first book publications. This volume also contains three stories published by Singer in translation but never collected in one of his books, along with ten stories not published in English during Singer's lifetime.

Singer wrote his stories in Yiddish, his native language, and published regularly in periodicals such as *Di tsukunft* (*The Future*), *Di goldene keyt* (*The Golden Chain*), and especially *Forverts* (*Jewish Daily Forward*), the newspaper to which he contributed stories and journalism as a freelance writer from 1935 through the early 1940s and thereafter as a salaried member of its staff. When Singer began publishing English versions of his stories in the 1950s, some were translated without his direct involvement. Soon, however, after his stories and novels began attracting interest in the United States outside of Yiddish-speaking circles, Singer began working closely with his translators (many of whom did not speak Yiddish) to produce English versions of his stories, revising and adapting the works for a new audience. Singer described the process of working with his collaborators to a *New York Times* reporter in 1975: "I dictate to them in English, my English, and they correct. They polish my English." Many of his later stories were translated through this sort of collaborative process. In the 1970s and 1980s the English versions of Singer's stories were often published in *The New Yorker* (and, less frequently, in other publications) before being collected in one of his short-story volumes. When preparing these volumes, Singer would continue to make or authorize changes while working with his editors at Farrar, Straus & Giroux.

Singer called English his "second original language," and the English versions of his fiction served as the basis for translations into languages such as French, German, and Italian. Although he would almost always publish a story in Yiddish soon after its completion, sometimes the English version of a story was published years or even decades after it was first written in Yiddish. For example, the story "Der yid fun Bovl" ("The Jew from Babylon"), first published in

1932 and revised for the 1943 collection *Der sotn in Goray: A mayse fun fartsaytns: un andere dertseylungen* (*Satan in Goray: A Story of Bygone Days: And Other Stories*), was not published in English translation until it was included in Singer's final collection of short stories, *The Death of Methuselah and Other Stories* (1988).

Several of Singer's stories included in books during the 1980s were published in more than one volume. Because of the overlap among collections, the present volume does not print the complete contents of Singer's books *The Collected Stories* (1982), *Gifts* (1985), and *The Death of Methuselah and Other Stories* (1988). For *Gifts* and *The Death of Methuselah and Other Stories*, the stories omitted are limited to those published by Singer in previous books, and are thus included elsewhere in the present volume. *The Collected Stories* is a compilation of 47 stories, all but five of which had already been published in one of Singer's books. The five previously uncollected stories are included in the section "from *The Collected Stories*"; the other 42 stories appear with the contents of the books in which they were first collected in English (in the present volume or in the two other volumes of The Library of America's edition of Singer's stories, *Collected Stories: Gimpel the Fool to The Letter Writer* and *Collected Stories: A Friend of Kafka to Passions*).

The list below provides information about the publication history of each story in Yiddish and in English. For Yiddish publication, the present volume has relied primarily on Roberta Saltzman's *Isaac Bashevis Singer: A Bibliography of His Works in Yiddish and English, 1960–1991* (Lanham, Md.: Scarecrow Press, 2002). David Neal Miller's two bibliographies covering Singer's early career, *A Bibliography of Isaac Bashevis Singer, 1924–1949* (New York: Peter Lang, 1984) and *A Bibliography of Isaac Bashevis Singer, January 1950–June 1952* (New York: Max Weinreich Center for Advanced Jewish Studies, YIVO Institute for Jewish Research, 1979), have also been consulted. These bibliographies, while thorough, are not complete (no bibliography exists for the period July 1952–December 1959); Singer published under at least six pseudonyms in Yiddish periodicals in New York, Warsaw, Paris, and perhaps elsewhere during his career, and it is unlikely there will ever be a comprehensive list of all his contributions to Yiddish publications. The English versions of Singer's works have been listed by Jackson R. Bryer and Paul E. Rockwell in "Isaac Bashevis Singer in English: A Bibliography" in *Critical Views of Isaac Bashevis Singer*, edited by Irving Malin (New York: NYU Press, 1969), as well as in articles published in the *Bulletin of Bibliography* by Bonniejean McGuire Christensen (January–March 1969) and David S. Hornbeck (March 1982). The list below includes the Yiddish title of each story and translates the title only if significantly different from the title of

the English version. If no Yiddish title is given, the story does not
appear in Saltzman's or Miller's bibliographies. Book publications
are abbreviated as follows:

SG   *Der sotn in Goray: a mayse fun fartsaytns: un andere dertsey-*
      lungen. New York: Farlag Matones, 1943. (*Satan in Goray: A*
      Story of Bygone Days: And Other Stories.)
DS   *Der shpigl un andere dertseylungen.* Jerusalem: Hebrew Uni-
      versity of Jerusalem, 1975. (*The Mirror and Other Stories.*)
OL   *Old Love* (New York: Farrar, Straus & Giroux, 1979).
CS   *The Collected Stories of Isaac Bashevis Singer* (New York: Farrar,
      Straus & Giroux, 1982).
I   *The Image and Other Stories* (New York: Farrar, Straus &
      Giroux, 1985).
G   *Gifts* (Philadelphia: Jewish Publication Society, 1985).
DM   *The Death of Methuselah and Other Stories* (New York: Farrar,
      Straus & Giroux, 1988).

As stated above, the present volume prints the texts of Singer's
English-language collections, in which the English versions of his
stories were published for the first time in book form (based on the
listing that appears in Saltzman's bibliography, pp. 149–162). The
source of each story printed here is indicated by bold type.

One Night in Brazil. "A gast oyf eyn nakht" (A Guest for One Night).
   Forverts, November 17, 18, 24, and 25, and December 1, 1977. English ver-
   sion: *The New Yorker*, April 3, 1978. **OL.**
Yochna and Shmelke. "Yakhne un Shmelkne." *Forverts*, October 1, 7, and 8,
   1976. English version: *The New Yorker*, February 14, 1977. **OL.**
Two. *The New Yorker*, December 20, 1976. **OL.**
The Psychic Journey. "Di psikhishe rayze." *Di goldene keyt* 90 (1976). English
   version: *The New Yorker*, October 18, 1976. **OL,** CS.
Elka and Meier. "Elke un Meir." *Forverts*, April 15, 16, 22, and 23, 1976. En-
   glish version: *The New Yorker*, May 23, 1977. **OL.**
A Party in Miami Beach "Di parti" (The Party; also the Yiddish title of the
   story translated as "There Are No Coincidences," below). *Forverts*, Febru-
   ary 26 and 27, and March 4, 5, 11, and 12, 1976. English version: **OL.**
Two Weddings and One Divorce. "Tsvey hasenes un eyn get." *Forverts*, April
   24, 1977. English version: *The New Yorker*, August 29, 1977. **OL.**
A Cage for Satan. *New Yorker*, May 24, 1976. **OL.**
Brother Beetle. "Bruder Zshuk." *Forverts*, October 1 and 2, 1965. English version: **OL,** CS.
The Boy Knows the Truth. "Dos yingl veyst dem emes." *Di tsukunft*, Octo-
   ber 1972. English version: *The New Yorker*, October 17, 1977. **OL.**
There Are No Coincidences. "Di parti" (The Party; also the Yiddish title of

the story translated as "A Party in Miami Beach," above). *Forverts*, December 3, 9, 10, and 16, 1966. English version: **OL.**

Not for the Sabbath. "Nisht far Shabes." *Forverts*, February 15, 21, and 28, 1974. English version: *The New Yorker*, November 27, 1978. **OL.**

The Safe Deposit. *The New Yorker*, April 16, 1979. **OL.**

The Betrayer of Israel. "Der oykher Yisroel." *Forverts*, December 24, 1978. English version: *The New Yorker*, July 23, 1979. **OL, CS.**

Tanhum. "Tanhum." *Di goldene keyt* 61 (1967). English version: *The New Yorker*, November 17, 1975. **OL.**

The Bus. "Der oytobus." *Forverts*, October 29, November 4, 5, 11, 12, 18, 19, 25, and 26, and December 2, 3, 1976. English version: *The New Yorker*, August 28, 1978. **OL, CS.**

The Manuscript. "Der manuskript." *Forverts*, January 23 and 24, 1975. English version: **OL, CS.**

The Power of Darkness. "Der koyeh fun finsternish." *Forverts*, August 21, 22, and 28, 1975. English version: *The New Yorker*, February 2, 1976. **OL, CS.**

A Night in the Poorhouse. "A vinter-nakht in hekdesh" (A Winter Night in the Poorhouse). *Di tsukunft*, February 1979. English version: *The New Yorker*, December 24, 1979. **CS.**

Escape from Civilization. "Antloyf fun tsivilizatsye." *Forverts*, August 29 and September 4, 1975. English version: *The New Yorker*, May 6, 1972. **CS.**

Vanvild Kava. *The Atlantic*, March 1980. **CS.**

The Reencounter. *The Atlantic*, July 1979. **CS.**

Moon and Madness. *The New Yorker*, October 6, 1980. **CS.**

Advice. "Di eytse." *Di goldene keyt* 104 (1981). English version: *The New Yorker*, December 28, 1981. **I.**

One Day of Happiness. "Eyn tog glik." *Forverts*, October 15, 21, and 22, 1966. English version: *Cavalier*, September 1965. **I.**

The Bond. "Petsh" (Slaps). *Forverts*, September 30 and October 1, 1966. English version: **I.**

The Interview. *The New Yorker*, May 13, 1983. **I.**

The Divorce. "Der get." *Forverts*, February 25 and March 4 and 11, 1983. English version: *The New Yorker*, June 13, 1983. **I.**

Strong as Death Is Love. "Shtark vi der toyt iz libe." *Forverts*, December 29 and 30, 1972. English version: *Partisan Review* 51:4–52:1 (1984–1985). **I.**

Why Heisherik Was Born. **I.**

The Enemy. "Der soyne." *Forverts*, January 30 and 31, 1970. English version: **I.**

Remnants. **I.**

On the Way to the Poorhouse. "Dos gehintekhts" (Riffraff). *Forverts*, March 28 and 29, 1969. English version: *Playboy*, October 1969. **I.**

Loshikl. *Partisan Review* 52:2 (1985). **I.**

The Pocket Remembered. "Di keshene hot gedenckt." *Forverts*, March 18 and 25, and April 1, 8, and 15, 1983. English version: **I, G.**

The Secret. "Der sod." *Forverts*, June 17 and 24, and July 1, 8, and 15, 1983. English version: **I, G.**

A Nest Egg for Paradise. "A knipl oylem habe." *Forverts*, April 22 and 29, and May 6, 13, 20, and 27, 1983. English version: **I, G.**

The Conference. "Di konferents." *Forverts*, January 2 and 8, 1981. English version: **I.**

Miracles. "Nisim." *Forverts*, August 24, 30, and 31, and September 6 and 7, 1968. English version: *Israel Magazine* 2:5 (1970). **I.**

The Litigants. "Der protses." *Forverts*, January 6, 1984. English version: **I.**

A Telephone Call on Yom Kippur. "A telefon in Yom-Kiper." *Forverts*, March 19, 20, 26, and 27, and April 2, 1981. English version: *The New Yorker*, September 6, 1982. **I.**

Strangers. "Fremde." *Forverts*, April 3 and 4, 1970. English version: **I.**

The Mistake. "Der toes." *Forverts*, February 19, 20, 26, and 27, 1981. English version: *The New Yorker*, February 4, 1985. **I.**

Confused. "Tsemisht." *Forverts*, September 19, 25, and 26, and October 2, 3, 9, and 10, 1975. English version: **I.**

The Image. "Der geshtalt." *Forverts*, July 22 and 29, and August 5, 12, and 19, 1983. English version: *The New Yorker*, October 8, 1984. **I.**

Introduction to *Gifts*. **G.**

The Trap. "Di pastke." *Forverts*, September 2, 7, 16, 21, and 28. English version: **G, DM.**

The Smuggler. **G, DM.**

Gifts. "Matones." *Forverts*, February 11 and 18, 1983. English version: **G, DM.**

The Jew from Babylon. "Der Yid fun Bovl." SG. English version: **DM.**

The House Friend. *The New Yorker*, July 1, 1985. **DM.**

Burial at Sea. "Dray" (Three). *Forverts*, June 3, 10, and 17, 1983. English version: *The New Yorker*, October 14, 1985. **DM.**

The Recluse. *The New Yorker*, July 21, 1986. **DM.**

Disguised. *The New Yorker*, September 22, 1986. **DM.**

The Accuser and the Accused. "Der bashuldiker un der bashuldikter." *Forverts*, August 19 and 26, 1983. English version: **DM.**

A Peephole in the Gate. "Oyf a shif" (On a Ship). *Forverts*, February 13, 14, 20, and 21, 1970. DS (as "A fentsterl in toyer"). English version: *Esquire*, April 1971. **DM.**

The Bitter Truth. **DM.**

The Impresario. "Di forlezung in Brazil" (The Lecture in Brazil). *Forverts*, October 21 and 28, and November 4, 11, 18, and 25, 1983. English version: *Harper's*, April 1986. **DM.**

Logarithms. **DM.**

Runners to Nowhere. "Di loyfers" (The Runners). *Forverts*, November 25 and December 2, 9, and 16, 1983. **DM.**

The Missing Line. *Partisan Review*, Spring 1988. **DM.**

The Hotel. "Der hotel." *Forverts*, September 10, 1961. English version: **DM.**

Dazzled. "Farblendt" (Blinded). *Forverts*, December 16, 23, and 30, 1983. English version: *The New Yorker*, March 18, 1985. **DM.**

Sabbath in Gehenna. "Shabes in Gehenem." *Forverts*, December 16, 1972. English version: *Central Conference of American Rabbis*, Winter 1974. **DM.**

The Last Gaze. *Partisan Review*, Spring 1988. **DM.**
The Death of Methuselah. **DM.**

Singer's uncollected stories fall into two categories: those published in translation in magazines but not collected in his books, and those not published in English. The first three stories in the "Uncollected Stories" section of the present volume were published in the following magazines: "The Bird," originally published in Yiddish as "Dos feygele" in *Di goldene keyt 36* (1960), English version in *The Jewish World*, September 1964; "'My Adventures as an Idealist'" originally published in Yiddish as "Der mehaber" ("The Author") in *Forverts* (October 8, 9, and 15, 1965), English version in *The Saturday Evening Post*, November 18, 1967; and "Exes" in *Confrontation*, Fall 1977–1978. The texts of these stories are taken from the English-language periodicals. The remaining ten stories were not published in English and are based on typescripts that are part of the collection of Singer's papers at the Harry Ransom Humanities Research Center, University of Texas at Austin. These typescripts are polished translations of stories that may have been sent to magazines for consideration; some obvious typographical errors have been corrected, but otherwise the texts printed here follow the Ransom Center typescripts. Most of these stories were published in Yiddish in *Forverts*: "The Angry Man" (as "Der kaysn," February 4, 1966); "Two" (as "Tsvey," April 17 and 18, 1970); "The Mathematician" (as "Der matematiker," March 22 and 28, 1974); "Hershele and Hanele, or the Power of a Dream" (as "Hershele un Hanale, oder der koyeh fun a holem," December 12, 18, and 19, 1975); and "Morris and Timna" (as "Moris un Timna," March 26 and April 22 and 23, 1976).

This volume presents the texts of the original printings chosen for inclusion here, but it does not attempt to reproduce features of their typographic design. The texts printed here are presented without change, except for the correction of typographical errors. Spelling, punctuation, and capitalization are often expressive features and are not altered, even when inconsistent or irregular. Transliteration of Yiddish and Hebrew words appear as presented in the source texts, even if the same words are rendered differently elsewhere in the volume. The translation credits are those given by Singer, and no attempt has been made to verify the accuracy of these credits or to identify translators for stories in which no credit line appears. The following is a list of typographical errors corrected, cited by page and line number: 103.29, attempt; 168.16, teamed; 170.37–38, occured; 173.2, then; 189.17, *rotzah?*; 205.32, Breathing; 407.13, Amran,"; 430.20, holidy; 457.34, his body; 466.28–29, "It's . . . funeral.";

467.30, Spinoza's; 468.18–19, "Lord . . . hands."; 468.22, "Jew . . . Palestine."; 468.27–28, "The . . . you."; 468.29–30, "Why . . . him."; 469.5–6, "Ye . . . Lord."; 469.27, "What . . . man?"; 470.16, *"Ostjude."*; 472.27–28, "Better . . . death."; 529.5, feel; 581.19, this wife; 683.27–28, "Where . . . Warsaw?"; 739.14, Its; 739.20–21, occured; 756.11, on for; 759.13, Terry's both; 765.29, as an.

Glossary and Notes

The glossary below provides basic definitions of terms that occur more than once in Singer's stories. The spellings follow the usage in Singer's texts (variant spellings used in the stories printed in this volume are listed in parenthesis).

Angel Raziel: Anonymous collection of kabbalistic texts published as a book in Amsterdam in 1701 but compiled centuries earlier.

Asmodeus (Ashmodai): According to some Jewish legends, king of the demons and husband of Lilith.

Beth Midrash: House of study.

Book of Creation: Sefer Yezirah, one of the fundamental kabbalistic books.

Britska: Carriage long enough to recline in.

Chalutz (pl. *chalutzim*)*:* Literally, pioneer; member of an organization of agricultural settlers in Israel.

Cheder (heder): Religious primary school.

Cholent: Stew made during the week for consumption on the Sabbath.

Days of Awe: Days of repentance between Rosh Hashana and Yom Kippur.

Dumah: Angel who demands the name of a person shortly after death and makes an accounting of that person's good and evil deeds.

Dybbuk: The spirit of a dead person who possesses the bodies of the living.

Ethics of the Fathers: Tractate of the Talmud.

Ethrog: A citron, used in the celebration of Sukkoth.

Feast of Booths: Sukkoth, the harvest festival following Yom Kippur.

Feast of Omer: Harvest festival between Passover and Shavuoth.

Feast of Tabernacles: Sukkoth.

Feast of the Rejoicing of the Law: Simkhat Torah.

Gemara: One of the two parts of the Talmud, primarily an elaboration of the first part, the Mishnah.

Great Poland (Greater Poland): Wielkopolska, historical region in west-central Poland around the city of Poznan; annexed by Prussia in 1793.

Guide of the Perplexed: Theological treatise (1190) by Maimonides.

Hashanah Raba (Hoshana Rabbah): Seventh day of Sukkoth.

Ketev Mriri: Chief of the devils in Jewish folklore.

Ketuba: Marriage certificate.

Kol Nidre: Prayer repeated three times at the opening of the evening service on Yom Kippur.

Landsman (pl. *landsleit*): Fellow-countryman.

Lilith: In kabbalistic literature and Jewish legend, a demon who was Adam's wife before Eve. After abandoning Adam, she mated with Asmodeus and other demons. She and her many offspring, the *lilin*, were believed to prey on children.

Litvak: Lithuanian Jew.

Machlath: Demon who rules one of the levels of hell with Lilith and the demons Namah and Hurmizah.

Metatron: In the Kabbalah, the highest archangel, seated beside God in heaven.

Midrash Talpioth: Book (1698) of commentaries and glosses by the Smyrna kabbalist Elijah ben Solomon Abraham ha-Kohen (d. 1720).

Mikveh: Ritual bath.

Minyan: The minimum number of ten adult Jews required to conduct a prayer service.

Mishnah: The first of the Talmud's two parts (the other is the Gemara).

Misnagdim (*Mitnaggedim*): Literally "the opponents," sect opposed to Hasidism.

Mohel: Man who performs a ritual circumcision.

Naamah: Demon who rules one of the levels of hell with Lilith and the demons Machlath and Hurmizah.

Ne'ila (*Nilah*): Prayer at the end of the Yom Kippur service.

Orchard of Pomegranates: Pardes Rimmonim, kabbalistic treatise by 16th-century mystic Moses ben Jacob Cordovero.

Panienka: Miss, young lady.

Rashi: French Talmudist (1040–1105), known especially for his commentaries.

Rebbetzin: Rabbi's wife.

Responsa (sing. *Responsum*): A form of commentary in which a rabbi answers a specific question addressed to him.

Samael: Lucifer, prince of demons in the Talmud and Kabbalah.

Sambation: Mythical river whose turbulent waters are supposed to rest on the Sabbath.

Sanhedrin: Supreme council and tribunal of the Jews during the Maccabean period (before the destruction of the Second Temple in Jerusalem in 70 C.E.) dealing with civil, criminal, and religious matters.

Shames: Synagogue-keeper.

Shavuot (*Shevuot, Shevuouth*): Feast, also called Pentecost, celebrating the revelation of the Law to Moses on Mount Sinai.

Shechinah (*Shechina*): Female aspect of divinity.

Shema: Prayer recited twice daily as an affirmation of faith; the first
   of its three scriptural citations is "Hear, O Israel: the Lord our
   God is one Lord."

Simkhat Torah (*Simchas Torah, Simkhas Torah*): Feast of the Rejoicing of the Law, holiday marking the end of the yearly cycle
   of weekly Torah readings.

Selichoth (*Selichot*) *prayers:* Prayers for forgiveness recited in the early
   morning on the days leading up to Yom Kippur, as well as on
   several other fast days throughout the year.

Shadai (*Shaddai*): One of the names of God.

Shokhet (*shochet*): Ritual slaughterer.

Shulchan Aruch: Codification of Jewish law by Spanish-born Talmudist Joseph ben Ephraim Karo (1488–1575).

Tishe b'Av (*Tisha b'Av*): Holiday marked by fasting to commemorate
   the destruction of the Temple in Jerusalem.

Tree of Life: *'Etz Hayyim* (1346), by Aaron ben Elijah (c. 1328–1369),
   Karaite theologian who lived in Constantinople.

Treif (*tref*): Not kosher.

Wonder Rabbi: Hasidic rabbi believed to have healing powers.

Zohar: Kabbalistic book probably compiled in the 13th century; its
   authorship was attributed by tradition to 1st-cenutry mystic
   Simon ben Yochi.

In the notes below, the reference numbers denote page and line of
this volume (the line count includes headings). No note is made for
material included in standard desk-reference books. For further biographical background than is contained in the Chronology, see
Richard Burgin, *Conversations with Isaac Bashevis Singer* (New York:
Noonday Press, 1986); Grace Farrell (ed.), *Isaac Bashevis Singer:
Conversations* (Jackson: University Press of Mississippi, 1992); Janet
Hadda, *Isaac Bashevis Singer: A Life* (New York: Oxford University
Press, 1997); Paul Kresh, *Isaac Bashevis Singer: The Magician of West
86th Street* (New York: Dial, 1979); David Neal Miller, *A Bibliogra-
phy of Isaac Bashevis Singer 1924–1949* (New York: Peter Lang, 1984),
and *A Bibliography of Isaac Bashevis Singer, January 1950–June 1952*
(New York: Max Weinreich Center for Advanced Jewish Studies,
YIVO Institute for Jewish Research, 1979); Roberta Saltzman, *Isaac
Bashevis Singer: A Bibliography of His Works in Yiddish and English,
1960–1991* (Lanham, Md.: Scarecrow Press, 2002); Clive Sinclair, *The
Brothers Singer* (London: Allison & Busby, 1983). Seth L. Wolitz

(ed.), *The Hidden Isaac Bashevis Singer* (Austin: University of Texas Press, 2001); Israel Zamir, *Journey to My Father, Isaac Bashevis Singer,* translated by Barbara Harshav (New York: Arcade, 1995).

OLD LOVE

12.27   Yehupetz]   Kiev.

12.27   Boiberik]   Boyberik (Bobrka) is a Galician town (in present-day Ukraine) near L'viv.

30.30   *Ze'enah u-Re'enah*]   Yiddish translation of the Pentateuch and commentary by 16th-century rabbi Jacob ben Issac Ashkenazi.

30.30–31   *The Lamp of Light*]   *Menorat ha-Maor*, popular treatise on ethics by 14th-century Spanish rabbi Isaac Aboab.

84.19   Zeromski]   Polish novelist (1864–1925).

92.7   ceremony of Chalitzah]   Ritual ending the bond of levirate marriage.

98.16   the famous saint Joseph della Reyna]   Versions of the legend of Joseph della Reyna are told in Singer's stories "Moon and Madness" (page 274) and "Miracles" (page 465).

115.31   tannaim and amoraim]   The sages of the Mishnah (70–200) and the Talmud (200–500), respectively.

152.5   *nachalniks*]   Local prefects.

154.12   *Ostjude*]   Eastern Jew, a term of contempt.

163.4   *Yetzer Hora*]   Evil inclination.

165.15   NKVD]   Soviet secret police.

183.6   *The Breastplate of Judgment . . .*]   Fourth section of *Arba'ah Turim* (*The Tur* or *The Four Columns*), treatise on Jewish law by Toledo rabbi Jacob ben Asher (1270–1340).

183.7–8   the text . . . Isserles]   Ben Isserles' *Mappa* (1571) contained commentary on the *Shulchan Aruch*, codification of Jewish law by Spanish-born Talmudist Joseph ben Ephraim Karo (1488–1575).

183.11–12   Korah . . . Abiram]   Korah and his followers, who included the brothers Dathan and Abiram, rebelled against Moses and Aaron (see Numbers 16).

212.38   Dubnow's]   Russian-born Jewish historian Simon Dubnow (1860–1941), author of *World History of the Jewish People* (1925–1929).

212.39   Klausner's *Jesus of Nazareth*]   Study (1922) of the life of Jesus written in Hebrew by historian Joseph Klausner (1874–1958).

230.14   Abdul-Hamid's]   Ottoman sultan Abdulhamid II (1842–1918).

THE COLLECTED STORIES

239.2–3   forty-seven stories]   42 of the 47 stories had been published in Singer's previous English-language collections; the five stories printed in this section of the present volume were published for the first time in book form in *The Collected Stories*.

242.18   Vilna Gaon]   Elijah ben Solomon (1720–1797), Lithuanian rabbi who opposed Hasidism.

254.21   Sven Hedin, Nansen]   Swedish explorer (1865–1972) of Central Asia and Tibet; Norwegian Fridtjof Nansen (1861–1930), explorer of Greenland and the Arctic.

254.21–22   Captain Scott, Amundsen]   The expedition of Norwegian explorer Roald Amundsen reached the South Pole on December 14, 1911, five weeks ahead of a competing expedition led by British explorer Robert Falcon Scott.

283.28   Cozbi, the daughter of Zur]   In Numbers 25, Phineas, grandson of Aaron, killed Simeonite prince Zimri and Midianite princess Cozbi for their lustful acts and appeased God's wrath.

THE IMAGE AND OTHER STORIES

296.16   *amor dei intellectualis*]   Intellectual love of God.

297.4   Birobidzhan]   Soviet area near the Chinese border established by Stalin as an ostensibly autonomous region for Jews. Although some Soviet Jews settled there, its Jewish population never exceeded one third of the remote region's population, and Stalinist purges attacked Jewish residents and institutions.

297.7–8   the Jewish doctors . . . Russian leaders.]   Nine doctors, seven of whom were Jewish, were publicly accused in January 1953 of murdering two of Stalin's aides and planning to poison many members of the Soviet political and military leadership. Shortly after Stalin's death in May 1953, the Soviet government admitted that the charges had been fabricated.

297.26   Sir Moses Montefiore]   British Jewish financier and philanthropist (1784–1885).

299.19   Czernowitz conference]   1908 meeting devoted to issues of Yiddish language and culture.

311.19–20   Heine's poem . . . love.']   In Heine's poem "Der Asra," the Asra are a tribe of slaves "welche sterben, wenn sie lieben" (who die, when they love).

327.15–16   poem about a cloud in pants]   Mayakovsky's long poem

"Oblako v shtanakh" ("A Cloud in Pants"), published when he was 22, helped establish his reputation as a poet.

327.19–20   Something like Lasker.] German-Jewish novelist and poet Else Lasker-Schüler (1869–1945).

327.33   Hermann Cohen] German neo-Kantian philosopher (1842–1918).

328.11   Professor Forel's book about sex] *Die sexuelle Frage* (*The Sexual Question*, 1905) by Swiss psychiatrist and entomologist Auguste-Henri Forel (1848–1931).

332.36   Cohen] Member of a priestly caste.

341.28   schmegegge] Dope.

376.9   *sephira*] An emanation of God.

405.3–4   Bloody Wednesday] In his story "Old Love," Singer explained that on Bloody Wednesday, 1905, "the Cossacks killed dozens of revolutionaries who had converged on the town hall to demand a constitution from the czar."

409.22   Amorites] Ancient Jewish sages.

413.28   Cave of Machpelah] Used for the tomb of the patriarchs.

425.27   Isaac Meir Dick] Popular writer (1814–1893) who wrote in Yiddish and Hebrew.

425.28   Mendele Mocher Sephorim] "Mendele the Itinerant Bookseller," pen name of Minsk-born novelist, short-story writer, and playwright Shalom Jacob Abramovich (1835–1917), who wrote in Yiddish and Hebrew.

425.35   Shomer's] Pseudonym of popular Yiddish novelist.

428.32   Haman] Persecutor of the Jews in the Book of Esther.

430.6–7   King Sobieski's time] Old-fashioned, anachronistic. John III Sobieski (1629–1696) was king of Poland from 1674 to 1696.

439.17   Gog . . . Magog] In Jewish eschatological tradition, Israel's battle against barbarian enemies led by the tribes Gog and Magog was prophesied to be one of the major events preceding the reign of the Messiah.

439.33   kashruth] Dietary regulations.

441.11   'And Manoach . . . wife.'] In the Berakhot tractate of the Talmud.

446.13–15   depraved . . . Phinehas] See note 283.28.

449.12   Sheol] Underworld.

449.34–36   Nebuzaradan . . . deeds] Nebuzaradan, captain of the guard under Nebuchanezzar who led the capture of Jerusalem, later set Jeremiah free.

453.10 Maggid] Preacher.

454.8 gabbai] Collector of money.

457.32 *Reshit Chochmah*] *The Beginning of Wisdom*, book on morals compiled and written by the 16th-century kabbalist Elijah ben Moses de Vidas.

469.30 Wyspianski] Polish poet, playwright, and painter Stanislaw Wyspianski (1869–1907).

470.7 Hermann Cohen] German neo-Kantian philosopher (1842–1918).

471.4 Otto Weininger] Austrian philosopher (1880–1903), author of *Geschlecht und Charakter* (*Sex and Character*, 1902).

499.36 Cave of Machpelah] See note 413.28.

517.14 *Gleichgeschaltet*] In German, "coordinated"; the Nazis used the word to describe a policy that consolidated their power and eliminated their opponents.

GIFTS

553.35–36 "The Jew from Babylon"] See pp. 593–99.

554.5 Professor Rhine] Joseph B. Rhine (1895–1980), Duke University professor who conducted research into paranormal phenomena and established the Institute for Parapsychology.

557.12 Melechavitch] The Yiddish poet Melekh Ravitch, one of the founders of *Literarishe bleter* (*Literary Pages*), journal that published Singer's early stories.

561.30 Sabbatai Zevi] Smyrna-born kabbalist (1626–1676) who declared himself the Messiah in 1648 and attracted a large following of believers throughout the Middle East, Europe, and North Africa. His movement weakened after he was forced to convert to Islam to save his life in Constantinople in 1666. He continued to assert messianic claims while observing the outward forms of Islam. A sect of his followers, the Donmeh, still exists.

568.5 Birobidzhan and such similar fakes] See note 297.4.

580.1 Khmelnetski] At least 100,000 and perhaps more than 1,000,000 Jews were massacred in 1648 and 1649 at the instigation of Cossack leader Bohdan Chmielnitzski (c. 1595–1657).

580.1 Petlyura] Ukrainian nationalist leader Simon Petlyura (1879–1926) was responsible for pogroms.

THE DEATH OF METHUSELAH AND OTHER STORIES

594.6 the cursed Sabbatai Zevi] See note 561.30.

605.7 the Moscow trials] Three public show trials were held in Moscow in August 1936, January 1937, and March 1938, during which prominent

Soviet Communists were falsely accused of conspiring with the exiled Leon Trotsky against Joseph Stalin and his regime.

605.9   Chekist]   Agent of the Soviet secret police.

635.2   Professor MacDougal]   William McDougall (1871–1938), English-born American psychologist, whose books included *Body and Mind* (1911) and *Outline of Abnormal Psychology* (1926).

664.40   Goldfaden's and Latteiner's]   Yiddish playwrights Abraham Goldfaden (1840–1908) and Joseph Latteiner (1853–1935).

676.33   Jacob Frank]   Polish Jewish false messiah and founder (1726–1791) of a heretical sect, the Frankists. He claimed to be the reincarnation of Sabbatai Zevi, made an ostensible conversion to Roman Catholicism but continued to practice his own religion, was imprisoned by the Inquisition, and eventually settled in the German village of Offenbach.

680.3   Baron Hirsch's . . . Argentina]   A settlement project bringing Eastern European Jews to agricultural colonies in Argentina was funded by German-Jewish Baron Maurice de Hirsch (1831–1896), primary backer of the Jewish Colonization Association.

714.22   *Migdal Oz*]   Allegrorical drama (1727) by Italian Jewish poet, playwright, and kabbalist Moshe Chaim Luzzato (1707–1847).

714.39   Sarah bas Tovim]   Daughter of a Lithuanian rabbi who wrote women's devotional prayers.

729.21   *tohu* and *vohu*]   Unformed and void, an allusion to Hebrew words in the account of creation in Genesis.

UNCOLLECTED STORIES

737.9   Sukkah]   Small enclosed structure or "booth" constructed for the celebration of Sukkoth.

740.27   *multum in parvo*]   Much in little.

742.4   Baal Shem]   Shortened form of Baal Shem Tov (Master of the Good Name), name of Israel ben Eliezer (c. 1700–1760), founder of Hasidism.

794.12   *Babba Batra*]   Tractate of the Talmud.

825.8   Gabriela Zapolska]   Pseudonym of Maria Korwin-Piotrowska (1860–1921), Polish playwright and naturalist novelist.

825.9   Marguerite and Dekobra]   French novelist brothers Paul (1860–1918) and Victor (1866–1942) Margueritte, who published collaborative works *Femmes nouvelles* (*New Women*, 1899) and *La Commune* (*The Commune*, 1904); Maurice Dekobra (1885–1973), French author of novels such as *La Madone des Sleepings* (*The Madonna of the Sleeping-Cars*, 1925).

847.25   Maydanek and Stuthoff] Nazi concentration camps located near the cities of Lublin and Gdansk, respectively.

851.31   *Szmalcownik*] Someone who extorted protection money from Jews and then turned them in.

851.34   Jambul] Region in Kazakhstan, then part of the Soviet Union.

Library of Congress Cataloging-in-Publication Data

Singer, Isaac Bashevis, 1904–1991
  [Short stories. English. Selections]
  Collected stories : One night in Brazil to The death of
  Methuselah / Isaac Bashevis Singer.
    p. cm. — (Library of America ; 151)
ISBN 1–931082–63–4 (alk. paper)
  1. Singer, Isaac Bashevis, 1904–1991—Translations into En-
glish. I. Stavans, Ilan. II. Title. III. Series.

PJ5129.S49 A2   2004
839'.133—dc22   2003066081

THE LIBRARY OF AMERICA SERIES

The Library of America fosters appreciation and pride in America's literary heritage by publishing, and keeping permanently in print, authoritative editions of America's best and most significant writing. An independent nonprofit organization, it was founded in 1979 with seed money from the National Endowment for the Humanities and the Ford Foundation.

1. Herman Melville, *Typee, Omoo, Mardi* (1982)
2. Nathaniel Hawthorne, *Tales and Sketches* (1982)
3. Walt Whitman, *Poetry and Prose* (1982)
4. Harriet Beecher Stowe, *Three Novels* (1982)
5. Mark Twain, *Mississippi Writings* (1982)
6. Jack London, *Novels and Stories* (1982)
7. Jack London, *Novels and Social Writings* (1982)
8. William Dean Howells, *Novels 1875–1886* (1982)
9. Herman Melville, *Redburn, White-Jacket, Moby-Dick* (1983)
10. Nathaniel Hawthorne, *Collected Novels* (1983)
11. Francis Parkman, *France and England in North America*, vol. I (1983)
12. Francis Parkman, *France and England in North America*, vol. II (1983)
13. Henry James, *Novels 1871–1880* (1983)
14. Henry Adams, *Novels, Mont Saint Michel, The Education* (1983)
15. Ralph Waldo Emerson, *Essays and Lectures* (1983)
16. Washington Irving, *History, Tales and Sketches* (1983)
17. Thomas Jefferson, *Writings* (1984)
18. Stephen Crane, *Prose and Poetry* (1984)
19. Edgar Allan Poe, *Poetry and Tales* (1984)
20. Edgar Allan Poe, *Essays and Reviews* (1984)
21. Mark Twain, *The Innocents Abroad, Roughing It* (1984)
22. Henry James, *Literary Criticism: Essays, American & English Writers* (1984)
23. Henry James, *Literary Criticism: European Writers & The Prefaces* (1984)
24. Herman Melville, *Pierre, Israel Potter, The Confidence-Man, Tales & Billy Budd* (1985)
25. William Faulkner, *Novels 1930–1935* (1985)
26. James Fenimore Cooper, *The Leatherstocking Tales*, vol. I (1985)
27. James Fenimore Cooper, *The Leatherstocking Tales*, vol. II (1985)
28. Henry David Thoreau, *A Week, Walden, The Maine Woods, Cape Cod* (1985)
29. Henry James, *Novels 1881–1886* (1985)
30. Edith Wharton, *Novels* (1986)
31. Henry Adams, *History of the U.S. during the Administrations of Jefferson* (1986)
32. Henry Adams, *History of the U.S. during the Administrations of Madison* (1986)
33. Frank Norris, *Novels and Essays* (1986)
34. W.E.B. Du Bois, *Writings* (1986)
35. Willa Cather, *Early Novels and Stories* (1987)
36. Theodore Dreiser, *Sister Carrie, Jennie Gerhardt, Twelve Men* (1987)
37. Benjamin Franklin, *Writings* (1987)
38. William James, *Writings 1902–1910* (1987)
39. Flannery O'Connor, *Collected Works* (1988)
40. Eugene O'Neill, *Complete Plays 1913–1920* (1988)
41. Eugene O'Neill, *Complete Plays 1920–1931* (1988)
42. Eugene O'Neill, *Complete Plays 1932–1943* (1988)
43. Henry James, *Novels 1886–1890* (1989)
44. William Dean Howells, *Novels 1886–1888* (1989)
45. Abraham Lincoln, *Speeches and Writings 1832–1858* (1989)
46. Abraham Lincoln, *Speeches and Writings 1859–1865* (1989)
47. Edith Wharton, *Novellas and Other Writings* (1990)
48. William Faulkner, *Novels 1936–1940* (1990)
49. Willa Cather, *Later Novels* (1990)
50. Ulysses S. Grant, *Memoirs and Selected Letters* (1990)

51. William Tecumseh Sherman, *Memoirs* (1990)
52. Washington Irving, *Bracebridge Hall, Tales of a Traveller, The Alhambra* (1991)
53. Francis Parkman, *The Oregon Trail, The Conspiracy of Pontiac* (1991)
54. James Fenimore Cooper, *Sea Tales: The Pilot, The Red Rover* (1991)
55. Richard Wright, *Early Works* (1991)
56. Richard Wright, *Later Works* (1991)
57. Willa Cather, *Stories, Poems, and Other Writings* (1992)
58. William James, *Writings 1878–1899* (1992)
59. Sinclair Lewis, *Main Street & Babbitt* (1992)
60. Mark Twain, *Collected Tales, Sketches, Speeches, & Essays 1852–1890* (1992)
61. Mark Twain, *Collected Tales, Sketches, Speeches, & Essays 1891–1910* (1992)
62. *The Debate on the Constitution: Part One* (1993)
63. *The Debate on the Constitution: Part Two* (1993)
64. Henry James, *Collected Travel Writings: Great Britain & America* (1993)
65. Henry James, *Collected Travel Writings: The Continent* (1993)
66. *American Poetry: The Nineteenth Century*, Vol. 1 (1993)
67. *American Poetry: The Nineteenth Century*, Vol. 2 (1993)
68. Frederick Douglass, *Autobiographies* (1994)
69. Sarah Orne Jewett, *Novels and Stories* (1994)
70. Ralph Waldo Emerson, *Collected Poems and Translations* (1994)
71. Mark Twain, *Historical Romances* (1994)
72. John Steinbeck, *Novels and Stories 1932–1937* (1994)
73. William Faulkner, *Novels 1942–1954* (1994)
74. Zora Neale Hurston, *Novels and Stories* (1995)
75. Zora Neale Hurston, *Folklore, Memoirs, and Other Writings* (1995)
76. Thomas Paine, *Collected Writings* (1995)
77. *Reporting World War II: American Journalism 1938–1944* (1995)
78. *Reporting World War II: American Journalism 1944–1946* (1995)
79. Raymond Chandler, *Stories and Early Novels* (1995)
80. Raymond Chandler, *Later Novels and Other Writings* (1995)
81. Robert Frost, *Collected Poems, Prose, & Plays* (1995)
82. Henry James, *Complete Stories 1892–1898* (1996)
83. Henry James, *Complete Stories 1898–1910* (1996)
84. William Bartram, *Travels and Other Writings* (1996)
85. John Dos Passos, *U.S.A.* (1996)
86. John Steinbeck, *The Grapes of Wrath and Other Writings 1936–1941* (1996)
87. Vladimir Nabokov, *Novels and Memoirs 1941–1951* (1996)
88. Vladimir Nabokov, *Novels 1955–1962* (1996)
89. Vladimir Nabokov, *Novels 1969–1974* (1996)
90. James Thurber, *Writings and Drawings* (1996)
91. George Washington, *Writings* (1997)
92. John Muir, *Nature Writings* (1997)
93. Nathanael West, *Novels and Other Writings* (1997)
94. *Crime Novels: American Noir of the 1930s and 40s* (1997)
95. *Crime Novels: American Noir of the 1950s* (1997)
96. Wallace Stevens, *Collected Poetry and Prose* (1997)
97. James Baldwin, *Early Novels and Stories* (1998)
98. James Baldwin, *Collected Essays* (1998)
99. Gertrude Stein, *Writings 1903–1932* (1998)
100. Gertrude Stein, *Writings 1932–1946* (1998)
101. Eudora Welty, *Complete Novels* (1998)
102. Eudora Welty, *Stories, Essays, & Memoir* (1998)
103. Charles Brockden Brown, *Three Gothic Novels* (1998)
104. *Reporting Vietnam: American Journalism 1959–1969* (1998)
105. *Reporting Vietnam: American Journalism 1969–1975* (1998)
106. Henry James, *Complete Stories 1874–1884* (1999)
107. Henry James, *Complete Stories 1884–1891* (1999)

108. *American Sermons: The Pilgrims to Martin Luther King Jr.* (1999)
109. James Madison, *Writings* (1999)
110. Dashiell Hammett, *Complete Novels* (1999)
111. Henry James, *Complete Stories 1864–1874* (1999)
112. William Faulkner, *Novels 1957–1962* (1999)
113. John James Audubon, *Writings & Drawings* (1999)
114. *Slave Narratives* (2000)
115. *American Poetry: The Twentieth Century*, Vol. 1 (2000)
116. *American Poetry: The Twentieth Century*, Vol. 2 (2000)
117. F. Scott Fitzgerald, *Novels and Stories 1920–1922* (2000)
118. Henry Wadsworth Longfellow, *Poems and Other Writings* (2000)
119. Tennessee Williams, *Plays 1937–1955* (2000)
120. Tennessee Williams, *Plays 1957–1980* (2000)
121. Edith Wharton, *Collected Stories 1891–1910* (2001)
122. Edith Wharton, *Collected Stories 1911–1937* (2001)
123. *The American Revolution: Writings from the War of Independence* (2001)
124. Henry David Thoreau, *Collected Essays and Poems* (2001)
125. Dashiell Hammett, *Crime Stories and Other Writings* (2001)
126. Dawn Powell, *Novels 1930–1942* (2001)
127. Dawn Powell, *Novels 1944–1962* (2001)
128. Carson McCullers, *Complete Novels* (2001)
129. Alexander Hamilton, *Writings* (2001)
130. Mark Twain, *The Gilded Age and Later Novels* (2002)
131. Charles W. Chesnutt, *Stories, Novels, and Essays* (2002)
132. John Steinbeck, *Novels 1942–1952* (2002)
133. Sinclair Lewis, *Arrowsmith, Elmer Gantry, Dodsworth* (2002)
134. Paul Bowles, *The Sheltering Sky, Let It Come Down, The Spider's House* (2002)
135. Paul Bowles, *Collected Stories & Later Writings* (2002)
136. Kate Chopin, *Complete Novels & Stories* (2002)
137. *Reporting Civil Rights: American Journalism 1941–1963* (2003)
138. *Reporting Civil Rights: American Journalism 1963–1973* (2003)
139. Henry James, *Novels 1896–1899* (2003)
140. Theodore Dreiser, *An American Tragedy* (2003)
141. Saul Bellow, *Novels 1944–1953* (2003)
142. John Dos Passos, *Novels 1920–1925* (2003)
143. John Dos Passos, *Travel Books and Other Writings* (2003)
144. Ezra Pound, *Poems and Translations* (2003)
145. James Weldon Johnson, *Writings* (2004)
146. Washington Irving, *Three Western Narratives* (2004)
147. Alexis de Tocqueville, *Democracy in America* (2004)
148. James T. Farrell, *Studs Lonigan: A Trilogy* (2004)
149. Isaac Bashevis Singer, *Collected Stories I* (2004)
150. Isaac Bashevis Singer, *Collected Stories II* (2004)
151. Isaac Bashevis Singer, *Collected Stories III* (2004)

*This book is set in 10 point Linotron Galliard,
a face designed for photocomposition by Matthew Carter
and based on the sixteenth-century face Granjon. The paper
is acid-free Domtar Literary Opaque and meets the requirements
for permanence of the American National Standards Institute. The
binding material is Brillianta, a woven rayon cloth made by
Van Heek-Scholco Textielfabrieken, Holland. Composition
by Dedicated Business Services. Printing and binding
by R.R.Donnelley & Sons Company.
Designed by Bruce Campbell.*